SOULMARKED

Book Three of the Fatemarked Epic

David Estes

For the page-turners I know and love.

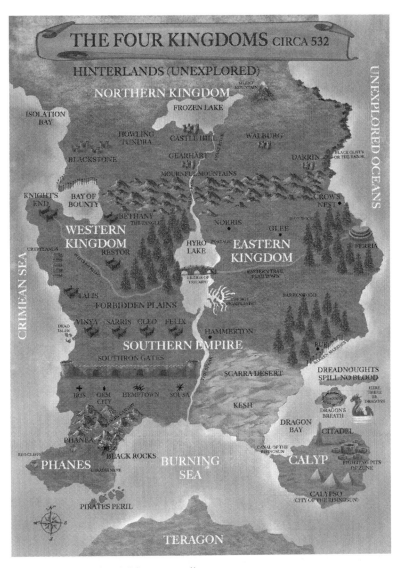

To view a downloadable map online:
http://davidestesbooks.blogspot.com/p/fatemarked-map-of-four-kingdoms.html

The story so far...

IN FATEMARKED...

The Hundred Years War has stretched over a century, ravaging the nations of the Four Kingdoms. Before the war began, a prophecy was made by a woman now known as the Western Oracle. The prophecy, which promised the coming of the fatemarked, who would bring peace to the lands, has been forgotten by many, while others believe it to be naught but a legend. Still, the truth of the ancient words has begun to come to pass, as there are those being born with strange markings that grant the bearers unusual powers. In some lands, the marked are revered; in others, hated, even put to death.

One of the fatemarked, the Kings' Bane, has his own prophecy: to bring death to eight rulers across the Four Kingdoms, which will usher in a time of peace. His work has already begun—three rulers have been killed in swift succession: King Wolfric Gäric, known as the Dread King of the North, King Gill Loren of the West, and King Oren Ironclad, the Juggernaut of the East, have all fallen. But Bane's task is far from finished, and now he plans to turn his attention to the south...

Little is known of what has been transpiring in the southern empires of Calyp and Phanes, except that the two nations have been embroiled in a civil war caused by the marriage dissolution of the two main sovereigns, Empress Sun Sandes and Emperor Vin Hoza....

In the kingdoms, however, time has marched ever onwards...

To the west:

With the death of King Gill Loren at the hand of the Kings' Bane, his eldest nephew, Jove Loren, attempts to usurp the throne from the true heir, Princess Rhea Loren. To accomplish this, Rhea is charged by the furia with breaking her vow of purity with a common thief known as Grease Jolly, an alias for his true name—Grey Arris. As punishment, a "W" for *whore* is carved on her face, leaving permanent scars. In her mind, her greatest attribute, her beauty, has been stripped from her, leaving her with nothing left but revenge.

When her horror and sadness turn to white-hot anger, she murders her cousin Jove and reclaims her crown, vowing next to win the war and defeat her enemies on all sides...

Meanwhile, Grey Arris's sister, Shae Arris, who is fatemarked, is abducted by the furia and taken south to a chain of islands called the Dead Isles, which are rumored to be haunted. Grey, charged with thievery, has his hand cut off as punishment, but manages to escape Knight's End with some help from Rhea. Grey follows the furia, eventually hiring onto a ship, *The Jewel*, which is headed south. His goal: find his sister and rescue her...

To the north:

After Bane murders the Dread King, the crown shifts to Archer Gäric. However, before he can claim it, his uncle, Lord

Griswold, swoops in, accusing he and his mother, Sabria Loren, of conspiring to kill the king. The eldest of the king's heirs, Annise, feels powerless as she watches the execution of her mother. When Archer is brought to be executed, however, the executioner suddenly makes himself known as a famous warrior known as the Armored Knight. They escape through the sewers along with another knight, Sir Dietrich.

While they travel to the southern part of the realm, Annise realizes she has turned eighteen and now has the primary claim on the throne. She refuses to tell her brother, though she confides in the Armored Knight, who turns out to be her long-lost friend from childhood, Tarin Sheary, believed to be dead, but now cursed by the witch's potion that saved his life. They also meet up with their eccentric aunt, Lady Zelda, who reveals that the Kings' Bane is actually their younger brother, who was smuggled from the north immediately after birth.

When the easterners attack Raider's Pass, Archer is knocked unconscious by the Kings' Bane, his own brother, who turns up to try to kill Annise, who is now the lawful queen of the north. However, Sir Dietrich manages to fight Bane off, showcasing his uncanny skills with the blade. Bane, exhausted from the ordeal, vanishes. Annise and the others seize victory from the east, killing King Ironclad and others.

Now, with Annise having declared herself the true queen and with Archer comatose, the Gärics and their allies are marching north toward Castle Hill to reclaim the throne from the usurper, Lord Griswold…

To the east:

When a young man named Roan, who grew up in Calypso, contracts the plague from a mysterious beggar on the street, he's sent to quarantine on an island called Dragon's Breath.

There he reveals his own fatemark, called the lifemark, which allows him to heal himself and escape the island, which is guarded by two-headed dragons. Fateful currents pull him to the east, where a chance meeting makes him the prisoner of Prince Gareth Ironclad, who immediately brings him to Ironwood and the eastern capital of Ferria, the Iron City, where humans live in harmony with the Orians, a mystical people who can channel the ore that lies beneath the forest.

With the help of one of the Orians, a fatemarked named Gwendolyn Storm, King Ironclad swiftly learns of Roan's marking, and forces him into helping their armies as they march on Raider's Pass to exact revenge on the north for the killing of the queen. Roan reluctantly agrees, and soon learns that the east has another of the fatemarked, a mighty warrior named Beorn Stonesledge, the ironmarked. Roan also discovers that, as the first-born son, Gareth is "the Shield," which means his life is forfeit, to be given to protect the second-born son, Guy, the true heir to the eastern throne.

Along the way, Roan begins to grow close to both Gwen and Gareth...

At Raider's Pass, the north defeats them, killing King Ironclad, Prince Guy Ironclad, and injuring Beorn Stonesledge. Gareth Ironclad is nearly killed by the Kings' Bane as he tries to protect Guy, but Roan saves him by using his lifemark.

In the aftermath of defeat, Gwendolyn Storm realizes who Roan really is: Roan Loren, prince of the west and true heir to the Western Kingdom. She helps him escape and together they slip away, crossing the border between nations and into the Tangle, the largest western forest, known to be almost impassable...

IN TRUTHMARKED...

To the north:

While her brother, Archer, continues his slumber, Queen Annise Gäric leads her forces against Castle Hill. Before they reach their destination, they encounter a knight, Sir Metz, who has just come from the castle. He brings tidings of an army of monsters, created from men by an elixir contrived by Lord Griswold's potionmaster, Darkspell. Though the news shakes Annise, she refuses to back down from the fight.

During the battle, the monsters are killed one by one, but not without a heavy toll: Annise loses almost her entire army, including Lady Zelda's husband, Sir Craig. However, they do make one ally during the bloodbath—Sir Jonius, in the form of a monstrous bear, who, by sheer will of heart, manages to maintain control and switches sides, helping them achieve victory, killing the Ice Lord and Lord Griswold, both of whom are monsters themselves.

Tarin Sheary, the Armored Knight, also survives, but is overcome by his bloodlust. Fearing he might be capable of harming Annise, he sneaks away while she is held captive by her queenly duties...

With her army annihilated and having learned that her uncle had lost the rest of the northern forces in the Bay of Bounty, Annise knows the north is ripe for invasion. Sir Jonius comes forward with a map only recently discovered. The map shows the location of an ancient group of mighty warriors known as the Sleeping Knights, who, as legend tells, will awaken in the north's time of need. Annise immediately begans making plans to lead a small expedition into the Hinterlands to locate these knights, who may be the north's only hope...

To the west:

Queen Rhea Loren, much to the chagrin of her cousin and advisor, Ennis Loren, enlists the help of a man known as the Summoner, long considered to be a practitioner of old magic forbidden by their deity, Wrath. When the northern armada sails out from Blackstone, Rhea commands him to summon an ancient monster of the deep called Wrathos. He does, and is killed a moment later, but not before Wrathos obliterates the northern ships, leaving none alive. During the melee, Ennis disobeys a direct command from his sovereign, saving Rhea rather than the Summoner.

With no other choice, Rhea charges Ennis with treason and plans his execution. In the end, however, her conscience makes a reappearance and she fakes his death, giving him a disguise and false name in her guard...

Meanwhile, in the Tangle, Roan and Gwen struggle to navigate through the insufferable forest. Soon they are joined by Gareth Ironclad, who tracks them after fleeing the east as the failed Shield. Together, they overcome an unexpected attack by a wood nymph queen, who tries to enslave Roan and Gareth. Gwen saves them with help from a half-man, half-bear who calls himself Bear Blackboots and then disappears.

Eventually they reach Knight's End, where Roan decides to take a risk and reveal himself to his sister. Rhea swiftly betrays him, imprisoning Gwen and Gareth. Gareth tries to commit suicide so he can't be ransomed to the east, but Roan saves his life yet again.

When Roan and Rhea uncover information that implies either the Western Oracle or her son might still be alive, she forces him to go south, to the Calypsian city of Citadel, to bring them back in chains. If he doesn't, she promises to kill Gwendolyn Storm...

To the south...

In Calypso, the Beggar who infected Roan allows himself to be captured by the empress, Sun Sandes, but is then pushed into her by Bane, who shows up unexpectedly. She dies of the plague, Bane's fourth kill under the prophecy.

The Calypsian throne is fought for by two of her daughters, Raven and Fire, but it is Fire, one of the fatemarked, who emerges with the empire. She immediately plans a mission to Phanes to attack the Southron Gates, taking most of her elite warriors, the guanero, led by Goggin. They cross the desert, stopping only in the oasis of Kesh, where Fire is nearly assassinated. From there they ford the Spear, marching on the Gates, managing to melt two of the four massive doors before Phanecian forces repel them. Fire is killed, her body exploding in a firestorm that incinerates the remaining enemies and lights the Tangle, far to the north, on fire.

The Unburning Tree finally burns to ash.

Raven Sandes becomes empress without challenge from her youngest sister, Whisper, who is heartbroken by the death of her mother and sister. Raven learns it was the easterners that plotted to assassinate Fire at Kesh, and she immediately begins considering revenge...

In Phanes, Jai Jiroux is a slave master bearing the justicemark. He is intent on freeing his slaves in Garadia Mine and helping them escape across the border. His opportunity comes when the mine is attacked by a group of rebels known as the Black Tears. They are led by Sonika Vaid, although it is another of them, Shanti Parthena Laude, who Jai becomes closest with. Together, they lead five thousand slaves across the arid wasteland, barely surviving an attack from a feared red pyzon, before reaching the Southron Gates at the same moment as the attack by the Calypsians.

At the same moment, the Beggar, who has been befriended by Bane, appears before Jai. Bane has charged him with spreading the plague in Phanes to eradicate any warmongers. However, the Beggar refuses, remembering who he once was, a boy named Chavos. Instead, he stabs himself in the gut, though Bane manages to save him.

In the confusion, Jai, the Black Tears, and the surviving slaves breach the wall and emerge into western territory—free at last! However, in a horrifying twist of fate, one of the slaves, an ex-master named Axa, betrays them with a magic mirror, which allows the emperor, Vin Hoza, who bears the slavemark, to reenslave them all.

They are brought back to Garadia, where Jai, along with most of the Black Tears, is now a slave in the very mine he once controlled. Shanti, however, is taken to Phanea to slave away in the palace. Jai is in despair until Bane kills Emperor Hoza, thus releasing every slave across Phanes from his magic...

And now, the story continues...

PART I

Lisbeth ⚜ Annise ⚜ Tarin
Rhea ⚜ Gwen ⚜ Gareth
Ennis ⚜ Christoff ⚜ Zelda

Their fates are moveable, changeable;
none can foresee that which is as fluid as the
forever-shifting rivers of time.
The Western Oracle

One

The Hinterlands, Circa 532
Lisbeth Lorne

She arrived in the midst of a storm, in the deepest throes of night.

Born of thunder and lightning and howling wind and needles of sleet, she was a spell incarnated, the product of magic and faith and a power beyond human understanding. She was the daughter of Absence and Wrath and Surai, the many-named gods of the south, the Creator, the One responsible for Life and all those who claimed it.

You shall be Lisbeth Lorne, a voice said. It wasn't a shout, but a whisper, nearly lost on the wind.

"Lisbeth Lorne," the girl tried. She laughed at the way it sounded on her tongue. She laughed at the coolness of the snow settling on her face and hands. She laughed at how the fabric of her pale blue dress felt against her smooth skin. She laughed because she was, inexplicably, alive.

Unlike the other humans that walked the face of the planet, she remembered the time before; a time when she was naught but a soul, a ribbon of light, free from the bounds of gravity and human nature, free from deception and violence and disappointment and foolish decisions. In those days, those eternities, she sang with the stars, laughed with the sun, slept with the moons.

She was free.

And yet now, trapped in this body, held fast to the ground, there was something liberating, astonishingly exciting—a giddy feeling in her lungs and chest, the simultaneous cold of snow against the warmth of the blood running through her veins.

I am alive.

The truth of the thought echoed through her, and she took off, stumbling over the drifts at first, her new knees knocking together, her new arms awkward at her sides. As the wind splashed against her smile, she fell less and less as she learned, as she found her balance.

Instinctively, she knew she saw the world differently than others. Some would call her blind, but that wasn't exactly true. She might not be able to see the outward physical nature of her surroundings, but what she saw held far more truth; for she saw the *soul* of every living thing, pulsing, alive, the truth behind a wall of lies, a single grain of sand amongst billions.

She relished the joy of dancing across the soul of the world, feeling it breathe beneath her feet.

Hours later, the night began to fall away, her star-friends fading one by one, and she stopped, tumbling to the snow, breathing ghosts into the lightening sky.

A wolf howled. Then another.

She sat up, looking around. They weren't wolves—for they didn't have the cool blue souls of wolves, ever stalwart—but something else, something larger, their inner beings red slashes of lightning, hungry, ever hungry. There were ten, twenty, a hundred, a sea of predators racing over the snowy hills, cresting one and descending another, starting up the final slope to where Lisbeth sat catching her breath.

Riding each beast were other souls, a combination of light and dark, bold and fearless and intense. They were violent shadows that had tasted blood.

Something pulsed through her: Not fear, exactly; more like curiosity.

The first of them reached the hill's apex, skidding to a halt. Though blind in the typical sense, she sensed the weapons: spears raised, shoved forward, their blades surrounding her.

"Uz nom nath kahlia!" one of them said, a grunt that seemed to come from the deepest part of his throat. *You have broken the pact*, Lisbeth understood.

"Iz nom klar," she spoke, the rough words hurting her throat. *I have just arrived.*

The one who spoke, perhaps the leader, cocked his head to the side, his soul displaying the gray tide of confusion. "Uz Gurz hom shuf? Cut?" *You speak Garzi? How?*

"I don't know," Lisbeth said, instinctively reverting back to the language that felt more comfortable.

"Filth language," the creature said. "Now you must die."

He raised his spear over his head just as the sun appeared, orange rays reflecting tongues of flame across the blade. This Lisbeth could see, though it was naught but flashes of light on the edge of her vision.

Lisbeth closed her eyes. She wasn't ready to die; she had only just arrived.

Bright blue light burst from her forehead, piercing the vision of the multitude gathered before her, both riders and beasts. The Garzi cried out, their voices raised together, their weapons dropped as they tried to cover their eyes.

In that moment, she revealed their souls at all their extremes. The darkness. The lightness. The pain. The betrayal. The fear. The joy.

The light died away, leaving only the mark on Lisbeth's head: a single, blue eye.

The Garzi warriors crashed from their mounts, screaming, scrubbing at their ears, at their eyes, at their heads. The beasts fled, abandoning their masters, knocking into each other in their haste to escape.

Rivulets of blood streamed from noses and ears, streaking the snow.

Even once it was over, the fallen warriors continued to shake, wracked with shivers though they were not cold.

Lisbeth opened her eyes. Her other eye, marked on her forehead, vanished, leaving her skin as pristine as freshly fallen snow.

She saw what she had done—hundreds of souls, cracked, wracked with pain—placed her face in her hands, and wept.

Two

The Northern Kingdom, Castle Hill
Annise Gäric

The night was a snow-haired queen wearing a crown of stars.

The queen's eyes were the moons, one green, half open, and the other red, just a sliver peeking out from behind a dark eyelid.

Annise sighed, wishing that being a real queen was as magical as the false one in the sky. Instead it was full of impossible decisions, unbearable sacrifices, and a lifetime's worth of heartache.

Frozen Lake stretched out in front of her, disappearing on the horizon, reflecting moon and starlight. *What secrets do you hold?* Annise wondered to the night.

The urge to relinquish the crown back to her younger brother, Archer, and depart Castle Hill to find Tarin still arose from time to time, but she tamped it down. That was something the old Annise would do. The new Annise would fight for her people, her kingdom. The new Annise wasn't selfish.

Then why do I have to keep telling myself?

She turned away from the night, shivering despite the warm blanket wrapped around her shoulders. The temperature had dropped the last few days, ever since that night when Archer finally opened his eyes. With his awakening, it seemed, winter had awakened as well.

Annise slipped back inside, closing the door to her balcony behind her. Warmth from the hearth instantly unfroze her bones, causing her skin to tingle.

Archer was sitting up in bed, staring at her.

She couldn't help it—she flinched. Though, for the last three days, her brother had been waking up more and more and for longer periods of time, it was still a shock whenever he did. It was like she'd grown so accustomed to his unconsciousness that him sleeping seemed more natural than him being awake.

"Does my face truly scare you, sister?" Arch said, smiling weakly.

I remember when his smile used to light up the entire kingdom, Annise thought. *Now it doesn't even light up his face.*

She released a breathy laugh, pulling her blanket tighter against her skin. "Only the awakeness of it." In truth, his face *did* scare her a little. His skin was far too pale, save for the dark half-moons under each eye. Worse, his cheeks were too skinny, the bones protruding at sharp angles. The sum of the changes was that he looked even more like their younger brother, Bane, than she'd like to admit. *Bane, the same brother who'd sent Archer into unconsciousness in the first place,* she reminded herself, not losing the irony.

He yawned. "Shall I go back to sleep?"

"No," Annise said quickly. "Well, yes. That is, if you're tired, you should sleep." The healer was strict in her instructions: Archer should continue to sleep for long periods to allow his body to fully recover from the injuries suffered at Raider's Pass.

"I'm tired, but I don't want to sleep ever again," Arch said. "I've got bedsores all over my body—my back, my legs, my—"

"I'm sure your many admirers will rub a soothing balm on them for you," Annise cut in.

"If you'd let me see them," Arch said, and Annise was glad the quickness was returning to his mind. He'd always been one of the few in the castle who could rival the speed of her tongue.

"It's for your own good. We don't want you to overexert yourself."

Archer narrowed his eyes and chewed his lip, not looking convinced. His tone turned serious. "What I really want to know is: How did I get knocked out in Raider's Pass and wake up in Castle Hill?"

Annise cringed. It was the question she was hoping he wouldn't ask for a good long while. She'd received a three-day respite, as he'd been too weak to do more than slurp soup, sip water, and sleep, but now there was no dodging it. She decided to face it head on.

"Well, there was a horse attached to a cart. And you were in the cart. The horse pulled the cart, and here we are."

"I see you haven't lost your sense of humor, sister."

"It's a permanent attachment to my body, lest I fall into despair."

"Annise."

"Archer."

"I'm the king, I need to know what I missed. I'm ready to lead again. To rule."

"About that…"

She was saved by a knock on the door. "You may enter," Arch said, sounding kinglier than he had since reawakening.

Sir Metz entered, bowing at the waist. As usual, his silver armor was so well-polished Annise could see her wobbly reflection in it.

"Good evening, Sir Metz," Annise said. "Allow me to formally introduce you to my brother, Archer. Archer, this knight was responsible for your protection many times while you slept. May I present Sir Christoff Metz."

"Well met, Sir," Archer said. "Thank you for your service. Now what can we do for you?"

"Do for me?" Metz asked. "Nothing. I serve the kingdom."

Arch cocked his head to the side and glanced at Annise. She shook her head. She could explain the knight's eccentricities later. "What my brother meant was: Why have you disturbed us so late?"

"That's a rude way of putting it," Arch muttered.

Metz looked right at Annise when he said, "Apologies, Your Highness, may I have a word?"

Frozen hell, Annise thought. *Could he be any less subtle?* The answer, of course, was no. Sir Metz was about as subtle as a stampeding mamoothen trying to enter a castle by a small door.

"Of course," Arch said, sitting up straighter. Annise saw a flash of pain cross his face, but then it was gone, hidden behind her brother's calm, confident expression. "Whatever you need to say, you can say in front of my sister."

Metz looked at Arch, then back at Annise. "Yes," Annise said, hoping to salvage the situation. "Speak freely in front of both of us."

The knight raised an eyebrow, but then said, "A stream has been received from Darrin. There is a storm gathering strength in the east. It looks to hit Castle Hill directly."

"We have weathered many storms before," Arch said. "Why are you telling us this?"

"Because we have delayed depart—"

"Thank you, Sir," Annise said. "That will be all."

The knight, seeming almost relieved, bowed again and departed the way he'd come, leaving them alone once more. Annise avoided Archer's stare as it bore into her from the side.

"Why did he stop answering my question upon your command?" he asked.

Annise said, "There is much I need to tell you."

"Then tell me."

Just like ripping off a bandage…

"I had a name day, Archer. I'm eighteen now."

"And?" He still didn't get it, still hadn't thought things through enough to understand. *I guess that's what happens when you're brought up assuming you will be king someday.*

"And you've been unconscious for more than a fortnight."

"A fortnight? That long? I suspected, but I couldn't be certain. I think I understand what you are saying."

"You do?" Annise was surprised at the lightness in his tone.

23

"Of course, sister, my injury didn't dim my wits. You've been leading my soldiers, haven't you? Knights like Sir Metz have been obeying your commands while I slept. They're in the habit now, and we haven't formally returned the torch to its rightful holder."

"Archer—"

"Tell me everything. The sooner the details are filled in, the sooner I can return to the throne and decide the next course of action."

"It has already been decided. I will be going north, into the Hinterlands, along with Sir Metz, Sir Dietrich, Sir Jonius, and maybe some others. We are going to find the Sleeping Knights."

Arch frowned. "Enough japes. I'm no longer in the mood."

Annise sighed. She could understand why her brother would think it a joke. The one-thousand Sleeping Knights were said to have been the elite soldiers of the early northern kingdom, established shortly after the first Gärics had splintered off from western rule, declaring their independence. Annise's ancestor, the fourth Gäric ruler, King Brown Gäric, was said to be a strange man, a superstitious recluse who dabbled in sorcery. After his elite squad was formed and trained, he'd supposedly found a way to grant them immortality, so they would always protect the north from invasion. However, what he didn't know was that once they were made immortal, they would leave him for the Hinterlands. According to legend, they'd left because they were not truly needed, and only when they were called upon in the north's true time of need would they awake from their slumber. That was hundreds of years ago.

Annise sighed again. "It was no jest."

His frown deepened. "The first thing I will do is revisit this decision. On whose authority was it reached?"

"On mine," Annise said, rising to her full height and jutting out her jaw. "Under northern law, you have not yet reached the age of rule. I have. I am the queen now."

Three
The Northern Kingdom,
East of Castle Hill
Tarin Sheary

Tarin, the man known by most as the Armored Knight, wished he wasn't so good at killing.

Maybe then I wouldn't have had to leave. Maybe then I could've been happy.

"You look like you want to curl up in a ball and sleep," Fay said.

He glanced at her sharply, but the blacksmith who'd designed both his armor and weapon, the enormous spiked ball attached to a chain, known as Morningstar, wasn't looking at him. Instead, she peered forward through the wall of lazy, fat snowflakes that obscured much of their vision.

Tarin sighed. He should've kept his helmet on—he wasn't used to his emotions being so easily deciphered. But, back at Castle Hill, he'd finally grown used to having it off, to people seeing the *real* him, the monster.

Fay, much to his chagrin, was undaunted by his pale, translucent skin, nor the dark, protruding veins filled with blood as black as tar. When he'd removed his helmet, she'd given him the barest of glances before nodding like she'd suspected as much.

"Sleep does not come easily to me these days," Tarin admitted.

Because of her. Because of what I did to her. Tarin, in his heart, knew Annise would be better off without him. Safer. She was strong, the strongest woman he'd ever met. Stronger than him in a lot of ways, despite the supernatural blood running through his veins. Then again, if harm were to befall her when he could've protected her by staying...

He would never forgive himself. He didn't know what he would do, the very idea sucking away his breath and spreading poison through his black veins.

The memory of the last night they'd spent together felt like needles in his skull.

"Nor to me," Fay said, washing away his thoughts. Tarin immediately felt bad. Since the moment they'd departed Castle Hill, he'd made this journey all about him. Well, about Annise, too, but mostly about him. About his self-loathing, his anger, his fear.

His pain.

But Fay, he knew, had demons, too, else she wouldn't have left with him.

"Why can't you sleep?" he asked.

"I—" She stopped abruptly, clamping her mouth shut. Tarin stopped, too, watching her, waiting patiently. Her boy-short hair was hidden beneath a woolen cap, her gray eyes darker than usual in the waning light. It was so quiet he could hear the soft rustle of snowflakes landing on the ground. It was the calm before a major storm, he suspected, an unintended metaphor for whatever was to come.

Fay started walking again, silent.

Tarin fell in beside her. He knew what it was like to have secrets—he wouldn't push her to reveal them.

Though he'd intended to make this journey alone, slipping away from the castle surreptitiously, Fay had caught him on the way out. Without having to ask, she'd known exactly what he was doing. *I'm going with you*, she'd said, and he didn't have the energy to argue. It was like the entirety of his reserves had been spent writing his goodbye note to Annise.

"Where are we going?" Fay asked now. He was surprised she hadn't asked sooner, but for a while she seemed content with simply knowing they were going *away*.

"Darrin," Tarin said. It was the first time he'd admitted it aloud.

Fay frowned. "Why? There is nothing there. Most of the soldiers were sent to Blackstone to die. It is an empty city. The easterners will take it, perhaps sooner than anyone thinks. Long have they coveted the Castle of Blades."

Tarin didn't answer, focusing on one trudging step after another.

"You're going there to die," Fay said.

"No," Tarin said quickly. Truthfully, when he'd first made the decision, he *had* wondered whether this was an attempt to kill himself. But no—"It's the only way I know how to protect her from afar," he explained.

"She doesn't need protection."

"I know, but that doesn't mean I can stop trying." And there it was: the truth of the matter. So long as Annise had breath in her lungs and blood in her veins, he would never stop trying to protect her. *I can't be near her, but I can't be away from her either.* It was an irony he knew he might never make sense of. Thus, they were headed to Darrin, rather than simply disappearing from the face of the earth forever, like Tarin had originally intended.

"You're a good man," Fay said.

"Not good enough."

"For what? For Annise? Did you think to ask *her?* Did you consider *her* feelings on the matter?"

Tarin stopped, whirling around. "She doesn't know what's inside me, no one does! I'm dangerous! I *hit* her! In my bloodlust, the monster raging inside me, I couldn't recognize her, I hurt her, I could've—I might've—I couldn't control…" He sank to his knees, the heat cooling in his chest, the sting of tears pricking his eyes.

Fay kneeled beside him, roped an arm around his shoulders, and rested her cheek on his armored shoulder. "And yet sometimes you're as dangerous as a puppy," she said.

An exhausted laugh burst from Tarin's lips. "A rabid puppy perhaps."

"Look, Annise isn't dead and neither are you. In this world, during this time of war, that's more fortune than most of us get. Don't give up on yourself when no one else has."

With that said, she stood and walked away, into the building storm.

Her shadow trailed behind her, seeming to darken more with each step.

Four

The Western Kingdom, Knight's End
Rhea Loren

Queen Rhea Loren, first of her name, felt as if she'd lived three lives:

First, her childhood, a time that felt happy but wasn't. Back then, she'd thought she was strong, beautiful, untouchable. Unbetrayable. Rebellious but innocent. But she wasn't any of those things. She was young and naïve. She'd fooled even herself.

Second, the shortest of her three lives, passed in an instant, a time of pain and fear and brokenness and anger. And then, like a match struck in the dark, enlightenment. Truth. Transformation. In that second life, as short as it was, she'd grown up. She'd become strong, powerful. She'd killed without remorse. She'd tortured without guilt.

Third was her current life. In this life she was a woman, a queen, a unifier, a battlefield general, the commander of monsters, the defender of the west. She was strong, confident.

And she was broken. So broken.

None knew the truth about what she felt on the inside. None could see that weakness, or she feared they would smash her into a million pieces. None could see the child growing inside her.

Without her mother, without her father, without Grey-rutting-Arris, she was alone. Even with the child in her belly, she was alone.

At least I still have Ennis, she thought now. *At least I saved him.*

That was good, right? That was merciful, wasn't it?

Even she didn't know anymore, her childhood beliefs flipped upside-down and drowned in the sparkling waters of the Bay of Bounty, pulled under by a thousand-tentacled monster known as Wrathos.

Ennis stood nearby now, just another one of her guardsmen. His disguise was effective. His blond beard was thick, covering his Loren jawline and cheekbones. His hair had been shorn close to his scalp, and was covered by a helmet. Two scars had been cut into each cheek—he did it himself. It was those scars people would see when they looked upon him—not the resemblance to her executed cousin, Ennis Loren. He was Bern Gentry now, a lifetime soldier who'd been promoted to royal guardsman after most of them had been killed by the Kings' Bane. None would suspect his true identity.

She turned her thoughts away from Ennis—Bern. Her people were waiting, whispering to each other, pointing at the three red-clad women standing in a line beside her. Rhea let the moment simmer just a little longer, and then said, "This is an auspicious occasion. Though we are saddened by the deaths of the Three, we know they have gone to meet Wrath in the seventh heaven. Our God's Furies shall receive the rewards they earned during their lives of righteousness and service."

The growing child inside her kicked, and she almost cried out. *Soon*, she thought. *Soon I will tell them about you.* At least the morning sickness had largely disappeared, thank Wrath.

She refocused on the heads nodding in the crowd. Her people believed her. They trusted her. *The Savior of the West*, some were beginning to call her. It was possible she'd had several of the furia spread the nickname around the city.

"But alas, this is a time of threats and war, of sin and fear. A time of dark magic. The rumors many of you have heard are true: our largest forest, the Tangle, burns. Some say it was caused by the evil power of the south, but I reject this! The largest fires are caused by a single spark—that is all. The fires will smolder down to nothing, and we will survive, as we always have. We cannot dwell on rumors, or rumors of rumors. We cannot dwell on the deaths of the Three. We must move on and honor their sacrifice with our actions, with our devotion to Wrath. Thus, today we will anoint the new Three, before Wrath and the people of the Holy City, not as replacements, but as sisters in righteousness."

More heads nodding, more looks of awe, craned necks to stare up at the dais. Before today, this kind of ceremony had been conducted behind closed doors, but not anymore. Rhea knew it was another opportunity to be seen, to gain favor amongst her people.

"These Three Furies have taken the oaths, and now need only a royal blessing, which I shall offer humbly before Wrath. Approach."

The chosen Three—women Rhea had handpicked from the Furium, three warriors who had fought for her in the Bay of Bounty—kneeled before her, heads bowed. They all had red hair, though that was not the natural color—all furia used the same hair dye when they entered the Furium. They were all strong, their muscles taut under their red clothes.

Annise touched the tops of their heads in succession and whispered the blessing. "You are the Three, the Chosen, Wrath's warriors in this land. You are One and the Same. You will have God's strength in your bodies, and wisdom in your minds, and courage in your hearts. You shall not fear death. You shall serve Wrath for all your days. Amen."

As each of the Three's heads raised, the people said, "Amen."

Rhea knew this solemn occasion was not the time for another war speech, and sometimes less was more. She turned on her heels and walked back into the castle, her guardsmen shadowing her footsteps. Somewhere off to the left she could feel Ennis's presence, feel his eyes burning into her. She refused to meet his gaze. She avoided the temptation to rest her hand on her swollen belly hidden beneath the shapeless purity dress she wore.

Earlier, she'd sent a stream to Ferria, a message for Grian Ironclad:

I have your brother, Gareth. But I'm willing to trade him for another. Give me Beorn Stonesledge, the ironmarked, and you may have Gareth. If not, he dies.

Rhea held her breath as she entered the royal stream, a narrow, slow-moving body of water that was fed by the Crimean Sea via an inlet on the western shores, near the Cryptlands. The stream passed via a hole in the castle wall and flowed all the way through the palace grounds. Along this portion of the stream, a thick grove of inkreeds grew, making it the perfect location for sending and receiving messages. Years earlier, the method of communication known as *streaming* had been discovered, and was now used throughout most of the Four Kingdoms.

Several of the stream workers straightened up when they saw her enter, looking nervous and uncomfortable. It was unusual for a lady or lord of the court to enter the stream, much less a queen. Most received their messages by royal couriers, who delivered scrolls all day long.

Rhea breathed out, looking at the clear waters of the stream, which burbled along happily. "What news from the east?" she asked, to no one in particular.

The nervous-looking stream workers glanced at each other. Finally, a woman, slender-looking despite the thick purity frock she wore, stepped forward. "We have received no response, Your Highness."

It took all of Rhea's efforts to hide her reaction. Anger and frustration burned beneath her neutral expression. "Pity," she said. "Please keep me apprised of any news."

She thought of the burning Tangle, how her scouts had said the flames were creeping from tree to tree, bush to bush, vine to vine, slowly consuming the forest, almost like the sands of an hourglass tumbling into the abyss.

"Of course, Your Highness."

She started to turn away to leave, but then the woman said, "Incoming stream."

Slowly, Rhea twisted her head back to look. Sure enough, dark, inky symbols were forming on the surface of the clear water. Words. Sentences. Sent from somewhere, a sheet of parchment dipped into the water, a message written with ink from the reeds harvested in this exact location, disappearing only to reappear right here, right now, almost instantaneously. On another day, at another time, Rhea might have been amazed, but not today.

She watched the slender stream worker wade into the creek carrying a blank sheet of parchment, which she sank into the water over the still-forming words. The words clarified, soaking into the paper. With trembling hands, the woman lifted it, clambering back onto dry ground.

Though she was buzzing with anticipation, Rhea pretended to wait patiently as the woman dabbed the wet sheet with a dry cloth.

"It's a message for you," the woman announced. "From Grian Ironclad."

"Please," Rhea said, her voice even. "Bring it here."

Obediently, the woman handed her the flattened scroll. Rhea scanned it, her excitement building with each line:

Queen Rhea Loren, First of Your Name,

Although I am surprised to hear of Gareth's appearance in the west, perhaps I shouldn't be. After our defeat at Raider's Pass, his mind became addled. He is of no value to me, but he is my brother all the same. I will make this trade. Bring Gareth to the Bridge of Triumph three days hence. I will deliver Beorn Stonesledge, the ironmarked. A man for a man, though I fear you shall receive the better end of the deal.

Your Eastern Counterpart,

King Grian Ironclad

"Yes," Rhea said.

"Your Highness?" the stream worker said, but Rhea wasn't listening, already turning away.

For the first time in history, the west would have one of the fatemarked.

Rhea was going to celebrate. It was time to carve her new Furies' faces.

Five

The Western Kingdom, Knight's End
Gwendolyn Storm

I don't love him, Gwen thought.

The thought made her angry. She shoved to her feet, stalking in one direction, hitting a wall, turning, and pacing back the other way. In her tiny dungeon cell, she repeated this process again and again, her frustration mounting with each stride. She was an ore hawk trapped in a cage, unable to spread its wings and fly.

And I don't even love him, she thought again. Lying to herself should've gotten easier, but it hadn't.

I am forged from ore, strong, unbroken, and to ore I shall return.

It was a mantra she'd recited for years, decades. It was truth mixed with lies.

She slammed her fist against the stone wall, which crumbled upon impact. Pain shot through her knuckles into her hand, shivering up her forearm. She gritted her teeth, relishing the mind-numbing distraction.

Her heromark pulsed on her cheek. *Fat lot of good you'll do me stuck in here.*

Within the bounds of Ironwood, she would have no trouble channeling the ore in the iron bars to escape, but here…the ore was as distant to her as light from a night star.

Footsteps in the corridor, an orange light flickering on the walls. Quickly, she sank back down in the shadows, cradling her bruised hand. *Don't show them your strength. You are broken. You are weak. You are a prisoner, no threat to anyone.*

"Et," a garbled voice said, stopping in front of her cell. *Eat,* she translated. The dungeon master was a squat man with no ears. Each day, he ambled along, past each cell, saying *Et. Et, et, et,* like it was the only word he knew. Maybe it was.

Now, he held a rusty, iron tray with a hard heel of bread and something mashed on a wooden plate. A small tin of brownish water completed the unappetizing fare.

"Can you push it inside?" Gwen asked, forcing a breathless rasp into her voice. She reached out a hand, letting it falter in midair before dropping. "Don't have the strength to get up."

Though the man was clearly deaf—kind of hard to hear with no ears—Gwen knew he was a master at reading lips. She'd seen him do it often enough, and he was looking at her now, soaking up every word.

He laughed, the choking sound of a man expelling phlegm from his throat. "Ol' tricks," he muttered. "Seen 'em all."

He left the tray on the ground just outside the cell, stood, and limped away.

Gwen exploded to her feet, slamming against the bars, grabbing the tray, pulling it inside the cell, and throwing it against the wall. Hard bread and mush flew through the air.

She sank back down, her chest heaving, the tray spinning circles before her, slowly coming to rest. She sat like that for a few moments before standing. First, she retrieved the bread, biting off hunks and trying not to chip a tooth as she chewed each piece a thousand times, forcing it down her throat. Then she scraped as much of the mush as she could from the wall, sucking it from her fingers. Last, she found the tin cup, which was on its side. It only held a few drops of brackish water, but she dribbled them on her tongue.

Her anger had faded.

Her thoughts returned. *I don't love him. I don't I don't I don't...* Why not?

Because I'm not capable of love. A woman with no heart cannot love, cannot care.

This was the truth she'd held onto for the long years since her bondmate was taken from her too soon. The hardest part was the fact that even if Alastair hadn't been killed during the Dragon Massacre in Ferria, he would still be dead today, of old age or something else. From the beginning, she was destined to outlive him, a truth that now seemed like a great injustice.

Furthermore, even if she *did* love Roan Loren—but she didn't—she could never act on her feelings because she would most likely outlive him, too.

She sighed. *I'm a fool. I'm thinking of love and death and history when I should be plotting how to escape this confounded dungeon.*

Her mind ticked over this thought for a long while, her injured knuckles throbbing in accompaniment to her beating heart.

40

An idea took shape, fuzzy around the edges at first, but then clarifying, striking her brain like a hard punch.

I'm getting out of here, she thought. *And I'm taking Gareth with me.*

Six

The Western Kingdom, Knight's End
Gareth Ironclad

"Go to hell," Gareth said.

Rhea raised her eyebrows. "We call it the first heaven, not hell."

"You can go there, too." Despite his bravado, Gareth's heart was pounding away in his chest, seeming to chip at the inside of his bones. *I can't let this happen. I can't.*

"This is going to happen," Rhea said. "Your dear brother, Grian, has agreed to trade for you. We ride out first thing tomorrow."

"I'll kill myself," Gareth said.

"You already tried that, remember?" Rhea motioned to the thick planks hammered over the window he'd shattered. The same window he'd tried to leap from, until…

He swallowed thickly. *He saved me. Roan saved me. How had he done that? Why had he done that? He said he loved me.*

He lied. He only said it to save me.

Gareth was tired of thinking, tired of the questions with no answers. He'd vowed not to allow himself to be used against the east, and yet here he was, still alive, about to be ransomed.

"Anything else to say for yourself?" Rhea said, filling the silence.

Gareth shook his head. What was there to say?

"Good. Now get some rest."

She left, leaving two guards behind. One of them was new, a fellow named Bern Gentry. He seemed different than the other guards, in that he didn't yell or threaten so much. For that very reason, Gareth didn't trust him.

The guards watched him like a hawk as he moved about the room, which was located high in a tower. A prison fit for a king, the space was large and fitted with a comfortable bed, a table and chair with several quills and scrolls of parchment for writing, a large map of the Four Kingdoms on one wall, and even a bookshelf with sixteen books.

Thus far, Gareth had built a tower out of the books, crumpled up all the sheets of parchment, and broken two of the quills in half. He had, however, slept in the bed, which was every bit as comfortable as it looked. He was frustrated, but not a fool.

"I'm hungry," Gareth said.

"Then eat something," the mean-tempered guard snapped. Gareth didn't know his name—he hadn't bothered to introduce himself like Bern Gentry had.

Gareth eyed the untouched tray of food that had been brought in earlier. The eggs were certainly cold, the toast dried out, and the apple, well, Gareth planned to explode it on the wall later for amusement.

"I'd prefer a side of bacon, a jellied roll with a drizzle of honey, and a bowl of strawberries, not too ripe. Some white sugar sprinkled on top, if the royal kitchens have any."

The guard glared at him. The edge of Bern's lip, however, seemed to curl a little. Was that a smile? The unnamed guard said, "Coming right up, Your Majesty," but didn't move from his position.

"The service is rather slow here, isn't it?" Gareth quipped.

Bern finally spoke. "Jarv, just put in the order or he'll never shut up."

So he *does* have a name, Gareth thought. "Jarv?" He snickered.

Jarv looked like he wanted to explode Gareth's head against the wall for amusement, but Gareth knew he wouldn't dare. Rhea needed him fully intact so she could ransom him.

Shaking his head, Jarv left. Gareth suspected he would get exactly what he ordered, though he wouldn't eat any of it—Jarv was certain to spit in it, and not just a little.

Gareth said, "Thank you, Bern Gentry."

Bern didn't respond, his lips pursed.

"'You're welcome' is the appropriate response," Gareth said.

Bern opened his mouth, closed it, and then opened it again. "I'm not who you think I am."

Gareth wasn't often surprised, but this time he was. He hid it behind another quip. "And I am not truly Gareth Ironclad, but Montoya, dragon rider of Calypso!" He raised a finger in the air.

"I am Ennis Loren," Bern said.

44

Gareth's hand fell back to his side. "He's dead." All of Knight's End had been talking about how Queen Rhea had executed her own cousin. Personally.

"We faked it," Bern said.

"Why?"

"She couldn't bring herself to kill me, and I couldn't allow myself to be banished. This was the only option in between."

"Why are you telling me this?"

"Because Rhea is making mistakes. She is too set on war. She's going to destroy the west."

"Sounds good to me," Gareth said, feigning a look of disinterest in the entire conversation. Truthfully, his mind was whirring through this new information, the true identity of the man standing before him.

"She'll destroy the Four Kingdoms in the process, starting with the east."

Gareth sighed. "What is your point, *Ennis Loren*? I can't control the fate of the kingdoms any more than you."

"Your friend, Roan Loren, he wants peace, right?" Bern asked.

Hearing Roan's name spoken so directly caused Gareth's stomach to squeeze into a knot. "Yes, but he's also the fool who thinks lions can lay down with lambs without taking a bite or two."

"What if I told you they could?"

"I'd say you're madder than a blind man who wants to become an archer."

"Rhea cannot get her hands on Beorn Stonesledge. It will only encourage her to march to war sooner."

"Then you'll have to convince my brother to refuse her ransom," Gareth said.

"What if I can do better?"

"I'm listening."

"I'll help you escape, if you promise to sign a treaty with the west."

Gareth scoffed. "Rhea will never agree to peace."

"Leave Rhea to me. As long as *you* are open to peace, I will help you."

Seven

The Hinterlands
Lisbeth Lorne

She hadn't killed the Garzi riders, nor their wolfish steeds, though she knew she could have.

But still, having probed into their minds, into their darkest dreams and fears, having used that against them, to subdue them...

Lisbeth felt sick.

In her mind's eyes, she'd seen great violence—a man killing another, stabbing him in the heart—and she'd seen great love—a child being born, cradled between its parents, who nuzzled its cheeks, its head. She'd seen a slaughter: long ago, hundreds of years past but as clearly remembered as if it had occurred yesterday, a story passed from generation to generation. There was a storm, and a group of bearded men, running for their lives, caught—and killed. The Garzi had killed them.

They came now, women—bright yellow souls filled with great strength—marching across the field of fallen warriors. The wolf-like beasts with the red-lightning souls were tethered to soulless contraptions. Each unconscious warrior was hefted up, set down, and then dragged away by the beasts, sliding across the snow.

Lisbeth followed them. She couldn't *not* follow them, the compulsion as strong as anything she'd felt in this short life or the long one before.

A long time later they stopped. Squat, unmoving souls rose on each side, some dark, some light. Lisbeth couldn't discern what they were, except they were sleeping, their heavy exhalations breaking the silence.

Somehow, she understood where they were: a city. *The Garzi live here.* She stood in the midst of the city, watching as the unconscious warriors—*not dead, at least they're not dead*—were tended to by the womenfolk. The souls of the unconscious men were now blue, frozen, while the women were as yellow as sunflowers, tinged with orange.

The women kept their distance, some of them muttering curses at her in Garzi, each of which she understood all too clearly. They thought she was some sort of demon from their myths and legends, a girl who would enslave their minds and bring them to their knees.

Is that who I am? Is that why I'm here?

And if so, can I change the course of my fate?

Lisbeth didn't know why she'd followed them at all—clearly she wasn't wanted here, and she might even still be in danger. And yet her feet had had other plans. Even now, the invisible eye on her forehead pulsed with satisfaction, seeming to speak to her: *You are meant to be here. You have a purpose.*

She hadn't really considered that. The gift of life was so new to her that she couldn't see beyond her arms, her legs, the sensations of cold and warmth and *existing* as more than a streak of light in the heavens.

"Girl is not what they say girl is," a voice said, close by. It was a woman's voice, rough and ancient, speaking the common tongue.

Lisbeth turned to find the strangest soul she'd seen yet, a shifting, pulsing orb of white light that seemed to radiate heat. She longed to touch it, to feel it, to experience the mysteries it must surely contain. Her hidden eye throbbed faster, hungry.

She held back, afraid of what would happen to this woman if she unleashed herself.

"I don't know what I am," she responded. "And I understand Garzi."

"Common tongue is yours to speak. Even here. Girl is reminder."

"Of what?"

"Of truth. Of fate. Of broken promises and false beliefs."

"I—I don't understand."

"Girl will. I am called Crone. Girl can stay with me."

The bright soul—Crone—turned away, and Lisbeth found herself following. Shapes rose up on each side, some kind of structures made of snow. She couldn't see them clearly, but they contained souls. *Homes*, she thought. *Each home has a soul of its own, a melding of the souls of those who live inside it.*

All around the homes, souls of varying shapes, sizes, and colors moved, going about their daily work.

They passed something taller, impossibly tall, rising up and casting a shadow over all the souls surrounding it. The tower had no soul, a black empty void. And yet, something pulsed from within. *No, many somethings*, Lisbeth thought. *What are those?*

"What is that place?" Lisbeth asked.

"Hall of War," Crone replied. "Dark place. Angry place. Sad place."

Lisbeth could feel all of that in her bones, an aching weariness that threatened to pull her into the throes of despair.

And then they were past and the feeling vanished. Lisbeth could breathe again.

Something else seemed to cast a shadow across the entirety of the city, a looming block of strength. *Cliffs*, Lisbeth thought. Something lived inside the cliffs, this she knew, as she could see the souls, small and wiry, moving like predatory insects. The creatures wanted to leave the caves they lived in, to descend upon the Garzi village, but they would not. They feared the outside world.

Eventually, they came to a dwelling that was small, but filled to the brim with a bright white soul that matched the soul of Crone. "Warmer here," Crone said.

Lisbeth laughed at the sensation as they entered the dwelling. Despite being surrounded by packed snow—ice really—it *was* warmer inside. Much warmer. Out of the icy wind and biting snowfall, Lisbeth's skin burned.

"Why are you doing this? Why are you helping me?"

"I can," Crone replied. Her words, though always cryptic, seemed so full of truth Lisbeth felt tears prick her eyes.

Am I crying? she wondered, reaching up to brush away the stray tears. It was a strange feeling, and yet not necessarily a bad one. If anything, it only made her feel more alive.

Another new feeling hit her as something gnawed at her stomach. She clutched her abdomen, frowning.

"Need food," Crone said. "Prefer fire meat?"

Lisbeth wasn't sure. "Do you?"

The woman laughed. "Mostly can't wait. Too hungry. Fire meat take longer."

"Hungry." Lisbeth tried out the word—was that what she was feeling?

"Girl wait here. Bring fire meat."

Lisbeth waited, listening to the sound of Crone's footsteps crunching away. In the distance, words were spoken in Garzi, but she couldn't make them out, only that it sounded like an argument. Moments later Crone appeared. She held something in her hands, a blackened, charred piece of a soul.

Bile rose in Lisbeth's throat and she threw up. Her mouth tasted…what was the right word? Bitter. Yes, bitter. "I'm sorry. I can't."

"Girl must eat."

"But the soul…" And then it was gone, fading away, slowly at first, and then faster, until it shot toward the sky in a streak of light. "Ahh," Lisbeth murmured. *It has returned home.*

She probed forward toward Crone, and the woman pressed the meat into her hands, though Lisbeth couldn't see it anymore. It felt both crusty and rubbery at the same time. She bit into it, juices bursting between her teeth, running down her chin.

"Mmm," she murmured, the taste vanquishing the bitterness on her tongue.

51

She ate the rest and then asked for more.

When they'd finished eating, Lisbeth's eyelids drifted downwards. *They are mine*, she thought. *I control them.* And yet, try as she might, she couldn't seem to keep them open. Her mouth opened involuntarily and she released a funny noise, like a deep-toned sigh.

Crone chuckled. "Girl tired. Long night. Many new experiences."

"How do you know?" Lisbeth asked, her chin falling to her chest.

"Answers later. Sleep now. Blankets warm."

Strong but gentle hands helped her crawl into a nook in the space. Something soft surrounded her: a blanket. She nuzzled her face into it, almost able to believe she was back in the heavens. She sighed.

And then she was gone.

Voices awoke her, arguing in Garzi. They were familiar, but seemed distant, as if shouted from a lonely star. Crone, her tone raspy and fierce. And the warrior who'd threatened her the night before. *He's awake. He's alive.*

She rolled over and opened her eyes, relishing the gentle pulsing soul of Crone's home all around her. Crawling, she probed against the soul, searching for a way out, finding an empty space and a breath of cool wind.

The voices stopped.

"I will leave," Lisbeth said.

"Girl no leave," Crone said.

"Silence!" the warrior snapped, using the common tongue. "Girl leave. Girl go south. Girl never return." Upon hearing his voice, images flashed in Lisbeth's mind:

A young Garzi girl with beautiful brown eyes filled with tears. Walking toward a lake, sparkling under the noonday sun. She was young—younger than Lisbeth—and wore naught but a white dress, far too thin for the snow and ice that surrounded her. The warrior was beside her, holding her by the elbow, guiding her. He was crying, too, though only a single tear tracked from his eyes to his chin. He blinked the rest away.

Others followed, hundreds and hundreds of Garzi. They chanted a song, their hands raised skyward. It almost sounded like a prayer.

"Father?" the girl said. She spoke in Garzi, though Lisbeth's mind translated it to the common tongue. "I'm scared."

The warrior stopped, holding both of her shoulders. "I'm sorry, my star, there is no other choice." The words broke from his lips like waves crashing on rocks.

"No. Zur does not speak for everyone," Crone said in the present, chasing the images away. Her voice was soft but filled with as much command as the warrior's, the male she'd called Zur. "Girl is guest. She stays." Lisbeth blinked, trying to reclaim the images, to see what happened to the girl, but they were gone.

They are not mine to claim, she realized.

The soul of the warrior rocked back and forth. "Foolish woman," Zur said. "Girl is dangerous. Unnatural."

"Leave us," Crone said.

Lisbeth held her breath, waiting for him to refuse, to bring his warriors, their weapons, to use force. *Please don't—I don't know what I will do if you try to hurt me.*

The moment shattered like crystals of ice, and the warrior turned away, muttering under his breath.

Lisbeth released a sigh, watching tendrils of her soul drift out, before being sucked back in as she took another breath. "He's right. I should leave," Lisbeth said.

"Girl choose what girl choose," Crone said, and then went back inside.

After a moment's hesitation, Lisbeth followed her.

Eight

The Northern Kingdom, Castle Hill
Annise Gäric

Archer was sulking, refusing to leave his room, taking his meals in bed, if he took them at all.

After she'd told him the truth, he hadn't lashed out in anger, as she'd expected. Instead, he'd sunken within himself, not speaking, not looking at her.

It was a stark reminder that her brother was only sixteen, despite how strong and king-like he'd acted before the battle at Raider's Pass. She would try to talk to him again later, but now she had mountains of frustration to chip away at.

Clang! Sir Dietrich's sword jarred against hers so solidly she lost her grip, her blade flipping away and sinking into the snow, which was ankle deep.

"Again," Dietrich said. "Try to hang onto your sword this time."

Annise glared at him, which wasn't particularly fair. She was the one who'd asked *him* to teach her a thing or two about sword fighting. "Sorry if I'm not *swordmarked* like you."

"That has nothing to do with it," Dietrich said. "I wasn't even trying. I've seen a child fare better."

Annise seethed, determination coursing through her. She strode to her sword, grabbed the hilt, gripping it so tightly her fingers ached, not caring, whirled back around, and charged. She swung the sword like a club, slamming blow after mighty blow, pounding away as if trying to hammer a metal stake into frozen rock.

Dietrich danced back, deflecting each attack with graceful ease, not so much blocking them as *accepting* them. The kiss of steel on steel, far too romantic for Annise's taste. For her, a fight should be brutal and rough.

Growing impatient, she retracted her sword back as far as it would go, building momentum, and then swung as hard as she could, the blow that would end the contest.

Dietrich ducked, simultaneously thrusting his own blade up, throwing her off balance as, still gripping her hilt tightly, refusing to let go, she toppled backwards, landing on her arse. Her opponent stood on the broad side of her sword. "Better, but you're still dead. Try not to hold onto your sword so tightly or you might choke it."

Annise gritted her teeth. Not only did she hate losing, but she hated losing so badly. "You told me to hang on tighter," she growled.

Dietrich chuckled, which only made her angrier. "Yes, but not *that* tight. Somewhere in between is better."

"Get off my sword."

"I think you've had enough for one day."

"Frozen hell, I don't need the damn thing anyway," Annise said, releasing her grip, rolling over and kicking out Dietrich's legs in the process. Surprised, the expert swordsman lost his own weapon as he tumbled to the ground. And then Annise was on top of him, pounding away with both fists, rubbing snow in his eyes, pinning his arms behind his back and hissing, "Do you submit?"

Gasping, Dietrich said, "You're going to break my arms!"

"Then submit."

"I submit, woman! Frozen gods of the north!"

Annise released him, smacking him across the back of his helmet for good measure. "I think you meant *Your Highness*," she said as she stood up, smiling.

"I meant *woman*," Dietrich said as he sat up and began massaging his arms. "And it's not my fault your paramour ran off with some other woman."

Annise froze. *What did he mean 'other woman'?* "He left because he's afraid of himself," she said. "He left alone."

"Then why is that friend of his missing? You know, the blacksmith? Kay or Lay or something."

"Fay," Annise murmured.

"Aye, her. She's gone. No one's seen her since the day Tarin vanished."

The adrenaline left Annise, and she felt cold seep into the gaping hole that had opened in her chest. "It doesn't mean anything. And anyway, even if she accompanied him, they are just friends."

"Traveling companions have a way of turning into more than friends," Dietrich said. "Isn't that how you and Tarin became involved in the first place?"

Annise knew he was just goading her. She had nothing to worry about from Fay. If anything, the blacksmith was her friend, too. After all, she'd designed her weapon, the Evenstar, a miniature version of Tarin's Morningstar. In a way, she was glad Tarin was not alone. "Sorry I rubbed snow in your face," Annise said, walking away. Over her shoulder, she added, "Though I did enjoy it."

She was tired of waiting for her enemies to come to her, tired of treading lightly on everyone's feelings, Archer's included. *My own included*, she reminded herself. *I've been as coddled as anyone. If anything, Dietrich did me a favor.* It was time to face reality and move forward.

She passed Sir Jonius in the corridor, but she silenced his greeting with a raised hand. "Later. We leave on the morrow. We cannot risk the storm hitting before we go."

He nodded. "Good."

She continued her path, past the entrance to the stairway that led to Darkspell's old chambers. *The last place I saw Tarin. The last place we kissed.* The place where she'd found his farewell letter and the thick sheaf of parchment with his stories written down. The same stories she'd refused to read, out of concern that her fragile heart would shatter into a billion pieces or some such nonsense. She stopped. Enough was enough. She'd been avoiding the place like she'd avoided the winter ball growing up.

The stairwell was dark as she descended, but she didn't bother going to fetch a light. There was nothing to see anyway. When she reached the bottom landing, she felt for the door, shoving it open and striding inside. Complete darkness surrounded her. Her fingers trailed along the rough stone as she made her way over to THE CORNER. The last place she'd seen him, kissed him, felt him. She sat down, inhabiting the space with her body. Claiming it for her own. It was no longer a bitter memory, but a victory. *I kissed him. I conquered him. And he is mine, regardless of his worries and fears. Either way, I will survive without him, as I have always done.*

Though that memory burned as bright as a torch, she now knew the truth of why Tarin had let her touch him, only to leave immediately after. *It was his way of saying goodbye. He wanted our last memory to be beautiful.*

And it was.

The thought left her warm and cold at the same time.

There was no jealousy in her heart at the thought of Fay traveling with him. She knew Tarin would be faithful to her the same way she knew the sun would rise on the morrow and the day after that and on and on into the eternities. In some ways, she wished he wouldn't, that he would find another, someone to make him happy again.

In some ways, she didn't want him to be alone, even if it wasn't she who filled the space beside him.

"I will always love you, Tarin Sheary, until the day I die," she said aloud. "But now I must say goodbye. There's too much work to do."

She rose, and the chamber was just a chamber again, cold and dark, holding no power over her anymore or ever again.

"You are coming with me," Annise said, sitting on the end of the bed. It wasn't a request or an option, but a command.

Archer opened his eyes, finding hers. "What?"

"We leave tomorrow. We will find the Sleeping Knights together. That is, if you feel strong enough."

Archer narrowed his eyes. "I am. But you're still the queen?"

"Yes, so get used to it. When you are eighteen I will relinquish the crown to you, if you wish. But for now, you are still the prince and heir to the throne."

"And if you marry?"

The question took Annise by surprise. Under northern law, if she were to marry before Archer came of age, her husband would become the king, and her brother would no longer have the first claim, not unless she and her theoretical husband died. "There's little chance of that happening."

"Because Tarin left. I still don't understand why."

"All that matters is that he's gone."

Archer nodded. "Fine. I can accept that. And I can accept your claim on the throne. After all, it is the law. I was just surprised, is all. I'm sorry I reacted the way I did."

Annise scooted closer, wrapping him in a bear hug, squeezing hard.

"I submit, I submit!" he said, his voice muffled.

"What? Can't hear you." She squeezed harder.

"Can't...breathe..."

She released him and he swung his feet over her head, twisting them to the side so she was pulled onto the bed. He hit her with a pillow for good measure. Archer said, "You know, just because you're bigger—"

"And stronger," Annise chimed in.

"And stronger," Arch admitted, "doesn't mean you can bully me. I'm a champion jouster, I'll have you know."

"The next time we ride into battle, I'll tell our enemy to set up a tournament," Annise quipped.

"That won't be necessary," Arch said. "I don't believe those living in the Hinterlands are much for sport. Plus, you have my charm and good looks to fall back on. With any luck, I will seduce one of their princesses and form an alliance with naught but a smile and a wink."

"I feel ill," Annise said, holding her stomach and making a choking sound.

Arch hit her with the pillow again, but then his eyes grew serious. "Before we go north, there's something you should know."

Annise frowned. "I already know about the storm. It's less than a week away."

"Not that. I was the heir to the throne growing up," Arch said. "Not you. Father told me things he never told you."

"Like how to rule with terror and an iron fist?"

"No, like what we might find in the north. The...people who live in the Hinterlands. And why we can never go there."

Annise chewed her lip, trying to discern whether this was a sibling ploy, but there was only truth in her brother's eyes. "I'll bite. Why can't we travel into the Hinterlands?"

"Because of the pact," Arch said. "Because they'll kill us if we do."

Nine

The Northern Kingdom, Darrin
Tarin Sheary

Although Tarin's memories of Darrin were that it was a harsh city, built from stone and mortar and the blood of the soldiers who'd inhabited it for centuries, he had to admit that, from afar, it held a certain amount of cruel beauty. The castle's spires rose like giant black swords, earning its nickname the City of Blades. Beyond, almost like a mirrored reflection, were the dark, jagged teeth of the Black Cliffs, more commonly known as the Razor, the easternmost bounds of the Northern Kingdom, which descended into rough ocean waters that tirelessly pounded waves into the stone barrier, as if attempting to break through. To the south were the snowcapped Mournful Mountains, the range that ran from one end of the kingdom to the other, broken only by the narrow river canyon known as Raider's Pass.

"It's been a long time," Fay said.

"Not long enough," Tarin said, though he wasn't sure he meant it. In this city he had found a home, a purpose, fighting in battle after bloody battle against the easterners. In this city, his true nature was celebrated, not feared.

Here I can be myself, he thought, *for better or worse.* In agreement, the monster inside him purred.

And yet, standing on the snowy hill overlooking the city he'd spent five long years defending, something seemed different.

"Where are all the people?" he wondered aloud. Not a soldier was in sight. Where were the marching soldiers wearing gleaming armor and swords in their belts?

"Gone to Blackstone on Lord Griswold's orders," Fay said.

In other words, dead, Tarin thought. "But surely he left a battalion or two. Enough to hold the border. They should be patrolling the streets. Or in the snowfields training." He scanned the flat, empty expanse between the castle bounds and the teeth-like cliffs. Not a human nor creature moved, though a stiff wind blew the freshly fallen snow in tornadic swirls. The fury of the early winter's storm had passed the night before, forcing them to settle down in the midst of a thick copse of pine trees, providing a natural shelter. Tarin had been worried the branches might break under the weight of the heavy snow, crushing them in the night, but, other than a few creaks and groans, the trees had withstood the onslaught.

Just like the north, Tarin though. *Cracked but not broken.*

Now the land almost looked peaceful. Too peaceful.

"Perhaps the storm drove them inside," Fay suggested.

It certainly would have, Tarin knew. While in Darrin, he'd seen half a hundred major snowstorms, perhaps more, and each time the soldiers hunkered inside thick stone bunkers to ride it out, telling exaggerated stories of battles long past, heroic victories and tragic defeats. But, after being cooped up for hours and hours, or sometimes even days on end, the moment the storm abated, the bored men would swarm the streets like bees emerging from a hive, filling the city to overflowing.

"They should've come out by now," Tarin said. "It's mid-morning."

"Regardless. We can't see all the streets. They could be congregating somewhere hidden."

Tarin conceded the point and they moved onward, striding down the hill toward the empty, silent city. Up close, Darrin looked much the same as it had from afar. The stone buildings and walls were snow-capped and icy with frost, but as solid as the day Tarin had left for Castle Hill after being summoned by Lady Zelda. It seemed like a lifetime ago, perhaps two lifetimes. But now he was back, and the City of Blades was a ghost town.

They walked along the cobblestoned streets, unspeaking, their eyes darting furtively about, seeking any signs of habitation. There were none.

As they approached the familiar barracks, Tarin said, "Wait here." He donned his helmet and face mask. Though he'd spent many years here, he'd never shown his face to his fellow soldiers.

Fay said, "No."

Tarin sighed. He didn't have the energy to argue. He rested his ear against the wooden door, listening. A frown creased his forehead.

"What is it?" Fay asked.

Tarin wasn't certain. It sounded almost like a buzzing, as if a beehive was just behind the door. But it wasn't consistent either. Strange. He opened the door, peering inside the gloomy stone barracks.

Frozen hell, was his first thought.

A few dozen soldiers lay askew on every available surface, forming awkward angles. Some were on the bunkbeds, backwards and forwards and sideways, legs and arms hanging off. Others were on the floor, nestled together head to head, feet to feet, head to feet, and every other possible combination. Tarin even spotted a soldier with no pants lying on the floor with his pale feet up on a bed, creating a tunnel. Underneath his bony legs another soldier lay on his stomach, peaceful as could be. There were women, too, most of them wearing the typical garb of serving wenches—low-cut dresses displaying ample cleavage, their hair tied up into varying formations atop their heads. All sleeping.

And many of them snoring; hence, the buzzing sound he'd heard through the door.

The strong smell of stale ale permeated the air, which was as thick as woolen knickers.

Despite the raggedy uniforms the men wore, Tarin didn't think they looked much like soldiers. Many were too skinny, their bodies more like those of boys than men, while others were rotund, their flabby jowls quivering as they snored. One man was so ancient-looking, his face weathered and spliced with wrinkles, Tarin might've though him to be dead rather than sleeping were his stomach not rising and falling with each breath. *The leftovers*, Tarin thought. Lord Griswold had sent the best of Darrin's men to Blackstone to die, leaving these sorry excuses for soldiers to guard his easternmost stronghold.

Behind him, Fay said, "They must've had a late night."

Tarin didn't respond, wondering what to do. In the end, he didn't have to decide as Fay decided for him.

"WAKE UP!" she screamed at the top of her lungs. Right in Tarin's ear.

He ducked as if a dragon was swooping down from above, firing a glare back at her. She only smiled and nodded toward the room.

Tarin swiveled around to find tired eyes opening and heads bobbing. Mouths yawning and arms stretching. The women woke up the fastest, covering their cleavage with their hands, picking up their skirts and slipping from the barracks before Tarin could count to five.

"Who the frozen 'ell are you?" one of the men asked. The geezer, his eyes milky with cataracts.

Fay stepped around Tarin. "Who is your captain?"

The old man laughed, but it quickly transformed into a wet cough. One of the other men, a stork-like man with a long horse face, slapped the geezer's back until he dispelled a ball of phlegm, hacking it into a filthy rag obtained from his shirt sleeve.

A rotund soldier attempted to descend the ladder from the top bunk but slipped, landing with a thud. He stood quickly, saluting with a hand over his heart. "Captain Morris at your service, uh, Sir." It wasn't clear whether he was speaking to Fay or Tarin, his eyes flitting back and forth between them.

"What kind of operation are you running here, Captain?" Fay said.

He shrugged. "Haven't had orders in days," he said, as if that explained everything. "And the storms have been fierce. We're on an extended holiday, you might say."

This is pointless, Tarin thought. It was clear these men weren't interested in being soldiers. He'd made a grave mistake coming to Darrin thinking it would be the same as it had always been, that he'd join a battalion and defend the border. He touched Fay's shoulder. "We should leave."

But she ignored him. "When the easterners come, what's going to happen then?" she asked. "What's going to happen when they find you drunk and asleep?"

"I'm planning to surrender the city," Morris admitted.

"Shall I inform Lord Darrin?" Lord Darrin was the ruling lord of the city, the castle passed down over generations.

"If he's still here," Morris said.

"What is that supposed to mean? He lives here. This is his city."

The old man interjected with another wheezing chuckle. "Soon as the streams about the impending attack came in, Darrin and his group o' fancypants started packing up. He declared the city and castle forfeit."

Tarin's interest piqued. "What streams?" The latest streams back at Castle Hill had advised that the easterners had turned their attention to the south, attacking nomadic tribes on the edge of the Scarra Desert. It was just the reprieve Annise had been hoping for, which was why she would head north to attempt to find the legendary Sleeping Knights.

Captain Morris said, "You haven't heard? The easterners have amassed six battalions at Crow's Nest. They're preparing to attack Darrin."

"What?" Tarin couldn't help his surprise. He knew an eastern attack was inevitable, but he didn't expect it so soon. And yet, that's why he'd come here in the first place. To protect the border. *To protect Annise in the only way I know how.*

The stork piped up. "Aye. That's when we started drinking. Luckily a few of the wenches decided to stick around for another night. The rest of the townsfolk fled west."

"And you did nothing?" Fay sounded incredulous.

"Fay," Tarin said, trying to control the anger in his voice. "We should go." A bitter stew of rage was boiling in his stomach, rising into his chest, pouring into his muscles, his bones. He had the urge to crush these men's skulls between his hands.

She wasn't listening, arguing with the captain and his pathetic group of soldiers. But Tarin didn't hear any of that, a roaring tide rushing through his head, and a voice, at first a whisper, but then louder, more commanding, LOUDER:

KILL.

Tarin whirled and stumbled from the barracks, his armor clanking as he rebounded off the doorframe, slipping in the snow, righting himself, tearing off his helmet, cold rushing in, twisting toward the stone exterior, cocking his fist, and slamming his knuckles into the wall.

And again.

And again.

Pain shrieked through him, vibrating from his fist to his forearms to his elbow.

But still he punched at the stone, trying to pound a hole through it, to crack the mortar, to tear the barracks down one brick at a time.

Destroying himself and the soldiers' quarters was better than ripping the captain's head from his shoulders.

"Tarin!" a voice shouted, piercing the rushing water in his head. He ignored it. He continued with his other fist. *Thud! Thud! THUD!*

Someone attempted to tackle him around the legs, but he barely felt it, a gnat annoying a giant. And then his legs were forced together, sliding on the ice, throwing him off balance. He toppled into a snowdrift, his bloody hands sinking deep, crimson tendrils snaking outwards like red starbursts.

Something lashed across his face. A hand. He shook his head, seeing a form over him, a slender hand closing in and then—

Smack!

Upon impact, a shred of awareness burst through the fog, and Tarin caught the next blow, holding Fay's wrist tightly, but not too tightly. Blood ran down his fingers, streaming along her wrist. He knew he could snap her bones as easily as a piece of string—and that's what the monster inside him wanted— but Tarin was in command of himself again. Barely. The pain had helped, the throbbing pain in his knuckles, the stinging on his cheek.

"I'm here," Fay said.

He released her wrist, dropping his bloody fist back to the snow.

Behind her, the ragtag group of soldiers stood barefoot in the snow. One of them was still without pants, but didn't seem to mind the cold. They were all staring at him. "You're that

Armored Knight guy they always talk about, aren't you?"
Captain Morris said.

Tarin shook his head. "No. I'm just a man without a purpose." He stood and walked away, hearing Fay following behind.

Ten

The Western Kingdom, Knight's End
Rhea Loren

She felt empty inside, like a waterskin drained of liquid, squeezed free of every last drop.

She thought it strange to feel empty considering the child inside her. *My heir.*

Rhea hated this feeling, and yet she seemed to be feeling it more and more. Before, she'd filled the hole with the burning fires of revenge. She remembered how strong, how alive, she'd felt when she'd killed her cousin Jove and taken back that which was hers. She'd felt a similar energy as she'd carved the face of the Fury who had taken her own beauty from her.

But now:

The screams of her three new Furies had only made the empty feeling worse. When they'd left, their faces torn and bloody, she'd wanted to turn the knife on herself and cut away.

What is wrong with me? she wondered, staring into the mirror. *I am the queen, I am loved by my people, respected by the furia and the guardsmen. Ennis is alive; I saved him. I captured the prince of the east, and I'm about to ransom him for a warrior more powerful than any in the Four Kingdoms. I'm with child…Grey's child…oh Grey, where are you?*

A tear trickled from her eye, changing direction as it funneled into her ragged scar line.

She hated this feeling, this emptiness. She hated thinking about the man who'd bedded her and abandoned her, like she was a common whore. She hated that she still loved him.

My child, she thought. *Will I be enough?*

She needed distractions. Something to focus her mind on other than the past.

Her Furies would ride out on the morrow with her prisoner, Gareth Ironclad, in chains. They would exchange him for Beorn Stonesledge. But until then, she was stuck waiting, bored and alone.

A knock on the door startled her. Hurriedly, she wiped the tear from her cheek with the sleeve of her dress. "You may enter."

One of her servant women slipped inside soundlessly. She was old, her bland face featureless, her long hair gray and tied into a knot atop her head. Rhea had specifically chosen her servants based on appearance. The more plain-looking the better. She couldn't have them outshining her every time they entered her room.

"Your midday meal is being prepared, Your Highness," the woman said.

72

Rhea smiled, which seemed to unnerve the woman. *Do I rarely smile?* She vowed to smile more. "Thank you."

"May I help with anything else, Your Highness?" she asked.

Rhea considered. A distraction. Yes. "Please fetch the twins. Bring them here."

"My queen?" the woman said, looking confused.

"Was my request unclear?"

"Prince Leo and Princess Bea are confined to the dungeons, Your Highness. By your own orders."

"Indeed," Rhea said. "And now, by my own orders, they are to be released, cleaned up, and brought here. Understood?"

"Yes, of course, my apologies, my queen. Right away." She bowed graciously and departed, closing the door silently behind her.

What am I going to do exactly? Rhea wondered to herself. Her reflection caught her eye. As she looked at herself—the perfect shape of her chin, the periwinkle color of her eyes, the golden gloss of her hair; all the features she had once coveted, now dwarfed by the ragged scars—she felt a chill run through her, though it was not cold. *I'm going to be their eldest sister. That's all.*

There was another knock. *The twins are here already?* She would have to compliment the servant woman on her efficiency. "Please come in," she said.

Instead, it was Ennis who popped his head in.

Rhea said, "Get out."

"I am here on official business, I swear it," Ennis said.

"What business?"

Ennis took it as an invitation to enter and close the door, though it was not. "Rhea, can I speak with you?"

"Bern Gentry, right?" Rhea said. "You will address me as Your Highness or I shall see you rot in the dungeons." Her heart broke just a little when Ennis flinched at her tone. It couldn't be helped. Coddling him could only lead to a disaster for them both.

Ennis stuck his bearded chin out. "Very well, Your Highness. There is someone here to see you. A man named Darkspell, do you know the name?"

"Yes," Rhea breathed. The streams had been full of news of the monsters Lord Griswold had unleashed at Castle Hill. Though they'd eventually been defeated by a much larger force led by Rhea's cousin, Annise Gäric, the monsters had killed hundreds of soldiers. It was rumored to be the royal potionmaster, Darkspell, who had brewed the concoction that created the monsters from average men. Her heart pounded. "I know of him."

"May I speak freely?" Ennis asked.

"If you must," Rhea replied tiredly, still processing the news. *What could Darkspell possibly expect by showing up on the enemy's doorstep?* There was only one answer.

"Turn him away without speaking to him," Ennis said, taking a step forward. "Or have him imprisoned. This man is dangerous."

"Like the Summoner?"

"Yes, exactly, he will only bring about destruct—"

"I think you mean victory. If not for the Summoner, who you advised me to ignore, we would already be destroyed and the northerners would be swarming across our kingdom like cockroaches. Now leave me, and don't return."

"Your Highness, please—"

"Go!"

Ennis shut his mouth, turned, and left. Rhea stood, smoothed out the wrinkles in her dress, and prepared herself for court. She would listen to what the talented potionmaster had to say. He was another weapon at her disposal, and she wouldn't waste him.

For a moment, the hole in her chest was filled once more.

Her hands stroked her belly, and then she slipped from the room.

Darkspell looked exactly as Rhea expected him to, a fact that pleased her greatly. He was a hunched, wizened man with feet that turned inward as he walked. He wore a navy robe that covered all but his feet and hands. His hair was a ring of black surrounding a bald, spotted head. As he approached, he looked up at her on the throne, one of his eyes falling open more than the other, which was locked in a permanent squint.

If I passed him on the street, I would think him a beggar, Rhea thought.

He stopped before her, continuing to meet her stare. "I am Darkspell," he said.

She didn't bother to reprimand him for his lack of formalities. There was no point—until this moment, he had served the kings of the north.

"How do I know you are who you claim?" Rhea asked. It was a necessary question, though she already believed he was who he said he was.

"A demonstration might be of help," he said. As he began to reach inside his robe, the Fury stepped forward, her hand on the hilt of her blade. Bandages were stuck to her damaged face, lines of blood weeping through. The other two new Furies were conducting other furia business throughout

Knight's End, but Rhea always required at least one to be present in court.

"It's fine," Rhea said. "Be on your guard, but allow him his demonstration." The Fury nodded and took a step back. Her hand, however, remained on her weapon, at the ready.

Darkspell extracted a small vial of amber liquid from a hidden pocket, pulled out the cork stopper, and sniffed. "Yes," he said. "This will do."

"What is it?" Rhea asked, curious. Was she about to see a monster created from a human?

"You shall see. May I use one of your guardsmen as a volunteer?"

Rhea knew she could easily request he perform his demonstration on a servant, but she wanted to see what it would do to a true soldier. "Will it harm him?"

"Not exactly," he said. "He will not die."

Not the most comforting thought. She scanned her line of guardsmen, all of whom stared straight ahead, ignoring her gaze. All except one of them. "Bern Gentry," she said. "Come forward." *Sometimes even those we love need to be punished.*

Ennis's jaw twitched as he moved out of line, approaching the potionmaster, but he didn't protest. "Your Highness," he said. "How may I serve?"

"Drink the elixir," she said.

"Just a drop will do," Darkspell said. "Stick out your tongue."

Ennis's eyes never left Rhea's as he obeyed. She hoped everyone else was so focused on the demonstration that they didn't notice his insolence.

Darkspell tipped the vial forward and a single drop oozed out, splashing onto Ennis's tongue. A spout of steam wafted up and he sucked in his breath. "It burns," he said.

"Yes," Darkspell said, sounding pleased.

"How long will it take to work—"

Ennis's eyes rolled back, his body shuddered, and he collapsed in a heap on the floor, hitting his head. Luckily he was wearing a helmet. As Rhea watched, fascinated, his joints locked up and his limbs stuck out as straight as wooden planks. His eyes rolled forward, unblinking, unmoving, staring at nothing. His jaw looked frozen, jutting out like a rock from a shoreline.

A shiver of fear rippled through Rhea. He looked...dead. "He's not..."

"No," Darkspell confirmed, guessing the end of her question. "This potion is called Paralyze. Useful in a pinch, particularly for disobedient servants or prisoners."

"How long will the effect last?"

"A day perhaps. Maybe less given the size of our subject."

"And if you'd given him more?"

"Two drops would've put him down for a fortnight," he said. "Three drops and the effect is permanent."

Wrath, Rhea thought. *If the old man's hand had flinched, Ennis might be paralyzed for life.* But it hadn't, the aging potionmaster's hand as steady as that of a man half his years.

"I hear you can create monsters," Rhea said, getting right to the point.

"Sadly, I cannot," Darkspell said, sounding like a man in mourning. "I've used up the raw materials and obtaining more would require a trip north, one with no guarantee of success."

Disappointment flooded through Rhea, followed swiftly by anger. "Then why have you wasted my time?" she snapped.

"I might be able to offer you another potion, one that could help you win the war with the east."

Rhea tamped down the flash of excitement she felt. "Why should I trust you? You've abandoned your loyalties to the north."

The man smiled, and Rhea noticed he was missing several teeth. "Queen Rhea Loren, I have no loyalties. All I wish is to be provided the resources to create new potions. If that helps you reach your goals, so be it."

Good enough for me, Rhea thought. "What potion do you offer?"

"A plague of sorts," he said cryptically.

Rhea frowned. It wasn't what she'd expected him to say. "The south already has a plague, and it's brought them nothing but misery. Plagues are unpredictable and hard to control."

"Not this one."

"How can you be so certain?"

"Because it will only kill Orians."

Rhea licked her lips. *Yes*, she thought. *This is just what I've been waiting for.* "What do you need to get started?"

"I have a sample I've been developing. It should be finished soon. Then I will need an Orian to test it on."

Rhea immediately thought of Gwendolyn Storm, the fatemarked Orian warrior in the dungeons. "I think I can arrange that," she said, her lips curling wickedly.

Eleven

The Western Kingdom, Knight's End
Gareth Ironclad

He finally had a way out that didn't involve suicide.

Then why am I so reluctant to take it? Gareth wondered. He knew the answer, though it was a blow to his pride to admit it: *Because I'm a damn coward.*

It was true—he was scared to face his brother, scared to face his people. He was, after all, a failed Shield. He'd failed his other brother, Guy, who'd been killed on his watch. But now, things had changed. Ennis Loren—who was decidedly *not* dead, like everyone thought—had offered him a chance to redeem himself. If he helped Gareth escape, maybe he could still protect the east, be the Shield he was born to be.

In the end, he'd consented to Ennis's proposition, on only one condition: Ennis had to help Gwendolyn Storm escape, too.

At first Ennis had balked—"What you ask is impossible!"—but when pressed, he'd relented. They would all flee the west together.

Only one problem: Ennis had disappeared since their conversation. Different guards kept appearing in his tower cell, changing shifts. *Come on come on come on...where are you?*

Gareth sat still, staring at the wall, *willing* Ennis to return. If the brightening light around the edge of his boarded-up window was any indication, dawn was fast approaching. Soon he would be hauled from this room and forced to travel east, where he would be ransomed for Beorn Stonesledge. It would be a mighty blow to his people, indeed, to lose their last skinmarked, their mightiest warrior to boot.

I will take my own life before I will allow that to happen, Gareth pledged.

The moment the thought took hold in his mind, the door opened and Rhea appeared. She wore a long white dress with sleeves to her wrists, and a smug expression.

"Where's my usual guardsman?" Gareth asked without greeting. "Bern Gentry."

Rhea blinked. "He's presently indisposed, not that it's any of your concern. Why do you ask?"

Gareth chewed his lip. What was that supposed to mean—indisposed? "He's not as ugly as the rest of the lot," Gareth said. "I was hoping he would accompany us to the east."

There was something behind Rhea's expression—curiosity perhaps—but she cloaked it well. "Us? *You* are going east. I am the queen, my place is here with my people, ruling, preparing."

Gareth was surprised, though perhaps he shouldn't have been. "Preparing for what?"

"For war, of course. Now I bid you Wrathspeed. When next we meet, may it be with your head on a spike." With that lovely farewell, she spun on her heel and departed. Three furia replaced her, marching in, their red cloaks swirling about them. One was clearly the leader, probably a member of the Three, standing in the center. Her face was scarred, recently it appeared, with a ragged W, similar to Rhea's.

"I see your master has branded you," Gareth said.

"Don't. Speak," the Fury said.

"Sorry, it's a habit of mine I've never been able to break."

The Fury glared at him, but he didn't look away. He knew she was all threats and no follow through, if only because he was too valuable to be harmed. "Take him," she said.

Her two furia—cold-faced girls who'd seen no more than twenty name days—each grabbed one of his elbows and roughly dragged him to the door.

He considered his options, which were few. *Throw myself down the steps and hope I suffer a mortal head injury? Wait until I'm outside and then "accidentally" get kicked in the face by a horse?* He searched his captors for weapons, but didn't see any, unless they were well hidden.

He chose another option: bide his time. A chance would come later, of that he was certain. And anyway, perhaps Ennis—*he's currently indisposed*—had a plan to rescue him in transit. For all he knew, Rhea's cousin had already freed Gwendolyn and was now plotting to attack his guards as they rode east.

81

So he did nothing. Nothing at all.

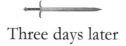

Three days later

I should have thrown myself down the steps when I had the chance, Gareth thought. He was tied to a horse, which was galloping at full tilt along the bumpy Western Road. A dozen furia surrounded him, each riding at the same pace, almost like a flock of birds in formation. They'd been riding like this for three days solid, the distance falling away in chunks beneath their horses' hooves. They stopped only to sleep and eat, and Gareth was never without at least six sets of eyes on him. When they halted, they stopped not in the rest villages along the road, but off to the side, hidden behind thick copses of vegetation or trees. Gareth had tried japes, insults and kindness, but none of the furia had spoken to him—they were too well-trained. *Or they've had their tongues cut out,* he thought. It was clearly one or the other.

He'd given up speaking after the second day.

He wasn't in denial, not anymore: Ennis wouldn't save him. Something had happened to him, that much was certain. Whatever plans he'd had, they'd failed.

I am on my own, Gareth thought.

He tried to calculate the distance in his head. Though he, Roan, and Gwen hadn't traveled the entirety of the Western Road, they'd traversed a good portion of it, probably more than half. It had taken them three days, but they'd been on foot and in no particular hurry. And he was almost certain he'd seen the lights of Restor—the largest village along the way—as they rode through the night on day two. Which meant…

A day, maybe two, before they reached the Bridge of Triumph.

"I'm thirsty," Roan said.

No one looked at him; no one spoke. It was as if he didn't exist.

"I have to piss."

Same response; or, rather, lack of response.

"I just pissed my britches."

At this point, he was mostly speaking for his own amusement.

"Have you ever heard the story of the furia who wore only green dresses?" he asked. Wait, was that a flinch on one of their faces? "Aye, she was shunned by the rest of her sisters for days and days and days, until eventually they killed her for disobeying their laws."

"What is the point of this story, prisoner?" the Fury said.

"She speaks!" Gareth said. "The point is that the woman they killed *was* wearing a red dress, while the others wore green. They were colorblind! Have you ever considered you might be colorblind?"

It was a stupid story, Roan knew, but on the spot it was the best he could come up with. And, apparently, it had worked, unsealing the Fury's lips at long last. "It's not the color of our garb, nor our hair, that matters," she said. "It is our uniformity, our solidity. None of us is above another. We stand together. We fight together. We serve Wrath together."

"Is that why only you bear a scar on your face?"

"As one of the Three, I am held to a higher standard."

"By whom? Wrath or Rhea?"

"Do not address the queen as a familiar."

"*Rhea* is a spoiled child angry at the world. *Rhea* is the one commanding, not Wrath."

"A righteous queen is the mouthpiece of Wrath."

Orion, this woman is frustrating. "You're lying to yourself. Queen Rhea Loren, First of Her Name, wants nothing but power. In her mind, she's already more powerful than your deity. And you know it."

After that, the Fury went silent. The drumbeat of hooves provided the only sound.

Hyro Lake was a dark pool of spilled ink under the cloudless night sky. Millions of stars were reflected in its surface, almost like fireflies captured in a glass jar. The lights of Portage, the eastern village nestled against the banks of the lake, twinkled in the distance. Somewhere to the north, Gareth could make out the flickering orange and red of a great fire. *What is that?* he wondered. *Has the entire world been cast aflame?*

He didn't have time to consider the anomaly, however, as they were approaching the Bridge of Triumph.

The bridge spanning the lake had been built in the year 400, when western forces drove the easterners back across the water, prematurely declaring victory in what would become the first year of the Hundred Years War. In honor of this "victory," the western king at the time, Fenrys Loren, had the Bridge of Triumph built to ensure he could maintain control of the east. The counterattack had been swift, as the held-back legions of eastern warriors, which included thousands of armored Orian soldiers, shattered the western forces, pushing them back across the bridge and into a full retreat. Rather than extending their line into western territory, however, the Ironclad-led army pulled back, destroying the bridge.

The bridge had remained shattered for over a hundred years. Until now. Five years ago, Gareth's father, King Oren Ironclad, had ordered the bridge to be rebuilt. Like the ill-will harbored against the north, he had long wanted revenge against the westerners for their mistreatment of Orians. The bridge would provide an easy means for a full-scale assault in which he hoped to end the East-West War once and for all.

Last Gareth had seen the bridge—about a year ago—it had been half-completed, though progress was slow due to daily attacks by western archers.

Now, Gareth marveled at the solid walled bridge that spanned the lake. Its stone walls and columns were plated with iron sheets, transported one at a time from Ironwood, where skilled Orians channeled the natural ore deposits provided by their ancient forest. His brother, Grian, who now stood as the King of the East, had been responsible for the project. *Perhaps he will be a great king*, Gareth thought. *If he can achieve something like this, perhaps he will one day lead us to victory.*

Perhaps this is why I failed to save Guy. If Grian was meant *to be king...*

He shook his head at his own foolishness. *Now I sound like Roan and Gwen*, he mused. Talk of fate and destiny was naught but an attempt to explain the randomness of bad luck and ill fortune. *No, I failed because I wasn't strong enough. I failed because I was too slow. But I shall not fail again, not on this night.*

The furia began funneling onto the bridge, forming a wall in front of him. Two remained at each side, ensuring he didn't attempt anything reckless. Anyway, he was tied firmly to his

85

mount, his hands secured behind his back. *I can barely move, much less throw myself over the side of the bridge.*

But that doesn't mean I can't do something, he thought. *The fools should've sealed my lips when they had the chance...*

He stared ahead, pretending his fear was naught but excitement, the tingling thrill most soldiers felt the night before a battle.

Near the center of the bridge, the furia stopped, their horses stamping and snorting.

Where? Gareth wondered, for he saw nothing but dark waters lapping against the stone columns, the twinkling lights of Portage, a path of darkness running from the bridge and across the border into the east...

And then they were there, dozens of riders in full metal, both human and Orian. In their midst, one held a flag, which snapped as a strong wind blew from the south. The flag bore the crossed iron swords of the east, the royal Ironclad sigil. A symbol of strength and you-shall-not-pass and—

I am the Shield, not the Sword, Gareth thought. *The sigil is no longer mine to claim.*

He saw him, riding up the field toward the front. His brother, Grian. The youngest of the triplets, but now a man grown, a born leader, decisive. Gareth immediately noticed the changes in his brother. His typically messy hair was combed neatly, poking out in clean strands from the helm he wore. His riding stance was more erect, prouder, not the brash, charge-into-battle position he used to prefer. Though his face was once identical to Gareth's, now it seemed like the face of a stranger, the jaw firmer, the eyes sharper and wiser, the eyebrows narrowed in determination.

He looked every bit like the king he was meant to be the moment Guy was killed in battle. *And yet I'm older, the next in line for the throne.* Gareth gritted his teeth and forced away the thought the moment it appeared. No matter what Roan said, he would never be king.

Immediately behind Grian was a figure nearly half again as large as the king, an imposing warrior Gareth had seen kill hundreds of lesser men in battle. A descendant of the mountain men of the north, Beorn Stonesledge stood over eight feet tall, his legs as thick as small trees, his arms battering rams. He rode a horse stolen in battle from the Phanecians, who bred the largest steeds in the Four Kingdoms, the only ones large enough to carry his weight.

He wore an iron pendant shaped like a fist around his neck. An exact replica of the skinmark he bore on his flesh, the source of his incredible strength and prowess in battle.

As awe-inspiring as Beorn was, Gareth had once called him a friend.

Now the man refused to look at him. Grian also avoided Gareth's stare, as if he didn't exist.

They're ashamed of me. They think I'm here to ruin them, to fail all over again.

I won't. I promise. He formed the words in his head, ready to scream them as soon as he was certain his brother would hear.

But Roan. But Gwen.

Though the thought of never seeing them again broke his heart into dagger-like shards, this was what he had to do. His chance at redemption. His final chance to be the Shield he became the moment he emerged from his mother's womb ahead of his brothers.

He opened his mouth, knowing the furia on each side would be too slow to stop him—*Do not ransom me, brother! Archers! Shoot me! Shoot me! Shoot me! For the east, I am the Shield!*— but his words never emerged, for his brother, King Grian Ironclad, spoke first.

His words were like knives. "It seems you have come a long way for nothing," he said, speaking directly to the Fury.

Gareth squinted, trying to make sense of his brother's words. Wait. Does he mean...

"There shall be no ransom for Gareth, not today, not tomorrow, not ever. The moment he failed to protect my brother, Guy Ironclad, heir to the eastern throne, the moment he *failed* as Shield...that was the moment he stopped being my brother. And when he fled from the east like the coward he is? He showed us his true colors, a pale shade of yellow."

A pit formed in Gareth's stomach. Bitterness coated his tongue. *I want to die*, he thought.

"You would dare go back on your agreement with Queen Loren?" the Fury asked, her words filled with venom.

"Oh yes, I dare," Grian said. "If you want to contend it, we can do battle here, on the bridge that once represented the strength of the west, now rebuilt by the strength of the east. Perhaps you will kill me. Perhaps you will kill Beorn. But you will not kill all of us. You and your sisters will die, and then you won't be able to deliver our message."

"What message?" A growled question.

"That we are coming for your queen. Knight's End will fall, and you and your false god will fade into history, lost to all but memory."

Gareth knew he could still say the words, still call for the archers to end him; now more than ever he was certain his brother would allow it, even command it. But instead he breathed in a ragged, quavering breath, refusing to cry. Refusing to give Grian the satisfaction.

A few grains of sand trickled through the hourglass of time, settling silently. In some ways Gareth hoped the Fury would attack, would force his brother's hand. But in a million other ways he wanted her to walk away.

Yes, I want to die, he admitted again to himself. *But not like this. Not for a brother who hates me. Not for a kingdom that shuns me.*

Without another word, the Fury wheeled her horse around and retreated across the bridge, heading westward. Her furia followed, occasionally flicking dark stares in Gareth's direction.

Now that he was useless as a prisoner, he knew Rhea would kill him.

Twelve

The Western Kingdom, Knight's End
Ennis Loren

Wrath-damn Darkspell and his Wrath-forsaken potion!

And Wrath-damn my stubborn cousin and her arrogant ways.

Three days earlier, Ennis had been rendered helpless by a single drop of Darkspell's potion. He'd stared, seeing all, but unable to do anything, not even to change the direction his eyes faced. His mind had been fully functioning, which was perhaps the cruelest truth of all, for he was a prisoner in his own paralyzed body, his thoughts spinning wildly like a tornado as he was carried to his quarters, set on his bed, and left to stare at the ceiling.

He had slept on and off, off and on, for what felt like days and days, though, according to the potionmaster, the effects should only last for a day.

Even that amount of time was too long, he had known.

Still, he'd clung to hope that he wouldn't be too late. As soon as his stiff legs and sore arms had become his own to command once more, he'd rushed from the guards' quarters, not even bothering to wait for the mechanical lift to carry him up, instead taking the steps around and around and around, his stiff muscles burning, screaming, his lungs heaving, throwing open the door to the tower cell, which was...

Empty.

Gareth was gone.

"No," he'd breathed, nearly breaking his neck as he'd flown down the steps three at a time, stumbling from the staircase and rushing to the palace gates, hoping against hope that they hadn't left for the Bridge of Triumph yet...

For the last two days, Ennis had been sleepwalking, going about his guard duties with numb disconnect. In the past, he'd tried reasoning with his cousin, tried appealing to the girl he knew she once was. And now he'd tried to commit treason, and had once more failed. He was but a man, while Rhea seemed almost supernatural in her ability to stay ahead of him, to forge a new path across the Four Kingdoms, riddled with corpses and bloodstains.

She didn't kill you, he reminded himself. It was that single truth that had sustained him thus far, but even that fact seemed to matter less and less with each of his failures.

Now, a stream had arrived from Restor, and Ennis could guess it was from the Fury, confirmation of Gareth being traded for Beorn Stonesledge. He watched as Rhea's eyes gleamed when she snatched the still-wet parchment from the messenger.

Her lips moved as she read.

Ennis dropped his head, wallowing in the muck of failure, as potent as sewer sludge.

Rhea screamed an obscenity and Ennis's head jerked up. In typical Rhea fashion, she was tearing the parchment to shreds, one ragged piece at a time.

No one spoke, though Ennis was desperate to know what the message said. Anything that sent Rhea into a rage like the one she was in now was worth knowing.

Finally, after the message lay in wet tatters at her feet, Rhea said, "Gareth will be rejoining us in Knight's End; Beorn Stonesledge will not."

Ennis's heart leapt. He didn't know how it was possible, but something had caused the ransom to fail. There was still hope. The moment Gareth returned to the city, he could lay plans to help him esc—

"I will execute Gareth Ironclad myself," Rhea growled.

"What?" The question burst from Ennis's lips before he could stop it.

Rhea's head turned slowly toward him, her eyes narrowing. He could see the recognition in her expression as soon as she realized who had spoken. "Guard?" she said. "Do you have something to say? Bern Gentry, correct? The subject of Darkspell's little experiment. Nice to see you're back in control of your own arms and legs." The scathing look she fired at him was almost a threat: *Cross me and you will pay dearly.*

"Yes. I mean no. I have nothing to say." Ennis hated that he had to play this game, that he no longer had the ear of his own queen, the cousin who he'd played with when she was just a little girl. Innocent. Unbroken. Full of vibrancy and life. She started to turn away. "Wait," he said. Her head swiveled back to him, her eyes flashing. "I was just wondering whether the prince might still have value. Perhaps one of our enemies might want him." It was a longshot, but—

"No," Rhea said. "If Gareth cannot be ransomed, he is of no use to me. He dies." Those two words ended the conversation before it ever really started.

And Ennis knew he was down to only one option:

He would rescue Gwendolyn Storm instead, then Rhea couldn't kill Gareth, as she would need him to force her brother, Roan, to do her will.

Thirteen

The Western Kingdom, Knight's End
Gwendolyn Storm

She waited like a predator in the dark, her eyes closed, her mouth, too. She controlled her breathing, slow and even, the rise and fall of her chest hidden beneath her breastplate. She hung from the wall by her neck, her feet dangling, her head slumped forward.

The façade hadn't been particularly difficult to create, though Gwen had had to be creative with raw materials. First, she'd torn seven strips of fabric from the trousers she wore beneath her armor. It had been difficult without removing her armor, but she'd managed, digging her fingernails between gaps in the plate, tearing with hands that were made for tasks requiring strength of grip. Why seven strips? No particular reason, except it felt right to do while imprisoned in Knight's

End, where the seventh heaven was the ultimate goal for its citizens.

Next she'd tied the strips together, and then created a noose, double thick all the way around and triple-tied where it would secure the back of her neck to the wall. The ill-maintained stone wall of her dungeon cell was ripe with holes and crevasses in which a rope could be tied. Still, she wanted to ensure the location she chose wouldn't crumble away under the weight of her armored body. The hole she'd finally discovered was the size of a fist, but still had enough of a stone bridge overtop that it would hold her weight. The only challenge was the height—it was nearly to the dank, dripping ceiling, a good jump for a mere mortal.

Luckily, Gwendolyn Storm was no mere mortal. Even for her kind, the Orians, she was an anomaly, her heromark adding height and distance to her leaps, power to her strikes, precision to her every move. She'd jumped, grabbing the thinnest of handholds with the tips of her fingers, clinging to it like an ore monkey. *Ha.* Gareth would've appreciate the reference. Quickly, she'd tied her noose with one hand, using her teeth to pull it taut.

Lastly, she'd stuck her head through and let gravity and her weight do the rest, pulling the double-layered cloth noose tight against her throat, which was protected by iron plate.

Now, she waited, as still as stone, letting a cool draft shift her slowly from side to side.

She heard a door creak open. Footsteps on stone. Heavy boots. Different than the sound of the earless dungeonmaster's typical approach, which was scraping and scuffling and less heavy by half.

She squinted, peering through the strands of silvery hair that had fallen over her face.

A shadow holding a too-bright lantern stopped in front of her cell, releasing a gasp the moment he saw her. "Oh Wrath," a male voice hissed. Frantically, he slung the lantern to the ground with a clank. Fumbled at the keys jingling in his hands. Tried one key, then another.

Gwendolyn took the opportunity to study him now that the lantern illuminated much of the newcomer's form. He was tall, with light hair poking out from a helmet. A thick blond beard covered much of his face. She couldn't make out the color of his eyes, but he wore hefty guardsman armor; the left breastplate was ornamented with the royal stallion of the west. Gwen could almost imagine the horse as it stood atop the cliff, its legs kicking as it reared in triumph. The sigil was a symbol of the original defeat of the Crimeans in the First Independence War.

Who is this man? she wondered. *And why is he here?*

Finally, the lock clicked as the man—*my prey*, she reminded herself—found the correct key. Had she truly been hanging herself, she would've died long before this fool got the door open. He shoved the door inward, letting it clang against the inside of the bars.

Wait.

He scampered through, reaching for her feet.

Wait.

She felt her body rise, the pressure on the armor around her throat releasing.

Wait.

She'd intentionally made the loop of the noose too large by half, making it easier to pull it over her head. When he lifted her further, she ducked her head and the makeshift rope fell away perfectly.

Wait.

He began to lower her to the ground, slowly, delicately, as if afraid she would shatter into a thousand pieces if he moved too swiftly.

Now.

Gwen snapped her feet over his head, locking them together as tightly as an ore panther's jaws. He released a muffled cry just before she somersaulted backwards, springing off her hands and launching him crashing into the wall.

And then she was on him, slipping his own sword from its sheath and pressing the tip into his throat. *I should kill him*, she thought, but for some reason she paused.

After all, he'd tried to save her from hanging herself.

"Why did you come here?" she hissed instead. For days and days, she'd seen only the dungeonmaster, heard nothing but his scuffling footsteps, ragged cough, and grunts, and the whimpers of the other prisoners.

Though his eyes were wide as he scanned her face, she sensed no fear in them. *This man is not afraid of death.* The realization surprised her—it's not what she expected from a mere castle guardsman. "To rescue you," he said matter-of-factly.

For just a moment, she released the pressure of the blade against his throat. He might've sensed it, might've taken advantage of the opportunity to counterattack, but instead he only slumped back, rubbing his neck. "Nice trick," he said.

"Why would you rescue me?"

"Because I made a promise."

"To whom?"

"Gareth Ironclad."

She jammed the blade back against his flesh. The edge pierced his skin, drawing a single drop of blood. "You lie."

"I wouldn't expect you to believe me, but it's true. I spoke to him, offered to free him. His only condition was that I release you at the same time."

Some instinct made her think she should believe him. Why would he lie? To save his own skin, possibly, but that wouldn't explain why he was here in the first place. What he was saying would.

"Where is Gareth?"

The man shook his head and there was a sadness in the gesture, a resignation.

"Tell me."

He told her what he knew, how Gareth had been sent to be ransomed, how something had gone wrong and that he was being brought back to Knight's End. How Rhea had vowed to kill him now that he had no value to her.

"If I rescue you, then Rhea cannot kill Gareth. She'll need him as leverage over Roan."

It all made sense, except for the fact that this man was helping them. "Who are you really?" she asked.

"I'm Ennis Loren," he said. Before she could laugh, he explained everything—his faked death, his false identity, the appointment as a guardsman.

Gwen hid her surprise. From her experiences with Rhea Loren, she wasn't the type to spare the life of someone who'd crossed her. This man, her cousin, must mean a great deal to her. Still, even if Ennis's heart was pure, he was still looking out for the best interests of the west, not the east. "I'm leaving," she said. "You're staying."

He nodded, as if he'd been expecting her to say exactly that. "I don't blame you. But if I leave with you, we may be able to help Gareth escape, too."

She chewed on that. Yes, her mark made her ideal for just such a rescue operation, but it *would* be easier with an inside man. "You weren't seen coming here?"

He shook his head. "I took the dungeonmaster from behind."

"You killed him?"

Another headshake. "Paralyzed him using a potion concocted by Darkspell. I stole it from his chambers."

She frowned, trying to recall where she'd heard that name before, but he cut her off. "It's a long story. I'll tell it to you once we're away from here. Rhea could visit at any moment. You're her most valuable prisoner now, or at least that's what she thinks."

Gwen's mind ticked over the facts, weighing the risks and rewards. If she locked him up and left, she could return to the east and rejoin her people. Gareth would be safe, for a time, as leverage over Roan. *But can I really abandon him when there might be a way to save him now?* If what this man—Ennis Loren—had said was true, then Gareth had attempted to rescue her *before* himself.

She growled her frustration. Each option carried an equal number of risks, and none of them pleasant. "Lead the way, Loren," she said. "But we better find a certain paralyzed dungeonmaster on the way out."

Gwen might have kicked the dungeonmaster in the ribs as they passed his stiff body. It also might have been unjustified, considering he'd been the one to feed her every day.

But it had felt so good.

Afterwards, they dragged him into her cell and locked the door. Gwen left her makeshift noose on his chest. With any luck, Rhea would believe Gwen had escaped completely on her own, fooling the master. The only problem was the paralyzing potion Ennis had used to knock him out. One way or another, however, the clues would lead to Darkspell, not to him. Hopefully by the time Rhea learned the truth, the three of them would be long gone.

Now, Ennis guided her away from the main stairs to a shadowy side exit. She wasn't too concerned that he would spin around and try to kill her; after all, she still had his sword. Plus, he hadn't lied about the dungeonmaster. Then again, the best liars wove some truth into their deceptions. Thus, Gwen remained alert, prepared to shove Ennis's blade through his spine if he led her astray.

The lantern cast an orange halo as they ascended, the light bouncing with each step. At the top was a wooden trapdoor.

"Where does it lead?" Gwen asked in a hushed voice.

"Storeroom. Food is brought down for the prisoners."

"I wouldn't call it food, exactly."

Ennis had no response to that. He raised a hand in the air, and she understood his meaning: *Wait here.*

Though she was reluctant to leave his side, she had no other option. If he raised the alarm, she could always fight her way through, or flee back down the steps and find an alternate escape route.

He pushed open the trapdoor, climbing out.

Darkness and silence greeted him.

He poked his head back inside the stairwell and said, "Come on."

Through a small room they went, the shelves on either side full of sacks and baskets of dry foods. Gwen ignored the ache in her stomach.

Ennis had timed it well—which Gwen was certain was no coincidence. The kitchen was empty of staff, the stone oven unlit, the dishes from the day's final meal washed and set out to dry. Ennis blew out his lantern and set it on a table.

From there they exited through a door that led outside, where it was dark. The clouds were allies, white ships sailing across an ocean of night, obliterating the light from the moons and stars. Lush foliage—elm and spruce trees, holly bushes, and square-cut hedges—provided excellent cover from any lookouts who might be watching from the castle walls. Pink bougainvillea crept up the sides of the squat stone building that housed the kitchens, storerooms, and, apparently, the dungeons.

Ennis reached inside a thick bush. Gwen watched him curiously, until he retrieved a long, white, hooded purity dress, which he handed to her. "Put this on."

If she'd had any doubt about his intentions before, they were chased away by this final part of his planning. Still, she placed the sword on the ground, standing on the broad side with both feet, and then rapidly pulled the dress over her head, tucking her silver hair beneath the hood. It didn't fit particularly well; then again, based on the other women she'd seen wearing them throughout the city, she didn't think it was meant to hug her form. No, it was meant to cover, a thought that made her teeth grind together.

She picked up the sword. "I'm keeping this," she said, just in case there was any doubt.

Ennis didn't argue. "Hide it under the dress."

She did, and he said, "You'll have to wait in the gardens until morning, when they reopen the castle gates. Unless, of course, you can scale a sheer stone wall without a rope." He chuckled softly.

Gwen did not. "I'll take the wall," she said. "I don't want to spend another moment inside this place. Not tonight."

He gawked at her. "They say the forest dwellers of the east are unusual, but I'd never met one until you."

"And?"

"You *are* unusual, but not so different as I expected."

"Right. Anyway…"

"If you truly can scale the wall by hand, return to the gardens on the morrow, when the moons approach each other in the night sky. I will be here, waiting."

She nodded. "When will Gareth return to Knight's End?"

"We received a stream from Restor today. The way the furia ride, he could arrive as early as tomorrow afternoon. If not, the following morning."

Gwen didn't know what else to say, except, "Thank you. And I'm sorry I attacked you."

"Like I said, it was a good trick. You had me fooled. And you're welcome, but I'm not doing this for you, nor Gareth. I only want peace and prosperity for the west. Unlike my young, misguided cousin, I'm willing to consider an alliance with the east to achieve that. Gareth is an opportunity I refuse to waste."

"Fair enough. Until we meet again."

With a burst of leaves, Gwen slipped through the bushes.

Fourteen
The Hinterlands
Lisbeth Lorne

Lisbeth awoke to a rough hand on her neck. Instinctively, she sucked in a breath before the hand began to squeeze.

Her attacker's soul was shadowy, but the white, pulsing soul of Crone appeared behind as she leaped atop his back, releasing a guttural scream. The male was strong—likely one of the warriors—and easily bucked the old female away, sending her crashing into the snow-packed walls of her dwelling.

He squeezed Lisbeth's throat harder.

No, she thought. At the same moment, she saw his soul clarify, illuminated by the light that swarmed from the glowing eye on her forehead, probing into him, feeling around in his skull, gripping his soul as tightly as he squeezed her throat.

It was Zur, the warrior who'd twice threatened her.

His grip lost all strength and he howled, falling back.

The young girl wearing the white dress waded into the water. Despite the snow and ice covering the land around the lake, the water flowed freely. Lisbeth could feel it—it was strangely warm—could feel the fluttering fear as the girl's heart beat too rapidly in her chest. She turned and looked back, tears sparkling in her wide brown eyes. "Father?" she said.

A question in that single word; a question without an answer.

The male Garzi warrior—her father, Zur—said, "Be free, my star, and then he turned his back on her, his only child.

The girl didn't see the tears dripping from his eyes, freezing on his cheeks in silvery lines. She didn't see the way his breath choked him, nor how he stumbled over feet that had always been sure in the past, now devoid of all strength and coordination.

No, she didn't see any of that, because his back was to her and she'd already turned around to face the water, crying, pushing off with both feet and letting the current surround her.

"No!" Lisbeth screamed, clawing at her own face, as if she could drag the images from her skull the way she'd forced them from his.

"Girl should hush," Crone said, cradling Lisbeth's head in the crook of her arm. The ancient woman winced as she spoke, and she was carrying her other arm strangely—too tight against her ribs. *She's injured,* Lisbeth thought, the realization chasing away the images she'd seen in Zur's head.

Zur! she remembered. The warrior was on the ground, his boots scuffing trenches in the snow as he writhed and twisted, clutching his head. Blood flowed freely from his nose, his ears, his mouth.

"What have I done?" she whispered.

"Girl does nothing Zur would not do," Crone said. When the woman tried to move, she hissed in pain, clutching her shoulder.

Lisbeth barely noticed, however, her eyes focused on Zur, who had finally stopped squirming, his eyes closed, his body unnaturally still. *Oh sun, oh moon, oh stars...* "Is he...dead?" she asked. To answer her own question, she reached forward to touch his chest, to feel for a heartbeat...

Zur jolted up with such abruptness Lisbeth fell backward, releasing a yelp of surprise. His eyes were wide, darting around, as if searching for something but seeing nothing, unable to focus. He scratched at his head, tearing at the strands of black hair, ripping them out. He shouted something in Garzi, spit flying from his lips: "Gash nom zuf dari!" He repeated the same phrase again and again and again, before collapsing from exhaustion, his chest rising and falling in huge waves.

Lisbeth didn't need Crone to translate his words: *Girl steal soul. Girl steal soul. Girl steal...*

Lisbeth ran, into a storm-filled night, afraid of herself, afraid of what she'd done to the warrior Zur, afraid of what she'd seen in his head, that girl in the water.

At any moment she expected strong hands to grab her, to go for her throat—she didn't fear them, but what *she* might *do* to them—but none appeared, ghostly hands of snow her only companion as she raced onwards, past snow structures nearly invisible in the storm.

Her plan was to get as far away from the Garzi city as she could, as fast as she could. It was what they wanted. She would miss Crone, her first and only real friend and ally, but that couldn't be helped.

An enormous shadow rose up on her right, and Lisbeth skidded to a stop, panting, icy nettles pelting her face, melting on her now-warm skin. She remembered what Crone had called this soulless place: Hall of War.

And yet, despite the emptiness she felt as she looked upon it, despite the shadows that seemed to surround its icy flanks, which rose into the sky like a snow-covered mountain, she could see the pulses of color within, like hundreds of beating hearts.

Souls, she knew.

The urge was still there to flee this place, to leave forever and never return, but she also felt drawn to the Hall of War, to the souls within, which were...sleeping? *No. Not sleeping, but not awake either. Something else. Something in between, like the place between living and dying, a void filled with ribbons of light.*

A place all too familiar to Lisbeth.

She could feel their wills pressing against the walls, their resistance to leave this world.

She walked toward the Hall, its open entrance the dark yawn of a slumbering beast. She stepped inside, feeling as if she was being swallowed whole.

The inside, however, didn't feel soulless or empty or dark. Though she was aware that, in the stormy night, there was no outward light in this place, light was all she could see. Pulsing forms of souls—crimson, lilac, jade...turquoise, amber, sapphire.

The sight took her breath away, not only because of the kaleidoscope of colors beating in perfect sync with each other, like separate parts of the same heart, but because she could hear them speaking to her in the deepest recesses of her mind.

The time has come, they said, as one. *The north will soon fall.*

"Who are you?" she asked aloud, for they did not speak Garzi, and their mastery of the common language was flawless.

Silence. Silence. And then: *We are those who sleep, warriors from another age, another land. The soulmarked seeks what we offer.*

It wasn't the clearest of answers, and yet Lisbeth felt the truth of their words thrumming through her. She felt the honor in their souls, the devotion to a cause that was a part of them, each one of them, as well as the collective whole. "And what do you offer?"

Their response was a single word: *War.*

Fifteen
The Northern Kingdom, Castle Hill
Annise Gäric

The pact was an ancient agreement between anyone residing south of Frozen Lake and the peoples of the Hinterlands. According to what Archer had been told growing up, the pact had been signed thousands of years ago, well before the Crimean explorers ever set foot on the lands now known as the Four Kingdoms.

The pact was a promise: No one in the Hinterlands shall travel south, and no one south shall travel north. In essence, don't cross the line.

Men had died for breaking the pact, including one of Annise's most famous relatives, Heinrich Gäric, the great explorer who'd led the voyage that discovered these lands in the first place. The story had been passed down from generation to generation by his son, Tomas, who was the first Gäric to declare independence from the Crimeans.

Tomas had seen his father die at the hands of the people who lived north—the Garzi they were called. Riding vicious beasts, they claimed all lands north of Frozen Lake.

Exactly where Annise's map indicated she would find the Sleeping Knights.

The night was still and silent, but Annise couldn't sleep, much weighing on her mind. Would she truly lead the hand-picked group into the Hinterlands, breaking the pact and sealing their dooms? Archer and Sir Dietrich and Sir Jonius and Sir Metz. Good men who had fought and miraculously survived by her side. Did she have any other choice? *I could go alone*, she thought. *The risk would be all mine to bear.*

She knew they wouldn't let her, and even if she snuck away, they would follow.

And anyway, the north was ripe for the taking, and she knew their enemies would arrive to pluck it from the branch soon enough. She had no way to stop them. The legendary Sleeping Knights were a chance. A hope.

We will risk it. I will risk it.

The decision made, she knew sleep would continue to elude her, so finally—finally—she unraveled the scrolls Tarin had left for her before he slipped away. *His stories*, Annise thought. *The parts of his life I know little to nothing about.*

And finally she was strong enough to read them.

Tarin's stories had made her laugh, cry, want to break things, and urged her to race off into the night to find him, to hold him, to tell him she was sorry for not understanding the depths of his fears, his sorrows, his doubts.

In the name of war, he had done terrible things. Things he hadn't even wanted to do, but which he'd *enjoyed*—or at least the monster living inside him had enjoyed. He'd killed without mercy. He'd shattered foes by the hundreds, singlehandedly winning several crucial battles for the north. He remembered all.

At times, he hated himself.

At times, he wanted to die.

He feared being close to anyone, feared to love, to desire, for he knew, in the end he would destroy anyone and everyone around him.

And yet, he'd tried for Annise. He loved her so much he had risked her life, just something else he regretted, hated himself for. He called it his "greatest act of selfishness," a phrase that made it hard for Annise to swallow. *How could what we have be anything but selfless?*

When she was finished reading, Annise rolled the parchment into a single, thick scroll, tied a bit of twine around it, and hid it in a box under blankets and pillows.

When she closed the lid, she knew, Tarin was gone.

Now, finally, she could sleep.

Her hands traced the taut lines of his muscled arms; had they been forged of iron they would not be any stronger. His back, shoulders, and chest might've been chiseled by a master stone carver. His face, his jaw, speckled with half a day of stubble, were as strong as the rest of him. And they were *hers*—they were all hers.

Oh Tarin.

She arched into him, thinking this moment could slide into eternity—wishing it would. His hands were gentle but greedy, rolling over her as they melted into each other. As they became one.

And the things he whispered into her ear, his gravelly tone full of desperation and longing...

I prefer your eyes to the stars, your tongue to the sweetest wine, your lips to breathing...

...they left her breathless and alive and trembling with desire.

And when he said her name—*Annise*—like a word carried on a warm wind...

All she could do was gasp and—

She did—gasp, that is—shooting up in bed, her heart pounding, her sleep-tangled hair streaking her vision, her lungs heaving.

Bloody frozen hell below, she thought. *Did I really just have a sex dream?*

For a second she felt rather foolish, but then, remembering how it had been with Tarin in real life, how good it had been, how right, she felt less foolish. She sank back into her pillows, wishing she could close her eyes and have that dream again and again and forget about the madness of today's venture into the Hinterlands and her shattered kingdom and just, for once, perhaps she could be truly happy.

All that was chased away when the sun rose a moment later, blades of orange light slashing through her window. The sky immediately above Castle Hill was clear and blue and free of snow. However, to the east she saw the towers of thick gray clouds building, crossing toward her like the great warships of her enemies.

With an exhausted groan, she dragged herself out of bed. She could delay the fate of the kingdom no longer.

"You understand the risks?" Annise asked.

She'd told them everything Arch had told her about the pact, with him correcting or filling in blanks where necessary. Despite that, each of her party of five nodded in turn, wearing grave expressions.

"I will not command you to accompany me into the Hinterlands, especially given this new information. I will go alone, if necessary. It is a great risk, but I believe we have no other option, not if we want our great kingdom to survive the coming storm. Regardless of whether the Sleeping Knights are naught but a legend, I need to know the truth. We must seek out allies in every nook and corner we can."

Aunt Zelda was there to see them off. She said, "Bring our knights home." She spoke around a thick sour roll she was chewing.

Annise nodded. "In my absence, I hereby grant you, Lady Zelda Gäric, all the powers, authority and determination of law that I hold as Queen of the North."

Zelda took another bite of her roll, and then said, "The Dread King of the North is rolling over in his grave."

Annise couldn't help the laugh that slipped out. After all, if she couldn't laugh under the gravest of circumstances, what was the point of any of this?

She turned to Sir Metz. She had one more order of business before they left. "Sir Metz," she said.

"Your Highness?" He stood a little straighter, his armor gleaming in the rare northern sunlight.

"You will not accompany us north."

He stared at her, and though he controlled his expression, she could see the disappointment flashing in his eyes. "Have I done something wrong?" he asked.

"No," she said quickly. That was the last thing she wanted him to think, but she needed to make this very clear, or else the knight would figure out a way to interpret her response in such a way that he could follow them. "I trust your honor above all others, even my own. I need you to continue the soldier training program started by Sir Dietrich. I can think of no other who would better serve in this regard. You will remain in Castle Hill, continuing to recruit soldiers and train them to the highest standards. You will take further commands from Lady Zelda."

His disappointment morphed to pride. "I will do this thing."

"You will not follow us into the Hinterlands. That is a command. Do you understand?"

"Yes, Your Highness," he said.

A twinge of regret spiked inside Annise, surprising her. She would miss having this loyal man. Not only was he a firstclass swordsman, but she now considered him a friend, though he might not think the same.

May we meet again, she thought, turning away from two people she cared for greatly. She aimed her face to the north, to the ice-sheathed surface of Frozen Lake and the rolling snowdunes of the Hinterlands beyond.

The first winter storm of the season hit before the sun reached its peak.

Sixteen

The Northern Kingdom, Darrin
Tarin Sheary

The blade-like towers of the castle seemed poised to fall, slashing Darrin, and those who remained in the city, to ribbons.

The torn flesh covering Tarin's knuckles continued to weep blood, dripping in the snow, which was packed down hard and alive with prints from horses' hooves.

Tarin raised his eyes to the sky, squinting at the brightness of the thin white clouds. *What now?* he thought.

Fay said, "The horses are gone."

It was as Tarin feared—the lord of the castle, Lord Darrin, had fled the city, abandoning it to the east. Any hope of mustering a force large enough to defend the city had left with him.

Tarin turned when he heard footsteps approaching from behind. The soldiers from the barracks, now all fully dressed and in somewhat rumpled uniforms, stopped in a ragged line, Captain Morris at their head. "You're leaving us, too, aren't you?" he said. His round cheeks were ruddy from the cold.

"Aye," Tarin said. "I'm leaving you." He walked past them without looking back.

Fay caught up to him just as he passed the barracks on the way out of the city.

"Coward," she muttered.

He didn't stop, couldn't stop. "How do you figure?" he said as he lengthened his strides. "Lord Darrin is a coward. Captain Morris and his so-called soldiers are cowards. I am merely being realistic. This city is forfeit, along with what's left of its defenses."

"Excuses," Fay said, stopping.

Tarin whirled around. "Just because we're old acquaintances doesn't mean that you know me," he said. "So stop pretending like you do."

"Fair enough," Fay said. "You best be on your way. It's a long march to the next city, which I'm certain will be more hospitable than Darrin. I'm certain you will find plenty of walls to crush your fists against there."

He stared at her. "What will you do?"

"Stay here. Stand against the east."

"That's suicide. Morris and the others are planning to surrender."

"Then I shall fight alone."

116

"You're not even a soldier," Tarin said, though he immediately regretted the words. Annise hadn't been a soldier either, and yet she was a warrior all the same, as formidable in battle as a hundred Captain Morrises. Nay, a thousand.

"The Dread King didn't *allow* women in his army, remember? Though clearly he favored fools based on present company."

I deserve that, Tarin thought. "You can fight?"

"Don't sound so surprised. You think someone with no experience in combat can design and forge the weaponry I do?"

Tarin took a guess. "Your father taught you to fight?"

Fay blew out a disgusted breath. "Men of the north are so narrowminded. My father left my mother and I before I could walk. My *mother* taught me. She was once a she-knight, one of less than a dozen in the last two centuries."

Tarin couldn't hide his surprise. Nor his shame. He *was* narrowminded, though he didn't mean to be. He just wasn't used to seeing women in battle. And he'd never seen a she-knight in his life, though he'd heard of them. Supposedly there was one in Blackstone, but she'd likely died in the assault on Knight's End.

"I'm sorry. I didn't know."

"You never asked." When he opened his mouth to respond, she held up a hand to stop him. "I know. I get it. When I first met you, you were still figuring out who *you* were. There wasn't exactly time to get to know me or Bart. But now you know. I *can* fight. I *can* forge weapons for the men here. I *can* try to convince them not to surrender."

"Then you will die," Tarin said.

117

"Perhaps. Perhaps not. But I will die defending this kingdom, as Annise and her aunt are doing. If the men won't protect these lands, the women will."

Tarin closed his eyes. One way or another, he had to *do* something. He couldn't stop moving, not for one minute longer. To stop was to think, to dwell, to remember. Action was the only way to silence the voice, to blur the memories. Whatever path he chose, he would throw himself into it with the entirety of his being—it was the only way he knew how to live inside his own skin.

"I'll stay. I'll help you," he said.

As Fay's lips curled into a broad grin, he wondered whether he'd just made the biggest mistake of his life.

Grudgingly, Captain Morris and his men had scoured the city, locating all remaining soldiers—most of whom were still drunk from the night before—and gathering them in the castle courtyard. Though their training and abilities remained in doubt, Tarin was pleased to find more than two hundred men still occupied the city.

The leftovers, he reminded himself. Still, leftovers could satisfy if heated and salted and stirred. Several of the men began arguing, shoving each other and uttering curses about mothers. *Maybe not* these *leftovers*, Tarin thought.

Captain Morris approached. "That's as many as we could find. There might be another dozen or so hiding, but they'll poke their heads out of the snow eventually."

"Good. Thank you," Tarin said, scanning the men for Fay's familiar slender form. He spotted her as she emerged from a dark-stoned building with iron bars over the windows. He frowned. Why was she in the prison? Realization set in when he saw four men appear behind her, their arms and legs shackled together.

Fay grinned and waved.

Tarin pinched the skin between his eyes, where a headache had begun to throb. *Criminals and castaways*, he thought. He released the skin, which continued to ache. *Doesn't matter. Keep moving, keep doing. That's all I have left.*

Fay brought the shackled men past the soldiers, many of whom jeered and shouted insults at them. "Four more recruits," she said when she reached Tarin.

Tarin eyed them each in turn. Two stared at their feet. One stared at the sky, like he hadn't seen it in a long time. And the fourth met Tarin's eyes with a steel gaze, nodding once in his direction.

"Do you want to know their crimes?" Fay asked.

"No," Tarin said. "We have all done things we regret, but today is a new beginning."

The two who'd been staring at their feet looked up through tendrils of long, dirty hair. The one staring at the sky continued to stare. And the fourth blinked, as if surprised.

Tarin accepted a key from Fay and unshackled them one at a time. Three of them, rubbing their ankles and wrists, melted into the crowd, which parted in the middle. Not to accept them, but to avoid them, or so it seemed.

The fourth, the man with the steel eyes, didn't move, didn't massage his raw skin. He wasn't young, but not old either, and his expression didn't contain the same defeat nor brokenness that most prisoners, in Tarin's experience, had.

"Do you not remember me?" he asked.

Tarin frowned. He'd spent many years at Darrin, but this man didn't strike him as someone he knew. His jet-black hair hung in long ringlets to his shoulders, his smudged face partially obscured by a patchy beard…

It hit him. Behind the changes prison had wrought on him was a man Tarin should've recognized immediately.

"Sir Jonathan?"

"In the flesh," the man said. And then he punched Tarin in the chest as hard as he could.

A dull clang rang out, silencing the murmur of conversation amongst the soldiers. Sir Jonathan's hand snapped back and he sucked on his knuckles, which were already starting to bruise from punching Tarin's armor. He laughed, pulling in a sharp breath at the pain. "That's for being a brutish bastard," the knight said. *Is he still a knight?* Tarin wondered. Depending on the severity of his crimes, Lord Darrin may have stripped him of his knighthood.

"Good to see you, too," Tarin said.

"We'll catch up later," Jonathan promised, finally stepping away and into the mob of soldiers.

Tarin shook his head. Darrin was full of surprises, and he was glad one of them had finally been positive. Sir Jonathan *was* a mighty warrior, one he'd known for all five of the years he'd spent in Darrin. *I will promote him first to a leadership position. Captain Morris will gladly be replaced.*

What am I talking about? Tarin had never been a commander before, always refusing offered promotions, content to keep his head down, follow orders, march wherever he was told to march, fight whomever he was told to fight…

But if not me, then who? Captain Morris? The thought almost made him laugh—gallows humor and all that. If he didn't lead, the city was doomed. Well, *more* doomed than it already was. No, Fay was right; she might not have said it, but this was his penance, his way to protect the north. And by protecting the north, he was protecting Annise in the only way he knew how.

Tarin turned to face the crowd, not certain of exactly what he would say. "As most of you know, the east has rallied six battalions to take this city."

"Only six?" someone in the crowd japed. Pockets of laughter.

"Aye, and we should consider ourselves fortunate. I was here when the full might of the east—half a hundred battalions—assaulted the Razor, when the cliffs ran red with the blood of my comrades and enemies alike, when pain was but a reminder that we weren't dead, when corpses were piled to—"

"Tarin," Fay hissed. He glanced at her. The barest shake of her head.

He took a deep breath. Right. Scaring these men was no way to convince them to fight for him. No, he needed to *inspire* them. How had his previous leaders convinced him to fight? *They hadn't needed to*, was the obvious answer. But these men were not him, and the next words he chose could make all the difference.

"The past is the past," he said, changing tact, waving it away with one of his monstrous hands. "All we have is the present and the future. The great city of Darrin is being threatened. I plan to defend it."

"Who are you again?" someone shouted.

"The Armored Knight, you dolt," another voice cried in response.

Tarin realized none of these men had ever seen his face, the truth of who—what—he was. All they knew was his armor, which had become a symbol of him as a warrior, a stalwart soldier responsible for the deaths of hundreds of enemies.

I am not that man anymore, not if I want to truly help my queen. I have to be more. *I cannot hide from myself any longer.*

It was a risk, but at this point he had little to lose.

He reached up with both hands, gripping the iron base of the helmet Fay had forged all those years ago, when he was just a scared little boy in a monster's body.

And he removed his helmet.

Muttering curses and whispering words like demon, sorcery, and witchcraft, half the men left. Maybe more. Tarin hadn't exactly had time to conduct a rollcall.

Half of nothing is still nothing, Tarin thought. *Dammit, I must stop thinking like that or I might as well leave with them.* Half of them had *stayed,* even after seeing the true face of the man who planned to lead them into battle. Fay nodded at him encouragingly.

"I am a man just like the rest of you," he said. He remembered how Annise had given her victory speech atop the wall at Castle Hill, how she'd met each soldier's eyes individually. He tried to do the same, scanning the crowd. Truth, that was all he had left. "I almost died as a boy. The act that saved my life changed me. That is a truth I cannot deny, cannot change, even if I wanted to.

"You all have the same choice as the men who left. Stay or go. When the Dread King ruled, you did not have that choice.

122

To desert meant you'd be hunted down and executed. Now his daughter rules, as your queen, and she is just as strong, but fair too. You can go where you will go, be with your families, find a place to hide…" He let the idea float for a moment, before continuing. "Or…you can stand and you can fight. You can reject the notion that the north can be conquered. You can shout at the top of your lungs that the north, even in its weakest state, is the shield that can be cracked but never broken. You can laugh in the face of six battalions and remember that this is *our* territory and the snow and ice and storms of winter are when we are at our strongest. We are the rock that cannot be moved, the stream that cannot be dammed, the sword that cannot be parried." Tarin's fists were clenched at his sides, his chin jutted out, his dark eyes gleaming with fire and determination. He felt…good, right, powerful, almost like he was rising off the ground. "What say you?" he bellowed.

Silence. Shuffling feet. Shifting eyes, most refusing to meet his.

And then: "Do we get breakfast?"

Tarin gaped at the man who'd spoken, none other than the old geezer from the barracks, the one with the infernal cough.

"Aye," another man said. "If there's hot food involved, count me in."

A chorus of agreement rippled through the group of men who remained. *Food*, Tarin thought, like it was a magical word. *I'll have to remember that.* "Yes," he said. "There will be food. We just have to find it first."

The men cheered and slapped each other's backs.

As it turned out, finding food wasn't a major challenge, at least not in the short term. In Lord Darrin's haste to flee the city, he'd left much of the castle's enormous store of provisions behind. There were lumpy sacks of oats, flour, and beans. There were baskets of potatoes growing fresh green shoots. There was a larder hanging with salted meats—antelope and deer and even several sides of mamoothen rump.

And there was ale—*frozen hell*, Tarin thought, *there's enough ale to keep the soldiers inebriated for the entire winter.*

His first order as Lord Commander—the men had unanimously agreed on the position being his—was to command Sir Jonathan to guard the mead. His next order was for every man to take a bath before breakfast; he could barely breathe because of the stale stink in the air.

The men dove into the task with remarkable energy, almost as if they'd been starved for something to do, but Tarin knew they were just starving for breakfast. In any case, they gathered large tin tubs, filled them with armfuls of snow, and then built fires beneath them to melt the snow. Some of them were so keen to get to breakfast that they didn't even wait for the water to heat, screaming as they scrubbed themselves in the icy water.

The entire scene might've been amusing if Tarin wasn't so busy thinking about what to do *after* breakfast. While Tarin was considering his plans, Fay snagged several of the first soldiers out of the tubs and conscripted them to organize the castle storerooms and prepare food. At first they'd balked at her barked command—"Don't take no orders from a woman!"— but when Tarin shot a glare in their direction they hopped right to it.

Once a vat of porridge was well on its way to being ready to eat, Fay plopped down next to where Tarin sat on his helmet. "You did good," she said.

Tarin laughed, thinking he hadn't done anything so far, but then said, "You too."

She echoed his laughter, and he wondered whether she felt the same way he did: that this was all some strange dream, the kind you get after eating something that had gone off.

"You know," she said, "we need to do something about your armor."

This was one of his least favorite topics of conversation, and yet he knew she was right. "Aye, it's snug around my hips and teats," he japed.

"More like everywhere," she said. "How does a man as large as you manage to grow even larger?"

He was tempted to speak openly to her, but the words stuck in his throat. Jokes were easier. "By eating enough for three men every chance I get." In truth, Tarin probably ate *less* than most of the skinny soldiers who were putting away two or three bowls of porridge and still going back for more.

No, he thought. *The violence feeds me, the bloodlust, the screams of those who fall beneath my Morningstar…*

Yes, the voice inside him answered. *And I grow hungry again.*

Tarin bit down hard on his lip, until he tasted blood, until the voice faded away once more.

"Tarin?" Fay said. "Are you well?"

"I'm fine."

"You look rather pale." A smile flitted across her lips.

"Hilarious."

"I'll build you new armor," she promised.

"We will need the forges firing day and night," he said, trying to push the focus away from him. "Armor, weapons...we may have a small force, but they must be well-equipped."

Fay nodded in agreement. "I'll speak to the men, find out if any of them have smith experience. If any of them deny me, I'll send them to you."

Tarin offered her a grim smile. "Don't let the men work on my armor until the rest of the company is outfitted with weapons and plate."

Fay narrowed her eyes, but didn't contradict his order. Instead she asked, "How long do you think we have before the east attacks?"

"A fortnight, if we're lucky. Half of the time to march to the Black Cliffs. The other half to scale them."

"These men need months, if not years, of training."

Tarin didn't argue with that. "It will have to be enough time," he said.

He stood, strode to the line of men waiting for porridge, towering over them like an ice bear over wolf pups, accepted his bowl, and then sat beside them in the snow.

Everyone was fresh and well rested and would soon have warm, full bellies.

Aye, he thought. *This is good.*

Because next he would work them until they could no longer stand.

Tarin embraced his old friend, their arms clasped.

Sir Jonathan's eyes never left Tarin's face, seeming to take in every detail. "You're handsomer than I expected," he said, taking a seat by the fire.

Tarin tensed at the jape, but then relaxed. He needed to get used to people seeing the real him—especially the soldiers he hoped to fight alongside. He sat down as well, sipping water from a tin. A light rain had begun to fall, very strange for the season. Typically any moisture in the air was frozen this time of year, puffy flakes of snow or stinging bullets of sleet. This misting rain was...odd...to say the least.

"And you could use a second bath," Tarin said, recoiling, pretending to hold his breath. In truth, the knight now looked much the same as Tarin remembered, having trimmed his scraggly beard, cut his tangled hair, and scrubbed the dirt from his skin. Even the gaunt, bruised look his cheeks had held was swiftly fading. "What were you in the dungeons for, anyway?" It was a question that had been itching at him ever since he realized who the man was. The man he knew would never even consider committing a crime, a model soldier.

"You know, this and that," Sir Jonathan said. "Mostly it was the murder that did it."

Tarin gaped. "What?"

The knight looked away, and that's when Tarin realized what was truly different about this man. It had never been the unkempt appearance of a prisoner, nor the weariness in his expression. No, it was the haunted look that never seemed to leave his eyes, even when he forced a smile onto his face. Something had happened to this man. Something worse than prison.

"It's not a happy story," Jonathan said.

Tarin said, "It's yours to tell."

"And mine to keep."

Tarin nodded. "I'll tell you my sad story if you tell me yours."

So they did, speaking in low voices deep into the night, two ghosts sitting around a fire, watching as puddles of color gathered rain.

Seventeen

The Western Kingdom, Knight's End
Rhea Loren

Rhea was working on controlling her emotions, though it was proving difficult considering the incompetence she was surrounded with.

"What in Wrath's name do you mean she escaped?" she said.

The nameless guardsman looked ready to wet his britches. "I found, uh, well, Your Highness, you see, when I made my rounds through the dungeons, the master was unconscious in Gwendolyn Storm's cell. The Orian's cell was locked up with him inside. And I found this." He held up what appeared to be a noose fashioned from lengths of ripped fabric.

She faked suicide, Rhea thought. When the dungeonmaster came inside the cell to cut her down, she'd sprung her trap.

Clever, she had to admit. She'd underestimated the Orian, a mistake she wouldn't make again.

"Is that all?" Rhea asked.

"No. After closer inspection, I found the dungeonmaster wasn't really unconscious."

"Dead?"

"Not exactly. His eyes were open. His body was stiff. He was like Bern Gentry—you know, paralyzed."

Rhea breathed, seething. First her attempt to ransom Gareth Ironclad for one of the skinmarked failed, and now the only other skinmarked in the west, Gwendolyn Storm, had *escaped*? And she'd been double-crossed by Darkspell in the process? For the first time since she'd become queen, Rhea felt like things were completely and utterly out of her control.

"Get. Out," she said, pointing toward the exit from the throne room.

"Your Highness, if I may, a thorough search will be conduct—"

"Out!" Rhea screamed, her voice rising. "And find Darkspell. Bring him to me!" The guardsman's eyes widened and he scuttled away, leaving her alone once more. Any moment her Fury would return with Gareth Ironclad. She'd planned to execute him immediately, to make a spectacle of it, to show her people they were already winning the war against the sinners of the east. But now…

He was her only bargaining chip to keep her brother, Roan, on the straight and narrow path back to Knight's End, hopefully with the Western Oracle or her long lost son in tow.

Yes, until Rhea recaptured the Orian…Gareth Ironclad would live.

Approaching footsteps chased her thoughts away. *Well, at least the decision is made*, she thought. *For now.*

When she saw who had arrived, she stood, pushing a broad smile onto her face. "Children!" she said, opening her arms wide for a hug.

Bea and Leo, her twin siblings, froze when they saw her. Her chambermaid stood behind them, trying to coax them forward, to little effect. The twins' feet were planted firmly—not defiantly, but with fear.

They're afraid of me, Rhea thought, and the realization saddened her for some reason. Something about having a soul growing within her had made her care more about the family she'd once despised.

Unlike the last time she'd seen them, with their filthy faces and hair, they'd been cleaned up and dressed in fresh linens—a white purity dress for Bea and long, grey woolen trousers and a white shirt for Leo. They were much skinnier now, on account of the lean diet offered in the dungeons.

"Approach your queen," Rhea said.

Bea's lip quivered. "You locked us in the dungeons for days." Leo nodded his agreement.

"As I told you, it was for your own protection," Rhea said lightly. "We have many enemies, more than ever before."

"They say Cousin Jove is dead," Leo said, finally taking a step forward. He blocked his sister—he'd always been protective of his twin, though she tended to be the feistier one.

"He is. Tragic. First Bane killed Father, and then our cousin. I should tell you, Ennis is dead, too, though it was me who killed him—he committed treason, after all."

"You killed Cousin Ennis?" Bea practically shrieked, stepping from behind her brother.

Here we go, Rhea thought. *Well, the silence was good while it lasted.* "Executed is probably a better word to use," she said. "But yes. A queen must be strong and obey the law, just like everyone else. We all have to make sacrifices."

"You're a monster," Bea said.

"Don't say that," Leo hissed. Rhea was fairly certain he didn't mean because it wasn't true; rather, he was scared of what she might do to them.

Good. Let him be scared. Fear will ensure his silence, that he will keep my secrets. Bea on the other hand...

"Would you prefer to stay safe in the dungeons?" Rhea asked them.

"No!" they answered in unison, doing that annoying twin thing.

"Please," Leo begged. "We'll do anything."

Bea nodded earnestly, though Rhea could see it was an act. Wrath, her sister was breathtakingly beautiful. When she was older, perhaps, Rhea would force her to carve the mark of Wrath on her face.

"All I ask is that you love me, like you once did. Can you do that?"

Leo and Bea exchanged a glance, an unspoken agreement passing between them. They turned back to her. Leo nodded. Bea said, "Yes, we can do that."

"And what does the scar on my face represent?" Rhea asked.

Another glance. Bea, always the actress, answered, "Your devotion to Wrath, my queen."

"Very good. And what do you know about Grey Arris?"

"Who?" This time, Bea was being genuine, and Rhea was happy to know she could tell the difference.

"Sorry. You would know him as Grease Jolly."

"Oh, *him*. He was a common thief, and his sister was sinmarked. Your Highness brought them both to justice."

Rhea smiled. "Leo, do you agree with everything your sister said?"

He nodded, apparently unable to speak.

"Good. Now come give your elder sister a hug."

They did, and while they embraced, Rhea was surprised how truly happy she felt. She had a family again.

Still, she was no fool. As soon as the twins had departed to get reacquainted with their royal bedrooms, she instructed her chambermaid to watch them like a hawk. "Tell me everything they do, everything they say, everyone they meet."

Her chambermaid nodded and then curtseyed. "Yes, Your Highness. I will not fail you."

Gareth Ironclad was back in his tower cell. Gwendolyn Storm was still missing, though all of the furia were scouring the streets of Knight's End. The Orian would've been smart to slip away from the city as soon as possible, but Rhea's instincts told her she was still here, and would stay until Gareth was either dead or liberated.

At least he's still useful as bait, Rhea mused. Perhaps this was the way Wrath intended it to be. Had she ransomed Gareth and then Gwendolyn had escaped, she would have nothing left to hold over Roan to bend him to her will. Then all her plans would be ruined. Without the Western Oracle's ability to create fatemarks...

She tried not to think about it.

Instead, she focused on the next matter at hand. Darkspell had been found—not hiding, but in his laboratory, of all places. Mixing vile concoctions, attempting to create the potion he'd promised her.

And now he was being shoved to his knees before her.

"Gwendolyn Storm, our Orian prisoner, escaped," Rhea said.

Darkspell, wincing, said, "This is a setback. We shall require another subject for experimentation."

Either he was a very good actor, or he had no clue *how* the prisoner had escaped. "Her dungeonmaster was found paralyzed."

He cocked his head to the side, birdlike. Again, the performance was topnotch; unless it wasn't a performance. "A vial went missing. I thought I'd misplaced it, I do that sometimes…"

"Are you saying it was stolen?"

"Clearly."

"Clearly, *Your Highness*," Rhea corrected.

The man, to her surprise, snarled at her. "If you think I would help an easterner—an Orian at that—escape, then I have just the potion to clear your addled mind."

"Watch your tongue—" Rhea started to say, but one of her new Furies was already striding forward, lashing out, snapping a backhand across the potionmaster's face. His head jerked to the side and he fell back.

When he swiveled back around, slowly, his cheek was inflamed and blood wept from a gash opened by one of the Fury's sharp fingernails. Despite that and the dangerous position he was in, his expression remained defiant, the old man's eyes as sharp as his tongue. "Kill me if you must. But it's the traitor in your midst you should be worried about. I came here offering you an advantage over your eastern rivals. After your decisive victory in the Bay of Bounty, I believed you were the horse to back in this contest. But perhaps I was mistaken."

Rhea didn't know who or what to believe anymore. She thought after she'd destroyed the north and captured Roan, Gareth, and Gwendolyn, that things would fall into place, like a well-positioned row of dominoes. Instead, the tangled web of her plans seemed to be unravelling before her very eyes.

Still, something about the potionmaster's story rang true. Why else would he not have fled after freeing the Orian prisoner? Unless it was a slick double maneuver, this man was innocent of everything but guarding his potions. And he was right, her time was better spent finding the true traitor in her court.

"I believe you," she said. "And I would continue to have your services. The Orian's escape is no matter. We will simply release your potion directly into the Spear and hope it works. If not, we shall try again and again and again, until they're all dead."

It had taken Bea no more than a day to betray Rhea, a truth that concerned her greatly. The speed and confidence of her sister's treachery shouldn't have surprised Rhea, but it did. Bea, despite the risk of going back to the dungeons, was made of stronger mettle than she'd given her credit for.

Rhea would melt her down and remake her.

According to Rhea's chambermaid, upon reaching her quarters, Bea had requested quill, ink, and parchment. She'd written a letter, sealed it the old-fashioned way, with wax printed with the royal sigil, and then called for a messenger, not to send the note via stream, but to hand-deliver it to one of the rival lords in Knight's End. Lord Thorne, Rhea's grandfather on her mother's side. It was well-known that the Thornes had long coveted the throne, though the closest they had come was wedding their daughter—Rhea's mother, Cecilia—to the crown prince, who'd later become the king and Rhea's father. Now, of course, Cecilia was dead, along with House Thorne's chances at ever ascending to the top of the royal food chain.

Rhea's chambermaid had intercepted the message and brought it directly to her. Rhea's lips had pursed and her blood had boiled as she'd read the letter, which was essentially a list of her "crimes" against Wrath and the west, enough ammunition to have her brought to trial, her rule overturned and denounced.

It was the darkest of treacheries, plain and simple.

But now it was time to put an end to Bea's never ending attempts to undermine Rhea's rule. She'd tried threatening captivity. She'd tried kindness. Fear was next.

"Thank you for joining me, brother, *sister*," Rhea said as her siblings approached, wearing wary expressions. Well, at least Leo looked wary, uncertain, while Bea looked as smug as a dog with both paws clamped atop a bone.

Rhea stood in a secure location along the banks of the Bay of Bounty, well out of sight of the royal docks, which were, as always, bustling with activity. Each of the Three Furies stood guard, in case some fool stumbled into the area and saw something he shouldn't.

In these sorts of situations, Rhea had learned, it was better to get right to things. Beating around a bush only gave the bush time to grow gnarled branches, thorns, and thick roots. It was better to hack down the bush, pull up the roots, and toss it all into the hottest part of the fire.

"You committed treason, Bea," Rhea said.

"What?" Bea said, placing a hand over her heart. "I would never do that."

Rhea held up the message, which fluttered open, the wax seal broken.

"I've never seen that before in my life."

The nerve of this girl. Even now, to deny her betrayal.

"I have a firsthand witness. And the message is in your handwriting." Rhea showed no anger, only certainty.

Still, Bea showed no fear, defiance coursing across her doll-like face. "You aren't above the law," she hissed. "We are the heirs now, Leo and I." Upon her mention of his name, Leo seemed to shrink into the collar of his shirt, as if he wanted no part in whatever was to come. "You have sinned, sister, no matter what you tell our people. You know it, we know it, and Wrath knows it. The scars on your face stand for *whore*, not *Wrath*. Father would be ashamed of you."

"Enough!" Rhea said, her temper finally reaching the end of its leash. "This is not a discussion. I could have you executed for less." Rhea didn't actually plan to kill her sister, only to scare her into submission. She'd done it with a far stronger woman—her first Fury, who had died to save Rhea's life during the battle they eventually went on to win. And now,

Rhea would do it with Bea, recreating her into the sister she wanted—submissive, loyal, scared.

"You would never execute me," Bea said. "I'm your *sister.*" As if that meant something in war.

Softening her tone, Rhea said, "Have you heard the stories of how *I* won the battle against the north?"

Bea's hands moved to her hips. "We were in the dungeons, remember? We know nothing about nothing."

"Well, let me be the first to tell you the tale..."

When she'd finished, Bea laughed. "You used to make up stories when we were children, too. Used to try to scare us. It worked then. Not now. A sea monster? That's the best story you've got?"

Ignoring her sister's outburst, Rhea turned to the calm waters of the bay, which lapped against the rocky shoreline. *Let this work, let this work, let this work...*

She didn't know for certain whether she could Summon Wrathos at will, not without the Summoner's help (and he, of course, was dead), but Rhea *believed* she could, and she thought that was the important thing.

She didn't know the words to say, or what to do with her hands, so she simply acted on instinct, raising her hands over her head, opening her palms to the sea, and shouted, "Wrathos! Your Queen commands your presence!"

Bea giggled. Leo didn't make a noise, but Rhea could sense his amusement, too.

Nothing happened. And yet the still waters seemed even calmer now, like a sheet of ice...and Rhea couldn't so much as see but *feel* a presence approaching.

Yes, she thought. *Oh yes.*

Wrathos exploded from the water in a spray of moisture, salty rain pouring upon their heads. Bea screamed. Leo gasped. And Rhea continued to stand, soaked to the skin, her arms raised to the monster rising before her. *My monster*, she thought. *Mine to command.*

The giant squid's skin was red, dotted with algae and slime and barnacles, a hundred tentacles writhing from the center. A single giant eye stared out from the bulbous body as it snapped its beaklike maw.

Rhea looked back at her siblings, who were frozen in terror. Bea tried to take a step back, but stumbled, falling. "Do you believe me now?" Rhea said, her lip curled.

Turning back to Wrathos, she said, "I shall have need of you soon. Your hunger shall be sated and Wrath shall smile upon you."

The squid seemed to bob its head in understanding. "Now go, return to the depths from whence you came, I shall call upon you in my time of need."

Slowly, the squid began to descend, slipping beneath the surface.

However, just as Rhea began to turn her back so she could steal another look at her sister's fear, a lone tentacle snapped out like a whip, slithering past Rhea.

No, Rhea thought, ice coating her skin.

Her sister's scream was a bright flame as Bea was dragged through the air, her purity dress flapping like a bird's broken wing. A flame that was snuffed out only when Wrathos crunched its beak down on her slender, lithe body, swallowing her before vanishing into the bay.

Rhea couldn't breathe, couldn't think, could do nothing but sink to her knees and stare at her hands—the hands that had helped command the squid. She felt numb, like she was stuck in a nightmare, the air thick and heavy. *No, this isn't real, isn't real, isn't—*

I didn't mean for this to happen, for her to…I'd only meant to scare her into obedience.

Right?

Or was that my true command, deep inside my core? Is that what I am, a monster, the very same Bea accused me of?

Will my child have a monster for a mother?

Leo's gasping sobs startled her; she'd forgotten he was here. Slowly, she stood, blinking away tears. She turned, plastering on the face of an emotionally distant queen.

Leo looked shattered as he stared at her, his red eyes brimming with tears, streaming like rivers down his cheeks. His hair was plastered to his head from when Wrathos had soaked them. In this state, he really did appear as a child, and not thirteen name days old, almost a man grown by the reckoning of the west.

She was vaguely aware of the Three, each turned in her direction, staring—just staring. She ignored them.

"Will you keep my secrets, brother?" Rhea asked, her voice as even as she could make it, though it trembled on the edges. Her bottom lip shook, but she clamped her teeth upon it until it stopped.

Leo nodded, his head collapsing into his hands.

Eighteen

The Western Kingdom, Knight's End
Ennis Loren

Ennis paced the gardens in the dark, his shadowy form hidden by the thick branches of a juniper tree, blotting out a sky full of stars.

He'd just received the news: Princess Bea was dead. Two had gone down to meet Rhea by the seaside, and only one had returned. The castle was buzzing with rumors and gossip:

The queen executed her for treason, just as she did Ennis.

No, I heard it was an accident, the girl stumbled on the rocks and drowned.

You're both wrong! Wrathos emerged from the sea and swallowed the girl whole. I swear it!

Ennis didn't know what to believe, only that there were no coincidences anymore. Bea came out of the dungeons only this morning, and now she was dead? Sure, he'd never felt the closeness to the twins he'd felt for Rhea as a child. They were bratty, insolent, conniving little urchins, but that didn't mean he wanted them to die.

And Rhea wasn't Rhea anymore, not the princess he once knew. She'd been broken by terrible circumstances out of her control, and when she'd been put back together she was a different woman entirely.

She killed Jove. She killed my brother. It was a truth he'd been hiding from for a long time, because he'd wanted to believe in her goodness, wanted to have someone to follow, to give his loyalty to. But all along he'd known.

Again, Jove and he had never really gotten along, and his brother had deserved to be punished for what he did to Rhea, but still...the fact that Rhea could murder him in cold blood and then act as if she was distraught, a scared little girl...she was as dangerous as a snake.

So he paced, a shadow amongst shadows, hoping against hope that Gwendolyn Storm would meet him as promised.

She won't, he thought. Why would she? She'd escaped from the dungeons and was likely halfway to Restor by now. In a month, she'd be in Ferria, spilling her guts to Grian Ironclad.

I shall rescue Gareth Ironclad myself. Now more than ever, he knew he needed to do whatever it took to overthrow his cousin before she shattered the Loren name forever.

"Soon there won't be any grass left under your feet," a voice said from behind.

He whirled around to find Gwendolyn Storm perched on a low-hanging branch, her yellow eyes gleaming like a wildcat staring down its prey.

"You came."

"I came. I assume our plan worked as there has been no announcement of plans for Gareth's execution?"

"Yes," Ennis said. "But something else has happened. Bea is dead."

Gwen frowned. "She died in the dungeons?"

Ennis shook his head. "No, Rhea released her. And then she was dead. I don't know what happened."

"Rhea killed her," Gwen said with certainty.

"Probably," Ennis agreed. He had to face the truths about his cousin he'd avoided for too long.

"This changes nothing. We rescue Gareth tonight."

"Impossible. I'm not on duty in the tower. And even if I was, now there is always one of the furia posted along with a guardsman."

"So you'll kill her," Gwen said. "The furia are evil."

Ennis said, "They are hard women, that much I'll admit, but they've been trained to be that way. They're only trying to enforce Wrath's will."

"Your god is a narrowminded god," Gwen said.

"Wrath is a just god."

"Hmm," Gwen said. "So you believe I am a demon, a witch, a dark sorceress of the forest, worshipping iron idols and seducing human men?"

"I didn't say that. I didn't say the furia are perfect, nor the westerners. Wrath is perfect, but our interpretation of God's will can be flawed. We are only human, after all."

"You are not what I expected for a Loren," Gwen said, tapping her teeth with long fingernails.

"Roan is a Loren," Ennis pointed out.

"Aye, and he's not what I expected either, but he also wasn't raised in Knight's End. Your lost cousin practically raised himself, from what he's told me."

"But you love him, don't you?"

"I love no one."

Silence bloomed like a flower, settling in and growing roots. Ennis looked away, unable to hold Gwen's unfaltering cat-like stare. Finally, he looked back and said, "I'm on duty in a week's time in the tower. If I handle the furia, what then? It's not like I'll be able to just parade Gareth out the front door. There are at least a dozen guards between the tower and the exit. Are we going to kill all of them too?"

Gwen smiled. "We're not leaving through the door. The window will suffice."

"Unless Gareth grows wings…"

"I'll handle that part. You handle the furia. Deal?"

Ennis looked away, considering. He had a bad feeling about this, but he didn't have a better plan. "Deal," he said, but when he looked back, she was already gone.

Nineteen

The Western Kingdom, Knight's End
Gwendolyn Storm

Although Gwen had been alive for nearly nine decades, the week felt even longer, the longest of her life.

She tried to stay busy, sleeping during the day in the cryptlands, beside embalmed corpses and monuments to lords and ladies, kings and queens, rulers who had despised her people in life, who had, in their hate and ignorance, issued commands to kill them for no reason other than that her people had been born different.

She didn't hate these people, however; no, she felt sorry for them. For she knew what it was like to hate, the feeling like a flesh-eating insect devouring her from the inside, gnawing away at everything that made her Gwendolyn Storm, the woman her father had raised.

Aye, that was how much she hated the Calypsians, their dragons, their emperors and empresses. Aye, that was how much she hated the Sandes, they who had taken everything from her, who had turned her into a bitter closed-hearted person.

Until Roan came along. Grudgingly, she had to admit he'd been slowly bringing her back to life, giving her hope for a better world, a better future. For as long as she'd tried to hold back her feelings for him, he was like ocean waves battering against a shore—relentless.

In the nights, she kept busy. First she stole twenty long coils of rope. There were many places she could've obtained the rope, but she chose to procure it from the castle, which seemed to create a sort of beautiful symmetry to the last few months. Next, she tied ten of the cords together, testing the knots again and again under her own weight plus several large stones while hanging from a thick tree branch. Then she repeated the process with the other ten ropes, until she had two exceptionally long ropes, which she tied together and tested a third time.

From there she stole supplies: food, water, satchels. It was enough to get all three of them to the Bridge of Triumph, at least. From there they would rely on the kindness of the easterners, who should be more than happy to resupply an Ironclad prince, or king, or whatever Gareth was now.

On the predetermined night, Gwen slung the three full satchels onto one shoulder, and the heavy coiled rope on the other, and then scaled the castle wall once more. By the time she reached the top, she was sweaty under her armor, but not tired in the least. It might be a different story once she climbed to the top of the tower, but she would make it—that much she knew. Gwen didn't know how to fail, her determination like a weapon in its own right.

Silently, she dropped into the gardens, repositioning the rope over both shoulders for balance, while hiding the provisions in a thick bush.

A scuffle in the typically quiet gardens put her senses on high alert. "Gwen?" a voice hissed.

Shite. It was Ennis, who was supposed to be high in the tower, guarding Gareth, along with a furia he should be preparing to knock out or kill.

She stepped out from behind the bush to find him peering into the shadows that surrounded her. "I'm not on duty," he said, his eyes flicking to the coils of rope on her shoulders.

"That much is obvious. What I'm trying to discern, is why not."

"Rhea has begun changing the schedule at the last moment. I've been trying to find you, to tell you. We don't know who will be guarding the tower until moments before."

"She suspects."

"Of course she does. You escaped. Even if there weren't shadows circling her, she'd still see them in every corner."

"I'll rescue him myself," Gwen said, gritting her teeth. She preferred to work alone, anyway.

"The window is boarded up. They'll be alerted the second you try to break through." She tried to interrupt, but he hurried on. "I know what you are capable of—I don't doubt that. But you won't have a chance. One of the Furies are posted tonight. One of the Three."

"I don't care who—"

"She'll stab you between the slats in the boards."

"I have armor."

"It won't be enough."

"What are you saying?"

"I will go to the tower. I will handle the Fury and the guardsman." The look he gave her was so sharp she felt as if her own determination was being reflected back at her. But—

"You said it yourself, getting through all the guardsmen between here and the tower is impossible, even if you come up with a good enough excuse. And the Fury won't fall for some hare-brained trick. You'll be caught for certain."

"Yes," he said, as if he'd already thought of all that.

"You would sacrifice yourself for Gareth Ironclad? For me?"

He raised his fist to his chest. "Aye. I was thinking before you arrived. I've lived a long life, a good life, but I've never really done anything that matters. For some reason, I think this might matter, might make a difference. It's a worthy sacrifice."

Gwen shook her head, but it wasn't a denial. "I don't know what to say, except thank you."

"It's not your thanks I want. Promise me you'll do what you can to forge peace between our kingdoms." His eyes shone in the alternating streaks of green and red moonlight filtering through the branches.

Gwendolyn extended her hand and he clasped it. "I promise," she said. "May Orion be with you."

"And Wrath with you," he said.

She slipped past him and headed for the base of the tower.

Gareth Ironclad

"I'd prefer if you didn't stare at me as I slept," Gareth said, his head stuffed under a pillow. Ever since they'd returned to Knight's End, Rhea had used a different man to guard him each night. But the guard was always paired with one of the Furies.

At least I still have my head, Gareth thought wryly. Why, he wasn't certain. All he knew was that Rhea had glared at him when they'd arrived, muttered, "Useless Ironclad," and then had him hauled back to the top of the tower, where he'd been bored out of his mind ever since.

Perhaps she plans to try to sell me to one of my enemies, he thought. *The Calypsians or Phanecians…they would pay richly for a living prince of the east.*

"It's my job," the guardsman replied gruffly.

Gareth pushed the pillow away to catch the Fury rolling her eyes.

"How about you?" he said. "Are you planning to stare at me all night, too?"

As usual, she didn't rise to the bait, her eyes on him but not; like the other Three, she wore her indifference like an armor.

"Do not speak to her," the guardsman said.

"Fine. Then I'll speak to you. What's the weather been like? Cold. Warm. Wet. Dry."

"Don't talk to me either."

Gareth sighed. "I suppose I'll have to speak to myself then. Cooped up like this, it was always inevitable I'd go mad anyway, I might as well speed up the process. Gareth, how would you rate the food in Knight's End? Superb! And the service? Superb! And the guards? Lacking."

The guard took a step forward. "Just. Go. To. Sleep."

"I will if you will."

The guard opened his mouth for another retort, but the Fury beat him to it, speaking for the first time since she'd entered. "Fool. The more you talk, the more he's encouraged to continue talking."

The guard went beet-red, but didn't say another word, stepping back.

Gareth laughed. "You're not as dumb as you look," he said to the Fury, whose eyes pinned him to his bed, before roving away. Disinterested.

He sighed. It was going to be a long night.

Gwendolyn Storm

She was perhaps halfway to the top, a shadow clinging to the exterior stone blocks of the tower. The coils of rope were feeling heavier on her shoulders by the moment, the sweat streaming down her arms and legs and back, her muscles burning...

It felt good. Like she was doing something other than waiting and preparing. If they could pull this off, if both of them could truly escape...

They could find a way to contact Roan, to let him know that he didn't need to obey his sister anymore. And then they could continue their quest to discover the origins of the fatemarks, what they meant.

The thought pushed Gwen higher and higher, the green and red moons a mere handbreadth away from each other in the night sky. The wind picked up, whipping past her, pulling several strands of silver hair from her plait and snapping them across her face.

Still, she climbed, her strong, nimble fingers finding cracks, her toes burrowing into the smallest of crevices. The ground was far distant, and the slightest misstep would send her hurtling to her death.

The thought would scare most humans, but Orians were built differently. Gwen had grown up climbing the highest trees, flinging herself from branch to branch, befriending ore cats and ore hawks.

She felt alive. And free.

She looked up, gauging the distance she had left. She spotted the boarded-up window, behind which Gareth was likely sleeping. She wondered whether Ennis had made it, whether he'd found a way to defeat the guard and the Fury. The man, she had to admit, had surprised her in a lot of ways. His courage. His dedication to his kingdom. His desire for peace.

He would make a great king, she thought.

Resting for a moment, she watched the wooden planks for a moment longer, for any sign of someone breaking through them.

"Where are you, Ennis?" she said to the wind.

The wind howled in response, pinning her to the tower.

Ennis Loren

Making excuses was easy, though it would've been simpler if he was still Ennis Loren, and not Bern Gentry. Regardless, the first several guards bought his lie about a change in plans— that the queen herself had asked him to replace the guard on duty in the tower.

The three guards positioned in front of the lift and staircase, however, were less stupid.

"We received no word of a guard change," one of them said, his hand resting casually on the sword hilted on his hip.

"That's the point," Ennis said. "Rhea doesn't want any of us to know who will be guarding the prisoner. There's a traitor in our midst." Perhaps mentioning the last part was a mistake, but Ennis suspected it wasn't. What true traitor would actually say the word *traitor*, drawing attention to himself?

"Still, I'll have to confirm it with the queen."

"Feel free," Ennis said nonchalantly. "Though she's gone to bed."

The guard chewed on his lip for a moment, considering. Waking the queen was clearly not his idea of a good time. "Change of plans," he said. "We'll keep the guard that's on duty."

Wrath. Gwen is probably halfway to the top by now, Ennis thought. *The woman climbs better than a monkey.*

"Fine by me," Ennis said. "I'm happy to get some shuteye. But I'll have to inform the queen in the morning. Heads will roll."

"Don't you mean inform *Rhea*?" the guard said.

Ennis frowned. There was something about the man's tone. "What?"

"You called her Rhea just a moment ago, like she was your lover and not your queen."

"Did I?"

Wrath, Wrath, Wrath! It was a fatal mistake, one that had foiled his lie before it had had a chance.

"Yes," the guard said, taking a step forward. "Your name is Bern Gentry, isn't it? There are a lot of guards around this place and I'm bad with names and faces, but I wouldn't forget yours, not after the queen chose you for Darkspell's little demonstration."

Ennis turned away, panicking, trying to shadow his face. "Nah. Name's Jack. Mother said I just had one of those faces..."

Footsteps approached from behind.

These men are innocent, he thought. *They are only following orders.*

Ennis had killed in battle before, but never like this, never his allies.

Something Rhea had said to him before the battle in the Bay of Bounty came back to him, as if it had been floating on the edge of his mind for some time. *We all must sacrifice ourselves for that which we believe in.* But was betraying his queen, his kingdom, something he believed in?

Yes, he thought. *As it stands now, yes.*

"Nothing else to say for yourself, *Bern*?" the guard said. "Not that you've been seeking revenge for what the queen did to you? Not that you're a liar and a traitor?"

Surreptitiously, Ennis closed his hand on his sword's hilt, his muscles tensing.

He spun, slashing the man's throat before he could utter another accusation. Warm blood spurted out, splashing him across the face.

He thought, *It is done; I have crossed a line I can never uncross.*

From there everything seemed easier.

While the next guard came at him, the third man fled, probably off to sound the alarm, to gather reinforcements. Ennis ducked under his foe's blade, simultaneously throwing his sword down the corridor. He was many years from his days of entering tourneys to show off his rare sword-throwing ability, but it wasn't something he could unlearn—the sword flew straight and true.

Bullseye. The blade impaled the fleeing guard in the back, likely severing his spine. He collapsed like a dropped sack of potatoes.

Weaponless, Ennis threw his elbow backwards blindly, landing an awkward blow on his opponent's shoulder. Unfortunately, it wasn't the arm holding the sword, or he might've dropped his weapon. Instead, the guard raked his arm back across his body, forcing Ennis to jerk away. The edge of the sword brushed past, and Ennis felt the sting of a slash opening up on his cheek.

I was lucky. It's naught but a flesh wound.

Ennis knew he wouldn't get lucky again, so he did what any wise warrior would do in a situation like this, weaponless with his foe advancing upon him:

He kicked him in the groin.

The guard buckled over, groaning, his blade finally slipping from his fingers and clattering to the floor. Ennis kicked him again, this time in the head, and the man landed hard, rolling over once before going still. He contemplated finishing him off, but there was no honor in murdering an unconscious man, and anyway, by the time the guard came to this would be long over.

Let him tell Rhea the truth.

Wiping the blood—his own mixed with that of the first guard he'd killed, the suspicious one—from his face with his sleeve, Ennis stalked over to the man with the sword in his back. Grunting, he pulled it out, swallowing the bile in the back of his throat. He felt ill; not because he'd killed, but the *way* he'd killed. A slashed throat before the man had time to defend himself; a sword in the back: *We all make sacrifices…*

Yes, he had sacrificed. His soul, his honor, any chance of achieving the seventh heaven and looking upon Wrath's face…

It wasn't the time or place to think about it, and anyway, Ennis had always been a practical man. *What's done is done, move on. Focus on the task at hand.*

His next order of business was to sever the chains attached to the pulleys, which were used to haul the lift to the top of the tower. Without someone to pull them, he couldn't use it anyway, and he didn't want anyone else to be able to.

He ran for the staircase, taking the steps two at a time.

Gareth Ironclad

Sleep wasn't coming easy for Gareth. He couldn't stop thinking about how that guard was probably still staring at him. He couldn't stop thinking about why he was still alive. He couldn't stop thinking about where Roan might be, whether Gwendolyn was still alive in the dungeons, and finally, whether

Ennis Loren would ever follow through on his promise to help them escape.

Since he'd returned to Knight's End, Gareth hadn't seen so much as a glimpse of the man now disguised as Bern Gentry, lowly guardsman.

A sound drew him away from his thoughts.

His eyes flashed opened; he faced away from his guards, in view of the boarded-over window.

A bird, he thought. *Pecking at the wood.* They did that sometimes, trying to get in. One of the boards rattled as the wind picked up, whistling between the slats. A dark eye stared in at him, a circular knot in the wood that had fallen out, the inky night sky peering through. Sometimes Gareth stuck his eye to the hole just to see something different than the inside of the tower cell. Usually the rare glimpses of the outside world were short-lived, however, as most of his guards discouraged such activities.

What the hell? he thought, flinching suddenly. The eye had changed, lightened, a yellow orb gleaming in the dark. And then it was gone.

Had he imagined it? The guards hadn't reacted, so either they hadn't seen it or it hadn't truly happened. He blinked. Pinched himself, felt the throb of pain on his arm. *I'm awake.* Still, his eyes might've been playing tricks on him—that happened when you were imprisoned sometimes, almost like a mirage in the desert.

Because only one person he knew had yellow eyes that shined as brightly as that in the dark. And she was supposed to be locked up, too, in the dungeons.

Gwendolyn.

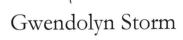

Gwendolyn Storm

Looking through that hole in the wood probably hadn't been the smartest move, but everything was so still and silent inside the tower that she couldn't not take a peek. Gareth, lying on a bed, had stared right back at her, had flinched at the sight of her eye, had *seen* her. Which meant it was possible the guards standing by the door—a bored-looking man who seemed more muscle than brains and a red-clad Fury, so still she might've been sleeping with her eyes open—might have seen her too.

Gwendolyn held her breath, clinging to the edge of the sill.

When no alarm was raised and Gareth—cleverer than he acted sometimes—didn't blow her cover, she exhaled slowly, considering the situation.

Ennis should have arrived by now. Climbing steps takes less time than scaling a sheer tower wall...

Then again, he might've had guards to deal with. Gwen wondered whether, when it came down to it, he would be able to do what needed to be done. She had a feeling killing guards who were only following orders would pose a challenge for the man, who seemed to have more honor than good sense. Not that she was against honor, just when it got in the way of doing the right thing.

Still, the determination she'd seen coursing across his face in the gardens, almost like a living, breathing thing...she needed to give him a little more time, a chance to come through on his side of the mission.

She waited, listening to the night, hoping, praying to Orion.

A voice broke the silence, muffled through the wood and yet as clear as a ringing bell to Gwen's ears.

"I was sent to relieve you of your post," Ennis said.

"What?" the guardsman's gruff voice replied.

"So..." a third voice cut in, a woman's voice, as sharp as a knife. "...the traitor has finally revealed himself."

Steel rang on steel.

A man grunted in pain.

A body fell.

Gwendolyn began frantically prying at the wooden boards.

Ennis Loren

He could never have let the guard live, even if both he and the Fury had bought his story.

The man's blood dripped from his sword as he circled the Fury, whose sharp stare had him pinned like a fly on a board. This woman was not only trained in the art of killing, but she relished it. This was her purpose in life: To be Wrath's enforcer, God's Fury incarnate, a way to punish sinners without requiring god-like power to be spent frivolously. Once, Ennis would've thought killing her was the equivalent of killing Wrath, but now...

The W carved into her face made him wonder whether this woman was truly ordained by Wrath, or merely by his cousin, a murderer, a sinner, a young woman consumed with power and control. A human, imperfect and prone to error.

If so, I can kill her. I will kill her.

The Fury didn't speak, didn't taunt, didn't wave her blade, which was painted red, as if stained in blood, around pointlessly. Each step was as cold and calculated as her stare, which never wavered from her prey.

Ennis had fought seasoned warriors before, mostly easterners trying to ford the Spear. The Hundred Years War had given him too much experience. He knew when to strike and when to sit back and let them come. But this woman...she was a spider in a web, as cunning as she was well-trained.

As it turned out, the choice was made for him, for at that moment there was a sound off to the right, the splintering of wood being pried from its moorings.

The Fury's head snapped toward the sound, while Ennis remained focused, slashing out while she was distracted.

Clang! She blocked his strike blindly, dancing deftly to the left and leaping his next blow. Whirling around, she resembled a tornado garbed in a red dress, her skirts swirling. Her sword was like lightning bursting from a cyclone.

He was too slow by half, her blade shrieking along the edge of his sword and deflecting off his armor. His plate served its purpose, but the force of the hit threw him off balance, stumbling over an ottoman, of all things.

And then her sword was upon him again, whipping for his neck as he dropped a hand to steady himself on the floor. He jerked his head sharply to the side, taking the blow on the helm, which popped off, clanking into the wall.

He rolled right sharply, raising his sword as he emerged from the somersault, ready for the attack he knew would come.

Which didn't come.

Instead, the Fury had taken the time to sprint in the opposite direction, circling around him on feet as silent as a mouse, her sword arcing on the edge of his peripheral vision.

He ducked, and the edge of the blade was so close he felt the displaced air as it whistled by.

Crack! The sound of the board breaking and clattering inside the tower only seemed to spur the Fury on more, as if she knew she needed to end him before help arrived. In truth, Ennis had to admit, he could use the help. At best, he was on equal footing with this woman; more likely, however, he was outmatched.

And then reinforcements arrived, though not from Gwendolyn, whose arm was struggling to squeeze through the narrow gap provided by the broken board.

From Gareth Ironclad.

Gareth Ironclad

Gareth, though surprised by the sudden appearance of Ennis Loren, had not been idle during the fight. Generally, his preferred weapon was a well-channeled Orian sword, but he was no stranger to improvising. Growing up with two brothers the same age had ensured he knew the ins and outs of an old-fashioned no-holds-barred brawl.

First he'd grabbed a pillow, more to use as a distraction than an effective shield. Then he'd raced for the chair. It would be heavy to wield, but it was the best weapon he had. But then the wooden board had snapped in half, two ragged halves clattering to the floor—*she's here, Gwen is really, truly here*—and Gareth had turned his attention away from the chair and snagged one of the boards.

Now, he wasn't a moment too soon. Ennis had lost his helmet, backpedaling like mad, basically trying *not to die*.

Also having learned from fighting with his brothers growing up, Gareth attacked from behind, slamming the board down on the Fury's back with all the force he could muster.

The blow never connected, the Fury dodging to the side at the last moment.

She has eyes in the back of her head, Gareth thought. When this was over, assuming they won, he would be sorely tempted to cut away her red hair to check for a second set of eyes.

Pincered between them, the Fury trained one eye on each foe. Gareth's eyes met Ennis's, and a plan passed between them. Gareth hoped they were thinking the same thing.

He threw his pillow.

The Fury's eyes widened in surprise, as did Ennis's—apparently they hadn't had the same plan after all—as Gareth shoved the jagged end of the board at the warrior woman's face.

She caught it with one hand, splinters stabbing into her palm, drawing blood. The pillow, on the other hand, landed harmlessly on the floor. It was a nice distraction but did little actual damage, unless, of course, the Fury had a severe allergy to goose feathers.

Gareth, now weaponless, waited to have his head removed from his shoulders, wondering whether it would hurt less or more than being rejected by his brother at the Bridge of Triumph.

The strike never came.

Instead, the Fury's eyes widened further, her mouth gaped open, and something shimmered from her stomach, protruding between two ribs.

The tip of a blade.

Her mouth, now dribbling blood, transformed into a snarl. "May you rot in the first heaven," she said. Ennis wrenched his sword back through the way it had entered, and the Fury died, landing facedown and likely ruining a rather expensive-looking Crimean rug with her blood. All week Gareth had been considering relieving himself on the same rug, but it seemed she had taken care of it for him, a fact that held a certain irony.

Ennis looked at Gareth, his light-colored beard speckled with drying blood. He said, "I don't make promises lightly."

"I can see that," Gareth said.

Another board cracked, and they both pivoted to face the figure stepping through the now-open window. "Gwen," Gareth said. "Thanks for the help, but we've got it covered."

Her armor shone in the starlight, her eyes as bright as twin yellow moons. Over her shoulders hung thick coils of rope. She eyed the two men before her eyes flitted to the two dead bodies littering the floor. She almost looked surprised, something that sent a flash of annoyance through Gareth. *We don't* always *need your help*, he thought. *Usually, but not always.*

Her gaze seemed to settle on the random pillow lying beside the Fury, soaking up her pooling blood. Gareth explained: "I guess they don't teach pillow fighting in the Furium."

A surprised cough-chuckle exploded from Ennis. "You are full of tricks, prince of the east."

"You don't know the half of it," Gwen said. "You should've seen the stunt he pulled in Restor on the way here."

"My friends love to ruin a good time," Gareth said, though he felt his cheeks burning. The Restor Incident had not been one of his finer moments.

"You don't have long," Ennis said, snapping them all back to reality. "I left one guard unconscious but alive, and other patrols might pass the base of the tower and see the bodies."

Gwen slung the rope to the floor. "Right. Secure it to something immovable. I'll feed it down the side."

While Ennis located one end and hustled out the door, presumably to tie it to one of the tower's permanent fixtures, Gareth said, "We're going through the window?"

Gwen didn't look at him. "From what I heard, you already tried it once, only without the rope." Her tone was cold. Hard. Angry.

"I had no choice," Gareth said. "Rhea Loren was going to use me against my brother, ransom me for Beorn Stonesledge. I failed my people once, I won't fail them again."

Gwen didn't look up. "One, there is always a choice; and two, you're only failing yourself with this attitude." He was surprised at the sincerity he heard in her words. She stood and hauled the rope to the window, easing it over the side, releasing it in segments, presumably so it wouldn't draw attention from the ground as it unfurled.

"You sound like Roan," Gareth said, feeling a bulge of warmth in his chest.

"He's a wise man when he's not being a fool," Gwen said, finally turning to look at him. "And I believe I owe you a thank you."

"For what?"

"Ennis told me what you said when he offered you a chance at escape. He came for me first, just like you asked."

"He busted you out of the dungeons?"

163

Ennis returned then. "She almost broke my neck in the process," he said. "Truthfully, she had the situation well in hand. But yes, I tried to help."

"Thank you," Gareth said. "I don't know what else to say." *Strange,* he thought, *the way friends could be made in the unlikeliest of places.*

"There's something you need to know," Ennis said. He was looking at Gwen.

"There's no time; you can tell us—"

"Darkspell is creating a potion for Rhea that will kill only Orians," he blurted out.

"What?" Gareth and Gwen said at the same time.

"It's true," Ennis said. "She was planning to experiment with it on you, but now...she's going to release this plague directly into the waters of the Spear."

Gareth said, "But half of the eastern water supply is connected to that river." If the potion spread...

"Thousands will die," Gwen said, her voice barely above a whisper.

Ennis nodded. "Which is why you need to stop it."

Gareth nodded. This man was a true ally. "Thank you," he said. "For everything."

"Enough talk," Gwen said. "There will be time for cuddling and planning later, once the city is well behind us."

As if to add emphasis to her statement, shouts echoed from the stairwell, followed by the thunder of dozens of boots on stone.

A temple bell, which doubled as a castle alarm system, pealed in response, cracking open the silent night.

The guards at the base of the tower had been discovered.

"Now!" Gwen said, sprinting for the window and flinging herself over the sill. She hung from the edge, leaving enough room for Gareth and Ennis to descend first. Gareth positioned himself on the sill, grasping the rope with both hands; he turned to face the wall, planting both feet firmly on the stone.

"Use these," Gwen said, handing him a pair of thick leather gloves. He quickly slipped them on one at a time, and then began to slide down the rope, clamping it between his feet and squeezing with the leather gloves to slow his speed.

Above him, Gwen said, "You next," the volume of her voice fading away.

Before Gareth dropped out of range, he heard Ennis say, "I'll be right behind you. I need to make certain none of the guards hack through the rope."

Gareth could hear the lie in the man's voice.

Ennis Loren was staying to protect them to the end. And, Gareth knew, it would finally, at long last, cost the man his life.

Twenty

The Western Kingdom, Knight's End
Ennis Loren

This was his penance, Ennis knew. It wasn't that he thought he'd been dishonorable. No, it was far worse. At least a dishonorable act was an act. Instead, he'd done nothing while his cousin had made rash decisions and destroyed so much of herself even as she was destroying everything he loved about the west. Yes, he'd argued with her and provided opposing counsel, but those were just words.

Action felt so much better, even if his every breath was treason.

They came in waves, rushing up the winding staircase with blood in their eyes. Ennis's only advantages were maintaining the high ground and the fact that the stairs were so narrow only two men could attack at once.

He used these advantages for a time, slashing throats and kicking the corpses down the steps, where they crashed into the reinforcements just behind them. He fought not for Gwendolyn or Gareth, not for Rhea or the west, not even for his own life. No, he fought for something more difficult to describe. It was muddled hope and a hazy future and the fuzzy image of children running through the streets, laughing and playing and knowing nothing of war or violence.

He fought for those unnamed children, even as blood streamed down his arms, both his and his enemies'. He fought for those future children as, eventually, several guards broke through, forcing him back. He tripped over the rope, the rope that was still taut with the weight of Gwendolyn Storm and Gareth Ironclad, creaking slightly as they slid down it.

One of the guards spotted the cord, realization dawning in his eyes, and he swung his sword...

Ennis lunged, extending his weapon to the end of his reach, barely managing to deflect the guard's blade. Rather than slicing through the rope, it slashed across the top of it, severing a half-dozen threads in the process.

The rope twisted, feeling the pressure of losing a portion of its strength, shuddering slightly as the weight on its end jerked violently.

And then the guard was swinging again and Ennis was finding his balance and blocking the blow, even as another guard sprang forward and aimed his own blade for the rope...

Clang! Clang! Clang! Ennis deflected three separate attempts from three separate guards, spinning and pivoting, a maelstrom of last-ditch effort.

One finally got through, and that was all it took.

The rope snapped, one end dropping harmlessly to the floor while the other whipped away, through the window, and out of sight.

Ennis, a prayer for his unexpected friends on his lips, dropped his sword, sank to his knees, and said, "I surrender."

Gwendolyn Storm

Although what Ennis had told them about Darkspell's potion was still ringing through Gwen's mind, she pushed it away—there would be time to process it all later.

Now, she had to focus, because something was wrong.

As they dangled, still halfway up the side of the tower, the ground a distant nothing below, the rope shuddered and then began twisting.

And she knew.

She knew.

Ennis had saved their lives by staying behind. But that didn't mean they were safe—not even close. "Go!" she screamed at Gareth, who, in his obvious humanness, seemed to move down the rope at a trickle while she was ready to be a cascading waterfall.

Gareth looked up, the fear clear in his eyes. This wasn't the time for it, and yet Gwendolyn felt a shred of relief pass through her when she saw it. Because if he was scared of falling to his death, that meant he didn't want to die anymore. She could use that.

"I'll show you," she said quickly, clambering past him. She hooked her feet around the rope for balance and then let the thick threads slide through, slowly at first and then faster and faster, her heromark flaring on her cheek, providing a supernatural level of strength, speed, and agility.

She glanced up and was buoyed to see Gareth following in her wake, barreling slightly out of control, his mouth open in a silent scream. When she looked back down, the ground grew larger and larger, like a giant black mouth yawning open.

Closer.

Closer.

With a jerk, the rope snapped, launching her downwards at double the speed. Her body, stretched tight as a bowstring, reacted instantly, changing position in the air so that she was horizontal rather than vertical, her feet churning beneath her as she sprinted *down* the wall.

When she neared the bottom, she leapt, throwing herself forward into a somersault, tumbling across the soft grass of the gardens, coming out of the roll in a crouch. *Holy Orion*, she thought, impressing even herself. Even after nine decades of learning about the abilities bestowed upon her by her fatemark, she could still be surprised by what she could do.

That thought, however, flashed past in less than a second, as she was already pushing off, charging back for the base of the tower, craning her head skyward, following the sound of Gareth's scream to its source, a deadweight body plummeting for the ground like a bird clipped of its wings.

She caught him in both arms, swinging downwards in an arc to prevent breaking his spine upon impact. Still, the force of his momentum coupled with her swinging catch sent them both sprawling end over end, a tangle of arms and legs.

When they came to a halt, Gareth said, "Whoa," as he released his breath.

And then the archers arrived on the garden walls.

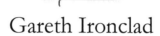

Gareth Ironclad

Why can't anything ever be easy? Gareth thought as the first arrow whizzed past, embedding itself in a tree.

He'd almost died from the fright of the fall and now he was about to be turned into a human pincushion. It wasn't his best day, and the sun hadn't even breached the horizon.

Of course, the damn Orian wasn't about to let either of them stop to catch their breaths. She was up in an instant, grabbing his arm and hauling him to his feet, yanking him into a forced run.

He supposed he should be thankful to have such a capable warrior helping him, but right now he just felt doomed, which was slightly better than the boredom of being locked in the tower for days on end.

"Faster," Gwen hissed, although Gareth was fairly certain he was already moving at maximum speed, arrows zipping past much too close for comfort.

And then she slammed to a stop and said another word he didn't want to hear. "Up."

It wasn't a command so much as a preview of what was coming next. Because she picked him up with arms much stronger than they looked and threw him into the air, a place he really wasn't keen to revisit after his last experience.

"Grab!" she said next, and Gareth did, wrapping his arms around a thick branch well off the ground. A moment later Gwen was beside him, although he wasn't certain how— whether she'd jumped or simply run up the tree.

She grabbed him and threw him again, almost as if it had all become a game and he was naught but an object to be tossed about. At least this time he was ready for it, was already looking up to catch the next branch, which was nearly halfway to the top of the tree. This continued twice more, until the thin uppermost branches bent precariously under his weight as he caught them.

"Hell no," he said when he realized what the only possible next move was. The top of the wall was an insane distance away, perhaps thrice his own height. And six or seven archers were already racing along the wall toward the closest spot, fitting bows to strings, preparing to stop, turn, and—

Gwen picked him up and stuffed him under her arm like a child, ran down the edge of the narrow branch like it was as broad as a road, and, the branch bowing under their combined weight, leapt.

The archers were so surprised by the move that they froze, only able to watch as the pair flew through the air, Gwen landing softly on both feet.

"Ready?" she asked as she set Gareth back on his feet.

Gareth thought she might be speaking a foreign language, but he nodded anyway, waiting to be jerked, yanked, or thrown into whatever the next step was in her plan.

To his surprise, however, she did none of those things, taking off along the wall at a sprint, right toward where three of the archers were kneeling, retracting their arrows…

She rolled and Gareth ducked and the darts flew past, stopping only when they slammed into the chests of the other three archers, who, screaming, toppled from the wall.

Ahead of him, Gwen came up in a full sprint, crashing into two of the archers, flinging them to the sides, where there was nothing but empty air. The third archer tried to run, but Gwen launched herself up and over him, twisting in midair so that when she landed she was facing him. He tried to draw a knife from his belt, but she was faster, landing three consecutive blows to his head. He wobbled on his feet and Gwen flicked him with a single finger.

Like the others, he toppled from the wall.

"You scare me sometimes," Gareth said. That's when he noticed an arrow protruding from a gap in the plate along her thigh. "What happened?"

"I'm getting slow in my old age," she said. "Come on, I'll deal with it later."

They raced along the wall toward the back of the castle, where it would be quieter.

The peal of alarm bells from the temple faded away.

Twenty-One
The Hinterlands
Lisbeth Lorne

The single word, spoken deep in the core of Lisbeth's soul, seemed to echo:

War war war war...

Though she was new to her body, new to this world and the actions of humans, Garzi, animals, and all the other creatures inhabiting this continent, Lisbeth knew what war meant. Violence. Destruction. Death. Spoils. Victors. Prisoners. Pain. Glory. Fear.

She didn't know how she knew, only that the word made her want to race back out into the night, to run and run and run until her legs failed her, until her breaths came in rolling waves, until she was so utterly exhausted she couldn't think couldn't feel couldn't hear anything but the beat of her own heart as she drifted off into a peaceful sleep.

A sleep without war.

"I don't—I won't—I'm not here for that," she finally got out.

The pulsing souls spread through the enormous tower built of snow and ice—*The Hall of War it is called*, a fact she only now remembered—buzzed with confusion. And she finally understood what they were: souls, very much alive, trapped in sleeping bodies. Their sleep felt unnatural, just as the hollow voice ringing in her head felt unnatural. *Then why have you come to us? Why has the sky spit you forth and planted you here, if not to awaken us, to call us to war?*

She found her words. "Coincidence. Misfortune. A random turn of events." She turned away, hearing their screams in her head, their anger at her abandonment, the pent-up violence twisting through their ancient souls.

The moment she stepped back out into the frozen night, the voices fell away, stolen by a blast of icy wind.

All was calm. All was quiet.

A figure stumbled through the snow, lurching toward her.

Zur crashed into her, his long, muscled arms slamming her to the hard-packed snow, his stringy hair bristling over her face.

She felt like screaming, but could only gasp as the air left her lungs.

She knew she could invade his mind again, could snuff out the last of his soul, that weak, barely-there pulse, throbbing like a dying heartbeat.

I can't I can't I can't
She stole my soul…

And then she was there, in that faded place that Lisbeth was beginning to realize was many years ago, before she had even contemplated the idea of being more than a ribbon of light, inhabiting a body in this world of sound and color and beauty and pain. This time, she didn't float above the memory like a gust of wind; rather, she *was* the memory—she *was* the girl in the white dress, understanding her hopes, her dreams, her fears, her thoughts. Her truths:

The current carried the young girl into the water, tears streaming down her face. She didn't sink, but floated, her white dress heavy but not enough to drag her into the depths. No, it was her fear that was the true anchor, pulling, pulling…

She whipped around, and her father was but a lone shadow in the distance, still retreating, unwilling to watch what was to come next. The other Garzi remained, however, staring silently at her in the water. Her people. Familiar faces. Friends. Loved ones.

She could swim back to shore, but what was the point? They would only force her back in, and her life was forfeit anyway. She'd carried the disease for three long years, and it would consume her any day.

So she'd been chosen.

A sacrifice to son-son-Matho, great hunter of the warm waters of Venus.

She'd seen the lake monster before, once, during the last Time of Sacrifice. Then, her father had been by her side, holding her steady, explaining what was happening. Not so she could learn, but so she could be prepared for when it was her turn. On that day, it had been an old man, Nero, the bulk of his life long past, his face calm and steady and free of tears.

Why me? *she wondered now.* Why me, a girl who has barely seen life, much less lived it?

She didn't have time to consider the mysteries of life and fate, however, because she felt it. It was surprisingly calm, gentle, the slightest displacement of water, a ripple uncoiling like a snake through the water, brushing against her. It almost tickled, the sensation like feathers on skin.

That sensation turned the buzz of fear into a spike up her spine.

Why me why me why me—

Son-son-Matho burst from the water, its sleek, scale-armored flesh beautiful in the light of the sun, changing color—red, green, yellow, blue...

She saw its red eye, and in it was contained a depth she hadn't expected, an all-consuming understanding of the world around it. She could see the hunger in that look, but also the appreciation, that she would come to it, a willing sacrifice.

And though her fear refused to fade away, she thought: I can do this.

She remembered that old man, who'd eventually panicked, attempting to swim for shore as the monster's fin closed in from behind. She remembered how she'd watched breathlessly as he'd been taken in a single gulp, his body vanishing in a splash so large it had created breaking waves on the shoreline.

She didn't want to be that man, running from reality.

I am going to die, *she thought.* Even if it wasn't today, it would be tomorrow, or the day after that. Not years, but weeks. Months at best.

This is what I can do to make my life meaningful...I can sacrifice for my people, for those loved ones watching. *She looked back once more—just once—and found her father standing in the distance, watching, his hands covering his mouth.*

She did not scream, did not cry, did not panic. A warm calm set in and she raised her hand high to her father. Do not mourn me, *the gesture said.* Do not cry for me, for I am safe, Father, your little star is safe in the heavens.

She turned back, saw the humped, bone-hard skull of son-son-Matho as it closed in, slicing through the water like a knife through snow. She raised her hands above her head, whispering a prayer to Venus, to the god that gave her these years of life and would now reclaim her.

The monster opened its maw, its shining teeth like bone daggers set all in a row. It was darkness. It was light. It was truth.

"Take me," she said, and then it did.

Why why why why why why why why why WHY WHY WHY WHY WHY WHY

Why

Please. Please. Please. Lisbeth knew she was begging those who couldn't hear her, who wouldn't hear her. For begging to change the past was as pointless as trying to turn stone into gold.

Zur's soul was fading, sliding away like the girl, his daughter, had drifted into darkness. Willingly and without regret.

I took everything from this man, Lisbeth thought. *His memories, his dreams, his fears, his soul...*

I am evil. I am death. I am—

An idea sprung forth, bursting through the contours of her mind like a green shoot through the dirt after a rainfall.

I can give it all back.

Though she wasn't certain whether the thought was a foolish lie, the naivete of her newness to this world, she clung to the idea like a rope dangling from a cliff, thinking it over and over and over again, until it wasn't a thought, but a belief.

She felt the third eye on her forehead burn, flashing in the dark, its blue light slamming into Zur's chest. He screamed, but she didn't stop, forcing her will upon him, expanding, shredding through flesh and muscle and bone, and then pouring into that last speck of soul that remained, a twinkling ember in the darkness. Repairing. Joining. Healing.

Images flashed: His daughter, laughing as he chased her around their dwelling; her face glowing with light from a fire as she told him a story while eating supper; the excitement in her eyes when she found a tiny pink flower growing, against all odds, in a snowdrift.

Memories poured forth, a hundred, a thousand, a brief lifetime flashing in a moment.

Zur groaned and rolled over, facefirst in the snow. Slowly, Lisbeth turned him over, watching his soul sleep for a moment.

She slumped beside him, exhausted, staring up at the sky, at the billions of stars overhead. The red ones soared past, leaving behind fiery trails. The gold ones twinkled like flipped coins. The green ones exploded again and again.

A vibrant, shifting soul blotted out the sky.

Crone.

"So now girl understands."

Lisbeth didn't have the energy to respond, so she merely nodded. *Yes. I understand.*

For she was not a destroyer of souls, but a strengthener, a forger, a bringer.

And though the thought of war scared her, she knew it was her purpose.

Twenty-Two
The Northern Kingdom, Darrin
Tarin Sheary

The leftover soldiers of Darrin were quickly learning that the Armored Knight was a man of his word. By the end of the third day, they collapsed in ragged piles, barely taking the time to stuff their mouths with sustenance before falling into their bunks.

After day four, dozens left in droves, marching from the city in groups. Tarin didn't try to stop them—he only wanted the strong ones anyway.

He laughed at his own thoughts. *None of them are warriors, save perhaps Sir Jonathan.*

Just as quickly, he chided himself for being unfair. *They are still here. They are still trying. And so are you. That has to count for something.* Tarin only hoped that when the enemy finally arrived, those left wouldn't turn tail and run. Regardless, he knew he would stand and fight, even if it was only him and his monster to defend the city. He would defend Annise's kingdom to the bitter end, one way or another.

And anyway, despite their faults, the men had talents of a different nature. Captain Morris, who was just Morris now that he'd been demoted—he'd almost looked relieved when Tarin told him—had a remarkable ability to make self-deprecating jokes at the exact moment when the men seemed on the verge of giving up. They would laugh and continue on, having forgotten their struggles. It was a skill Tarin had yet to master. The skinny old geezer, who everyone called Creak on account of the sound his knees made when he ambled past, could shoot an arrow as straight and true as any man Tarin had ever met. "I used to win every tourney I entered," the man said. Tarin had charged him with training the archers. They wouldn't get that much better in the short time they had, but any improvement was better than none. Fay, as she'd promised, had managed to find enough blacksmiths to keep the forges going day and night, the sounds of hammers meeting anvils providing a raucous accompaniment to every other activity.

Tarin stood watching Sir Jonathan drilling the men on the snowfields, which had begun to turn to slush under the strangely warm winter temperatures. Like Tarin, ever since that night of unhappy stories, Sir Jonathan had thrown all his strength into the task at hand—training a bunch of green soldiers who'd spent more time drinking in the last year than fighting.

But Sir Jonathan's story…Tarin shook his head. It was worse than he'd ever expected. Cruel soldiers had broken into his home, had taken advantage of his wife, and had lied about it later when accused by the knight. Without proof other than her word against theirs, the charges had been dropped. His wife had descended into a dark place, and Sir Jonathan an even darker one, a place of shadows and sorrow and pain.

And anger.

Tarin understood that part more than any of the others.

Sir Jonathan had snapped. He'd cornered each of the three soldiers separately, disarming them and cutting off their manhood with their own blades. Then he'd killed them, slowly. Painfully. He'd relished every cut, every scream of pain, every drop of blood that spilled out.

When finally, his hands stained with the blood of a trio of evil men, he returned home, he found his wife dead, an empty vial with the distinctly bitter smell of darkweed lying beside her body on the floor.

He'd carried her outside, his expression frozen, his mind blank, marching her through Darrin in his arms, forcing everyone to see the unfair justice of the world they lived in. He knocked on the door of his commanding officer and told him everything, including his own crimes.

He'd been in the dungeons ever since, having to daily make the decision not to kill himself—"She wouldn't have wanted that…"—until Fay had shown up and released him.

Frozen hell, Tarin thought. *What is wrong with this world and the people who live in it?*

Snapping him from his thoughts, a man approached—one of Fay's charges. Well, Tarin was being generous thinking of him as a man, for Lucky was half his size and a third his width and looked as if a stiff breeze might knock him flat on his back. Still, Fay said the boy was a hard worker, and kept the fires burning hot. The boy was struggling under the weight of a large metal plate, which he carried with both arms. Somehow, he managed to reach Tarin before dropping it awkwardly in the slush with a slight splash.

"Begging your apologies, Lord Commander," Lucky said. "Shoulda used a cart for that one." The boy, like many of the others, refused to look directly upon Tarin's face, except when they thought he wasn't aware of their stares.

Tarin frowned. He wasn't sure any of his men would be able to carry the plate of metal, much less use it for anything. "What is it—some kind of shield?"

Before Lucky could answer, Tarin casually flipped it over with one arm, as if it weighed nothing. The boy gawked at him.

Tarin ignored him, his breath hitching. For, carved into the opposite side was the image of a large knight wielding a long length of chain attached to a spiked ball—what could only be Tarin's weapon, designed by Fay herself—the Morningstar.

Anger plumed from Tarin's mouth as he grabbed up what he now realized was a chest plate—*his* chest plate. He shoved past Lucky, who yelped and dodged away, and marched for the forges, his own fires stoked by each step. *Damn woman!* he thought, kicking up slush as he stomped.

He knew he should stop, should try to calm his temper before confronting Fay, but his feet just kept moving on their own. He burst into the sweltering area, the *ching! ching! ching!* of hammers ringing in his ears, stalked to the back, where the largest fire of all was raging. That's where he found Fay, sheathed in sweat, her muscles taut and rippling, using a massive sledge to pound away at a piece of red-hot iron.

"What the frozen hell is this?" Tarin roared.

He felt the monster inside him stir, try to rise up, but he gritted his teeth and pushed it back down.

182

Fay drove her hammer down twice more, sparks flying, before setting it gently on the bench, turning to face him. "Your new chest plate," she said. "I thought that was obvious."

Tarin felt his face flush, felt the monster probing at his weak spots. It wanted blood. "No," he growled, low and dangerous.

Fay's eyebrows narrowed. "No what?"

Tarin shook his head, not wanting to explain. "I explicitly ordered you not to work on my new plate until my men had been outfitted with weapons and armor."

"No," Fay said slowly, drawing out the word with a roundness that made it sound to Tarin like she was speaking to a misguided child. "You said not to have any of the *men* work on your armor until after the rest of the work was done. Thankfully, I am no man; we've got too many of them around here as it is." Tarin tried to rebuff her, but she went on. "And, you need armor as much as anyone. You're beginning to resemble a sardine in an old tin can. A very large sardine, yes, but not a look fit for the Lord Commander."

Tarin growled again, but Fay refused to back down. "I will continue with this project. If you don't like it, you'll have to restrain me."

He was aware that several of the other smiths had stopped what they were doing to watch the commotion. "Fine," he grunted, hefting the plate with one arm over his shoulder and turning to leave.

"Did you even try it on?" Fay said to his back. "I need to know whether you need any alterations."

"I'll let you know." Tarin left, feeling frustrated.

Is the north full of stubborn women? he wondered. *No,* he thought, *just stubborn people in general.* It was their greatest strength and weakness. They didn't know when to give up.

He stopped outside in the slush, trying to slow his breathing, trying to stop the thoughts of broken bodies, rivers of blood, severed—

"Argh!" he roared, sprinting back toward the fields.

He had to sate the monster's appetite, and there was only one way he knew how, other than violence:

Action. Movement. Work.

He slung the chest plate to the ground and whipped out Morningstar, unleashing it into the clear sky, cutting silver arcs, sweat dripping from his face, his men—having long finished their own training—gawking at their Lord Commander with jaws open, mouths agape.

He fought invisible enemies long into the night, until his soldiers left to take their evening meal, until he was alone...

You are never alone, the monster reminded him, purring in the dark.

Toward the south, well past the peaks of the Mournful Mountains, gray clouds of smoke blotted out the sky as the Tangle continued to burn.

The next day, Tarin awoke to a headache, which was exacerbated by the clang of metal against metal. He groaned, squinting when he opened his eyes to bright light hitting them.

"Top of the morning," a voice croaked, descending into a choking laugh-cough.

One eye open just a slit, Tarin gazed at Creak, who was sitting on the bottom bunk across the aisle, staring at him. "What time is it?"

"Noonday, I'd say."

"Why aren't you training the archers?"

"The woman told me to watch you. Make sure you're okay."

"What woman?" Tarin said, though he only needed one guess.

"The blacksmith. The one with the big mouth."

"Do I give the orders or does she?"

"Most think it's near on the same thing."

Tarin groaned again. It was hard enough organizing this strange assortment of castaways without Fay pulling stunts like this.

"May I speak freely?" Creak asked.

"Don't you always?"

Creak chuckled. "Good point. The blacksmith woman might be a stone-cold heartbreaker, but she's only worried about you. Truth be told, we all are. Since the day you showed up, you've hardly said more than a word to anyone. You stomp around like some beast from the Hinterlands that looks like it wants to rip someone's head off, and then you go mad in an instant, working like a dog for an entire day without stopping. Leaves us all a little...unsettled."

Tarin jerked back. *Worried? His men were worried about* him?

"Everyone watched you last night. I almost skipped dinner because of it, and that's saying a lot. We finally dispersed when we couldn't keep our eyes open any longer."

Tarin tried to remember last night, but it was all foggy, like it had been a dream. He remembered swinging Morningstar,

185

again and again and again; he remembered feeling the wind on his face, the slippery ground beneath him...

He remembered the men watching him, but at some point they'd faded away, disappeared into the background, and all that existed was his weapon, his beating heart, and the thing purring inside him.

"Gather the men on the fields. I want to speak to them."

"Good idea," Creak said, his joints crackling as he rose and limped outside.

Tarin rubbed his face, trying to chase the sleep away. He hadn't slept that long in years. He started to stand, but cracked his head on the underside of the top bunk. He cringed, massaging his scalp. Lately, he'd begun to feel like a real life giant. Fay was right—his armor was so tight against his skin it was bruising him. His entire body ached.

After taking some time to clean his face in the washbin, he headed for the forge. When he arrived, it was deserted—Creak had followed his orders efficiently. He was about to turn away, when he heard a noise in the back.

"Hello?" he said.

Fay eased around a wooden shelf full of raw materials, raising an eyebrow when she saw him. "Welcome back to the land of the living. Want to tell me what that was all about last night?"

"No," Tarin said.

"I didn't think so. Let me know if you do."

"Look, Fay, I'm sor—"

She waved him away before he could finish. "Nothing to be sorry about. You're damn right I circumvented your orders. But I'm not sorry about that either. You *will* have a fresh suit of armor—one that fits."

186

That's when he noticed the dark circles under her eyes. "How late were you up?"

"As late as you," she said. "Wanted to make sure you found your way back into your bunk. Figured I might as well get some work done."

"Let me guess, you were up at the crack of dawn." Something about one of his own working harder and longer than him didn't sit well with Tarin. He'd served under good leaders and bad leaders, mean sons of bitches and kind-hearted souls, but the ones he respected most were those who toiled alongside their men. That was the kind of leader Tarin wished to be, not a hot-tempered giant that everyone worried about.

Fay smiled. "I don't need much sleep. Heard you called a little meeting."

"Aye, the man you ordered to watch me sleep is organizing it."

Fay's smile broadened. "I got these men wrapped around my small finger."

"Perhaps I could learn a thing or two from you," Tarin said. He turned away, then looked back. "Coming?"

"Wouldn't miss it."

Most of the men were looking at his feet. The few brave souls who managed to meet his stare quickly looked away, flinching.

"Look at me," he said.

Some looked. Some didn't. None held his gaze, except Fay, Creak, and Sir Jonathan, who seemed immune to his strange appearance.

"Look at me!" he shouted.

All eyes flicked to him. Held, barely. "Don't look away," he ordered, tracking across each line of men, holding each set of eyes for a moment or two before moving on. He met all one-hundred-and-twenty-six pairs of eyes before he was finished. Fay's held sparkling amusement. Creak's curiosity. Morris's were bloodshot, likely from sneaking a bottle or ten of ale. Sir Jonathan's were steel, as if forged by one of Fay's smiths. In between those familiar eyes were eyes of all shapes, colors, and temperaments. Individuals, each with their own hopes and dreams, fears and insecurities.

"I am just a man," Tarin finally said, when the silence had almost become another soldier, standing amongst them. "Just as each of you are." Fay coughed. Tarin rephrased. "A human like you. Something happened to me a long time ago, when I was a boy. It changed how I look. It changed something inside of me, too, but I hope it didn't change everything." He paused, remembering why he wanted them all here in the first place. "Why are you here?" he asked.

"For the food!" Creak shouted immediately. The man had a quick tongue, Tarin had to admit.

"Aye," Tarin said. "Castle food isn't half bad, but it won't last. So you have to find another reason, a bigger reason. Or else you shouldn't be here."

Fay warned him away from the topic of leaving with her eyes, but Tarin ignored her. No, he wouldn't hide from the steady flow of deserters, he would face them head on. It was the only way to stem the tide.

"I will tell you my reason," Tarin said.

The men shifted from foot to foot, like a habit, a way of keeping warm. They waited. Some had averted their eyes the moment they were no longer being ordered to stare at him, but most had not. Tarin continued to meet their eyes, treating them like the individuals that they were.

"I came here to try to protect someone," he said. "That first day, when I saw you lot, I almost left." A few chuckles rolled across the crowd. "But someone convinced me to stay, and she was right." Eyes shifted toward Fay, and Tarin enjoyed watching her squirm in discomfort. "My reason for staying is my own—to protect Queen Annise Gäric, our lawful ruler, from the eastern invaders who would murder her and smash her throne. But that is only *my* reason. You each need your own. We don't have time to sit around and think about it, we have to keep training, but I want you to consider this question. If you don't have an answer by the time we see our enemies' weapons flashing over the cliffs, then you should leave. But even if you all leave, I shall stay. I shall fight. And I shall spill the blood of my foes across the land of our fathers and mothers, sisters and brothers."

Silence fell once more, the sun glittering through the clouds, which were thickening once more.

Someone thumped their chest. Sir Jonathan, his expression coursing with determination. "I fight for my wife, may she rest in peace. That is my reason."

Several men nodded, gaining confidence from the knight, who Tarin had appointed as their new captain. More fists thumped chests, and voices spoke over each other, stating their reasons for staying. *I got nothing better to do...I just like a good fight...I hate those damn easterners...I always wanted to earn me knighthood...I really am here for the food (Creak's answer)...*and many, many more, none better than another.

As if in response, dark clouds assembled overhead, blotting out the sun. The temperature dropped, infusing the air with an

189

icy chill. Snow began to fall in earnest once more, huge flakes that stuck to everything they touched, the men included.

The soldiers thumped their chests and stomped their feet. Winter had returned, and with it their advantage.

Twenty-Three
The Hinterlands
Annise Gäric

"I should have stayed unconscious," Archer said, rubbing his gloved hands together.

And I should've stayed in bed, Annise thought. Why had she ever wanted to flee into the Hinterlands anyway? They'd only traveled a day north of Castle Hill and already the temperature had become colder than she'd ever experienced, which was saying something for someone who'd lived their entire life on this side of the Mournful Mountains.

The storm had moved in so fast they'd barely had time to erect their shelters before it was upon them. With the howling wind and sleet, a fire was impossible. Cold, half-frozen water, hard bread and tough meat made for unsatisfying dinner fare.

Annise longed for Tarin, not for his humor or heart, but for his heat. *Frozen hell, I would love his warmth wrapped around me right now.*

But longing and wishing was pointless. At least they were out of the wind, having dug a bunker deep into the snow to construct their thick tents. And they had plenty of warm, woolen blankets, which they wrapped themselves in.

In some ways, it was humorous, the four of them in one medium-sized tent. Archer and Annise occupied one half, while Sir Dietrich and Sir Jonius crammed into the other. Before her father's death, she could never have envisioned such a scene.

Annise giggled.

"Ha ha," Archer said. "I must've missed the part where any of this was funny."

She giggled again as the wind howled.

Sir Jonius looked at her strangely. Sir Dietrich opened his mouth as if to speak, but then shut it, shaking his head. Perhaps he was remembering the beating she'd given him a day earlier.

Annise said, "I was just thinking how amusing it is that the four of us are here right now."

Archer made a face. Sir Jonius raised an eyebrow. Sir Dietrich said, "My queen is in a queer mood."

"We're searching for *the Sleeping Knights*. Doesn't that strike any of you as funny?"

No one replied. Annise groaned. Tarin would've gotten it. He understood her eccentricities like no one else ever had— including her Aunt Zelda. "Fine," she huffed. "I shall wallow in self-pity like the rest of you. Good night." She blew out the lantern, casting them all into complete darkness.

Arch said, "If I was still king, I'd have sent you lot on this mission while I stayed warm in Castle Hill."

"I'll let you have a chance to be king," Annise said.

"Really?"

"You have to fight me for it. No weapons."

Sir Jonius chuckled. "I'd like to see that."

"Well you're not going to," Archer said. "She fights dirty. I won't stoop to that level. Now if we jousted…"

"Forget it," Annise said. "Horses are evil beasts intent on tossing me in the snow."

Dietrich said, "If I were king, I would declare winter a long holiday. No work. No war. Just warm fires and food."

"If you were king," Annise said, "hell would freeze over…again."

Archer finally laughed. Dietrich did not.

Sir Jonius said, "Sir Dietrich, I remember all too well being bested by you in the tourney. You are a fine swordsman, though I hear your hidden mark gains you quite an advantage."

"Your point, Sir?" There was an edge to his voice; Annise knew from experience that the knight did not enjoy talking about his skinmark.

"I do not intend to offend. I'm merely curious as to your background. Why did you avoid serving the Dread King for so long?"

When Dietrich didn't answer right away, Sir Jonius added, "In truth, I wish I could've hidden myself as well. Unfortunately, I had no choice but to serve King Gäric."

Annise remembered the day she learned why Sir Jonius had been such an enigma to her for so long. How his wife had been sick for years. How only an elixir provided by her father's potionmaster, Darkspell, had kept her alive. In exchange for

193

the potion, Sir Jonius had been forced to carry out all manner of atrocities in the king's name, a fact that continued to haunt him.

Sir Dietrich sighed. "Why is everyone so nosy?" Though he sounded exasperated, Annise could tell it wasn't a refusal to answer the question. They waited. He said, "My father was a simple man, a stoneworker in Gearhärt. He'd been born there, and he always planned to die there. He didn't give much credence to the wars and territorial pissings of kings and queens. He lived for my mother. For me."

He paused, and Annise could hear him swallow in the dark. The patter of snow rustled against the tent. She wondered whether they'd need to awaken in the middle of the night to dig themselves out before it got too deep. She hoped not.

Dietrich continued. "When the war front began to intensify at Raider's Pass, the Dread King himself rode through Gearhärt, stopping briefly before marching to the border. Now, his father, the Undefeated King, had always been supportive of Gearhärt's role in the war—providing brick and mortar, weapons, and provisions to his soldiers. Your father, however, wanted men. He recruited in Gearhärt before continuing south. And by recruited, I mean forced every last man over the age of twelve to take up arms in defense of the kingdom.

"My father refused. Like I said, he was a simple man who didn't like to be bullied, not even by a king. Your father, as you might expect, didn't appreciate his ideals."

"Frozen hell," Sir Jonius said. "I remember him. I remember your father."

"You should," Dietrich growled. "You helped tie him up in the street, so his friends could see what happened to those who defied the king. I was only eight years old."

Sir Jonius was silent for a moment. And then: "I'm sorry. I had no choice."

"So you keep saying," Dietrich said. "But there is always a choice. Your wife was dying, while my father was a strong, healthy man with many years left in his life. He was a *good* man. The best. Do you want to tell the queen and prince what their father did to my father?"

A rustle of blankets. Sir Jonius said, "He killed him. Stabbed him through the heart. Left him to bleed in the streets. Everyone else joined the army, marching south with the king and I. We defeated the easterners as they tried to battle through the pass. I was—" His voice caught, trembled, and then found the words. "I was *thankful* he hadn't made me kill him—your father. I was *thankful* that he had done it himself. I didn't think about who he was, or who he'd left behind, or whether he had a family, children…no, I never allowed myself to think about such things. I had to stay numb, or else I would never have been able to do the things I did."

Dietrich said, "After the army moved on, having cleaned out the city of able-bodied men, my mother and I cut the ropes from my father, cleaned the blood off his face and clothes, and buried him. We piled stones he had cut with his own two hands atop his grave. I cried for a long time. But eventually I stopped. And I vowed never to work for the Dread King, even if it meant my own death. I never broke that promise."

"And then you met Tarin," Annise said, the pieces to an old puzzle finally coming together. She was surprised at how easily

195

his name slipped off her tongue, like it had been resting there the whole time.

"Aye," Dietrich said. "We faced each other at several tourneys. He even defeated my sword once, something no one had ever done. We became friends. He opened up to me about his…past…and I reciprocated. He wasn't even bothered that I'd defeated him numerous times using my swordmark, and—"

"Wait," Annise said, her temper sparking. "You're saying he *knew* about your mark?"

"Oops," Dietrich said, realizing his error.

Annise gritted her teeth. All those times she'd complained about Sir Dietrich to Tarin, how he wouldn't tell her the truth…he'd known the whole time. And yet, she realized, he hadn't lied. He'd only advised her to give the knight time to explain himself. *Because he was a true friend. Is a true friend.*

No, she couldn't blame him for that.

"Go on," she said. "How did you end up in Castle Hill working for my mother?"

"The tourney was a good excuse to be there, but our true purpose was far more cunning. Queen Sabria had been searching for Tarin Sheary for some time, eventually realizing he was the same person as the Armored Knight, who had gained quite a lot of fame. Through Zelda, she brought him into her inner circle, and he vouched for me. We became her secret guard, you might say."

A loop was finally closed, explaining so much about the last few months, how they'd gotten to this point.

"Thank you," Annise said. "For telling us. For helping my mother and Tarin. I'm sorry I've been so hard on you."

196

"So you'll stop throwing boots at me and rubbing snow in my face?" She could hear the smile in his tone.

Archer said, "Boots? Sounds *just* like something my sister would do. I told you, she fights dirty."

Ignoring the quip, Annise said, "I can't make any promises. But I'll try. Now get some rest. We move at first light, storm or not."

Surprisingly, the storm had moved on during the night, leaving behind an enormous white blanket in its wake.

Jonius had gone out twice while they slept to shovel snow away from their tent, piling it in huge drifts that now resembled castle ramparts—a miniature version of Castle Hill. Twice he'd told them to sleep, that this act was part of his penance for crimes of the past. Annise tried arguing with him, to no avail. He was a man in a pit, and he would need to climb out of it on his own.

There was no sign of dry wood, which meant no fire. They ate more cold meat and bread and used their armpits to melt enough snow to drink.

From there, the going was slow through the snow, which reached Annise's waist, so they veered off toward the east, to where the Frozen Lake very much lived up to its name. Though it was also covered in snow, the drifts were mostly piled along the edges, the howling wind driving them into domed walls. On the frozen water, the snow reached only to their ankles, allowing them to travel much faster. The ice wouldn't break—not in winter. The only negative was the lack of protection from the wind, which seemed to have teeth, biting through cloth and armor.

No one spoke, as their faces were covered by thick, triple-wrapped scarves.

A day passed, then another. They camped right on the ice, without fire, without any heat other than that of their own bodies inside their tent. It wasn't enough. Annise could feel the ice settling into her bones, threatening to take her fingers, her toes.

They would need fire soon or they would all lose even more than that.

Still, they pressed on, trying to cross as much of the Frozen Lake as possible before being forced to angle westward, to a spot marked on an old map that none of them knew whether to trust. With each frozen, weary step, Annise wondered more and more whether she was leading them on a fool's mission.

We have no other option, she reminded herself. *War is coming, and we have no army. I have to give my people a chance to defend themselves. Risking my life, the life of my brother, and the lives of these two knights is the price of hope.*

Still, doubt crept in, day by day, night by night.

Then, something changed.

"What is that?" Archer said, his voice muffled through his scarf. Annise looked at him; he was pointing into the distance. She followed his gaze. Something sparkled. Shifted. *Flowed.*

"Is that…" Her question trailed away, because it was impossible. This far north in the dead of winter, it was *impossible.*

And yet… "Water?" Dietrich said.

The moment he uttered the word, the ice beneath his feet began to crack.

Twenty-Four
The Northern Kingdom, Darrin
Tarin Sheary

Tarin froze mid step, dread coiling through his gut.

Annise. Inexplicably, impossibly, he knew she was in mortal danger.

Fay, always by his side, always supporting, stopped too. "Tarin?" she said.

He didn't see her, didn't hear her, as he whirled around, scanning the flat, empty expanse separating the castle of Darrin from both the Mournful Mountains and the Razor, half-expecting to find Annise standing there, surrounded by enemies.

Wind whipped across the barren snowfields. The snow had been falling continuously since it started, garbing Darrin in a thick, white coat. Hundreds of soldiers were working hard, as they had been for several days, digging pits, lining them with spikes, covering them with flimsy branches and snow, smoothing them out. Others built walls at odd angles, wrapping them with coils of spiked metal wire. Those not digging or building drilled with Sir Jonathan nearby. None of it was done to Tarin's standards, the way it would have been if he had a platoon of seasoned soldiers. But it would have to be enough. It had to be.

But that was the last thing on Tarin's mind at this moment, the fear lingering, clinging to him like a thick fog.

"Tarin?" Fay said again. "What is it? What's wrong?"

Tarin didn't look at her, chewing his bottom lip as he tried to decide how to explain the unexplainable. *She'll think me paranoid*, he thought.

And maybe I am…

No, a voice hissed from the deepest, darkest recesses of his mind.

Tarin cringed. For the last few days he'd avoided that voice, that *thing* inside him, by moving, working from dawn till dusk, throwing himself into each task with a furious fervor none of his men could come close to matching. He barely stopped to sleep, eat and relieve himself, and even when he did, he kept his mind focused on anything and everything but the monster in his core.

But now…

What do you mean, no? Tarin thought back. He was distantly aware of Fay grabbing his arm and trying to force him to look at her, but he shrugged her off, focusing, focusing, focusing—

I mean you're not going mad. I mean Annise is in danger.

Shut your filthy mouth, Tarin snapped back. *You don't know that—you can't.*

You are connected to her now. A part of me is in her. In Castle Hill, on the battlefield...your blood mixed with hers...

What? No. What have I done? he thought, feeling ill in the core of his being. Could his curse truly be spread so easily? Would her blood turn black? Would fire and bloodlust war inside her heart?

He'd left to protect her, but that meant that he couldn't protect her from any other dangers. Which was worse? It was an impossible decision, but he'd made the only choice he thought he had at the time. But if he'd left a part of the monster inside of her...

If anything happened to the one person that mattered the most to him in this world, Tarin knew he couldn't live with himself.

If you hurt her... he thought, leaving the threat unfinished.

The monster had the nerve to laugh, boiling Tarin's blood in the process. *Your anger is misplaced. She isn't like us. I can't change her the way I can you. I can only feel what she feels. This is my gift to you.*

Which brought everything full circle, to that feeling of dread, the danger she was in. "I have to go," Tarin said. "I have to find her."

Fay grabbed his face, on both sides, forcing him to look at her. "I don't know what war you are fighting in your own head, but you must focus. You are here. You are the Lord Commander. These men *need* you. Everything falls apart without you."

Tarin felt like everything was falling apart anyway, like chunks of him were being ripped off by birds. He couldn't get his breath, couldn't find the air, his chest sucked in, gasping, gasping...

Fay hit him, hard, and the monster responded, snarling from the back of his throat.

"Better," Fay said. "You'll need that anger when you face your enemies."

Tarin threw his shovel down. The last pit was finished. Several men skittered past him, sliding ladders into the hole, dropping sharpened wooden poles that would be shoved into the ground, business end facing up. Others hauled thin branches to thread across the gap, which would then be covered with snow. They were crude traps, Tarin knew, but anything to slow the enemy down was worth the time and effort.

From there Tarin strode to the wall builders, crouching to lift a large tree trunk stripped of branches and bark. Other, similar trees were being lifted and carried by teams of half a dozen men. Tarin grunted, relishing the burn in his legs, the slight ache in his back, the flex of his biceps and chest. His anger had burned out long ago, but still he toiled alongside his men, even as the shadows lengthened and the sun dipped precariously toward the top of the Razor.

Balancing the tree on his massive shoulder while he waited his turn, Tarin considered their chances. If the easterners came with less than half a thousand, thinking their enemy was weak and ill-prepared, perhaps they could put up a fight. But if their enemy brought a force greater than that...

He didn't want to think about it. All he could do was prepare them the best he could, both physically and mentally. He needed them to *believe* they could seize victory, even if everything else pointed to the opposite. And he needed them to be able to stuff their fear and doubt into a place where they wouldn't see it.

Maybe you should do the same, he thought, slinging his trunk down onto the half-finished barrier of wood and mud and mortar. *Annise is fine.* He clung to that belief, because he would know if she was dead, wouldn't he? If what the monster inside him said was true—and he believed it was, for the monster had never lied to him—then he would know without a shadow of a doubt the moment she passed from this world and into whatever came next.

And he hadn't felt that, even as the feeling of dread lingered all day while he tried to distract himself from it by working his body to its fullest.

He wasn't scared for her, not anymore, because she was the strongest woman he knew, a fighter, a survivor, and he believed that, whatever she faced now, she would prevail. She would conquer.

And so shall you, the voice hissed, slithering from whatever hole in his soul it had been hiding in.

Twenty-Five
The Hinterlands
Annise Gäric

Before their eyes, the ice began to shred, cracks forming like spider webs, radiating outwards at an alarming rate. The ice beneath Annise's feet wobbled slightly, and she was forced to drop to a knee to keep from falling.

Archer, his eyes wide brown orbs, said, "Annise, you have to get off the ice." She heard the meaning in his tone: *You first. Only one can move at a time or we're all getting wet.*

"He's right," Sir Jonius said, his teeth locked. His arms were out to maintain his balance as the ice continued to shift below.

"Brute strength and queens before beauty and finesse," Sir Dietrich said.

In any other situation, Annise would've thrown something at the knight for such a remark, but right now she feared the slightest twitch would shatter the ground. "We go together," Annise said. There was no time to even contemplate *how* the ice was cracking. The air temperature had only gotten colder as they'd traveled north. If anything, the ice should be thicker, stronger.

"No," Arch said. "You are the hell-frozen queen, and you *will* get to safety."

"I *am* the hell-frozen queen and I command you all to go together," she growled back. *Damn these chivalrous men and their honor.* "We'll move apart, keep our weight spread out. Dietrich left, Jonius right, Arch straight down the center."

"And what about you?" Arch said.

"I'll head even further south, where the ice should be thicker. Like you said, I'm the queen and I should get special treatment." She forced a grin onto her face. "Now move!"

They looked unconvinced, but obeyed. Arch, with his usual grace, practically danced across the ice on his tiptoes. The ice groaned with the first two steps but then he passed the point of true danger, flashing a smile behind him as he made for shore.

Dietrich had little trouble, too, his movements agile and swift, slipping over the breaches in the ice like wind over bumps on the ground.

Jonius, however, immediately found himself in trouble. His very first step sank *through* the ice with a splash. He let out a cry and retracted his foot, but the damage was done. The crack gaped open as the ice tore apart, growing dark, watery arms and legs. He slipped, and when he landed on the floating chunk of ice, it flipped, dumping him headlong into the icy lake.

Annise hissed a curse. Arch and Dietrich both stopped and turned, and were about to head back, but Annise shouted, "I command you to get to shore." When they hesitated, she growled. They turned tail and ran.

Annise stepped as lightly as she could to the edge of the chasm that had opened up in the ice, dropping to her knees to scan the lapping water for signs of movement...

A hand shot from the water, grasping for something to hang onto. Annise grabbed it, shocked at how...there was no other word for it...*warm* Jonius's skin was, despite being in the icy waters.

She tried to pull him out, but his fingers were wet and slippery and the ice offered little purchase for her feet and knees.

He sank back in, clawing at the ice.

Annise went in after him, grabbing for his armor, which shone like a beacon now that the sun was piercing the water.

The moment she sank beneath the lake's surface, she thought she'd gone into shock. Where she'd expected water as cold as melted snow, she instead got lukewarm bathwater. Still, it was dangerous, the current threatening to suck them beneath the ice, the water soaking her clothes and pulling her into the depths.

The knight was in even worse shape, sinking far too fast, his armor like an anchor.

Her fingers closed around the lip of his chest plate and she kicked as hard as she could, reaching for the sparkling surface with her other hand.

Crack!

Her knuckles met ice, pain shooting through her hand. She nearly dropped Jonius, but managed to cling to him, searching the underside of the ice for the breach they'd entered through.

She saw nothing but a shimmering blue-white ceiling in all directions.

Her lungs heaved, desperate for air.

Jonius became her anchor, threatening to pull her below even as he writhed and kicked.

There! She finally spotted the hole in the ice, slightly brighter than the rest of the surface, like a real diamond in a pile of imposters. The current had pulled them much further than she expected, a sucking force of nature.

Go! she urged herself, kicking for that diamond, fighting her clothes and the pull of the strangely warm water and the anchor dragging her down, down, down.

Bubbles burst from her lips, the last of her air expelled as her lungs tried to force her to breathe, not knowing there was nothing for them outside of certain death. Her chest screaming, she reached for that hole in the ice...

The frozen air was a shock as it met her wet skin, pricking like hundreds of needles. Her face burst from the water, her throat sucking in a tunnel of icy air, burning beautifully the whole way down, filling her lungs. The current tore at her, but she managed to grab the edge of the ice, where two sets of strong hands clutched her, pulling her skyward.

The fingers on her other hand ached, hooked like claws around the edge of Jonius's armor, but she refused to let go, refused to weaken, even as his weight truly became an anchor as he emerged from the water. And then her fingers were pried from his armor and she was airborne, slung over a hard back, the world tipping until she could see nothing but a sodden gray sky, webs of sunlight splintering through a crack in the clouds, like a reflection of the shattered ice below.

Spots dancing before her vision, she was dimly aware of the ice creaking and groaning and the jostling of heavy footsteps made heavier by the weight they carried.

"Hurry," a voice said. Archer's. "We need fire or they'll freeze to death."

"Get her out of these wet clothes," Dietrich replied, the world spinning once more as she was placed on the ground— the cold, cold, snow-blanketed ground.

She tried to protest, but her throat felt constricted, only the thinnest stream of air squeezing through. Gentle hands probed at her clothing, peeling them away, one layer at a time. Her eyes found Archer's, which were haunted but determined.

She found her voice. "Jonius?" she croaked.

"He spat up a bunch of water, but now he's breathing. Dietrich is taking care of him."

Good. That is good.

Another gulp of icy air. The needles in her skin were getting worse, probing into her bones, trying to carve her apart. "You disobeyed my command," she rasped.

His eyes were moist. "I disobeyed my sister, and you're the only one I have, so I wasn't about to let you die."

"I thought...you wanted to be king."

"I do," he said, "but not like this. Not if it meant you wouldn't be by my side."

He was down to the last layer, but as he peeled it away he replaced her underclothes with a warm, dry blanket. So caring, so thoughtful. It almost made her feel ashamed at stealing his throne. Still, the cold pressed in, surrounding her, chasing away her thoughts.

Her eyelids suddenly felt heavy.

"Don't fall asleep," Arch said, pinching her cheek.

She barely felt it, because she was so warm now, so warm so warm so warm...

"Annise?" *Annise Annise Annise*

Annise?

The voice was so distant now that it might have been calling from one of the stars.

Sleep was good. So good. Annise felt as if she could sleep and never wake up.

So she did. She slept.

Twenty-Six
The Northern Kingdom, Darrin
Tarin Sheary

For a while the feeling of dread had intensified, growing stronger and stronger as Tarin tried to sleep. Eventually, he rose, heading for the forge to see if Fay was still awake. He needed a distraction, anything to take his mind off of whatever danger Annise was in. Even if he trusted her capabilities, he still worried.

He found Fay right where he expected to, except she was asleep on a bench, her hands curled under her head. The largest forge still glowed with molten embers, pulsing like a living, breathing creature in the dark. Several more pieces of huge armor hung cooling on a rack. A gauntlet. A greave. A shin plate.

He sighed and headed back out into the night. Just because he couldn't sleep on this night didn't mean others should be forced to endure the same.

With no particular purpose in mind, he passed through the quiet, snow-wrapped city streets, marveling at how the night changed everything, almost like a disguise. The stone city had turned from nondescript gray to jet-black. Even the blade-like spires of the castle were as dark as shadows, piercing the sky, which had been granted what would most likely be a brief reprieve from the incessant snowfall.

Tarin felt like he was wearing a disguise, too. Anyone who saw him now would call him the Lord Commander, bowing slightly, their mannerisms full of reverence. But was that really who he was? Could a title and a few barked commands really chase away the true monster that lived in his core?

The monster laughed, a sound like knives scraping against stone.

And yet better than its usual screams of bloodthirsty glee.

He emerged from the city onto the snowfields, frowning. Not because he disliked what he saw, but because he was surprised how good everything looked. Their preparations were nearly complete. Even the war machines were in place and stocked with ball and oil, torches ready to be lit, projectiles ready to be launched.

The men had performed remarkably well. "Too bad it won't be enough," he murmured aloud, letting the wind steal his words, his doubts, and take them away to another place, where they couldn't haunt him.

"If that's what you think, then why don'tcha leave?" a voice asked, startling him.

Nearby, a shadow shifted, white teeth grinning in the dark. A tiny pinprick of fire pierced the night, tendrils of wispy gray smoke rising from the end of the pipe.

"You weren't supposed to hear that," Tarin said. He approached Creak, who didn't rise to bow to him, didn't offer the same reverence and fear most of the other men did.

Something about the man's irreverence was refreshing. "Don't matter," the man said. "I *did* hear it, and words are just words, as numerous as flakes of snow. And I can squish them under my boots the same way."

"You won't tell the other men?"

Creak laughed, breathing out a puff of smoke. "I won't, not that it makes a difference."

"Why's that?"

"They're all thinkin' the same thing!" He laughed again, slapping his knee, eventually having to pull the stem of his pipe from his mouth so he could cough for a minute.

"Then why are any of you still here?" Tarin asked. "If we all believe the situation is so dire, why don't we all get the frozen hell out and live to fight another day?" *And then I can stop being a fool and go find Annise...*

The old man took another drag from his pipe, contemplating the question. Then said, "I'm not really here for the food." He shifted position, straightening one leg, the joint popping. "Truth be told, I'm not even much of an eater."

Tarin gaped at him. "Then why..."

"Why do I keep talking about food?"

Tarin nodded.

"Because it means something else." He sighed. "When I talk about food, what I really mean is my wife."

"I didn't know you were married."

He nodded, glancing up at the sky. "She was a real beauty, my Greta. Not sure how she picked me, but I wasn't about to question her decision. We had a good life, even in a world without a lot of goodness. She died five years ago, but it could've been yesterday. I can still see her face…"

"I'm sorry," Tarin said. He was—he couldn't imagine the one he loved dying.

"It's fine," Creak said. "I'll see her again one day."

"You believe that?" It was strange talk for a northerner.

"Aye. Why not? We all need hope, and she's mine."

"And she's why you stay in a city that's about to be sacked? She's your food?"

He shrugged. "Something like that. It's not that she's buried here—though she is—but that we lived our whole life here. My happiest memories are in this city. The day after she passed on, I joined the army. They laughed at me on account of my age, but they needed bodies, so they didn't refuse me. I would do whatever it took to protect this place."

Tarin stared at him.

"Don't you be lookin' at me like that. I ain't no hero."

"There aren't any heroes," Tarin said, but just as quickly regretted it. Just because he was the villain in his own story didn't mean others had to be.

"Are you good?" Creak asked, tilting his pipe in Tarin's direction.

Tarin considered it. The feeling of dread had passed. Whatever had happened to Annise, she was safe again, at least for now. "I'm good."

Tarin stood and began to walk away, but stopped on the outskirts of the city. Turned around. "Thank you," he said.

Creak only took another drag from his pipe, sending a cloud drifting into the sky. The smoke met the first of thousands of lazy snowflakes descending from the sky.

For some reason, the scene struck Tarin as utterly beautiful. *Beautiful like her.*

A horrifying thought sprang into his head. *Wait...*

Does Annise know a part of you is inside her? he asked the monster.

The monster cackled with glee. *She will,* it said.

She will.

Twenty-Seven
The Hinterlands
Annise Gäric

Annise.

The voice was a hiss in the dark, long and drawn out—*Anniiissse*—and yet as clear as if it was shouted directly into her ear. It was not Sir Jonius or Archer or Sir Dietrich. *Then who?*

Anniiissse. You are alivvvve.

Good to know, she thought. Something soft and warm whispered against her skin, tucked all the way under her chin. And for a second she was back there, trapped under the ice, being dragged into the abyss by a swift current and the dead weight of a knight in full plate.

"No!" she shouted, clawing at the warm water, trying to fight through it, to breach the surface, to breathe, *please just let me breathe!*

Strong hands grasped hers, and a voice said, "You are safe now, Your Highness." This voice she knew. She opened her eyes to find Sir Dietrich holding her hands between his, tenderly. He was on his knees, and such was his position that, from afar, he might be mistaken for praying.

"The water," she gasped.

"You escaped," he confirmed.

She remembered. The water had pushed at her lips and her lips had *wanted* to open, had desperately wanted to drink. And Sir Jonius— "Jonius?" she said.

"He awoke a while ago, but is sleeping again. He is shaken, but well enough."

Annise's eyes found a pile of blankets nearby. They swelled and shrunk as the knight breathed somewhere beneath them. She glanced back at Dietrich and then at their hands clasped together, and he quickly released her. "Thank you," she said. "For coming back. For comforting me now."

"You're not angry?"

"No."

"I suppose I can give you these back then." He slid her boots toward her.

She laughed, but then cut off suddenly when she realized what she was wearing:

Nothing.

Only a nest of blankets covered her nakedness. A fire crackled happily nearby, the snow melted in a wet circle around it.

"Umm…my clothes?"

"Just about dry by now," Dietrich said, grinning.

"Wipe that look off your face."

"It's just my face," Dietrich said. If anything, his grin grew broader.

"Then cut it off."

The smile vanished.

"A jape," Annise said. Then, casually, "Who removed my clothes?"

Dietrich winked.

She reached for her boot—

"Your brother!" the knight said, scooting back and holding up his hands. "He was very respectful about it and I turned away to tend to Sir Jonius. I swear it."

She laughed. Something echoed her mirth, but deeper, more snakelike. *What the frozen hell?*

Annüissse.

She shook her head, and the voice faded. Had she swallowed too much lake water? Had the loss of oxygen addled her mind?

No. But now you know.

"What?" Annise said aloud. "Know what?"

Dietrich looked at her strangely. "I was just saying how Jonius informed us of the unusual water. How it is warm. That explains the melting ice. The prince is down by the lake feeling it for himself."

Annise blinked. Right. The water. "Yes. I felt it, too." There was snow on the ground, meaning the temperature was freezing, and yet the water had felt as warm as bathwater. "It doesn't make sense. The Hinterlands are a frozen wasteland. Frozen Lake should be, well, *more* frozen."

217

Dietrich nodded. His lips moved as he said something else, but Annise didn't hear it. All she heard was that whisper in her mind.

You know what Tarin hears.

Despite the warmth of the fire and the blankets wrapped around her, Annise shivered. And she knew.

She knew.

The voice was Tarin's monster.

Annise had requested more sleep and Dietrich had gone off to help Arch gather water down by the lake.

But Annise wasn't sleeping. No, she was trying to communicate with that voice in her head.

The voice that had now disappeared, as if it never existed at all.

Did I imagine it? Annise wondered. She thought perhaps this might be her way of coping with Tarin's departure, a way of connecting with him on some level.

Hello? Monster? Are you there?

When nothing responded, she sighed, feeling foolish. Then again…

Tarin had told her that the monster came and went as it pleased. And if it was somehow inside her…was it going to change her, too, the way it had Tarin?

For her own sanity, she opened her eyes and glanced at her arm. Her skin was pale, but not unusually so, not like the chalk-white complexion Tarin bore. And her veins were hidden, not black and raised. No, so far she was unchanged.

She almost felt awful for the relief she felt. She wondered what Tarin must feel all the time. She wondered whether she'd tried hard enough to understand what he was feeling. *Is it my fault he left? Did my ignorance chase him away? If I had delved deeper into what he'd been through, what he was going through, could I have changed his mind?*

She sat up, pulling the blankets around her. Gritted her teeth. "No," she breathed. She couldn't think this way, couldn't second-guess, couldn't doubt. She was the queen, and she had to move forward. Tarin was gone, she might never see him again, and that voice inside her was—

Yesss. Oh yesss. You are interesting. More interesting than that armored hunk of flesh you can't stop thinking about.

Annise froze. *How is this possible?*

When, on the battlefield, your blood mixed with his...with Tarin's, I slipped inside you.

Her cold shock turned to hot anger. *How dare you? You ripped us apart! You ruined everything!*

I saved him. There would've been no us, no everything to destroy.

The truth was a slap in the face. She'd told Tarin as much herself. She took a deep breath, refocusing her energy. She needed information. *How can you be in both of us at once?* she asked.

I don't know.

Not helpful. *Is he hearing this conversation?*

No.

What does he hear? How does this work?

He hears nothing except what I tell him. All I can pass to him are your most powerful emotions. Fear. Love. Agony. Sorrow.

219

The thought of weighing Tarin down with any of those things tightened Annise's chest. *Does he know about this? That you are talking to me? That you are...with me?*

A purr. *Yes. He knows.*

Shite. Tarin already hated himself for, while in the throes of his bloodlust, hitting her. If he also knew his monster had somehow slipped a part of itself into her...

She tried not to think about it. There was no point in thinking about it.

Will you change me? she asked, holding her breath.

That's for you to decide, it hissed. She felt the moment the monster slipped away, disappearing like an eel into an underwater hideaway.

There was no doubt in her mind the monster would return.

Twenty-Eight
The Northern Kingdom, Castle Hill
Sir Christoff Metz

The men were laughing at him, that much he knew.

It hurt sometimes, but Sir Christoff Metz was used to it. His entire life he'd been laughed at. He didn't take offense, however, for he knew most people were afraid of what they didn't understand. They only japed to make themselves feel better.

Christoff hated japes. Hated dry humor. Hated sarcasm. He didn't understand why someone would say something that wasn't real, hiding secrets between their words like lies whispered on the wind.

And these men he'd been charged to train liked to joke quite a lot. The latest was some absurd story about the time the Ice Lord walked into a tavern, and how his heart had melted from the heat of the fire whiskey, or some such nonsense. Instinctively, Christoff knew the story wasn't true, that the Ice Lord hadn't truly become made of ice until he'd drunk Darkspell's monster potion and fought them in the castle. He also knew fire whiskey wasn't actually made of fire. However, when he tried to point these errors out to the soldiers-in-training, they laughed, shaking their heads.

He liked the women better, however. They were more serious about the training, watching him with keen, observant eyes and mimicking his motions with precision as they learned how to wield a sword in combat. It was unusual seeing women training with swords, but then again the queen and her aunt, Lady Zelda, who was now the queen regent, had fought bravely against her uncle in order to retake Castle Hill. And anyway, once he got used to seeing them dressed in tight-fitting garb, moving and whirling, parrying each other's swords, he got past the fact that a few of them made him stir inside something fierce.

One of the most attractive ones—her hair black, her eyes green, her eyebrows sharp and thin, her nose small and well-shaped—approached him now, sheathing her dull-edged practice sword. "Don't let them get to you," she said.

Sir Metz's heart pattered in his chest. These feelings had always been strange to him, and when he had them he usually found his mouth dry and his senses trembling. "Get to me? Why would they get to me?"

She laughed softly, a beautiful, musical tone, and though Christoff hadn't intended it as a jape, he found himself glad he'd said it.

"I only meant they can be mean, but they shouldn't be. You're doing a fine job training us." Those green eyes, sparkling as she met his...

He looked away; direct eye contact had always been hard for him. It almost felt like he was being touched, which was even worse. If he could choose between being touched by a human hand—hands touched all kinds of things and were almost always dirty, even if they'd just been cleaned—or have a thousand spiders crawl all over him, Christoff would take the spiders.

"I know," he said, and she laughed again.

"Have you ever held back something that was in your head?" she asked. Her hand was still gripping her sheathed sword, and the pose—the way her hips sat atop her legs, the lines of her arms, the way the sun hit her jawline just right—seemed to make his blood run a little faster through his veins, though he knew that was quite impossible.

"Why would I do that?" he asked, frowning.

She raised one of those delicate eyebrows, paused, and then said, "After training today, can you help me with the basic dueling positions?"

He couldn't say anything but "Yes."

"Thank you." She strode away, back to her training partner.

By then, the brief break was over, and the men had finally stopped laughing at his expense. He took them through the drills, correcting errors in their positioning until they were more precise in the angles of their swords and the placement of their feet.

Still, even after three hours, they were far from perfect, something that rubbed on Christoff's nerves. If it was up to him, he would stop the sun from sinking below the horizon so they could train for a few hours more, until they were up to his standards. But, of course, that was impossible, and he didn't like to waste time on foolish hopes and dreams.

It didn't help that new recruits continued to arrive each day, having heard about the open call to join the Queen's Army. Lately, most of them were women, a steady flow of femininity and strength that seemed to bother some of the men, who muttered inappropriate things under their breaths. When Christoff heard such nonsense, he punished them with kitchen duty, polishing armor—though that hardly felt like punishment to him—or scrubbing leathers. On occasion, one of the women would take offense to something one of the men had said, and he would punish them, too.

All of his soldiers were treated equally, as it was meant to be, even the green-eyed beauty now approaching him once more as the rest of the men and women headed for the barracks to get cleaned up and locate supper.

He knew the woman's name—Private Sheary—as he knew all of his soldier's surnames. Remembering names had always come easily to him, just as easily as remembering numbers or facts or anything else most people considered useless. But to Christoff, it wasn't useless—it was order. He created order from chaos, like setting up a bunch of fallen-over boots in a perfect line. It was only this order that allowed him to remain calm in a world that always seemed to be changing.

Christoff also liked making connections between things. Like how when the wind blew from a certain direction at a certain time of year at a certain speed, it almost always meant a storm was brewing. He could pretty much predict the timing and intensity of a storm down to the day, if not the hour.

Another example was the name of the woman who now stood before him expectantly, as if waiting for him to say something. Her surname—Sheary—was the same as that of Tarin Sheary, the Armored Knight, who'd left Castle Hill in secret a while ago. (He tried not to fault the man for shirking his duty, especially after how hard he'd fought for his queen, but it was hard for him not to.) His thoughts spilled to his mouth, as they often did.

"Are you related to Tarin Sheary?"

The woman blinked. He'd surprised her. "Not that I know of," she said. "I was born in Blackstone, grew up there. When my parents died several years back, my auntie raised me. She died a year ago and I've been making my own way in the world ever since."

"Oh."

She stared at him, like she expected him to say something else. But what?

After a brief silence, where he could feel her eyes on his, where he directed his stare to her earlobe—which was quite nice, Christoff noted, for an earlobe—she said, "Are you ready?"

"For what?"

The edge of her lip quirked. "To help me with my basic positions. Remember, like we agreed before?"

"Of course I remember," he said. And then: "First position!"

She flinched, as if surprised by his barked command. *Though she shouldn't have been,* Christoff thought, *the whole thing had been her idea in the first place.*

She unsheathed her sword and assumed the position. Badly. Christoff cringed. Her feet were all wrong, the angle of her sword so poorly placed that an enemy strike would rattle it right out of her hands. She was looking him in the eyes, Christoff noticed, which was the one *right* thing she was doing—an enemy's eyes were the windows to predicting his next move. In fact, combat was the only time Christoff ever managed to look anyone in the eyes for an extended period of time.

He talked her through her mistakes. "Widen your stance. No, wider. Yes, that's correct. Now your feet are off-center. Good, better. Still not perfect though. Now your sword. Lift it by a hand. A little higher. Yes. Straighten it out. Straighter. No, no, no!"

Private Sheary threw her sword down in frustration. "You know, you could be a little nicer about it," she muttered, bending down to retrieve her sword from off the packed snow.

Christoff licked his lips, which he knew was a bad habit, especially in the north where his saliva would likely freeze. "I was just being honest," he said.

She took a deep breath. "I know. I'm sorry. I feel like I'm falling behind the other women."

"And the men," Christoff chimed in.

"Thanks," she said.

"For what?"

"I was being droll."

"Oh." *I hate droll.*

"Maybe if you helped me," she said, stepping closer. Too close, too suffocatingly close.

Christoff stepped back. He could breathe again. He said, "I *am* helping you."

Her eyes narrowed slyly, and she said, "No, I mean *help* help me. Like move my arms where you want them to go. My legs. My hips. That sort of thing."

"I—" His mother always told him to choose his words carefully, so he wouldn't come across as rude, but Christoff had never really understood what she meant. He only knew one way to explain things. Directly. "I'd rather not."

He managed to meet her eyes for a bare moment, and he saw something flicker in them, though he couldn't discern what. This time, it was she who looked away. "I'll get cleaned up." She started to leave.

"But I thought you wanted help with the basic positions. We haven't even finished with the first one yet."

She turned back. "It's fine. Really."

"I'm sorry," he said, though he wasn't certain what he was apologizing for. However, he suspected he'd offended her in some way, unintentionally.

Private Sheary frowned. "I don't know what to make of you."

"Make?"

Her amused smile was back, and Christoff realized how much he preferred it to that other, shadowed look. "I don't understand you."

"The feeling is mutual," Christoff muttered.

She breathed out an airy laugh, shaking her head. "Shall we continue?"

"Yes. First position!"

Christoff wasn't certain what he was feeling, exactly. Private Sheary had improved her basic positions, but she was still far from perfect.

Yet, all things considered, it had been a fine day, as far as days went. It had been a week since his queen had departed with the others on their mission to the Hinterlands, and he finally felt like he was settling into a good routine.

He sat on the bench in his private captain's quarters and got to work.

After a few minutes of hard polishing, his armor was gleaming. In fact, he could see his own wobbly refection in it, the dark shadow of red-brown stubble on his chin and cheeks. He would have to shave before bed, and then again in the morning. The captain of the Queen's Army couldn't look sloppy; he needed to set a good example for his soldiers, both men and women.

Though, from experience, Christoff knew most would've stopped polishing at this point, he did not. No, he sought out the nooks and crannies, the secret places where dirt and grime liked to hide, to fester, to build up. He polished until his forearms burned, his dirty cloths piling up beside him…

He polished until his armor was perfection.

And then he polished some more, just to be certain.

His brother, Jordo, had been just a baby when he fell down the well.

Christoff, only eight years old himself, was supposed to be watching him while his mother finished sweeping the floors. Jordo was playing with some rocks behind their house, and anyway, he had only barely learned how to walk. Plus, Christoff had been distracted by the older boys with the wooden swords play-fighting nearby. He forgot about Jordo, watching as the boys moved, how they shifted their feet, the positions of their swords, counting their strokes. Christoff focused his attention on the boys who were winning, soaking in their movements like a sponge drawing water from a washbasin. Learning. Wishing he didn't have to watch his brother so he could join in the fun.

His brother! he remembered with a hint of alarm. How long had he left him alone? The sun hadn't moved much overhead so it could only have been a few minutes. Still, Christoff raced back, calling, "Jordo! Jordo!"

He found the rocks scattered nearby, but the baby was nowhere to be seen. Christoff whirled around, searching the yard for any sign of his brother, but nothing moved. Nothing breathed. Not even Christoff.

The house! he told himself, feeling foolish. Either the baby had gone back inside on his own or, more likely, his mother had come out and found Jordo alone, so she'd taken him. Oh boy, Christoph knew he was going to get in big trouble for leaving the baby like that. He willed it to be true, wanting to get in trouble—because that would mean his brother was safe.

His mother was still sweeping, her back to him. Jordo wasn't there, the floor empty.

Christoff backed out quietly, thinking, panicking, desperately searching the yard for any clue he might've missed.

Then he saw it, his breath rushing out of him in a gasp.

The well.

The bucket, which he definitively remembered resting on the circular stone ledge, was gone.

He raced over, giving up any idea of keeping this a secret as he screamed "Jordoooooo!"

He barely heard the door slam as, presumably, his mother came outside to see what the commotion was all about. He reached the well, slamming into its stone side, heaving his head over the lip, staring down into the inky gloom.

229

Dark, so dark, the sound of moving water lapping against the sides, the long rope, slick with moisture, trailing into the shadows.

And then a whimper.

"Jordo! Jordo!"

A spluttering scream and more splashing. "I'm going to save you!" Christoff called. A promise to his brother. A promise to himself.

He yanked at the rope, hauling it as fast as he could, watching as the tin bucket emerged from the dark, spilling water from its edges, tear-like drops cascading below.

Save for the water, the bucket was empty. No no no no!

His mother arrived just then, her face awash with fear, having realized what had happened. She grabbed the bucket, tossing the water out while shouting, "Get in, Christoff!"

*He didn't hesitate, fully understanding the situation and the only solution—the only hope—they had left. The moment he squeezed into the too-small bucket, his mother began lowering it into the darkness, the air around him growing colder with each passing moment. He craned his ear, listening for his brother's whimpering, listening for his splashes, listening for anything to tell him there was still time—*please let there be time...

Toward the bottom, the pace of his descent slowed and the bucket hit the water with a soft goosh *sound. He looked around him, his eyes slowly adjusting to the dark.* Where is he where is he where is he...

There! Small pale fingers drifting beneath the dark...

He grabbed them, pulling, feeling the wet hand slip from his, falling away, submerging...

He dunked his entire head, shoulders, and arms, reaching blindly into the murky water...

Finding...nothing.

And then, Jordo! Bubbles exploded from Christoff's mouth as he tried to scream his brother's name, pulling him up up up grasping him under

230

the arms hauling him into the bucket where there was barely room for either of them his brother's eyes closed no they need to open please open them screaming something to his mother who got the message and began hauling the bucket up but his brother wasn't breathing Jordo you have to breathe you have to try you can't die please don't let him die.

As they ascended, Christoff held his brother's limp body and counted his own heartbeats, for Jordo had none to count.

Christoff awoke soaked in sweat, lying in his bed in his captain's quarters.

Someone was knocking on his door. Loudly, hammer blows that seemed to go *through* the door and directly into his skull, which was pounding with a headache.

He's already gone too late the past the past the past can never change the past can only try harder save them all change the future...

The words streamed through Christoff's head, as they always did after one of his nightmares that weren't nightmares, but memories, a decade-old past that could never be altered.

Jordo is dead, he reminded himself, the truth steadying him, slowing the raucous pounding in his skull.

"Coming," he said, sliding out of bed. His pristinely polished armor was laid out perfectly, ready to be donned as part of his morning routine. But this was decidedly *not* part of his routine, this caller hammering his door before first light.

He slung a cloak over his shoulders, unconsciously trying to smooth out the wrinkles, though there were few, as he strode to the door, pulling it open.

A woman stood at the door. He blinked. Private Sheary. Her pale cheeks were flushed pink, her dark hair frosted with snow.

"Good morning," she said.

"Good morning," he replied.

"A stream has arrived in the night. The Queen Regent asked me to fetch you."

"Oh? Where is it from, who is it to, what does it say?" Christoff rattled off. He hoped he hadn't missed anything pertinent. He hated having to ask more questions.

"Can I come in?" she asked.

"No. And you didn't answer my questions. A question is never an answer to a question."

She raised her eyebrows. "Fine. I shall stand out in the cold." She hugged herself, shivering slightly, but Christoff thought it looked rather staged.

"You're not 'out', you're in the corridor. And it's not particularly cold, especially when compared to the actual outside."

"So I truly can't come in?"

"It wouldn't be appropriate," Sir Metz said. *Nor would I want your dirty boots on my floor.* He almost said it, but his mother's admonitions about not being rude stopped his tongue. For once.

"Because you're my captain?"

"Is that a question?"

"Not really."

"Good."

"So are you coming with me to see the queen? She's waiting."

"Yes, but you haven't answered my questions."

"I don't know. I don't know. And I don't know. Does that cover it?"

"Yes," he said. "Thank you." Then he shut the door.

He turned toward the washbasin, but there was another knock at the door. He opened it.

Private Sheary scowled at him. "You shut the door."

"Yes. Our conversation was finished, was it not?"

"In. My. Face."

It was Christoff's turn to frown. "I'm fairly certain that's impossible."

"You're impossible."

"Now you're just speaking nonsense. I am right here, which makes me entirely possible."

She huffed. "You can find your own way to Lady Zelda," she said.

"That's true," Christoff said, once more closing the door. *Strange girl.* And yet he couldn't help but to find her incredibly appealing. More than once he'd had the strange urge to touch her hair, a thought that made him want to cut off his own hand before he tried. He shuddered once, and then went back to getting ready for the day.

"We received a stream in the middle of the night," Lady Zelda said.

"I know, Queen Regent," Christoff said. "Private Sheary told me."

Private Sheary stood nearby, refusing to look at him. *Strange girl,* he thought again.

Lady Zelda wore a frizzy fur cape across her broad shoulders. She balanced a plate of breakfast across her knees. She wasn't sitting on the throne, but next to it. On the floor.

Christoff tried not to stare.

Lady Zelda said, "The private also said you were quite rude to her."

Christoff glanced at Private Sheary and her cheeks flushed.

Christoff said, "I might have been. I'm not sure. Mother always said I struggled with social niceties."

Private Sheary's eyes met his and he was forced to look away, but not before seeing the shadow of a smile that ghosted across her face. Something about that smile made his heart pitter-patter a little faster, a fact that bothered him. Smiles should *not* affect automatic bodily activity.

Zelda waved away the topic with a hand gripped around an exceptionally thick slice of buttered toast. "It's fine. Captains should be tough with their underlings. I respect that. Back to the stream we received…"

"Where is it from, who is it to, what does it say?" Christoff asked.

Zelda chuckled, flecks of toast flying from her lips. She licked them off and bit into a hardboiled egg. Christoff's stomach began to rumble. He was supposed to be eating breakfast now, not watching someone else eat it. "It's from Darrin to me. More specifically, from the blacksmith woman, Fay. Do you remember her?"

"Of course." *Why wouldn't I?* he added in his head, proud of himself for keeping that thought from spilling from his lips. "Some believed she left with Tarin Sheary."

"Yes," Zelda said, smiling. She licked her fingers, an act that chased away Christoff's appetite. Human saliva was something

234

he detested. He detested a lot of things, but spittle was definitely near the top of the list. He managed to keep his expression neutral as Zelda continued, though he couldn't stop looking at those spit-moistened fingers. "And it turns out, she did. Her stream states that Tarin Sheary is now the temporary Lord Commander at Darrin, as Lord Darrin himself has fled the castle. They are preparing for war. They expect the easterners assembled at Crow's Nest to descend from the cliffs before the next full green moon, if not earlier."

Christoff said nothing, waiting for her to continue. Instead, she bit into an apple, crunching loudly. He hoped the fruit had been washed. Thoroughly.

Lady Zelda placed the apple back on the plate, which meant it touched the leftover egg and toast crumbs. Christoff cringed. He hated when food touched. It wasn't as bad as saliva, but still…

"Fay also requested any assistance we could provide," Zelda said. "She stated that without assistance they will likely all perish during the battle."

Christoff straightened up. Darrin needed their help? "We are early on in our training still, but I can have several of the more prepared groups leave at once. I will leave training instructions behind for everyone else, and when I return, we shall continue."

"No," Zelda said.

"No? I don't understand."

She shook her head. "While I am sympathetic to their plight, we simply can't afford to send any men at this time. We are in the rebuilding stage and defending Castle Hill must be the priority."

"They will all die," Christoff said. "Including Tarin Sheary."

Zelda closed her eyes. Reopened them slowly. There was no mistaking the look of sadness that pulled at the edges of her eyes. "These are hard times. We all must make sacrifices for the greater good. Lord Commander Sheary and his soldiers will help give us the time we need to defend ourselves. With luck, Annise will be back with our army before the easterners reach Castle Hill."

Christoff simply could not accept that. No. Whenever he saw someone in need, someone *he* could save, everything else seemed to fall away and he was in that well again, was watching his brother's fingers slip beneath the water, was watching the life drain out of his kin. *Because of me. My fault, all my fault.* That was why he counted the number of people he had saved. One-hundred-and-seventy-four. It wasn't nearly enough, but he hoped one day the number would be enough to make up for the one boy he couldn't save. Jordo.

And yet his honor made it impossible for him to refuse to obey an order from the Queen Regent. Luckily, he had a plan around that. "So I cannot send any of my men to Darrin?" he asked, just to make things clear with Private Sheary as his witness.

"Correct. I'm sorry. Training will continue as planned. But I wanted you to be aware that Darrin will soon be under siege. Our eastern stronghold will surely fall, and then our enemies will march on Castle Hill. Will your soldiers be ready in time?"

"We will be ready," he said. "I will not fail you." *Nor Darrin.*

"I know," Lady Zelda said.

Christoff spun on his heel and strode toward the exit. "Private Sheary!" he barked. "To breakfast, the day is wasting away."

And we have a long road ahead of us if we're going to make it to Darrin in three days.

Twenty-Nine
The Northern Kingdom, Darrin
Tarin Sheary

Tarin was furious. "How dare you go over my head and send a stream to Castle Hill?" he growled, eyeing the table separating him from Fay. The urge to grab the table and flip it over sang through his blood, but he tamped it down, cursing at the monster inside him to remain silent. *Stay out of this!*

"How *dare* I?" Fay shot back. "My apologies, I would hate to undermine our self-appointed Lord Commander who is too stubborn to realize when he needs help."

"Self-appointed? I was voted in by the men!"

"They were scared half to death of you."

"You're the one who convinced me to stay!"

"Because I thought you would listen to reason. Castle Hill will have bodies they can send. We need more men or we'll be annihilated."

"I refuse to let you weaken the defenses at Castle Hill."

"It's already done," Fay said.

"It's not," Tarin countered. "I will send a second stream right now telling them to disregard the first."

"You wouldn't."

"Watch me." Tarin turned to leave the forge and head for the nearest stream, but stopped when a soldier approached. He was carrying a wet scroll between two pinched fingers, waving it dry.

"What is it?" he demanded.

"A reply from the Queen Regent," the soldier said.

"Give it to me." When the man held the wet parchment out, Tarin snatched it, scanning the words still drying on the paper.

He felt Fay hovering beside him. "Frozen hell," she muttered.

"Like you said, it is done," Tarin said, crumpling the paper and tossing it into the embers of one of the forges, watching it crackle, smoke, and then burn.

The final two sentences of the message burned simultaneously in his head.

Unfortunately, we can spare no soldiers at this time. I am truly sorry.
It was signed by Lady Zelda herself.

Thirty
The Northern Kingdom, Blackstone
Dirk Gäric

Dirk Gäric's father, the self-declared King of the North, Lord Griswold, had ruined everything in his haste for war. And now Dirk had to be the one to pick up the pieces.

He turned away from the sparkling waters of the Bay of Bounty, wiping away the snow that had melted on his face.

(Because his father was really, truly dead.)

He *hated* his cousins, Annise and Archer. Hated the way the residents of Castle Hill always cheered for Archer and not him. Hated how Annise always had a quicker tongue than he, getting the last laugh whenever they traded quips. Hated that they'd wrested the crown back from his side of the family, stomping on his future with heavy steel-toed boots. (He hated that they'd killed his father, but he tried not to think about that.)

He hated the western queen, Rhea Loren, too, who had decimated their warships, killing thousands of soldiers, the entire strength of the north in one fell swoop, like a hawk hunting a nest of baby pigeons. He'd watched from his hiding spot in the bushes as that damn creature rose from the depths, cleaving bodies in two.

(He hated that he'd been too cowardly to fight, but again, he pushed that thought as far from his mind as he could. Being alive was more important than being brave.)

Yes, Dirk Gäric, in his present condition, hated a lot of things.

But that didn't make him weak. No, on the contrary, he was stronger than he'd ever been. His father's secret training regimen had been brutal, fueled by a diet that consisted mainly of raw egg yolks, barely cooked meat, and jugs and jugs of water. His personal trainers had been a group of combat experts known as the Brotherhood, who'd been hired by his father to guard their household and to teach Dirk to fight. He knew they were little more than sellswords, mercenaries, willing to trade their services to the highest bidder. For a while that was his father, but when they'd traveled with him to Blackstone to be a part of the Battle at Bounty, Dirk had made them a better offer. So, when he didn't board one of the warships, neither did they.

As long as he could keep paying them in gold, they would do as he commanded.

The only problem: He was swiftly running out of coin.

Those were the thoughts swirling like snowflakes through his mind as he moved along the deserted streets of Blackstone, the westernmost city in the north.

It was eerie, this cold, empty city, once teeming with life, with vigor, soldiers marching and merchants hawking wares and scantily clad women hanging from windows trying to entice the men.

Now, Dirk could almost still *feel* their presence, passing through him with a chill, ghosts of a recent past, not yet having passed over into frozen hell.

He hurried on, anxious to get to his destination.

Of course, with the fall of Blackstone, there were plenty of castles ripe for the picking. Yes, at first the lords and ladies were still in residence, hunkering down with their food and wine and warm hearths, but the riots had quickly ridded them of their wealth. Those who weren't killed by the mobs were chased from the city with barely more than the clothes on their backs. Most would likely perish on the Howling Tundra as they tried to get to Castle Hill. Those who did, by some miracle, make it to the northern capital, wouldn't find the hospitality they expected—previous allies of Dirk's father would likely be hung for treason.

Which was why Dirk wouldn't be stumbling into the frozen city weak and exhausted, begging for mercy. No, he would march in with weapons and strength, reclaiming what was rightfully his.

At least that was the plan, if today went well.

Finally, he reached the meeting place: Blackguard itself, with its dark, savage walls and shadowy gate, almost like the maw of an undead beast. Once, there would've been mail-clad guards bearing the royal crest, who, of course, would've let

Dirk inside without question—he was a Gäric after all. Now, however, the guards wore only black cloaks bearing no symbol, which, Dirk knew, hid all manner of weaponry. There were two of them, both members of the Brotherhood. They nodded at Dirk as he entered, dangerous gleams in their eyes.

He heard them close the gate in his wake and then fall in behind him. None would be absent from this meeting to decide their future.

The meeting was held in court, a broad windowless room adorned with enormous tapestries depicting some of the bloodiest battles in history. There were black-eyed mamoothen rampaging across a frozen wasteland, Orian bodies hanging from their tusks; there were red-clad furia spiked with arrows; there were eastern battalions crushed under enormous flaming boulders. Though Dirk had always been fascinated by the images contained within this castle, he was also scared of them. If this was what war was, he wanted no part of it, which was one of the reasons he'd avoided the disaster in the Bay of Bounty.

And I'm alive, he reminded himself, striding to the front of the room.

There the Brotherhood waited, lined up in a curving arc, like the edge of a black scythe. Though Dirk's heart was thundering and his legs wobbled beneath him, he hid his anxiety the way he'd been taught. This was *his* domain, a lordling having been taught all about political maneuvering from the time he was a young boy. He'd learned two important things: Coin spoke louder than swords, and swords gave you coin and power and women and all you could ever desire. It was something of a circle, one he could complete with a few fancy words and promises to these violent, capable men.

He opened his mouth to speak first, to set the tone for the meeting, but one of the Brotherhood cut him off, stepping forward. "Lord Gäric," he said, "we've been awaiting your arrival." It was Severon, the unofficial leader of the group. What the man lacked in beauty—his face a miasma of scars, his hair long and stringy, his eyes a strange shade of green that seemed to pierce both shadow and stone—he made up for with raw strength. He was a valuable man to have on one's side.

Being addressed by his father's title sent a warm thrill through Dirk's chest, but he refused to let his excitement show on his face. "Thank you." He began the speech he'd planned in his head. "The Brotherhood has long been an ally of my father's, and I—"

"Ally?" the man said.

Dirk blinked. Something about the man's tone gave him pause. It was...off...somehow. Almost mocking.

"The Brotherhood has no allies," Severon said. "Only employers."

Ah. A minor word-choice error, Dirk realized. He knew the importance of words. He selected his next ones more carefully. "Indeed. I would like to continue to employ you to my house. All we must agree on is the terms."

"You mean the gold," Severon said, a wicked gleam in those emerald eyes. "The last payment has nearly run out."

Frozen hell. He had paid them only a week ago. Where was the gold going? There wasn't anywhere to spend it. The only currency in Blackstone at the moment was looting and theft.

"We will require double that amount if you would like us to continue to serve you."

"Double?" Dirk practically shrieked. He was down to less than half of what he'd paid before.

"Aye. Rates have gone up on account of the war."

Dirk set his chin, refusing to back down. These men responded only to strength, power, and wealth. Dirk didn't have any of those anymore, but he couldn't let them know that. "You will receive the *same* payment, half now, and half after we've retaken Castle Hill. I can also offer you land and titles—"

Severon started laughing, a grating sound echoed by the men around him.

Dirk felt a chill run through him, but also a slice of anger, a natural response bred into him by a life of wealth and power. "Did I inadvertently jest?"

"Aye," Severon said. "Your every word is a jest. You have nothing. Your gold is nearly gone. Your house is destroyed. You have no lands or titles to give, and we'd have no interest in them even if you did. You are a spoiled brat lordling used to getting his way." Dirk was frozen in place, unable to breathe, his lips clamped together. "But the world has changed *Lord Gäric*"—that mocking tone again—"and you are no longer the breed who controls the north. The Brotherhood *will* march on Castle Hill..."

Dirk released a sigh of relief. The man was simply jostling for a better position, trying to squeeze the promise of more coin from him. "Good. And I will double your payment—no, triple it. Will that be sufficient?"

Again, that laugh, like sword grinding against shield. "No." Severon took a step closer to Dirk. His men followed.

Dirk's façade crumbled the instant he realized this meeting had been a farce from the beginning, a trap. And he'd stumbled headlong into it like a blind mouse. *Father would be ashamed at my foolishness*, he thought, whirling around to race for the exit.

He stopped.

Black-cloaked men blocked his escape, having shifted behind him on silent feet while he talked with their leader.

"What is this?" he said, spinning back to face Severon, forcing a growl into his voice. A growl that quivered around the edges, descending into a whimper. Then a plea as he dropped to his knees. "Please, I'll do anything. I'll join your ranks, I'll help you, all the spoils will be yours and yours alon—"

He gasped as the first blade pierced his back, severing his spine, bursting from the front of his chest. Paralyzed, he collapsed, spots of color bursting across his vision as blood pooled around him.

What had happened? What had gone wrong? He'd avoided the death trap in the Bay of Bounty only to die at the hands of the men who'd worked for his father?

This is a new world, he realized, *just as Severon said. A world I no longer understand.*

Dirk Gäric, just like his father, died, alone and outnumbered.

The Brotherhood dispersed, off to loot and pillage and prepare to leave Blackstone. For they'd intercepted a stream from Castle Hill requesting all able-bodied men *and* women seeking employment to report to the capital to begin training in the Queen's Army.

After all these long years of being told what to do, they were finally masters of their own destinies. The north was ripe for the picking, and they would be the first to reach for the fruit.

Thirty-One

The Western Kingdom, Knight's End
Ennis Loren

Ennis Loren didn't want to be taken alive, but before he could turn his sword on himself, the castle guardsmen were upon him, grappling his weapon from his grip, slamming him to the floor, holding him there. A dozen blades were aimed at him, and a single thrust would end it all.

Do it, he thought, still struggling, trying to give them a reason to finish things.

"I'm disappointed," a voice said, emerging from the stairwell.

The last voice Ennis wanted to hear. He closed his eyes. Refused to open them even when Rhea said, "Look at me, guardsman."

"The prisoners escaped through the window," one of the guards said. "Gentry killed several guards and a"—the word seemed to stick in his throat—"Fury…before we could stop him."

"Leave us," Rhea said, and Ennis's eyes finally flashed open. She was staring at him, and for a moment Ennis couldn't discern the look in her eyes, so foreign to his cousin's face that it almost felt like an intruder.

"Your Highness, this man is danger—"

"Leave. Us." A command with all the authority of a queen, but without emotion.

As the guards shuffled away, looking uncertain, Ennis realized exactly how Rhea looked:

Lost.

Alone.

Sad.

She was his cousin again, the girl whose face had been carved by the Furies, a princess without a throne.

As he stared at her in wonderment, the look seemed to fade, but not entirely. Once the guards were gone, Rhea said, "You will leave the west at once."

Defiance coursed through him. "I will not. You will have to really kill me this time. No more lies."

"I will not," she said, her voice trembling. Were those tears shining in her eyes? She blinked them away before he could be certain. "I have lost too much already."

"What happened to Bea?"

A sob choked her and she almost collapsed, gripping a table to keep her feet.

This was not a woman who had killed her own sister in cold blood—at least not intentionally. "I—I thought I had control." That look again. Lost. Broken. Defeated.

"Rhea…"

"No." She shook her head. "No more words. You are leaving the west, Ennis."

"I allowed your prisoners to escape. I killed your guardsmen and Fury. I committed treason of the highest order. And you would let me live?"

"Yes." A single word that seemed to span the canyon that had opened between them.

"Why?"

She shook her head.

Ennis sighed. "Rhea, you pushed the light away from you, so why does it surprise you when you're left alone in the dark?"

She gritted her teeth and, finally, a tear trickled from the corner of her eye. "I'm not alone. I have my guards, my furia, my people. They're going to fight for me. All of them. They want what I want."

Ennis didn't know if he was overstepping, but he reached forward and held her shoulders gently. "None of it is *real*, Rhea. None of it *matters*. You can kill all your enemies, raze their cities to the ground, claim the entirety of the Four Kingdoms for yourself, and you'll still be alone."

She fell into him, sobbing into his chest, a lifetime of tears soaking his armor, running in rivulets along the etched, blood-spattered lines of the rearing stallion atop a high cliff. He held her for a long time, until long after the sun had crept over the horizon, casting the entire room in a mystical yellow haze, her blond locks shining. This was the real girl inside the monster,

Ennis believed. Her armor and mask had hidden her for a while, but they'd fallen away at last.

Words hovered on his lips, and Ennis couldn't hold them back any longer. "I love you," he whispered into her hair.

She froze. "Ennis," she said, and that word seemed to close a door, turn a key. "Ennis, I'm pregnant."

He left at once. Several of the furia had forced a thick cloak over his head and hustled him out the rear of the castle, where horses were waiting, stamping in the morning light.

Ennis wondered whether Gareth and Gwendolyn had escaped. He hoped so.

He tried not to think about Rhea, about what she'd taken from him, the pieces of his soul carved away only to become carrion tossed to the scavengers cawing and swirling overhead. He'd rather she'd have taken a knife to his face.

He knew he was a fool for feeling this way. He was decades older than her and she was the queen and he was supposed to be dead and she'd done horrible *horrible* things.

A heart wants what a heart wants, he thought, as he was tied to the horse, a dark-eyed furia behind him.

They took the coastal route, riding along the banks of the bay before turning southward. When Rhea had informed him of his fate, it had felt almost poetic. He'd almost laughed.

Within a fortnight he would either be dead at the hands of the Phanecians, or sold into slavery. He hadn't yet decided which he preferred.

Thirty-Two

The Western Kingdom, the Western Road
Gwendolyn Storm

Gwen was already regretting having saved Gareth Ironclad.

After escaping the castle, they'd raced through the deserted city streets. Not south, like would be expected—they wouldn't leave through the main gates—but east, directly for the enormous wall surrounding Knight's End.

"Ore save me," Gareth had said, eyeing the climb he'd faced.

"Your whining will be the death of me," Gwen had replied, and then tossed him onto her back.

His complaining hadn't ceased since, even as they raced through the darkness along the Western Road, only stopping when day broke, sleeping off the road in a thick copse of trees. *My feet hurt. I'm tired. I'm hungry. And on and on.*

Ore! Princes are impossible, Gwen thought now, ignoring whatever Gareth was saying. It was dark again, and so on they went, a race against Darkspell and his blasted potion. They needed to reach the Spear first, and then hopefully stop the potion master from ever dumping it into the river...

Finally, she could take it no longer. "Would you shut that sorry trap of yours?" she said.

Gareth said, "No."

She groaned. "Look, compared to the hell I've been living in since we were captured, your so-called cell was luxurious. I saw that plush bed of yours. You know what I've been sleeping on? Stones and rat droppings."

Gareth crinkled his nose. "I thought I smelled something. Perhaps we should find a stream..."

Gwen continued. "You had a table and chair, for Ore's sake! If I wanted to sit, I pressed my back up against the rough wall and bent my—"

"Now who's complaining?" Gareth said, grinning like he'd just made the cleverest jape of his life.

Ore grant me patience, Gwen thought. *Else I murder the prince before we reach the bridge.*

They walked in silence for a while, the dark covering all. Even the stars were blotted out by thick gray smoke. *So it's true,* Gwen thought. *The Tangle burns.* She thought of the nymph she'd battled there—Felicity. She thought of the nymph's sisters, whose lockets Gwen still wore around her neck, hidden beneath her armor. They were the only possessions besides her plate that Rhea's guards had been unable to take from her. She wondered whether the nymphs had the strength to leave the fiery wood, moving on somewhere safer.

"I need to rest for a while," Gareth said, stopping and falling to the ground where he stood.

"No," Gwen growled. "We can only move at night, and we need to reach the bridge before—"

"You think I don't know that?" Gareth fired back.

"It's not your people being threatened."

"You're damn right about that," Gareth said, looking away. "I have no people, not easterner or Orian."

"This again," Gwen said. "You know, I am so sick and tired of your nonstop woe-is-me horse dung. Roan and his soft heart might've fallen for it, but I won't. So get up, and quit being stubborn."

"That's like telling a skunk not to stink," Gareth said. Then, intentionally slowly, he worked his way back to his feet, grimacing like an old man with half a hundred ailments and a bone disease to boot.

They walked on, and Gwen let her anger fade away. She took a deep breath. "Sorry I said that about Roan."

He glanced at her sharply, but then seeing something in her expression, genuineness perhaps, he sighed. "It's fine. It's not like we weren't at each other's throats half the time. Or all the time."

"Seems a common theme in your relationships," Gwen quipped.

"Sad, but true." The melancholy in Gareth's tone reminded Gwen of what he'd said a moment ago, about not having people.

"You have people, you know. Me. Roan. Ennis."

"Roan is out of reach. And Ennis?" Gareth laughed. "That fool is dead by now. I still can't believe he helped rescue us. As if we can really forge an alliance between our kingdoms."

"So you're not even going to try?"

"My brother told me the east doesn't want me. So what can I do?"

"Roll over, shove your face into a hole, and stop breathing."

Gareth gaped at her.

"I'm kidding. You fight. You go to Ferria and demand to be a part of any decisions that are made."

"You want me to try to reclaim the throne?"

"No. Yes. I don't know, maybe. It is technically still yours. You were injured and confused when you relinquished your rights."

"Injured, yes. Confused, no."

"They don't know that. If you can forge a peace between kingdoms, it's worth trying."

"Don't you see?" Gareth said. "No one wants peace. Except Roan, and he's off chasing a dead oracle and her dead son, who you claim is a skinshifter."

"*I* want peace."

Gareth laughed again. "So if Empress Raven Sandes showed up right now, on this very road, and offered an alliance between Ferria and Calypso, you would…what? Invite her to a feast and break bread and drink mead with her?"

Damn, she thought. *Never argue with a prince, or king, or whatever he is.* The faces of those she'd lost at the hands of their desert neighbors cycled through her mind. "Not Calypso," she growled. "Never Calypso."

"And that, my friend, is the very problem we face—the problem Roan faces. Everyone hates someone. Which means there will never be peace in the Four Kingdoms."

"Then that leaves only one other option," she said, finally realizing the truth. Gareth looked at her, his eyebrows arched in the dark. "We win the Hundred Years War."

Thirty-Three
The Western Kingdom, the Western Road
Gareth Ironclad

"Do you really love Roan?" Gareth asked on the third day since they'd fled Knight's End. The question had been weighing on his mind the entire time, but he'd been afraid of the answer. But with each passing day his fears seemed less and less important.

"No," Gwen said. It was too fast, too automatic, like she'd *planned* to say it if he ever mustered the nerve to ask the question.

"Orion," he sighed. "You do love him."

Gwen set her jaw, her teeth jammed together. Though the smoke still roiled overhead, even blacker and thicker than before, occasionally there was a break in it, one of the moons slicing through, red or green, casting trails of light across their path.

"This is awkward," Gareth said, chuckling. "An Orian-king-king love triangle, and two of us fatemarked to boot. Ha!"

"So you admit you're a king?"

"You're trying to change the subject."

Silence, her graceful footsteps drowned out by his own stomps.

"What do you love about him?" Gareth asked.

"We shouldn't talk about this."

"Why not? What else is there to talk about?"

"It's...strange."

"Damn right it's strange," Gareth said. "Which is exactly why we need to make jokes about it and do everything but take it too seriously, or else we might go crazy and then one of us will end up strangling the other in their sleep, and the strangler will likely be you because you're freakishly strong."

Gwen blurted out, "I love how when Roan talks about the idea of peace his eyes seem to light up from within, how *real* it is to him."

"Naïve bastard," Gareth said, but he couldn't disagree. He loved that about him too. "I love his quick tongue. It's rare I meet my match, but he tested me from the moment I met him."

"Aye!" Gwen said. "For the longest time I tried to hate him for it, but half the time I had to look away so he wouldn't see that I was amused."

"He thought you were giving him the cold shoulder," Gareth said, smiling at the memory. "I thought so too."

"Why does he have to be so damn amusing?"

"At least he's not charming, like me," Gareth said.

Gwen made a vomiting sound.

Gareth laughed. This felt like the most normal conversation they'd had since they left. Which said a lot, considering they were talking about the man they both loved. "Half the time I wanted to hit him and the other half kiss him."

"Did you?" Gwen said. "Kiss him?"

There goes our "normal" conversation, Gareth thought.

"Yes. Sort of."

"Sort of?" Gwen's eyes twinkled as they were highlighted by a green moonbeam. "Well, I kissed him."

Gareth couldn't help the twinge of jealousy that struck him. He fought if off. It wasn't her or Roan's fault. *I was the one to reject Roan originally*, he reminded himself.

"What did you think?" he asked instead.

"About the kiss? I've had better."

"But he's a damn good kisser, right?"

"You think so?" The moonbeam passed on, but her yellow eyes continued to shine in the darkness.

"Better than any women I've kissed," Gareth said. There hadn't been many, not as many as he made everyone think. And he'd forced himself to kiss each and every one of them, for appearance's sake, later coming up with some excuse why he had to break it off with them. His brothers, his father, would never have understood where his true attractions lay.

Gwen said, "Fine. He's a good kisser."

For some reason, neither of them could find words after that.

Thirty-Four
The Hinterlands
Annise Gäric

The rage was a living, breathing monster, ringed with fire, filled with storms and ice and power—so much power. The monster saw through different eyes, the world a dark place full of mist and danger and enemies on every side. Those around it were wraiths, ghost-like forms whose voices seemed to come from a faraway place, as if spoken underwater, or from deep inside a cave. Annise could *feel* what that monster felt: the fury, the bloodlust, the violence.

The monster was Tarin. Tarin was the monster. In the throes of battle, the line between them faded to nothing and it was impossible to tell where one ended and the other began.

They—for there was no longer Tarin and the monster— swung the Morningstar, crushing skulls, felling the wraiths around them without compassion, without mercy, feeling nothing but desire to end. To destroy.

She was there, a pale ghost before him, her voice rising and falling in waves. *Tarin. Tarin. It's me. Me me me me... Your Annise. Please stop. Please please please...*

They stopped, confused, and for a moment the monster separated from the man, still reaching for him, trying to grab him, to claw him back. *Do I know her?* Tarin said in his mind. *She is...familiar.*

No! the monster hissed, in that snakelike voice Annise was now familiar with. *She will kill you. She is the enemy. They all are. Kill kill kill KILL*

The Annise before him reached out, tried to touch him, to comfort him, but in Tarin's eyes *she* was the monster, and her fingers were claws and she would destroy him if he did not destroy her first.

He swung, his hand slamming against her jaw, twisting her head around, throwing her back. The pain she felt, the pain Annise remembered as distinctly now as the moment he'd hit her—a red hot flash that struck all the way to the core of her heart—trembled not only through her, but through him too. The monster was thrown out, tumbling across the ground, and Tarin fell to his knees. *What have I done?*

"Tarin!" Annise shouted, her eyes exploding open from the dream, the cold air immediately stinging them. Her blanket had fallen away and she shivered.

And then Archer was there, and Dietrich, and even Sir Jonius, though he looked paler than she'd ever seen him look. "Annise," one of them said, though she could not discern whom. "What happened? Are you hurt?"

She looked at each of them in turn, not really seeing them, looking *through* them to that dream, that nightmare made real. And though she preferred the *other* dream she'd had of Tarin, this one provided her with more insight into him than any conversation ever had. Finally she understood how he felt—the fear, the pain, and, above all, the anger—and why he'd had to leave.

And yet...at the core of the dream was something else, something Annise clung to now, her breath misting before her.

It was hope.

My pain dispelled the monster, she thought. *His love for me. That is the answer.*

"Annise?" This time she was certain is was Arch who had spoken, his face laced with concern.

She gathered her strength, letting it wash over her, straightening out her bent nerves one by one. "I am fine. My strength is back. We push onwards."

And push on they did, the calm between winter storms like a held breath, passing the time in silence, the crunch of their boots on frozen snow a drumbeat to the whistle of the winds across the barren Hinterlands.

For a while, the not-so-frozen Frozen Lake flanked them, its dark waters lapping against the bleak and empty shore, but eventually they were forced to angle away, toward that hell-frozen spot on an old map that could be more farce than fact. Before they'd veered away to the west, Sir Dietrich had suggested they take advantage of the strangely warm waters of the lake to bathe, but Sir Jonius had warned against it. "'Tis not natural," he'd said. Annise had not disagreed, and they'd not dipped foot nor hand in the lake.

Now, as they stopped to rest, Annise searched the east for any sign of the large body of water. All she saw, however, were snow-covered mountain peaks turning silvery orange in the light of the dying day. If she didn't know better, she could almost believe the enormous lake had vanished completely, sucked into a crack in the earth.

Sir Dietrich muttered curses as he struck a flint against stone, trying fruitlessly to generate a spark beneath Sir Jonius's cupped hands. Arch searched for anything that might be used as kindling, though dry vegetation was sparse on the tundra.

Annise turned away, watching the glow of the sun behind the clouds as it sunk lower, lower, casting the north into murky darkness. And then, like a vision of light through fog, the thick clouds parted to reveal a sky drunk with stars. Twinkling golds, exploding greens, streaking reds. The moons, however, were noticeably absent, hidden behind the mountains perhaps.

You look upon the same sky as him, the voice hissed. *I see it twice. Through you. Through him.*

"Shut your pie hole," Annise growled, though the damage was already done. Tarin filled her mind, sapping the strength from her knees, forcing her to crouch to avoid falling. She pretended to busy herself with the tent poles and canvas covering, though she could feel Arch's eyes on her back.

"Who were you talking to?" he asked.

"This cursed tundra," she lied, working the flexible poles into their fittings.

"Annise, I'm—"

"I'm fine," Annise interrupted. *Aren't I?*

Yes. Of course she was. If anything, she understood Tarin—truly understood him—for the first time in her life, save perhaps when they were children playing Snow Wars in the castle courtyard.

"You don't always have to be the strong one, you know," Arch said, his boots crunching closer. He was so near she could see his breath now, curling wisps of vapor passing overhead. A hand on her shoulder. Warm, tender, so different than the way they usually treated each other—the shoves, the playful punches, the trips and barges and elbows.

The honesty behind the simple touch made her resolve begin to crack.

She shrank away, refusing to let herself fall into the yawning chasm that was forever threatening to drag her down into darkness. She stood, hauling the poles with one hand and the heavy canvas with the other. Her legs were strong, well-muscled from long treks across the harshest terrain in the Four Kingdoms. Her back and shoulders were broad and firm, capable of carrying the weight of a man—though not a man as large as Tarin, who weighed as much as a small bull—for several leagues. No, she would not do more than crack. She would become the northern sigil, a shield forged of steel, sometimes cracked, never broken. Unless she died first, she would shield her people from their enemies, even if the entire world was amassed against them.

Ignoring Arch's stares, she raised a hammer and began pounding the first stake into the rock-hard ground, inch by inch, relishing the feeling of progress as the metal disappeared beneath the surface.

Progress. Aye. That's what each day was, each step, each rise and fall of the sun.

Toward what, she wasn't certain.

Yesss, Tarin's monster hissed, and this time she didn't respond, content to let its voice be carried away by the wind.

The next day dawned bright and warm. Well, not *warm* exactly, but relative to the frigid temperatures they'd endured thus far, anything that made her fingertips tingle was as welcome as a hot bath.

A hot bath, Annise mused. She could almost feel the water rushing over her, soothing her aching muscles, shrinking the ice sheathing her bones. Perhaps they had been too hasty to reject Dietrich's notion of swimming in the queerly warm northern waters of the Frozen Lake.

She yawned, rolled over, and crawled from the tent, making a true effort to avoid waking the three men, who remained deep in slumber. Outside, she blinked against the shards of sunlight piercing the clumps of cloud cover. She scooped up a handful of snow, letting it melt in her cupped hand, and then slurped it greedily.

Next she reached back inside the tent and felt around for their provisions, grasping a satchel heavy with salted beef and half-frozen potatoes. Without fire, the duo would make for a meager breakfast, but food was the last thing on her mind this morning. Not when the white cliffs seemed so much closer in the morning light than they had the night before. Not when that spot on the map might be directly behind them. Yes, the climb would be steep and treacherous and test the limits of their strength and endurance, but they would make it. Of that Annise was certain.

She realized she was gritting her teeth, clamping them down on a mangled leather-stiff chunk of salt beef. She relaxed her jaw, feeling the ache in her teeth. Laughing at it. Pain was an old friend now, and she wouldn't fear it nor avoid it.

She was pulled from her revelry when the flaps of canvas fluttered and Sir Jonius emerged. He squinted, surprised by the burst of sunlight across a landscape that had been cloaked in gray for several days. While he adjusted to the brightness, she studied his face. As a child, she'd thought of him as old; but now, the signs of his age were even more evident: the crow's feet fanned on either side of his eyes, the frown marks creasing his forehead, the droop of his lips and the streaks of gray in his hair. This was a man who'd been through frozen hell and back, who'd done horrible things and wonderfully heroic things, who'd served a tyrant and emerged from the fire unburnt. Not unchanged, however, just as a blade could not pass through the forge without being affected.

"Top of the morning," he said, still squinting, looking at her.

"And we're nearly to the top of the world," Annise said, gesturing to the towering cliffs.

His eyes widened as he took in the view. "And here I thought those cliffs were retreating."

"A trick of the light," Dietrich said, scrambling from the tent on all fours.

Annise faked a kick at his midsection and he flinched. Jonius chuckled. Annise said, "Says the man who claimed, just last night, that those selfsame cliffs were—how did you put it again? Ah, yes, 'bewitched by ice faeries.'"

Arch yelled from inside the tent. "Is there a point to this prattle? Some of us still need their beauty rest."

Annise grinned. Something about this morning felt so…normal. Like the world had finally, after a long hiatus, spun back into its proper position.

Only one thing was missing: Tarin.

She swallowed the thought away and met Arch's eyes when he pushed through the tent. If anything, he looked *more* handsome than ever, the dark stubble of his cheeks suiting him the way everything seemed to suit him. She remembered the way he'd touched her shoulder the night before, the concern evident in his voice. On this morning, a thousand thoughts seemed to pass between them, as they only can in a shared look between a brother and sister born to a monster of a man.

"You look tired," Annise japed.

"See? I had at least another hour of sleep in me," Arch said. He targeted his stare on the cliffs. "Whoa."

"Eat up," Annise said. "If the weather holds, today we shall mount the north."

"I have a better idea," Sir Jonius said, pointing toward the base of the cliffs, where a jagged triangle of black marred the otherwise white-blue face. "We cut *through* to our destiny."

Sir Jonius was correct. The black slash in the cliffs was a cave mouth. As they stared into the infinite blackness, Annise couldn't help but feel like they were looking into the maw and throat of an enormous beast—one of the legendary hintermonsters they'd told scary stories about as bored children with vivid imaginations.

She weighed the pros and cons in her mind. "Thoughts?" she said, to no one in particular.

"I'd rather be swallowed by an ice bear," Dietrich said.

"Perhaps I can find you one," Annise said. Dietrich grimaced.

Jonius said, "We will be free of the cold and wind. If we bring along enough kindling, fire will come easy and we can keep torches burning the entire way."

"What if it dead-ends halfway through?" Arch said. "Or curves around on itself so that we walk in circles? For all we know, it could be a labyrinthine series of tunnels no better than a maze. I say we take our chances with the cliffs."

"I'd rather scale the towers of Castle Hill," Dietrich noted helpfully.

"Again, I will arrange it upon our return," Annise said. Despite her quip, she was seriously considering all opinions at this point. In truth, none of them could predict what either the cliffs or caves would bring. More likely, they were equally dangerous, as most paths in the north were.

"We could all use a break from the snow," she said. "And if a storm hits…"

Arch frowned, but didn't argue. "We are overdue for the next one," he conceded.

"Atop the cliffs we'll be unprotected," Jonius said, hammering the final stake into his argument.

"We go through," Annise said.

As it turned out, Archer's concerns were unwarranted. The tunnel, though narrow, was impressively straight, as though a giant had thrust his spear through the cliffs and then withdrawn it. Occasionally the shaft would widen into caverns spiked with teethlike stalactites and stalagmites, some so large it would've taken all four of them joined hand to hand to reach around their bases.

In one such cavern, Dietrich cast down his bundle of unlit torches and kindling with a rattle. "The path ascends without end. I can scarcely breathe in this place."

"Did you try opening your mouth?" Annise said. Despite the joke, her lungs were heaving as well. And he was correct. Though, at times, it was difficult to discern, the burn in her calves and lungs made it clear the tunnel was rising gently with each step.

Jonius waved a torch along the wall, chasing away the shadows cast by the unfinished columns of stalagmites. "We are not the first to pass this way," he said.

Annise followed the light, immediately noticing the markings on the rock walls. The depictions were rough, drawn in red ink—or at least Annise hoped it was ink—and yet not difficult to interpret:

Legions of plate-clad soldiers bearing arms, marching through a tunnel. Strangely pale creatures surrounded them, wearing nothing but thin cloths about their loins. Some might've been female, but it was impossible to tell. They didn't walk upright, but were more crouched, their fingertips almost brushing the ground. Others clung to the walls and ceiling like spiders.

"Frozen hell," Archer said. "What are those things?"

He was referring to the creatures, Annise thought.

"Are those the Sleeping Knights?" Dietrich said, running his fingers along the lines of soldiers.

"They are knights, alright," Jonius said, "but they look very much awake to me."

"They were attacked," Annise said, a chill settling into her bones. "We've all heard stories about how the finest knights of the north marched into the Hinterlands to await the time when they would be called forth. But what if they never made it to their destination? What if these…" The right word eluded her. "…killed them first?"

"It depends on who drew these pictures," Arch said. "If these were drawn by the knights, then they emerged victorious. But if it was the…*natives*…" That felt like the right word to Annise. After all, in these lands they were the invaders, having broken a pact signed long before any of them were born.

She swallowed a deep breath. Let it out. "It doesn't matter," she said. "We aren't turning back. We will find the truth of these markings one way or another."

"Unless the truth finds us first," Dietrich muttered.

After a brief rest, they marched onwards. Annise knew they'd been walking for hours, but she had no grasp of the time of day in this place. If not for their torches, it would be blacker than the blackest night, even if it was midday outside. In some ways, she felt like they were violating the very nature of the tunnels by filling them with torchlight, by breaking the silence with the scuff and thud of their boots, by clouding the air with their exhalations and torch smoke.

She had hoped to pass through the cliffs without stopping to sleep, but as the tunnel wore on, never ending, never changing, she worried it would take days, if not weeks, to emerge back into the light and cold.

Along the way, they passed more paintings, drawn in red. They were battle scenes, filled with as much violence as the famous paintings at Blackguard, the ruling castle in Blackstone. The pale creatures were clearly attacking the armored knights, coming in waves, throwing themselves from the ceiling, from the walls, biting at their feet, clamping their claws around their wrists. The color of the drawings made perfect sense now, each scene splattered with more blood and gore than the one before.

Interestingly, none of the knights were shown as dead or dying. Instead, it was the pale creatures that fell along the way, a few at first, and then in droves, their fleshy half-naked bodies piling up around the knights, who marched onward, ever onward, slicing off their enemies' limbs, stabbing through hearts.

And then, abruptly, the paintings stopped, the walls bare and nondescript once more.

Dark tunnels began to emerge on either side, small at first—perhaps large enough to shove a fist through—but growing larger, until several were passable if one stooped.

She remembered how the pale creatures depicted on the cavern walls had been drawn walking stooped over.

"What if we reach a fork?" Archer said.

"We go right," Dietrich said immediately.

Though Annise wasn't fond of what-if scenarios, she frowned even more at the knight's quick answer. "Why right?"

"Because it is right," he said, grinning.

She rolled her eyes. "If it comes to it, we will judge each fork individually. We need to keep moving in the same approximate direction if possible." She hoped they wouldn't encounter any forks. Or pale creatures that climbed on walls and ceilings.

"A logical response," Jonius said, winking at Annise. Despite the aged weariness that seemed to surround the old knight these days, something about this journey had chased the shadows from his eyes. That, more than anything else, made him seem younger than his age.

In a way, it reminded her of Tarin—how action and movement kept his demons at bay. Distractions were a powerful tool for anyone with a past.

"Thank you, Sir," she said, firing a childish smirk at Archer. She might be a queen, but he was still her baby brother, and she was entitled to a bit of gloating now and then.

When they started forward again, however, Archer brushed the tip of his boot against her heel and she stumbled. It was just the sort of prank she had liked to pull as children, but in the reverse. As she fell, she grabbed at anything available to catch her balance. Worse, it was Dietrich's arm that she caught, steadying herself.

"Thank you," she said, forcing the words out as he grinned at her.

"No thanks are necessary," he said, beaming. "As a knight of the realm, it is my pleasure serve you, Your Highness."

"Still, I will refrain from causing you bodily harm for the next day," she promised.

"A royal gift," he japed back. "I was hoping for a kiss, but..."

"Don't tempt me. These days my fists do the kissing."

"I would relish the bruising of my lips."

Annise had the urge to punch herself. "Frozen hell, the women of the north must be desperate indeed if they fall for such silver words."

"Not desperate," Arch said. "*Cold.* A man warming their beds is the only way to survive winter."

"Not for me," Annise said. "I make my own heat these days."

Arch touched her arm, recoiling sharply as if he'd been burned. "She speaks the truth!" he announced. "The Frozen Queen is now the Fire Queen!"

"And we're all carrying kindling," Dietrich said with mock-fear, hastening his steps to distance himself from her.

Annise couldn't help the laugh that slipped from her lips. These men might be fools, but they were *her* fools, and she was glad to be in their company in this dark place. Else she might've already gone mad with fear and trepidation.

Up ahead, Jonius, who had been ignoring their youthful banter, stopped, raising an arm to silence them. He cocked his head to the side, as if listening. "Do you hear that?" he asked.

Annise frowned, hearing nothing but the echo of the knight's words as they skipped down the tunnel, fading into the dark. "I don't hear—" She clamped her mouth shut abruptly as a burst of sound shot from one of the side passageways. It was high-pitched, an eerie keening that reverberated off the walls before changing pitch, stopping and starting, staccato-like.

Almost like a strange laugh. A strange, maniacal laugh.

"What the frozen *hell* is that?" Annise said.

Jonius shoved his torch into the tunnel entrance, revealing slightly more of the stony corridor, which curved to the left and out of sight.

"Oh gods," Dietrich said. Annise's blood ran cold. Instinctively, they all took a step back from the side tunnel, the torchlight retreating with them.

They could no longer see the passage, but Annise didn't need to—the image would be burned in her memory for the rest of her life.

Bones. Some whole, some cracked and splintered—all picked clean. She recognized some of them: ribs, feet, entire skulls, while others she couldn't place. Though it was unclear as to the origins of most, she was almost certain some were human.

"Run," Jonius breathed, and that single word seemed to break them all out of a trance, pushing them to move.

They threw themselves down the tunnel, finding a reserve of energy none of them probably knew they had, brought out only by fear of whatever was making the spine-tingling sound that now chased them from behind.

Another peal of laughter burst from a side tunnel that opened on the right. Annise flinched away as if the sound had substance, crashing into the wall, scraping her shoulder but ignoring the sting of pain, racing onwards, kindling scattering from her satchel, crackling under her feet as she crushed it to splinters.

More side tunnels appeared, more frequently now, each full of the raucous sound of pursuit, a clamor of frivolity and pent up violence that seemed to encapsulate the violent images they'd left far behind them. More bones spilled from each corridor, crunching under their trod as they fled.

So the pale creatures had prevailed in the end, she thought. *The knights are dead. And so, soon, shall we.*

273

Not me, the monster inside her hissed. Annise didn't know whether it meant because it would live inside Tarin, or something else. In this moment, she didn't care about anything but finding the end to this infernal tunnel, to avoid seeing those pale creatures that clung to walls and ceilings, biting, clawing, dying, and yes, killing.

But her wish was not to be granted. Just as she passed a dark tunnel, something flew from its maw, a flash of white skin, all bony arms and legs and big round eyes, each as pink as a sunrise.

Dietrich, who was bringing up the rear, cried out; not in pain, but surprise, or so Annise hoped. She spun around, but he was already pushing her forward—"Move move move!"— her eyes barely able to comprehend the decapitated creature lying dead in a pool of a glowing white substance she assumed was its spilled blood. Dietrich's sword flashed beside her as they ran, his other hand resting firmly on the small of her back, lending her speed.

More white forms scrambled from more tunnels, some along the ceiling, some along the walls, some launching themselves through the air. Annise punched one in the face and was shocked by how soft and rubbery its flesh was, almost like that of a fish. It squealed and fell away, disappearing into the gloom they left in their wake. Dietrich hacked at several others, slashing them in half or removing heads from necks.

There were too many, however, and soon they began to emerge from tunnels ahead of them, their peals of laughter arriving first, a strange battle cry far worse than the gruff shouts of a man or the beat of powerful drums. Soon, Annise knew, they would be overwhelmed.

Jonius ground to a stop, flanked by Archer. Annise and Dietrich halted in turn, whirling around to face the creatures in pursuit. Cackling with glee, the cave dwellers slowed their pace, creeping forward, sticking to every surface like insects.

Annise noticed the flaps of skin between their long pale fingers, webs that presumably allowed them to climb walls and hang upside down. Similar web-like flaps held their toes together as well. The sound they were making sounded like it came from twin holes on either side of their heads, where their ears should have been. They were hairless, their skin as smooth as fresh ice. From a slit on the tops of their heads, they seemed to sniff the air, which was when Annise realized their pink eyes were blind, filled with milky cataracts.

They attack by smell, and perhaps sound, she thought, even as they closed in.

She turned back to determine the positioning of the creatures that had cut off their escape, but instead her eyes settled on Archer, who met her gaze. There was no fear in his expression, no youth—not in this moment. Only determination. The same determination she felt in her own steely gaze, and running hot through her veins. This life that had been thrust upon them had changed them both, a blacksmith's fire stoked with pain and sadness, trust and companionship, experience and strength, melting them down and reforming them into what they had become. Yes, they would die, this they both already knew, but it would be a glorious death, even if the bards would never sing of it.

"We stand together," Annise said. "We die together." The others nodded in turn, angling away to face the enemy.

Annise started to turn, too, but the voice in her head stopped her. *Look*, it said. *See*. Somehow she managed to pry

275

her stare away from the creatures ahead of them, noticing something beyond, a pinprick of color she might not have noticed if she hadn't managed to focus her vision forward, past the immediate threat.

A small triangle of light amidst the dark stone walls of the tunnel. Straight ahead. An end and a beginning.

"There!" she cried. "Our escape is there! We fight forward!"

Thirty-Five
The Hinterlands
Lisbeth Lorne

After Crone had assured her that Zur was not dead and only sleeping, his breath as soft as a whisper on his lips, Lisbeth returned to their dwelling. Exhaustion took her immediately, a monster of the deep pulling her down into the depths.

She slept a dreamless sleep, the first of her short life as a human.

A few hours later she awoke with a start, her pulse pounding between her temples.

No. It's something else, she realized. There it was again, a dull thumping reverberating through the night:

THUM-THUM

Other sounds accompanied it—snarled shouts, stamping feet, mournful howls.

"What is happening?" she said, more to herself than to anyone else.

Still, Crone heard her, sticking her long head inside the ice dwelling. "A call to arms. Garzi ride to war."

War? "Why? Who?"

"This thing I do not know."

Lisbeth remembered the revelation she'd received earlier that night, what felt like an instant ago, a half an instant, a crucial part of her returned after having been missing for eons. *My purpose for coming to this place. My purpose for having this body, in this place, in this time.*

War. The word no longer felt like a declaration of doom but an opportunity for change. She was not a destroyer herself— though she knew she was capable of great destruction—but a forger, a strengthener, a harbinger of great violence, of the war that was destined to come.

THUM-THUM

The drumbeat reminded her that such a fate was perhaps not a distant twinkling light like she'd hoped, but an approaching dawn brighter and colder than any before it.

Is it here already? she wondered. *Have I caused this?* Then she thought of those powerful souls frozen in the Hall of War, of the pent-up violence she felt in her bones as she spoke to them, the centuries of stored purpose and aggression.

If they were the lock, then she was the key. And if she opened this door...

I can never close it. Somehow she knew this, the same way she knew her name, her purpose, like the knowledge was a part of her—had *always* been a part of her, even as she slid through the fabric of time and space, a silvery ribbon of light.

"I have to go," Lisbeth said.

THUM-THUM

Crone said nothing, stepping aside. Letting her pass.

Lisbeth drifted more than walked into the night, like a feather blown on a breeze, her feet barely seeming to brush the snow-crusted ground.

The Garzi were gathering in droves, spears bristling from their backs like a porcupine's quills. Some held spiked clubs over their heads menacingly, as if they were tempted to hit each other, too impatient to wait for whatever foe threatened them. Their wolfish steeds prowled around, their rough fur bristling, their mouths forming eternal snarls.

Lisbeth scanned the mob for Zur, but he was noticeably absent. Instead, another stood at their head, a powerful being that rose a head taller than any others, his shoulders broad, the skin of his triangular face as rough as sundried leather.

"Warriors!" he shouted, raising a spear in the air. "At long last the pact has been broken again. Filth invaders have come to our lands, seeking to sneak past our defenses." He spoke in Garzi, but Lisbeth understood every word. "It started with her. The spy."

All heads turned toward Lisbeth as the great warrior pointed in her direction. She could see the hostility in their eyes, but also the fear. None would touch her; not after what she'd done to Zur, to the legions that had been unable to kill her on the snowy hills.

"We cannot kill the blind witch, but we will string up those who follow her!" A roar of approval. "Tonight we will feast upon their flesh and remind all others that the pact is as strong as ever!" More cries, and the drums started up again, louder and faster than before.

The warriors mounted up, digging their heels into the beasts, though it wasn't necessary. The creatures snarled, charging away, past the dwellings, past the Hall of War, toward the frozen cliffs that cast a long shadow over the village.

Lisbeth watched them go, uncertain, but then gave chase, running on her toes, feeling a rush of energy, of purpose. *Yes. I am meant to do this thing—whatever this thing is.*

Atop their steeds, the warriors reached the base of the cliffs well ahead of her, immediately charging through a gap that led to a switchback trail, narrow and treacherous. The animals, however, were as sure-footed as goats, clambering up the path, snow blasting over the edge as they rounded the first bend.

A few moments later, Lisbeth reached the trail, but didn't take it. No, it would be too slow and she would be too late. Though she'd only spent days with these people, she knew what they were capable of, the violence they wore like a badge of honor. Instead, she ascended the cliffs. She didn't fly, nor climb—not exactly—but something else. She just moved up the sheer rock face because she wanted to, her fingertips and toes occasionally brushing the ice.

Despite her more direct path, she continued to fall behind; the beasts and their riders knew these cliffs well, making short work of them.

Hurry hurry hurry! Lisbeth urged herself as she climbed higher and higher, but a strange force seemed to push against her, thwarting her momentum, holding her back.

I will be too late, she thought.

From high above, someone spoke, and though she couldn't make out the words, she could tell it wasn't spoken in Garzi.

No. This was spoken in the common tongue.

Annise Gäric

There are too many, Annise thought, swinging her Evenstar around and around, feeling the satisfying but somewhat sickening smack of metal on soft flesh. Their enemies' glowing white blood was everywhere—the ground, the walls, on their clothes and skin—but still they came, emerging from the side tunnels like water pouring from pipes, an endless supply that made every inch forward as difficult as wading through quicksand.

Jonius, at the front, had taken several wounds—a claw across his cheek, a bite to the hand, a mangled ear—but had killed many, his sword moving from opponent to opponent in that graceful way of his that reminded Annise of a dance. Archer, considering his lack of true battle experience, had done remarkably well thus far, killing several of the cave dwellers and only suffering a bloodied nose.

Dietrich, protecting their rear, had killed dozens of the creatures already, and more fell moment by moment on his sword, which spun, slashed, and stabbed like tornadoes and lightning, a storm of his own making.

The bodies were piling up, just like in the images they'd seen painted on the walls, but that didn't mean they would emerge victorious, not when their foes seemed as innumerable as grains of sand on the edges of the ocean.

Still, the light—the hope!—Annise had spotted in the distance, continued to grow closer, larger. Step by hard-fought step, they made progress toward the escape that moments earlier had seemed improbable if not impossible.

As Annise passed the dark maw of yet another side tunnel, a blob of pale flesh flung itself at her. Instinctively, she shoved her torch in its direction. They'd quickly learned the creatures feared and despised fire, something they'd used to their advantage. Hissing, the creature twisted in midair to avoid being burned.

Which was exactly what Annise had been expecting.

Crunch!

Her Evenstar connected solidly with its face, ripping through its blind eyes and sinking deep into its skull.

The creature dropped at her feet with a squishing sound, pulsing white blood pumping from the mortal wound she'd inflicted.

Annise didn't have time to contemplate what it meant to kill a living creature, nor her feelings on the subject, for another was already clambering across the ceiling to attack from above. No, there was no time to think, or consider, or fathom the fathomless—there was only time to act. To do. To survive.

The creature dropped so quickly it took her breath away. Her weapon was still ensconced in her previous foe's skull, and she was too slow by half in bringing her torch up. She only had one option, and she took it, pushing off from the balls of her feet, leaping upwards to meet the attack head on.

Literally.

As she headbutted it in the jaw, she felt its fangs sink into her flesh, its claws rake across her cheeks. Pain flared through her skin like a series of hot pokers thrust under her flesh, but she managed to lurch forward and land atop it, shoving her torch in its face.

The howl was so close to her ears she could hear nothing else for several moments, even as she watched it writhe and twist, its face burned black and bubbling, until it went still.

She whirled around, seeking her next foe, but then realized how close they were to the light. In fact, Sir Jonius was already *out* of the cave, his body drenched in moonlight that seemed— after so long in the dark—as bright as a noonday sun. Archer was a mere step behind him, turning back to beckon to Annise and Dietrich, his mouth forming a soundless cry: *Hurry!*

Behind Annise, Dietrich stood completely still, holding his torch aloft, peering into the gloom. The still, silent gloom.

"Sir?" Annise said, dumbfounded. Where was the enemy? Just a moment ago she'd sworn the creatures were everywhere, on all sides. But now...

"Something scared them off," Dietrich said. Instead of sounding victorious, he sounded worried.

"That's a good thing, right?"

"Depends on what scared them off," he said, turning and ushering her toward the exit, where the others were waiting.

When Annise stepped into the moonlight, she was forced to shield her eyes against the bright green and red orbs shining from opposite sides of the sky, their long beams of light crisscrossing on the cliffs. This far north, the moons seemed closer somehow. Bigger. Brighter. In this midst of certain death, Annise had assumed she'd never see them again, and now she relished the way the light washed over her like a winter storm.

Archer seemed to be doing the same, holding his blood-soaked arms to either side as a light breeze blew across the cliffs. Jonius was already moving down a narrow path that led away from the tunnel, scouting the terrain for weaknesses, where the ice and snow might fall away. Dietrich, however, had slid onto his belly, peering over the edge.

"Damn," was all he said.

That's when Annise heard the drums.

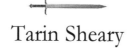

Tarin Sheary

Any possibility of sleep was vanquished the moment he felt the danger. Not to him, but to *her*, channeled through him by whatever dark magic the monster had conjured.

Tarin sat up sharply in bed, all weariness chased away in an instant, his muscles flexing, his body urging him to *Find Her*.

She is out of reach, the monster hissed.

It was a truth he already knew, but still, it was like a bucket of cold water had been thrown over his head. Tarin had never felt so helpless in his life, save perhaps for when he'd contracted the bone disease that had eventually led him to this very place. *Everything comes full circle*, he thought, even as he concentrated on that feeling inside him, that connection to Annise.

He could *feel* her action, her fear, her desperation. Something was trying to hurt her, maybe even kill her, but she wasn't dead yet.

For a long time, Tarin just sat there, ragged breaths pushing between his clenched teeth, blood pumping through his veins, his heart pounding as if he was the one in grave peril.

And then, abruptly, the feeling passed, leaving him exhausted and breathless, though he'd barely moved.

At first, he thought, *No. No no no*… Because the emptiness he felt could only mean one thing…

284

She lives, the monster purred.

Upon hearing those two words, he collapsed on the ground, the sense of relief as powerful an emotion as he'd ever felt before.

But then—

Like a hot knife shoved into his heart, the rush of danger, of fear, returned in an instant.

Annise was under attack once more.

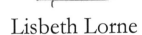

Lisbeth Lorne

Lisbeth crested the cliff, which was packed full of Garzi nestled shoulder to shoulder, spears shoved forward. Their tall spokesperson was barking in their rough language, spitting the words like darts through a blow gun. "You have broken the pact. There is only one sentence: death."

The chant went up through the crowd. "Death! Death! Death!"

Somewhere beyond the warriors, a voice spoke in the common tongue, calm and placating. "We don't understand what you're saying. We come to your lands in peace."

The Garzi reverted to the common tongue. "Filth language. I make understand. Pact broken. Now die."

"No!" Lisbeth shouted in Garzi.

Several heads turned, but not all. Instead of shoving through the crowd, she spoke to those in her direct path, where only they could hear her. Their souls were like soft clay to the invisible hands she molded them with. The precision of her power was improving; rather than collapsing, they simply moved aside, pressing closer against their brethren.

A path was opened, and through it Lisbeth saw the exhausted, bedraggled souls of four strangers, three men and a woman.

Lisbeth moved through the Garzi toward them, her eyes cast forward.

The tall Garzi leader stepped across her path, for she had not yet touched his soul. If he was surprised at her sudden appearance, his soul—a roiling mixture of black and gray, almost like smoke—didn't show it. He spoke to her in the common tongue. "Leave us. This not your concern."

"My concern is my own," she said.

"Leave us!" the Garzi repeated. "The pact broken! Punishment death!" At that, dozens of warriors pointed their spears at the strangers once more.

One of the humans, a tall man wearing dented armor, his face scarred, said, "Let's dance."

"No!" Lisbeth said again, louder. "There shall be no violence on this night."

In reply, the warriors screamed "Death!" and attacked.

Annise Gäric

Annise's head was still spinning from the turn of events. Evidently they'd stumbled from the fire and into the maw of an even greater danger. After she'd heard the beat of their drums, the strange-looking warriors had rushed up the incline toward them. Jonius had danced back, Dietrich had found his feet, and the four of them had knotted together, weapons at the ready. As the enemy had approached, Annise had taken in their unusual appearance: They were hairy, their exposed arms hidden beneath dark bristly fur. Over their broad chests they wore spiked bone armor, long wispy hair falling from their scalps to their shoulders. Their faces were bone-hard and shaped like upside-down triangles, wide at the top and narrow and pointy at the bottom. Their eyes were too far apart, dark and intense, boring into them. More fearsome than any of that, however, were the steeds they rode, wolf-like in appearance, but much larger, with all-white coats and long snouts gaped open in snarls of fangs and dark gums.

And then, in stark contrast to the enormous spear-wielding warriors and their beasts, a wisp of a girl had approached like a light in the dark, the sea of death parting for her like flaps of skin split by a sharp knife. A blue eye glowed on her forehead. A third eye, not real, but a marking. *A skinmark*, Annise immediately recognized.

The girl had seemed to argue with one of the warriors, the tallest of the bunch, but whatever she'd said had made no difference.

Now the spears closed in, jabbing toward them from all sides, cutting off any hope of escape, herding them toward the edge of the cliff. Dietrich lashed out with his sword, severing several of the sharp tips. More spear points immediately took their place. Annise shifted back, trying to gain some breathing room. The others retreated as well, though there was nowhere to go but off the cliff or back into the tunnels. Both options felt like certain death. Annise clutched Archer on one side and Jonius on the other.

As they stumbled back, the spears followed. Annise glanced behind, dizziness swarming as she took in the sheer drop they faced. She tripped as the ice cracked along the edge. Archer grasped her arm, pulling her back from the brink. He nodded, and his expression seemed stripped down, all arrogance and bravado gone; it was the most real look he'd ever given her. In this moment, he was simply her brother, her kin. They'd survived much together, and it felt right that the end would come by his side.

As if to echo her thoughts, the tall warrior spoke. "Now you die," he said, meeting her eyes with his, which seemed to burn with dark fire.

Goodbye, Tarin, Annise thought, hoping the monster was still there to hear, that it would pass her final words to the only man she'd ever truly loved. *I will always love you.*

Thirty-Six
The Northern Kingdom, Darrin
Tarin Sheary

Her words tore through him like a thousand knives. Tarin could hear her voice, its richness, its truth, a voice he could listen to all day, a voice with a half a hundred different aspects, each of which he loved for different reasons: her contagious laugh, quick to rise and fall; the sharpness of her "queen voice" as she issued orders that couldn't not be followed; the dry tone of her quick-witted quips and japes; the rough textured voice that only he knew, whispered in the dark as they melted into each other's arms. Dozens of others sprang to mind, too, but Tarin swallowed them away.

He was split in two.

Tarin dropped to his knees, tears pricking at his eyes. Inside, he felt empty, his innards scooped out, his bones cut away and tossed aside. *I am a husk*, he thought.

You are death, the monster purred.

Tarin didn't rise to the bait, didn't try to argue. He had no strength left to do so, no desire to fight. The belief that had driven him these last days was gone, vanquished by Annise's final words to him, words that would once have sent his spirits flying.

I love you, he thought back. *Annise? Annise? Are you there? I love you. Please don't leave me. Please come back to me. I will never leave you again. I promise I promise I—*

The monster's laughter grated inside his head. *She cannot hear you. Not anymore.*

Something twisted inside him. Pain. Agony. The knife that had stabbed him awake was now being turned, measure by measure, destroying anything left of his soul. Anything and everything that made him human.

I hate you, Tarin thought.

Lies, the monster returned.

"If I kill myself, I will kill you, too," he said aloud.

You won't kill yourself.

Tarin hated that the monster knew him better than he knew himself. Even as lost as he now felt, as alone, the monster was right. Tarin would fight to the bitter end, even if the entirety of the world collapsed around him, which, perhaps, it already had.

Dashing away tears with his hand, Tarin stood. The enemy was coming—there was no time to waste. Only after the battle was decided would he grieve for the love he had lost.

Thirty-Seven
The Hinterlands
Annise Gäric

"Stop."

That single word was spoken and the world froze. The spears' progress halted in midair, their wielders' unblinking stares seeing nothing, though Annise could sense the hate in their eyes.

They hated the girl who had spoken, the girl who now approached from their midst. They hated that she had the power to halt their violence.

Though the girl's feet moved toward them, she seemed to float rather than walk, such was the grace of her movements. Her eyes were devoid of color, pale unseeing orbs, while her third eye, the glowing blue skinmark on her forehead, seemed to see right through them. Her skin was unnaturally smooth, like fine porcelain. Her dark hair hung in silken waves upon her shoulders.

Annise felt a sense of comfort that was remarkable given the precipice upon which they stood.

"Who are you?" Annise said, unable to hold back the question.

"I am She Who Brings," the girl said. She waved a hand and the warriors and their steeds began to shift back, away from them. Annise stepped forward, glad to be free of the cliff's edge once more.

"Why did you save us?" Annise asked, watching in awe as those that had threatened their lives a moment earlier moved back and away, down the trail, as easily as one moved pieces on a game board.

"It was not your time to be taken," the girl said. Though Annise was certain she was blind, the girl's white eyes seemed to pierce her directly. She wondered if her companions felt the same way.

"Thank you."

"You have come for the Sleeping Souls," the girl said.

"How did you—"

"I don't know. I am learning still, as we all are. My time here has been short."

By Annise's estimation, the girl was perhaps eighteen name days old. Maybe nineteen, it was hard to tell because of how sleight she was. Slender and graceful, like a wisp of smoke, but still a woman grown, her small breasts hidden beneath the thick furs she wore.

"You're…beautiful," Dietrich said, and the girl's cheeks flushed pink.

Thanks for your contribution, Sir, Annise thought, though she couldn't argue with the truth of his words. "The Sleeping Knights are dead," Annise said. "We saw their story. We saw how it ended."

"No. They live."

That single word: a spark of light in the darkness.

"How do you know?"

"I have seen them."

Annise's breath caught. "Where?"

"Hold on," Sir Jonius said. "What of the warriors? Those are the Garzi, correct? They seem to want us dead. Thank you for protecting us, for *saving* us, but you must sleep some time. You cannot defend us forever."

A thin smile formed on her lips. "My name is Lisbeth Lorne," she said. "And I think I was meant to meet you."

"Me?" Dietrich said. "I was thinking the same thing."

"No," the girl said, which almost made Annise laugh. Until she added, "Her. I was meant to meet the Queen of the North."

They didn't exactly receive a royal welcome into the Garzi village. More like stares tipped with poisoned barbs and mouths filled with disgust. Several of the males, and even one of the females, spat in their general direction.

Still, it was better than the reception they'd received from the pale, web-fingered cave dwellers. At least no one was trying to gnaw on them—at least not yet. Annise considered it a victory.

A mob of Garzi blocked their path, headed by the tall warrior who'd made their deaths such a priority atop the cliffs. This time, however, no weapons were drawn, the long spears sheathed on their backs.

"This wrong," the male said. "Pact broken. Blood must pay." Though he spoke the common tongue, his accent was strong, each word short and clipped, like he was clearing his throat.

"Your traditions must be changed," Lisbeth said. "A new pact must be forged."

"Never."

"Step aside."

The small, thin girl continued to impress Annise with her mettle. There was something about her, something powerful, despite her small stature. She was a force of nature.

"I no fear you. Zur might—I do not."

"Zur doesn't fear me, but he does *understand* me better now. Soon you will, too. Now step aside, or I will make you."

The great warrior stepped aside, as did the rest of them. Annise tried not to stare at them as they passed through. "Do you ever get the feeling you're being watched?" Arch whispered in her ear.

Annise snorted, but didn't respond, her eyes taking in the dwellings formed of snow and ice. An ancient-looking woman watched them from outside one of them. "Welcome to true north, Your Highness," she said with a nod.

"Thank you," Annise said, surprised by the genuineness in the woman's tone.

"She is a friend," Lisbeth explained. "Perhaps my only one."

"In saving us you earned four more," Annise said. The girl only nodded, turning her flawless face forward.

They continued on, and Annise didn't need to look back to know the Garzi warriors were following them—their footsteps were the rumble of thunder. The constant threat of peril served only to heighten her senses. Though she should've been exhausted from their march through the tunnels and fight for their lives, she wasn't, the adrenaline continuing to course through her veins.

I have seen them. Lisbeth's words from earlier came back to her, sending a buzz of excitement through her chest. Unless there was some sort of miscommunication, the girl had just confirmed the Sleeping Knights not only existed, but were nearby. *The north is not lost. Not yet.*

They stopped before an enormous ice structure, at least ten times larger than any others they'd seen so far. "The Hall of War," Lisbeth said, beckoning them forward.

"What is inside?" Archer asked, taking a step forward.

"Truth. Destiny." Though the words were cryptic, Annise felt the rightness in them, like everything about the girl standing before her was right.

"I don't know about the rest of you," Dietrich said, "but I don't mind a bit of truth and destiny. Shall we?" He started forward, but Lisbeth suddenly extended her hand and he collapsed to a knee, cradling his head in his hands. A deep groan rumbled from the back of his throat.

Lisbeth's eyes widened even as the eye marked on her forehead faded, and she retracted her hand. Dietrich toppled over, still holding his skull. "I'm sorry!" the girl said, bending over to touch him. He shuddered at her touch. "I only meant to say you cannot enter this place. It is forbidden."

Dietrich turned his head, wincing. He used a hand to shield his eyes from the moonlight as if it was too bright for him. "What did you do to me? I saw…" He trailed off, shaking his head.

"I—I touched your soul. I'm sorry. I'm still learning."

Annise had no idea what to make of Lisbeth's words. *Touched his soul?* It obviously had something to do with her skinmark, her power. The way she had controlled the Garzi earlier…

Her power almost seemed godlike.

"Try throwing a snowball the next time instead," Annise said. "Are you hurt, Sir?"

"No, I—no. I don't think so." He sat up, massaging his forehead.

"Then there is no harm."

Dietrich nodded, pushing back to his feet, his cheeks slightly pink, either from the cold or whatever the girl had done to him.

"Who *can* enter the Hall of War?" Annise asked.

"You. The Queen of the North."

"Annise," Jonius warned. "We know nothing of this place or what dangers it contains."

Annise turned to the man who'd, at times, felt like a father figure to her. "Thank you for your concern, Sir, but considering we have escaped death's grasp twice in one night, I'm willing to risk it." Jonius nodded, duly chastened.

Archer said, "May I pass inside? I am still a prince of the north."

"I'm sorry," Lisbeth said. "This magic was forged centuries ago."

Archer bit his lip, appearing frustrated.

Sorry, Annise mouthed. "Fine." She glanced at the Garzi gathered around them. "Will they be safe outside?"

The girl's easy, almost childlike, smile was back. "As safe as any of us," she said.

The Hall of War, though beautiful in its own way, was a forlorn place, the ice so thick it was almost black under the moonlight. The ceiling was high, vaulted to several points, a marvel of construction Annise couldn't fathom as being possible from the spear-wielding people outside.

Her gaze travelled along the angles to the thick walls, passing to the center of the large space, where icy columns rose from floor to ceiling. Not one or two, but dozens, perhaps hundreds. They were spaced an arm's length from each other, each identical, their glassy surfaces smooth and round.

Something dark stared out from each of them.

Annise's blood curdled.

"Do you see them, too?" Lisbeth asked. "Do you see the many colors?"

As they approached, Annise didn't see anything but darkness, armor as black as midnight, swords of obsidian steel, helmets like carved granite. And then:

Frozen pale faces, staring out at her with unseeing eyes.

"Frozen hell," Annise whispered.

"A good description, perhaps," Lisbeth said, seeming to seriously consider her words. "But sometimes hell forges the way for heaven, and the angels are only called upon when demons rise."

Like everything else the girl said, her words sounded more profound in sum than when taken individually.

Annise shifted closer to one of the ice columns, her fingers trembling as she reached out to touch it.

"Careful," Lisbeth warned.

Annise glanced at her, considered, and then touched the ice. *Rise o' queen! RISE RISE RISE RISE!*

Annise fell back, stunned by the power, the sheer volume of the voice that burst inside her skull. If Lisbeth heard the voice, too, she showed no evidence of it, standing as straight and stoic as before. "They have waited centuries for this night," she said. "It's no surprise they should be slightly overeager."

"You can hear them?"

"The moment we entered they began their shouting. I hear them still. It makes it hard to have a conversation with you."

Once more, Annise was amazed by Lisbeth Lorne. Annise knew she wouldn't be able to think, much less speak, with that voice in her head. And Lisbeth was hearing hundreds of shouts, a cacophony of raw sound energy. She approached the column once more, but this time made no move to touch it. Staring into the ancient knight's eyes, she searched for any sign of him still being in there, still being alive.

"What do we do?" she asked.

Lisbeth turned toward her, and those blind eyes of hers once more seemed to pierce her flesh, her heart. "First, you must understand."

"Understand what?"

"This." The glowing blue eye began to form on the girl's forehead, slowly at first, but then brighter and brighter, until Annise was forced to squint or else be blinded.

And then the Hall of War was gone, vanishing in an instant, replaced by a field of red flowers, blooming on every surface, glistening under the bright sun rising overhead. Hundreds— no, thousands—lay amongst them, bathing under the perfectly cloudless sky.

Overcome by weariness, Annise wanted desperately to join them, to lie down, to rest amongst the scarlet bouquets. To sleep and sleep and sleep some more.

And then she saw him, his sheer size unmistakable next to the other normal-sized people.

Tarin.

He, too, slept, his hands folded across his chest, his expression one of complete tranquility.

A smile burst upon her lips, and Annise ran through the flowers, mindless of how she trampled them underfoot. She weaved through the sleeping people until she was by his side, falling upon him, touching his face—his real, real face—with its protruding veins, which were no longer black but devoid of color, snakes of pale flesh. She frowned, not understanding, shouting his name, kissing his lips with hers, pulling back sharply when she felt the iciness of his flesh. The unnatural cold.

The world changed around her. The field turned to snow, the flowers to blood, the sleeping people to corpses marred with dozens of wounds, their blank stares trained skyward at the thick blankets of gray clouds that replaced the clear blue expanse.

And she couldn't breathe couldn't breathe couldn't—

"Tarin!" she screamed. Her voice bounced from icy wall to icy ceiling and back again, and she found herself back inside the Hall of War, only Lisbeth Lorne and the Sleeping Knights there to hear her cry. She gasped, her eyes wide, trying to catch her breath. "What...was...that? What did you show me?"

The girl didn't answer her question. "Once you release these souls, you cannot recall them. Their violence will be complete. Their destruction total. Those who threaten the north will die."

"Will *he* die?" She couldn't say his name, not after feeling those cold lips, his unbeating heart beneath his chest, which refused to rise and fall.

"I am not a soothsayer nor fortune teller," Lisbeth said. "Your soul speaks for itself, as does mine."

Annise felt like crying. Felt like throwing things. Felt like running away, fleeing north, never looking back. At least that way she would never have to face this decision. If she didn't release the Sleeping Knights, the north would fall. And if she did, Tarin would. Love or kingdom? Happiness or responsibility? Passion or honor?

Why did she have to choose? Why couldn't it be both? Why couldn't she be both?

Because I am queen. Because I chose this. For my people. For my mother. For Archer.

The words were there, but they stuck in her throat.

Oh, Tarin. Oh, Tarin. I'm sorry. So sorry.

She swallowed. Licked her lips. Spoke.

"Release them. Release them all."

"A queen has chosen," Lisbeth said.

Her skinmark began to glow, blinding blue light radiating outwards as the eye formed.

Voices rose as if in response, a hundred speaking at once, unified in their message:

Time, time, defend the north, defend, fight, war, victory, VICTORY!

Annise looked away from the light, plugging her ears against the cacophony.

The ground began to shake, and the blue ice pillars began to crack, sparkling crystals tinkling across the white floor of the Hall of War. Annise stared at the knights, each of whom stood atop their pedestals, unmoving, unblinking, their limbs frozen in place and time.

In a strange way, Annise felt relief. It hadn't worked. They'd waited too long to find the knights, and they were beyond recovery, their slumber eternal. At the same time, she felt a sense of failure. Those two warring feelings did battle in her chest and mind.

But then:

One by one, the knights broke free of their pedestals, their movements jerky at first, but smoothing out as they shook off the haze of centuries of disuse. The knights were tall and strong, each clad in mail and adorned with fine weapons that seemed as equally preserved as they. Whatever magic had kept these men alive over the years was powerful indeed, perhaps as strong as Lisbeth's skinmark.

"We know our orders," they said, as one, though Annise had not spoken.

"We march for Darrin at once," Annise said, waiting for some sign that they agreed.

Instead of a sign, the knights fell into line, marching from the Hall of War and out into the night. The Garzi, gathered outside, backed away, staring in awe at the scene before them. None moved to follow them, save for Annise and her travelling companions, each of whose jaws hung open. "How?" Archer said.

"The girl," Annise answered.

She noticed Lisbeth Lorne hanging back, conferring with one of the Garzi—the old woman who had welcomed them to the village. The girl looked shaken, weakened, clutching the woman's shoulder. Lisbeth noticed her gaze. "I will follow you," she said. "I promise. But I must attend to something first."

Annise nodded, gesturing for her companions to stride to the head of the knight army.

None looked back as they started south by another, longer route, avoiding the cliffs and their deadly tunnels.

Thirty-Eight
The Hinterlands
Lisbeth Lorne

Lisbeth's entire body was shaking like a leaf. Crone held her, rubbing her hands along her sides, trying to warm her. The woman didn't understand that it wasn't the cold. It was what she'd heard as she released the Sleeping Souls. What she'd *seen*.

A single word, repeated over and over in succession: HORDE. The word in and of itself meant nothing to her, but when combined with the fragments of images that flashed through her mind—horrific scenes of war and bloodshed, entire nations thrown down by their enemies, their cities burned, their people annihilated—Lisbeth could hardly breathe.

What is this new threat? she wondered. The images had been so fleeting, so full of destruction but lacking detail.

And then Zur was there, the warrior's soul very much alive and conscious as he stood in the doorway. "Girl saw my daughter," he said. Rather than an accusation, he sounded defeated. Exhausted.

Lisbeth could not deny it. "Yes."

His soul bobbed, nodding. "Zur saw her too. Saw what girl saw. Never knew she was strong at the end. Brave. Proud of her."

Lisbeth didn't know what to say. She'd thought she'd broken the man by touching his soul; instead, it seemed, she'd enlightened him.

Crone said, "Girl tell Zur what told me."

Lisbeth hesitated, but Zur encouraged her. "Girl is no enemy, Zur knows that now."

Lisbeth pursed her lips. "Thank you." And then she told him what she'd seen and heard in the Hall of War.

When she finished, Crone said, "Zur knows what girl speaks of?"

"Yes," Zur said, without hesitation. "The Fall of All Things. It has been foretold for centuries. That is why we honor the pact. That is why Garzi must never leave these lands. Cold lands safe."

Lisbeth's heart hammered in her chest. "I have to go," she said. She needed to catch up with the queen and her knight army. Needed to warn them of what was coming, even if she didn't fully understand it herself. She stood and moved toward the door, but Zur blocked her. "Garzi do not fight below the lake. Girl knows that?"

"Yes," Lisbeth said.

"Good." He stepped aside. "Wish girl luck. Never return to these lands."

"I won't," Lisbeth said. "I promise." With that, she flew outside, following the churned-up path of marching warriors through the snow. None of the Garzi tried to stop her.

Thirty-Nine
The Northern Kingdom,
on the road to Darrin
Sir Christoff Metz

Since departing Castle Hill for Darrin with only his battalion of female soldiers—in strict obedience of Zelda's command: *None of your* men *shall go to Darrin's aid*—Sir Christoff Metz had learned something important:

Women complained less and worked harder than men.

It was because of this truth that they were ahead of schedule, a fact that helped comfort his orderly mind, even as he counted their continued steps toward Darrin.

Back in Castle Hill, he'd left several of his more experienced men in charge, to continue training and to await his return. By now, Queen Regent Zelda would have learned of his deception. Though he'd not broken the letter of her orders, he'd certainly shattered the spirit of them, and he wasn't so naïve to believe there wouldn't be consequences. He could be stripped of his position as captain, or even have his knighthood revoked. However, to him, these risks were worth it. The people of Darrin needed help, and he was in a position to give it.

He'd appointed Private Sheary as his aide for the journey, and she'd been a great help thus far, organizing camp in accordance with his very specific orders. She'd even come to him late the night before, appearing at his tent with a simple question: *Do you need anything else from me?* For a moment he'd hesitated, tongue-tied, for something about the look in her eyes took his breath away, but then he'd said, "No, thank you, Private. That will be all."

Why she'd looked disappointed at his response continued to confound him the next day, as they rode eastward through the snow.

Inexplicably, she appeared beside him now, riding her brown-speckled white mare. "Private Sheary," he said formally.

"Captain Metz," she said, lowering her voice sternly, as if imitating him.

"Did I call for you?" He knew he hadn't, but there was no other reason for her sudden appearance. Strict riding formation was necessary in the event of an unexpected enemy attack.

"No," she said. Nothing else, just *No*.

He frowned, trying to decide what to say next without coming across as rude. Nothing sprang to mind, so he said nothing, the words of his mother guiding the decision: *When in doubt, say nothing.*

Private Sheary laughed, removing her helmet to run a hand through her silky dark hair, her jade eyes glittering in the sun.

Christoff's frown deepened. "Did I miss a jape? That happens to me a lot."

She shook her head. "You miss more than just japes," she said.

He looked at her. Well, more like at her lips, which were pink and moist and almost more uncomfortable to look at than her eyes. "Explain."

"Last night," she said.

"Last night?"

"When I came to your tent?"

"You asked if I needed anything."

"Yes. And you turned me away."

"Yes. Because I didn't need anything."

She laughed again. "You're the queerest man I've ever met."

"I get that a lot," he muttered.

"And yet I continue to find myself drawn to you—why is that?"

He stared at the path ahead, afraid to meet her eyes. No woman had ever spoken to him this way. Most just got angry with him and slapped him or threw water in his face. "Perhaps it's my magnetic personality," he blurted out, having no idea where the words had come from. *Ah yes.* A jape he'd once heard another knight make. He still didn't understand it, not truly, but the collection of people gathered in the tavern had laughed loudly.

And so, to his pleasure, did Private Sheary. "You surprise me at every turn," she said. "May I visit your tent again tonight?"

"For what purpose?" His cheeks felt hot, though the temperature was anything but.

"To talk."

"About what? We cannot determine the strategy for Darrin until we reach the castle and assess the situation."

"Not about strategy. Just about life. About you. About me."

Something about those last two sentences felt strange, like she had joined them together in her mind. *Women are a mystery I shall never understand*, Christoff thought, which almost made him laugh considering he was now leading an entire platoon of them to battle.

"I'm certain I don't understand what you mean," he said. "I have little and less to say about myself."

"Then I shall do the talking," she said. "I will tell you stories to lighten your mood."

"An example please."

She looked away, seeming to consider his request for a moment. Then she spoke:

"Last night, while we slept on the cold, hard ground, I imagined it was something else."

"What do you mean?" Besides women and jokes, *imagination* was yet another thing Christoff had yet to fully understand. *Your imagination was removed before you were born*, his mother always liked to say.

"Well, before I joined the Queen's Army, I was a maidservant for a lady in Blackstone. Not one of the major ones, but a rich one nonetheless. She wasn't a particularly pleasant woman, but she paid me well and I never wanted for food, clothing or shelter. Anyway, she had this enormous bed—it was so big I swear the entire city could've slept on it."

309

Christoff had the strong urge to inform her of the impossibility of her statement—no bed could be that large—but managed, barely, to hold his tongue. His mother would've been proud.

She continued. "This bed was crafted of the finest goose down, an entire mountain of it that must've cost a small fortune to procure from the west, back before the trade was cut off. When she slept on it, I swear she looked dead—that's how peaceful she looked."

Metz didn't comment—he understood comparisons as well as anyone. Private Sheary looked at him expectantly, and he remembered that at this point in a story, most people had this strange habit. Rather than argue the point, he complied, feeling like a sheep being herded. "Then what happened?"

She smiled, as if reacting to her own private little joke. "Well, my mistress went out for the day, as she did sometimes. She didn't require my services on this particular outing, so I was left to my own devices. What do you suppose I did?"

Christoff was certain he didn't have the faintest idea. He shrugged.

"Take a guess."

Christoff hated guessing games. "Took a nap."

She clapped her hands, dropping the reins. "Exactly! On my mistress's bed!"

Christoff's eyes widened, surprised. In retrospect, he should've connected the two halves of the story, but establishing these kinds of relationships between facts were hard for him, especially when an action was such a clear breach of honor, duty, and etiquette. "She should've terminated your service," he said.

Private Sheary was fully laughing now. "She did, you dolt! When she found me sleeping atop her goose down bed, nestled in the covers, hugging her pillow to my chest, she canned me on the spot. But it was *worth it*, Captain Metz. I've never slept so well in my life. If I didn't know better, I'd have thought I was sleeping on a cloud."

The knight could hold his tongue no longer. "But a cloud is a gaseous vapor, like smoke. If you slept on a cloud you would likely fall to a violent death."

"Thank you for that lovely image."

"You're welcome?"

"My point is, last night as we slept on this awful, awful ground, I imagined I was sleeping on my old mistress's bed. And you know what?"

He shook his head, as baffled as ever.

"I awoke this morning as refreshed as the day I was terminated from my lady's service."

"That's impossible," Christoff said automatically.

"It's true."

"You must've found a soft spot, a bed of soft snow, or winter moss. Something."

"No," she said. "I checked. My resting place was as hard as everyone else's. My imagination fooled my body."

Christoff struggled to make sense of the senseless. The facts, if indeed they were facts, spread out before him, refusing to come into alignment. "But how?

"Sometimes belief is more powerful than truth," she said. "Sometimes imagination rules logic and wisdom."

She flashed a final grin, and, with that said, rode away, back into line.

Christoff realized the distraction had made him lose count of his steps.

More importantly, he didn't care.

When, as she'd promised, Private Sheary came to his tent that night, he didn't turn her away when she asked, "Captain, do you need anything?"

Instead, he said, "Yes, please. A story, if you will."

She smiled as she entered, sitting cross-legged across from him. "Of course. It shall be my pleasure."

Forty

The Western Kingdom, Knight's End
Rhea Loren

As she stood on her balcony gripping the railing, Rhea realized that the city of her childhood, the Holy City, the city to end all cities, Knight's End, had become her own personal prison. She hated its endless walls, its cobblestoned streets, its purity dresses and temples and righteous warriors garbed in red.

For here, in this place, in this castle, lived only ghosts, each and every one seeming to haunt her every waking step and the hollows of her dreamless sleep.

Everyone she had ever loved. Her father. Her mother. Grey Arris. Ennis Loren. And, yes, even Bea. She'd loved her once, a long time ago. The memories of her youngest sister were like pins in her skull. *When did I grow to hate her? Why did we push each other away at every turn?*

Even her unborn child felt like a ghost inside her, a lost soul.

In some ways, the losses humbled her, made her want to change, to finally listen to Ennis's advice and seek peace with their eastern and southern neighbors.

I can heal you. Roan's words before he left; words that she now clung to like the only thread keeping her from tumbling off a precipice and into the void. Though she'd been no saint before the furia had marred her beauty, her worst sins had come after. It was no excuse, but perhaps it was an opportunity to start over. If Roan healed her, maybe she could use it as an excuse to rescind her previous proclamations.

The child growing in her belly stirred. *Wrath, what would you have me do?* It was the first time in years she'd directly addressed the god of the west. *Are you there?*

Nothing answered her but silence and the rush of a cool wind through her hair.

I am empty. I am lost. I am broken.

Ennis. Oh, Ennis. Come back to me.

Come back.

But he wouldn't. He couldn't. She'd cast him away with her words, her truth.

Could she change? Would it make a difference?

No, the course she'd set herself on was a leap from a cliff into a dark sea, and nothing could arrest her fall now. She would leave this city, ride with Darkspell east. She would see this done personally. The Orians would die and the east would fall. After that, the Four Kingdoms would be hers for the taking. This vision, this goal, was the only thing she had left.

It was a week later, and for the first time in her life, Rhea looked upon the east. Though it was still far off in the distance, obscured by the clouds of smoke that cast a haze over everything—the Tangle continued to burn out of control—she could see the green countryside, emerald grass and tall trees and farmsteads dotting the plains. Only the great silver line of the Spear separated the kingdoms. *Such a small barrier*, she thought.

Thus far, Rhea, Darkspell, and her retinue of furia had traveled primarily along the Western Road, but in the last day had shifted southeast. The purpose was to avoid Hyro Lake and the recently rebuilt Bridge of Triumph. This wouldn't be a mission of force, but of stealth.

Now, as they approached the end of their journey, Rhea had to swallow away the second thoughts that continued to plague her.

Why do I care what happens to the Orians? she wondered. For years they'd killed her people without compassion, using their Wrath-damn ore magic against the west.

She knew the reason: Ennis. She could almost feel him looking at her in that judging, serious way of his. Yes, he was far too old for her—he'd been more of an uncle figure than a cousin growing up—and yet something about how he treated her made Rhea feel...good, wanted. Like she was beautiful, despite her scars, despite her sins.

The way he'd looked at her always made her want to be *better*, even if she'd fought the feeling at every turn.

"Your Highness?"

Rhea shook her head, the past fading like ink from an inkreed, pulled from the waters of her mind.

The old potionmaster, Darkspell, was staring at her, his wrinkled head cocked to the side.

"Yes," she said. "It is time."

He licked his chapped lips eagerly, as if the thought of the deaths of thousands of Orians gave him pleasure without measure. "There are two potions that, when mixed, will create something beautiful."

She grimaced. This man had a strange definition of beauty. Rhea wondered if that was why he was drawn to her in the first place.

He held up two small vials. It was odd to think that something so small and seemingly insignificant could cause unimaginable destruction.

The moment was yet another threshold in her life. Thus far, she hadn't hesitated to cross any of those that came before. But this time she paused, seeing her sister's death pass before her eyes, the dark, disappointed look in Ennis's expression as he rode away, the bright, blue eyes she imagined her child would wear, so observant, watching her every move, learning from her. And, finally, the maw of the oceanic monster she'd twice summoned.

And, once again, she allowed the world to be crushed by it.

"Do it," she said.

Forty-One

The Eastern Kingdom, the Rot
Gwendolyn Storm

Though she'd spent the last fortnight hiding in the Rot, the festering swamplands on the southeastern edge of Hyro Lake, Gwendolyn had not grown used to any of it. Not the swarms of insects biting day and night; not the smell, a sweet, moldy odor that reminded her of rotting meat; and, especially, not the dead stares of the corpses resting at the bottom of the dark waters.

It was unnerving, those stares. Even when Gwen forced her chin to remain raised, her eyes fixed above eye level, she could *feel* their wide, empty gazes.

Per legend, the Rot was not always a swampland, but simply one of Hyro Lake's numerous inlets, teeming with plant life and the wildlife that flocked to it. A hundred years after the

Crimean expansion into the Four Kingdoms, however, a great battle was said to have been fought on the banks of what would later become the Rot. Thousands were killed on both sides—Orians and humans alike—and the survivors were so few that digging graves would be impossible. Instead, the corpses were tossed haphazardly into the waters of the lake. Rather than decomposing, the bodies remained intact, preserved by some strange magic no one understood, not even the natives. The nature of the inlet changed, the plants shriveling and dying, the waters unmoving, the animals steering clear. A swamp, the Rot, was born.

Gwen peered over the edge. A dozen sets of eyes stared back.

"*Ore,*" she muttered.

Gareth chuckled. "What? You haven't made friends with our neighbors yet?"

"You shouldn't jape about the dead. It's irreverent."

Gareth pulled his oar around, turning them toward the west. "Since when have you known me to be reverent? Anyway, the dead don't seem to mind. Whether I jape or not, they will continue to stare."

Gwen couldn't argue with that. After stealing a cheap fisherman's boat that he didn't seem to be using—it leaked in several places—they'd been patrolling the edges of Hyro Lake for over a week, and, to Gwen's knowledge, none of the corpses had so much as blinked. Generally, they set out in the morning, early, heading northward against the gentle current, crossing the lake well before reaching the Bridge of Triumph, and then drifting south until they reached the mouth of the Spear.

As each day passed, Gwen felt more and more like their endeavor was pointless, like searching for a diamond amongst chips of ice. If Rhea Loren and Darkspell were going to unleash an Orian-killing plague on the east, there were plenty of other ways to do it.

At the same time, she knew they couldn't give up. If there was any chance she could stop this atrocity from being carried out, she had to try.

They emerged from the swamplands, the broad expanse of Hyro Lake spreading out like a sparkling ocean, so wide it was difficult to see the far side. Gareth handed her the oars. "Your turn," he said.

She grabbed the oars, settled into position, and began pulling, using her breaths and the beat of her heart to establish a rhythm. It felt good, doing something, the consistency of the work calming her nerves, which seemed to fray a little more each time the sun set. Now that they were out of the Rot, she felt calmer, more like herself.

The current that fought her every stroke wasn't particularly strong, and she made swift progress northward. Gareth used a spyglass they'd "acquired" to scan the bank for anything suspicious. They didn't expect Rhea Loren to show up with a platoon of red-garbed furia surrounding her, but that didn't mean they couldn't spot a small group of out-of-place westerners sneaking about.

By lunchtime, Gwen's muscles were burning and she handed the oars back over to Gareth, who turned their path westward, crossing the lake with long pulls while she ate an unsatisfying meal comprised of edible leaves fit for rabbits, and crunchy bark. "Mmm," she murmured, in jest.

"Good, eh?" Gareth said. "I was tempted to eat your portion, too, but I didn't want to deprive you of life's simple pleasures."

"Thank you. The bark is to die for."

"Now who's making jokes about death?"

She snorted. Though Gareth and she fought like close siblings at times, he wasn't the worst traveling companion she could have. After all, they had Roan in common, which, for some reason, had brought them closer together rather than put them at odds.

Strange, she thought, *the way the world works.*

Gareth was as capable an oarsman as she, and he made short work of the lake's width, steering them close to the western shore. Here, the air was thicker, filled with the drifting smog of the burning forest to the north. She wondered whether the forest would burn forever, regrowing and burning and repeating for eternity. The thought didn't seem so impossible, not when the Four Kingdoms had done the same for five centuries.

Gwen's gaze coasted along the shore, seeing nothing but specks of white and gray—birds come to drink.

"See anything?" Gareth asked. He rowed backwards to stop their progress, and then slowly turned them so the craft would slide into the current.

"Birds," Gwen said.

"I hate birds," Gareth said. "Especially when they shite on my head."

"I like them. Especially when they shite on your head."

Gareth feigned like he would hit her with an oar, but she didn't flinch. "Sometimes I think your nerves are forged of the same steel armor you wear across your loins."

Gwen raised the spyglass to her eye, pushing her scope further south, past where the lake gave way to a narrow strip of silver, shooting away perfectly straight, like a gossamer thread. The Spear. "One, it's just *you* I'm not scared of; and two, don't speak of my 'loins' ever again."

Gareth opened his mouth to respond, probably with another pointless quip, but Gwen quickly shushed him. "Wait."

"What is it?"

She squinted, trying to magnify her vision further. It worked, and suddenly the smudges she'd thought were moving across the land took shape:

People. *Lots of them.* They were on the eastern riverbank, not quite to its edge, but swiftly approaching.

"Gwen?" Gareth said.

There was no time to explain—she snatched the oars from him, shoving him off the bench.

"What are you—"

"They're here!" she hissed, splashing the tips of the oars back into the water, pulling as hard as she could to quickly gain momentum, the current lending additional speed as they funneled toward the entrance to the Spear.

Gareth rose to a kneeling position, grabbing the spyglass from the boat's bed, where Gwen had dropped it. Gwen pulled harder. The fatemark on her cheek flared, sending additional strength to her arms, her abdomen, her legs. The boat sprang forward with a lurch, cutting through the water, sending waves from its bow.

"What do you see?" Gwen asked. "Tell me."

"Holy Ore!" Gareth said. "It's *her.*"

A shockwave shivered through Gwen and she nearly dropped the oars. She quickly recovered, sending the boat shooting forward once more. "Queen Loren is here?"

"Yes. I can see her. And him, too. Darkspell. They've got several furia with them as protection."

The nerve of that woman, Gwen thought. "How much time do we have?"

"Not long," Gareth said. "You'll have to go faster."

To anyone else, it might sound like an impossible request, but not to Gwen. She redoubled her efforts, her cheek burning, the light nearly blinding her left eye. As the oars cut through the water again and again and again, the boat seemed to lift from the water, sliding over it rather than through it.

"You're a force of nature, you know that?" Gareth said.

"So I've been told," she said, grunting from the strain.

"Assuming Roan picks you—and let's face it, he probably will—please be careful with him. He might have a fatemark, but he's fragile."

Gwen ignored the comment, using every ounce of her breath to pull, pull, pull—

The rickety boat swept into the Spear, which seemed to grab it from the front, drawing it along faster and faster and faster still.

And then she saw them: A dozen travelers on horseback. Rhea, her white purity dress swirling around her feet as she rode; Darkspell, his dark cloak covering his hunched form. The furia just ahead and just behind. The group was trotting along at a reasonable pace, unsuspecting that they were being hunted by their own escaped prisoners.

Even if we make it in time...the furia are worthy foes. Gwen had fought them several times before, and though she'd managed

322

to kill them, the battles were long and drawn out. If they distracted her long enough for Darkspell to empty his potion into the Spear...

It's over.

I can't let that happen.

A shout—they'd been spotted. The horses were spurred on, sprinting across the plains now, angling further south to add distance between them and their pursuers.

"Dammit!" Gwen growled. Her entire body was rocking back and forth as she strained against water and distance and time, the old boat rattling as if it might break apart at any moment.

"We're not going to make it," Gareth said.

"We. Are." Gwen hated being defied, hated losing, hated seeing innocent people die. She wouldn't give in until the act was complete.

Gareth grabbed her shoulder. "Gwen, this potion will kill you. We need to get you somewhere safe."

She shrugged him off. "The waters are connected! Nowhere is safe!" Anyway, she didn't care about herself, but about her people. The young, the old, the unborn. All of them deserved life and she refused to let Rhea Loren take it from them.

Ahead, the riders had dismounted near the river and were running toward it. Rhea Loren was at their head, while Darkspell and his shorter legs fell behind. She was flanked by her furia, their blades drawn, flashing in the afternoon light as their arms pumped at their sides.

"No," Gwen gasped. Their foe was so close she could see their eyes, and yet too far away to be stopped. Gareth was right, this she knew, but still she rowed.

Rhea looked at her, and Gwen was surprised to see she wasn't smiling, wasn't wearing her victory like a mask, but simply staring in her direction, motionless, patiently waiting for the potionmaster to reach her side.

And then the old man was there, his chest heaving, his hands fumbling at two small vials, prying the corks from their mouths, tipping them forward—

Rhea Loren

Rhea's heart was in her throat as she launched herself at Darkspell, backhanding both vials from his grasp. They flew back, colliding with his chest and splashing their dark, tar-like contents onto his face, his lips, entering his mouth.

The man tumbled backwards, his face awash with horror, his hands scrubbing at his skin.

Something clarified in Rhea's mind, a seed of an idea, a truth, quickly growing a stem and leaves, flowering into reality.

The potion was never meant to kill just Orians. He was going to destroy us all.

As if to prove her point, the potionmaster's back arched and he gasped, his pink tongue flopping from the side of his mouth. He writhed from side to side like a fish out of water, struggling for breath, clutching at his throat.

With a final jerk, he went still.

Rhea stared in horror, not at the speedy and violent death of the man who'd tried to stab her in the back, but at the fact that she'd foiled his plans with her sudden change of heart.

Why did I do that? Why did I stop him?

She thought of Ennis, of how his declaration and departure had felt, the final look of disappointment searing through her with the force of a lightning strike. She thought of the gaping hole that had opened when Bea was murdered by Wrathos—*no, by* me, she thought. *I did it. I did it all.* She thought of Grey Arris, how she'd longed for him to hold her before he'd left—how she longed for him to hold her now. Missing his touch for so long was like a throat deprived of water, lungs denied air.

And she thought of the child growing inside her, a future prince or princess of the west. And she knew:

I did it for him. Or for her. I want to be better for my child. I must be better.

On the edge of her vision, movement caught her attention. She turned. The small boat skated past on the current. Gareth Ironclad knelt while the Orian, Gwendolyn Storm, stood. Both were staring at her in shock, their eyes dancing between her and Darkspell's corpse.

And then the most surprising thing happened:

Gareth tapped his chest, right over where his heart was.

Gwen offered a single nod.

That was all, the boat disappearing downstream faster than it had appeared.

Warmth flooded Rhea's chest as she watched them go, her vision blurring. *Wrath*, she thought. *What am I doing? Who am I? These are the enemy and I'm wishing they would return, that I could break bread with them, that I could speak to them like friends.*

But then they were gone, and Rhea, tear-streaked and windblown, felt more alone than ever.

"Your Highness?" one of her furia said from behind.

She stiffened at the voice—she'd forgotten anyone else was with her. Blinking rapidly, she cleared her vision, feigning a sneeze to wipe the tears from her cheeks.

She turned, composed once more, her eyes like steel, her chin raised. Queenly. "Ready the horses. We ride for Knight's End at once."

Forty-Two

The Eastern Kingdom, the Rot
Gareth Ironclad

Forlorn vines hung from the fungus-afflicted trees of the Rot. Mournful howls burst through the swamp from time to time, shattering the silence.

Gareth Ironclad distracted his mind with anything and everything. *Look*, he thought, crouching by the dark, fetid waters. *Even here, inkreeds grow.* He plucked one from the mossy riverbank, cracking it open and letting the ink spill across his fingers, staining them black. He pulled out another, and another, and another, counting them, breaking them, splotching his clothes, his skin, smearing streaks on his face.

Gwen sat nearby, her back to a rotting stump. Her eyes were closed, though Gareth was certain she wasn't sleeping. Neither of them had said a thing after what happened on the banks of the Spear. They were both trying to process what it meant.

No, Gareth thought. *It means nothing.*

Didn't it?

Yes, they hadn't expected Rhea Loren, the tyrant in a young woman's body, to create a threat and then save them from it, but that didn't mean she was on their side. One act did not a saint make. Gareth had seen what Darkspell's potion had done to the man—clearly it was meant for a far broader group of people than just Orians. Perhaps Rhea had sensed his treachery at the penultimate moment, leaping into action, saving her own skin and the lives of her people. A noble act, yes, heroic even, but not entirely selfless.

The lies we tell ourselves are the basest of all deceptions.

It was something Gareth's mother liked to say whenever Gareth or one of his brothers tried to justify their mistakes. It was usually followed with:

Those who own their actions shall rule the world.

Gareth threw down the last of the inkreeds, its broken stem still leaking dark fluid. He'd ripped every single one from the soft earth, and now his skin and clothes were stained, almost like a reminder of his lies.

Because the truth had shone on Rhea Loren's face, sparkled in the unshed tears in her eyes, rang like a bell calling shepherds home from pasture:

Peace. We can have peace.

That truth shuddered through Gareth, and something made him turn to look at Gwendolyn, whose eyes were now open, staring right at him. "It's time to go home," she said.

"I—" *I can't.* Memories flared like red stars streaking across the night sky:

The disgust in Grian's eyes as he refused to pay the ransom for his own brother's release.

His father's words to him when he was eight name days old: *You are the Shield, son; that is your purpose, your calling. Do not fail your brothers, nor your people.*

I won't, Father. I won't.

The light pouring from Roan's chest, from his body, as he saved him from the mortal wound Gareth had sustained at the hands of the Kings' Bane.

It was all for a purpose. A greater purpose. And I've been running away like a petulant child avoiding his chores.

Self-loathing roiled up inside him, but Gareth tamped it down, gritted his teeth. Stood, his hands black with ink. "The king shall return to Ferria. I shall return. The throne is mine."

It might've been Gareth's imagination, but the dead eyes peering up from the swamp's depths seemed to narrow, hardening their eternal stares.

Forty-Three
The Eastern Kingdom, approaching Ironwood
Gwendolyn Storm

They'd set out from the Rot a week earlier, disguising themselves before entering each village along the way. They gathered gossip and stole supplies, including a pair of purebred stallions keen to run. Though she hated doing it, procuring mounts was a matter of necessity, and Gwen vowed to send double the horses' value back to the owner once they reached the castle.

Gwendolyn's initial optimism had swiftly waned as the story had gotten worse with each town they passed through:

The legions march for Darrin. War is inevitable with Calypso; it's only a matter of time. The Bridge of Triumph will soon be crossed into the west. Our armies shall fight our enemies on three sides. King Grian predicts complete victory. Revenge shall be ours.

And then there shall be peace.

Gwen spurred her horse onwards, charging across the plains. There was no time to lose. She needed to deliver Gareth to the castle before it was too late, before Grian's reckless actions destroyed their people.

Gareth's horse maintained pace beside her, though he lolled in the saddle, half-asleep; he didn't have the boundless energy she possessed when in the throes of her heromark, which continued to flare on her cheek. A few days earlier she'd tied him into the saddle so he could sleep. She was glad for his slumber—he would need his rest before facing his brother.

Somewhere in the distance, a silver light sparked, the reflection of the sun on steel.

Ironwood.

Gwen dug her heels into her stallion's sides and raced on.

The night was cloaked in a blanket stitched with stars. To the west, the horizon glowed—the Tangle burning. And before them, Ironwood drew closer, as if hauled in by an enormous rope.

As the distance fell away, the feeling of a great weight pressing on Gwen's chest intensified, until breathing became laborious. It was a feeling she'd had before, a sense of foreboding provided by her heromark. She felt as if a noose was about her neck, tightening, tightening, cutting off her airways.

Beside her, Gareth stirred in the saddle. "I'll have some mince pie with a side of roast potatoes," he murmured. At first Gwen thought he was still dreaming, but then his eyes flew open and he smirked. "Wouldn't that be nice? A warm meal. A soft bed."

"The last time you said such things you got drunk in Restor and challenged passersby to a drinking duel."

"Thank you. Lest I forget."

"I'm here to serve," Gwen said.

Gareth turned his gaze forward, peering into the night. "Those aren't stars," he said, pointing at the lights of Ironwood.

"No," Gwen said. Orelights they were called. Orian channelers captured firelight within the ore as it was formed, causing the metal to twinkle in the dark.

"Another village?" He almost sounded hopeful. Though the prince—*no, the king*, she reminded herself—was resigned to the fact that he would return to Ironwood, he was clearly hoping to delay his homecoming as long as possible.

"No," Gwen said again.

"Damn."

"Not damn. Destiny. Roan would be proud of you."

"If he's alive," Gareth muttered.

Gwen pulled back on her reins, pulling her horse to a stop. Gareth's horse, used to following her commands rather than his, halted as well. "Don't say that. He *is* alive, and so are we. That means something. You mean something."

Gareth seemed surprised by the seriousness of her words, her tone. "I...yes, you're right. It's just hard with this whole failed-Shield thing hanging over my head. It feels like a blade about to fall."

"You are not the Shield—not anymore," Gwen said.

Gareth frowned. "Then what am I, if not the very thing I was born to be?"

Gwen drew her horse closer, until she was near enough to rest a hand on his shoulder. He met her gaze, and for perhaps the first time since she'd known Gareth Ironclad, First of His Name, Shield of the East, she saw the true man behind the façade. *Is this what Roan sees in him? If so, I understand their connection.* For this was not a man of arrogance and bravado, of quick japes and meaningless banter; no, this was a man of substance, of worth, of strength—even in his self-doubt and unbelief.

Gwen chose her words carefully. "None of us are born to be one thing, but many. You were a Shield for a time, but as the seasons change, so shall you. For now, you must be the Sword."

She turned away from him and rode on, eventually hearing him fall into stride beside her as the clouds devoured the stars, one by one at first, and then in large swallows, casting the world into abject darkness.

Forty-Four

The Northern Kingdom, Darrin
Tarin Sheary

The monster inside him had been silent for days, and Tarin was beginning to wonder whether it had died with Annise, her final gift to him.

He jammed his teeth together until his jaws began to ache, and threw himself back into his work. Lingering on such thoughts would cause him to collapse, to curl up in a ball. He wouldn't do that—*couldn't* do that. No, he owed Annise so much more than that. His strength. His commitment. His life.

And he would give it, gladly, for the hope she'd harbored for the north, for her people.

With a grunt, he leaned back against the load, straightening his knees, his back, hauling the enormous stone across the castle courtyard. Other men tumbled away, unable to keep up with his pace. Step by painstaking step, the boulder closed the distance, eventually skidding into position beside the others. It would be painted with oil, prepared to be lighted and launched at the enemy as they charged across the frozen expanse riddled with traps and blockades.

It would not be enough—this Tarin knew—but that didn't matter, especially now. No, his death, whenever it came, would be welcome, the ground around him littered with his dead enemies.

Yesss, the monster finally hissed.

What happened to her? he demanded. *Who killed her?*

She was on a mountain, on the edge of a cliff. And then she wasn't.

Tears threatened, like the air before a summer rain, but Tarin blinked them away. Could it be? Could the magnificent woman he loved truly have died in a terrible accident? The truth hurt him more than anything else, because it meant there was no one to punish, no one to seek revenge on. You couldn't fight a mountain any more than you could the moons or the sun.

He roared, slinging the thick rope to the ground, stalking back toward the next boulder, his men scattering to either side to avoid being crushed by his rage.

Except one. Fay. She stood before him, her hands extended. "Tarin, stop," she said.

"No," he growled, changing direction to brush past her. She stepped to the side, forcing him to stop or bash into her. He stopped.

"Talk to me. What is happening to you?"

"Nothing that hasn't happened before," he said. *I lost her once, and it nearly destroyed me. This time it will strengthen me against my enemies.*

"Not good enough," Fay said. "But it will have to do. Come with me."

"There's work to be——"

"The others will finish it. Come."

Tarin sighed. Sometimes arguing with Fay was like arguing with an ice bear. No wonder Annise had been so fond of the blacksmith woman. "Fine."

She led him past his men as they started hauling the next stone to the pile. Through the castle gates. Past the prison and the barracks. Veering from their path only when she reached the forge, which, for once, was eerily silent.

"Why have the fires been doused?" Tarin said, an annoyed edge to his voice.

"We're finished," Fay said matter-of-factly.

Finished? Comprehending that word was a challenge at first, but then he took in the dark circles under Fay's eyes, the bloodshot gleam in her gaze. While he'd sunk inside the darkness of his own mind, Fay had continued to shine the way she always did. "Good," he said, a sad understatement he had meant as a compliment.

Fay laughed. "Yes. It is good. My fingers are covered in burns. Maybe now they can heal."

Heal. Another word that seemed to have no meaning anymore. Perhaps some wounds could heal, but not all. Not the one he had suffered. Tarin knew his heart would limp for the rest of his life, regardless of how long or short.

She brought him to the back of the area, where she'd been toiling for days and nights on end. Like the others, the fires of the enormous forge were extinguished, naught but smoldering coals giving off no light.

A thick blanket hung on the wall, lumpy with whatever was hidden beneath it.

"Do the honors," Fay said, gesturing to the blanket.

"Fay, I'm not really in the mood."

"Neither am I," she said, her hands on her hips.

Not wanting to argue, he strode forward, whipping the blanket away in one swift motion.

His breath blew from his lungs.

The monster hissed its protest, but Tarin silenced it with a growl.

"Do you like it?" Fay asked.

It wasn't a matter of liking it or not. It was a matter of truth. The armor plate hanging before him was magnificent—no one could deny that, not with its spit-polished faces, sharp-angled joints, and iron fittings made for weapons—but it was a lie.

For the armor was painted white.

The color of purity. The color of goodness.

"I can't wear that, I'm sorry." There was a reason Tarin had always worn black armor, a reason the very color he bled was that of darkness, a reason that he was so capable of destruction and little else.

"You *will* wear it, else I will be forced to shove three soldiers in it to fit the size."

It was meant as a light-hearted jape, but Tarin could hear the desperation in her voice. This suit of armor wasn't just about protecting him in battle, but something more, hidden in the quiver in her voice, the tears that threatened to spill from her eyes. To this strong woman, Tarin sensed, everything hinged on what he did next.

"I will wear it for this battle only," he said.

The weight seemed to leave the room and Fay smiled. "Good. And after you're victorious, we'll talk about the next battle."

Standing alone atop the wall, Tarin was thinking about the inevitability of time. Even the strongest of men, the greatest of warriors, could not stop its ceaseless march. It devoured, it stole, it pierced stone and steel and skin.

It shattered mountains and dried up oceans and knocked stars from their seats in the night sky.

And now, as was inevitable, time had brought their enemies to their doorstep.

Hundreds of torches danced over the cliffs as the eastern soldiers descended on ropes. Tarin's forward scouts were rushing across the snowscape, dancing around each trap and barrier, falling back behind the safety of the castle walls. They did this on his direct orders—they couldn't afford to lose a single soldier until the real siege began.

"It's time," Fay said, coming up from behind. Her words seemed to echo his own thoughts.

He nodded, spreading his arms and legs. Behind her, it took three soldiers to haul his armor up the steps. Plate by perfectly forged plate, Fay slotted his white armor around him. The fit was exquisite, so customized he barely felt as if he was wearing steel.

The fires continued to gather to the east, building to an inferno as their enemies amassed.

"Thank you," he said when she finished. He waited a moment for the soldiers to leave, speaking only when they were out of earshot. "Your work here is done. And now it's time for you to depart the city. Flee toward Castle Hill. Tell Lady Zelda what happened here. Tell them we fought valiantly but failed."

"Tarin—"

He wasn't finished, rushing on. "Tell her Annise is dead. Archer is king now, if he returns."

"You can't know—"

"I do."

Fay shook her head. "I'm not leaving."

"You must. Someone must speak for us."

"You can speak for yourself."

"The dead don't speak."

"You've never failed," she said. "You won't now."

"No, I won't," he said, but he didn't mean they would be victorious either.

She shook her head, biting her lip.

"You're my friend," he said. "This doesn't change that."

"I know," she said, managing a smile. "I'm mourning the loss of this perfect suit of armor, not the buffoon who wears it."

For the first time in days, Tarin smiled back. "I don't blame you, it really is beautiful. I'll try to do it justice."

Suddenly, she hugged him, her arms barely reaching to his back. Surprised, he slowly wrapped one arm around her, pulling her head to his chest.

Screams burned through the night as brightly as the torches carried by the enemy. Dozens perished in the pits they'd dug.

Others were slowed by the barbed-wire walls, only to be crushed by flaming boulders shot from the catapults hidden behind the walls. Creak and his newly trained archers rained arrows down upon the killing fields. Most missed, but enough hit their marks to throw the eastern army into chaos.

The enemy, however, pushed forward, as Tarin knew they would. Though their numbers had been culled, they still had at least a five to one advantage, even as they approached the final barriers; and then, the wall.

The eastern legions were led by a familiar foe—Beorn Stonesledge, his broadsword flashing in the firelight as he hacked through each barrier, arrows glancing off his armor. The last time they'd faced off, Tarin had emerged victorious, almost killing the man; but tonight, he knew, the story could be very different.

He glanced down the steps at his men, his *soldiers*—for they truly deserved that title now, regardless of what happened henceforth—who were rallying at the gates, even as the first battering-ram blows rattled the great doors on their hinges. Though he could see the fear in their eyes, none fled—the cowards had all left the city days ago. These were the stalwart, the chosen, the heroes in human bodies. A swell of nostalgia took Tarin by surprise. Not a fortnight ago he would've written them off as a lost cause; now, however, these were his people, his soldiers, his friends.

He strode down to meet them, a battle cry on his tongue. All heads turned his way. The monster roared inside him, but he growled, "No," and chased it away. In the throes of battle, perhaps, he would need the strength the monster afforded him, but not now. Not in this naked moment of glory and honor.

The door shook as another heavy blow battered it. But it held. There was still time for a speech.

"Tonight, we defend the north as wolves defend their caves. Tonight, we rain hellfire and steel on our enemies. Tonight, we live and die in honor, men unbroken, souls of stone."

Rattling hinges. Splintering wood. Creaking timber.

Time marches with our enemy. Annise, oh Annise. I'm fighting. I'm here, till the end. "We are the chosen defenders. We are the chosen warriors of our time, men who will be sung of by the bards a hundred years from now—nay, a thousand years. What say ye?"

The men roared in the face of the next blow, which blew the doors inward.

The real fight began in earnest.

Annise!

The battle was not going well, Tarin noted as he swung Morningstar, smashing it into the helm of two foes in short succession.

Tarin's men were determined, aye, but a few ill weeks of training were nothing against years of battle experience. And the easterners had a platoon of Orians, too, the fierce forest dwellers clad in pristine iron armor, their movements nimble and efficient, their eyes shining in the dark—yellow, orange, lavender.

In short, the men of Darrin were outmatched and outnumbered.

And yet, none had retreated, none had fled from the threat of death. Even when Beorn Stonesledge himself marched through the courtyard, his sword slashing, stabbing, hacking at everything in sight, Tarin's men held the line.

He was proud of them, almost like a father to a son.

Annise. I have done good. I think you would be proud of me, too. The monster inside is silent. The monster inside is imprisoned. I am fighting on my own.

And then a new sound arose, distant and foreign. Voices raised, slightly higher pitched than the standard battlefield cries he'd grown accustomed to over the years. He turned, seeking the source of the sound and then they were there. A hundred armor-clad soldiers, all of whom appeared to be women, marching in perfect formation, their voices raised in challenge to the attackers.

At their head, a familiar face, his plate so thoroughly polished it was gleaming under the starlight.

Sir Metz.

"Division one—right flank!" he ordered. "Two—left flank! Three—with me! With me!" With that said, he charged right up the middle into the heart of the battle.

Tarin didn't consider the *how* of the situation—only caring that Zelda had apparently changed her mind, sending reinforcements to Darrin at the last moment, perhaps saving the city. *A hope, a chance*, Tarin thought, vowing not to waste it.

He redoubled his efforts, commanding his last remaining group of soldiers to support Metz's push into the center while the knight's other two divisions harried them from the sides.

Due to the unexpected appearance of Metz and his women warriors, the battlefield tilted for a few moments as the easterners struggled to cope. The women fought like wildcats, without fear, throwing themselves with reckless abandon at the enemy. *We should've permitted women into the army centuries ago*, Tarin thought.

Still, Darrin was outnumbered two to one, and inch by bloody inch, Stonesledge and his soldiers regained their advantage.

Enemies closed in, slashing his men and Metz's women to the ground. Tarin tried to protect them, hated seeing them perish under his watch, but he was only one man. He fought and killed, bodies piling up around him, staining the hard-packed snow scarlet. Dead eyes were the only spectators now, watching, observing, counting down the seconds until Darrin fell.

Metz fought valiantly, too, a master swordsman, but it wasn't enough—couldn't have been enough even if the battle was waged a hundred times.

Beorn Stonesledge burst through the line, his sword spraying blood in a crimson arc. He gripped the ironmark amulet he wore around his neck with one hand, while swinging his sword with powerful strikes with the other.

Several of Tarin's men and Metz's women released a cry, charging to meet Beorn, to defend their leaders. There were so few left, perhaps two dozen. Two dozen souls. Tarin, for the first time, cried, "Fall back! Back!"

Surprised, the men and women whirled and looked at him. He shouted again and the men turned to run. Metz's women hesitated, waiting for confirmation from their captain. The knight's eyes flicked from Tarin to one of the women and then back again. "Retreat!" he echoed, and his soldiers fled.

Tarin strode forward as they passed, swinging Morningstar in long slow arcs above his head, gaining momentum with each rotation. "You, too, Metz," he said. "Save yourself."

"No," the knight said.

"I am the lord commander of this castle, and I order you to retreat, Sir."

He saw the moment of hesitation on the man's face, the point of indecision as he grappled between his sense of honor and the innate need to protect the lives of others. Finally, he nodded, striding after what was left of his platoon.

Tarin turned to meet his foe's gaze.

"We meet again," Stonesledge said, a grim smile creasing his bearded face.

"It shall be the last time," Tarin said.

"Yes." Legionnaires crowded around the enormous man, Orians and humans alike.

Tarin stepped into their midst, unafraid.

Annise, I come to you.

The voice burst through the calm of his mind like a punch through an ice wall. *Tarin, no!*

Her.

How? Tarin shook his head, trying to understand, even as the first attack came, from his left flank. He blocked two swords with his chain, jabbing his elbow backwards into the jaw of the soldier who leapt in from the right. At the same time, he probed through his mind for that voice, that connection, the one he thought was lost, the woman he believed was dead.

Annise?

I'm here.

How? I heard your goodbye. The monster implied you'd fallen from a cliff.

I almost did. I thought I was dead.

Tarin's first thought was: a trick. But no, the monster could never impersonate her—he would know the difference.

His Morningstar crushed another man's skull. Invigorated, Tarin kicked out a huge boot, knocking another man back. Two Orians leapt in, their movements lithe, sliding beneath the chain, jabbing at his midsection. He turned sharply, avoiding one blow while taking the other one on his plate. Using his momentum, he punched one in the face and wrapped his chain around the other's throat, dispatching her with a twist of his wrist.

Tarin, it is time. Release the monster. It's the only hope.

No. Anything but that.

Please. You must. For me. Do it for me.

Anything. He would do anything for her. So he did. He released the monster.

The hiss was so loud it was a shout, a growl, a roar of delight, of freedom.

Tarin felt his body expand, grow, strengthen even more. The monster's roar exploded from his own mouth as he charged.

Men, women, and Orians alike scattered as he bashed through them. Several blades rang off his plate, one knife wedging itself into one of the paper-thin gaps. His Morningstar destroyed at will, cutting a path to Beorn Stonesledge, who waited, his mouth opened slightly in surprise.

"What devilry is this?" he muttered.

"Now you die," Tarin said.

It was easier said than done, for Stonesledge was a devil in his own regard. His broadsword lashed out, and though Tarin blocked it with his chain, the impact shivered through him, rattling his white armor.

And then Stonesledge was there, ducking under the chain, hammering blows upon his face, his helm, grabbing his armor with monstrous hands, trying to wrench each plate free.

Tarin responded in kind, snagging his spiked metal ball and slamming it into Beorn's head, again and again and again. He was vaguely aware that he was fighting more than one foe—pinpricks of pain flared in his legs, back, arms...

Annise's voice was there still, but fading, like a distant memory: *Hang on, Tarin. Hang on, my love. I am here. I am coming. Hang on...*

He roared, spinning in a circle, crushing bones, rending flesh, a reaper of souls. Bodies flew, shattered, broken. Dozens more charged in to take their place. So many, *too* many.

Annise?

Hang on.

Annise?

Gaps in his armor, filled by blades. His skin punctured, his black blood flowing, tasting it in his mouth.

The night faded into a world of pain.

Forty-Five

The Northern Kingdom,
the outskirts of Darrin
Annise Gäric

Annise could feel the beat of his heart in her chest; his ragged breaths flowed past her lips.

He was dying, she could feel it, could feel each spike of pain. *Hurry!* she urged herself as her boots struggled to find purchase on the icy city streets. The gray walls of Darrin seemed to close in with each step.

Behind her, an ancient army, having marched with barely any rest or sustenance—*We have slept long enough*, the Sleeping Knights had said, their voices unified—from the Garzi village to Darrin. Twice the knights had carried Annise and her comrades while they slept, the rhythms of their footfalls a strange but effective lullaby.

She still remembered the moment Lisbeth Lorne awakened the knights from their slumber, still remembered how weak the girl had looked afterward. And yet the girl had caught up to them on the second day, her face as pale as the snow, like she'd seen a ghost.

Annise had asked her if she was alright, and she'd said, "Yes," and that was it.

The memory faded and Annise realized the city had passed by in a blur. Forms were running toward them, and at first she thought the enemy had come to meet them, but then she noticed the northern sigil each of them bore. *They're retreating,* she thought, at the same time realizing at least half the soldiers were women.

Sir Metz almost collided with her, his eyes wide. For some reason, the knight's presence didn't in any way surprise her. "Sir Sheary," he said, breathing heavily. "He ordered our retreat. He is facing the enemy alone."

No. "As your queen, I order you back to the battle, all of you!" They didn't have to be commanded twice. Metz, almost too eager, whirled and headed in the direction he'd come, flanked by two small groups of soldiers—one all men, one all women.

"With me!" Annise cried, racing after them. The satisfying clomp of hundreds of ancient boots fell in behind her.

Annise hoped they weren't too late.

Tarin?

Tarin?

Answer me!

No reply came as she charged through the wide-open gate and into the castle courtyard, which was a mess of ruined bodies. She was forced to step on several just to get through

348

to where the enemy stood, waiting for them. She was dimly aware of a commotion behind them—was Tarin still standing, still fighting?

Parallels between the reality she now saw and the vision Lisbeth had given her of the killing fields fell into place. *No, it cannot be. There is still time. There must be.*

Tarin?

Her knights poured around her, meeting the enemy with sword and shield, strength on strength. Though the legends said the knights were the most capable warriors in the realm, even the stories had underestimated them. They were like a many-limbed beast, hacking, stabbing, piercing the enemies' defenses like rain through a sieve.

In a way, their violence was beautiful. Frighteningly beautiful, like an eagle swooping down to devour a rodent.

And then the enemy lines broke, opening to a view of the commotion beyond. A large man, still on his feet, but staggering, dark fluid covering his armor, his exposed face, pooling beneath his boots.

Tarin!

At that thought, his gaze jerked up and his eyes met hers. They were weary but determined, the look of the man Annise had known, had loved, had never—not truly—given up on.

With renewed vigor, he threw himself at the enemy, joining Annise's knights and Metz's soldiers. Annise ran toward him, slamming her own Evenstar against any easterner that moved. It didn't matter their size or their skill—she was not to be denied, not when she was this close.

As she approached, a man nearly as large as Tarin swung a sword toward him. Beorn Stonesledge, apparently recovered from his injuries at Raider's Pass. Tarin blocked the attack but was thrown back, stumbling. Annise reached him just before he fell, jamming her shoulder under his arm, holding him up, supporting him. Tears bit at her eyes as she growled, "End this."

Tarin looked back, surprised, and it broke her heart to see the wounds on his face, which were likely nothing compared to what was surely hidden beneath his armor—the white plates that suited him even more than the black had.

With a roar, she flung him forward, providing a burst of momentum. Simultaneously, he swung his Morningstar, which slammed into Stonesledge's helm, cracking it in two. But Tarin didn't stop there, completing another arc of the spiked ball.

Annise looked away before the blow landed.

With a grunt, Tarin fell back. She caught him under the arms, using every bit of her strength to draw him slowly to the ground, resting his head in the crook of her shoulder. "Oh, Tarin," she said as his eyes fluttered, his gaze piercing her as it focused.

The battle raged around them, the knights sweeping over their foes in a relentless dance of death, but she barely noticed, her world boiling down to a single drop of life: this man. This big, beautiful man.

"You're alive?" he said. He sounded almost as if he believed this was a dream.

"Of course, I am, you big ice bear. You think the Hinterlands could kill me?"

"I thought…I heard your last words to me. The monster gave them to me. It implied you fell from a cliff."

Annise frowned. "We almost did. I thought we were finished," she admitted. "I spoke them in haste, but then we survived. A girl saved us. The monster didn't tell you that?"

"No," Tarin said, his voice a rasp.

"No more speaking," Annise said. "Rest. Take my strength." She kissed him on the lips, breathing into him, not caring that she tasted blood. All that was his felt like hers anyway, the separation between them fading away into a meaningless nothingness.

Swords rang out, shields clashed, men and women fought, and Annise kissed Tarin.

She felt the moment he drifted away into unconsciousness, a little piece of her breaking.

Forty-Six

The Northern Kingdom, Darrin
Tarin Sheary

Tarin felt as if he was sinking. It wasn't a particularly bad sensation, especially because he could still taste her on his lips, but still, he fought against it, knowing instinctively that he should.

Her voice was somewhere above him, but he couldn't make out her words. He could, however, hear her sobs, which made him realize:

I am drowning in her tears.

The thought made him unbearably sad, because *she* was unbearably sad.

A new voice came to him through the dark waters, taking form as a spark of light, as blue as the ocean or the summer sky. Changing, shaping itself into something familiar: an eye.

Rise, the voice said. It was that of a girl, pleasant and soothing and yet full of command. It was a voice not to be denied, and with it came a cascading avalanche of memories:

A witch pouring vile potion down his throat; fighting in endless tourneys, inflicting pain as he seized victory; countless battles, the lives of strangers snuffed out by his strength; the first time he saw Annise again, the way his heart seemed to open like a flower for the first time in a decade; their first kiss, a dazzling gesture full of urgency and need and passion; walking away from her to protect her…

He gasped, his eyes shooting open. Fuzzy images projected overhead, blanketed by smatters of winking stars peeking through the gray cloud cover. Clarifying, becoming truth. Becoming her.

My Annise.

He tried to speak the words but didn't have the strength. "Shh," Annise said, cupping his chin. "Save your strength."

"I can heal his soul, but not his body," another voice said, that pleasant-soothing-commanding voice he'd heard in the water. A girl, kneeling, pressed in tight beside Annise, her eyes pale white orbs without sight, flanking the blue All-Seeing eye marked on her forehead.

"I can tend to his wounds," another familiar voice said. Sir Metz, his blond straw-like hair as ruffled and out of place as Tarin had ever seen it.

A woman was beside him, and there was something familiar about her, too, like she was more than a woman—a memory. She said, "I will help. I have training in healing, too. From the time I looked after my mistress as she aged."

Tarin's lips tried to move again—*Do I know you?*—but Annise shushed him. "Later," she said.

353

Forty-Seven
The Northern Kingdom, Darrin
Sir Christoff Metz

Private Sheary had been a great help tending to Tarin's wounds, which were numerous. He wasn't out of the blizzard yet, but he had a fighting chance—the man's strength would serve him well now.

Although the queen had hovered like a concerned hummingbird the entire time they treated the knight, he'd eventually had to insist she leave and let the man sleep. He'd promised to inform her of any change to his condition, or if he woke up.

Private Sheary slumped down in a chair, looking exhausted. Sir Metz had the urge to do the same, but he knew *slumping* wasn't an action befitting a captain. Plus, there was more work to do—he needed to take roll of the dead members of his battalion, who were many. The thought of so many dead because of his decision made his heart ache, but at the same time he felt an odd sense of relief that Private Sheary had come out on the other end without serious injury.

"Can you stay with our patient while I tend to other business?" he asked, maintaining a formal tone. He was growing more accustomed to hearing her speak to him informally, in private, but still wasn't that comfortable doing so himself.

"Christoff," she said, her voice low and raspy.

"Captain Metz, please," he said, though he felt tingly all over when she called him by his first name.

"I need you to be Christoff right now," she said. "Please."

Though he didn't exactly understand what she meant, he could not refuse her, not in this moment. "Yes..."—he recalled her first name, though he'd never used it—"Mona." The name tasted good on his tongue, almost sweet. *Strange*, he thought. *Names shouldn't have a taste.*

"Hold me," she said.

He froze. "I—I shouldn't. I can't."

She stood. Stepped closer, her hands bridging the chasm between them. He tensed, waiting for her touch, that feeling of spiders on his skin, trying to bear it without flinching so he wouldn't offend the woman who was beginning to mean a lot to him.

And then her arms were around him, her warmth sliding against his, her dark hair brushing his cheeks, the crown of her head nestled against his neck. She tilted her head back and kissed the soft skin there tenderly, sending electricity through the whole of his body.

There was no feeling of spiders.

And then, even more to his surprise, he wrapped his arms around her and pulled her to him, his lips brushing her hair.

"Thank you," she said into the hollow in his neck.

"You're welcome," he said, though he felt, perhaps, he should be the one thanking her.

Forty-Eight
The Northern Kingdom, Darrin
Tarin Sheary

Tarin awoke to darkness, wearing a broad smile on his face. He'd had the most wonderful dream…

A sound snapped him away from his thoughts: a creak. A scuff. The release of a breath.

"Tarin?"

That voice. *That voice.*

Everything came back in a rush: How he'd been on the verge of defeat, floating in a sea of enemies; the voice he'd heard in his head—*her* voice; the way he'd clung to it like a stone; how suddenly there were warriors around him, knights, their swords flashing, his enemies falling; and then her face, her beautiful face, and her tears falling like life-giving rain…

"Annise," he breathed, drawing her name out like a prayer.

"I'm here." And then she was, her hands clasped in his, which hurt slightly because of the cuts and bruises he bore. But he didn't care—he squeezed back harder.

Her lips found his, and he leaned forward into them eagerly, drinking from the only well that could possibly sate his great thirst. Her hands cupped his chin, sliding along his smooth skin tenderly. "I love you," she said into his mouth, and they were the sweetest words he'd ever heard, ever tasted on his tongue. "Move over."

He did, very slowly, very gingerly, and she squeezed onto the bed beside him. He turned into her, her hips pressing against him, her body folding into him like time and distance had never separated them, like they were *always* this close.

He winced as she groped at his chest, pain flashing from one of a dozen wounds.

"Sorry," she mumbled, "perhaps we should wait."

Wait? That word was the enemy now, and Tarin wouldn't be defeated by it. "No," he growled. "We'll be careful. We'll go slow."

She nodded, her eyes burning in the shadowy darkness.

Time melted into the night, and as their passion flowed like a river, one second could've been an eternity, a lifetime. In those stolen moments, Tarin lived many lifetimes with Annise, and those he hadn't faded into the darkness of the past.

Sometime later, Annise nestled into his shoulder, one hand resting lightly on his chest. Groggy, satisfied sighs slipped from her lips. "I thought I might never see you again," she said, after a few brief moments of silence.

Tarin knew the feeling. Worse, it was he who had made her feel that way. There was nothing else to say but "I'm sorry."

"Don't be sorry," Annise said. "Just don't do it again."

"I won't." It was more than a promise—it was a vow pledged on everything he'd ever cared about. He paused, and then said, "Did you ever wish you could strip everything else away?"

Tarin knew it was a cryptic thing to say, but Annise immediately laughed and said, "All the hell-frozen time."

"Really?"

"More than anything. Have you forgotten I was the princess who wanted to flee to the Hinterlands?"

He had. He could hardly imagine such a thing now. It felt as if Annise was always the queen. "So you wouldn't drift away if you could? Live a simple life?"

Annise's lips brushed his chin, his neck, and for those brief moments he forgot what he'd asked. When Annise spoke, he struggled to concentrate. "There's no such thing as a simple life," she said. "Life, by its very definition, is a complex creature. Anyone who believes otherwise is a fool."

Tarin laughed, which made him hurt. He groaned. "Then I count myself lucky, for I'm as complicated as they come."

"Can I ask you something?" Annise asked.

Who was he to deny her a question; even if she wasn't the queen, he would deny her nothing, not ever again. "Of course."

"Is it my imagination or have you grown even larger?"

He laughed again, louder, which hurt even more. But he relished the pain, for it meant he was alive. Perhaps more alive than he'd ever been. "Possibly. It's hard to tell. Everyone just looks little to me these days."

359

"Well, perhaps you could put in a request to that monster of yours to stop the growing."

"Why?"

"Because if you get much bigger, this"—she pulled him into her, grasped his hands, tugging them to her hips—"will become far too difficult."

"Good point," he said, but his words were lost against her lips.

"One more question," she said, after they lay, exhausted once more.

He laughed. "I should start charging."

"I'll pay you in *favors*," she purred.

"Ask away!" he said with boyish eagerness that belied the man's body he wore.

"The monster…" she started. Something rumbled deep in his core, but he held it back with sheer force of will. "Is it gone? I don't feel its claws in me anymore."

He hated to tell the truth, but he wouldn't lie to Annise. Not ever again. "No," he said. "It will never be gone."

"Good."

He frowned, a difficult expression to form considering her hands had begun to slide along his abdomen, exploring. "Good? How is that good?"

"It's a part of you," she said. "You wouldn't be the same without it. And it saved me. Twice. Out on the ice and in the tunnels. And in the midst of the battle, it saved you. You cannot deny it."

No, he couldn't. As much as he despised the violent creature inside him at times, he couldn't rebuff the connection he felt to it. Nor the fact that it had, in a way, strengthened his connection to Annise even more. Fooling him into believing she was dead was a nasty trick, but it only made him realize that he couldn't live without her, even if it meant endangering her with his very presence. All he replied, however, was, "On the ice? In the tunnels?"

"Oh, do I have a story to tell you," she said. "And just wait until you hear about how the Garzi almost shoved us off a cliff!"

Before he could respond, her lips whisked him away to another place, a place only the two of them could exist, for the third time in a night.

And he didn't mind one bit—they had the rest of their lives to tell stories.

Forty-Nine
The Northern Kingdom, Darrin
Lisbeth Lorne

Lisbeth stood on the killing fields, her breaths coming in waves, her hands on her knees, her entire body wracked with agony. She wasn't injured, no—the pain was *theirs*. The fallen. She could hear their souls crying out to her as they left their bodies, mournful wails that seemed to cut her to the quick.

I did this, she thought. *I came to this place. I brought death. I am war.* Yes, the queen had made the decision in the end, but to pass blame was to deny the truth of the matter: that she had a choice.

Why am I here? To kill? To end lives? To destroy cities? Why? Please, tell me!

She didn't know who, exactly, the question was meant for—the universe perhaps—but it was the knights who answered. The Sleeping Knights ceased their prowling through the corpses—they were seeking enemies who still lived to put them out of their misery—each turning toward her. Their soundless voices joined as one. *You are the bringer*, they said, thunder in those four words.

Bringer of what?

You already know, they said, turning away, going back to the business of death.

She remembered that word she'd heard before—HORDE. *Am I the one bringing the Fall of All Things?* she wondered.

Lisbeth looked away, up toward the heavens from whence she came. Gold stars glittered. Green stars exploded. Red stars streaked across the cold, dark expanse of eternity. And she knew:

No. I am the bringer of hope. Whatever is coming, I am here to help. My work is not yet accomplished.

She closed her sightless eyes, but that provided no comfort, not when her third eye continued seeing—was always seeing.

Just then, a man ran up, his soul pearlescent blue and weary, his hands trembling. His soul was young—far too young for war, and yet she could smell the coppery tinge of bloodstains on his hands. He held a scroll of wet parchment, which had a green soul of its own, a remnant of the tree from which it was harvested, rolled up and dripping. "Where is the queen?" he asked Lisbeth.

"Sleeping," she said. "What is it?"

He paused, as if trying to decide whether the news should be shared with anyone other than the queen herself. In the end, he seemed eager to shift the weight of the information from his shoulders alone. "Castle Hill is under attack," he said.

Lisbeth froze. "By whom? The eastern legions?" Had the easterners attacked through the Pass, using the siege of Darrin as a distraction? And if so, why hadn't she discerned this truth from the stars?

"No. Northerners," he said, and her heart sank. "They call themselves the Brotherhood."

Lisbeth said, "Thank you." The boy turned away and she suddenly felt very tired. Her legs gave way and she would've fell if not for the strong arms that caught her, lifting her up easily.

A man with a familiar faded blue soul looked down at her. Sir Dietrich, one of Annise's companions on her quest into the Hinterlands. The amusing, charming one. Or at least he tried to be. "Thank you," she said, suddenly breathless.

"Are you unwell?" he asked, his soul fluttering with concern.

She shook her head. "Just tired."

"Can you walk?"

She didn't think so. "I just need to rest for a while."

"Nonsense. I will find you a bed."

"No," she said. "Please. Take me to the queen."

Fifty

The Northern Kingdom, Castle Hill
Zelda Gäric

Due to the invasion, Lady Zelda had missed breakfast. She hated missing meals.

Then again, for the first time in her life, she had no appetite.

She'd fought alongside her men, but it was a losing cause from the beginning. Though they had the numbers, the dark-cloaked attackers had the experience, the skill.

It was a slaughter.

Sir Christoff Metz and the other half of their army—the women—were, of course, nowhere to be found. The funny thing was, she'd expected him to go to Darrin's aid. Though, as the temporary queen, she'd been unable to give him the order, she'd offered him plenty of latitude with her command. She'd even watched him leave with his women soldiers.

Moments before the battle began, Zelda had sent a stream to Darrin warning them of Castle Hill's fall.

The Brotherhood had left no man alive. Zelda would rather they'd killed the women too. *I wish they'd killed me*, she thought now, as the sellsword leader, Severon, approached her cell. He wore a fine suit of armor, likely stolen from a lord somewhere, the gleaming plate partially hidden beneath his dark cloak. He was flanked by two other cloaked men.

"You killed one of my men," Severon said without greeting.

"Two actually," Zelda said. "You just haven't found the second one yet. Follow the trail of blood. Shouldn't be too difficult, even for a yak-brain like you."

He grunted, but not in anger. It was more a sound of amusement. He pushed several tendrils of stringy black hair away from his face, tucking them behind his ears. They immediately fell back across his sharp green eyes. "Your entire pathetic army was decimated by my fifty-nine men, and—"

"Fifty-seven men now," she reminded him.

A smirk. "Yes. Fifty-seven. None of your men could kill a single one of us, but you managed to kill two. Your reputation doesn't do you justice."

The only reputation she was aware of was that she was a reclusive mad woman, but she didn't mention that. Instead, she said, "Let the women go. They have nothing to do with this."

It was a fruitless request to make of a soulless man such as him, but she had to try.

"No. Who else will clean the blood from our clothes? Prepare our food? Pamper us like the lords we now are, like the *king* I have become."

Zelda laughed. Loudly.

He frowned, the scars on his face shifting, darkening. "Something amusing?"

"Besides the smallness of your mind? Your arrogance, for one."

"How so?"

"You're a *sellsword*, Severon. Nothing more, nothing less. You and your men are a fungus on this land. Small, sad men like my brothers have kept you in business, but your days are numbered. When Annise returns…"

"I'm trembling in my boots," Severon said. "The real soldiers are all dead. I watched them perish until the waters of the Bay of Bounty ran red with their blood. The north died with them. A child queen is the least of my worries, especially one who's run off on a fool's errand."

So he knows. Zelda had heard the screams as they tortured a few survivors for information. But it didn't matter, a man like him would never understand women like she and her niece. And he would *always* underestimate them, which was exactly the sort of advantage they could use.

Zelda knew she would be smart to say nothing more, but she couldn't help herself. "Do you really think the other kingdoms will recognize your claim on the throne?" she scoffed. "They'll read your streams while counting their coin, and then come for you with their armies, and you will die the same way you lived—friendless and with nothing to call your own."

Severon, to his credit, didn't rise to her bait. Instead, he only smiled. "We shall see," he said, starting to leave.

After a few steps, he turned back. Almost as an afterthought, he said, "I'll let you watch as I slit Annise's throat. And then I'll slit yours."

Fifty-One

The Northern Kingdom, Darrin
Sir Christoff Metz

The news had spread like wildfire, eventually reaching Christoff's door in the form of a hard knock, jarring him awake.

He stood, instantly alert, sensing something important had happened.

When he pulled the door open, he was surprised to find Private Sheary there. The memory of their fleeting moment of closeness from the night before sprang to mind. He'd ruined it by pushing her away, by asking her to leave. He still didn't know why he did it, only that as she began to kiss his neck he'd felt like the walls were closing in, trying to crush him.

Now, embarrassment roiled through him for a second, until he saw the troubled look on her face. "What is it? What has happened?"

"Castle Hill," she said.

"What about it?"

She shook her head.

"*Tell me.*"

"It's fallen," she said.

"How?"

She told him.

He thanked her, closed the door, and slumped into a chair. Holding his head in his arms, he rocked back and forth, murmuring under his breath.

My fault my fault my fault my fault...

My fault.

Fifty-Two
The Northern Kingdom, Darrin
Lisbeth Lorne

They stood before her in perfect lines, their backs straight, their heads held high. Their souls were coiled with unspent violence.

She did not fear the knights, though she'd seen them kill without mercy. If anything, she feared *herself*, for she was the one who had unleashed them on these lands. She was the one who might not be able to stop them.

We may need you again, she said now, on orders from Queen Annise.

We know, the knights said in unison, their voices echoing in her head.

You serve the queen? she asked.

Yes. For now, they said, a qualification that sent a shiver of fear through her. *For as long as the queen serves the north.*

Lisbeth thought it was a strange thing to say, but didn't comment. Now was not the time to anger their strongest ally. *Good. At first light, we march for Castle Hill. Your mission is to defeat the invaders.*

It shall be done, they said, stamping their feet, a hundred sets of boots thundering in unison. *The Brotherhood shall die.*

Not for the first or last time, Lisbeth wondered whether she was doing the right thing. She hadn't told Annise about her visions of the Horde. She didn't fully understand them herself. She would, eventually, but not until after Castle Hill was retaken.

Briefly, she touched her soulmark, which pulsed faintly on her forehead.

Fifty-Three
The Northern Kingdom, Darrin
Tarin Sheary

Tarin wouldn't have planned his reunion with Annise to involve a major battle in which he almost died, plus an invasion of Castle Hill, but he wouldn't complain. No, he would take whatever he could get. Never again would he waste one single moment with this woman. And he would follow her to frozen hell and back if she asked.

For now, what she required was comfort. Companionship. His arm was around her, her head tucked against his broad chest. Her work for the day was done, her commands given. The injured would remain behind, to be cared for by those with healing experience. The rest would march on Castle Hill. Tarin knew the monster would heal him swiftly, as it always did, and that he would be ready to march beside his queen when the time came.

"Zelda is alive," Tarin said now, because it felt like the right thing to say. It felt true.

Annise's head dipped back and she looked up at him. He could see the worry in her eyes, and it broke his heart. He would take it all away if he could. If she would let him. "How can you know that?" she asked

"The same way I know I love you," he said.

She smiled and, briefly, kissed his cheek. She pulled away, and her sudden absence made him feel cold. He knew what she was doing, and he would endure an eternity of ice if it allowed her to be the woman she'd become. The strong queen.

Standing before him, the worry was gone, chased away by that stubborn Gäric jaw and those fierce, beautiful Gäric eyes. "I love you, Tarin. And I love my kingdom, my people. I will retake Castle Hill. I've done it before and I'll do it again."

There was nothing else to say but, "I know you will."

She nodded and left, slipping out into the night. The queen would not find sleep on a night like this.

Fifty-Four

The Northern Kingdom, Darrin
Annise Gäric

It was immensely difficult leaving the warmth of Tarin for the chill of the frozen night. Difficult, but not impossible. By now, Annise knew impossible didn't apply to her. Not anymore.

Leaving Tarin tonight was necessary. She had responsibilities. She had duties. People who looked to her for leadership. People who were willing to die for her.

She swept through Darrin, checking on the injured, trading quips with the soldiers eating around campfires. She considered locating Lisbeth and the knights, but decided against it. Something about them made her uneasy. It was natural, she supposed, considering they were from another place and time, suddenly thrust back into a world they'd been away from for a long time.

Instead, she found Archer, who was sitting with Sir Dietrich and Sir Jonius, watching red stars shoot across the sky. "Couldn't sleep?" Archer asked, raising an eyebrow.

She shook her head.

"There are far more interesting things to do than sleep anyway," Dietrich said. "I figured after you forgave that metal-head for running away you'd be shacked up with him every chance—"

"*Sir*," Jonius interrupted sharply. "You are speaking of Her Highness."

"And my *sister*," Archer added.

Dietrich said, "You're right. I apologize. But you should still consider my advice. Go back to Tarin and *have fun*."

Annise shook her head as the knight left, likely off to cause trouble elsewhere.

"How is the big tin can anyway?" Arch asked. "I trust you're taking good care of him?"

"Almost fully healed," Annise said. "He'll have scars, but his blood serves him well."

"Who would've thought there were advantages to being cursed?" Arch quipped.

Exasperated, Annise said, "Perhaps I *should've* stayed with him. And he's not cursed. He's just…himself." She thought of the way the monster had tricked him into thinking she was dead. Had it been playing games with him? Was it evil? Something told her the ploy had, in the end, been to help him, to fill him with enough pain and anger to keep him alive until she could arrive.

Thank you, she said.

You're welcome, the monster answered. *Do you see now?*

Yes, she thought. *I think I do.*

Now if you could just get that stubborn man to understand.

Annise laughed, and both Archer and Sir Jonius looked at her strangely.

If only, she thought. But sometimes a person had to discover a thing on their own in order to fully appreciate it.

She'd come a long way—they all had—but they still had a long way to go. The next stop was Castle Hill. *I'm coming, Auntie*, she thought. *You saved me once. It's my turn to return the favor.*

Another scarlet star arced overhead, soaring westward, in the direction of Castle Hill.

Fifty-Five

The Western Kingdom, Knight's End
Rhea Loren

Something had changed in Rhea ever since she'd foiled Darkspell's nefarious plans on the banks of the Spear. *Or was it earlier?*

This thing inside of me.

No, not a thing—a child. My child.

She had looked into the eyes of her enemy—a prince of the east and his Orian companion—and had not found the vile monsters she'd expected to find. No, to her utmost surprise, she'd felt a kinship amongst those with a shared purpose. But what purpose? Peace?

She laughed at the thought as she brushed the tangles out of her golden hair. No, there could never be peace—not on this war-torn continent. But perhaps alliances could be forged.

Word had reached her ears of a great battle in the north, in Darrin. The streams were alive with the news. The north, despite all odds stacked against them, had emerged victorious. They weren't dead yet, and perhaps the offer of an alliance from Rhea's cousin, Annise Gäric, still stood. Better yet, with the easterners licking their wounds, she could play both sides, forging a second alliance with Gareth Ironclad and Gwendolyn Storm. *Yes! A northern alliance!* The thought suddenly excited her, as nothing had for weeks.

All we need is a common enemy, she thought, placing her brush on the table. And, of course, they already had one:

The Southron nations of Calyp and Phanes, embroiled in a civil war that would make them an even easier target.

She glided toward the open doors to the balcony, a cool breeze rushing over her. As she stared into the blustery night, she considered.

She could paint it as a war of good versus evil, but she knew an ulterior motive slid like a shadow around the fringes of her mind.

Ennis.

Though she would never be able to love him the way he wanted her to, she still loved him like a father, a brother, a friend. He'd been nothing but good to her, even in her darkest hours, and she'd ruined everything between them. But if she could find him, show him she was finally listening to his advice...that she had *changed*, then perhaps...

She slammed her doors against the cold. Turned away. Folded herself under the warm blankets atop her bed.

Closed her eyes.

A common enemy. Phanes. The rutting Calypsians had already opened the Wrath-damn gates for them. All they had to do was march through.

Yes. The slavemasters would fall, and she would be the one to push them.

A plan formed in her mind.

Her people were gathered, eyes turned expectantly toward her. It was time.

They have no idea what's coming.

Her past speeches had been delivered within the castle walls, her citizens packed inside shoulder to shoulder, sardines in a can. On the broad banks of the Bay of Bounty, however, there was room to spread out, and her people did just that. The furthest spectators were nearly three quarters of the way up the gradual incline to the castle. She would have to shout to be heard by all ears.

This was the exact spot where Wrathos had taken her sister, Bea.

It was poetic, in a way, regardless of the outcome.

A chill running through her, Rhea took a deep breath. It was time. She turned to the side for effect, tightening the folds of her bulky purity dress against her belly. "I am big with child," she declared.

Gasps. Whispers. Angry voices. Fists raised.

She raised her hand, and despite their righteous anger, the crowd quieted. "I continue to wear this purity dress with honor," she said. "For I have never lain with a man." *Well, not on a bed anyway. She and Grey had been on the mossy ground within the walls of her family's cryptlands.*

More gasps, this time alongside confused expressions.

"Your humble servant, your committed queen, has been chosen by Wrath to bear this fatherless child. I was as shocked as any of you. I still am. I am but a lonely woman; who am I to claim this responsibility? However, it is not we who choose our destinies but Wrath above. But please, the truth of my words must not be believed on faith alone. I will put my words to the test and let Wrath decide."

The people were curious now, leaning forward eagerly. A typical trial of crimes was conducted by the Furies, but, purposely, Rhea had left them far away from this morning's festivities. *No man nor woman shall decide my fate*, she thought. *Only Wrath and Wrath alone.*

Her knees trembled in anticipation. Everything that had happened since the moment Grey had abandoned her in the cryptlands, leaving only his seed behind, seemed to lead to this single moment in her life.

She locked her knees, steeled her nerves, and raised her hands. This time, Rhea didn't have to say a word, nor did she have to look. She heard the churning waters, felt the waves sloshing against the shore, saw the monster's great eye reflected in the horrified stares of the onlookers, most of whom gasped or screamed or backed away, or did all three in short succession. Children cried. Men drew makeshift weapons. Women prayed to Wrath to deliver them.

Wrathos had come.

Still refusing to look back, Rhea raised her voice above the din. "With Wrath as my witness, this child is mine and mine alone! If I bear falsehood, let Wrath's servant swoop upon me

380

and break my bones, crush my heart, devour my soul, send me to the first heaven to burn!"

Silence fell across the crowd. Bubbling water lapped against Rhea's ankles, overflowing the rocky embankment. She closed her eyes. *Guilty*, she thought. *I am guilty. By my own words I have condemned myself.*

Screams poured from a thousand mouths and her eyes shot open. A thick, slimy tentacle flew past, curling around her, squeezing her pregnant belly slightly as it lifted her into the sky. The ground fell away as she ascended, the wind in her mouth, her heart in her throat. Though the instinct to scream was there, she refused. *I will go quietly. I am not afraid.*

The great Eye appeared before her, and as she looked into it, Rhea felt as if she was staring into the eternities, a fathomless pit with no beginning and no end. Her judge. Her jury.

Slowly, Wrathos pulled her away from its stare and toward its beaked maw, which opened wide, a black void sucking her into it. *So this is it*, she thought. *This is what Bea saw, this is what she felt. Her fate is mine.*

The beak crunched down, making a raucous cracking sound.

And then she was spinning away, the tentacle uncurling, ratcheting her back toward the shore. It set her back on the ground with surprising tenderness, sliding away, leaving her slick with slime.

Grimy and soiled, yes, but alive. Something felt different, and she reached up to touch her hair. It was shorter, her long golden locks snipped away by the monster's beak.

A warning from Wrath, she knew. A recognition of her lies, but a willingness to ignore them if she did what was required of her.

381

Though she felt heavy with the child growing inside her, energy rolled off her in waves. Purpose, too. She'd stared into Wrath's Eye and been deemed worthy, her sins forgiven.

I'm coming, Ennis, she thought. *Wherever you are, I shall find you.*

She watched as the monster sank back into the depths; concentric, churning ripples widened as it descended. When she turned back to meet the stares of her people, no one blinked, no one breathed.

Until she raised her hands.

And then they cheered.

Oh yes, how they cheered.

After all, who could argue with the mother of Wrath's child?

Fifty-Six

The Western Kingdom,
the Southron Gates
Ennis Loren

The journey had been long and tiresome, but at long last they'd reached the last place in the Four Kingdoms Ennis Loren ever thought he would see. The Southron Gates.

The wall rose high and thick, an impenetrable barrier against an attack from the west. And yet, between the jutting mountains of solid stone was a wide gap. The steel hinges were still in place, but the doors were gone, melted down into shapeless lumps of steel having cooled on the dusty ground. It was said that the Calypsians, led by Empress Fire Sandes herself, had destroyed two of the four Gates before being stopped by a large contingent of Phanecian soldiers, masters of the martial art of phen ru.

The two furia who had chaperoned him this far, pointed to the gap in the wall. "Go," one of them said. "If you try to flee anywhere but south, we will kill you."

Ennis was certain it was a bluff—Rhea would never have ordered his death, this he was certain of—but he didn't want to run. He was ready, and he had made his choice, perhaps the final one of his life.

He dismounted, the cracked ground beneath his feet nothing like the green plush lands of the west he was so accustomed to. Step by step, he walked forward, refusing to look back, to show his fear. No, he wouldn't give Rhea's vicious servants the satisfaction.

The wall cast a long, angled shadow across him as he approached. He expected shouts from atop the wall, archers leveling arrows in his direction, swords raised. Instead, he got the one thing he hadn't expected: nothing.

Standing between the Gates on that mound of melted and then cooled steel, all he saw was dust and sand and burned land. *I have entered the first heaven,* he thought. *I am being punished for my numerous failures. I receive nothing less than I deserve.*

The moment he stepped into Phanes, he got everything he'd expected:

Shouts from above, loud and fierce. Arrows protruded from holes in the wall, aimed his way. Boots slapped stone steps as narrow-eyed Phanecians garbed in flexible leather armor charged toward him. Strapped to their wrists were long knives, leaving their hands free to perform acrobatic maneuvers—flips and cartwheels and gravity-defying aerial twists—as they surrounded him. Attached to each boot were long knives, which Ennis was certain could slash open his throat with a single kick.

With that thought, he knew it was time. He thought of young Rhea as a child, the mischievous gleam in her eyes, her quick-to-laughter sense of humor. He remembered how, after being apart from her for several years in the army, how surprised he was to return to Knight's End to find her a woman grown, flowered and beautiful. At first his unexpected romantic feelings toward his cousin had felt wrong considering their age difference, but little by little, over time, he'd become comfortable with them, like a stiff new pair of boots requiring breaking in.

He thought of how she'd shattered his heart with her news of the child inside her.

Yes, he thought. *I am tired of fighting, of losing. I am tired of it all.*

"Kill me," he said.

To his surprise, the Phanecians laughed.

Anger coursed through him. They would not deny him this final wish. "Kill me!" he roared, lowering his head and charging toward one of them, his eyes never leaving the gleam of the knives strapped to each limb.

The man didn't move until the last moment, leaping away and slamming an elbow across the back of Ennis's head. Stars burst across his vision as he tumbled headfirst into the dust, scraping his nose and cheek.

Voices, dull and muted, as if spoken from underground, drifted to his ears. "Foolish westerners," one said. "Always thinking we want to kill them. Far more valuable as slaves, they are. A strong western slave like this one will make a valuable gift to Emperor Falcon Hoza."

No. Ennis gritted his teeth, the stars fading. Fought to his knees, trying to push to his feet. Someone lifted him up and he swayed as the world spun. "Sleep, slave," the spinning Phanecian said.

He slammed his head into Ennis's face and everything went black.

Fifty-Seven
The Eastern Kingdom, Ironwood
Gareth Ironclad

Gareth was surprised when they entered the iron-sheathed trees of Ironwood to discover it still felt like home. For some reason he thought he'd feel like a stranger here now. An outsider.

But no. If anything, it felt like he'd never left, a thrill running through him.

"You feel it too," Gwen said, glancing at him. "This is our home. Time and distance and the twisting pathways of life cannot change that."

He nodded, and for once didn't feel like joking. He felt more like crying than anything. But he didn't; the last thing he wanted was to be seen weeping as he returned. His brother would only use it against him, take it as another sign of his weakness.

Having a heart is not weakness, he thought, remembering something Roan had once said to him. At the time, he'd laughed it away as overemotional drivel, but now the statement seemed almost prophetic.

He was aware of the eyes that watched them as they slowly rode along the broad forest corridors that led to the city. They were Orians mostly, Gwen's people, perched on airborne bridges and platforms, their bright eyes staring intently. He didn't look at them. Though the urge was there to spur his horse to a gallop, he fought it off. A returning king must always remain composed.

Is that what I am? he wondered. *A returning king.* Dressed in the torn, ink-stained, dirty clothing of a pauper, he felt like a fraud.

No, he thought, gritting his teeth. *This is my birthright, regardless of what happened at Raider's Pass.*

As if sensing his inner turmoil, Gwen said, "Steady, Your Highness. The throne will not be reclaimed in a day."

Her words comforted him. For one, it was the first time she'd used his honorific without sounding amused. She believed he was the rightful king—that was something wasn't it? Secondly, he wasn't alone. It was an unusual feeling for Gareth, one he wasn't used to. Even growing up surrounded by his brothers and parents, he'd never felt like he was part of the family. His title—Shield—had hung over his head from the day he was born, even if he wasn't aware of it until he was slightly older.

I am not alone anymore, he thought. *I have Gwen. I have Roan, wherever he is.*

The thought made him sit up straighter, and all his fears and doubts seemed to fall away.

Just ahead, the beautiful iron structures of Ferria rose like great angular sculptures built to be a *part* of the forest, rather than something separate. Each plate of metal gleamed as sunlight breached the forest canopy.

Aye, this is where I belong. This is home.

Though butterflies fluttered through his stomach, Gareth ignored them. Before, when he'd entered the city of his youth, he would've done so with princely bravado, trading quips with his citizens, purchasing a sausage and onion sandwich, chewing irreverently and laughing with his mouth open.

Not this time.

Now he rode straight-backed and silent, poised, nodding to those he passed, most of whom gawked at him openly. More than likely, he'd been the subject of many a rumor and juicy morsel of gossip over the last month. *Let them stare*, he thought. *They know nothing of what I've been through.*

The city's main thoroughfare fell away behind them, and soon they reached the castle's enormous iron gates. Several large guards defended them. Notably missing was Beorn Stonesledge, their ironmarked leader.

Though the guards, as they were trained, tried to hide their surprise, most of them visibly flinched when they realized who he was. One of them stepped forward to address him, one finger twirling his long red mustache nervously. "Sir, uh, I mean, prince, we didn't expect...no one told us you were coming."

"Need a king of the east announce his arrival?" Gareth said.

"Beggin' your pardon, but the king holds court on the throne at this very time."

"Not anymore," Gareth said. "Step aside!"

The guard flinched again, but didn't refuse him. A gap opened as the guard shouted, "Make way for Prince Gareth Ironclad!" Without a creak or jangle of chains, the iron doors opened, melting away to either side, controlled by one of the Orians, who channeled the ore.

As usual, the outer castle circle was abuzz with activity. Archers trained using strawmen targets. Legionnaires conducted mock battles with dull-edged swords. Grooms brushed down black and white horses. Armor was polished.

Gareth ignored it all, even when he heard the whispers, saw the fingers pointed his way as all activity ceased, like he'd entered the calm, silent eye of a storm.

They rode in a curving path around the outer circle, entering another gate and reversing direction. More stares. More whispers. After several more gates and direction changes, they reached the great iron stairs. Here, they dismounted.

"Are you ready?" Gwen asked.

"I am the king," Gareth said. "I was born ready."

Gwen grinned. "I almost believe you."

With Orian speed, she took the stairs two at a time—it wouldn't do for a king to arrive at court without a caller preceding him. He took them more slowly, relishing how his muscles remembered these steps.

He reached the top just as he heard his brother say, "Gwendolyn Storm? I'll be damned."

Instead of responding, Gwen said, "You're sitting in the king's seat."

To his credit, Grian laughed. He stopped when he saw Gareth standing behind her. "Brother? Is it truly you? I wouldn't have thought you'd have the nerve to crawl back to the country you failed."

Gareth stepped forward, refusing to rise to the bait. In his youth, he'd have charged his brother, settled this with fisticuffs and much scratching and clawing. But that boy was gone now, leaving behind the man he'd been forced to become.

"Prince Grian," Gareth said. "You shall address me as 'Your Highness' from this moment forward."

His brother tried to hide his discomfort behind a smirk, but a twitch in his eye gave him away. "*Prince* Gareth," he said. "You stepped down from the throne. You spoke the words. You did the honorable thing; don't ruin it now."

"I was *injured*, Grian. There were a dozen witnesses, including Gwen. I was coerced into speaking the words against my will."

"Liar!"

Gareth finally noticed something: the others in the room were all legionnaires. Generals. Advisers. This wasn't just any meeting. This was a council of war.

"What has happened?" Gareth said.

"It is not your concern," Grian said. But again, the quiver in his voice gave away his unease.

"Beorn Stonesledge wasn't at the gate," Gareth said.

"The ironmarked has many responsibilities." Grian refused to meet his eyes as he said this.

A man cleared his throat, looking equally uncomfortable. General Jorgundium, a man who'd been appointed to his position by Gareth's father almost a decade ago.

"Do you have something to say, General?" Gareth asked.

"Not a word," Grian said, firing daggers at the man.

"I cannot let this farce go on a moment longer," the man said. "Throw me in the stocks if you must." He turned to Gareth. "The ironmarked is dead."

"What?" Gareth and Gwen said at the same time.

"*General.*" The warning was still in Grian's tone, but it had lost its sharpness.

The general went on. "It's true. He fell at Darrin. We thought the city would be all but undefended, so only a small force was sent over the Black Cliffs. I was against it from the beginning, but I was overruled."

"Speak another word, General, and you'll be *wishing* for death!" Grian roared, pushing to his feet. His face was beet-red.

The general ignored the outburst. "Instead, the northerners had two sets of reinforcements. We were decimated. Stonesledge fell."

Grian was livid. "Arrest him. For subordination and treachery of the highest order."

None moved.

The general said, "We are spread too thin. We wage wars on three sides, but they are ill-planned and overly hasty."

"We are *winning* in the south," Grian said, his jaw set. "And the western forces have retreated back toward Knight's End. What happened in the north was a minor setback."

It was Gwen's turn to speak. "The south? What progress have you made against Calypso? Have you crossed the Scarra? Have you set foot on the Southron peninsula?"

"Well, no," Grian said. "But we have defeated several bands of Calypsian savages on the edges of the desert. They were the guanero, their mightiest warriors."

"You *fool*." Even Gareth was shocked by the venom in her tone. Had it been directed at him, his legs would've turned to rubber.

"Excuse me?" Grian said, not backing down. "You dare speak to your king that way? Just because my father gave you a long rope doesn't mean that I will."

"Your father was a wise man, a great warrior. You are but a *child* next to the lifetimes I've lived. I knew another Ironclad king like you, full of arrogance. He poked the Southron bear, too. Do you know what happened?"

Stunned silence.

"No? Well I was there. It was my bonding day, in fact. Do you know your history, child? The Dragon Massacre was a day I will never forget."

"The dragons are *dead*," Grian countered, though his confidence was fading. He looked pale now.

"A sleeping dragon isn't the same as a dead one," Gwen said. "They will return, and it will be because of you. Now step down with our thanks. You've done little but keep the throne warm for Gareth."

"I will not." Grian turned toward Gareth, an eerie calm entering his voice. "You are a *failed Shield*, brother. You have no place here. The people will never accept you as their king, and without the people, you cannot rule."

In the past, his brother's words would've cut into him like a hundred knives, but now they bounced off his skin. He was wearing a different kind of armor. The armor of truth and purpose.

"I may have failed as a Shield, but I am the Shield no longer." He remembered Gwen's words, back amongst the decaying stumps of the Rot. "Now I am the Sword."

Gwendolyn Storm

The feeling started on her skin, a faint buzzing, almost like the precognition that comes before the arrival of a still-distant storm.

No.

Her heart sped up, fleeting memories long buried rising to the surface. Fire. Claws. Death.

Please, no.

She'd spoken the words before as a warning, not a prophecy, and yet now she knew they were both.

Grian was screaming at his brother, at the generals, crying for arrests and trials, clinging to the throne like a fly to a leaf amidst a gale force wind.

She barely heard any of it, her keen ears trained skyward, listening.

She heard the shouts first. Then the bells, clanging their warning. Their call to arms.

Ferria was under attack.

That's when she heard a sound she hadn't heard in eight decades:

The beating of powerful wings.

394

PART II

Raven ⚜ Grey ⚜ Jai
Falcon ⚜ Bane ⚜ Roan
Bear ⚜ Windy

The halfmarked are joined; a key is complete.
A lock is opened; their fates are sealed.
The Western Oracle

Fifty-Eight
The Southern Empire, Calypso, Circa 532
Raven Sandes

"What are our options?" Raven asked her war council. For the moment, the civil war with Phanes had been put on hold. The more immediate threat came from the east.

Father, are you truly dead? she wondered. Thus far, they'd only heard rumors of his passing. Until it was confirmed, Raven refused to let herself feel anything.

As heads bobbed and turned to look at each other, Raven felt an eerie sense of déjà vu. Like her sister, Fire, her first act as empress was the consideration of war.

These are dark times we live in, she thought.

"I'll speak if no one else will," Rider said. The dark-eyed dragon master had long been a friend and ally to Raven.

Though Rider was at least twenty years older and had been training the *dragonia* for years, she had a timeless complexion, her dark-skinned face unweathered by wind or sand, stress or battle. She wore a black cloak that typically flapped in the wind as she rode the dragons, but which now hung lifelessly behind her back.

"Thank you," Raven said. "What do you propose?"

The dragon master stepped forward, past the rest of the council. There were five others invited to the meeting: Goggin, the commander of the *guanero*, the legion of elite warriors who rode their reptilian steeds, the *guanik*, into battle; Ponjut, a brute of a woman and Goggin's second-in-command—she would go along with whatever he said; Shanolin, a narrow-eyed dragon master with thirty years of experience; Whisper, Raven's sister and the Third Daughter, who was heir to the Calypsian throne in the event Raven perished; and, of course, Rider, who spoke now.

"My position has not changed. The dragonia are almost a year from maturity, and their development cannot be forced. These attacks by the easterners are not a major threat to the empire. We should wait. Do nothing."

Raven gritted her teeth, but not because she disagreed— she'd made almost the exact same argument in Fire's war council, in regards to the civil war with Phanes. Was this really any different? Yes, the Ironclad monarchy, which was now ruled by Grian Ironclad, was attacking the nomadic border villages along the edge of the Scarra Desert, but they were still hundreds of leagues from the southern peninsula. If anything, King Ironclad seemed to be goading Raven into taking drastic action when none was needed.

Raven shifted in her uncomfortable throne. The dragon throne was intentionally full of spikes and hard edges, so that the ruler never got too comfortable in it. As her maata had always said, *Ruling is a privilege not a right.* "Goggin?" Raven said. "Any thoughts?" She was surprised she had to ask at all; the man was usually the most outspoken of her leaders.

"We can't do nothing," he said. One hand played with the mangled stub of ear he'd recently acquired in battle; he was fortunate the Phanecian arrow had only taken his ear, and not his life. "That is no option. The people will see you as weak. They may rebel. Send a portion of the guanero. We will clean up this mess with the east."

Goggin would ask to be sent into battle against a gang of bloodthirsty rabbits if he had the chance. He thrived on battle. Raven sighed. "You lost half your forces at the Southron Gates. Your new recruits have never seen battle and are not fully trained. You would have me send them to the border?"

Goggin pounded his broad chest. "We do not fear death. We serve the empire with our strength, and our blood if necessary. All members of the guanero have taken their oaths, and they will do as I command."

"I am not questioning their honor, only whether we should spend more lives."

"What other option is there?" Shanolin asked, though he didn't make it sound like a question. He paused, licking his dark lips. "Goggin spoke truly when he said we cannot do nothing. The Sandes have always been strong; Calypso has always been strong. To do nothing would expose you to threats both inside and outside the empire."

To Raven's ears, it almost sounded like a threat, though it was probably true. She nodded toward Rider. "What say you?"

"I agree with that," Rider said slowly.

"I doubt you'll agree with the rest of my proposal, however," Shanolin continued, giving his fellow dragon master a pointed look. Raven knew from experience that the two most experienced dragon masters rarely saw eye to eye on such matters. "We should conduct the testing of the dragonia early."

"Absolutely not," Rider said, shooting a glare at Shanolin. She turned back to Raven. "Empress, it has only been three months since they were last tested, and only one of the dragons came anywhere close to passing."

Raven already knew this—she had been there. In fact, she was the only one of her sisters who had bothered to attend. *Heiron*, the largest of the brood, had put on a spectacle, passing all but one of the tests and making the rest of the dragonia look utterly inadequate.

"I've been spending extra hours with the weakest dragons," Shanolin offered. "They might surprise you. Anyway, what's the harm in testing them again? If they don't pass, it will make this decision much simpler."

"Empress, if I may—" Rider started to say, but Raven raised her hand to cut her off.

"Shanolin's right, Rider. It won't hurt anything."

"It will waste time that would be better spent *training* them."

"True, but only a half a day—perhaps a day at the most. In any case, I would prefer to know exactly where their abilities stand."

"As you wish," Rider said. Raven could tell from her tone that she was offended by the decision, but too loyal to speak out further.

"What about the guanero?" Goggin said. "While you're playing with your dragons, we could still send a small force to the border. Let us be your fist against the east."

Raven glanced at her sister, but Whisper seemed not to be listening, staring at her feet and playing with a lock of her flawless chestnut hair, which was so long now it kissed her hips. Her long silk dress was dark, as it had been for days, and lacked any of the usual adornments she adored. Raven wanted so badly to reassure her that she wouldn't die like their mother had, like Fire had, but she couldn't. Not now.

As Raven considered, her hand absently moved to play with her long black hair, a habit of hers, but found nothing but empty air. She was still getting used to her short hair, which was in the awkward stage of regrowth after it had been burned off in the arena while she fought Fire for the dragon throne. "Send thirty guanero," Raven said, dropping her hand.

"I will lead them myself," Goggin said.

"No. Ponjut shall lead them. I need you here."

Goggin nodded, though there was disappointment in his expression. He would sorely miss another stop in Kesh, the oasis in the desert, renowned for its hospitality and spirit. Raven, however, would not miss Kesh—the last and only time she'd ever visited the desert village Fire had almost been murdered in her sleep.

In the end, Fire died anyway, she reminded herself.

"Thank you. That is all," Raven said. Everyone filed out, save for Whisper, who continued playing with her hair, oblivious to anything but her own thoughts. Raven watched her for a moment and then cleared her throat. Nothing. Her sister's huge brown eyes were glazed over, staring at something only she could see.

"Whisper," Raven said.

"Hmm?" She turned her head in Raven's general direction, but didn't make eye contact.

"I—" What did she want to say? What *could* she say? She couldn't bring her maata or sister back from the dead. Nor their father, who had seemed dead for a long time. And maybe now he really was. She also couldn't promise that she would never leave. Nor should she. Whisper was next in line for the empire, and babying her now would only cripple her. "I miss them," she said instead.

Whisper's eyes finally met hers. "I can't breathe sometimes," she said breathlessly.

"I know."

"Do you really?" Whisper snapped, her voice turning to steel—well, at least as much as it could. "You're talking of *war*, Raven. You sound just like them. Maata. Faata. Fire. That's all they cared about. And where did that get them? It got them dead."

"I'm not them. I'm being more cautious."

Whisper shook her head, pursing her butterfly lips. "You're *not*. You just agreed that if the dragonia pass the testing that they'll be ready for battle, even if they're not fully grown."

So she was *listening*, Raven thought, surprised. "I didn't make any decision other than to test the dragons. And they won't pass."

"You can't know that. And anyway, you sent thirty guanero to the border."

"To stop a war!"

"To *start* a war!" Whisper fired back. When had her youngest sister become so tenacious? "This is how it happens—this is how it always happens. One side attacks, the other side counters with a larger force, and on and on until everyone is dead and I'm alone again." The fight left her and Whisper's head slumped into her lap. Her shoulders began to shake, the soft sound of muffled weeping rising to fill the sudden silence.

If someone entered the room now…Raven couldn't let anyone see her sister like this. Sandes women did not cry or show weakness in public, if ever.

Raven slipped off her throne, roping an arm around her sister's shoulders. "Come, let us return to our quarters. A cold drink and a bath will serve you well."

Whisper squirmed away. "Stop coddling me," she said, dashing her hand across the tears on her cheeks. Her eyes were wet and red, but still sharp. "I'll go myself."

As Raven gaped at her, she stalked off, the hem of her dark dress brushing the floor behind her. Raven shook her head, still trying to come to terms with this new fierier version of Whisper.

Just then, one of the empire messengers entered, bowing slightly at the waist. He wore baggy white pants cinched at his knees and a gray vest with three silver buttons. "Two messages have arrived," he said, handing her a freshly streamed note on moist parchment. He stepped back twice, giving her space to read in private.

What now? Raven thought.

She scanned the letter, her eyes widening when she noticed the sender. *Aunt Viper.* The strangeness wasn't in the message itself, which was of a mundane nature—a recent profit report from the fighting fits of Zune, of which Viper was the mistress overlord—but the fact it was sent at all. She hadn't heard from her aunt in years, not even after her mother's death.

She realized the messenger was still standing, waiting, another message in hand. She folded her aunt's stream for later consideration.

"Where is the second message from?" she asked the messenger.

"I'm not sure."

Raven frowned. "To where was it streamed?" Generally certain senders used the same locations again and again.

"It wasn't streamed, Empress. It came via pigeon." The man held up a sealed scroll.

Raven's frown deepened. Since streaming—the instantaneous method of sending messages using inkreeds through the water network—was invented, people rarely used birds anymore. The messengers generally just ran from the stream locations to deliver their messages and back again.

"Approach." He strode forward once more and handed her the scroll. "Thank you. That is all."

The messenger left, but Raven barely noticed, because she was staring at the wax used to seal the rolled parchment. It was blood-red and printed with a strange symbol—a sickle. In the south, the sickle was associated with the god of the Void, or underworld, *Dragonus*.

She cracked the seal and unfurled the scroll. The succinct message was scrawled in red ink.

Stop war or Whisper dies.

Raven stared at the words, her breath stuck in her chest.

The ink smelled distinctly metallic, coppery. From experience, Raven knew that smell. The message was written in blood.

Fifty-Nine
The Southern Empire,
somewhere off the coast of Phanes
Grey Arris

Grey Arris was still getting used to this different version of his sister, Shae. Sure, she'd always been strong-willed, outspoken—stubborn as a mule, Shae was, if Grey was being honest.

But this Shae was all those things, and something else. Something *more*.

When she looked at him, as she was doing now, her gaze seemed to pierce him to the core, as if she was seeing his demons, his memories, his faults and his burdens.

"We are close," she said now, snapping him away from his ruminations.

"Close to what?" he asked, but her stare had already moved on, out to sea, settling on something perhaps only she could see.

She didn't respond, something else Grey was still getting used to. When she was like this, Grey knew it was fruitless to try to badger her further. It was like she'd folded into herself, a bat tucking its wings around its body, hiding in plain sight. On the Dead Isles, Shae had been through hell and back, and Grey wasn't about to push her until she was ready.

All he really knew was that she'd dreamed about a man, a pirate, who was marked with the other half of the symbol on her palm, the one she'd been born with. Together, their two symbols formed a key, apparently. A key to open what, neither of them knew. Solving the mystery was the primary reason why they were now heading on a southerly bearing, toward Pirate's Peril, an island off the southwestern coast of Phanes. As its name suggested, the isle was the known hideout of a notorious band of pirates operating in the Burning Sea.

Watching her stare out to sea, Grey had the urge to ask Shae more about her dreams, what the pirate looked like, why he, of all people, would bear the other half to her mark.

Instead, with the sun peeking over the horizon, he left her alone, off to see if Kyla, the captain's daughter, was awake yet. Stomping across the foredeck, he passed several seamen, each of whom greeted him with respectful nods and tipped caps. It was an abrupt change to the way they'd treated him before, back when he'd been known simply as "the cripple." Strangely, their newfound respect made him uncomfortable.

As he approached the stairs below decks, Captain Smithers himself emerged, blinking against the brightness of daybreak. Garbed in faded trousers held up by an old leather belt with a dull silver buckle, a stained button-down shirt, and a floppy brown cap, the captain could've been just another seaman starting work for the day.

But Grey knew better. When the captain barked orders, his men listened, else they face the stiff edge of his walking stick. Grey had known the captain's wrath in the past, though now the man generally looked at him with a similar respect to his men.

Thus far, the captain had promised to take them within rowing distance of Pirate's Peril. Smithers had said that any additional help beyond that was "to be discussed in good time." They also had yet to speak about where the captain's daughter's place in all this was. Grey had been avoiding the conversation for a week.

"Well met, Seaman Arris," the captain said now.

"Well met, Captain," Grey said, removing his cap, his unruly black hair spilling out.

"You're up early."

"Sleep is hard to find these days," Grey explained. In truth, he'd been up for several hours already, passing the early morning beside Shae, who seemed to sleep even less than he. Their predawn vigil had become somewhat of a ritual. As usual, they'd spoken little, watching the Phanecian coastline pass like the ghost of an enormous beast in the dark. A few days earlier, the smoke that had blanketed Phanes had dispersed, leaving the sky clear.

"For me as well." The captain squinted into the distance, searching the red Phanecian cliffs they'd been staring at for a week. "We'll all rest easier once we've passed the Southron peninsula."

Grey didn't know if that was true, but he agreed anyway, suddenly anxious to see Kyla. "Is your daughter awake yet?"

The captain grinned knowingly. He not only supported his daughter's interest in Grey, but openly encouraged it, an abrupt turnaround from when he'd forbidden them from seeing each other. Grey had showed her kindness, and to a father that was much the same as retrieving the moons for her. "Last I saw, she was dead to the world. Feel free to wake her though, else she'll sleep till midday."

"Thank you, Cap'n," Grey said over his shoulder, descending the steps.

Below decks the corridor was dim, the barest sliver of sunlight finding its way onto the landing. The first door on the right was the captain's quarters, which belonged to Smithers and Kyla. Grey smoothed his salt-stained shirt with his hand before raising his fist to knock.

The door opened before he could finish the gesture, a hand shooting out to grab his collar. Off-balance, he found himself being pulled inside the chamber by Kyla, who proceeded to kiss him hard on the lips, stealing his breath.

When she pulled away he gasped. "What was that for?" he asked. Not that he minded.

Her brown curls bouncing, Kyla said, "For being you. For being here." She had that telltale twinkle in her eyes, the barest of smiles on her lips. Combined with her button nose, rich brown skin, and sharp eyebrows, he found everything about her utterly attractive.

He leaned down to scoop a hand around her waist, using his stump to support her waist as he leaned her back and kissed her deeply. She came up giggling. "What was *that* for?"

"That was good morning," Grey said.

The entire exchange left him giddy. Though their brief but intense romance felt sweeter than his last relationship, it was no less passionate. His smile quickly faded, however, when he saw Kyla's bottom lip begin to quiver.

"Oh gods, Kyla," he said, pulling her into his chest. She nuzzled against him, unfurling her arms around his back. She didn't have to say anything. He knew. "You had the same dream?"

She shook her head, her voluminous hair tickling his chin. "Almost, except…" She trailed off.

"Take your time," Grey said, cupping her chin, lifting her gaze to his. "I have all day."

A shadow smile creased her lips. "What about your daily tasks? The decks won't scrub themselves."

"I could skip a week and your father would still think I walk on water."

"But you won't."

"I will if you need me to."

She dipped her head again, pressing her lips against his chest. He could feel the warmth as she kissed him through his shirt. "Where did you come from?" she asked.

"Knight's End," he said, though he knew that wasn't what she meant. Though he'd told her a lot about his past—about his parents' deaths, about Shae's sinmark, about the furia's capture of her and his subsequent mission to save her—he hadn't told her everything. He hadn't admitted to being a thief in a past life, nor that he'd bedded Princess Rhea under the false name Grease Jolly. He didn't know why, exactly, he'd withheld these things. It wasn't as if Kyla was naïve—she'd grown up a captain's daughter, spending her time amongst cursing, gambling, spitting seamen.

No, he thought. *I do know why. I'm ashamed.*

She believed him a hero, when he was nothing but a recovering crook and swindler.

Could present goodness wash away past badness? It was a question he'd struggled with for some time. In the end, he'd had to put it into the voluminous category of things he'd didn't know. All he could do was try his best to do *good* going forward, and protect his sister and Kyla and those he cared about.

Still, despite Kyla's strength, sometimes Grey felt she was as fragile as a crystalline swan, ready to shatter if the wind blew in the wrong direction.

Kyla began telling him about her dream. Much of it was the same as her previous ones had been: her daughter, Myree, who had arrived stillborn, drifting away on her floating casket; her eyes suddenly flashing open, as brown as Kyla's skin; the baby's sharp intake of breath; the crying…but from there the dream changed. The child stood, a babe no more, and its eyes were sparkling blue, its blond hair sunlit, its cheeks fair and rosy.

Grey frowned when her story ended. He'd seen her baby. Her skin was a rich brown, albeit not quite as a dark as Kyla's. And her head had been covered with a thin layer of black hair, plastered to its scalp by birthing fluid and blood.

"That doesn't make sense," Grey said.

"I know."

They held each other in silence for several minutes, both lost in their own thoughts. "Are you okay?" Grey finally asked. He might not be able to interpret the dream, but he could comfort its recipient.

"I don't know. It was hard enough losing her, but to have to see her again every night…and then to have her change like that? Into someone else's child? It feels like torture. Every time, I wake up out of breath, like I've run a great distance."

Grey raised an eyebrow. "Is that what you think? That you were seeing someone else's child?"

She looked up at him, her eyes shining with unshed tears. "Maybe. I don't know why I said that. But there was something else."

"What?"

"The child bore a strange marking."

Grey's blood turned to ice. The only skinmark he'd ever seen was Shae's—her half-key that didn't seem to do anything. "What marking?"

"Well, I don't know if it was a marking exactly. Five letters. A word. H-O-R-D-E."

"Horde?" Grey said. "What is that supposed to mean?"

Kyla shrugged, finally pulling away from him. "Probably nothing. But I felt scared when I saw it."

"Land ho!" the scout shouted from the crow's nest. As Grey looked up at him, he waved his hat wildly over his head. The other shipmen began to gather on deck, craning their heads over the railing and peering into the distance. Without the spyglass used by the scout, all they could see were endless waters.

Though Grey had expected to hear just such a cry for a few days now, it still sent a sensation through him. He didn't know why, exactly, except that something about it felt like he was turning another page in the book of his life. Thus far, every new chapter had brought massive changes, not just in scenery but in *him*. He wondered what kind of person would emerge at the end of this chapter, assuming he emerged at all.

The weather had grown steadily warmer as they'd sailed south, while the wind had slowly died down. He could feel the beads of sweat forming on his forehead, trickling down his cheeks, occasionally dripping from his chin.

He was also nervous, because he'd run out of time to talk to the captain about his daughter. He could imagine the conversation in his head:

What are your intentions toward my daughter?

Uh. I like her?

Is that a question, son?

I don't think so?

Grey groaned just thinking about it.

"Arris!" Smithers shouted now, as if reading his mind. "In my office!"

Grey scanned the deck for Kyla or Shae, but found neither of them. The men winked at him, smirking, as if he'd been caught with his hand in the coin box.

There was nothing for it. He headed below decks, passing the closed door to the captain's quarters. He wondered if Kyla was inside, awaiting to hear news of her fate. On the left were the seamen's bunks, where he'd slept for the last several weeks, ever since he'd talked his way onto *The Jewel* in the first place. Surprisingly, he felt a pang of melancholy in his chest. His top bunk was lumpy and uncomfortable, lacking even a proper pillow, but he would miss it all the same, especially since twice Kyla had snuck in for a midnight cuddle.

At the end of the corridor was a scratched oak door with a miniature version of a ship's wheel nailed into it. He collected his nerve, took a deep breath, and then knocked. "Git in here!" the captain's gruff voice shouted.

Grey cringed, but opened the door. Inside, Captain Smithers sat behind a scratched up old desk covered with various items typical in a merchant vessel's office: signed contracts, a brass compass, dozens of nautical maps, a tin lock box. His eyes narrowed at Grey as he entered. "You think me a damn fool!" the dark-skinned man bellowed.

Grey froze. This wasn't the beginning to the conversation he'd expected. "No, I—I don't know what you're talking about." He took a step into the cramped room, closing the door behind him, which was when he noticed two others in attendance—Kyla and Shae. They were side by side, stuffed into a corner. Shae refused to look at him. Kyla's eyes met his, and she mouthed *I'm sorry*.

Sorry for what?

The captain glared at him. "Kyla here was just telling me how you've been boasting about stealing her away, whisking her off on some foolbrained adventure in the land of the pirates."

Grey's jaw fell open. Not only had he and Kyla not discussed anything of the sort, but he didn't take her for the type to tell such a lie, especially to her father. He turned to meet her eyes, but she'd looked away.

"I—no, I'm not planning to steal your daughter away. I never said that."

"Then what *are* you planning?" Here it was: the conversation.

Grey collected his thoughts, determined not to say anything he would regret later. "The truth is, Cap'n, I barely know what I'm going to eat for breakfast, much less my plans for the future. All I know is that I care about your daughter deeply, more than I've cared about anyone in my life, save my sister, I suppose. And I know I must, once more, thrust myself into danger for the sake of learning about Shae's marking, as I've told you. If I may have a rowboat, I will make the attempt on my own, asking only that you protect Shae and Kyla in my absence. If I manage to escape the isle at some point, I will seek you out, along your merchant route."

"Is that all?" the captain growled, as if Grey was asking for the clothes off his very back.

Grey nodded, holding his breath.

The captain leaned forward, his jaw trembling with what appeared to be rage. And then he coughed, his face changing, a laugh bursting from his mouth, spluttering out with a splash of spittle. Grey raised his eyebrows as Smithers slapped both knees with vigor, all the while laughing so hard Grey thought the captain's head might fall from his neck.

Grey turned to Kyla and Shae to find them both laughing, too, though not nearly as hard as the captain. He felt like the butt of a jape he'd completely missed the punchline for.

"I shoulda bin a play actor," Smithers finally said, wiping his eyes, which were moist with amused tears. "You shoulda seen yer face, sailor! White as a ghost, 'twas!"

Grey was still trying to catch up, but he thought maybe the reaction was a good thing? "So you're loaning me the rowboat?"

That spurred another round of laughter. "After what ye did ta the last boat I loaned ye? Never again," Smithers said. "No, I don' trust ye with me stuff. My daughter, aye, but not me vessels."

"What are you saying?" Grey said slowly.

"Tell him, lass," Smithers said, gesturing to Kyla.

She was beaming. "We're coming with you, Grey."

What? "No. You can't." This, of all things, was not what he wanted. Pirate's Peril was a danger he and he alone would face.

The captain stood, moving around the desk to slap him hard on the back. "We can and we will. That's the deal, unless ye'd rather swim."

Grey groaned. "Sailing a merchant vessel into Pirate's Peril is like..." He searched for the right comparison.

"Like a lamb wanderin' into a lion's den?" the captain offered, looking all too pleased with himself. "'Bout right, I esspect."

"But the other men," Grey said.

"They've already agreed to it. Days ago."

Grey shook his head, trying to make sense of the nonsensical. "Kyla?"

Kyla said, "I'm going, Grey. I told you you're stuck with me. Get used to it."

"Shae?"

Shae, still grinning, said, "This was always my path. I think we both know that."

Grey did. Though he'd had the best intentions of slipping away on his own to seek answers on her behalf, in the honest part of his heart he always knew she wouldn't allow it. Nor was it his place to do so.

"Why?" Grey asked the captain, who'd stuffed a plug of tobacco under his lip.

He chewed for a minute and then spit in a tin cup. "Boredom, I guess. Me and me men, we've bin sailin' this route fer a long time. Too long. It's exhaustin'. We barely turn a profit as 'tis. A bit of a pirate adventure seems jest the thing we need."

Grey didn't know about that, but he also knew having a ship would offer them a much greater chance of escape, when the time came. He had nothing else to say, other than, "Thank you, Captain. For everything."

The man's smile faded away as he said, "Don' make me regret it, son."

Sixty
The Southern Empire, Phanes
Jai Jiroux

Vin Hoza, the Slave Master, was dead.

And yet, nothing had changed. After that fateful night in which it felt as if *everything* had changed, when the metaphorical chains were broken, the slave marks vanishing from thousands of slaves' necks across Phanes, Garadia Mine, Jai's prison, had erupted in cheers. Men, women, and children, most of Teran or Dreadnoughter origin, had rushed through the tunnels, racing for the mine's entrance. They could smell freedom, sweet and fragrant. Finally, at long last, within their reach.

The masters, including Mine Master Axa, had reacted swiftly, slipping from the cavern and dropping the steel gate, barricading the mob inside. One of the masters had been too slow—there wasn't much left of him when the mob had finished. The previously docile slaves had raged, screaming threats and curses through the bars, but their words were empty, lost on the wind.

A day later the reinforcements arrived from the canyon city of Phanea. Hundreds of armed soldiers trained in the martial art of phen ru marched on the mine. By then, hungry and exhausted, the slaves had had no choice but to succumb to the force gathered against them.

The few who had fought back were killed, an example set for the remaining slaves.

It was at that moment that Jai Jiroux, previous Garadia Mine Master, realized two things:

First, that it had never been Vin Hoza and his slavemark alone that had enslaved the people.

Second, that true escape was impossible so long as a Hoza ruled the empire.

It was these two truths that fed him now, day by day, as he toiled alongside his people in the mines, chiseling away rock to uncover enough raw diamonds to make the new emperor of Phanes, Vin's son, Falcon, a very rich man. All the while, Jai was making plans.

Not to escape, no, such notions had been futile, pointless. Childish dreams as unattainable as touching the stars in the night sky.

Weighed down by ball and chain and a heavy axe he swung again and again and again, he glanced down the line of slaves. There was poor Jig with his gimpy foot, gathering rock dust to be sifted. There was Sonika Vaid, the previous leader of the all-female rebel group known as the Black Tears, her eyes as dark and sly as ever, hammering away. Twice since her slave mark vanished, she'd attempted to escape. Now her strong back bore the scars from the beatings. In private, out of earshot from the mine masters, she told Jai she would keep trying until she succeeded, or died in the attempt.

One didn't cage someone like Sonika Vaid and expect a good result.

Jai had other plans.

This time he would fight back. Gods help anyone who tried to stop him.

"We're leaving tonight," Sonika hissed. Her smooth brown skin was dotted with black tears, permanently etched in her flesh. A reminder. Once Jai had believed the rumors—that each tear was for someone she'd killed. Instead, each tear was for someone she'd lost.

Sonika Vaid had a lot of tears. Too many.

Jai shook his head. "It's too soon. The masters are watching you and the Black Tears like vulzures."

Sonika looked away, scanning the cavern they ate in, slept in, bathed in, lived in. She'd been the one to give these slaves freedom once, even if it wasn't permanent, and Jai wouldn't be surprised if she accomplished the same thing a second time.

If she didn't get herself killed first.

When she looked back at Jai, her face was determined. "I can't stay another night in this place. I have to try. The Tears are ready. It's already planned."

Jai knew there was no point arguing further; it would only draw attention, and when Sonika had made up her mind about something, there was no changing it. "May Surai's light shine upon you."

"Thank you, but the Goddess of Light can shine on you, too, Jai. Come with us."

A swell of sadness rose inside him. In truth, he wanted nothing more than to escape this place. And he would, eventually, but under his own terms, in his own way. The wheels were already turning, just in a different direction. "We will meet again," he said. "I promise. It will be a beautiful day indeed." He lifted her fingers to his lips and kissed them. She was the sister Jai had never had.

When he met her eyes again, he was surprised to see tears sparkling in them, more beautiful than the diamonds speckling the mine walls. And then she was gone, carrying her lead ball on her shoulder, her chains clanking.

He hoped he wouldn't see her again, but feared he would, fresh scars etched into her back.

"You're not eating," Marella said, nodding toward Jai's plate.

He flushed. He hadn't even realized she'd filled his plate with the day-old bread and mushy beans. His mind had been elsewhere, wondering where Sonika and her Tears were. The mine had been abuzz ever since they escaped the night before.

She did it, Jai thought. *She really did it.* He knew he shouldn't be surprised—she was the most capable woman he'd ever met, save perhaps for Shanti—but he was. Garadia was a fortress these days, with more mine masters than Jai had ever seen in one place in his life.

Other slaves were talking about revolting, but they were a minority. Since the escape, the guards had used their whips more. Jai knew an outright revolution wasn't the answer.

Sonika would do her part, he was certain. But it still wouldn't be enough.

The only answer was to fight from within. It was something he'd believed in as a mine master, and he still did, only a new approach was necessary.

"Jai?" Marella's wide eyes were narrowed into a look of concern.

Oh gods, he'd done it again.

"Sorry, Marella. My mind is heavy on this night."

"Is it because of the Black Tears' escape?" Jig, Marella's son, asked. The straw-haired boy was literally bouncing with excitement.

"No, idiot, it's because of his arm!" Viola, Jig's older sister, said. The young girl was the spitting image of her mother, from the coppery hair to the round blue eyes to her heart-shaped face. Her hair was beginning to grow long again, a requirement for all female slaves, while Jig's was chopped short. The family was of Teran descent, and in their culture it was the males who usually wore their hair long.

Jai was only half-Teran, his mother having been a slave, but his eyes had none of the narrowness typical of Phanecians.

"I'm not an idiot! You're an idiot!" Jig retorted, pushing his sister.

Marella cleared her throat and raised a single finger, and that was all it took for the siblings to quiet down. "Viola, you *will not* call your brother any names, is that clear?"

The girl nodded meekly, while Jig beamed.

The boy's grin faltered, however, when Marella turned her wrath on her son. "And you *will not* push your sister. Correct?"

"Yes, Mother."

"Good." Jai smiled in appreciation of the stern but warm woman he'd been friends with for more than five years. She'd faced enough heartache and tragedy to make the strongest of souls falter, but she hadn't. Nor would she ever, Jai knew. "How *is* your arm?" she asked now.

Viola leaned closer to Jai, batting her eyes at him. The girl was naught but twelve but she'd been infatuated with Jai since she was nine.

Jai cradled his left arm against his body, while using his right to use the bread to scoop up some mushed beans. "Could be better, but it won't kill me."

"Now you're like me," Jig said. "Except with your arm instead of a leg." The comparison seemed to make the boy happy.

"Correct you are, young Emperor," Jai said. The nickname made Jig giggle and Viola roll her eyes.

The leg will be next, Jai thought. If his plan was to work, the injuries needed to believable, if temporary. Earlier that day, he'd thrown down his pick in sight of Garadia's Mine Master, Axa. Axa, who was in on the plan, had reacted the only way he could: with extreme violence. He'd thrown Jai to the ground and kicked him repeatedly in the arm. Jai had to hand it to him—the man could kick. He thought it might be broken, but he wasn't certain.

Axa's eyes had met his for a spare moment as the master walked away, and Jai had seen the self-loathing in the man's expression. Jai *relished* seeing that look, because it gave him hope. Not in the world—but in *people*. Axa had once been the nastiest, most violent of Jai's mine masters, and yet he had changed for the better. All it took was his enslavement—seeing what it was like. He'd walked many miles in the shoes of his

421

victims and found compassion in his heart somewhere during the journey. Even the sting of his betrayal at the Southron Gates had faded; after all, Jai knew it wasn't his fault—Axa had been cursed with a slave mark at the time.

And now he was helping Jai in the exact manner Jai had requested: By beating the living rock dust out of him.

If Sonika and her Tears could escape, so could he. He would walk right out the front door, none the wiser.

Sixty-One

The Southern Empire, Phanea
Falcon Hoza

Falcon Hoza, newly anointed Phanecian Emperor, had a real mess on his hands.

And he felt utterly unprepared for it. His father, the Slave Master, was supposed to live forever. He now realized how ridiculously foolish that belief had been. How childish.

I am no emperor, he thought now, sitting in the very chair that said the opposite. The plush throne was so big, and yet his father had always seemed to fill it so completely.

Falcon was positively swimming in it. *More like drowning*, he thought, as the three generals approached. *No, not the generals*, he thought. My *generals*.

As they approached, he glanced back at his younger brothers, Fang and Fox, each of whom looked utterly unperturbed by the situation, their white-powdered faces and narrow eyes expressionless. Behind them, the Three Great Pillars rose to the ceiling, seeming to bear the weight of the world upon their backs. Each was etched with a different marking: the Fist, the Sword, and the Whip. Symbols of violence and justice; at least that was what he'd been taught as a young boy. The Fist for brothers, the Sword for enemies, and the Whip for slaves.

Falcon turned to face his generals, using the one talent that had served him better than any thus far: faking it.

Growing up a Hoza had forced Falcon to either pretend to be like his father and brothers, or be stomped beneath their collective trod. So he did, day after day. As a young boy, he'd mastered phen ru before either of his younger siblings, and then he'd used it to defeat them in hand-to-hand combat again and again, until they knew he couldn't be beaten.

Sometimes, afterwards, as he rinsed the blood from his hands and feet, he would dry heave into the wash basin.

When he turned twelve, Falcon had his head shaved, save for a narrow scythe of hair down the center. Gaudy emeralds were supposedly sewn into his scalp. He pierced his ears and adorned them with diamonds. He powdered his face daily, in the way of his people.

And now, just yesterday, in the traditions of Phanecian emperors of the past, he'd had his eyebrows permanently removed, "sewing" jewels in their stead.

To anyone who couldn't see into his heart, he was a Phanecian emperor, haughty, powerful, and absurdly wealthy.

"Speak," he said now, addressing the general in the center, a grizzled veteran of war named Killorn.

The man stood up straight, his dark eyes devoid of fear. He wore leather battle armor, flexible enough to flip and spring in. His chest bore the four-eyed lioness, the symbol of Phanes. Strapped to his footwear were blades. Similar blades were lashed to his wrists. This man had killed hundreds, if not thousands, of foes in battle. He was violence in the body of a man, and he bore the scars to prove it.

"Before he died, your father chose not to repair the two destroyed Gates," General Killorn said.

"I know this," Falcon said. "He wanted to welcome our enemies across the border. He wanted war."

The general nodded. "We are prepared. Those north of us believe our defenses have been weakened, but it is the opposite. The slave army is stronger than ever, ten thousand strong. Prepared. Trained."

Falcon shook his head, trying to hide his discomfort at all this talk of war. "But not loyal. Before, my father controlled them with magic. Now they could easily drop their weapons on the battlefield and join the ranks of those who march upon us."

The general smiled, which made Falcon frown. What was this man not telling him? "Your father was a man of secrets, even from you," he said.

Falcon's frown deepened. This was not what he had expected. He'd been ready to declare that the Gates be rebuilt, that war be averted, or at least delayed. "What secrets?"

"The slave army was never marked by chains—your father never controlled them the way he did the other slaves."

Falcon didn't need to ask why—it all became clear in an instant. "He knew he'd be killed eventually."

It wasn't a question, but the general said, "Yes. His life was threatened daily. He pretended it didn't affect him, but he prepared for his eventual death. He wasn't willing to risk his army's loyalty on his *tatooya* alone. For his army, he only used child slaves, those he could mold into warriors, those he could influence, those he could *break*. This army is his legacy."

"You're saying the slaves are loyal to Phanes?"

"They are obedient, which is almost the same thing. If you're asking whether they will fight for you, the answer is yes."

Deep inside himself, Falcon sighed. On the exterior, he forced steel into his eyes, his expression. He said, "Good. Then we shall plan for war. May our enemies' blood run like rivers through the desert."

Falcon was preparing for bed. First, he wiped the powder from his face. Then he removed the jewels from his scalp, eyebrows, and ears. He couldn't bear the weight of them any longer; not the weight on his skin, but on his soul. For he had seen the mines, the slaves toiling in those horrid places. None knew the gems weren't truly sewn into his skin, but only stuck on each day, using the adhesive sap from the lyptus tree.

His father was a man of secrets, yes, but so was he.

Beside his father's enormous bed—the same bed Vin Hoza had been murdered in—Falcon prepared a thin mattress and pillow. He needed no blanket as the Southron air was hot and thick. The first night after being made emperor, he had tried lying in the bed, but tossed and turned uncomfortably for several hours before shifting to the floor. He'd slept there ever since.

Hidden in his bedroll was a book, one he'd procured in secret. He'd read it half a dozen times already, as he did with most books, before eventually getting a new one. According to his father, literature was for women, whereas men should focus on things of substance, like training, power, and wealth. His father only made exceptions for true works, which he had read to his sons so they could learn from the past failures and successes of their ancestors.

This particular book would've turned his father's face red in anger.

It was fiction, for one, a story invented by a famous Dreadnoughter storyteller. The story was centered around a forbidden love between a man and woman on opposite sides of a bitter war between kingdoms. The man was a prince, the woman a princess. Their fathers hated each other. Their people killed each other.

Falcon eagerly turned the pages, soaking in the author's words, the growing suspense as the young lovers were nearly discovered in the throes of rapture on numerous occasions. And yet, despite the risks they faced, they refused to let their love be consumed by the hate between their families.

In the end, he knew, they would die because of their beliefs, their love. Still, each time he approached those final pages, Falcon hoped their story might change. That they might escape, sail to a faraway land where they could live in peace and happiness.

And each time he was disappointed as they died in each other's arms, killed by their own kin.

Sixty-Two

Unknown location
Bane Gäric

Bane, Killer of Kings, Destroyer of Empires, Bringer of Peace, knew the man would eventually try to kill him.

Even as they sat across from each other breaking bread, drinking wine, he could see it in Chavos's red eyes. The man no longer called himself "the Beggar," for one. No, he insisted on reassuming his childhood name—Chavos. That was a bad sign. A beggar might need what he had to give. A Chavos, well, he didn't know what a Chavos might need.

In truth, Bane didn't know much about people, considering his upbringing had been limited to a cold cave and a man named Bear Blackboots. A man who, he was now beginning to realize, wasn't exactly who he had pretended to be.

Bane had finally found the man hiding in the vast archives of Citadel, the northernmost Calypsian city. He was hidden among the stacks, muttering under his breath, searching thick tomes, his fat fingers brushing the pages with unexpected tenderness, as though caressing a lover's hair.

Bane, for some reason, felt disgusted by the man he'd once called Father. For a long time, he considered stealing up behind him, slitting his throat, ending his mutterings.

But he didn't. Something about it didn't feel right, and Bane had learned over the course of the last few months to always trust his instincts.

After all, they'd gotten him this far—six dead rulers with still four to go.

"Can you pass the butter, my friend?" Chavos said, gesturing toward a silver plate set between them.

"Of course, my *friend*," Bane said with a smile. Rather than hand it to him and risk being touched by the plague-riddled man, he slid it across the floor.

"Thank you."

"You're welcome."

Bane hated that he couldn't seem to convince anyone of his mission, the justness of it, the *rightness*. He was ordained by the Western Oracle, wasn't he? He was *created* by her. Surely that should mean something. Where others saw only a trail of blood and corpses in his wake, he saw a glowing red path to peace. The rulers of the Four Kingdoms had become far too bloodthirsty, drunk on their power. He was simply the equalizer.

Why couldn't anyone seem to see that?

The urge to slash open the man in front of him rose bitterly in the back of his throat, but something stayed his hand.

It was need. Pathetic human need. For companionship. For a friend. Even a false friend felt better than none at all.

And so he smiled and ate, waiting for that inevitable moment when one of them would need to kill the other.

Sixty-Three
The Southern Empire, Calyp
Roan Loren

Roan Loren, having grown up under the vicious glare of the Southron sun, knew better than to attempt to cross the Scarra on his own. Instead, after parting ways with his furia escort on the banks of the Spear, he swam across, taking a few moments to wring out his sodden clothes, and then turned directly south, following the arrow-straight river toward its end: the Burning Sea.

The Burning Sea suited its name well. In the brightness of midday, it appeared to be not water, but a roiling, ever-shifting bed of flames, stretching from horizon to horizon. To the west was a burnt wasteland that eventually reached the towering red-rock spires that were home to a large colony of vulzures, the bloodthirsty sky hunters known to scoop up small children, sinking their claws into the scruffs of their necks.

To the east, the land angled southward, forming the narrowest portion of the desert, brown and sun-speckled. Here, along the coast, the Scarra wasn't nearly as formidable. The winds were cooler, and the sea provided plenty of food in the form of crabs skittering across the wet rocks. Roan, of course, wouldn't eat any living thing, instead relying on the bare rations afforded him by Rhea Loren before she sent him away.

Rhea Loren, he thought. *My sister, the tyrant.*

He shook his head, still in disbelief that he was back in the empire of his childhood. *How had everything gotten so turned around?* he wondered. Then again, at the same time there was a certain symmetry to it all, like his life had come full circle. At least that was what he told himself, because if fate had brought him here, then perhaps he could still find a way to achieve his goals—namely, find the ancient sorceress known as the Western Oracle, or locate her son, a man who now went by the name Bear Blackboots. And if he could do that, then maybe he could still save his friends, Gareth Ironclad and Gwendolyn Storm.

Friends. That word seemed like a lie. Because what he felt for each of them went far beyond the bounds of friendship. With Gareth, his love had been like a vial of poison turned over abruptly, spilling its contents, which turned out to be the sweetest wine. With Gwendolyn, the love had grown more slowly, building like a storm on the horizon: roiling clouds, pattering rain, strikes of lightning, rolling thunder.

Gods.

Each love was different in a thousand ways, but the same in one; and that one was what drove Roan now. If his sister wanted the Western Oracle or her son, he would give them to her to save those he loved. But perhaps Rhea would get more than she bargained for.

The evening faded into morning, and Roan stopped to eat and sleep. The sun was too harsh, forcing him to travel at night—risking a deadly sting from a scorpion or a poisonous bite from a snake—and take refuge under the sparse vegetation during the day.

He rose again when the sun set, continuing this pattern for two days, until the landscape began to change, his passage cutting sharply toward the east, where a narrow stretch of land jutted out toward the sea.

Where he saw a remarkable bridge, a long, curving scythe of stone connecting the desert to the peninsula known as Calyp.

My home.

He strode forward, unafraid.

Though it had seemed a much shorter distance, it had taken Roan the better part of the night to cross the windswept bridge. It was a harrying experience, each breath of wind threatening to blast him into the roiling whitecaps churning far beneath.

As expected, dark-skinned Calypsian soldiers blocked his path at the end of the bridge, the final gatekeepers to Calyp. They were frowning at him—at his dusty but pale skin, his blond-streaked hair, his pale-blue eyes. *A foreigner,* their expressions said, even as their hands closed on the weapons hanging from their belts. Only one of them was a guanero, his bulky frame resting atop a scaled guanik, the beast's pink tongue flicking restlessly from its black lips.

He was the one who spoke first: "You're a long way from home, westerner."

"I grew up in Calypso," Roan said. He held out his hands in a gesture that said *I'm unarmed and harmless.*

The guanero laughed without breaking his stare. "And I am Empress Raven Sandes. You're no more Calypsian than a gray-skinned Dreadnoughter."

"I didn't say I was Calypsian. Only that I grew up here. I've lived in many places, including, most recently, the east."

Although Roan had been expecting a reaction, it came far swifter and more powerfully than he was prepared for. Weapons screamed from their scabbards, rough hands grabbed him and slung him to the hard ground, and he found himself staring at the tip of a sword, which hovered a finger's breadth from his eye.

"Something I said?" he managed to quip.

"Why were you living in the east?" the guanero man said, his voice even, all humor sucked from it.

Roan's strategy had made sense up until now. Apparently even mentioning the word "east" could get you a sword through the eye. He chose his next words more carefully. "I was a prisoner," he said. "The Ironclad's took me captive. They thought I was a Calypsian spy."

The man's gaze narrowed. "How did you escape?"

"I didn't."

"They let you go?"

"Sort of. Let's just say I earned their trust."

"Meaning?"

"Meaning I have information."

"Information about what?"

"Remove your sword and I'll tell you."

The man bit his lip, considering. Then, slowly, he drew the blade back. Not all the way, but far enough that Roan felt like he could breathe again. "Speak."

"I know all about Ferria's defenses. I'll save the details for Empress Raven."

The man's lips curled as he showed his teeth. He shoved his blade downward. Roan flinched as the steel bit into the cracked ground just beside his face.

"Come with me," the guanero said, hefting Roan up by his collar.

Sixty-Four
The Southern Empire, Calypso
Raven Sandes

Nestled beneath the shadow of the three massive pyramids, all of Calypso, as well as many of the outlying villages, had gathered for the testing of the dragonia. This was remarkable as Raven had explicitly asked that it be kept secret.

Rumors and gossip swirl like winds upon this land, she thought.

If nothing else, the testing was a welcome distraction. She'd scarcely been able to think of anything but the words of the message delivered a day earlier.

Stop war or Whisper dies.

It was those five words that had shaken her awake in the middle of the night, her entire body trembling. She'd thrust the covers away, feeling suffocated, cold beads of sweat forming on her forehead and running down her spine. Frantically, she'd rushed from her room, bursting through the tinkling barrier of threaded guanik bones and into Whisper's quarters. At first, she'd thought the bed was empty, so small was her sister's form beneath the sheets. At first, she'd thought, *oh gods, what have I done?* but then she saw her chestnut hair spilling out, saw the rise and fall of her sister's chest beneath her coverings. Raven had stood there for a long time, just watching Whisper sleep, just enjoying the *aliveness* of her. And when she'd finally left, sleep had been impossible.

Still, now, outside amongst her people, the air of excitement was contagious, and she felt herself leaning forward in anticipation. The threat on the note was still there, somewhere in the back of her mind, but she managed to lock it away, at least until she had more time to consider the source.

It was hard not to be down there with the dragons, considering she was almost a dragon master herself given how much time she'd spent with the dragonia as a child and as she'd reached womanhood.

But she was empress now, and needed to separate herself from individual pursuits, and that included day-to-day monitoring of the dragons.

That being said, it was nearly impossible for her not to think of them as her children. The dragonia numbered twelve in total, as they always did. Six male, six female. No one knew exactly why that was, except that each generation of mates only bore two eggs each. Their parents were well past their prime, having descended into madness as their long lives wore on. Some of them had even grown a second head, or, in rare cases, a third. The thought made Raven sad—she hated the way the dragons, like humans, deteriorated with age. Not their bodies, which never stopped growing, but their minds.

She shook away the thought as she spotted Heiron, the largest male of the brood, with his dark, sleek scales and insatiable love of cured bacon. He had been the only dragon that had passed the last testing. Screams burst from the crowd as he snorted a gout of flames from his snout, so close to them that they could probably feel the heat. He wouldn't hurt them, of course; he just had a sense of humor.

Raven chuckled, watching Rider and Shanolin begin the testing.

First were flying challenges, each dragon beating its powerful wings, kicking up dust and small stones, commanded by their masters to perform various tasks. Hover in place. Rise at sharp angles, bursting through clouds. Swoop down sharply, brushing the ground without crashing. Fly in formation. Other, more junior dragon masters rode them as they performed, and Raven found herself envious of them—it had been over a fortnight since she'd been able to fly.

There was Siri, the red-backed female covered in spikes, the smallest but most agile of the brood. She'd long been Raven's favorite, her temperament as prickly as her hide, and yet easily subdued by a belly rub and brace of roasted coney. Beside her was Cronus, the dragon usually ridden by Shanolin. The hot-tempered beast was almost as large as Heiron, his grey scales shimmering like silver plate. He obeyed none of the dragon masters but Shanolin, a fact that had always frustrated Raven. No dragon master should have that kind of power. In the center of the formation was the bacon-loving Heiron, Rider's steed of choice. The enormous male struggled with the flying exercises—his own girth getting in his way—but he still managed to pass.

In fact, all twelve of the dragonia performed extremely well during the flying portion of the testing, each passing. This was no surprise. Flying was to dragons what walking was to humans.

Shanolin and Rider marked each dragon's scores on a large board, a line drawn for the passing mark.

Next, they began fire-breathing, which had been the only part of the testing Raven's sister, Fire, had ever really shown interest in. Raven's mouth suddenly felt dry at the memory, and she wished Whisper were here. Her sister, however, still garbed in all black, had refused to attend, calling the event "a farce of epic proportions."

Fire-breathing involved the destruction of various objects, from as small as human dummies, to as large as huge stone structures meant to represent enemy buildings or walls. The larger dragons, like Heiron and Cronus, tended to dominate the destruction of the larger structures, their fires as hot as the sun, oceans of eternal flame, while smaller dragons, like Siri, could form more precise streams of flame, capable of obliterating a smaller object from great distances.

Again, the dragonia as a whole performed well—only one didn't pass. Raven realized that at some point she'd folded her hands together, her dueling grips locked together in a sweaty embrace so tight it was beginning to ache. Slowly, she released them, though her fingers continued to throb.

Was Whisper right? Had she unintentionally agreed to a war if the dragonia passed the testing? As the dragons continued to perform at a high level with each new phase of the examination—ground battle, aerial battle, defense against projectiles, etc.—her unease grew.

And then it was over. Raven was biting her lip so hard she could taste blood. The crowd was roaring, whipped into a frenzy by the monstrous beasts' performance. The dust began to settle as Shanolin and Rider completed the final tallies, taking into account each dragon's performance in each area of testing.

Raven saw the moment Rider realized the truth, her dark cheeks paling.

They'd passed. Not just Heiron, who had, once again, achieved the highest score.

All of them.

They'd all passed.

Before Raven could consider the ramifications of such a surprising result, a messenger approached, marching up the steps and whispering something to Goggin. The large man turned toward her, raising an eyebrow in question: *Can I let him through?*

She nodded, immediately recognizing the young messenger who had delivered the last message. As he approached, his hands holding out another scroll sealed with red wax, her blood ran cold.

The wax, as before, was marked with a sickle.

Sixty-Five

The Southern Empire, Calypso
Roan Loren

As he dismounted, Roan added 'ride on a guanik' to his mental list of Things I Never Want to Do Again. Gingerly, he rubbed his backside, wondering whether he should use his lifemark to heal the numerous bruises. He opted not to, remembering how easily Gwen had discerned his power from just such a frivolous act. At the same time, he wondered whether he would ever be able to sit down again.

Stretching, he scanned the streets of Calypso, surprised at the swell of nostalgia he felt, as if being reunited with an old friend—not that he had any of those, of course. This wasn't just the place he grew up, but the place he'd found himself, the place that started it all. A strange urge to aimlessly wander the streets, haggling with nut roasters and other merchants, tugged at him, but was swiftly chased away by the guanero's firm grip on his elbow, steering him toward the palace gates.

A barked command by two more mounted guanero, and the gates were hauled open by enormous guanik pulling chains.

Inside, the dusty ground was marred and churned by hundreds of guanik footprints. Thick columns set with mosaic tiles of many colors supported a wraparound shelter that offered protection from the harsh sun as one made their way from the gates to the palace entrance. At that point, there were a dozen more pillars, each a work of art. Not gaudy, but beautiful, tasteful, the tiles hand-cut and individually set within the mortar, each placed at the perfect angle to catch the sunlight, giving them the appearance of sparkling drops of dew.

Roan wondered whether anyone ever appreciated them anymore. He suspected not. From his experience, Calypsian royalty were like that, aloof, arrogant to a fault, not of the people, but *above* the people.

He hoped to use this weakness against the empress.

Inside the atrium, the art continued. Each sandstone wall was inlaid with tiles, forming images from Calypsian life: the guanero astride their guanik, marching through the streets; an empress standing atop one of the pyramids, kneeling in prayer to the gods; the Unburning Tree, radiant, gods-blessed.

Roan looked away, focusing on the alternating black and white tiles beneath his feet. They turned left, the open-air corridor providing a stunning view of the pyramids, which rose like perfectly formed mountain peaks stabbing at the sky. In the red afternoon light, their shadows stretched long and thin, dark fangs splitting the Southron peninsula to shreds.

They turned left again, and the guanero stopped, holding Roan back by tightening his grip. Before him was a broad area ending at three steps and a small dais. Atop the platform were four chairs—thrones. The one in the direct center was the largest and most impressive, scaled like dragon's hide, the maw of a winged beast rising from the back.

The dragon throne, Roan thought.

It was also the only seat occupied, its resident studying an unfurled sheet of parchment intently, her blue-black hair cut short.

The guanero cleared his throat, and the woman looked up, her dark eyes darting to Roan. For the briefest of moments, Empress Raven Sandes looked deeply perturbed. The moment passed as she sat up, straightening her back, rolling the scroll and tucking it away at her side. "Who is this?" she asked. She studied him with interest, as one might inspect an unusual insect alighting on a flower. Her eyes were intelligent, and Roan noticed how she picked out details: the guanero's grip on Roan's elbow; his lack of belongings, other than a small satchel; the dust on his boots and trousers, evidence of a long journey.

The guanero spoke: "He crossed the bridge early this morning. I was tempted to toss him in the dungeons, but he claims to have information you might be interested in."

"What information?"

"He was unwilling to share the details with anyone save you, but it's in regards to the eastern defenses at Ferria. I don't know whether to believe him, but I didn't want to risk it given the present…situation."

"You've done well in bringing him to me. Thank you." Her gaze drifted back to Roan. "Approach."

In tandem, they moved forward, the short distance feeling like a great journey under the shrewd stare of the empress. A few steps before the dais, they stopped. "Your name?" the empress asked.

In the unpredictable manner of memories, Roan was unexpectedly taken back to the first time he encountered Gareth Ironclad, how he'd dodged the very same question with quips and ridiculous banter. It almost made him laugh. Instinctively, however, he knew that such a tactic would not be nearly as effective with this ruler. The Sandes were known to be serious women, quick to anger and action. "May we speak alone?" Roan asked.

Raven Sandes' eyebrows slowly stretched toward her brow. "You would leave me without the protection of my man?"

"I am unarmed and not prone to violence—in fact, I abhor it. And, from what I hear, you are more than capable of defending yourself."

"True, but I am also no fool. If you prefer to speak in privacy, there are other ways. He will stopper his ears." The man didn't look happy about it, but he marched over to a small stone shelf secured to the wall, where a clay dish sat. From it he withdrew two balls of a waxy material, twirling them between his thumb and forefinger. He plugged each ball into his ears, pressing them firmly to flatten them.

"Does that satisfy you?" Raven asked.

Roan nodded. "I am Roan Loren," he said, angling his lips away from his chaperone so they couldn't be read.

He'd expected shock, or denial maybe, or even anger. Instead, all Roan got was a thin smile and a raised eyebrow. "Indeed," Raven said. "You certainly fit the profile. And there have been rumors…"

"There have?" Roan immediately wished the words back—any control of the conversation he'd begun with was now lost.

"Of course. With the stream network expanding every day, word travels fast across the realm. You have been missing for a long time, son of Gill."

"I was here, in Calypso. Well, for most of my life."

"Right under our noses, it seems. And then?"

He'd have to leave some gaps in the narrative, but hopefully they would go unnoticed. "I decided to see the world. I headed east."

"You crossed the Scarra?"

He shook his head. "Via boat. I ended up in the Barren Marshes, accidentally. It was there I was taken prisoner."

"By whom?"

"Gareth Ironclad."

She pursed her lips, as if he'd spoken a vile word. "Go on."

He continued with his story, leaving out crucial details, like his fatemark and what he'd done at Raider's Pass—how he'd saved Gareth. He ended with the same lie about how the easterners had released him to spy for them, first in the west and then the south.

Raven said, "You lie well. There is truth to your story, but not all of it. Why should I believe anything you say next?"

"You are a wise empress," Roan said, trying to mask his surprise at having been discovered so easily. Where was the Sandes' arrogance he'd been counting on? Thus far he'd seen only a shrewd, reasonable young woman. A different tactic was necessary. "I have no love for the easterners. They are warmongering bastards intent on controlling the land from east to west, north to south."

"And what would you call the Calypsians? We don't exactly have a history of peace either."

Time to test the waters. "I choose the lesser of evils whenever I can."

His words, as he'd suspected they would, had the intended result. Raven laughed loudly. "An unusual strategy, that one. Insulting the Empress of Calypso."

"I only want to save Calypso from utter annihilation."

Her laugh dried up. "Speak your mind or be gone!" she said, anger blazing across her face. *Ahh*, he thought. *There you are.*

"You are planning to attack Ferria, correct?" It was a guess, perhaps a longshot, but with the east harassing the Calypsian borders, eventually the empire would have no choice but to hit back, and they weren't the kind of people to pull punches. They would go for the heart.

She blinked and he knew his conjecture was on point. Even if the decision to go to war hadn't been made, it *had* been discussed. "You know nothing."

"I know that an attack on Ferria is the worst decision you can make." Even as Roan spoke the words he felt the futility of them. Had words ever stopped a war? The violence that had become a part of daily life in the Four Kingdoms felt like a wriggling snake in his grasp.

"Why?"

Roan held his breath for a second, then slowly released it. "I'm willing to trade my information."

She licked her lips thoughtfully. "I could have you locked up. An enemy prince falls into my lap, what did you expect me to do?"

"You won't do that. If you've heard rumors of my reappearance in the west, then you also know Rhea's stranglehold on the throne is complete. I have been away from Knight's End for too long—I have no power there. And my sister would rather hang herself than pay a ransom for my life. If you lock me up, the information will be locked up with me."

"You sound very certain of yourself."

The comment gave Roan pause. It was true. *When did I become so confident? When I healed Gareth? When, against all odds, Rhea released me to find my destiny in the south?* Roan knew there was an unseen hand at work, both in his life and in the broader Four Kingdoms. For some reason, that knowledge calmed the inner storm that had raged inside him from the moment he ran away from the only home he'd ever known. With a start, he realized the empress was staring at him, waiting for a response. She was frowning.

"I, well, yes. There is little certainty in this world, but I know I have a place in it, just not the one everyone expects from a prince."

Her eyes drilled into him, and Roan got the distinct impression she was looking at him like a puzzle to be solved. "What do you desire? Wealth? Land? A position in my empire? Those are mere trifles to an empress of Calyp."

Roan shook his head. "I care not for such things. I require nothing so grandiose. Simply safe passage to Citadel and an irrevocable pass to enter the archives, coming and going as I please."

Again, that look. "A strange request, prince of the west, but one I can hardly deny. There is nothing in Citadel but dusty, moth-eaten tomes and my dusty, moth-eaten Aunt Windy. It is done. But know one thing: If you cross me, there will be consequences. The Sandes have long memories. Now tell me what you know."

Roan paused for effect, clinging to this penultimate moment, where, once again, fate or luck or something greater seemed to push him forward, either toward victory or a great precipice. Then he said, "If you attack Ferria, your entire force will be destroyed."

Sixty-Six

The Southern Empire, Calypso
Raven Sandes

Raven felt like her enemies were encircling her, their blades jabbing for her throat. More concerning was the fact that each of her foes seemed to be cloaked in mist, unidentifiable.

The second note she'd received had been more specific than the last:

Renounce the war with the east before the moons kiss or Whisper's life is forfeit.

She hid her feelings, however, behind a mask of indifference, flicking a bored hand in Roan Loren's direction, as if talk of the annihilation of her people was as uninteresting as talk of the weather. "Ever heard of the Dragon Massacre?" she asked.

"Of course," Roan said. "More than half a century ago. The Calypsians were defeated in Ferria."

"Pushed back, yes. Defeated, no. Our dragonia laid waste to the Iron City. Thousands of easterners—humans and Orians alike—were slaughtered. It was one of the single greatest military victories in modern history."

Though he tried to hide it, Raven could see the disgust written all over his face. *I abhor violence*, he'd said. "Exactly," Roan said, and something about the calm with which he spoke gave her pause. Did he truly know something she did not? "It was because of the Dragon Massacre that Ferria's defenses were improved."

"Improved how?"

"Traps. Dragon-proofing. That sort of thing."

"Dragon-*proofing*?" This fool had clearly never seen a dragon in action.

"I can give you all the boring details if you want. But the moral of the story is that attacking Ferria is a bad idea."

Whisper's life is forfeit...renounce the war...before the moons kiss...

If only it was that easy. "What would you have me do?"

"Be patient. Let the easterners come to you. Fight them on your terms." She could see the tension in Roan's body, like his very existence hinged on her decision. Why was he so intent on delaying war? It felt strange that this western prince's goals seemed precariously close to aligning with her own. She wanted more than anything to hold back the Calypsian strength, to force the easterners to enter the desert, which would surely become their tomb. But, despite being a Sandes, a Southron empress, sometimes her actions were out of her control.

"Thank you," she said evenly. "I shall consider your advice. Now take your leave of Calypso. I shall have orders prepared for your safe arrival in Citadel."

Roan looked surprised at her response, almost like he'd expected the entire encounter to be fraught with risk. *Let him be surprised. I shall have him watched like a hawk. Whatever he seeks in the City of Wisdom will be mine.* "Thank you," he said, turning stiffly.

The guanero seemed to realize the private conversation was over, fumbling to retrieve the wax from his ears. He looked disappointed when the empress handed down her orders, but didn't argue. "As you wish."

With that, they departed, Roan offering a final glance over his shoulder before vanishing around the bend.

Exhausted by her façade of self-control, Raven slumped into the seat, wishing, not for the first time, that the throne was more comfortable. She reached back and plucked the scroll from her side, accidentally chipping away a portion of the bloody wax that was still affixed to its edge. She reread the message, though she'd already memorized it.

And, for the tenth time, she did the math in her head. The moon god and goddess would kiss soon, in just over a fortnight, sealing Whisper's fate if she didn't find a way to stop whomever was sending these messages.

In the meantime, she would delay the war as long as possible. A difficult task, especially now that the dragonia had passed the testing. The pressure was building; Raven could feel it like a great weight on her chest, forcing the air from her lungs.

The war council would meet again the following morning, but first Raven needed a distraction, else she would never be

451

able to sleep. She stood, heading for the largest of the great pyramids, known as Calyppa:

The home of the dragonia.

With ravenous delight, Siri gobbled up the morsels Raven tossed her. As each rabbit reached its peak, fire burst from the young dragon's maw, blackening the meat before it slipped between her rows of dark fangs. She stretched her sinewy red-scaled neck appreciatively, crunching loudly.

Raven smiled at the ease with which she could satisfy the dragon. Later she would give Siri a belly rub to complete her reward for performing so well in the testing. If only humans were as easily placated. Ever since the testing was complete, rallies had been held in the streets, most Calypsians in favor of war, swift and absolute. *First the east,* they shouted, *and then Phanes! Who can defeat the Dragon Empire? None!*

As if winning a war against nations that had stood for hundreds of years was as easily accomplished as crossing the road.

Rider approached, her day's work over; most of the dragons were sleeping or on the verge of it, having been fed and watered after a long day. Though the aging dragon master smiled, Raven had known her long enough to tell when it was forced. Lines of worry cut across Rider's forehead and sprung from the edges of her eyes, as if she'd been frowning for most of the day. She probably had. Raven wondered if she looked just as tired.

"I've been putting in extra time with her," Rider said, gesturing at Siri.

"Thank you," Raven said, genuinely appreciative. "It showed during the testing."

"She's a remarkable creature, as clever as any dragon I've ever trained. I'd bet on her against any of the others."

"Truly? Even Heiron?"

She nodded. "Yes. Don't get me wrong, sheer size and strength matter, but her intelligence is unmatched."

Raven couldn't argue with that. Her belly full, the magnificent beast lay down, her head resting against Raven's side. The message was clear: scratch my chin. Raven complied—one did not argue with a dragon—and soon Siri was purring in contentment.

"Shanolin has been pushing all of the dragons hard," Rider said. Although the dragon master said it casually, Raven could feel the weight behind her words.

"Is that a bad thing?"

Rider started to speak, stopped, and then started again. "No. Not exactly. But his bond with the dragons and their masters feels...different than it used to."

"Different how?"

Rider shook her head. "It's hard to explain. The dragonia favor him—except for Siri and Heiron, of course."

Raven's eyes narrowed. "What are you saying? Speak plainly."

"Keep him on a short tether," Rider said. "He's dangerous."

"That's absurd," Raven said. "He's worked for my family for three decades."

"Yes. For your mother."

"And then my sister. And now me."

"It's probably nothing," Rider said. "The testing has me on edge."

Raven sighed and rested her hand on the dragon master's arm. "I'm sorry. I trust your council. I will tread carefully around Shanolin. You need not fear: He will not pressure me into any decisions I do not want to make."

Rider's body language softened, as if satisfied by the response. "What are we going to do?" she said, a jarring reminder of the next day's war council.

Raven glanced around, making certain the other dragon masters had left for the day, especially Shanolin. She lowered her voice. "We delay," she said. "If the guanero succeed in the border skirmishes, that will give us reason enough to be patient."

Rider nodded. "And if they're not successful?"

"How long will it take to prepare the dragonia for war?"

Rider shrugged. "A week perhaps. A fortnight at the most. No one expected them to pass the testing this early, not even Shanolin. Battle armor must be constructed. Even finding enough leather will be a challenge."

"Good," Raven said, nodding. It would have to be enough time. Uncovering her sister's would-be assassins was her priority. Only then could she deal with Roan Loren's warning. Not that she was particularly concerned about the eastern defenses. There was only so much one could do to fortify against dragons.

Still, prudence told her to be cautious, even when everyone else, save Rider, seemed ready to rush to war.

Once more, she gave Siri a scratch.

The animal purred in delight.

Sixty-Seven

The Southern Empire, north of Calypso
Roan Loren

Truth be told, Roan hadn't expected his meeting with Raven Sandes to go as smoothly as it had. At best, he'd expected to be thrown into the dungeons, if only because he was a Loren. At worst, he thought he'd be killed on the spot.

Instead, he was, despite his objections, once again on the back of a guanik, its thick, bony hide adding bruises to his bruises. Unable to take it anymore, he slowly healed the wounds, letting his lifemark pulse slowly on his chest.

He'd been handed off to another guanero, a giant of a man who'd introduced himself as Goggin. "You must be an important man, indeed," he'd barked. When Roan had inquired why, the man had only laughed loudly. Goggin rode the most monstrous guanik Roan had ever seen, its clawed feet leaving deep impressions in the hard ground. Anytime the lizard looked at him, he had the distinct impression it was sizing him up, trying to decide whether it could swallow him whole.

Still, this companion was better than the last one. At least he didn't aim pointy objects at his eyes nor deal in thinly veiled threats. Instead, Goggin preferred stories and japes, most of which centered around his many failed marriages. "Did I ever tell you about my third wife?" the large man asked now, as if they were two old friends shooting the breeze.

Roan counted on his fingers, pretending to seriously consider the question. "No. Your second and fourth, yes, but not your third. That's a story I'd very much like to hear."

"Har! Good man!" Goggin bellowed, slapping his guanik's back. The beast opened its mouth and yawned, as if used to such behavior from its master. "Anyway, here's how we met…"

The long, convoluted story took the better part of the evening, until long after the sun had vanished behind the horizon, leaving a trail of purple-black in its wake. Despite himself, Roan had laughed loudly several times, most notably when wife number three had called Goggin "a bastard of the highest order" and chased him from their dwelling with a scimitar.

"A good woman, she was," Goggin finished, sniffing sadly. "That's one I wish hadn't gotten away." A moment of silence passed slowly. But then he clapped his large hands and said, "Time to make camp and drink the night away!"

Making camp was a loose term which basically involved unfurling bedrolls under the stars. "Too hot for a fire," Goggin declared, handing Roan a heel of warm, spicy bread and a leaf-wrapped strip of spiced meat.

Roan bit into the bread, relishing the yeasty, zesty taste he'd enjoyed as a youth. There were a lot of things about Calypso he could complain about, but not the food. "You can have my meat," he said handing the leaves back to Goggin.

The man looked as if he'd been given the sun itself. "Did I mention you're a good man?" he said.

"Once or twice," Roan said, though Goggin didn't seem to hear, already chewing loudly, washing down each bite with a swill from a water skin. Roan recognized the distinct odor, sharp and spicy as it filled his nostrils. *Simpre*, a strong drink served in most taverns. Most Calypsians enjoyed a taste or two with a meal, but this man slugged back mouthfuls like water. When he'd drained the last few drops, he burped loudly. Then he reached into his pack and retrieved a second skin. This one he emptied into a clay bowl, which he placed in front of his guanik. The beast lapped at the drink greedily.

"Monster likes a bit of simpre now and then," Goggin explained.

Although Roan thought this man's definition of "a bit" was a little off, he kept that to himself. Then, inexplicably, the guanero extracted a third skin of strong drink from his pack, handed it to Roan, and said, "Drink!" with all the gusto of a round-bellied tavern keeper.

Roan sniffed the skin, recoiling as the acrid smell assaulted his nostrils. If anything, this was even stronger than normal simpre.

Goggin bellowed out a laugh, slapping his thighs. "Good stuff, eh? My own recipe, brew it at home. My fifth wife grew tired of the smell, so she took off. Chased her all the way to

Teragon I did! Har!" His expression turned serious once again, and, in a lower voice, he said, "Now drink, son, the night's a-wasting."

As politely as he could, Roan said, "Thank you, but I'll stick with water."

"Bah! We're off duty now and you've been as dry a companion as the dust beneath our feet. Drink or wrestle me, those are your choices."

Roan gaped at him, uncertain as to whether he was being serious. Wrestling a man as large as Goggin would result in his bones breaking in several places, so, holding his breath, he took a small sip of the dark liquid.

fireburnscorchacidFIRE!

With a gasp, he spewed a thin stream of liquid into the dust.

Goggin roared with laughter.

Roan couldn't help his own laughter, which poured from him like rain from a gray cloud. And, he had to admit, Goggin's simpre recipe was damn good.

He took another sip; this time, he swallowed it, relishing the burn.

Half the night later, a large portion of the simpre was gone, but both men were very much awake.

"That group looks like an ore-monkey," Roan said, pointing at a cluster of stars in the southern portion of the night sky. He felt warm all over, both giddy and calm at the same time. He was fairly certain that if he were to cut his skin, he would bleed simpre rather than blood. The thought made him giggle and then hiccup, which made Goggin slap him on the back as if he were choking.

"It also looks like my ex-wife," Goggin declared.

"Which one?" Roan asked.

He'd meant it as a serious question, he was having trouble keeping track of all the ex-Lady Goggins, but his question only made the man burst into laughter once more. "I'm not sure," the large man said. "They all blur together these days. Strong women with angry faces. Har!"

Roan had learned much about the man he traveled with, though he wasn't certain how much he would remember in the morn. For one, Goggin wasn't just another guanero, but the captain of all guanero, a prestigious position on par with the shiva, or master of order in Calypso. No wonder he'd made the comment earlier about Roan being an important person. Still, it surprised him that the empress would provide him with such a high-ranking escort rather than just sending a low-level foot soldier.

The captain of the guanero slumped back onto his bedroll and yawned—it seemed the strange night had finally come to an end. A moment later, he was snoring.

Roan stretched and unleashed a yawn himself. Staring at the sky, he wondered whether Gareth, high in his tower prison, was looking out at the same stars. At the same time, he felt bad that Gwen, confined to the dank, dark dungeons of Knight's End, wouldn't be able to see any stars at all.

He sighed, watching the moons continue their nightly jaunt across the sky. Their paths would come close, but not cross. A near miss. Soon they would kiss, as the expression went. A week perhaps, or a fortnight at most.

By then I will be able to help my friends, Roan vowed, even as he drifted off into a simpre-induced sleep, as deep and restful as any in recent memory.

Sixty-Eight
The Southern Empire, Calypso
Raven Sandes

"Whisper," Raven said, gently stroking her sister's shoulder. Dancing lines of sunlight were just beginning to form between the hanging guanik bones threaded across the opening to the sleeping quarters.

Her sister stirred, her lips murmuring nonsense in her sleep.

She looked so...peaceful. Raven wished she could let her sleep, but they didn't live in that kind of a world. Plus, they were Sandes. Sleep was a luxury they could scarce afford.

I need to prepare her. She needs to be ready to rule. War was coming, and Raven couldn't ensure her own survival. The thought made her feel strangely calm. *Am I prepared to die for my people, my country, my sister?*

Yes, she knew. *Yes, yes, yes.*

Finally, Whisper's eyelids fluttered open. "What is it?"

"The war council will soon convene. You need to be there."

"No." The answer was swift, certain, final.

"Whisper—"

"I said no," Whisper said. "It's not up for discussion. You can force me if you wish. Otherwise, go away." Unlike the other day, when she'd sounded older than her years, now she came across as a petulant child. *She is caught between girlhood and womanhood*, Raven mused. She thought about how her maata had handled she and Fire growing up.

"You have a voice," she said. "All you have to do is use it."

Whisper blinked. Clearly, she'd expected to be forced. "I've made my opinions very clear," she said slowly.

Progress. "To me, yes, but not to the council. There, you've been as silent as a sleeping lamb. They all think you're in shock, voiceless and broken."

"My voice works fine. And I'm not broken. I'm hurt, but not shattered like everyone thinks."

"I know. I don't think that."

"Aren't you hurt?" The question was so simple, so innocent, and yet it burned through Raven like a hot knife.

She'd watched Fire die, watched her burst into flames in her final act. First their mother, then Fire...yes, she was hurt. The only difference was that an empress couldn't waver, not for one second—her mother had taught her that.

"Like you, I'm hurt but not broken."

"You don't look hurt."

"I'm a Sandes."

Whisper released an exasperated breath. "People love to say that. Like a name defines who a person is."

Raven frowned. "It does. It must."

462

Whisper shook her head, her slightly mussed hair shifting from side to side. "I reject that. We can be better. We can seek peace. There doesn't have to be any more death."

Raven's heart broke slightly. Despite all the tragedy Whisper had been forced to endure in the short years of her life, she still clung to the hope that they could simply live their lives. Sniffing flowers, painting, playing games, ruling with feather-soft wings and not the hardened, clawed wings of the dragonia. And although Raven knew her sister was being naïve, she allowed herself to dream of such a life. Just for a moment...

And then gone. "Speak your mind at the war council," Raven said. She stood and left.

"Shiva," Raven said as the man entered her quarters.

The dark-eyed master of order in Calypso bowed stiffly. "Your Magnificence, I received your orders to attend you in your quarters, but I must voice my objection. This is highly unusual. People will think—"

"Were you seen?" Raven asked.

"Of course I was seen, there are a hundred guards between—"

"Good. Let them think what they want. Rumors will shift with the desert sands no matter what we do."

But—"

She held up a hand and he snapped his mouth shut. "If the guards believe you are coming here for another reason, a more *scandalous* reason..."—she offered a seductive smile to illustrate her point—"...then they won't suspect the *real* reason."

His brows rose. "Which is?"

"I need you to be Whisper's personal guard, but secretly. No one can know that you're protecting her—she most of all."

The shiva shook his head. "I don't understand."

"Will you protect her?"

"Yes, of course, but it's highly unusual. I am bound to Calypso, not to the throne."

"Calypso *is* the throne."

"Why me? You have a thousand palace guards at your disposal."

"I don't trust them."

"Then Goggin..."

"The commander has another mission. You're my last option. Please."

His lips pursed, but it wasn't a rejection. "I will do this thing. Whisper is safe with me."

"Thank you." She spoke the last two words tersely, blasting from the room and into the hot morning air. Inside she was thinking *Thank the gods.*

Raven tapped her fingers on the scaled arm of her throne.

Her war council was smaller than before. Goggin was notably absent, escorting Roan Loren to Citadel, as she had commanded. His enormous form usually took up half the room. Ponjut was on her mission to the Scarra with her guanero. Also, Whisper had yet to arrive. Twice Shanolin had cleared her throat, anxious to begin the council. Twice Raven had ignored her. Whisper would come. She *had* to come.

And then she was there, sweeping through the private rear entrance and settling into her seat with all the grace of the princess that she was. Unlike the previous times she'd attended the council, her eyes settled not on her feet but on the eyes of each person in attendance, eventually alighting on Raven's.

Raven was barely able to conceal the smile that tried to bloom upon her lips. Whisper nodded once, and Raven returned the gesture before addressing the council.

"As you all know, the dragonia have passed the testing."

"With flying colors, it seems," Shanolin said, beaming. There was a gloating note to his tone.

"So it would seem."

"This changes everything," Shanolin said.

"Does it?"

"Of course, Your Magnificence. With a fully trained dragonia, none can oppose us. Surely you have heard the voices of your people in the streets."

"I have, but Sandes women refuse to be swayed by public opinion."

Shanolin shook his head. "What are you saying?"

"I'm saying we must be patient. Haste will only hasten our demise." Roan's words rattled around her head. *...your entire force will be destroyed.*

Whisper was staring at her, but she refused to meet her gaze, lest she give away the fear she felt every time she looked at her sister. *She thinks I might be killed if we go to war, when in reality it is her life in danger.*

Shanolin, as Raven had expected, refused to be rebuffed so easily. "Haste will catch our enemies off guard. They think they can poke and prod without retribution. They think Sun's and Fire's deaths have weakened us."

"Watch your tongue!"

Raven's eyes snapped to the side, for the rebuke came not from her, but from Whisper, who was on her feet, her eyes fiery and focused. "You will not use the dead as part of your argument for war. You, *dragon master*, do not rule this land. The Sandes do. And as long as we have breath in our lungs, we will not be bullied into action."

Raven would've kissed her sister if they didn't still have an audience. Instead, she watched Shanolin intently. At first, she thought the dragon master might push his luck, diving into another argument, but instead, he bowed his head slightly and said, "I apologize. I am merely anxious for the dragonia to serve the empire." Still, his eyes remained dark, and she thought she could detect a sneer in his tone.

"And they will," Raven said. "In good time. For now, we wait to hear from the guanero sent to the Scarra."

"As you wish—"

Shanolin's deferential response was cut off sharply when the sound of feet slapped the tile floor, coming closer.

All heads turned toward the entrance to the council chambers, where a messenger appeared, his eyes wild with a mixture of excitement and something else.

Fear, Raven realized. *Oh gods.* "Speak," she said. "Please."

He gulped down a breath and then said, "Word has arrived from Kesh. A stream." He paused, swallowing thickly, as if his next words were caught in his throat.

"What has happened?" Raven said, though she already knew.

"The defeat was complete. The guanero sent to the Scarra are dead."

Sixty-Nine
The Southern Empire,
between Calypso and Citadel
Roan Loren

When he opened his eyes, Roan released a sound more animal than human, halfway between a groan and a growl. He jammed his eyelids shut, though the sun, which was already a quarter of the way toward its peak, continued to burn across his vision. His head pounded. His muscles felt weak.

He groan-growled again, wondering whether Gwen would consider it an abuse of power to use his lifemark to cure the aftereffects of a night of drinking. Probably. And yet, there was nothing for it.

As warmth seeped from the three-leafed marking on his chest, the dull throbs in his skull began to lessen, before vanishing completely. His muscles and bones recovered, too, gathering strength like a bucket collects rainwater.

Why had he drunk so much anyway? Why had he drunk at all?

A chuckle answered his question, and when he opened his eyes, Goggin was grinning at him. His eyes were clear and he looked refreshed, seemingly unaffected by their night of madness. "We need to teach your body to hold its drink; I thought you would sleep the entire day. Har! Do not fear, my young friend, a few more nights like that and you will build a tolerance."

Roan didn't want to build a tolerance. He wanted to quit being a fool and get back on track. While he had been drinking himself into oblivion, Gwen and Gareth had been passing another night in captivity. *I'm a damn fool*, he thought. He could almost hear Gwen's answering response: *Yes. Yes, you are.* And Gareth's: *Next time you drink like that, I better get an invitation!*

"How many days until we reach Citadel?"

"Five," Goggin said, and Roan groaned again. "If we're lucky."

Roan massaged his temples, though his headache was long gone.

In the end, it took six days. Or perhaps five and a half, as they arrived at midday.

Each night, Roan had, barely, managed to fight off Goggin's pressure to partake of "the drink of the gods," as the guanero commander liked to call his homemade simpre. He was only granted a reprieve when, finally, on night three the drink ran out. Goggin had tipped the last skin upside-down, peering inside as if someone was playing a nasty trick on him— like maybe the simpre was not gone, but hiding.

"Pity," he'd said, before rolling over and going to sleep. After that, the journey had picked up pace, as they rose earlier and made camp later.

Now, sweat-sheened and dusty, the City of Wisdom appeared in the distance, almost like a mirage, the hot air making its white spires appear to shift and blur.

"Thank the gods," Roan muttered.

"No. Thank me," Goggin said, jabbing a finger in the air.

"Thank you," Roan said. Despite 'the simpre incident,' as he called it, the man had delivered him safely to Citadel, as promised. Twice they'd come across dangerous-looking men pulling carts filled with various knickknacks. But both times the men had given Goggin a quick look and then turned their path in the other direction.

"Banditos," Goggin had said. "Shame they didn't want a fight. I could use the practice."

Roan, on the other hand, had been relieved.

Now, he leaned forward, eager to reach the city that boasted the largest collection of history and books in all the Four Kingdoms. Compared to the Western Archives, it was a vast treasure trove that had the potential to solve the mysteries of Roan's very origin. Gwen's, too, as well as all the fatemarked. Would he learn what really happened to the Western Oracle? And her son? The very thought made him jab his ankles against his guanik's sides, urging it to go faster. The beast glanced back darkly; if anything, it slowed its pace just to spite him. He would be happy to be quit of the temperamental animal.

Slowly, pace by pace, Citadel began to come into focus:

Tall, narrow spires split the sky, their faces as white as the snowy mounts that flanked Raider's Pass in the north. Oddly, the first thought he had was: *I wonder who cleans the outside of those towers?* Beyond the city was a vast body of water, sparkling under the sun—Dragon Bay. His last memory of the sea involved nearly being eaten by dragons after narrowly escaping Plague Island. And then almost drowning. After all that, he'd met Gareth Ironclad. It was almost ironic, in a way, that he would find love so soon after dodging death.

He blinked away the memories, refocusing on the city. Beneath the spires were buildings with arched roofs—also white—an abrupt change to the blocky beige sandstone structures of Calypso with which Roan was so familiar. And then, set between the spires, an impossibly large dome of glass, catching the sun along its edge as it curved into a perfect hemisphere.

"The Citadellian Archives," Roan said, his voice taking on a note of awe.

"Aye," Goggin said. "Also known as A Whole Bunch of Parchment."

Roan glanced at the man, guessing he'd never opened a book in his entire life. "You aren't interested in history?"

"My history, yes. The history of a bunch of dead people? Not so much."

And this, Roan thought, *is the crux of the problem.* Those responsible for leading, for commanding armies, for *ruling,* had no interest in studying the mistakes of their ancestors. The scholars, on the other hand, had their noses stuck so far into their books that they barely noticed the passage of time. The world could be crumbling around them, and they would merely flip to the next page.

471

I must change that, Roan said. *I must be the bridge between the scholars and the leaders.* Only then would things change. Again, he was surprised at his own convictions—not his ideals, which were long-held, but his belief that he *could* change things. Somewhere between leaving Calypso and returning, he'd gone from being a jaded skeptic to a believer. A believer in what, he wasn't certain. But he was determined to find out.

They entered the city just as the sun began its long descent toward evening. Roan immediately noticed how different the city *felt*. There was still a sense of hustle and bustle, aye, but it was muted. People scurried hither and thither, many of them clutching crumpled scrolls to their chests or bags bursting with parchment. Most of them were dark-skinned Calypsians, but Roan also spied several gray-skinned, broad-foreheaded Dreadnoughters, as well as a red-skinned Teran. Some stopped to purchase sustenance from vendors, but they placed their orders with whispers rather than shouts. There was no haggling, only a brief handover of the required number of silver dragons, and then they were on their way.

Roan was shocked that this city was part of the Calypsian Empire. He might've been in a foreign land, for it held none of the familiarity from his childhood.

"Can't even find a decent watering hole," Goggin muttered.

"I'm not thirsty," Roan said. "Nor hungry."

"Nor fun," Goggin said. "Our stay here is going to be dismal indeed."

Roan frowned, tugging his gaze away from the exquisite white buildings long enough to consider Goggin's choice of words. *Our stay.* "You're, um, staying in Citadel? Don't you have training or battles to plan?"

"If only!" the man bellowed, drawing stares from several passersby. "I'm stuck with you for the foreseeable future. Truth be told, I'd rather be pitfighting in Zune!"

Roan looked away. This complicated things. He felt a fool for not realizing that the empress would never allow a western prince the luxury of wandering the archives unchaperoned. But Goggin?

"Do you know the way to the archives?" Roan asked. Now that they were in the city, the rounded buildings and tall spires blocked all view of the massive dome they'd seen from a distance.

Goggin gestured blandly at the people scurrying well clear of their vicious steeds. "Follow the book-heads," he said.

Roan nodded, just noticing that, other than the merchants, everyone was on the move, and all heading in the same direction. No one stopped to eat the food they bought, which all seemed to come attached to long wooden twigs—ideal for snacking on the move. In Calypso, such behavior would be the equivalent of sacrilege—food was meant to be enjoyed over the course of several hours, accompanied by simpre and good conversation.

Also unlike the Calypsian capital city, the roads of Citadel weren't laid out in even blocks, and they weren't sprinkled with dust. Instead, they were white stone blocks that somehow stayed clean, long curving roads occasionally intersected by straight narrow pathways that all seemed to angle in the same general direction. When they reached the first such alley, a bottleneck of pedestrians clogged the entrance, funneling from both directions.

"We'll never get the guanik through there," Goggin said. "At least not without someone losing a limb or two. Har!"

"We can go on foot," Roan suggested hopefully.

"And leave our guanik here? The bookish folk of the City of Wisdom are unaccustomed to handling these leathery monsters. There will be carnage." He paused thoughtfully, as if warming up to the idea because it involved destruction. "Nay. Empress Raven will have my hide."

Roan blew out in frustration. "Then how do we get to the city center?"

"We wait."

As they waited, Goggin procured several bottles of simpre—"Enough to pass a day of boredom," he said, tucking them away in his pouch—and enough food to feed an army. There were fried peppers (on wooden sticks, of course), chunks of braised meat and various grilled vegetables (also on sticks). There were loaves of spicy-sweet bread, a rice dish spiced with mixa and cinnamon, and a variety of nuts roasted with honey. The rice and nuts were the only items not speared by sticks; rather, they came in easy-to-carry paper funnels that could be tipped directly into one's mouth.

Despite his impatience, Roan enjoyed everything, feeling fuller than he had in a long time. To his surprise, Goggin didn't even offer him the simpre, knocking back two bottles on his own. Apparently, he'd finally given up on Roan as a drinking companion.

When they finished, the alleyway had nearly emptied out, like a thin river drying up after the sun comes out.

Goggin grunted. "Single file." He led, entering the road on his massive guanik's back, its sides a hairsbreadth from scraping against the walls. Roan's steed had more room to spare; but still, if anyone tried to pass in the other direction, the logistics would be impossible to manage. True to form, however, traffic seemed to flow only one way this time of day, and they cleared the passage quickly, spilling into a large circular courtyard. From other similar alleys around the edge, more pedestrians trickled forth, each aimed directly at the huge structure in the center.

The Citadellian Archives was a circular building constructed of enormous white stones mortared together. A shaded area ringed the structure, the overhang supported by smooth broad pillars. Above the overhanging stonework was the dome, rising like a giant eye, reaching a point higher than all other buildings in the area, save for the white spires piercing the clear, blue sky.

"Nothing for it," Goggin said, eyeing the archives with the wariness one might exhibit upon seeing an old enemy. His remaining simpre bottles clinked as he steered his guanik toward one of the many entrances. Rather than dismounting at the large, arched entrance, like Roan had expected, Goggin drove his steed inside, nearly trampling a squat, bald man as he skittered out of the way.

Roan, having no other choice—he still didn't truly know how to steer his guanik—fell in behind him.

Inside, wood-paneled walls blocked further entry. One of them slid closed behind the bald man as he slipped past. Sitting before the panels was another man, this one at a desk cluttered with numerous unrolled scrolls of parchment held down at their corners by smooth white stones.

He stood, looking deeply perturbed by the presence of two very large animals in his atrium. His dark head was ringed by a layer of gray hair.

"No beasts allowed," he said sternly, pushing a pair of spectacles down his nose to glare at them. He pointed at a sign, which, sure enough, echoed his sentiments. Roan wondered how often ignorant guanero rode their guanik inside the archives.

"I'm here on urgent business from the empress herself," Goggin said. He yawned, looking bored.

"I do not answer to the empress, but to her aunt."

"Aye. Windy," Goggin said. "Go get her."

"Excuse me?" The man removed his spectacles and waved them at the guanero commander. "There is protocol for such things. Appointments to be made, rooms to be prepared, preparations to be..."—he seemed to search for a word, coming up with nothing—"...prepared.

"Or you could just get her before Monster gets hungry." Hearing its name, the guanik licked its lips with its thin snake-like tongue.

The man's righteous anger shuddered away. "I cannot leave my post. I shall send her a message, though tracking Windy down is sometimes more difficult than lassoing the stars."

With that, he sat back down, replacing his glasses on his nose, peering at a paper with a complex-looking map with strange markings. He reached for one of the panels, opening it to reveal a mess of cords, each designated by a different letter and number. Searching through them, he found the one he was looking for, giving it a slight tug. Nothing happened, but he offered them a satisfied smirk, closed the panel, and then opened a book.

Goggin and Roan stared at him in silence for a moment. *Is something supposed to happen?* Roan wondered. A scholarly-looking woman entered behind them, flinched when she saw the guanik, and, thinking better of it, retreated. Casually,

Goggin extracted a bottle of simpre from his pack, popping the cork out. The man looked up from his book.

"No food or drink in the archives," he said.

Goggin ignored him, taking a swig, smacking his lips in satisfaction. He plugged the cap back in the bottle and returned it to his supply.

"I don't know who you think you are—"

"Tired of waiting," Goggin said, slinging himself off his mount, landing with a heavy thud. "Did I ever tell you about my first wife?" Roan couldn't tell whether he was talking to him or the gatekeeper, so he didn't respond.

The man stood again, blocking Goggin's path. "You can't go in there without a pass."

In one swift motion, Goggin yanked two creased sheets of parchment from his pouch, handing them to the man. From a distance, Roan could just make out sentences formed in stiff lettering and an official-looking hand-drawn symbol—the red sun rising over a dragon.

While the man perused the passes, Goggin slung open one of the wooden panels, which slid to the side to reveal a narrow staircase.

"Protocols!" the man screamed, his face darkening in anger. "You can't go in there until I have cleared your arrival and entered your names on the official register…"

He trailed off as footsteps announced the arrival of at least two newcomers from the stairway. Goggin stepped back to let them pass. They halted on the landing. A boy and a girl. There was something familiar about them…

"We're here to escort the commander and his guest to Second Daughter Windy," the girl said, seemingly unruffled by the beasts staring at her.

477

Roan's eyes narrowed as he tried to place her in his memory. She was taller than the boy, whose appearance was similar enough to hers that he had to be her brother, or at least a close relation. Her dark eyes were intense, steely, and her long arms emerging from her white tunic looked strong.

A flesh of memory, there and gone. A game played on a dusty field. A girl, faster than the others, kicking the sack toward the goal. Knocked over by a taller, bigger boy.

Oh gods.

Her broken leg.

I healed her.

But no. This is impossible. Impossible impossible impossible...

His guardian, Markin Swansea, had punished him. Had punished *them.*

Roan remembered the smell like it was yesterday, bile creeping up the back of his throat. He remembered the bones, set in a pit of ash.

For, standing before him in this most unexpected of places was the dead girl and her dead brother. The ghosts that had haunted him for years.

Seventy

The Southern Empire,
approaching Pirate's Peril
Grey Arris

Kyla aimed her kiss for his lips, but he turned his head, taking it on the cheek.

The ship was at anchor, bobbing slightly on a calm sea, the sails lowered and hanging limp. The sight of land was now visible without the spyglass, a large wall of rock cliffs flanked by a smaller rock isle beside it. As they stood beside each other against the railing, the sun dipped into the horizon, a perfect egg yolk about to be cracked.

A raucous laugh burst from the other end of the deck, likely because of some jape either the captain or Shae had made. The atmosphere was that of a carnival, as if they were about to drink and make merry, and not serve themselves up to a ruthless band of pirates.

"This is madness," Grey muttered.

Kyla grabbed his chin with a strong hand, turning his face toward her. This time her aim was true, and his defenses crumbled as he fell into it. *Gods* she tasted so good, of mint tea and rosewater. Grey could drink her in for the rest of his life and still be thirsty.

"You don't fight fair," he said, when they finally broke away, leaving him breathless.

"Would you rather I did?" Her lips curled seductively and he felt a stirring in his loins. Sometimes he hated how *easy* it was for her to manipulate him. Other times he loved it, relished it even.

"I just wish you'd discussed it with me first," he said. He tried not to look at her lips for fear that any resolve he had left would melt into a puddle.

"I didn't know until today, I swear it, Grey. The old man came up with the idea all on his own. Even got the sailors on board without my knowing."

He loved her earnestness, the way her words slipped out like gentle exhalations.

"This smells of Shae," he said.

Kyla laughed. "She's a clever one. Probably planted the thought in Da's head and made him think he came up with it on his own." More laughs from the men, accompanied by the clinking of bottles. He saw two of the seamen lift Shae onto their shoulders, parading her around as she giggled. Seeing her like this she looked so innocent, child-like. She was a girl caught between reality and dream, the simple pleasures of life and a destiny so mysterious Grey regularly pinched himself to ensure he was awake.

"She's too clever by half," he muttered. "I just want to keep her safe. I told you about the promise I made my parents. And this quest is the opposite of safe."

"Even a mama bird must eventually push her babies out of the nest."

"I'm not a bird nor a mother," Grey said.

Ignoring his negativity, Kyla said, "Besides, we have a plan, Grey."

His eyes darted to hers. "We do?"

"Of course. This time it was *my* idea." She kissed him on the cheek, her lips as warm as sunshine on his skin. "We're not going to be the lamb wandering into the lion's den."

"We're not?"

A laugh, like music. "No, Grey. We're going to be the lion."

The disguises were ridiculous. *And yet*, Grey thought, *they might just work.*

Faded belt buckles had been polished to a shine, stained britches and shirts had been cleaned and pressed, several eye patches had even been created from bits of old leather boots, tied with twine around the volunteering men's heads. Smithers's crew was also so weathered and hard-looking that they could easily pass for pirates, criminals. "Bailed most of 'em outta the stocks, I did," the captain had admitted to Grey.

The captain himself was an impressive sight, bearing a large patch over his left eye, his floppy cap replaced with a broad, tall captain's hat, his white shirt spotless, his silver buckles shining on his black belt, and his boots spit-polished. And, of course, he already had the bravado of a captain, the growled orders, the barked commands. "Man the decks, ye witless dogs!" he shouted, stomping about the decks to laughter. "Earn yer keep, ye lazy lubbards!"

Kyla hadn't been overlooked, though Grey was less comfortable with her attire. Her clothing had been altered, her blouse stretched to sit near the top of each arm, revealing her brown, glowing shoulders. The neckline had been cut, dipping precariously low. Her skirt had been shortened to display long, slender legs. Even her hair was remade, forced to obey a comb and brush, hanging lazily over her ears and eyes rather than springing out in all directions. Grey wasn't uncomfortable with her garb because it showed off her beauty—he could look at her all day—but because he feared what a lusty gang of pirates might do when they saw her.

Shae, on the other hand, was dressed differently, much to Grey's relief. Though she was fast becoming a woman, she donned a shapeless white frock (Kyla's purity dress for when they docked in major western cities, like Knight's End, where it was required) and pinned her hair chastely to her scalp. Grey figured she could pass for a maiden eleven name days old if she was a day. That suited him just fine.

"We don't have any weapons," Grey said, when all other preparations had been made.

"Course we do," Smithers growled, still fully immersed in his role as pirate captain. "We're bloodthirsty pirates."

As two men were sent below to retrieve whatever weapons he was referring to, Kyla explained. "Part of our trade route rounds the southern tip of Phanes. From there we make our way to the Spear so we can access several of the eastern villages along its banks. The risk of interest from pirates is small, but still possible, so we are prepared."

Grey soon saw what she meant, as the men returned lugging an enormous chest. They were breathing heavily and their faces were red. Smithers said, "There we are," and opened it. Inside were a dozen longswords, at least that many smaller blades, and even a long, curving scimitar, which the captain picked up. He was no longer using his stick, which seemed more of a *beating* rod than an aid to help him walk. He brandished the sword toward Grey, threateningly. "Cross me and I'll chop ye to bits an' feed ye to me sharks!"

Grey carefully arced his way around the captain; he was certain the man had never used such a weapon in his life and he was likely to lose his other hand if he got too close. The other men were raiding the chest, choosing their own weapons. Kyla found a small but sharp knife, which she sheathed and tucked away into her low-cut corset, which almost made Grey faint with desire. Shae found a shortsword and lifted the hem of her long dress to strap it to her calf.

Grey eyed the remaining weapons, which included one longsword, and a strange-looking knife no one had wanted. He grabbed the sword, but Kyla gripped his hand and said, "No," prying his fingers apart so he'd drop it back in the chest.

She reached down and handed him the knife. "Is this a comment on my manhood?" he quipped.

She leaned closer, brushing lightly against him. No one else was watching, too focused on getting a feel for their weapons. "Do you want it to be?" she whispered. When he leaned closer, desperate to taste her, she slapped him lightly on the cheek. "Don' git fresh with me, ye scoundrel!" she snapped.

He flinched back, so shocked by her reaction and the brilliant impersonation of her father that he couldn't hold back his laugh.

"See?" she said. "No reason to worry about me amongst the pirates. I'll be fine."

In a small way, it did comfort him. He nodded. More carefully this time, he inspected the blade she'd chosen for him, turning it over in his hand.

"It was my grandfather's," she said.

The knife, though short, had two blades, both in need of a sharpening, but strong and solid-looking. The handle was carved from some kind of bone. "Where did he get this?"

"It was a gift," she explained. "From a northerner. You might've heard of him. King Wilhelm Gäric."

Grey looked at the blade with newfound respect. "The Undefeated King? That is a royal gift indeed. Who was your grandfather to earn such a reward?"

She lowered her voice, her eyes darting to her father, who was still distracted by his scimitar. "Only one of the most well-regarded merchants in the Four Kingdoms," she said. "*The Jewel* was his ship. Though it might not look it now, it was once the pride of the merchant vessels. He was the preferred supplier for both the western and northern thrones, providing exotic spices from Teragon and many of the Crimean tapestries that still adorn their royal halls. King Gäric gave him this knife as a token of appreciation. The handle is carved from mamoothen tusk, the blade forged from Orian ore. A rare combination. Before he died, my grandfather passed it on to my father."

"Why is it gathering dust at the bottom of a chest?"

Once more, Kyla's eyes darted to her father. "For a while, my father maintained his father's reputation. But after my mother died..."

Grey remembered her stories about her mother, what her death had done to them both. He nodded. She didn't need to explain further. Smithers had struggled, his business faltering with him. Repairs to the ship had been ignored, his top sailors had left for higher-paying gigs, and Kyla had gotten pregnant.

Somewhere along the lines, he'd likely thrown the priceless knife into the chest, closing the lid on a legacy he'd rather not remember.

"I'm sorry," Grey said.

"It's fine," Kyla said, though it was clear by her expression that parts of her had been stripped away by the experience. She began to busy herself with a leather belt, wrapping it around the knife's bone handle.

"Hey," Grey said, trying to cheer her up. "At least it led us to this place, where we get to play pirates!"

Glancing once more at her father, she pecked Grey on the lips and said, "Thank you." She began strapping the knife to his stump, cinching it tightly.

"For what?" He watched her agile fingers work, longing to hold them, to kiss them.

"For saving me."

He wondered if she knew that she, in a way, had saved him too.

"There," she said, retracting her hands. "What do you think?"

He looked at his useless stump, which was now a weapon. He moved it around and the knife followed. "It's perfect," he said, though he hoped he wouldn't have to use it.

Grey cleared his throat, feeling awkward all of a sudden. He'd been meaning to talk to Kyla about his past, but the time had never felt right. Now they were almost out of time. She noticed his discomfort and said, "What is it?"

"Back in Knight's End…"

She straightened up, pinning him with a stare. "You *never* talk about Knight's End."

He forced out a laugh. "I know. I'm sorry. It's just…I'm embarrassed. I was a different person back then."

She took his hand, smiling. "We all *change*, Grey. I don't care about the past, only what I see in front of me. But if it would make you feel better to tell me something, I will listen without judgment."

So he told her the parts of the story he'd always left out. He told her about Grease Jolly, the thief he had once been. And, finally, he told her about Rhea, and how he and Shae had ended up in their situation in the first place.

When he finished, Kyla pulled back, dropping his hand. *Shite*, he thought. *Maybe that was a bad idea.* But then her eyes lit up and she said, "Grey! This is fantastic! I have a plan. But it'll involve you becoming Grease Jolly again, I hope that won't be a problem?"

Seventy-One

The Southern Empire, Phanes, Phanea
Bane Gäric

"Falcon Hoza," Bane whispered, gesturing surreptitiously at the young man riding a chariot through the sunken canyon streets of Phanea. Chavos followed the man with his eyes, but said nothing.

Bane watched the new emperor, too, trying to read him. Was he a bad man, like his father, Vin Hoza, had been? Was he a warmonger and a slave lover? Was he ravenous to expand his power and territory, as most of the rulers in the Four Kingdoms seemed to be?

His father certainly was, which was why Bane had been forced to kill him. Because Emperor Vin Hoza was slavemarked, his death had instantly released all of the slaves from the mystical nature of their bondage. Then again, it hadn't really changed anything—they were all still slaves—which told Bane much of what he needed to know about Falcon Hoza.

On his chariot, his face powdered, his skin gleaming with gemstones, he was an iron-fisted emperor in every sense of the word.

Bane was tempted to vanish and reappear on the chariot behind him and slit his throat, but something about it seemed too barbaric for this stage in his evolution. He was beginning to hone his skills, his methods, and he needed the people to start seeing him the way he saw himself—as a savior.

Chavos was so near to him now that Bane was beginning to get nervous. Then again, they'd slept for a week in close proximity and the plaguemarked man hadn't once tried to touch him.

"Can I ask you something, Chavos?" Bane said, turning to face his companion.

Chavos remained silent, offering only the slightest nod as a sign that he'd heard the question.

"What is your purpose?"

The young, pale-faced man blinked, surprised by the question. He licked his lips, looking uncomfortable. Finally, he said, "I have no purpose."

"That's why you tried to kill yourself at the Southron Gates?"

Chavos shook his head. "I didn't want to hurt anyone else. If you hadn't saved me, the world would be safe."

"From you, yes," Bane admitted. "But not from the greater evils that are out there. You have an excuse. When you touch someone, they get the plague and die. You were born like that.

But men like"—he spat the name out—"Falcon Hoza, kill hundreds or even thousands simply because *they can*."

Bane saw the look in Chavos's eyes—he'd seen it before, when he'd first met him. Like a lost lamb, wide-eyed and scared. *Maybe he isn't going to kill me after all. In fact, I don't think he has it in him.*

That thought comforted Bane greatly. Maybe he wouldn't have to be alone after all.

Chavos didn't say anything for a long time, watching the dust settle as the emperor's chariot faded away into the distance. Sweat dribbling down his face, forming tracks on his dry face, he said, "I want to help. I won't fail the kingdom this time. I swear it."

Bane smiled, feeling warm inside, and not from the heat. "I know you won't. Now let me show you something else."

Seventy-Two
The Southern Empire, Phanes
Jai Jiroux

Strong hands grabbed him, hauling Jai to his feet. He felt like he'd just fallen asleep, only to be jerked back awake by a force he was blind to comprehend.

And then he was falling, hitting the ground with a vicious thud, the wind bursting from his lips. "Sorry, old friend," a voice whispered in his ear.

Axa's.

Pain bloomed in his knee, radiating up his thigh and down his calf. He couldn't help it—he groaned in agony.

Other slaves were awakening now, asking what was happening. Tired heads turned in his direction. Jig was on his feet, trying to help, but one of the other mine masters held him back, his little arms swinging at nothing but air. *Don't hurt him. Please don't hurt him.*

Thankfully, they didn't, probably on direct orders from Axa. *Thank you, Axa,* Jai thought, just as the man kicked him again, in the same spot. Something crunched—his bone perhaps.

Stars erupted across Jai's vision, and he almost blacked out, only just managing to curl up in a ball to protect himself from the next kick, which glanced off the thickest part of his leg.

Axa grabbed the front of his tattered shirt and pulled Jai's face directly in front of his. He was feigning anger, red and hot, but Jai could see right through it, could see the deep sadness again. The regret. "*Never* drop your pick again, *slave,*" Axa growled.

A few slaves were crowding around now, but none tried to help him. There were three dozen mine masters, all heavily armed, there to dole out additional punishments if necessary. No one wanted to take a beating for no reason.

"Do you understand?" Axa said, when Jai said nothing.

"Yes," he breathed, another slash of pain erupting from his knee.

Axa shoved him down and stalked off.

Jai longed to tell so many people what he was planning, but he couldn't. The risk was simply too great. If his people, his friends, were questioned, he needed them to genuinely be able to say they knew nothing about what he was going to do.

At the same time, he didn't want them to think he'd abandoned them. *They know me,* he reminded himself. *They know I wouldn't do that.*

As he hobbled to the tunnels on one leg, hefting his axe over his shoulder, he prayed to every god and goddess in the sky and beneath the sea and on dry land that his and Axa's plan would work.

At his slow pace, other slaves passed him, most offering him pitying looks, some patting him on the back and urging him to "Stay strong." Some even offered him the three-fingered salute he'd invented. One finger for the masters, one for the slaves, and one for them, people who, at least in their own minds, were neither masters nor slaves.

At the entrance to the area of the mine currently being worked stood a despicable master named Carvin. Jai gritted his teeth, because Axa was supposed to be at this post on this morning. Axa was supposed to—

"Jai Jiroux," a commanding voice called from behind. Jai stopped, his knee almost buckling. Marella and Viola had cared for him the night before, using whatever materials they could find to bind his knee. It wasn't enough; Axa had done his job well.

Now Axa strode up to him, his eyes casting over Jai's shoulder to find Carvin on guard. "You're late," Jai whispered.

"You look incapable of mining today, slave," Axa said. Under his breath, he said, "The bird was here early. I had to ensure he stayed."

Jai said, loudly, "Even without a leg and an arm I can mine as well as any two slaves." It was all for show, of course, both for the other slaves and for Carvin. Several slaves laughed, but kept moving, flowing around him.

"I won't lose a slave because of your stubbornness. To the infirmary."

Jai didn't look back to see Carvin's reaction. He merely shrugged and said, "As you command," and headed back against the human flow.

The "infirmary" was a small cave with several dirty cots, a nasty healer nicknamed the Cutter, and a shelf full of surgical tools and vials of strange concoctions. Most of the supplies were used simply to ease a slave's pain and get him or her back on their feet and working as quickly as possible.

There were no other slaves in the infirmary today, another detail Axa had arranged.

"Lie down," the Cutter said. He was a short Phanecian man, his hair dark and plastered to his scalp. Though his face was powdered, he wore no jewelry—probably because he would only ruin it with the blood of his patients. He wore a bloodstained frock over his clothing.

Jai obeyed, easing back onto the cot. Though the bed was lumpy and hard, it was the softest thing he had laid upon for months, and an audible sigh of pleasure rose from his throat, unbidden.

"Don't get used to it," the Cutter said snidely, inspecting Jai's leg. "Savages," he muttered, sniffing at the dirty, makeshift bandages fashioned from bits of torn clothing. Jai wanted to point out that they'd done the best they could, but didn't think the healer would be interested. No, people like him had minds so closed they were like steel vaults. A statement like *The Terans are savages* was as much a fact as *The sky is blue* or *The emperor is rich.*

So Jai kept his mouth shut and persevered, as the man pushed and twisted, prodded and poked, until the pain was on the verge of making him pass out.

"Hurts, does it?" the Cutter said, and Jai wanted to slap him.

"A little," he said instead, gritting his teeth.

"Might need to amputate."

Hence, his nickname. It was his standard answer to most ailments. Jai thanked the gods Axa hadn't accidentally kicked him in the head. "Please. Don't take my leg." Jai said it blandly, with no emotion. The act was over—Axa would be there any moment.

The healer blinked. "I'll get my saw."

"Get out," Axa said, right on time.

"But—"

"Out."

"Yes, master." Though the healer wasn't technically a slave, he answered to Mine Master Axa just like everyone else in Garadia. Jai remembered those days, but didn't miss them one bit.

With the healer gone, Axa said, "I'll pay him to keep his silence. He will be a very rich man when the day is done." He got to work on the chains, unlocking them in four places using a thick iron key that hung on a chain around his neck.

"And the bird?" Jai asked when he finished. He massaged his wrists and ankles, which were raw and chafed from the constant rubbing of the manacles.

"Still here. He's anxious to get back to Phanea, as he is under strict orders to return, but I ordered him to stay. It'll hold him for a while."

Jai nodded. "What will you do to him?" This was the part he hadn't asked about—he thought he'd rather not know, but now that it came down to it, he couldn't not know.

"When you say it like that, you make it sound so sinister," Axa said.

"Just tell me."

"Nothing so bad. He's a slave. I'll simply redirect him to another city, another master. No one will care."

It was true, Jai knew. Slaves were traded and passed around like common collectibles. The bird had been their code name for a common slave, a cripple, whose place Jai was about to take. "What else do I need to know?"

"He walks hunched over, dragging his left leg behind him. His left arm doesn't work properly, so he curls it under, like this." Axa demonstrated the slave's mannerisms. Jai tried it out, finding it wasn't so difficult in his current condition. Having Axa injure two of his limbs had been Jai's idea—he wanted to be the most authentic cripple he could be. The fate of the empire might depend on it.

"What about my face?"

"He's young, about your age. His eyes are narrower than yours. His skin is redder. Here." Axa rummaged in the satchel before handing him a pouch of dye and two clear, thin pins.

Jai was beginning to hate their plan. However, he didn't complain, using a small mirror and the pins to pierce the skin of each eyelid, pulling them to each side and fixing them in place. It was harder to see, his vision blurred, but it would have to do.

Next he spilled the dye into a large basin Axa pointed out in the corner. The water turned bright red. "How long do I need to be in?" he asked.

495

"Just a few moments—the dye is potent. The effect will last several months."

Jai quickly stripped out of his slave clothing and stepped into the water, fully submerging himself. He held his breath for ten long heartbeats, and then rose above the surface. Axa handed him a towel, which he used to clear the dyed water from his eyes and lips, before drying the rest of his body, which was now a reasonable shade of Teran red.

"Wear this." Axa tossed Jai a satchel containing a white shirt and gray trousers. Considering they were meant for a slave, the clothing was in decent condition, free of holes or tears. Jai had been to the palace often enough to know that the slaves there were treated well, all things considered. Then again, not having one's freedom was the cruelest life of all, no matter the circumstances.

He quickly donned the new garb. Axa talked while he changed. "People see what they want to see, and a cripple is the most invisible of all. Everyone knows he's there, but no one actually sees him."

"And I'll be working for the Hozas?"

Axa grinned. "In the palace, yes. Not directly for them, but cleaning their messes and emptying their chamber pots. Should be fun."

"Thank you, Axa," Jai said. He wasn't being droll. The mine master had risked much to help him.

Axa, however, shook his head, unwilling to accept his appreciation. "My debts will never be repaid in this lifetime, but I will continue to try. And I *will* be there when you next need me. That is a promise."

Jai nodded, clasping the man's arm. He offered the three-fingered salute with the other hand. There was nothing left to say, so Jai left, falling into the role of a man known as Birdie.

And as he'd promised to himself, he finally escaped Garadia, a place that had once been his home, now his prison, by walking out the front door and into the light.

Seventy-Three
The Southern Empire, Phanes
Falcon Hoza

The slave woman had caught Falcon's eye a fortnight earlier. It wasn't so much her beauty—though she was beautiful—but the way she carried herself. Upright, proud, unbroken. There was something familiar about her too.

Her reddish skin and coppery hair gave her away as a Teran, as most slaves were, but the length of her hair—barely brushing her slender shoulders—made it clear she was a recent...acquisition. The black tears printed on her face marked her as a rebel, a member of the Black Tears, the group that had been trapped by his father at the Southron Gates, not long before he'd been assassinated.

Twice Falcon had tried to catch her gaze, but she refused to look at him, going about her work in an unhurried, methodical manner. Her ankles were chained together, as well as her wrists, and an additional tether bound her hands to her feet, decreasing her range of motion. Some form of restraint was necessary for all slaves now that Falcon's father was dead, his slavemark dying with him, but most only had leg irons. Watching this young woman walk about awkwardly, her strides cut in half, having to shuffle particularly close in order to grab things, left a bitter taste in Falcon's mouth.

He knew he shouldn't focus on one slave, but he couldn't help it.

"Who is that woman?" he finally asked one of his palace guards.

The man, a wiry fellow who'd been groomed to the position by his father—another guard—since birth, raised an amused eyebrow. "A rebel who is now a slave," he said, which didn't help. He threw up his hands, as if to say *What else is there to say?*

"I know that," Falcon said, growing impatient. He hated obvious answers. "But why is she *here?* It was my understanding all the Black Tears captured had been sent to Garadia."

"Not this one," the guard said. Falcon was considering changing the man's title to Master of the Obvious.

"*Why?*" he repeated.

Another shrug. Falcon stormed off. He considered asking one of his younger brothers, but they rarely spoke any more. He was certain they were hoping he would be killed next by the Kings' Bane. Then Phanes would be theirs.

Instead, he took a more direct approach. Whether he liked it or not, he was the emperor—he might as well take advantage. So, when he knew she would be in his quarters going about her daily chores, Falcon slipped away from court during an intermission and stole back to his room.

She was there, her back to him. Though he tried to enter quietly, he saw her back stiffen. He waited a moment, just watching her, but she said nothing. Nor did she turn.

Everything about this woman intrigued him. He'd learned long ago that everyone has a story, and most were good ones. He desperately wanted to know this woman's story. Perhaps it would help him escape his own awful life for a time.

"What is your name?" he asked.

Finally, she turned, her chains clanking. For the first time, her eyes met his and his breath caught. Now that the slavemarks had been shattered, most slaves' eyes were pools of sadness, exhaustion, resignation.

Not hers. They were full of fire, of barely concealed fury. Her stare seemed to pin him to the spot, his legs refusing to move. He had the urge to look away, and eventually did.

"My name is Slave," she said, when she'd forced his eyes to the ground.

Falcon chewed on this for a moment. It was an answer that would usually be used to appease, to show one's subservience, but this woman used it like a weapon, a stab in the gut. "Mine is Falcon Hoza," he said, looking up.

This time it was he who had caught her by surprise. She gave a mocking laugh. "Truly? I hadn't noticed you before. You're the emperor, are you not?"

"Not on purpose," he quipped.

Her eyebrows shot for the ceiling. "You would forsake your position?"

"I cannot," he said. "Do you know the law?"

"Which one? The one that allows Terans to be treated as dogs? Or the one that allows rivers of diamonds to flow into your coffers?"

"Neither of those," he said, trying to ignore the jab. "The one that says a Phanecian emperor can only be dismissed by death."

She offered a wolf's grin. "Would you like me to help?"

Coming from a member of the Black Tears, Falcon knew it was more than a jape. Closer to a threat. They were known to be mighty warriors, and if her chains were removed she would likely test his own abilities to their limits.

Also, one thing he'd learned by having three sisters was that women were not to be underestimated. It was a fact his father and brothers had never fully appreciated, which was one of the main reasons why the civil war with Calypso had dragged on for so long.

"Not today, but I'll let you know," Falcon said.

"Why did you return to your quarters?" the woman asked.

"An answer for an answer?" he offered.

"My true name?"

He shook his head. "Why are you here and not in Garadia?"

She snorted. "You're the emperor and you don't know?" She cocked her head, seeming to consider this new information. "Though I suppose it makes sense. Your father wouldn't want anyone, even his own sons, to know the limits on his power."

That caught Falcon off guard. "Limits?"

"He *tried* to mark me. He failed."

Falcon jolted. He'd never heard of that happening before. "What do you mean?"

"Just what I said. He couldn't mark me, so I was brought here, to be his plaything."

Oh gods. "What did he do to you?"

"An answer for an answer. I gave mine, now it's your turn. Why are you here?"

He considered lying. Maybe he forgot something. Maybe he was tired, wanted to lie down for a bit. However, his instincts told him this woman would smell the falsehood. "To see you," he said truthfully.

Her eyes narrowed, and he immediately regretted his vague word choice. "Not like that," he said. "I'm not like my father."

"You're *exactly* like your father," she spat, venom in her tone. "Else I wouldn't be here emptying your *godsdamn* chamber pot."

With that, she left, clanking past him.

The entire exchange left Falcon speechless, a thousand more questions racing through his mind.

Falcon barely made it back to court in time for his next meeting. Fang offered a raised eyebrow, but didn't say anything, while Fox said, "More important matters keeping you, *brother?*" Falcon ignored the comment, stepping between his brothers and before the throne. The meeting *was* an important one, requiring him to make decisions regarding the slave army.

Predictably, his generals were chomping at the bit.

"General Killorn," Falcon said as he sat on the throne. He tried to focus his thoughts; he was still rattled from his conversation with the rebel slave. "What is your recommendation?"

The general cleared his throat, the skin of his neck wobbling slightly. Though he was still hard and strong, the years hadn't been particularly kind to him. His powdered face made him so pale he might almost appear dead if he laid down.

Killorn said, "The last stream was clear—the west is distracted by the easterners. Though their army is preparing for battle, they will likely attack at the Bridge of Triumph, rather than the Southron Gates."

Falcon did his best to look perturbed by the news, while inwardly his heart did a flip. It was almost too good to be true. "So my father's little trap might not catch the mouse," he said. *And I won't be forced to use the slave army, nor fight a war I don't want.*

"If I may," Killorn said, "I would advise forcing their hand."

Falcon scoffed, doing his best impression of his father. Haughty and unimpressed. "You would have me march through the Southron Gates and leave Phanes unprotected?"

Fang, who had become more and more vocal in such meetings, interjected. "Who will attack us, brother?"

"Emperor," Falcon growled.

Somewhat cowed, Fang said, "Apologies, Emperor Falcon. The north is obliterated. The east and west are embroiled in their usual rivalry. And Calypso? Empress Sun and Empress Fire are both dead and—"

"You dare speak of the deaths of your mother and sister so casually?" Falcon bellowed, standing suddenly. Fang took a step back. This time, it was no act—Falcon was livid. Ever since his parents' union had been severed, both his brothers and father had acted as if their mother and sisters didn't exist.

503

"They've been dead to me for a long time," Fang said, trying to act cool.

"Not to me," Falcon said. "I plan to end this pointless civil war and reunite with Raven and Whisper."

"What?" Fang and Fox said at the same time.

General Killorn said, "I cannot advise that, Emperor. I know your heart still holds a place for your sisters, but they are shrewd women, Raven especially. May I remind you that Raven was *there* at the Southron Gates. She sought to destroy Phanes, too."

"On Fire's orders," Falcon said, firing a final dagger-filled stare at his brothers before taking his seat.

"True, but Raven is empress now, and she won't be a weak one. Also, their dragons are not far from maturity."

Dragons. Gods, how Falcon hated hearing about dragons. They came up almost every war council; the generals used dragons as their excuse to attack Calypso again and again.

"The Calypsians have never attacked Phanes with dragons," Falcon said. "Even before our marriage alliance."

"But what if they do?"

Falcon gritted his teeth. Time for the final act, which would delay the decision further and close the meeting. He slammed his fist down on the arm of his throne. "Then we will crush them!"

Falcon wanted to hurry back to his quarters to think, but luck was not with him on this day. Instead, Fang pulled him aside the moment the meeting had ended. Fox hovered nearby, his lip curled in an annoying manner.

"Have you heard the news, brother?" Fang said. His tone made it clear he *knew* his brother didn't know and that he was quite enjoying that fact.

"There is much news in Phanes these days," he hedged. "Be more specific."

"The slaves that escaped from Garadia, of course," Fang said, raising his eyebrows. From experience, Falcon knew his brother was holding something back in an attempt to make him look foolish.

"What care do I have for escaped slaves? Capture them and bring them back." He started to walk away.

"They were Black Tears."

The words stopped him in his tracks, even more so since he'd recently spoken to one of the Tears, the mysterious slave woman. He wondered if his brother knew he'd spoken to her, or if the timing was merely a coincidence. He didn't turn around. "How many of them?"

"All the Tears in Garadia."

Which meant all the captured Tears except for the woman in the palace. "How did this happen?" He tried to sound furious, the way his father would have, but it came out like he was curious.

"That's a mystery. None of the guards were injured, nor did they see anything suspicious. They even took their chains with them."

Though escaped rebels should've been of great concern to a sitting emperor, Falcon felt nothing at the news. He didn't hate the Black Tears the way his father had. He hated that their actions resulted in more deaths, but that was the nature of rebellion.

"That's not all," Fang said, while he was still processing the information.

Gods, Falcon thought. *Will this day never end?* "Speak, brother."

"They've already attacked one of the mines." Falcon's heart stood still. "One of the smaller ones. We visited it last year, you probably remember it. Hornhelm?"

Falcon *did* remember it—he remembered all the mines they visited, the despondent, broken expressions of the slaves burned in his memory—but he pretended to think. "Ah, sapphires, right?" *Rubies*, he thought in his head.

"Rubies," Fang corrected.

"That's right. I remember now. Not much more than a hole in the ground. Four mine masters, including the chief."

"All dead."

That news didn't surprise him. The Tears' attacks rarely left any survivors, except for the slaves, who were always gone. But, under his father's rule, the escaped slaves had always either been captured or killed. Sometimes both.

"How many slaves?" he asked.

"Forty-nine."

Gods be with them, he thought. Inwardly, he hoped they'd make it across the border. Outwardly, he said, "Find them. Try not to kill them. We need them for the mine."

Fang's eyes narrowed. "And the Tears?"

"Bring them to me in chains."

When Falcon returned to his quarters, he quietly closed the door, resting his back against it for a moment, his eyes closed.

He breathed in and out. Once more, he'd managed to delay war, but he couldn't hold off the generals, nor his brothers, for much longer. And the news of the resurgence of the Black Tears only complicated things further. It was true what he'd told the rebel slave woman earlier: a Phanecian emperor could only lose the throne through his own death. But he hadn't told her about the right of challenge that any Hoza heir could make at any time.

A fight to the death, the victor being the emperor. Thus far, neither of his brothers had the courage to challenge him, but it was only a matter of time if he sought peace with Calypso and their western neighbors.

A distraction, he thought. *I need a distraction.* Eagerly, he strode to his bed, dropped to all fours, and scrabbled underneath for his bedroll. Swiftly, he unrolled it, seeking the prize in the center—his new book.

When he finished, he frowned. The book was gone. He peeked under the bed, but didn't see anything. He distinctly remembered placing it in the bedroll this morning before he hid it beneath the massive bed.

"Looking for this?" a voice asked, startling him.

He whirled around to find the rebel slave woman standing inside his room, the door closed. He hadn't even heard her enter, such was her stealth. *All the clanking she did earlier was intentional*, Falcon realized.

In her hands was a book with a red leather cover—exactly the one he'd been seeking.

"You stole it from me?"

"Why do you sleep on the floor each night? Your bed looks more comfortable than most—far more comfortable than what I sleep on each night."

"I—" Why did he suddenly feel compelled to tell this woman the feelings in his heart? Because she was a slave and wouldn't be able to tell anyone else? Maybe. But that didn't feel quite right. "I can't sleep in that bed."

"Why not?"

"Because *he* slept there."

"Your father."

He nodded.

"Because he died there?"

"No. That's not it."

"Then what?" she asked. She took a step forward, holding out the book.

He stared at the book's cover. A golden dragon was etched in the leather. The writer was a Calypsian, which was practically sacrilege in Phanes. Falcon thought this was ridiculous—good writing was good writing. "He wasn't...a good man."

"And you are?"

He shook his head, but it wasn't an answer. In truth, he didn't know. He wanted to be a good man, but his position felt more like a prison each and every day.

"If you are a good man, you would release the slaves. Let them go home. Back to Teragon. Back to the Dreadnoughts. The Tears will not stop until they've destroyed you and the masters." Her eyes were dark blue, shadowed by her thick copper eyebrows and golden lashes. The expression on her face was so serious it shook his heart to the core.

His breath rushed in. She knew about the rebels' escape. "How do you know about that?" Even he hadn't known about it until a moment earlier.

"I have ears, and no one pays attention to a lowly slave. Except you, it seems."

He ignored the jab. "Will they come for you?"

She shrugged. "We are loyal to the cause, not to each other. But I will rejoin them eventually."

"You will try to escape?"

"I don't *try* at anything," she said, the implication of what she'd left unsaid echoing through his mind.

"I don't hate the Tears," he said, trying honesty.

"Good to know. But you'll kill them just the same if you catch them again."

"Not if I can help it."

She bowed low, the mocking clear in the unnecessary flourish of her sweeping hand. "Thank you for your mercy, oh Emperor."

"What do you want from me?"

She pinned him with a stare. "Absolutely nothing. I just wanted to know who I'm dealing with. A coward, obviously. You are unlike your father, and yet you won't change his horrific laws and traditions."

Her words hurt, but he refused to let it show. "It's not so simple."

"Why not? You're the emperor. Do you want slavery to continue?"

Again, the truth spilled from him as easily as water from a tipped over jug. "No." If one of his brothers heard him say such a thing, he would receive challenges from both of them, as well as dozens of cousins he didn't even know he had. "But if I tried to change things, I would be killed."

"Sometimes death is the only way," she said. By her tone, he knew without a shadow of a doubt that this rebel was willing to die for the cause she believed in. It made him feel...lesser.

For he didn't want to die, didn't want to meet a tragic ending like so many of the characters in the books he loved to read.

Once more, she offered the book. This time, he took it. She held onto her end for a moment, her eyes locked on his, their fingers a breath apart. "I read the last page," she said. "Do you want to know how it ends?"

He shook his head. He'd never read this one, and he didn't want it to be spoiled. "Fine," she said. "Then I'll tell you the end of your own story instead." She paused, letting the statement sink in. "In your story, you die."

She released the book, and his hand jerked back. He didn't realize he'd been gripping the cover so tightly. As quiet as the wind, she opened the door, slipping out. Before the door closed, however, she called back. "My name is Shanti Parthena Laude," she said.

The door closed without a sound and she was gone.

Falcon sank back to the floor clutching the book, feeling utterly miserable. Not because she'd spoken of his own death, which truly was inevitable—all men died, after all—but because he knew his life wouldn't matter, regardless of what he did.

Unlike the stories trapped between the pages of the books he read, his story was one without purpose, without meaning.

His was an empty life.

Seventy-Four
The Southern Empire, Phanes
Jai Jiroux

Axa had been right. Being a crippled slave had its advantages.

The first few days he'd gotten his bearings. Though, when he was Garadia Mine Master, he'd been to the palace in Phanea many times to meet with Emperor Hoza, his movements were always strictly monitored. One didn't waltz around the palace exploring.

Unless, of course, you were a slave.

Yes, he had duties—none of the guards had even noticed that the same crippled slave that left hadn't returned—but so long as he did them and kept out of the way, he was left alone. Several of the other slaves, however, had frowned at him, but they said nothing. Even if they knew he wasn't the real Birdie, they didn't seem overly concerned about it. Like Axa had said, slaves were moved around all the time.

Unlike the other slaves, Jai wasn't forced to wear chains, due to his withered arm and leg. His ailments were his chains, sufficient to prevent his escape. Not that he was trying to escape. Though his injuries were very much real—Axa had done his job well—they were beginning to heal somewhat. As it turned out, there were no broken bones, a major stroke of luck. His strength was already returning, and more and more each day he had to fake his limp and awkwardly hanging arm.

All in all, Jai managed to cover a fair portion of the palace, memorizing the layout, the way the narrow slave passages linked up with the major halls and broad corridors used by the royalty and their guards. He did as he was told, delivering washbasins to the slaves charged with cleaning, emptying the dirty ones and refilling them. Occasionally he had to clean, too, spending hours on his hands and knees. Sometimes when he arose, he really felt like a hunchback, his muscles spasming and his spine curled like a question mark. His body was more accustomed to the endless motion of swinging a pick, and he went to bed sore each night.

Most of all, as he worked, as he explored, he looked for Shanti.

Thus far, he hadn't seen her. He was tempted to ask some of the other slaves, but that would give him away—Birdie apparently didn't talk much, nor would he ask after another slave. The last thing he wanted to do was draw attention to himself unnecessarily. He needed to be a shadow, a ghost.

He didn't want Falcon Hoza to see it coming when he killed him.

Jai's plan was simple:

Kill Falcon. Kill Fang. Kill Fox. With the three ruling brothers gone, there would be a moment of confusion and chaos, which he would use to slip away and find Sonika and the other Black Tears, hopefully with Shanti in tow.

From there, they would begin a fullscale revolution. The palace was already abuzz with the return of the Black Tears, who had escaped from slavery in Garadia. Two mines had been hit already, both smaller ones. Both fully liberated. Thus far neither the escaped slaves nor the Tears had been caught. *A revolution*, Jai thought, relishing the sound of the word in his mind. This time it would be easier. They could rescue slaves from the mines, as Sonika was already doing, starting with the smallest and least protected ones first. Over time, they would grow their numbers, training the people in phen lu, phen ru, and phen sur. Building their army.

Looking back, Jai felt like a naïve fool. Prior to his first attempt to liberate the Garadia slaves, he hadn't wanted to train them to fight. If they fought, they would die. At least that was his reasoning. Sneaking away was better. Now he knew the truth: Sometimes fighting was the *only* way to survive.

Now, he lurched down the corridor, hauling a filthy, reeking chamber pot. He would empty it and then bring it back. Only this time he was going to pretend to be confused. For this pot belonged to a lesser noble in the household, but he was going to bring it to the emperor's quarters, a room he'd only just found in the palace maze.

The mission was simply reconnaissance at this point, but he felt a flutter of excitement at the thought of seeing the emperor's private space. He longed to stare upon its lavishness, to see the inequality of the world in the form of fine adornments and wealth unmatched.

It would only add logs to the growing fire in his belly.

By the time he finished with the pot and began hobbling back, the sun was creeping down toward the horizon. He longed to stop, to gaze at the beauty of the world, to appreciate a place he had once loved.

He kept his eyes trained forward; many years had passed since he was a boy. If, one day, he managed to free every slave in Phanes, only then would he look upon another sunset and be mesmerized by it.

The outside world fell behind him as he entered the palace, taking a route that wasn't the most direct, but which would be least likely to get him caught. As he limped, the empty pot jerking to and fro from the grasp of his "lame" arm, his eyes never left his shoes. Not making eye contact was one of the keys to being ignored—both in Garadia and here. For some strange reason, masters saw eye contact as an affront, a challenge, rather than the simple attempt at human connection that it truly was.

It was because of this that Jai didn't notice the form rounding the corner hurriedly, nearly bumping into him as he passed. His head jerked up and for a moment he forgot himself, his eyes meeting those of the woman who was moving in the opposite direction, her own head twisted around to look at him.

His own eyes widened, while she merely blinked, before turning away and moving on, like a ghost fading away around the next bend.

He almost ran after her, almost made the critical error that she was intelligent and quick-minded enough to avoid. He took one step in her direction and stopped himself. No matter how fast he limped, he wouldn't catch her, and he couldn't give up the disguise.

Still, the image of her face, of her night-dark tears on her cheeks, of her coppery hair brushing her soft brown shoulders, burned in his mind like a lit torch.

At long last he'd found her:

Shanti.

After seeing Shanti, Jai forgot the purpose of his mission, staring at the chamber pot dumbly. Had Shanti recognized him, or had she been fooled by his disguise, his red skin? He thought he'd seen recognition in her eyes, but it had been fleeting at best. If she had known it was him, her mastery of her mind and emotions was impressive.

As Jai considered what to do, a guard chose to patrol that particular corridor. "Cripple!" he barked.

Jai's breath was in his throat. He stared at his feet.

"Are you lost?"

Jai nodded.

The man released an exasperated sigh. "Fools, the lot of you. At least the Dreadnoughter slaves are a clever bunch. You Terans are useless. Back the way you came, turn right, another right, left, you'll find Lord Dramonos' quarters. That chamber pot you're holding, with the Dramonos' seal? Belongs there."

Jai nodded, his eyes fixed on his toes as he shuffled around. As he slowly hobbled away, he felt a powerful urge to bolt, but fought it off. Thus far, it was his closest brush with any palace master. He'd have to be more careful going forward.

The next day, Jai was assigned to an important gathering in the palace. His role was to be invisible, collecting dirty plates and silverware as they were discarded.

The gala was held in a long hall with an arched glass ceiling. Twice Jai had attended similar events at the emperor's request due to his prestigious position as Master of Garadia. He'd hated both nights, rubbing shoulders with men and women who he considered to be his enemies. The only solace he had taken was the knowledge that his slave miners were treated better than any others.

This particular gala was of a similar nature, with long tables set up around the walls, covered in the finest foods the empire had to offer. A long, roasted pyzon took up an entire wall, its thick body stripped of scales and mounted on dozens of metal skewers. The head had been kept on, its mouth purposely propped open to reveal its fierce fangs and wide throat, which was more than capable of swallowing a full-size male whole, even if he was wearing armor. Important Phanecians lined up to receive a slab of the snake meat, which was cut by a tall Teran slave with a carving knife. Jai watched the scene for a moment, noticing how none of the wealthy attendees so much as looked at the slave. In less time than it took him to carve each cut of meat, he could stab the knife through one of their hearts, but they didn't fear him. No, in their eyes, he was broken, of no concern.

Jai gritted his teeth and moved on. Though he kept his head down as he limped through the regaled royalty, he occasionally flicked his eyes up to seek Shanti's face. After all, he had seen her in the emperor's corridor, which might mean she would be assigned to his royal events.

His frustration mounted with each trip from the feast room with another stack of dirty dishes for the kitchen. Not only had he not seen Shanti, but the emperor had yet to make an appearance. He'd been in Phanea for more than a week and hadn't so much as caught a glimpse of Falcon. How could he kill a man he couldn't find?

When he returned to the hall, however, something had changed. There was a buzz in the air, which he noticed immediately. People were still chattering, but their voices had dropped lower, and all eyes were focused on the front of the room, where two familiar young men sat in large, high-backed chairs, their hands resting casually on armrests. They generally ignored the hubbub, speaking only to each other, waiting to be served.

That's when he saw her for the second time, her strong, capable form moving nimbly through the room, balancing large plates on the palm of each hand. Shanti handed a plate to each of the younger Hoza brothers, and they didn't even acknowledge her.

She was the most beautiful woman Jai had ever seen, and she might as well have been a ghost.

With a start, Jai realized he was still staring at her, watching as she spun on her heel, retreating to the food lines. Her eyes found his, and though she once again pretended not to notice him, her eyes gliding past like gusts of wind, this time she winked.

His heart swelled and it was all he could do to keep his feet moving, to gather the next stack of dirty plates. When he returned, he spotted her right away, because she was standing at the focal point of the entire room, handing a plate to one final newcomer.

Emperor Falcon, Jai thought, taking in his enemy in a glance. He and his two brothers were three of a kind with their powdered faces, jeweled scalps and brows, and upright, stern positioning.

The emperor's lips moved, but Jai was fairly certain he hadn't spoken, for his brothers didn't notice. *Thank you*, he mouthed, the words directed at Shanti. When she turned away, there was no mistaking the shallow smile on her lips.

Jai felt gut-punched. Everything about their interaction went against the standard slave-master system in place. Everything about it was far too casual, familiar.

The truth slapped him in the face and he almost dropped a dish. *She's gotten herself close enough to the emperor to kill him.*

Her eyes found his, and this time there was no mistaking the words she mouthed to him. *Be careful.*

And then she was gone. She didn't return to the gala that night.

Seventy-Five

The Southern Empire, Phanes
Falcon Hoza

He'd sent for Shanti three nights in a row, asking for her to deliver a sleeping draught to help him rest.

And all three nights, he'd dumped the draught in his chamber pot. Sleep was the last thing he was interested in.

The Teran woman had been all too willing to share her story, dumping it out like a box of broken ceramic figurines, her eyes stabbing daggers of accusation at Falcon the whole time. How her family had been enslaved in Teragon's capital city when she was just a child. How she'd been dragged from her home, abused, chained to a ship. How her father had been murdered protecting her sister. How her sister had been murdered anyway, her mother taken away from her. How she had escaped, somehow developing immunity to the Slave Master's powers.

The story was as tragic as the fiction he usually read, and it tugged at his heartstrings all the more because of who was telling it. Though her voice never wavered, her eyes as dry as the Scarra Desert, the pain she still felt was in every word, punctuated by the black tears etched on her cheeks.

When she finally finished her tale, Falcon felt as if nails had been driven into his chest. He always knew his father was a monster, but he'd avoided hearing about what he did as much as possible.

Something else nagged at him—the part about her mother, who was taken away. He also remembered how something about Shanti had been familiar to him, despite the strange tears on her cheeks.

A memory was unchained, breaking free in his mind. He winced visibly. His eyes closed.

"Do my words sorrow you?" Shanti said, cocking her head to the side mockingly. She was fearless, and he wondered if it was because she knew he was weak or if she simply no longer cared what happened to her.

"Yes," he said, his voice raspy.

"It is one of a million, and there are worse than mine."

Nails driven on top of nails. "I'm...sorry." Even as he said it, Falcon knew it was the weakest response of a plethora of weak responses that had sprung to mind.

"Sorry?" Shanti's lips had pulled into a tight line, and Falcon had the impression she was fighting back the urge to destroy him, chains or not.

In many ways, he wished she would, especially now that he knew he'd seen her mother before. That he knew what had happened to her. A stronger man would tell her, but he was no such man. Never would be.

He shook his head. "Yes. But more than that, I am ashamed."

"Save it for someone who believes you." She wheeled around, turning to leave in the same manner she had the previous two nights, like a whirlwind of fury.

"Why did you say I am going to die?" he asked. He'd wanted to ask since the moment she said it, but had been nervous, though he wasn't sure why.

She turned back for a moment, her eyes narrowing. "Haven't you finished that book I gave you yet?"

He shook his head. Each night when she left, he was so exhausted he'd fallen right to sleep, his dreams full of images from her ongoing story.

"Read it," she said, and then she was gone.

Falcon Hoza read all night, turning the pages with a vigor more driven by anxiety than a desire to finish the book. The story was a good one—about a misunderstood group of people with mottled flesh and long, clawed fingers, who were treated like nothing more than animals by the nation that had conquered them—but he didn't enjoy it the way he normally would. For one, the parallels to the realities of the Phanecians—of his father, his brothers, *himself*—were so numerous and obvious it was almost a fictional work of treason. Secondly, the last page was fast approaching, and he'd realized something:

Shanti had claimed to have *only* read the last page of the book. The urge to skip pages, to skim, to go straight to the final piece of parchment was powerful, but he continued reading, forcing himself not to miss a single word. She'd shared her story with him—he owed her that much at least.

The area around his window shades was lightening and his eyes were stinging when he did, finally, reach the last page. He'd read through the night, he realized.

Now that he was here, he didn't want to find out the ending, because there was no good outcome in sight. The enslaved people were broken, beaten down, each new generation less hopeful than the one before it until the word hope didn't even exist in their language.

The ruler of the dominant people had died, but he had three sons to continue ruling, to maintain their way of life. None had shown any signs of wanting to change. The last line on the second to last page felt like a black hole sucking him into it:

Those defeated, dream of escape. Their rulers die alone and heavy. The hourglass empties, the final grain of sand falling to the pile.

Change? Change does not exist in their world.

He took a deep breath, the edge of the page scraping loudly against the parchment as he turned it, grating his ears.

Numbly, he stared at the final page in the saddest story he'd ever read. It contained only one word:

Unless…

The ending had been so different to what Falcon had expected, what Shanti had insinuated, that the emperor couldn't stop thinking about it. Though another war council was scheduled for that very day, Falcon canceled it, making up an excuse about being unwell and needing a day to rest.

Most of the day, he lay on the floor, ignoring knocks on his locked door, his brothers' voices demanding him to let them in. Instead, he read the words again and again, trying to understand how the open-ended conclusion to the book was linked to his own death.

By the time the sun had set and his stomach was empty and clawing at him from the inside, his mouth dry from lack of water, he was about ready to tear out the page and fling the book across the room.

It clicked.

"She wasn't threatening me," he said aloud, the idea taking shape, dawning bright and gold. He shook his head, wondering how he'd been so foolish. His own fear of death had painted the worst possible outcome in his mind, but all she'd been telling him was what he already knew; what *every* man already knew:

That they would, one day, die.

But between birth and death, there was a whole lot of time that needed to be filled. Most referred to that time as "life," but to Falcon it had always felt like an infinite, black space, a countdown. Like the book said, the grains of sand flowing through an hourglass until none were left at the top.

The truth was, Falcon had never loved his life, despite the riches and status that came with it. *No, it's more than that*, he thought, his fingers tracing the letters printed in the book. *I loathe my life—always have.* The word hate rose to his mind so easily—*too* easily.

But that single word and the three dots of possibility that followed it—*Unless...*—seemed to emulate everything that was Shanti. She'd lived her life with purpose, fighting for a cause she believed in, a cause that *seemed* as hopeless as the plight of the broken people in the book.

She was no emperor, had no armies, had no wealth to back her efforts. None of the Black Tears did, as far as he knew. And yet the small measure of success they'd had—enough to make his father, the Slave Master himself, curse their names—was the very embodiment of hope.

And her message to him was clear:

You can do something.

The only problem was that he couldn't, not really.

But he *could* tell her the truth about her mother. Maybe then she would see reason. Maybe then she would give up.

Seventy-Six

The Southern Empire, Calypso
Raven Sandes

"I want to come with you," Whisper said. "Please."

Raven didn't look at her; couldn't look at her. Instead, she stayed busy, hastily packing supplies for the short trip she'd be making on dragonback. "No," she said.

"Sister." Whisper grabbed her arm. "*Sister.*"

Finally, Raven met Whisper's eyes, and was ashamed at what she saw there. Love. Need. Fear. "Whisper, I can't do this right now. I have to know. I have to be certain."

"You asked me to speak my mind. This is me speaking my mind. I'm coming with you." Not a request—not anymore. If Raven didn't feel so ill, she would've been proud of her sister. Whisper was growing in strength by the day, casting away her childhood like all Sandes women did eventually. *Yes, she will make a fine ruler once I am gone. Probably a better one than either Fire or I ever did.*

"Thank you for speaking out in the war council," Raven said. "You have done all I asked for and more. But sending the last two Daughters to the borderlands is too risky. I will not allow it. You must stay here as tradition requires."

Whisper's nose scrunched and her lips knotted together angrily. She shook her head, tears already beading along the bottom half of her eyelids. "Because you might *die*. Because you might *leave me*. Just like everyone else."

Raven wanted to hug her, to hold her, to tell her she wasn't going to die. To tell her she would never be alone, not ever again. But those were lies, and Raven couldn't treat her like a child anymore.

She turned away.

"Yes," she said. "I might die."

She turned back. Whisper dashed the unshed tears away with a knuckle. Raven said, "Any of us might die on any day— that is just life. But this is only a scouting mission. We will not engage the enemy unless absolutely necessary. They cannot hurt us in the sky."

"Fine," Whisper said. Her fierceness was back. "I will pray for you on Calyppa."

"Thank you, sister."

Raven strode away, afraid her resolve would shatter if she looked back.

As Raven prepared to depart Calypso, she received another stream from Zune, from her Aunt Viper. This was not a profit report. This was a personal message, informing the empress that the Second Daughter would be visiting the City of the Rising Sun within the fortnight.

Raven felt like crumping the note.

She didn't, breathing away her frustration. Of all the times for Viper to want to visit Calypso...this was the worst.

She froze, scanning the note once more with narrowed eyes. Something about the timing...what with the disaster in the Scarra, the testing of the dragonia, Roan Loren's sudden appearance...

Raven's mother had never believed in coincidences and neither did she. Her aunt was a shrewd woman with a long memory. Quickly, she penned a message using an inkreed harvested from the central stream in Zune. *Dear Aunt Viper...*

When she was finished, she found a messenger and sent him scurrying back to the royal stream with the message, which politely requested that her aunt remain in Zune to oversee the fighting pits, and that the empress would visit Zune soon.

I am the empress, she thought. *The sooner Viper remembers that, the better.*

Despite the maddening circumstances, Raven felt alive soaring above the clouds. Siri's leathery wings beat the hot air, creating her own wind. The dragon's spiked, scaly skin was alive beneath the saddle, cresting and crashing like oceanic waves. *A sea in the sky*, Raven thought, using her hand to shield her eyes from the sun.

Rider was on one side, astride Heiron; Shanolin on the other, riding Cronus . Though the dragon masters had offered the entire strength of the dragonia for the mission, Raven had declined. They needed speed and stealth, not strength. The plan was to make the three-day flight to the easternmost edge of the Scarra in two days, perform aerial reconnaissance to determine the situation at present, and then make for Kesh, the desert village from which they'd received the stream.

At first, Cronus had snapped at Siri, jealous of her position in the center of the formation, but after the tenacious female responded with a slap of her spiked tail in his face, the sleek, gray dragon had grudgingly settled into formation. Heiron, on the other hand, hadn't put up a fuss, assuming the left flank without so much as batting an eye. Despite his size and strength, the dark-scaled monster was an even-tempered creature.

This was day two of their journey, and beneath them the clouds looked as fluffy as giant pillows. Between them Raven spotted splashes of brown and white, the alternating sands of the Scarra. And to the east: the blue, diamond-speckled waters of Dragon Bay. Far to the north, the ground turned gray and then bright green, rolling out like a massive rug. Ironclad territory.

"How far?" Raven shouted over the beating of wings. She was growing more and more anxious as they closed the distance to the borderlands.

Rider and Shanolin looked past Raven to meet each other's eyes. "Half a day," they said at the same time. Though they disagreed on much, when it came to details about dragons— their speed, their abilities, their temperaments—the two masters found common ground.

Damn, Raven thought. She was hoping to make it before nightfall, when visibility would still be at its best. Instead the sun would be long gone, leaving them to scout by moons and starlight.

She ducked her head lower and shouted into the wind. "Yah!" Siri shot forward, instinctively searching for the air currents that would further increase her speed. The two larger dragons gave chase, though they swiftly fell behind. Raven could hear her dragon masters' cries drifting away behind her, lost on the wind.

Hours later, after the sun had sunk below the horizon, after the purple sky had given way to navy and then an ink-black plain speckled with stars, Raven and Siri descended toward the desert.

Under the light of Ruahi and Luahi, the two moons casting dueling bands of light across the sand, Raven saw them:

Dark slashes, some straight as arrows, others curled like question marks. Two dozen perhaps. *No, three dozen*, Raven remembered. After all, it was she who had given the order to thirty-six of her guanero. Thirty-six souls who had now left their bodies to seek the Halls of the Gods.

The pit she'd had in her stomach for the last two days grew into a fist, punching the inside of her abdomen.

Siri swooped lower, and Raven forced herself to look. She owed them that much. Most of the bodies were half-covered by the ever-shifting dunes, the desert trying to claim them before the birds could turn them into carrion. There a leg stuck out. Here an arm. She saw a few bits of leather armor bearing the Calypsian sigil. Several familiar faces, staring blankly toward the night sky.

The ill feeling continued, but she swallowed it down. She wouldn't lose her stomach. She would mourn these loyal, capable men and women with her every thought, and then she would clear her head and decide what to do next.

They deserved better. They deserved to live.

She brought Siri into a hover over the carnage. Her voice barely above a whisper, Raven spoke each of their names, for she knew every member of her guanero by name and face.

"Scarab, Jorg, Valia...."

About halfway through the list, Shanolin and Rider arrived, settling their own dragons into a hover. They didn't speak, listening to Raven's accounting of the dead in silence.

"Brin, Hez, Noura..."

And on and on, until Raven reached the end of the list, a final name—Goggin's second in command, a strong woman, an honorable Calypsian, a valiant warrior.

"Ponjut," she whispered. The wind blew, stealing the names. "Burn them."

Without so much as a huff, the dragons angled downward, shooting streams of fire at the dead, until they were each burned to ash.

Raven awoke with a start, trying to make sense of the bright blue world above her.

I'm flying. She recalled falling asleep astride Siri, who had continued her path across the desert toward Kesh. Dragons had the remarkable ability to sleep for days on end, and then wake up and remain that way for a week straight. As if reading her mind, Siri huffed out a hot breath. *About time you got up,* she seemed to be saying. *I'm hungry.*

"Sorry," Raven said, rubbing her eyes. She didn't just feel tired, but exhausted, like she'd walked across the desert rather than been carried by the fastest creatures on earth. The names she'd spoken the night before echoed through her head, silent memories of why she was here. She glanced to either side; both Shanolin and Rider continued to slumber, their chins resting against their chests.

"Oi," she said.

Rider's eyes fluttered open and she stretched. "Morning," she mumbled.

"The dragons have flown all night."

"They'll be hungry," Shanolin said, yawning.

"Down," Raven commanded.

On command, the dragons angled toward the desert, which stretched in every direction. As they approached the ground, their wings beat the sand into a frenzy, shifting the dunes slightly. The moment Raven dismounted, Siri rolled over and jerked her head toward her belly, demanding a scratch. Raven complied, using her opposite hand to untie a satchel of salted beef from Siri's underside. She tossed each chunk in the air, and her dragon seared them with a thin stream of fire before snapping her jaws around them.

Nearby, Heiron's towering form waited patiently as Rider added a sprinkle of the dragon's favorite spice, mixa, to each piece of bacon.

A further distance away, Cronus drank greedily from a bowl of water until it was gone. Then, instead of eating, he slumped down on his forepaws and went right to sleep.

Shanolin made his way over. "Kesh is close now," he said, glancing at the position of the sun.

"What will we find there?" Rider asked no one in particular.

"Information," Raven said. Despite how she'd mourned and honored all thirty-six guanero the night before, she knew one of them must have survived. It was the only way a stream could've been sent from Kesh with the news. She was anxious to meet the survivor, to hear the full story behind the attack on the borderlands.

Rider and Shanolin sat in the sand to eat and drink, but Raven couldn't; her blood felt supercharged with energy. She barely ate anything, the food tasting like dust in her mouth. She did, however, swallow an entire canteen of water—it could be refilled when they reached the desert oasis.

She clapped her hands and said, "We must move on."

Cronus burst from his haunches at the sound, looking as refreshed as if he'd slept for hours and not just a few minutes.

Siri lowered her head so Raven could climb on.

As the desert flowed under them like a white ocean, Raven scanned the area ahead for any signs of life.

Before anything else, she saw the smoke.

Her heart was exploding in her chest, her blood rushing like raging rivers through her veins. The second Siri landed, she leapt from her mount, racing toward the grove of palms, most of which had been felled, lying prone on the ground. They were charred and smoking, their leaves burned away. The sweet, delicious fruit they once bore littered the path, cracked, burnt husks. They crunched under Raven's heavy trod as she sprinted into Kesh, coughing as smoke poured into her lungs, her eyes burning.

Covering her mouth and nose with the top of her shirt, she dove low to the ground, whirling her head around in shock at the scene before her. Every structure was afire, some already having collapsed. There, the large tent she'd once slept in with her sister, Fire—now a desolation of burnt poles and smoking canvas. There, the table she'd dined at with their soldiers, with Goggin—now an inferno, shooting flames into the air, licking at the sun shades she'd once enjoyed so much.

There were no people, at least none she could see, neither enemy nor friend.

"We have to get you out of here," Rider said, grabbing her shoulder and pulling her back. The dragon master's eyes were wide, her mouth and nose covered with a wet piece of cloth.

Raven shrugged her off, twisting away. She darted forward, crawling for the nearest still-standing structure, a small doorless hut. Flames were dancing from the other tents, tiptoeing onto the hut's roof, climbing down the walls.

A scream rent the air.

Raven dove inside, scanning the space, squinting through the smoky haze.

There! A form lay on the floor, still resting against a toppled over chair. Smoke was pouring through a window and directly into the person's face.

Raven scrambled forward on hands and knees, grabbing the person by the legs, pulling. To her surprise, not only did the form slide across the floor, but the chair too. They were tethered together, locked inside a structure that had become an oven.

She hauled with all her strength, her muscles popping, her skin scraping the floor, the smoke sliding lower and lower. She was forced to use two hands, leaving her mouth and nose unprotected, but still she toiled.

I will not let another person die. Not today.

She reached the door, and then a second set of hands were there, helping. And a third, Shanolin having caught up. Between the three of them, they wrestled the chair across the village and down the path, spilling into the sand. They slumped in a pile, the chair falling onto its side, the occupant releasing a grunt.

Raven's lungs and throat burned. Her tongue tasted like ash. Her eyes stung. Her head swam, as if filled with saltwater. She rolled over, struggling to her knees, fighting to crawl over to the chair, which was facing away from her. Spots were dancing before her eyes, the world fading.

No, she thought. *I'll sleep when I'm dead.*

She rounded the chair, placing a hand on the person's chin, leaving a dark handprint before turning him to face her. For, indeed, it was a man. A man she recognized.

Guta, the proprietor of Kesh and its famed hospitality.

Her friend.

He seemed to recognize her, a surprised smile drifting across his lips. And then his eyes slipped closed.

Seventy-Seven

The Southern Empire, Citadel
Roan Loren

The dead girl was still staring at him; her brother, too. Their eyes seemed to core him like an apple, tearing his heart from his chest.

Roan opened his mouth to speak, closed it, opened it again. The words still wouldn't come.

"Do I know you?" the girl said, frowning.

Yes. Yes yes yes… Roan found the words pouring from his lips before he could stop them. "I'm from Calypso."

Her frown deepened for a moment and then, suddenly, vanished, her lips parting, her eyes widening, her eyebrows lifting. "By the gods," she said. "You can't be here. We can't talk to you."

Roan felt off-kilter, like he was attached to an invisible pendulum, swinging, swinging, rocking... "Why not?"

"He'll kill us. Your guardian will kill us." As the final word slipped from her lips, the girl turned and raced back up the steps, shepherding her brother before her.

Roan dropped from his mount, stumbled, and then gave chase, but Goggin blocked his path, holding him back with a single huge hand.

Roan stared daggers at him. "I need to find that girl," he said, hoping words could help where his muscles had failed him.

"No time for chasin' tail," Goggin said, "gotta find Lady Windy."

"I'm not..." Roan's words fell away. There was no way to adequately explain the situation. Plus, it seemed the girl and her brother—dead, dead, they were supposed to be dead—worked for Windy anyway. So finding her might help find them.

Goggin turned to face the gatekeeper, who was looking even more unsettled than before. "We're going up those steps," the guanero commander said. "Try to stop us."

Though the man protested, they left their mounts in the small entryway. "They'll sleep all day anyway," Goggin muttered as they ascended the steps. Roan tried to see past the large man, but he was like a lunar eclipse.

Eventually, however, they emerged through an arched doorway.

Roan blinked, his breath hitching. *Holy gods...*

The domed structure had been spectacular from the outside. Inside it was simply magnificent. The glass dome shimmered with sunlight, the midafternoon rays angling in and splashing light across one end while casting shadows on the other. At the dome's peak, a ladder descended to a white-marble platform, connected by a staircase to the highest of a dozen ringed walkways that followed the curving the walls of the immense structure.

At various intervals, a platform sprung from each walkway toward the center of the space, like cogs on a wheel. Each platform was supported by its own marble column, beautifully carved.

However, what truly captured Roan's attention was the inner section of the building, which was home to hundreds upon hundreds of circular bookshelves, each rising from the floor and high into the air, ending near the top walkway. The strangest thing, however, was that portions of these bookshelves appeared to be moving. Spinning, really.

Roan's gaze travelled along one of the spinning shelves to its adjacent column, and then upwards to the nearest platform, which, in this case, was situated on level six. Atop the platform was a scholar who was reaching beyond the banister to pull a series of handles attached to the shelving. With each pull, that particular section of the shelves rotated, the spines of thousands of books flying past so rapidly it was impossible to read their titles. The scholar was unfazed, spinning faster and faster until, finally, she slammed her heel into one of the handles, stopping the motion. Lightning-quick, she reached out and snatched a title from the top shelf, briskly flipped a few pages, and then placed it on a wheeled cart resting nearby. A dozen volumes later, she wheeled the cart away.

The whole event took only a few moments to transpire, and left Roan with several questions. *What sort of mechanism allowed the massive bookshelves to rotate like that? How many books were contained on each section of shelving? And, most importantly, how had the scholar located the books she desired so quickly?*

His inner thoughts were extinguished like a candle pinched between two moistened fingers when Goggin said, "It smells funny in here," wrinkling his nose.

Roan thought it smelled wonderful. Not dusty or old, like he had expected an ancient archive to smell, but like fresh parchment and ink with the subtle smell of glue. To Roan, it was the aroma of knowledge. For, somewhere amongst the thousands of books, were answers to the questions that had haunted him his entire life.

For a moment, he forgot all about the girl and boy from his past, the ghosts of his darkest nightmares.

But then, like a flash of light, they returned to the forefront of his mind, standing beside a wispy woman with sharp, intelligent eyes and a dark head of curly hair that resembled an old bird's nest. "Prince Roan," she said. "I am Windy Sandes, keeper of the Citadellian Archives. Would you like some tea?"

In hindsight, Roan should've said no to the tea. It was thick, more like beef stew than herbs steeped in water, with a taste like mud—or how Roan suspected mud would taste. But in the moment, he'd been so shocked by the question and the reappearance of the girl and boy that he'd been unable to utter anything but, "Yes, please. That would be lovely."

Now, as he tried to choke down the thick sludge, he fought off the urge to gag.

"Good?" Windy said, nodding in his direction.

"Delicious," he gasped.

They were in a private room—*My personal study*, Lady Windy had called it—which seemed to Roan to be more of a place to store junk. When they'd entered, Windy had used her hands to push books and scrolls and sheets of jumbled parchment away to clear a space for them to sit at the square stone table. The rest of the slab was hidden beneath various paraphernalia, including two maps of the Four Kingdoms, several iron talismans tied together with string, a half-dozen dirty teacups, stained brown, and, of course, the endless stacks of paper, among other oddities. The area around the table was also filled, and Roan had nearly knocked over three teetering towers of books on the way to his seat. The walls were adorned with paintings, each labeled with the name of the artist and the piece, as well as the year it was created. Most of them were crooked. Compared to the meticulous order of the archives themselves, this room was nothing short of a mess that might've been caused by a tornado passing through.

Goggin had given the room one look and said, "I'll be outside tending to the guanik."

And drinking simpre, Roan thought wryly, wishing he had some of the strong drink to wash down the taste of the horrid tea.

He smacked his lips several times, trying to generate some saliva, and then said, "Those two you sent to collect me at the entrance, the boy and the girl..."

"Yela and Daris," Windy said. "Two of my most prized students. What of them?"

"They're not from Citadel."

"That's not a question," Windy said. "But I'll answer anyway. No. They're from Calypso. I heard you grew up there."

"Yes, from before I can remember. My guardian raised me for a while, and then not."

"What happened to him?"

Roan remembered the fear in the girl's—Yela's—eyes when she said Markin Swansea would kill she and her brother if she spoke to Roan. Now that he had accepted they were really, truly alive, pieces of a puzzle were slowly coming together. Clearly, his guardian wasn't the monster he'd pretended to be. He hadn't killed the children, only scared them into leaving Calypso.

Because they knew my secrets, Roan thought. *No. They* know *my secrets.* Just as quickly, he wondered what they'd told Windy of his past, if anything.

He realized Windy was still awaiting an answer to her question. "My guardian died," he said.

"How?" The woman asked each question casually, sipping her tea, as if she cared not for the answers. Roan got the distinct impression it was an act, feigned indifference to hide her keen interest.

"I don't know. I'd already left home seeking my own path." Roan did know—his guardian was murdered—but didn't feel compelled to share the information with this stranger.

"Mmm-hmm."

"When did you come to know Yela and Daris?" Roan asked, trying to push the attention away from him.

"Their family arrived years ago, but I suspect you already know that. Who are they to you? Old friends?"

More like old ghosts, Roan thought. "Acquaintances," he said. Still, he couldn't help but be glad they were alive, that his guardian hadn't murdered them on his account. How many years he'd spent fearing his own powers because of what might happen to those around him if he used them. Wasted time.

He chided himself silently; there was no point dwelling on a past he couldn't change.

"My niece was terribly vague about your purpose here," Windy said.

"Scholarship," Roan said.

"Hmm, yes. Vague." She sucked down the rest of her tea and promptly refilled her cup from the kettle. The thick tea chugged from the spout slowly, almost oozing.

"I'm sorry, but I really must insist on privacy," Roan said. The last thing he wanted was a Sandes learning of his mission. If word got back to the empress…he suspected his irrevocable pass to the Citadellian Archives would become less…irrevocable.

"You have experience searching our bookshelves?" Windy asked. There was a hint of smugness behind her words.

"Well, no, but how hard can it be to find a book?" He remembered the ease of the scholar, how she'd spun the shelves and snatched volumes to stack on her cart.

"Indeed," Windy said. "Well then, I'll leave you to it." With that, she stood, taking her tea with her. Before she closed the door, she added, "I will arrange a private room for your scholarship. Only the best for a prince of the west."

Two days later Roan was at his wit's end.

He'd begun his search with excitement, starting on the first level and vigorously spinning the bookshelves, scanning the titles for anything referring to "the Western Oracle," or one of the various common names for fatemarks; namely, skinmarks, sinmarks, and tatooya. After being scolded by other scholars on several occasions, he quickly learned there were certain rules, the most important of which was first-come-first-served, meaning that whomever arrived on each platform first had rights to browse the shelves for as long as they wished without interruption. Hence the daily rush of people hurrying to enter the archives first.

Having to wait in line greatly slowed his progress, especially considering he didn't have the first clue where to start looking. Several times he tried to ask for assistance from other scholars, but they just shook their heads, muttered an apology, and swiftly walked away. Something about their reaction smelled of Windy's influence.

Goggin had popped in several times, his breath smelling of simpre. "Having fun yet?" the man had quipped, slapping Roan on the back. His raised voice and raucous laughter drew several annoyed looks from other scholars, but they all wisely kept their opinions to themselves, and Goggine didn't seem to notice.

Windy, however, was notably absent, presumably hunkering down in her private room.

The second day Roan decided to go all the way to the top level. It made sense to him that the most secret of information, the most *valuable* knowledge, would be housed at the apex of the towering shelves.

Goggin had joined him this time, surreptitiously sipping simpre from a hip flask and amusing himself by reading the titles of each book he spotted. Backwards. *Freemen Boronian the of History Tragic and Brief A. Sandes Sky Empress of Exoneration*

The. And on and on. Each time he read a title he'd crack up laughing. "Mebbe books aren't as bad as I thought," he'd said.

Roan ignored him, his frustration mounting. Each turn of the bookshelves was beginning to feel like a large step backwards.

Eventually, the guanero commander had left.

Twice Roan had seen Windy flitting about, her hair still a-tangle, wearing the same clothes as the day before. When she noticed him staring at her, a caterpillar smile had appeared on her lips. *The woman is mad,* Roan had thought.

Now, however, he was on the verge of swallowing his pride and risk bringing her into his confidence in order to get some help. Else he might be wandering the bookshelves until the war came to Citadel and all was lost.

Just as he made up his mind, Yela and her brother appeared, climbing a staircase and onto the top level. Roan stood, transfixed, unable to look away from either of them as they approached. It was like a window into the past, their forms changing to children and back to the present in an instant. The girl stopped immediately before him. She was still tall and wiry, but now had developed the curves of a woman, a narrow hourglass. Her brother, Daris, had shot up like a weed, his face pocked with acne.

She stuck out her hand. "Yela," she said.

Roan stared at her brown fingers, shocked for a moment, but then bent to kiss them lightly, remembering the Calypsian custom when meeting strangers. "Roan," he said.

Daris touched his chest and said, "Daris."

Roan nodded at him. "You're not scared of speaking to me anymore?"

She shook her head. "Windy told us your guardian is dead."

"He is. All those years ago…he threatened you?"

"Yes," Yela said. "Our very lives. I believed him."

"I'm sorry."

"Don't be." She laughed. Roan cocked his head to the side, trying to figure out what could possibly be amusing about a death threat. "He also *paid* for our silence, and for us to leave Calypso forever. Very richly, in fact. Your guardian wasn't a very good haggler."

Now Roan laughed too. It was true. Markin Swansea had been pitiful when it came to negotiating a fair price, always accepting the Calypsian merchants' initial exorbitant offer. "I thought you were dead. Both of you. He showed me your bones in the fire pit."

The girl's laughter fell away. "For that I am sorry. It must have been hard on you. We were just children then."

"I hated him for it. I ran away from home."

"Oh gods," Yela said. "I didn't know. While we were living like royalty you were living on the streets."

Roan didn't care about any of that. Not right now. His world had been turned upside-down in the best possible way. For once, a tragedy had been reversed. For once, peace had ruled the day. "I'm fine now," he said. "Did Lady Windy tell you who I really am?"

Yela nodded, her dark eyes suddenly shining. "A prince of the west. Roan Loren." She paused for a moment, as if trying to decide something. Then she said, "Well, Roan Loren, I never properly thanked you for what you did that day, when you healed my broken leg. You bear a tatooya, don't you?"

Once Roan might've lied, would've come up with some plausible explanation, and then made a run for it. Not anymore. "Yes," he said. "I do. The lifemark."

The girl nodded, as if he'd only confirmed something she'd known for a long time. "If not for your actions, I might've never walked again. And, to boot, we got paid for it. I am forever in your debt. Whatever you are looking for, I can help you find it."

After that, things went much more quickly. Even if Yela decided to tell Windy what he was looking for, Roan was willing to bear the risk. And she'd promised him she wouldn't, a promise he was inclined to believe. So he'd told her. Not everything—he didn't have time for a story that long—but the basics: how he believed the tatooya, or fatemarks, were the key to restoring peace to the Four Kingdoms; how knowledge was crucial, and that his search had led him to Citadel. He didn't mention Bear Blackboots, or the possibility that the Western Oracle or her son might still be alive—he didn't want her to think him mad.

Though it was well past sundown, or so Roan suspected, he poured over the stacks of tomes Yela continued to deliver every hour or so, the candlelight dancing across the pages. Goggin had returned once, but soon tired of reading titles backwards, and had left seeking sustenance. Roan didn't expect to see him again until the morning. *Late* morning, more than likely.

Thus far, he'd found six references to the fatemarks, most of which were firsthand accounts of the powers they gave certain individuals—people who became weapons used by their kingdoms.

"They only made things worse," Roan whispered.

"What?"

Roan hadn't realized Yela stood in the doorway. She looked exhausted from all her running around on his behalf, but she hadn't complained once. Daris had gone to bed hours earlier, but she had persevered.

"The first people bearing tatooya—fatemarks—were used to exacerbate the war. Their rulers made them into soldiers and they did battle for years."

"I know the stories," Yela said.

Of course she did. She was a scholar in training, after all. According to Windy herself, Yela was one of her prized students. "What else do you know?" Roan asked, feeling foolish for not having asked in the first place.

"I know nothing has changed. Those with...*fatemarks*, as you call them, are still weapons. The Ice Lord in the north, now dead. Beorn Stonesledge in the east. The Slave Master in Phanes, also dead. Even Lady Windy's niece, Fire, was a bringer of death and violence before she was killed."

Gwendolyn Storm, Roan added in his head. It was true of her as well. Though she tried to use her powers for good, to save lives, she was still thought of as a weapon by the ruling Ironclads. He nodded thoughtfully. "The mindset has to change."

"To what?"

"I don't know. I'm hoping if we can learn more about the Western Oracle and her purpose for creating the fatemarks..."

"We can learn how to use them to achieve peace," Yela filled in.

"Exactly."

Yela nodded, moving into the room, depositing her new stack of books onto the desk. "That's the last of them," she said.

The declaration sent a shiver of excitement tinged with fear through him. What if the answer he'd been looking for was sitting right in front of him? What if it wasn't? What then?

"And look at this," Yela said, interrupting his thoughts. She cracked open the book on the top of the pile, carefully turning the pages until she reached one she'd marked with a bit of string. Roan slid over as she pointed to the part she wanted to show him. A passage of text, supposedly spoken by the Western Oracle while being prepared for her fiery execution in Knight's End:

For they must put to bed their disputes, their hate, their anger at acts of the past, the traditions of their fathers and forefathers. Only the fatemarked can help them achieve this. Only the fatemarked can unite the Four Kingdoms before the day of commencement. If they do not, they shall be unprepared for the HORDE that shall sweep across the land, consuming all.

The words sent a shiver through Roan. "Horde?" he said. "Have you ever heard of that?"

Yela shook her head. "No. Never. I started to look for other references but didn't see anything. It will take a long time to search these books."

Roan chewed his lips, wondering what this horde was, in all capital letters. Something about the word resounded inside him, like a hammer striking again and again. It felt important. *Is this why you created us?* he thought. *Is this the purpose for everything? Will one of the kingdoms go too far, seeking the annihilation of all the others?* Given his experience with rulers like Rhea Loren and

547

Grian Ironclad, it certainly wasn't out of the realm of possibility.

"You should go to bed," he said. "I'll need to sleep eventually, and then you can take over the search."

"Not a chance." She grinned. "I want to be here."

Roan could see the fires of potential discovery in her eyes. She was a collector of knowledge, not to be denied. He understood the feeling. He waved at an empty chair. "Thank you," he said. "I could use your help."

Seventy-Eight
The Southern Empire, Citadel
Bear Blackboots

Roan Loren had shown up two days earlier, as he knew he would. The young man was determined, that was for certain.

He is the one, Bear Blackboots thought now, watching as Roan sat at the table with the scholar girl. Though they had a private study to work in, the door remained open—no one was left in the archives except them. And Bear, of course, but he had his ways. He hid behind one of the stacks, peering through a gap in the books—a gap he had created. His perfect vision magnified the open room beyond.

When you were as old as he was, you learned a few tricks.

Still, Bear knew that Roan could read every word in those books and he still wouldn't have the answer he craved. *Mother,*

I am here; I am fighting for the peace you believed in, the peace you died for.

Of course, she didn't answer. He wasn't sure whether the Western Oracle was gone forever, or if she was merely sleeping, her soul exhausted from the years of waiting.

But that didn't matter, because Bear *was* here. Bear *was* the answer, the truth of his mother's wisdom inked on his very skin, hidden beneath his dark cloak. He'd lived many lives, but this one was the only one that truly mattered. *I shall be the truthbringer*, he thought. *Mother, I will not fail you.*

He retrieved the book from his deep pocket; he'd removed it from the bookshelves days ago, safeguarding it until this very moment, when the time felt right. His large fingers brushed the tattered leather cover, tracing the letters etched into it. *The Death of Absence*, it was titled. *A Story of Woe, by the Western Oracle.* Despite the years, seeing his mother's title, the one that had condemned her in the end, brought a tear to his eye.

He dashed it away before it could fall on the book.

He opened the book to the last page, which contained only two sentences. Four words.

Absence lives. Find It.

A shiver ran down Bear's spine. He plucked a quill from the floor, dipping it carefully in a pot of ink. Slowly, he penned a brief message:

Find Absence. Find the Truth. And find me.

Bear Blackboots.

On silent feet, he travelled the arc of the top-level corridor, until he was immediately outside the room. No sounds arose but breathing and the occasional turning of pages.

He propped the book against the wall and left.

550

It was time for another voyage, the first he had taken since his childhood.

He'd departed Teragon a boy; he would return as a man.

Seventy-Nine
The Southern Empire, Citadel
Windy Sandes

The large, bearded man thought he was a ghost, floating in secret through the archives. But he wasn't, at least not to Windy. The archives were hers, and she knew everything that happened within their bounds.

Through a false mirror hanging on the wall, she saw the man write something in the old book and then leave it outside Roan Loren's study.

After the man left, and she assumed he was gone for good, she stole through the large, domed space, and took the book.

Hours later, her eyes burning from lack of sleep, she turned to the last page. Saw the message. *Bear Blackboots*, she thought. The name sounded familiar, and yet she couldn't place it. She'd read a lot of books over the years, more than she could count or keep track of. This was a fleeting name, one she'd probably come across in the midst of one scholarship or another.

"Who are you?" she wondered aloud. *And what have you to do with the Teran god, Absence?* Or with the Western Oracle, for that matter. For she knew it was information on the Oracle and her legendary fatemarks that Roan was seeking.

The urge to take the book to Roan Loren and demand answers rose inside her, but she tempered such hasty actions. She was a woman of patience, of wisdom. No, first she would see how this played out before offering the book in exchange for his story.

And then, perhaps, they would take a trip south, across the Burning Sea. Together.

Eighty

The Southern Empire, Calypso
Raven Sandes

Guta had lived for a few more hours, drifting in and out of consciousness, before eventually succumbing to the smoke inhalation.

Raven, more than ever before, wanted to sit down and cry. Instead, alongside Rider and Shanolin, she stared at Kesh as it burned all the day long and into the night. They didn't sleep; they didn't speak. Their dragons seemed to understand the gravity of the situation, remaining equally silent and calm.

At dawn, Raven buried Guta in the middle of the destroyed oasis. It's what he would've wanted, she knew. They picked through the still-hot rubble, finding dozens of other bodies. Guta's employees, probably. Travelers, maybe. One of the guanero perhaps, whomever had survived the battle on the borderlands only to die in Kesh.

Heavy footprints marred the sand to the north of the desert village, pushing northeast, back toward the border. *The eastern army*, Raven knew. It was the furthest they had ever ventured into the Scarra, a bold act that had struck a blow that might as well have been the heart of the empire.

Staring at the destruction around her, it felt strange. The last time Raven had been here, it had been a vibrant oasis of joy in the midst of a harsh desert landscape. Now, it was nothing but a burnt tangle of sticks and canvas, palm and brush. Despite the change, she no longer felt sick, her stomach formed of leather and fire.

No, she felt only anger, dragonfire in her blood.

Rider shook her head, while Shanolin said, "This was an act of war."

"Yes," Raven agreed. She could deny the dragon master no longer.

"We must return to Calypso immediately and convene the war council."

"Soon," Raven said. "First we must stop in Citadel."

Shanolin frowned. "Why? What is in the City of Wisdom that could possibly help us plan a war?"

Raven had not informed her of her guanero commander's secret mission. "Goggin, for one. And information. Something that could change everything. When we attack Ferria, our victory must be total this time. Next to what we are going to do, the Dragon Massacre will be remembered as a minor skirmish."

The City of Wisdom shone like a beacon in the midday light, flanked by an ocean so blue it might've been a painting.

It had been many years since Raven had traveled to Citadel. The last time was when she was ten years old, spending the summer with her Aunt Windy, the keeper of the vast archives housed within the bowels of the city. Though Raven wasn't much for books, except for the occasional tome regarding the history of dragonlore, she'd enjoyed her time there, swimming in Dragon Bay and exploring the library while her aunt studied books all the day long.

She'd been sad when her mother wouldn't allow her to return the following year. "You will soon be a woman. It's time you began preparing for the future," her mother had said.

Raven hadn't thought about Citadel much since then, throwing herself into training the dragonia and learning the art of combat.

Now, however, her good memories from summers spent in this city came rushing back. She blinked them away; it felt wrong thinking of happy times.

As they approached from the air, the scholars, as small as ants from this height, stopped their constant scurrying about the city to stare at the sky. Some pointed. Some began running for cover, as if they believed their own dragonia had come to destroy them.

Raven steered Siri toward an old dragon landing platform set at the peak of the enormous glass dome of the Citadellian Archives. Rarely used, the platform was still in good condition and free of dirt or bird droppings, as everything in this city was. *Aunt Windy still runs a tight ship*, Raven thought as Siri landed softly on the large platform. Cronus and Heiron dropped in beside her.

Briefly, Raven had told her dragon masters about Roan Loren's sudden appearance in Calypso, as well as the deal they'd made. "You should have told us before," Shanolin had said in response. "I'm telling you now," Raven had replied, leaving it at that. They hadn't spoken much since, each processing the events of the last few days in silence.

Now, Shanolin said, "I'll wait with the dragons."

"Good," Raven said. "Thank you. Rider, with me." It was better this way. Shanolin and Roan seemed to be at opposite ends of the spectrum and forcing them together would likely only cause trouble.

She strode over to a hatch in the platform, pulling on the handle. Its hinges didn't so much as squeak, well-oiled and maintained, despite having not been used in years. An iron ladder descended onto a marble platform, which was held up by a large column and connected to the rest of the enormous space by a series of shiny staircases.

Quickly, efficiently, Raven descended the ladder. When she reached the platform, hundreds of oval-shaped faces were staring up at her wearing shocked expressions. *They would've seen the dragons fly across the glass*, Raven thought. "The archives are closed until further notice," she announced. "Leave now."

Without complaint nor argument, the scholars turned away and filed toward the exits, of which there were many. A wry smile creased Raven's lips. For better or worse, the scholars of Citadel knew how to follow rules.

She clambered down the steps to the highest level, running her hand along the stone banister. Somewhere below, a voice called out. "Raven, First Daughter. Is it truly you?"

When she peered over the railing, Aunt Windy looked up at her wearing a wistful smile.

557

"Hello, Auntie," Raven said. "Roan Loren is still here, I trust?"

"You've changed so much, my dear. A girl flowers into her destiny…" She sounded as if she was quoting something, which Windy was known to do quite often.

"Auntie, please. We can catch up later. Right now I need to know: Is he here?"

"Oh, yes. We've spent a fair bit of time together already. A wonderful soul he is."

"Good. I need to speak to him. Immediately."

"He's already left for the day, I fear. He'll be back in the morning. Now come, have a cup of tea with me."

"Windy, I really must insist on seeking Roan Loren in the city," Raven said. "War is brewing and we must be ready."

"War is always brewing, my dear," Windy said, handing her a cup of a strong-smelling tea resembling boiled mud. "Hasty action serves no one. The empire will not fall while you enjoy a warm drink with your aunt."

Gods, Raven thought. *She hasn't changed a bit.* Yes, a few thin lines creased her forehead and crow's feet now limned the corners of her eyes, but that was to be expected for a woman who spent hours reading print so fine she at times required a magnifying glass. Other than that, she was the same as always, her brown frizzy hair sticking up in several places and interspersed with spots of gray, like woven spider webs. Her conservative clothes—a long-sleeved, high-collared shirt and mannish brown trousers—were wrinkled and dotted with old stains. She wore no shoes, her brown feet protruding like river trout poking their faces from the water. It was as if she reserved all her meticulous care for the archives and none for herself.

"It might," Raven replied. "Kesh is destroyed. I lost a tenth of my guanero in the desert. The world has gone mad."

Again, her aunt appeared unperturbed by the revelations, taking a sip of her tea, wrinkling her nose slightly. Taking another sip. "The world has always been mad. The degrees change, but the disease does not."

"Is that from a book?"

"No, my dear. It's from experience."

To Raven's knowledge, her aunt hadn't experienced much of anything, the entirety of her existence spent in a single city, most of it in this very building. But she wouldn't be rude, nor would she argue with her eccentric aunt. The urge to head out into the city, where she'd sent Rider on ahead, began to tug at her feet again.

"I have to go, Auntie. Thank you for the tea." She started to stand.

"You haven't drunk any of it, so it's odd you would thank me for it."

Raven sighed. She glanced at the tea. Though the memories had faded, she faintly remembered hating her aunt's tea. Still, the sooner she drank it, the sooner she could be quit of this place. She made the mistake of smelling it first, recoiling like she'd been stung. *Something is rotting in there*, she thought. Taking a deep breath, she threw it back, clamping her mouth shut to avoid spewing the thick noxious liquid back out.

"Mmm," Windy said, nodding. "You'll be alert for hours."

Raven swallowed, shivering slightly. A flip of a coin would decide whether she vomited it back up.

559

A moment passed, then another. When she didn't throw up, she said, "I must go now, Auntie, but I promise to return for a visit soon, when all of this is over."

"Oh, Raven," Windy said, shaking her head in such a way that Raven suddenly felt very small, "this will never be over. For this is life, as eternal as the paths of the moons in the sky."

Eighty-One
The Southern Empire, Citadel
Roan Loren

Roan had been in his private study when Empress Raven Sandes and her dragons had arrived. Like everyone else in the archives, he'd heard the beating of wings. His first thought was that Yela had betrayed him, but then he saw the fear in the girl's eyes. Perhaps Lady Windy then. She'd figured out his quest and sent a stream to Calypso, informing the empress.

However, as he and Yela had peeked through the doorway, he'd heard Windy *lie* for him. In truth, he hadn't left the archives since he arrived. Neither had Yela. When they got hungry, Daris would fetch them food. When they got tired, they slept on the floor, using stacks of paper as pillows.

Thus far, they'd found no other references to the horde. The fatemarked were mentioned numerous times, however, and Roan was learning much about his predecessors.

"What do we do?" Yela asked now, after the empress had followed Windy inside her private room.

Roan considered the question. Raven would eventually find them if they stayed here. Even if she didn't, Roan would never know why she'd followed him to the City of Wisdom. And he needed to know. Something was happening, and though he longed to tuck his head back into his shell like a turtle, continuing to study the pages and pages of century-old information at his fingertips, that wasn't a luxury he could afford.

The door to Windy's study opened, Raven's voice echoing out. "The moons do not interfere in the wars of women, Auntie. But thank you for the advice."

Wars? he thought, his eyes meeting Yela's. Were Calyp's troubles with the east moving even faster than he expected? Or was the reference related to the civil war with Phanes? One way or another, he needed to know.

He stepped from the room.

Down below, just past the edge of one of the rotating bookshelves, the empress stood, looking away from him. Windy, however, looked up, spotting him. Her head shook, an almost imperceptible movement. A warning. *Stay silent.*

Why was she protecting him? Why had she lied for him?

"Empress," he said, loudly enough that his voice would carry down several levels to her ears.

Raven Sandes slowly turned, her gaze lifting. "Ah, Roan Loren. Thank you for making your presence known despite my

Auntie's *lies*." If Windy felt anything at having been discovered, it didn't show on her face, her expression as smooth as glass.

"She was only trying to protect the privacy of my scholarship. Any falsehoods she told were at my request."

Raven chewed on this. "Back in Calypso you offered to provide details of Ferria's defenses."

Roan's heart skipped a beat. "I did. But you won't need them. Attacking the Iron City would be a fatal mistake."

"A mistake, no. Fatal, yes. But for my enemies, not me."

Roan shook his head. "What has happened?"

"An act of war," she said. "One that will be answered in kind."

Something had changed in the empress's eyes. They were the same—dark, intense—but different at the same time, the fires of revenge burning.

They sat in Windy's room—all of them. The dragon master, Rider, leaning casually against the wall. Goggin, mounting two chairs backwards to hold his bulk. Windy, pouring tea for everyone and attempting, without much success, to clear more space on the hopelessly cluttered table. Evidently there was another dragon master atop the dome, attending to the dragons.

Yela was the only one who had been dismissed. Roan had seen the disappointment in her eyes, but she hadn't argued, slipping away quietly.

Raven had already told him what had happened in the desert. The thought of so many dead at the hands of Grian

Ironclad's legionnaires—soldiers Roan had once travelled with—sickened him.

"Pull your forces back from the Scarra," Roan said.

"I already have," Raven said. "Before leaving Kesh, I sent a stream to Calypso with orders. Even now, my armies are assembling, awaiting further command."

"To march to war, you mean."

She shook her head. "There will be no marching. We go by sea and air, as we did once before. My dragonia will rain fire from the skies over Ferria."

"I told you—"

"Th eastern defenses are improved, aye, I heard. That's why I need to know the specifics. Otherwise, by your own words, we will be annihilated. Now speak, my patience grows thin."

Roan could see the crossroads before him. He remembered the day Gareth had given him a tour of the castle, given him a demonstration of just one of the new iron-based defenses they'd implemented. He'd mentioned others. But, when speaking to Raven, he'd bluffed. He didn't know much more than she. Now he would need to invent some "details" so fearsome as to change her mind, convince her to wait.

"The Ironclads have an army of Orians," he started.

"That is not news. The Orians have fought by their side for years."

"Not within their legions," Roan explained. "Within the castle. Atop the walls. Hidden in protected alcoves."

Raven frowned. "For what purpose?"

"Defense." Roan recalled how the blade had burst from the wall, giving him quite a scare. "They are expert channelers, each and every one of them."

He saw the moment the light of understanding entered Raven's eyes. "The castle itself will attack us?"

Roan nodded.

"Give me an example."

The blade from the wall trick was nothing. He needed to come up with something better. An idea struck him. "The walls rearrange themselves into iron knights as tall as trees. They will knock your dragons from the sky. Your ground forces will be crushed under their trod. Within the bounds of the forest, they are invincible."

A twitch of Raven's lips. Though she tried to hide it, his revelation had struck a chord. "Dragonfire is the hottest substance known to humans. We will melt them into iron puddles."

Roan didn't know if that was true or possible, but he had an answer. "They will reform instantly. They are not alive— not in the ways of men—so they can't be killed. Their god, Orion, holds great power within Ironwood."

She looked away, her eyes meeting those of each person, before returning to Roan. "Thank you. This is a matter for the war council," she said.

"But you will recommend patience?" Roan said.

Goggin snorted, the first sound he'd made since he arrived. When he'd heard the news of his guaneros' deaths in the Scarra, he'd bit his lip but said nothing. "You might be from Calypso, but you are not Calypsian," he said.

Windy slipped from the room, as if the truth had chased her away.

Rider said, "I'll tell Shanolin to prepare the dragons," and left as well.

Roan was missing something.

Raven said, "No, Roan Loren. Patience is the last thing I will be recommending."

No. Everything was happening too quickly. He'd barely arrived in Citadel, barely scratched the surface of the mysteries to be found here, and yet the world was crumbling around him. Once again, his fate seemed set before his feet, a path he had to follow to its bitter end. "I'm going with you to Calypso," he said.

"As you wish," Raven replied. "But it will not change anything."

Eighty-Two
The Southern Empire, Pirate's Peril
Grey Arris

As the anchor was hauled up from the depths and the sails were unfurled, Grey pulled Shae aside. "We need to discuss something," he said. His head was still buzzing from his conversation with Kyla, how well she'd taken his affair with Rhea, and the plan she'd come up with, which was so insane it just might work.

Shae nodded, though her eyes didn't meet his. They were locked on the sunlit rocks of Pirate's Peril, her head cocked slightly to the side, almost as if she were listening to some great call only she could hear.

The last words uttered by Grey's father drummed out a steady beat in his head. *Protect your sister above all else...all else...all else...* Thus far, he'd done a shite job of it, and sailing into a pirate's lair didn't seem to be any better. Then again, for the first time since their parents' deaths, he was letting *Shae* make the choice on where to go.

"Are you certain you want to do this?" Grey asked. "You've been through so much already—we both have. There's no reason we can't tell Captain Smithers we've changed our minds, that we want to stay on as members of the crew. We could have a good life, Shae. No more running. No more schemes."

He couldn't tell if she'd heard him, her expression as unchangeable as the face of the sun. After a few moments of silence, she said, "It's hard to explain, Grey. These dreams..."

"Tell me," Grey said.

She shook her head. "It's not the dreams themselves, but the feeling after them, when they've ended and I'm awake, aware of the piece of me that's missing."

"This pirate?" he said. There was a slash of frustration in his tone, and he instantly regretted it. Shae, however, didn't seem to notice.

"Not the pirate, not exactly, but the power locked inside him. His mark completes mine, and mine his."

"The key," Grey murmured.

She nodded.

"But what does it unlock? What is its purpose?"

Shae sighed. "That's what I must know. When I'm awake, I feel like a heavy weight is pushing on my chest and I can't breathe. The only way to remove the weight is to meet this pirate."

"Why him? Why you?" Grey knew these were questions Shae had probably battled with ever since the dreams started, but they forced their way out of his mouth, refusing to be silenced.

But Shae, to his surprise, answered, her eyes finally locking on his. "We've been chosen." Her gaze was like steel armor, impenetrable.

"For what?"

"We will soon know, Grey. It is all becoming clearer. My path, my purpose. Yours too. You're a part of this now, as is Captain Smithers and Kyla and the crew. That's why they're doing this—because they can feel it here." She pointed to her chest.

More than anything, Grey wanted to protect his sister from evil, from a dangerous world that could chew you up, swallow you, and then vomit you back up to be chewed and eaten again. However, it seemed he would have to go with the second best option, which was to follow her into danger and do whatever it took for her to emerge alive and unscathed on the other side.

"Alright," he said.

She nodded, and the ship lurched back into motion, pushed by a stiff, warm wind. She turned her head back to the ocean, to the approaching isles.

"Shae?" Grey said.

"Mmm?" she murmured.

"I don't tell you enough, but I love you."

The shadow of a smile. "I know, Grey. I know."

The cliffs of Pirate's Peril cast long shadows across the green sea, darkening *The Jewel's* sails.

Even in Knight's End, stories of the pirate-infested island were popular. How the island had gotten its name was a matter of constant debate. Some said it was because any pirate who stepped onto its shores risked being murdered by another pirate who wanted their ship and all its spoils. Others believed it was the island itself that was perilous, the powerful currents snatching even the most seaworthy vessels and smashing them onto the rocks. Of course, as stories generally went, there were darker versions, too. Whirlpools, sea monsters, ghosts...

Grey knew most of the stories were probably worth about the same as the contents of a chamber pot, but he wasn't so foolish as to ignore them. Staring at the cliffs that now towered over them, he was strung tightly, prepared for anything.

This close to the rocks, the sails had been lowered and tied. Each of the two-armed members of the crew—which included everyone but Grey—manned the oars, attempting to navigate the treacherous waters, which had, so far, included sudden shallows, unpredictable currents, and rocks that seemed to spring from the sea at a moment's notice. They'd hit one so far, a glancing blow, but it was only a scratch, almost indistinguishable amongst the hundreds of other similar markings on the prow.

By Grey's estimation, they were moving too fast by half, but the captain seemed to be in full control, standing on the foredeck, spinning the wheel back and forth while barking orders to his men.

Something thumped the bottom of the boat, and its progress stalled for a moment. "Halt!" Smithers shouted.

"What is it?" Grey asked aloud, to no one in particular.

"It's as if someone dropped the anchor," Kyla said, frowning.

The anchor, however, was resting in its berth, the chains coiled around the spool.

"We're stuck on something," Grey said. "Some coral?"

A sailor was sent below to check for leaks or other damage, but returned without any new information. Then, as swiftly as they'd stopped, the ship eased forward of its own volition. *The Jewel* moved slowly, drifting with a light current that was pulling them toward a channel between the main island and a nearby rock outcropping that, to Grey, resembled a human skull. Connecting the "skull" to the island was a long stone archway that might've been a spine. He groaned inwardly at his own imagination.

"Are we going to clear that?" Grey asked no one in particular. From this distance, it was hard to compare the height of the arch to top of the ship's mast.

Smithers leaned on the railing, his scimitar sheathed, though his hand had a habit of resting on the hilt, as if he might draw the blade at any moment. "I don' like this," he muttered under his breath. He spat a wad of tobacco juice into the water.

Grey understood what the captain meant. Something about the entire situation felt eerie, almost like they were being pulled by the island itself. He had the distinct feeling of being watched, though as he scanned the rocks he saw nothing, not even a bird.

From somewhere nearby, there was a sudden splash.

Grey turned his head to look, but whatever had caused it was gone, leaving behind only whitewater and ripples.

"Anyone see what that was?" the captain asked. No one had. "Prolly just a big fish," Smithers concluded, though it was clear from his tone he wasn't convinced himself.

571

They were almost to the archway, which, Grey could now see, was carved with images of strange creatures: half-women, half-fish, their fins and long tails giving way to slender human bodies. The depictions were so well done that clearly the stone had been chiseled away by an expert stoneworker. Grey wondered who would be mad enough to clamber up the narrow archway and hang over the side in order to carve the stone.

It's going to be close, he thought. If they cleared it, it would be by the barest of margins.

Another splash drew everyone's attention to the opposite side of the vessel. Again, there was no sign of what sort of creature had made it.

A third splash, then a fourth and fifth, resounded in short succession. Grey tried to follow the sounds, but every time he looked in one direction, the next splash came from the opposite side. The others were clearly having the same problem—panicked shouts and cries of alarm began popping up.

And then he heard it: the cry. It was somewhere between a child's wail and a piercing melodic note. Had there been glass, it surely would've shattered. Everyone on deck immediately covered their ears with both hands, but Grey was only able to cover one. Had he used his new blade-hand, he would've stabbed himself in the brain, which, in some ways, would've been better than the pain he felt in his skull as a result of the horrific sound.

The shriek seemed to come from all around them at once, impossible to pinpoint, but then someone shouted, "There!" and soon everyone was pointing to the rocks. Grey was certain they'd been empty a moment earlier, but not anymore. A woman sat on the edge, her legs and feet invisible beneath the green water, which lapped against her stomach. She was naked, at least as far as they could see, though her long hair covered all but a small portion of her breasts. In fact, "hair" didn't seem like the correct term, for it was different than human hair, thick, wet tendrils dangling with seaweed.

Her mouth was open—the source of the ear-shattering cry.

And then, abruptly, she cut it off. Slowly, one by one, the sailors uncovered their ears, staring in disbelief as she blew them a kiss.

There was something about those eyes...which glimmered, seeming to change color with the sea...

The attack came from behind, while everyone was focused on the single woman, who leapt into the water with a familiar splash. Instead of feet, it was a long, purple tail that burst from the water.

One sailor was hauled, screaming, from the deck and into the water, vanishing. No one had even seen what took him. But then they were all around, bursting from the water, landing on deck with wet thumps.

"To arms!" Smithers shouted.

They were like the woman on the rocks, except, up close, more horrifying than Grey could describe. Their hair was indeed formed of seaweed, saltwater clinging to it like dewdrops on grass. Their eyes were a moving target, swirling white and turquoise and green. Their breasts, Grey couldn't help but notice, were the closest resemblance to human, but even they flashed with scales, as did their firm bellies and backs. Below the waist were the long, finned tails depicted by the images on the archway. Their tails came in many different colors—green, purple, blue, yellow. Without legs, it should've given the humans an advantage on ship, but the fish-women moved far quicker than one could imagine, using their strong arms and clawed hands to haul themselves across deck, sliding on their tails.

Yet, none of that was as horrifying as the moment they began to open their mouths. Not only did their screams consume all other sound, but their fangs appeared, long sharp incisors protruding past their bottom lips. Their tongues were inhumanly long, flicking from their mouths, reaching a barbed point at the end.

Grey watched, dumbfounded, as one of the creatures leapt atop a sailor, ripping open his chest with a single swipe of her claws. Her fangs sank into his neck and he saw her tongue burrow its way into his skin. She seemed to sigh in satisfaction, her back arching in relief.

They're hungry, Grey thought. *Or, rather, thirsty. It's our blood they want.*

"Get behind me," he said to Shae and Kyla, a strange calm filling him. This was his purpose: to protect these two beautiful souls, and he was willing to die for them if necessary.

Captain Smithers appeared beside him, a grim look on his face. "With me!" he cried, leaping forward, scimitar raised.

A creature launched herself at him, knocking him to the deck with her tail. He did, however, manage to slash at her— one of her fins came free, flopping across the wood and over the side. She hissed at him, rearing up like a snake, preparing to attack.

Grey didn't think—only acted—throwing himself forward, trying to block the captain's body with his own. He was thinking of Kyla, of how much she'd already lost, how he couldn't let her lose anything more…

There was a sucking sound as the woman—fish—*thing*, landed atop him, her fangs so close to his face he could see the saliva glistening on their enamel. Her barbed tongue shot out, probing, slashing his cheek, but then went limp, as did her body. Grey was covered in something gray and wet and sticky.

As hard as he could—she was rutting heavy and he had only one arm to do the job—he shoved her away from him. Her skin was rough against his hand, even the portion that looked like normal skin. Again, there was that sucking sound and his blade came free, having been impaled in her stomach. She flopped onto the deck and lay still, her sticky, gray blood gushing from the wound, pooling around her.

Nearby, two other creatures lay dead, cut down by other sword-bearing sailors. Grey whirled to find Shae, who had drawn her knife and looked ready to use it, unharmed. Kyla, on the other hand, was straddling one of the creatures, her blade sunk into its neck. She was breathing hard, but appeared uninjured. With her hair askew and her lean, strong arms gripping the blade, Grey never thought she'd looked more beautiful.

The rest of the attackers crawled-slid across the deck, throwing themselves over the sides. Several of them were carrying the bodies of Smithers' seamen, while the rest hauled their own dead away.

Grey pushed himself to his feet, helping the captain up beside him. They stood, side by side, at the ready. The other sailors, white-faced and breathing heavily, had drifted toward them, until they were gathered in a knot in the center of the deck, forming a protective circle around Shae and Kyla, though Grey was beginning to wonder whether it was the women who should be protecting the men.

They stood like that for a long time, just breathing, waiting, anticipating.

The stone archway faded away as they drifted toward an inlet. As it turned out, clearing the barrier had been the least of their problems.

Finally, after what felt like an eternity, Smithers said, "I think it's over."

At final count, they'd lost ten men, almost half the crew. Twelve remained, not including the captain, Grey, Shae, and Kyla.

Once again, the stories hadn't done justice to the horrific realities.

Grey felt sick to his stomach. *This is my fault,* he thought, staring at the mismatched patches of human and sea-creature blood. He felt compelled to begin scrubbing, though he didn't. He felt even worse because of the relief knowing that Shae and Kyla had survived. He would've sacrificed each and every man on the ship, himself included, if it meant they were safe.

Kyla said, "I know what you're thinking." Her tight-fitting clothes were, like Grey's, slick with gore.

"That's because it's true."

"It's not. Each of the men knew this would be dangerous, but they agreed anyway. There was no pressure. Da even said he'd drop them off somewhere if they wanted him to." She roped an arm around him.

"You were incredible," Grey said, motioning toward her blade.

She picked it up nonchalantly, wiped it on the front of her shirt, and slipped it back inside her corset. Shrugged. "You learn a thing or two sailing with scoundrels."

If those men hadn't died, he might've laughed. But as it was, he could only thank the gods that some of them had made it through.

They made their way over to where Shae stood beside the captain. Smithers was back at the helm, steering them into the rock-walled inlet.

Shae was staring ahead, where the walls became shadows, gray at first and then as black as a starless, moonless night. "I feel it," she said.

"Shae," Grey said, touching her shoulder gently. "What do you feel?"

"The other half of the key," she said, wrinkling her brow. "I don't understand what it means, but things are clarifying. It's so warm." She looked down at her palm, which was bursting with light.

Her mark was shining, the back half of a golden key that could only be completed by a pirate.

Kyla stared at it in amazement. In fact, most of the crewmembers were doing the same. The captain, his voice barely above a whisper, said, "The darndest thing I ever seen."

The light began to fade, before disappearing completely, along with the marking. "So tired," Shae said. Her eyes rolled back and she fainted.

Grey barely managed to catch her with one arm before she hit the deck.

She was breathing, and Grey could feel the strong pulse in Shae's neck, but he was still concerned. Nothing like this had ever happened to her. In fact, he'd never seen her marking flare up like that unless a torch was shone across it.

She was changing, and he felt helpless.

"She'll be fine," Kyla said, holding Shae's hand, stroking her skin. "She is strong. She survived the Dead Isles, remember?"

Grey knew she was right, but that didn't help quell his fears. For all he knew, they were sailing right into a trap set by the pirates who came before them, if any had survived an attack by the deadly sea creatures.

Regardless, it was too late to change their minds now, the currents continuing to pull them into the inlet, straight for the shadowy maw of the cave. Stalactites hung from the ceiling, like enormous teeth. As the ship drifted into the shadows, he had the uneasy sense they were going to crack off and impale him. It was only after they'd passed under them did he manage to breathe normally again.

Smithers had had three of his surviving sailors light lanterns before they entered the cave, and now these men shone light on either side of the cavern, which was so broad and tall that Grey couldn't see its walls or ceiling. Instead, the wobbly yellow light only managed to reveal clear, shallow waters. The cave floor beneath it seemed to sparkle.

"Those are gold coins if I'm a captain," Smithers said.

Grey looked more closely, his eyes widening when he realized the captain was right. Thousands, if not hundreds of thousands, of gold coins covered the bottom. He wondered what kind of pirate would throw that much wealth over the side of his boat. *A very rich one*, he thought.

They eased forward, peering into the gloom, trying to see beyond the short arc of the lanternlight. "Dead ahead!" the eagle-eyed scout cried. "Steer to port!"

The captain didn't hesitate, trusting his man, spinning the wheel to the left. Sure enough, shadows took shape, emerging from the darkness. Grey's breath caught. A ship, at least twice as large as *The Jewel*, bobbing at anchor. They glided past it, so close they could've touched it if they'd reached out. The scout's eyes had saved them from certain collision.

Grey tried to make out an insignia on the sails, but they were down, the folds of cloth hiding any markings, if there were any to be found.

"To starboard!" the scout cried.

"I thought you said to port," Smithers replied, his hands gripping the wheel.

"And now to starboard," the scout insisted.

Once more, the captain spun the wheel, but this time to the right. Another shape loomed before them, twice as big as the first, a mammoth black-painted vessel with two masts. Their smaller ship was turning, but too slowly, the bow arcing through the black water. Grey had no experience with steering ships in tight quarters, but even his unseasoned eyes could tell a hit was imminent. He dropped to the deck, pulling Kyla with him. He threw his body atop Shae.

There was a raucous shriek and the ship shuddered, trembling from bow to stern, port to starboard. Everything went still.

The captain said, "Aye. That was close."

Grey stood, offering Kyla a hand. He glanced back. The enormous vessel hadn't moved, but now a long scrape ran down its side. He swallowed. The owner of the ship wouldn't be impressed. At least *The Jewel* was still floating, it could've been much, much wors—

"We're takin' on water, Cap'n!" a voice cried.

All heads turned to find a sailor frantically gesturing down the stairs, below decks.

"How bad?" Smithers said, his knuckles white on the wheel.

"'Tis sprayin' like a summer monsoon!" the seaman said, backing away.

The captain's face was grim as he faced forward once more. More shapes passed on either side. Ships of various sizes and shapes, but none as large as the one they'd collided with. Dozens of them.

Was it Grey's imagination, or did the water seem slightly closer now?

The captain nodded. "Always knew this ol' lady wuld fail me 'ventually," he said. "Was hopin' fer a few more good years..." His large, experienced hands seemed to handle the wheel almost lovingly, gently, finding a path through the other vessels. *The Jewel* continued to dip lower in the water.

We're sinking, Grey thought. He glanced back to see water bubbling overtop the last step and onto the deck. "Hurry," he said. He reached down and scooped up Shae in one arm, careful not to catch her with his blade hand. Kyla helped him sling her over his shoulder.

A broad wooden dock appeared. "To oars!" the captain bellowed. There was a moment of confusion, because the crew was missing so many of its members, but the veteran seamen quickly determined the best positioning, six on each side. "Reverse thrust!"

As one, the men pulled, and the ship slowed. "Pull! Pull! Pull!" they chanted. The ship continued to decrease its speed.

"Pull to port!" Smithers cried, simultaneously spinning the wheel hard to the left.

Less than a stone's throw from the dock, the ship began to turn, bubbles churning around its sides. Like a tender kiss, the starboard side met the wood.

Captain Smithers was a lot of things, but he was one helluva captain, Grey thought, his admiration for the man going up several notches.

"Not a moment to lose," Smithers said. "Everyone, disembark." The men scrambled from their positions at the oars, dropping anchor and sliding planks across to the dock. They helped Grey, who was still carrying Shae, across first. Then Kyla. Then, at the captain's insistence, each sailor clambered over.

The captain stood alone, water sloshing against his boots. His eyes were steely as he swept his eyes over the deck one last time. He kissed the tips of his fingers and then pressed them against the wheel.

He climbed across the planks. Behind him, the ship jolted, its prow dipping on a sharp angle, settling into the golden-coin bottom. Along the side beneath the surface of the water was a huge gash, ragged and deep.

Grey didn't know if it was fatal, but it certainly looked like it.

Footsteps pounded along the wood, echoing throughout the cavern. Dozens of blinding lights preceded them. "Who goes there?" a voice drawled.

Smithers took two steps forward, shielding his eyes from the light with one hand. After the bloodthirsty sea creatures they'd faced, Grey felt no fear. He was ready for a fight if necessary. The rest of the men seemed of similar mind, moving forward to flank their captain.

"I am Captain Darius Smithers," the captain said defiantly. "Acclaimed pirate of the Burning Sea." If Grey hadn't known the man, he would've believed him, such was the fervor in his tone.

The lights stopped, bobbing slightly, hiding the faces of those who hid behind them.

That's when the laughter began.

"Secure them," a man said, his voice low but commanding.

A roar of approval, and then the lights began to move forward once more.

They were trapped.

Wisely, Captain Smithers said, "Don' fight. Drop yer weapons."

So they did, all except Grey, who couldn't—Kyla's knots were almost impossible to untie. They were surrounded by pirates, who secured their weapons and lashed their hands behind their backs with thick, rough rope. The rogues came in all shapes and sizes, some short and as pot-bellied as pigs, and others tall and lean, the sleeves of their shirts cut off at the shoulders. To Grey's surprise, several of them were women, and, if anything, they were rougher than the men. Three had eye patches, one a peg for a leg, and two wore broad-brimmed hats and gave the orders. Ship captains, Grey assumed.

One of them said, "She dead?" pointing at Shae. He was a thickset man with a drooping red mustache and gold hoops in each ear. His head was as large as a watermelon.

"Just sleeping," Grey said. "You harm a hair on her head and you'll be the dead one."

The captain barked out a laugh. "Run me through with yer blade arm, will ye? I've bettered men twice yer size with twice yer skill."

Before Grey could voice a response that would likely get him into even more trouble, one of the pirates who had clambered onto the waterlogged ship, called, "There're bloodstains on deck, Cap'n."

"Been in a fight, have ye?" the man said. He eyed their clothing, which told a similar tale, spattered with blood, both rust-red and vomit-gray.

He peered closer, his brows knitting together. "Drahma blood," he breathed.

Swords shrieked from scabbards, their tips pointed at Grey and his companions.

"Is there a problem?" Captain Smithers asked.

The pirate captain's face had gone white, and for the first time Grey saw fear in his eyes. "You've doomed us all," he said.

Eighty-Three

The Southern Empire, Phanes,
in a remote part of Phanea
Bane Gäric

Chavos was pressed against the hot canyon wall staring at his hands.

Bane stood nearby, watching him out of the corner of his eye. Chavos's dark hood made it difficult for Bane to see his face, to read the myriad emotions that seemed to be streaming through the young man. All of his plans for Phanes hinged on what happened next.

Clearly, seeing the slave army had had an impact on Chavos. Hidden in an empty alcove cut into the rock wall high above the canyon floor, they'd watched the slave soldiers go through their daily training routine.

After an hour, Chavos had sunk back. "Doesn't make sense," he'd muttered. He hadn't said a damn thing since, and Bane hadn't pushed. He wanted whatever came next to be dictated by Chavos. He'd tried persuasion before, and it had failed. Now he would use a softer touch.

So he waited, until long after the sun had passed over the canyon and out of sight, finger-like shadows creeping into their alcove, eventually shrouding them in darkness. He could barely make out the pale glow of the uncovered portion of Chavos's face. His red eyes, however, had vanished into the growing gloom.

How long can the man just sit there, doing nothing, saying nothing? Bane wondered. He could be patient when necessary, but at this moment he felt antsy, his muscles twitching for something to do.

I could go kill Falcon Hoza and be back before Chavos gets bored. The thought amused him, but he didn't act on it. He was no longer frivolous. He was a spider in a web, planning, plotting, weaving intricate formations that would trap his prey before they knew what was happening. One moment they'd be flying along, and the next…

Thwap!

Bane smiled. Unable to take it any longer, he spoke. "Do you hunger?"

Chavos shifted, a slight groan rolling from his throat. "No."

"Do you want to stay here?"

"No."

Though Bane still had high hopes for Chavos as a companion, he was turning out to be as interesting as the dust caked on his feet. *Beggars can't be choosers*, Bane thought, once more amusing himself.

He touched Chavos's arm, which was covered by three thick layers of cloth, awful garb to have to wear in this heat. The man didn't take any chances though. Bane thought about another place to go, and then they were there.

Chavos gaped, stumbling back, which was exactly the reaction Bane was hoping for. "By the gods!" he hissed.

"No. By *me*," Bane corrected.

Beneath them, the sea crashed against the base of the cliffs. The rocks here were rust-red from afar, but almost pink up close. Bane stood on the edge, his balance perfect, unafraid of falling. A man with a fate such as his needn't worry about mundane things such as accidents. No, when he finally died it would be glorious indeed, his very death perhaps his final act in restoring peace to the Four Kingdoms. Not an unseen fall from a cliff.

On the other hand, these cliffs would suit Chavos's death perfectly, if he wanted them to.

"Why did you bring me here?" Chavos asked. "Why did you show me the slave army earlier?"

Bane liked a man who got right to the heart of the matter. "I showed you the slave army to prove that the disease running through these lands is deeper than any one man. I killed the Slave Master, and yet still there are slaves. And not just forced slaves, but ones whose minds have been so twisted that they don't even *know* they are slaves." He watched the pain return to Chavos's face as he spoke. Seeing the slaves had affected him deeply.

"I don't understand," Chavos admitted. "There are thousands of them, and only dozens of their masters. Vin Hoza no longer controls them by magic. Why don't they rise up? If they did, Phanes would be a different place. A *better* place."

"I agree," Bane said. "But they won't. You could tell them all this, and they'd still obey their masters. You see, these slaves have been raised to be Phanecian soldiers since the day they were born. It is the only life they know."

"It's not fair."

The look on Chavos's face made Bane feel a tinge of remorse. This young man had seen so much tragedy, and yet it had not jaded him, had not made him angry and violent. No, it had the opposite effect. *He's the best of us*, Bane thought. *He is the kind of person I am fighting for.*

"No, it's not fair," Bane said. "And I wasn't being fair when I pulled you from the brink of death—a death you'd chosen— and nursed you back to health. But I don't regret it. You deserved a second chance to think about your purpose."

"I have no purpose," Chavos said.

"The Western Oracle gave you that mark for a reason—I have to believe that. *You* have to believe that."

Chavos stared at him. "You never told me why you brought me here." His eyes wandered away, across the sea, as if looking for the better place he spoke of.

"So you can jump," Bane said simply.

Chavos's eyes snapped back to his. Bane could see the fear in them. *Good*, he thought. *If he still fears death, perhaps he may be able to help me.*

"I—I don't like heights," Chavos said, taking another step back from the brink. A particularly large wave exploded against the shore, spraying droplets so high the air filled with mist.

"I stole death from you!" Bane shouted, over the sound of crashing waves.

"You *saved* me," Chavos said, still backing away.

"What does that mean?" Bane said. He strode toward him forcefully. Chavos stumbled over his own feet, sprawling onto his rear. Bane grabbed him by the collar of his thick robe and hauled him to his feet, his deathmark pulsing, strengthening him. Slowly, he lifted Chavos into the air, carrying him toward the edge. "What does it mean to save a man with no purpose?"

"Please," Chavos said, his voice trembling as he stared down at the churning whitewater. "I don't want to die."

"What?" Bane shouted, thrusting him over the edge, dangling him like a worm on a hook.

"I DON'T WANT TO DIE!" Chavos bellowed.

Bane dropped him a bit, and the man yelped. He turned him to face him. If anything, Chavos's face had grown even paler. "What is your purpose?"

"I—I don't—"

"What is your purpose!?"

"Peace," Chavos screeched. "All of the fatemarked were created to bring peace to the Four Kingdoms."

Bane took a deep breath and smiled. "Yes," he said. "You understand at last." Very carefully, he set Chavos back down on the cliff. The man's legs collapsed and he lay in a ball for a long, long time, but that didn't matter. He'd finally gotten through to him.

Indeed, his methods had become refined, but that didn't mean that drastic measures weren't needed sometimes.

Eighty-Four
The Southern Empire, Phanes
Jai Jiroux

Jai wasn't about to be left behind. He didn't know where the emperor and his retinue of slaves were going, only that he needed to go with them. The first three chariots held the Hoza brothers and their drivers, while the fourth was larger, cramped with at least a dozen slaves.

His back laden with heavy jugs of water bound to him with rope, Jai clambered awkwardly onto the dented old slave chariot. He grunted and groaned and feigned more difficulty than it truly was—his injured arm and leg were both feeling much stronger now. As usual, he was supposed to be emptying chamber pots, but he could finish that work later.

Several other slaves shot him surprised looks as he slumped into a sitting position, but he ignored them. The chariot began to move, pulled by three enormous Phanecian stallions, and they soon lost interest, staring sightlessly at the canyon walls as they flashed past. Only one gaze remained fixed firmly on him, and Jai didn't need to look to know whose it was:

Shanti.

But look he did, and when their eyes met it felt much like being struck by a bolt of lightning, as if all the days since they'd last seen each other, all the pain and struggles and *anger*, were searing through the air, pushing into their bodies.

And then came the calm, the tenderness, the desire to rush to her, to pull her into his arms. Months ago, as they'd tried to liberate the slave miners of Garadia, they'd formed a connection stitched of shared interest, tragic pasts, and hope.

Now, as he looked into her fierce blue eyes, their connection seemed forged of fiery determination and unspent violence. She nodded and he nodded back, before they looked away, the connection released but not severed.

In another world, Jai thought wistfully, wondering what life they could've had.

Just as quickly, he tempered such dreams, for they floated on the clouds and he rode through a boiling canyon in an empire built on the backs of slaves.

Soon the busy thoroughfares of Phanea were behind them, the canyons narrower and darker, full of shadows. Jai frowned. He'd never been in this part of the canyons. Where were they going?

The journey took nearly half a day, and Jai's cramped muscles were screaming when they finally made a last turn, the narrow canyon spilling into a huge area nestled between the high rock walls.

Holy gods, Jai thought.

For there, in that enormous canyon, were hundreds—no, thousands—of slaves, each wearing flexible leather armor and performing the tell-tale aerial flips and leaps of masters of phen ru.

At long last, Jai knew, he was seeing Vin Hoza's slave army. *No*, he thought. *Not* Vin *Hoza's.* Falcon *Hoza's. This is his army now.*

Slaves shoved their way around Jai, but he didn't move, staring at the sea of red flesh, none of the young soldiers older than himself. His justicemark flared on his heel, pulsing energetically. An idea fought to the front of his mind, and it took all his self-control not to smile. Could it be? His mark never lied, and he knew it wasn't lying now.

This is our *army now. The rebel army.*

Shanti's eyes met his once more, and what he saw was a reflection of his own mind. The corners of her lips tugged upward for a bare moment, before she too mastered her emotions.

For a while, Jai's water-bearing services weren't needed, and he sat in the shade, continuing to watch the slave army train.

The more he watched, the more his hope slipped away, and his justicemark seemed to realize the same thing, its pulsing slowing and then stopping completely.

There was something off about them. Their eyes were too focused, for one. Focused on their masters, a handful of Phanecians who were taking them through their paces. The soldiers obeyed without question, never straying for a moment.

Though their masters had whips strapped to their belts, they didn't need to use them, not even once.

Jai stared intently at the slave army as they stood at attention, having just completed a vigorous set of coordinated movements to perfection. His eyes narrowed beyond what the translucent pins already caused. For, between the gaps in their leather armor, he saw them.

Scars. Ancient, hardened. White stripes drawn in their red skin. On their arms, their legs, their backs. He even saw scars on several of their cheeks, pale slashes that told the story of their breaking.

Jai's father had been an experienced horseman, and as a boy he'd watched him break several wild Phanecian stallions. It had been a long, arduous process, in which Jai repeatedly felt bad for the horses as their will had been slowly stripped away, until there was nothing left.

Nothing but obedience.

And once they were well and truly broken, the horses would obey none other but his father. Their master.

It was in that moment that Jai knew this slave army was useless to the rebel cause, unless…

No. I can't.

His justicemark burst back to life, warm against his heel.

I can't, not ever again.

Throbbing, throbbing.

I must.

His conflicting emotions warred for several long moments, until one of the Hoza brothers, Fang, flicked his fingers in Jai's general direction. A command. *Bring me water, crippled slave. Now.*

I must, Jai thought again.

592

Somehow, some way, he would need to become a master again, a master of this slave army.

His justicemark was on fire, and he knew the way.

A sinking feeling had grown in Jai's stomach during the journey back to Phanea. He could kill the emperor and his brothers without remorse—this he knew. But to command the slave army they'd bred, they'd *created*? That was an entirely different task, one that filled his heart with sickness.

Several times Shanti had tried to catch his eye, but he couldn't look at her, not knowing what he was going to have to do to her people. What he was going to have to make them do.

She brushed past him as they exited the chariot, her small finger curling around his, squeezing. There for a moment and then gone. It was as if she could feel the struggle inside of him, lending him a measure of her strength.

Watching her walk away was one of the hardest things he'd ever had to do.

He fell back into his act, hobbling into the palace, dropping his now-empty jugs back in the kitchen to be refilled for the next journey. Then he began making his rounds, entering the rooms, removing the foul-smelling chamber pots, emptying them, and returning for more. Though he was doing his work much later than usual, it was still early enough that each room's occupant would still be eating their evening meal.

Though the work was repugnant, there was something about its monotony that helped him clear his mind. A single word kept finding its way to the forefront of his thoughts.

Sacrifice.

It was a word he'd always hated in the past, because it felt like a badge of honor—and no one in this country, save the true slaves perhaps, deserved to wear such a badge, especially him. Yet now, he felt the truth of the word like a thick blanket on his shoulders. He *was* making a sacrifice. They all were. They had to, else nothing would change.

And that slave army he'd seen, those broken soldiers who followed orders without thought, without question, they had already sacrificed so much. But they would need to sacrifice more to overthrow their masters.

Jai was so focused on his thoughts and completing the task at hand, that he was more than halfway into the next room before realizing someone was in it.

He froze, hunched over, his eyes stuck on the woman whose back was to him, her body flowing like water from a cliff's edge, like wind through the clouds, like a dust storm across the desert.

As she danced, her movements lithe but powerful, graceful but forceful, her entire form seemed to glow, though the sun had given way to shadows at least an hour earlier.

The dance was phen sur, considered by the men to be the lowest of the martial arts, useful for nothing but entertainment. Jai might've thought the same once. But since meeting the Black Tears, who were all masters of the womanly dance, Shanti included, he'd changed his mind. He'd seen how it could be used to kill even more effectively than the manly arts of phen ru and phen lu.

However, he'd only seen one woman dance the way this woman danced now, her movements so perfect that the light of the sun goddess, *Surai*, was drawn into her. The memory sent a shiver through him, and he knew even before her maneuvers turned her face toward him who she would be.

Mother.

He turned and fled.

His heart refused to stop hammering in his chest.

Though he hadn't seen the woman's face, in his mind she was staring at him, her eyes full of tenderness and love, the way his mother had always looked upon him. In truth, he'd believed her to be dead, his father's final sacrifice.

This doesn't change anything, he thought. *It can't change anything. I need to stay focused on my mission. I can't think about her. Not until after she is safe. Not until I've done what I need to do.*

Gods, how he wanted to go back to that room, to spill through the door, to throw himself into the warmth of his mother's embrace like a love-starved child. To be held, to be comforted, to feel safe again.

All these years…how had he never seen her in the palace? He knew the answer: Because Vin Hoza had never *wanted* him to see her. It was part of his punishment, his own sacrifice.

But now that she was so close…the yearning was a force more powerful than anything he'd ever experienced, even the force that drew him to Shanti.

I've waited so long. I can wait a little longer. He clung to those thoughts like a man dangling over a cliff clutching a rope that was beginning to fray.

At least she is alive. It was that thought alone that anchored him, that allowed his heartbeat to return to normal.

He finished his work and went to bed, sleep fighting him until late into the night, long after the other slaves were breathing deeply, gentle susurrations in the dark.

Eighty-Five

The Southern Empire, Phanes
Falcon Hoza

Falcon felt torn in two pieces.

In some ways, he'd been in awe of the slave army, of the beauty of their movements, of the raw power their presence gave Phanes. The protection. None could attack them and hope to survive.

On the other hand, seeing their scars, the vacant expression in each of their eyes, had brought bile to the back of his throat. He could still taste the burning bitterness.

This is my father's legacy, he thought, sitting cross-legged on the floor on his bedroll. *Who am I to defy him? Even in death I can feel his presence.* The very fact that he was sleeping on the floor and not in his father's bed was proof enough.

Still, Shanti's message to him had had a powerful effect. That final word—*Unless...*

Unless what?

Unless he, the Emperor of Phanes, did something to change the world. To erase his father's legacy.

The faith the beautiful slave woman seemed to have in him only made things harder. He didn't want to disappoint her, even if he knew he would. Which was why he knew he needed to tell her the truth about her mother as soon as possible. Needed to tell her how his father had used her and abused her, eventually killing her in a fit of rage after he had learned of the Black Tears' latest attack—the one on Garadia.

If he shared such a horrible story with her, she would never believe in him again. It was better that way.

However, tonight she had not come to him as he'd expected. No, it seemed she was giving him a night to mull things over. To pass the time, he read the book again, his heart growing heavier with each page he turned.

Eventually, he shut the book loudly, called for a slave, and sent for her.

When the slave returned alone, he looked fearful. "The slave woman you requested to see refuses to leave the slave quarters," he said, flinching back as if expecting to be hit.

Falcon was so surprised by her refusal—who refuses an emperor?—that he brushed the slave away with a hand and shut the door.

She is testing me, he thought. *She is seeing what kind of man— what kind of ruler—I truly am.* The only problem was, he didn't know himself.

He could go back to reading, or he could simply go to sleep—the gods knew he was exhausted. But neither of those options appealed to him in the least. The desire to tell Shanti the truth about her mother was the only thing he could think about. He *needed* to see that look in her eyes, that hatred for him and his family. Only then could he forget about her and the last word in that book, a word that had nothing to do with him.

I am mad, he thought, even as he stole from his quarters, waving his guards away as they tried to follow him. They looked uncertain, but he pinned them with a commanding stare and they remained on either side of his door.

Alone, he made his way through the finest portion of the palace, across the courtyard, and into the slaves' quarters. The place the slaves slept wasn't the worst-looking building—his father wouldn't allow an eye-sore in the palace—but they were still forced together like cattle, dozens of women on one side, dozens of men on the other.

The guards there looked surprised, straightening up quickly, but he said, "At ease, this is a private matter," and they instantly relaxed, looking somewhat amused. Falcon wondered how many times his own father had done such a thing; probably more times than he could count.

He headed toward the women's quarters, feeling a growing sense of foolishness, but pushing through it, biting his lip.

In the darkness, he stared into the room, dozens of sleeping forms gathered in rows across the floor. He stole between them, peeking at faces, trying to find Shanti. She wasn't in the first row, nor the second. That's when he spotted a shadow sitting on a shelf by the window, her knees pulled to her chest, her strong arms roped around them.

Just watching him.

"I'm not going with you," she said. "I'm not a dog to be called by its master." She spoke with determination, loud enough for several of the women slaves to stir in their sleep, rolling over. One of them hit his leg and she cried out, her eyes flying open.

The noise drew others awake, the room shifting from silence to a clamor in a matter of moments. Falcon was frozen, cursing his own stupidity, trying to decide what to do.

He could flee, but his guards would almost certainly notice he'd been chased away by his own slaves. Rumors would spread, and his brothers would learn of what had happened. They would begin to circle like vulzures.

There was only one option, the very same he'd relied on for years. *Be what they expect you to be.*

"Out of the way," he growled, shoving women aside as he strode through the crowd of surprised slaves, his eyes focused on the form by the window.

Shanti didn't flinch, didn't appear surprised, watching him the whole way. If anything, she looked like she'd expected him to do exactly what he was doing, a thought that unsettled him.

He shook it away and continued, until he stood before her. "Slave," he said. "I command you to my quarters. Immediately."

Her eyes narrowed at his tone, one he'd practiced his entire life. He knew she'd heard him use it many times before, but never directed at her. Her lips parted, and in the green moonlight they were pale slivers. She formed a single word. "No."

Please, he pleaded with his eyes. *Don't make me do this.*

"You *will* come." He grabbed her arm.

600

With impressive speed, her casual posture twisted into action, her leg coming up in a high, rounded kick that caught him on the side of the head. He released his grip on her arm as he stumbled backwards, stars shooting across his vision.

Though the pain was significant, he'd taken hits before, and his entire focus was on the fact that a slave had just hit the emperor, a crime punishable by death. Stars still spiraling across his vision, his mind sought a solution. He could once more try to subdue her on his own, dragging her from the room like a possession, but he could tell from the look in her eyes that she would fight him every step of the way.

Why is she doing this? he wondered, but just as quickly the answer came: *She's forcing my hand. She's making me choose.*

The facts lined up as his vision cleared. He would have a mark on his face, but he could make excuses for that. He didn't need to force her to come with him—he could just as easily deliver his message with the other slaves watching. If anything, it would only make her hate him more.

He knew he had to hurry—the guards would've heard the noise and would be coming to investigate. He opened his mouth to tell her the truth.

Eighty-Six
The Southern Empire, Phanes
Jai Jiroux

A commotion in the women's quarters had Jai on his feet in an instant. He'd been only half-sleeping anyway, his eyes fluttering with the beginnings of a dream.

He jerked awake, immediately determining the location of the sound, listening for a recurrence. Another shriek, the high tone of a woman.

Shanti.

He knew it wasn't her screaming—she would never scream like that—but he needed to know what was happening, that she was safe. He sprang to his feet, his knee screaming in pain, almost buckling, but he managed to keep his balance. Other slaves groaned and complained as he raced between them, charging for the door between the gender-separate quarters and hauling it open.

The scene before him was chaos, and it took his mind several moments to pinpoint the focus of the action. *Shanti.*

Jai gaped as he saw who was standing before her, his face unpowdered, his skin free of his usual glittering jewels. *They weren't really sewn into his skin,* Jai realized with a start.

Still, Emperor Falcon was standing before Shanti, rubbing his head, his eyes completely focused on her. She was upright in one of phen sur's many stances, and looked like she wanted to hit him. *No,* he realized. *She already hit him. Or kicked him. Hence, the sorry state he's in.*

The puzzle pieces fit together in an instant. Images of what must've happened came to life in his head. She'd gotten close to him by leading him on. He wanted more. She denied him. He tried to force himself on her and she defended herself.

Suddenly, the revolution, the thousands of slaves, even his own mother, were forgotten. He was a man defending a woman he deeply cared for. She might not need defending—she'd already made that clear—but he would kill the dastardly man without remorse, even if it meant he would be killed for it later. At least the world would be a better place.

He strode toward the emperor, slave women parting before him. Falcon Hoza took a step toward Shanti, and at the same moment she noticed Jai storming toward him. Her eyes widened and she waved him off.

He didn't listen, was tired of waiting for justice. The mark on his heel told him as much, faintly pulsing with each step.

He grabbed the emperor from behind, twisting him around, his fingers surrounding his throat, squeezing. Falcon gasped, a look of shock swarming across his face, which had already begun turning red.

"No!" Shanti screamed, throwing herself at Jai, slamming a kick into his ribs, knocking the wind from him. His grip weakened, and the emperor managed to slip free, tumbling to the floor. Shanti stood in front of him like a wildcat defending her mate, a truth Jai didn't fail to notice.

"He tried…to force…you," Jai huffed out, trying to understand.

She shook her head. "He didn't," she said. "He only wanted to talk. He's not the man you think he is." The way she said it, the slight tenderness in her tone, sucked all the fight out of Jai, even as Falcon found his feet, rubbing his neck with his hands, which was red and beginning to bruise.

Before he could respond, however, pounding footsteps signaled the arrival of the guards. "Go!" Shanti said, urging Jai to flee back to the men's quarters, where several other male slaves were gathered in the open doorway, peeking through.

Jai didn't move. He was numb. The woman he was beginning to love cared for the emperor of the kingdom that had enslaved her parents. That had enslaved *her*. The world had twisted on its axis, and Jai felt exhausted by it. They could kill him—he didn't care.

So he just stood there and awaited his fate.

Eighty-Seven
The Southern Empire, Phanes
Falcon Hoza

Falcon didn't know who this Teran slave man was, only that he looked familiar.

And that the slave wanted him dead, the proof in the fierce red rings around his neck.

It also seemed that Shanti knew this man, and was trying to get him to leave before the guards arrived. But he was refusing, locked in place with a determined stare.

The guards burst into the room, their whips raised over their shoulders, ready to be used. Several women screamed, and, as a group, they dropped to the floor, leaving only Falcon, Shanti, and the bloodthirsty slave man standing.

"Emperor?" one of the guards said. "We heard noises. We came as fast as we could. Thank the gods you are—" His words dropped like a stone as he noticed Falcon's bruised jaw and neck. The other guard seemed to notice at the same instant, both of their bodies stiffening. "What did they do to you?" His words were full of accusation, and Falcon knew exactly what would happen next if he stood idle.

Shanti and the man would be bloodied and taken away, tried on the morrow for their crimes. Both would be executed. "Nothing," he said, forcing himself to laugh. "I'm very sorry to have concerned you. I merely tripped in the dark. Badly, it seems. I hit my head. My clumsiness startled the women and a few screamed. This man came running"—he gestured to the slave, who was staring at him with a dumbfounded look on his face—"and leapt atop me. He thought an intruder was here to violate the women."

"He tried to kill you?" one of the guards said, taking a step forward, his whip cocked.

Falcon held out his hands placatingly. "It was very dark. Once he realized who I was, he released me. It was all a misunderstanding. I feel a fool." Again, he tried to laugh it off.

"A misunderstanding?" the guard said, his eyes narrowing.

"Yes. Back to your posts. Thank you for your service."

The guards didn't look convinced, but they wouldn't refuse a direct command from their emperor. Shaking their heads, they departed.

Shanti said, "We would have been killed. Unless…"

With that, she stepped over to the man, placed a hand on his shoulder, and steered him toward the open door back to his quarters. He limped a little, but didn't argue. Before he closed the door, he cast a glance back, his eyes darting between Shanti and Falcon. *There is something there,* Falcon thought. *Something between him and Shanti.*

Shanti said, "You should return to your quarters, Emperor. It is late."

He considered asking her to return with him again, but thought better of it. He'd already caused too much trouble. And, despite the story he'd concocted, rumors would spread across the palace like a dust storm.

He nodded, casting his eyes over the room, across the dozens of women who were staring at him in fear. "I am sorry to have awakened you all. Please, be at peace and rest."

With that, he left, his jaw throbbing and the skin of his neck on fire.

Eighty-Eight
The Southern Empire, Phanes
Jai Jiroux

Jai was tempted to sneak back into the women's quarters and speak to Shanti. Fraternizing amongst the slaves wasn't forbidden—after all, it was necessary to make more slaves. In the end, however, he decided against it. Shanti had made it clear she didn't need his help. Whatever she was planning with Emperor Hoza didn't involve his hands around the man's neck. She was willing to risk Jai's *own* neck, a thought that brought blood to his face. He wasn't angry at her, just disappointed. And embarrassed. Whatever he'd thought they had between them was clearly not there.

As he lay awake, thinking, he felt lost and alone, a ship with no sails or oars or crew. His entire life had been driven by a desire to enact change, to help the Phanecian slaves. His mother's people. *My people*, he reminded himself.

What had changed? he asked himself. There were still slaves. There were still emperors and masters and mines. And he was still in a position to do something, as precarious as it was.

In fact, it was possible he was the *only one* who could do something, considering the justicemark he bore.

He forced all thoughts of Shanti from his mind. *I will do something, one way or another.*

The next chance he had, he wouldn't hesitate to kill Falcon Hoza, even if he had to go through Shanti to do so.

Eighty-Nine
The Southern Empire, Calypso
Roan Loren

Raven had explained to Roan that he would be included in the war council as her guest, and as an advisor on all things related to the Ferrian defenses. That was all. He'd agreed with his words, if not with his mind.

The last two days had been a blur. Saying goodbye to Windy and Yela had been bittersweet. He barely knew them, and yet felt like they were allies, swiftly on their way to becoming friends. He promised to return as soon as he could.

Then there had been the ride on dragonback, a harrying, thrilling experience that left him appreciating every second he spent back on the ground. He'd ridden behind Rider, while Goggin had traveled with the dark-eyed man called Shanolin. Their guanik would be driven back across the dustlands by the most experienced handlers they could find in Citadel. The speed of their trip back to Calypso had felt supernatural after the long road he'd ridden with Goggin.

Now, the war council was gathering. Shanolin and Rider. Goggin. The shiva, who was engaged in quiet conversation with the empress atop the dais. They were waiting for one more—Raven's sister, Whisper.

Roan leaned toward Goggin, lowering his voice. "I'm sorry about your warriors."

The big man seemed surprised by his words. "It should've been me," was all he said.

With a start, Roan realized that the man had been drinking simpre under starlight while his men and women were being slaughtered. He shook his head. The world was an unpredictable place in the best of times. In the worst, it was chaos.

Movement caught Roan's attention. A slender wisp of a girl entered the council from the rear. She had sad brown eyes and look of determination about her. Her skin was a few shades lighter than Raven's, her eyes narrower, more exotic, but the sisterly resemblance was obvious. Whisper Sandes, next in line to rule the empire. Instead of taking a seat beside her sister, she glided up to her and handed her a rolled scroll. The wax seal was red, but already broken.

Roan saw the way Raven reacted when she saw it—the fear that widened her eyes. Even without reading it, the empress knew who this note was from and what message it might contain. He watched her as she read, saw the way her jaw locked and her teeth ground together.

She rolled it back into a scroll, masked her feelings, and hid the message away at her side. Then she said, "We all know the situation. What are your recommendations?"

Rider said, "The dragonia may have passed the testing, but they are not yet full grown. Roan Loren has warned us of the dangers that await us in Ferria. It would be wise to be patient. In less than a year, an attack will have a greater chance of success."

Goggin swore under his breath. "I lost thirty-six guanero, Ponjut included," he said. "Their blood demands vengeance. *I* demand vengeance."

Shanolin spoke up. "I second the commander's sentiments. He is not wrong. A direct attack on Calyp has always been met with a swift and decisive response. Anything less would be weakness. I would understand a delay if the dragonia were not ready. But they are, they've proven themselves."

"Just to be clear," Raven said, "Goggin and Shanolin are recommending an attack on Ferria, correct?" Roan noticed how her words came out: monotone, devoid of emotion. Almost numb-sounding.

Goggin said, "Aye!" Shanolin nodded.

Rider said, "Nay."

A commotion at the front of the chamber drew Roan's attention. A young woman carrying a scroll approached the throne. "A message for the empress," she said.

"From?" Raven asked.

"A stream from our spies in the north."

"Please." Raven held out her hand. The messenger handed her the note, bowed, and departed.

All eyes watched the empress as she unfurled the scroll and read its contents. Her only reaction was a slight lifting of her eyebrows. "The northerners have some fight left in them after all," she said. "They've defeated the easterners at Darrin. They're saying Beorn Stonesledge was among the dead."

Goggin clapped his hands. "Some good news at last. My only regret is that it wasn't I who killed the ironmarked." He fired a look at Roan. "See, princeling? The easterners are not as invincible as you think."

Roan's head was spinning. How could Grian have bungled the attack on Darrin so badly? After what Rhea had done to the northerners in the Bay of Bounty, they should've been easily finished off. And yet, Annise Gäric, his own cousin, had demonstrated her mettle, defeating one of the fatemarked.

A swell of sadness washed over him; Beorn Stonesledge had only been kind to Roan.

"What say ye?" Raven asked Roan. He was surprised to find all eyes clamped down on him.

"I say this only supports what I said before. Fighting the east on your terms gives you a chance. A direct attack on Ferria is folly."

"Snakes and sand," Goggin muttered. "The ironmarked is *dead*. Without him, the easterners are nothing."

"Whisper?" Raven asked, turning to her sister. "I will hear your opinion, too. Given the attacks in the Scarra and Beorn Stonesledge's death, has your opinion changed?"

The girl had been staring at her shoes. Not bored, or scared, but thoughtful. Roan found himself holding his breath to hear what she would say. He was fully prepared to voice his own opinion again, if necessary, not that it would make any difference.

Now Whisper Sandes looked up, meeting her sister's eyes. "Yes," she said. "My position has changed. We attack the east immediately. Blood must be met with blood."

Roan's breath left him and he gathered his argument as he stood.

Ninety

The Southern Empire, Calypso
Raven Sandes

Raven stared at Whisper, her sister's gaze unwavering, unblinking, as steadfast as the Calypsian pyramids. *No*, she thought.

For her sister had read the same note she had, the threat having been sent directly to Whisper this time, marked with the sickle and penned in blood.

An army of dragons flies to war, wings as black as a raven's.

A bird with a broken wing falls from a nest, her whisper silenced forever.

Whisper had received the death threat and yet not quivered in fear, not backed down. At long last, her peaceful nature had been overcome by the Sandes' blood running through her veins.

The war council had spoken, her own sister in favor of war. What was she to do? *Perhaps the shiva can protect her in my absence. Perhaps we'll return in victory and she will still be alive, our enemies captured in their attempts to kill her.*

Or perhaps by declaring war she was sentencing her own sister to death.

She hadn't noticed Roan standing until he spoke. "I ask for a day to reconsider, when emotions aren't so high," he said.

"Sit down, westerner," Goggin growled. "You have no place here."

"It's fine," Raven said. "I invited him. His words may be heard."

Roan, looking surprised, offered her a thin smile. *Thank you,* it seemed to say. "Will a day make such a difference?"

"Every moment makes a difference in war," Shanolin said.

"But you are not *in* war," Roan said. "You are contemplating war. The second you declare war everything changes. Plan for war, but wait a day, perhaps even a week, to consider your actions before you make them."

"So now a day is a week, princeling?" Goggin said. "Your clever tongue is as slippery as a snake. But you forget that Calypsians eat snakes for breakfast."

"I am only offering a suggestion, as all of you have. In the end, it is the empress's decision."

Raven realized what he had done for her—the gift he had given her. Did he suspect what was on the note? Or was he simply doing what he'd done from the beginning—attempting to delay war.

She realized his motives didn't matter. She wouldn't look a gift horse in the mouth. "We prepare for war, but we shall not make a final decision for three days."

By then I may have caught Whisper's would-be assassin.

She ignored the way Goggin and Shanolin strode angrily from the room. She ignored Rider's nod of agreement. She ignored the way Roan slumped into his chair. No, she only had eyes for her sister, who seemed as calm as a spring day.

Raven's eyes narrowed. Something didn't make sense.

And she would find out what.

She watched Whisper as she swept across the courtyard, disappearing into her rooms. Something was amiss. Raven couldn't say how she knew, only that growing up with Whisper had taught her to read her moods and whims. Something had changed in her; it wasn't just her newfound confidence or the fire that seemed to burn in her eyes...

Suspicion seared through her, like venom from a snake bite. *I can't jump to conclusions. I need evidence.*

She didn't want to be right, but at the same time it would be a relief to no longer have her judgment clouded by fear.

She strode after her, pushing aside the guanik bones as she entered her sister's quarters.

"Raven?" Whisper said, glancing over at her. She was seated at her dressing table, running a guanik-bone comb through her long chestnut hair. Hurriedly, she placed the comb on the table and wrapped a silk scarf around her shoulders, which were bare.

Even under normal circumstances, it would've been an odd gesture among sisters.

And, in this case, it had been a heartbeat too late, the truth laid bare in the angry red lines carved into Whisper's arms.

Raven had every reason to be angry, furious even, but instead she felt only a deep melancholy set in. "Oh, Whisper," she said.

Whisper's gaze fell away, probing at the looking glass. Raven wondered what her sister saw when she looked at herself—a girl or a woman grown? "You left me no other choice," Whisper said.

"There is always a choice."

Her sister's eyes met hers again, filled with angry tears. "Not for me. It was always mother's way, or Fire's way, or *your* way. There was never room for *my* way."

"I was willing to listen, I swear it."

Whisper shook her head, the motion causing the first tear to fall, meandering down her smooth cheek. "No. I *made* you listen."

"By cutting yourself? By using your own blood to write your own death threats?"

"Yes. You never thought your sad, weak little sister could be so conniving. You never suspected me. You even thought I wouldn't notice the shiva hanging around all the time, watching over me? You thought me that foolish? That naïve?"

"I didn't want you to worry."

"Always so protective of your pathetic little sister, but never of yourself." Whisper spat the words, her scarf falling away to reveal her healing self-inflicted wounds.

"It's not like that," Raven said.

But Whisper wasn't listening. "You should've heard the gossip. The empress has taken the shiva for her lover! Ha! As if you have time for love. As if your cold, black heart could possibly love anything or anyone but your wars, your revenge."

The words stung, but Raven was willing to take them all if it made her sister feel better. And there was some truth to them. Raven hadn't loved anyone but her family members. She'd seen what love had done to her mother; she didn't want it or need it.

"Nothing to say, sister? Do my words ring true?"

"Yes," she breathed. "And the sickle?"

"Something I read in a book. The stamp was easy enough to procure."

"Why?"

The anger died in an instant. Tears streamed freely now, pouring down Whisper's face, dripping from her chin. "I couldn't lose you too."

The words were knives, each a reminder that she had failed Fire at the Southron Gates; in a way, she'd failed Whisper, too. More than anything, she wanted to go to Whisper, to hold her tight, as she had done when their mother died.

But she couldn't. Like Whisper had said, there was no room in her heart for love. Not now. Maybe not ever again.

"My decision is made," she said, turning away and striding from the room. She would convene the war council once more, and this time they would declare war on the east.

Ninety-One
The Southern Empire, Calypso
Roan Loren

The three days had evaporated under the hot Calypsian sun.

Roan shouldn't have been surprised when the empress reversed her decision, calling for a swift and immediate attack on Ferria, but he was. In all his dealings with her, he'd found the Sandes heir to a be a calculating, patient ruler.

Not anymore. Someone had changed.

Though he longed to return to Citadel to continue his research, he requested to travel with the army to Ferria. Perhaps he could use his lifemark to save lives, to do some good.

"Which side will you fight for?" Raven asked.

He could easily lie, pledge his nonexistent sword to the empire he'd spent most of his life in. But he wouldn't, not to a woman who'd been nothing but honest with him. "Neither."

She nodded. "I suspected as much. But what I don't understand is why a peacekeeper would attend a battlefield."

Roan grinned. "To keep the peace, of course."

Raven's eyes narrowed. "As you wish, princeling. But know that I cannot protect you once the fighting begins."

"I understand." *But I can protect you.*

Ninety-Two

The Southern Empire, Pirate's Peril
Grey Arris

As the pirates led them across the docks and onto the stone floor of the cavern, their weapons poked and prodded Grey's skin. His mates were getting similar treatment, all except for Kyla and Shae. Kyla, her eyes wide but defiant, was steered by the elbow. One of the pirates had tried to search her, but she'd said, "Ye touch me and I bite yer hand off." Though the man had laughed, Grey had noticed the way he'd darted his hand back. She'd winked at Grey afterwards, and mouthed *Stick to the plan.* Though this version of Kyla scared him a little, she also made his heart beat faster.

Shae, to Grey's appreciation, was handled delicately, carried in the arms of another pirate. She hadn't so much as stirred in her sleep.

The pirates refused to answer any of Captain Smithers's questions about the Drahma or how killing a few of the vicious sea creatures had "doomed us all," as they'd said.

The pirates, all now grim-faced and serious, marched them along at a swift pace, out of the cavern and into a tunnel lit with torches set into golden fixtures along the walls. Beneath their feet, coins clinked and scattered as they walked. *The wealth beneath our feet could feed every hungry urchin in Knight's End*, Grey thought. *And these pirates use it for paving and to decorate the bottom of the sea.*

As they walked, Captain Smithers asked, "Whose gold is this?"

The broad-headed pirate captain said, "If you don't know, then yer an even bigger fool than I thought." That shut Smithers up right quick.

A few minutes later, Kyla said, "This place is amazing." She practically purred the words out, and Grey noticed the way she pouted her lips. The pirate who was guiding her by the elbow drank her in with his eyes, and Grey felt a spike of anger, which he quickly tempered. She was playing a role, that was all. Their ability to act might mean the difference between life and death. Him included.

"You ain't seen nuthin' yet," the pirate said, easing closer to her, rubbing his fingertips along the smooth skin of her arm.

Kyla smiled seductively. "How many big, strong pirates are there on this island?" she asked.

"Only one," the man said. "Me!" He laughed at his own wit. "But all said there are three hundred or so at any time, give or take. Plus our wenches!" Another laugh, echoed by several of the other pirates, none of them women.

"Silence!" the pirate captain said. The man clamped his mouth shut. "No more questions and no more answers." Grey silently applauded Kyla for getting some valuable information. Then again, the news wasn't good. Three hundred pirates was more than Grey could have ever imagined. *Doesn't matter*, Grey thought, watching his sister's unconscious body bob in the pirate's arms. *The mission hasn't changed. Good men have died so we could get to this point. We cannot fail.*

Eventually, a light appeared up ahead, growing larger with each step. It was different than the torchlight, brighter and less orange, more white. *The end of the tunnel*, Grey thought. Though it had felt like a year had passed since they entered the darkness, it was still day outside.

The tunnel spilled out and Grey had to blink several times to adjust his eyes to the brightness. Once he could see again, he scanned the terrain in disbelief. Despite the pirate admitting there were three hundred pirates on the island, he still wasn't prepared for the bustling city unfolding before them.

The area was surrounded by towering cliffs, impossible to scale without plenty of rope and nerves of steel, and palm trees lined the edges, as well as the pathway leading from the tunnel to the village. Grey quickly took stock of whether there were any other tunnels carved into the cliffs, but found only sheer stone. Evidently the way they'd come was the only way in or out.

Gold coins continued to scatter beneath their feet, as if they were naught but pebbles to be kicked and trod on. Grey, curious as to the origin of such wealth, stooped to look more closely at them.

"On yer feet, ye mongrel," a pirate said, hauling him up by his underarm. "Ye'll not steal from the king."

King? Grey thought. Since when did pirates have a king? He'd managed to inspect several of the coins before being yanked back up. Two were golden dragons from Calyp, three were golden pythons from Phanes, and one was a golden stallion from Knight's End. These pirates clearly didn't discriminate when choosing their targets.

They reached the point where the pathway split the rows of buildings, which were of surprisingly fine workmanship, built from well-cut stone blocks, heavy timber, and slate roofing. The windows had glass panes and shutters, and the doors were painted in bright colors—blue, red, and yellow.

Dozens of pirates stared as they marched through the village, jeering at them. "Forgot to pay yer tax, did ye?" said one. "Newcomers, eh?" another commented. "Fresh meat." And on and on, some of the insults so full of creative profanity that Grey almost blushed. Almost. Kyla, on the hand, seemed immune to it. It wasn't much more than she heard on the ship every day of her life. Still, Grey was glad Shae wasn't conscious to hear it.

Even worse were the catcalls from the highest windows of the buildings they passed. Women hung over the sills, their ample bosoms barely covered by short-cut corsets and nothing else. *The wenches,* Grey assumed. Like the pirates, they came in all shapes and sizes and colors. There were even a few he-wenches, which Grey should've expected considering there were she-pirates.

Through a number of the windows, Grey saw more than he bargained for, lovers locked in intimate embraces, most of them without a thread of clothing.

"Hey, blade-arm," one of the women called to Grey, tossing her dark hair and pressing her pink lips together. "Once the king is done with you, I can nurse you back to health."

Kyla fired a deadly glare at the woman, but she didn't notice. Grey looked away, not knowing what to say. He wasn't accustomed to such...blatant sexuality—Knight's End had a dark underground, as all large cities did, but it was quiet and secret and didn't shake its bosoms out the window.

Along the way, Grey also saw great wealth, none of it hidden away. Gaudy jewelry seemed to hang from every limb, pierce every crevice, sparkling and shimmering in the sunlight. Men, women, even a few pirate children, showed off their wealth without fear of theft. It was a thief's dream city. He wondered how such behavior was possible amongst fellow thieves. Did these people actually *trust* each other? As a recovering thief himself, Grey didn't see how such an arrangement could work. He would never have trusted one of his thief acquaintances back in Knight's End. Not as far as he could throw them. And he didn't expect them to trust him.

He had so many questions about this place already, and they'd only just arrived.

The further into the row of buildings they got, the more chaotic the atmosphere became. Music was played by men and women with stringed instruments and flutes. Dancers flew around them, singing along. Pirates groped and kissed wenches against walls and barrels, in full view of everyone else. Not that anyone noticed. Vendors served roasted leg of cow and braised grilled chicken wings, smoked fish and fried octopus, baked potatoes swamped with rich, brown gravy and fire-roasted peppers on slabs of buttered bread. Coin seemed to change hands at the speed of light, and Grey wondered how many paid

626

by simply reaching down and grabbing the wealth beneath their feet. He watched carefully, but never saw a single hand reach for the ground.

He remembered the pirate's warning: *Ye'll not steal from the king.* Whoever this king was, Grey assumed he must be greatly feared to inspire such loyalty amongst criminals.

Eventually, they reached the end of the line, where a final structure sat at the end of the path, slightly apart from the rest. Two stone lions sat on their haunches on either side of a doorway, their mouths open in a silent roar. Other than that, the building was not so different to the others they'd passed. It had a red door with a golden lion painted on the front. The doorknob seemed to be made of pure gold, though it could just as easily have been gold-painted brass.

Two pirates, both broad-chested and tall, brimming with muscles, guarded it.

The pirate captain who had captured them strode up to one and whispered something in his ear. The guard's eyes widened and he swiftly opened the door, waving them inside. "The king's not gonna be happy 'bout that," he muttered.

The captain led them inside. They entered a wood-paneled parlor. In the center sat a long wooden table surrounded by a dozen padded wooden chairs. The walls were festooned with various nautical memorabilia—a full-size ship's wheel, bits of tattered sails and shreds of rope, three swords, two daggers, and even a captain's hat. On every horizontal surface there seemed to be at least one statue of a golden lion. The side tables, the bar, and the corner table each had one, while the long table had three, so that each seat was in direct view of at least one.

At one side, a winding wooden staircase spiraled upward. One of the pirates scurried up it.

"Sit," the captain commanded, when the man was gone.

"On our hands?" Captain Smithers said, mockingly. "Is this the way you treat all your pirate captains?"

The man flicked a finger in Smithers's direction, and one of the other pirates shoved him into a chair. More chairs were brought out until everyone had one. Shae was laid gently on a plush, red sofa nearby. Again, the pirate who took care of her was far gentler than Grey would've expected.

Grey was directly across from Kyla, who gently touched her foot to his leg. He offered her a small smile and a nod. It was time to begin their plan, the one they'd had to keep from her father to ensure he didn't accidentally spoil it.

Footsteps approached on wooden steps, bringing Grey's attention back to the situation at hand. He, along with the others, turned to face the newcomer, this pirate king. As the man came into view, Grey's eyebrows slowly rose. He wasn't sure what he'd expected, but not the man now descending the staircase. Grey looked behind him to see if another followed. Someone rougher. Someone *older*.

But no, the way the other pirates straightened up, their demeanors that of underlings in the presence of their leader, made it clear that this young man was, in fact, the king they'd spoken of.

Grey studied him intently. His garb was clean and ironed, from his long black trousers to his fresh, white shirt. His black belt was clasped with a silver buckle inlaid with gemstones— rubies, emeralds, sapphires. His boots were made from fine leather and not scuffed. He wore no hat, his long, sandy-brown hair tied in a ponytail. Unlike most of the other pirates they'd come across so far, he wasn't adorned with jewelry, the only exception being the priceless belt buckle. The pirate king was older than Grey, perhaps by two or three years, with sharp, intelligent green eyes that darted from person to person, seeming to analyze them in an instant before moving on. Grey had the urge to look away from his stare when it settled on him, but he didn't, holding his breath until the pirate's gaze had passed by.

Last of all, the pirate located Shae, her small form swallowed up by the large couch she slept on. Upon seeing her, his eyes widened. "By the winds," the pirate whispered.

"It was just like you said, King," the pirate captain said. "She was in the cave, unconscious. We thought she was dead."

The pirate king didn't seem to be listening, the entirety of his attention focused on Shae, on the rise and fall of her chest. He took a step closer to her, then another. He seemed almost...scared...like he was trying to corner a snake. Regardless, Grey wanted to scream, "Get away from her!" but knew an outburst like that would give him away. Instead, he nudged Kyla under the table. She nodded.

"She's not bin well since we passed the Phanecian tip," she said loudly. "First we thunk it might be the scurvy, but she'd et plenny of veg, it shoulda passed by now." Grey had to hold back a laugh at her accent.

Slowly, the king's head turned to face Kyla. "Who is this girl? How did she come to be on your ship?" The young man spoke crisply, enunciating each word.

"She's a servin' wench," Kyla said. "She ain't worth yer—"

"Silence!" Captain Smithers suddenly bellowed, standing. One of the pirates grabbed his shoulders and shoved him back down.

"And you are?" the king asked.

"Captain Darius Smithers, at yer service, Yer Highness," Smithers said, tipping his oversized hat.

"And you're a…pirate?" The king's tone made it clear he was suspicious.

Smithers recited the mixture of truth and lie easily. "Aye. As of a few months ago. I was a lowly merchant, scrapin' by on the skin o' me teeth. Ye see, me wife passed on into the Void 'bout that time. Not gonna lie, it tore me up. I'm not ashamed to say I 'bout drank meself into oblivion, I did. But then, after I sobered up, I decided I'd had enuff of fightin' fer ever' coin, fer ever' meal. So I took me first ship, a fellow merchant, one of me rivals. Made more coin from that one venture than I had in years. I was…*hooked*, if ye'll excuse the expression."

The pirate king did not look impressed.

Grey took advantage of the brief silence to make his move. He leapt up onto his chair, danced onto the table, and sprang over the head of one of the pirate guards. His goal wasn't to escape, of course, so when another pirate charged to block his path, he cut *toward* the man, bashing his shoulder into him, felling him like a tree. He landed atop him, careful not to stab him in the process, and then rolled deftly to the side, using his momentum to regain his feet. He probably could've done all this with his hand firmly tied behind his back, but it wasn't, not anymore. While sitting, he'd maneuvered his blade against the knots, slicing it back and forth until they'd snapped and fallen away.

Now, however, he was grabbed by two strong pirates, one man and one woman. He didn't fight them as they hauled him before the pirate king, who was studying him like a master jeweler might inspect a gem believed to be a fake.

"Who are you?" he asked.

"Grease Jolly," Grey answered. He was surprised how smoothly the words came out after all this time. He'd been loath to reassume the old nickname, but Kyla had insisted the name was important for the plan. He needed to look and act the part in order to convince these pirates.

The king said, "You weren't trying to escape." It was a statement of fact, by a man who trusted his instincts. "So what were you doing?"

Grey was impressed. "How did you know?"

The king didn't seem to mind being questioned by a prisoner. "You're surrounded, for one, so you'd have to be mad to attempt an escape, and you don't strike me as crazy. Secondly, you had a clear path to the door, but you chose to smash into my guard instead. Third, you didn't struggle as they retook you. Fourth, anyone who had the skill to escape their bounds would've been more selective at choosing their moment to flee." The king ticked off each point on his fingers, until all but his thumb was sticking out.

Grey nodded. "You're right to be suspicious of Captain Smithers," he said.

The king nodded. "You're the true captain, aren't you? Captain Jolly."

"Now wait just a minute—" Smithers started to say, but there was a loud thud as Kyla kicked him under the table, turning his protests into a howl.

"Yes. Many apologies for the act, but I needed to test your mind before I revealed myself," Grey said.

631

The king's eyes narrowed, but not in anger—more like he was trying to figure out the solution to a problem. "And what is the result of your test?"

"That you are not a rash man. That you are reasonable, logical. That we can negotiate what happens next without fear of bodily harm."

The pirate king said, "All of that might've been true *before* you stirred up our gatekeepers. Instead I must kill all of you."

Grey's breath caught as the king turned back toward Shae. "Except her. She is mine."

Ninety-Three
The Southern Empire, Pirate's Peril
Grey Arris

As swords were drawn, Grey knew that not only had his plan failed, but he'd sorely misjudged the pirate king. He'd expected a man who might be impressed by a fellow criminal as slippery and wily as he. So he blurted out the only thing that might change the course of events. "She's my sister."

The king held up a hand, and his pirates stopped, though their weapons remained drawn and at the ready.

"How do I know you're not lying?" the pirate king asked. "Everything has been a lie thus far. The lot of you are common *criminals.*"

The word stung, because Grey knew it was true. Regardless of everything he'd done as Grey Arris, Grease Jolly's sins would always haunt him. But what struck him harder was the fact that a notorious pirate seemed so affronted by it.

"Here's the truth…" Grey said. As quickly as possible, he came clean. He told them how they weren't really pirates, how they were here seeking a pirate with a marking on his hand, how Smithers was the true captain of *The Jewel*. He even revealed the gold coin and satchel of gems he'd stolen from the pirate he'd bashed into when he pretended to try to escape. "I was once a thief," Grey admitted. "But I'm not anymore. I am Shae's brother." He pointed at her. "My name is Grey Arris."

Throughout it all, the pirate king only listened, his expression neutral. When Grey finished, he said, "I am King Erric Clawborn, King of the Pirates. And I am the marked pirate you seek."

As Grey stared, thinking *Shae was dreaming of this pirate king the whole time*, a torch was brought, and waved over the king's hand. The golden marking shone forth, a beautiful shaft of color, ending in the tell-tale form of the end of a key.

At the same moment, rays of light burst from Shae's palm, revealing her mark.

"By the winds," King Erric said again, his tone full of awe. "It *is* her."

"What do you want with my sister?" Grey asked.

The pirate's eyes never left Shae's glowing palm. "The same thing she sought coming here. To know my purpose. To know what it all means, the dreams, the markings. I can feel it now, in my skin, in my bones—she calls to me."

"She's only eleven," Grey lied, his natural instinct to protect her flaring to life.

"You misunderstand me," Erric said, a look of disgust crossing his face. "I feel drawn to her like a brother to a sister. I feel the need to protect her the same way I suspect you do."

"But you don't even know her," Grey pointed out.

The pirate said, "I can't explain it, but I do. I knew the moment she collapsed on the deck of the ship. Before that, I felt the pain as she was tortured by the furia, on that windforsaken island. I *saw* through her eyes. It was as though I was in the throes of a waking dream, but I knew it was *real*."

It all sounded strange to Grey, but then again, most of what Shae had told him in the last fortnight had been hard to believe. The truth was here in front of him, in the marking on this man's hand.

"King," the pirate captain said to Erric. "I don't mean to interrupt, but all this talk is wasting time."

The king's eyes snapped to his captain's. "You're right," he said. "We will explore my connection to this girl, but after."

"After what?" Smithers blurted out.

"The Drahma," the king said. "They are coming to kill us all."

As they were being untied, King Erric Clawborn explained things. "The Drahma—which translates to 'Vipers of the Sea'—made an agreement with my father long ago. They would allow us shelter on this island so long as we paid their blood tax. Each time a ship passes through their archway, they claim two, the weakest of mind."

Grey remembered the way the vicious sea creatures had dragged the bodies from the ship. "The...*Drahma*...took *ten* of our men."

"Because you fought them. You broke the treaty, so they feasted."

"So if we hadn't done anything, they would've only killed two of us?"

The king nodded. "Correct, but they wouldn't have *killed* them. The Drahma are ancient creatures, as old as the dragons if they're a day. They recognize a good deal when they see one. Before my father came along, they would've had to swim further and further to find their food. Now their food comes to them, an endless supply so long as my fleet flourishes. It's our blood they want. And they always return the men, usually a day later, though they are pale and on the brink of death. We have experience nursing them back to health, and we rarely lose a man."

"Why do you come here?" Grey blurted out, trying to understand.

The king looked bemused. "A fair question. It's because of the Drahma, I suppose. My father was the first pirate king. He attacked only Phanecian ships, as do I. The Hoza empire would love to catch me, but they dare not approach Pirate's Peril because of the Drahma. We steal from the rich. We keep only enough to live a reasonable life. The rest we give to those who have been devastated by the Phanecians. Much of it goes to Teragon—or what's left of it."

"You *give away* the gold?" Grey said.

The king laughed. "Aye. It's more than we could spend in a thousand years anyway."

"But it paves your streets. Your people are covered in wealth."

"It's more of a recruiting tool than anything. When we bring new pirate blood to this island, their desire for wealth without measure usually convinces them to join our cause."

"And when they realize the wealth is given away?"

"Some leave, but most stay. The wealth beneath their very feet lowers its value, so they don't miss the gold we give away. And here we live a safe, easy life. We have plenty of food, shelter, clothing…it's more than most nations can boast for the entirety of their people. There is no poverty here. No classes. We are all equals."

The message tugged at something inside Grey, an ideal he never knew he longed for. Just as quickly, he smashed it with his fist. "Except you. The king."

The king shrugged. "Someone has to lead."

Grey said, "This is our fault. If we hadn't come, hadn't fought the Drahma, they wouldn't attack you." Inadvertently, he'd put his sister in the greatest danger imaginable. He knew what he needed to do. It would be the hardest thing he'd ever have to do. "I'll leave," he said. "I'll pay the blood price. I'll sate their hunger myself."

"No," Kyla said, but Grey refused to meet her eyes. He hated to hurt her like this, but the alternative was far worse.

"I will go," Smithers said, surprising Grey by breaking his silence. "My daughter needs you, but I'm an old man. I will pay the price."

"And I will follow my captain," one of the seamen said. Others echoed his words, nodding in Smithers's direction. The captain shook his head, but didn't say anything. For only the second time since Grey had met the man, his emotions seemed to overwhelm him into silence.

Grey said, "I don't know what to say. I can't let you make this sacrifice for us."

"You can and you will," Smithers said. "You are my son now, just as Kyla is my daughter. All I ask is that you care for her."

The king, who had been watching the exchange with thin-lipped interest, finally interrupted. "Your loyalty and willing sacrifice moves me," he said. "But it doesn't change anything. The Drahma believe the treaty has been broken by *pirates*. You dressed the part, you acted the part. Giving your lives to them will not satisfy them. They will still attack. They won't stop until there is no man or woman left on this island."

"King," the pirate captain urged once more. The man was practically shaking with anticipation. Or was it fear? "The day has wings. They will likely attack at nightfall. We need to prepare."

King Erric glanced at Shae longingly. Then he said, "Sound the alarm." Turning back to Grey, he said, "You and your companions, come with me."

"Where are we going?" Grey asked.

"You are the only living souls to have fought the Drahma in this generation. We need to know what to expect. And you may not be able to sail away to protect us, but you will fight. We all will."

More than three hundred pirates gathered before them, bearing beautiful weapons of fine workmanship. Sprinkled amongst them were the non-pirates who lived on Pirate's Peril, too. Cooks, merchants, even the women from the pleasure houses—now covered up and grim-faced—stood ready to fight. Grey's head was still spinning from his conversation with the king. Was there really such a thing as a *good* pirate?

He shook his head. It didn't matter; not now. All that mattered was the impending attack. If they lost…

Grey shuddered to think what would become of Kyla and Shae. At his side, Kyla linked her smallest finger in his. He squeezed back, relishing the closeness he felt to her. Their shared trust and the strength they borrowed from each other.

Shae had been left behind in the king's quarters, guarded by the two burly pirates. Though Grey had only just met King Erric Clawborn, he trusted him with his sister. They bore two halves of the same mark, after all. Like it or not, they were connected by a power greater than any of them.

As succinctly as possible, Grey and his companions related the attack they'd faced from the Drahma, fielding questions from the pirates. They wanted to know every detail—how they moved as they attacked, whether they struck in pairs or in bunches or one at a time. Whether they went for a killing bite first, or tried to incapacitate. These were men and women experienced in the art of battle, having defeated dozens— maybe hundreds—of ships over their collective lifetimes.

Erric seemed content to listen, though at times Grey had the impression his mind had wandered elsewhere.

After every question had been asked, the pirates dispersed, their orders to be provided by their pirate captains. Blades of sunlight still managed to sneak over the high cliffs, but they were swiftly decreasing in number and intensity as the day charged toward twilight. Grey said to Erric, "What now?"

"Now we wait," the king said.

They waited in the king's quarters, where Shae continued to sleep, oblivious to the danger she was in. That they were all in.

The king sat near her, his eyes focused on her face, occasionally darting to her hand, which lay palm up. Her skin was clear and smooth, her mark hidden, as was his.

"I recognize you," he said, though his head didn't turn.

Instinctively, Grey knew he meant him. "You saw me through her eyes on the Dead Isles?"

"Aye. And on the ship. But I couldn't hear anything. I didn't know you were her brother. I only saw flashes, the experiences she had that were the most intense."

Grey nodded. It made sense. If Shae dreamed of him, of course he would've known of her, too. "She spoke of you often," Grey admitted. "She believed meeting you was her destiny. Her purpose. Her responsibility."

Erric finally turned to meet Grey's eyes. "I've felt the same way in the last few months. Shame our meeting had to come under such dangerous circumstances."

"I'm sorry this happened," Grey said, though the king had already looked away, his gaze returning to Shae's sleeping form.

Silence fell, save for the crackling of the hearth fire and the whispers of Smithers's men. They were all untied and had been lent fine weapons. They would be the last line of defense against the Drahma. Grey still felt they should be the front line, but the king had insisted they stay with him and Shae.

Kyla stood up from where she'd been sitting with her father. She sat down next to Grey, their legs touching. "Seems your time as a fearsome pirate captain was short-lived," she said.

He smiled, thankful for the brief respite from the seriousness of the situation. "And your time as a pirate wench even shorter."

"And yet I'm still dressed as one," she said, pursing her lips seductively.

"If we survive this," Grey said, "I request you keep these clothes."

"I never knew you had a pirate fetish," she said, slapping him playfully on the shoulder.

"Me either." The moment of levity had run its course and Grey could no longer maintain the façade. He sighed, feeling exhausted.

Shae cupped his chin. "We are with you. You're not alone."

"I know," Grey said. "That only makes things worse. Aren't you scared?"

Kyla, staring into his eyes with an intensity that made him want to kiss her, seemed to consider the question. "When you face the loss of loved ones, you can either curl up in a ball and hide, or you can take it on the chin. With my mother, I chose the ball approach. My father did too. It served neither of us well. Hell, it almost killed us both. I thought it would, but guess what? It didn't. If anything, we're stronger now, because we got through it. Because we're still together, still fighting." A fierce look crossed her face. "With my Myree..." She pointed to her chin. "I *hate* that I lost Myree. I *hate* that I spent so much time with her inside me and didn't get to meet her. Sometimes

I curse any and every god I can think of for taking her from me. But I'm not going to be the ball again. Not. Ever. Again."

Grey loved the determination radiating from her words, from the way she stuck out her chin stubbornly. But it didn't change the fact that *he'd* brought them all here. It was on him.

Kyla seemed to read his mind. "You feel like you let everyone down," she said. Not a question. A statement, and an accurate one.

Grey nodded, wondering where she was going with this.

"First, Rhea Loren, your first love."

Grey's heart pounded as he tried to read her tone, her expression.

She continued. "Then, Shae, who was taken from you."

Yes yes yes.

"And now me, my father, his men. Hell, Grey, do you think you've failed this entire rutting island of people, too?"

He was taken aback by her words. Not because of the exasperation in her tone, but because the answer was a resounding yes. He nodded.

"*Wrath*, Grey. You're not *that* important a person." She shoved him in the chest. Not hard, but enough to make him rock back slightly. Her response and the gesture forced a ragged breath from his lips.

"I know I'm not," Grey said.

"Then why in Wrath's name do you think the entire world revolves around you?"

"I don't think that." *Do I?*

"Everything you've told me—all the awful things that have happened to you and your sister—were not caused by the mistakes you made."

642

Grey gaped. "Of course they were. *I* got tangled up with Rhea Loren. *I* crossed her. *I* lost Shae."

"*You* rescued her, you dolt. And from the sounds of Rhea Loren, she is the one who made a mistake in capturing you and your sister, and in the end she regretted it. Whatever attacked the palace, this Kings' Bane guy, started this, not you. Yes, you are a man I care about greatly, a good man most of the time, but you are not the master of all things, Grey Arris. You are just a man getting pushed by the winds of fate, just as we all are. And, by my estimation, you are doing your damn best to protect those you care about, which is exactly why I love you."

Grey didn't move. Didn't breathe. Had he misheard her? "I—I—don't know what to say."

"Say you love me too, you rutting fool."

"I love you too." She kissed him hard on the lips and then stood, returning to her father's side, where the old man was laughing his head off.

"You have a good woman there," King Erric said, apparently having overheard the entire conversation.

Grey, still stunned, said nothing.

A moment later, the alarm bells began clanking violently. The Drahma had arrived to claim their blood price.

Ninety-Four

The Southern Empire, Pirate's Peril
Grey Arris

The first screams announced the Drahma's arrival a moment after the alarm bells. They came in two forms: the ear-shattering shrieks of the sea creatures as they attacked; and the pained cries of pirates as they died. Together, they were a grim closing symphony on a brutally long day.

Grey knew tonight the ancient creatures weren't here just for blood—they wanted to end their lives. All of them.

Not on my watch. His conversation with Kyla had left him thrumming with energy and courage. She loved him and he loved her. Add Shae, Captain Smithers and his mates to the mix and he had plenty of compelling reasons to fight on this night.

The pirate king had not moved from Shae's side, and Grey got the impression he would die to protect her, their bond from the dream world as strong as anything that could've been forged in reality. *That makes two of us*, Grey thought.

Smithers was at the window, half his men huddled around him, while the other half guarded the door. Down below, there were also a dozen pirates protecting the front door.

Kyla grabbed Grey's hand and said, "Take it on the chin, and we'll emerge stronger than ever." The fervor in her tone was such that he couldn't not believe her.

Smithers said, "There are dozens..." There was a note of excitement in his voice, as if this was the best night of his life. He looked back, grinning. *He's lost his damn mind*, Grey thought.

"Incoming!" one of the sailors announced.

The group began backing away from the window, while Smithers took one large step back, brandishing his scimitar with a flourish. "Let 'em come," he growled.

For a frozen moment, there was near-silence, time seeming to crawl forward as the fire popped, as hearts beat, as breaths slid in and out of lungs...

The window exploded inward as if punched by a large stone, spraying glass shrapnel into Smithers' face and across the wooden floorboards. The Drahma shrieked through the ragged opening, claws flashing like a dozen knives in the orange light. Smithers ducked at the last moment, flipping the creature over his shoulder. It crashed into two of his men, writhing and squirming. One sailor's throat was slit open while another got a bath of sea slime in his face. The rest of the men dove atop the Drahma and began stabbing. Soon it was dead, but only just in time for them to face the next foe. Two slipped through the window with incredible speed considering their lack of feet, landing on tails and hands with a dull *thump-thump*. Somewhere down below, the sounds of a fight rose through the floorboards, while all around, the night was full of the cries of battle as the streets became killing fields.

One of the Drahma hissed at Smithers, who only said, "Whoa, girl. I don' wanna carve ye, but I will."

She swept her dark-green seaweed hair away from her face with a flick of her claws, revealing her scaled breasts and firm abdomen. Her partner shrieked a war cry and, as one, they attacked.

Not Smithers, who was ready for it, but King Erric, who was crouched by Shae, blocking her face from view. They launched themselves like thrown spears, using their strong tails to propel their powerful bodies up and over two chairs and a chest. Though clearly taken by surprise, Erric pushed to his feet, sword already drawn. He slashed, and Drahma blood sprayed as he opened her throat. The second one, however, had come in lower, driving its head into his midsection, slamming him back against the wall. Like a snake, she wriggled her way up and sank her fangs into the king's neck.

Grey sprang into action, the creature too close to where Shae slept for comfort. He felt Kyla right behind him. He leapt atop the Drahma's back, reaching around her head as she bucked and shrieked, sliding his blade-hand across her neck. She slammed back and forth violently several times before going still, slumping to the floor.

Erric stared at him with wide eyes. "You saved my life."

"I did it for Shae," Grey admitted. "But yes."

"Regardless of your reasons, I am in your debt."

"I'll call you on that if we survive the night."

The king offered a wry smile. "The bitch bit me."

"Will it kill you?"

He shook his head. "I'll be ill for a few days because of the venom, but that's all. She only got a gulp or two before you arrived."

Grey nodded, turning his head to listen. A few shrieks pierced the night, but compared to before it was quieter. "Is it almost over?"

The king laughed. "Captain Jolly, it's just beginning."

King Erric had spoken truthfully. The battle raged for half the night, the Drahma attacking in waves, never all at once. Usually they came in threes, with one coming through the door or window first, the other two close behind. They lost another three seamen, bringing their total to six crew. Smithers was bitten three times, but he refused to move to the back—"Used to have a hound named Biter that'd chomp on me all the time," he said several times. Kyla showed her mettle on at least three occasions, twice killing the creatures on her own, and once holding her foe at bay long enough for Grey to finish it off with a knife-hand to its heart.

Grey received multiple claw wounds—to his arms, his legs, his chest, and his back—but avoided the fangs.

Shae, with everyone working together to protect her, slept through the whole thing. That made Grey smile.

And then, when no attacks came for more than two hours, he fell asleep on the floor beside her, dead to the world. He was dimly aware of Kyla's warm body beside him, something he would've enjoyed immensely had sleep not pulled him under like a dark wave.

When he awoke, the sun was streaming through the broken window, Kyla was bustling about humming a sailing tune, Shae was still unconscious beside him, and everyone else was eating breakfast and sipping hot tea.

The king was nowhere to be seen.

"Any news?" Grey rasped, his mouth as dry as sand.

"Finally," Kyla said with feigned exasperation. "You slept as if you'd fought ancient sea creatures all night."

He pointed at a plate of food she was carrying. "That," he said, hoping it got his point across.

"Pirates are so demanding," she said. But she gave him the plate, which he immediately tucked into, using his fingers to push the food into his mouth. Scrambled eggs, pickled sardines, a thick slab of buttered toast—it was the best food he'd ever tasted. The warm tea, lemon with a hint of honeysuckle, washed it all down. Kyla watched him devour the plate with satisfaction. "Who said I can't cook?"

"I'm a lucky man," Grey said, already feeling better, though his wounds were weeping blood and pus. He grabbed her around the waist and pulled her into his lap. She squealed with delight, which made the seamen applaud raucously.

"Don' git too frisky, lad," Captain Smithers said from across the room. "Till ye wed her, she's still me little girl."

Duly chastised, Grey released her with a smile, which she returned, and pulled himself to his feet. They crossed the room hand in hand, dodging diners until they reached the captain. The man was clearly in a bad way, propped up against several large cushions, his dark-skinned face practically turning green. Sweat beaded on his forehead. Kyla used a wet cloth to dab his skin, and he smiled gratefully.

"Yer a good daughter," he said. "Don' deserve ye half the time."

"More like *all* the time," she said, helping him take a sip of water. Most of it dribbled down his chin, forming drops in his beard. "And quit being so dramatic—you're not dying. King Erric said you'll have a fever, chills, and plenty of achiness for a few days, but then you'll make a full recovery."

The captain winked at Grey. "Can't even milk a little special treatment these days."

"When you're not around, she speaks of you as if you hung the moons," Grey advised.

Kyla slapped him on the arm. "Stop giving away all my secrets."

The captain tried to laugh, but ended up clutching his sides in obvious pain. "Sleep, Da," Kyla said. "I'll be back to check on you later."

Grey said, "We should find Erric." Kyla nodded. Grey turned to the sailors, most of whom were onto their third or fourth helpings. "Keep an eye on the lass, will you, boys?" They nodded, their mouths full.

They started down the winding staircase, which looked freshly scrubbed, still moist and glossy. *To clean the blood*, Grey thought. On the first floor, several pirates were working, cleaning blood—both pirate and Drahma—from the floors, fixing broken furniture, and scraping the shards of broken glass from the window frames. One of them nodded at Grey and another tipped his cap to Kyla, then went on working.

Outside, things were even worse. Nearly every building had significant damage. Broken windows, scratched wood—where the Drahma had evidently clambered up the sides of buildings—shattered doors, and broken roofs. The streets were a mess of blood and ichor.

And then there were the bodies. Some of the carts were laden with piles of sea creatures, their flesh already turning gray in the midday light, but most were piled with pirates. Grey stopped counting when he reached thirty, feeling suddenly ill, as if he, like Smithers, had been bitten. He doubled over, clutching his stomach. "I should've warned you," Kyla said, rubbing his back.

"It's fine," Grey said. He remembered Kyla's words from the night before. This was not all his fault, was it? Yes, they'd broken the treaty, but it was by accident. And anyway, if the pirate king had known they were coming, why didn't he meet them at sea, thus preventing such a grievous error? The realization hit Grey so hard he straightened up.

At that same moment, he spotted Erric, who was conferring with several pirates about how best to reattach a door to its hinges.

Grey shrugged Kyla off and stalked up, anger coursing through him.

"Grey?" Kyla said.

But Grey didn't hear her, or didn't want to. He grabbed the pirate king by the shirt with one hand, flung him up against the side of the building, and growled in his face, "You could've prevented this. You could've prevented all these deaths, and the ones before, the other men we lost."

For a moment, the king looked surprised, his face ashen, and Grey remembered he'd been bitten, too. This man was ill, and yet he was still out here helping his men and women.

Strong hands grasped Grey's arms from behind, and he went airborne, slamming into the ground on his back, the breath rushing out of him. Two burly pirates, the same two he'd first encountered the day before, stood over him. They looked ready to run him through if their king commanded it.

"It's fine," Erric said, using the back of his sleeve to wipe sweat from his brow. "I deserved that." He walked over to Grey, looking down at him. "You think I don't know I could've saved them?" he said. "It's all I've thought about since you arrived ten men short. It's all I've thought about since I awoke this morning to find half my pirates dead or seriously injured. I will have to live with this mistake for the rest of my life."

It was the last response Grey had expected to get, and it took all the fight out of him. Well, if he had any left after being slammed to the ground, that is. But he still didn't understand. "Then why didn't you sail out to meet us?" he asked.

Erric sighed. "Because I thought I was losing my mind, for one," he said. "My men and women thought I was sick, because sometimes I would get dizzy in the middle of doing something. I couldn't tell them about the visions about some young girl I'd never met. They'd think me mad or perverted or worse. So I kept them to myself. It wasn't until I received word of a lone ship sailing into Pirate's Peril that I knew the dreams were real. I also couldn't know when you would arrive, if ever. It might've been days, or months, or years, or never. Still, looking back, I should've trusted my instincts. If I had, none of this would've happened. Good men and women would be alive. Their blood soaks my soul and drowns my conscience."

Grey felt awful for what he'd said, the judgment he'd passed. As if he had any right. "I know the feeling," he said. "Maybe we have more in common than either of us think."

The king extended a hand and Grey took it, allowing himself to be pulled to his feet. "We have Shae," Erric said. "I don't know what that means exactly, not yet, but I will."

Grey nodded, wondering when Shae would wake up. Now that the battle was over and things had calmed down, his worry for her began to grow. What if she never woke up? He knew it was pointless to think like that, but the thought wouldn't go away, like a rat gnawing at his insides. "We need to talk about something else," he said to the king, trying to distract himself.

Erric frowned. "What?"

"Leaving."

His frown deepened. "No one is leaving."

The argument had been in full swing for the better part of an hour. The king had refused to discuss the future until after each and every one of their dead comrades had been given a proper burial at sea—which basically meant they were dropped off the cliffs with large stones tied to their ankles. Even the Drahma were treated this way, though from a different cliff, with the stones tied to their tails.

Despite the brewing difference of opinion, Grey's respect for the pirate king had continued to grow. Now, however, they sat on opposite ends of the large table, staring daggers at each other.

"This is our home," King Erric said. "*My* home. And my father's before that. We're not just going to leave."

They'd gone around and around in circles, but Grey wasn't ready to back down. They couldn't stay here. It was suicide. "Pirate's Peril will never be a safe haven for you again," he argued. "You may have won the battle, but the war is far from over." Already several large splashes had been spotted by scouts. Although they hadn't seen what had caused them, it was almost certainly Drahma. In Grey's estimation, they would attack again, sooner rather than later.

"I will talk to them, as my father did before me. I can explain what happened. The circumstances. We can forge a new treaty." The determination on Erric's face was like steel armor, so strong that it almost made Grey want to believe him. Almost.

But he couldn't take the risk, not with those he loved still in danger. "They're not going to forget how many we killed."

"They attacked *us*!" Erric shouted, jumping to his feet.

"And *we* broke the treaty!" Grey countered. It didn't matter that it was ignorance that caused the breach, not anymore. Too much blood had been spilt.

As the two men stared at each other, the rest of the pirates at the table glanced back and forth between them, probably placing silent wagers on who would blink first. Kyla had left the meeting half an hour earlier, calling them both "stubborn pig-headed mules." Smithers, having been bitten thrice as many times as anyone else, was sleeping off his latest fever.

And then:

A voice from the seventh heaven:

"Grey?"

All heads turned to find Shae at the foot of the steps, her white purity dress wrinkled and creased, her eyes bright and focused. "I'm here, Shae," Grey said, his own voice a whisper.

Her eyes danced from person to person, making her way down the line, until they widened, settling on the pirate king. "It's you," she said with awe.

"Yes," he said. "It's so nice to finally meet you, Shae Arris. I am King Erric Clawborn."

Shae's awakening had delayed the decision, at least for a while. Grey was ecstatic, picking Shae up in a bear hug and spinning her around. She squeezed back, her small arms tight against his neck.

Erric ordered the other pirates to vacate the room, which they did, and offered Shae a seat by the hearth. Kyla had come down to watch, upon Shae's request, squeezing in between Grey and his sister as they sat across from the king. "My dear," he said, "I've been waiting so long to meet you."

In the firelight, Shae's eyes shone. "I've dreamed about this moment so often it feels as if I'm dreaming now," she said. "Does that make sense?"

"Yes," he said. "More than you can know. I can still hardly believe it." He shook his head in wonderment. Grey had never seen the pirate king look so unsure of himself.

"Can I see your mark?" Shae asked.

"Of course." He extended his hand toward the hearth. At first just the edges of the key appeared, but then, slowly, the entire mark burst to life, shining forth. Shae licked her lips and then mimicked his movements, until her half of the key appeared. Their hands moved closer, a mere hairsbreadth away.

"The key," Kyla murmured.

Grey, for the first time, realized it was the king's right hand, while it was Shae's left that held her mark. Almost as if they were meant to be clasped together. He shook the thought away; it made him uncomfortable. He cleared his throat. "We're still not any closer to understanding what the key is meant to unlock," he said.

"Grey," Shae said. "Thank you, for everything. Calm yourself. This is meant to be."

She grasped King Erric's hand.

Grey tried to pull her away, but it was too late, something was already happening. Clasped together, the light seemed to burn through their hands, revealing their bones, which looked like white, five-fingered trees. Shae's eyes rolled back in her head, until only the whites were showing; Erric's, too. Grey fought at their fingers, but they were locked tight. Their bodies were shaking, convulsing. Their lips moving, but not saying anything, as if they were engaged in a conversation only they could hear.

"Shae!" Grey cried, still fighting her fingers, but she had the strength of a much larger person. Erric's were equally powerful, clamped down like a metal vice.

Kyla touched his shoulder and he flinched. "Help me!" he said.

"Grey," she said, "leave them be."

"Wha-what?" Grey turned to look at her. "He's hurting her!"

She shook her head. "Look at her face. It's peaceful."

Grey did look, and he was surprised to find that despite the rolled back eyes, the rest of her face was as calm as the waters of a pond on a windless day.

"She's not in pain," Kyla said gently, pulling him back. He let her, falling back into her arms, his breath coming in waves.

"What is happening to them? Why are they like that?"

"I don't know," Kyla said, hugging him from behind. "But it's important. This is what *needs* to happen. I believe that now. Before, I wasn't certain. But now…this all has to *mean something.*"

Grey knew exactly what she meant. All those they'd lost, all the sacrifice, all the pain and broken hearts and sadness. The world might be a broken place, but that didn't mean it couldn't be fixed. Somehow. Watching his sister and the young pirate king holding hands made a shiver run through him.

And then it was over. Shae gasped, her fingers tearing free of the king's. The king fell from his chair, panting, his chest heaving. They were both staring at their palms, where their marks were slowly fading away, leaving only smooth skin behind.

Grey was at Shae's side in an instant, cradling her head against his chest. "Are you hurt?" he asked.

Her eyes were wide with wonder and something else as she looked at him. Something she tried to hide, but was unable to from someone who'd known her as long as Grey had.

And he knew:

What she hid, was fear.

Ninety-Five

The Southern Empire, Pirate's Peril
Grey Arris

"We saw them," King Erric said, once he'd caught his breath.

"Saw who?" Kyla asked. She was on her knees, sandwiched in between Grey and the king.

"Others," Shae said. "Ones like us."

"Marked?" Grey said.

Shae nodded gravely.

Erric said, "There are more than I think anyone knows. Two in Phanes. One in Calyp. There were two in the east, but then one died. A huge man—Beorn Stonesledge."

The easterner's legend was known even in the west. "The ironmarked," Grey said.

Shae nodded, picking up the thread. "In the north there is only one, but she is powerful. A young girl, like me. But she is blind."

"Blind?" Kyla said. "But how could a blind girl have any sort of power?"

"Those who see with more than their eyes, see more than any of us," Shae said. The words sounded almost like a quote, but Grey didn't know where from. She continued. "In the west there were none like us." She said the last part sadly, like she was part of a unique group of creatures slowly becoming extinct.

"There were two others, too," Erric said. "They stood together. One shone with the brightness of the sun; it poured from his chest. All around him were saved, their injuries and afflictions healed. The other was pure darkness, created from shadow and death."

"Kings' Bane," Grey said, remembering the bodies in Knight's End. All the guards. The king, his throat opened up.

Shae nodded. "Bane is threatening to undo everything the fatemarked have done."

Kyla said, "I don't understand. What have the fatemarked done?"

"Peace," Shae and Erric said at the same time. They smiled at each other, but it reached neither of their eyes.

Grey said, "There can be no peace. All four kingdoms are at war. Even the empires of the south are embroiled in a civil war. Peace is a fool's errand." He could hear the cynicism in his own voice, but he couldn't help it. What did any of this have to do with his sister anyway? Or this pirate king?

"What does it all mean? What does your key do?" Kyla asked.

Grey's eyes snapped to hers; he'd forgotten about the key.

Shae said, "We can use it to change things, if we choose."

Grey frowned. "Change things how?"

Shae looked at Erric, as if afraid to meet her brother's eyes. He could sense that fear again, armored by the determined set of her jaw.

"We can kill Bane," the king said. He raised a hand before either of them could ask another question. "Let me just get this all out before you ask any questions. If we choose to turn the key to the right, Bane will die. We could do it right now if we wanted to."

Grey couldn't hold his tongue any longer. "But that's fantastic. Do it, I say. That murderer deserves whatever comes to him."

"*Grey*," Shae said.

His eyes darted between his sister and Erric. There was something they weren't telling him. Erric opened his mouth to speak, but Shae beat him to it. "I'll tell him. He's my brother; it should be me."

"Tell me what?"

Shae opened her lips, closed them. Opened them again. "If we turn the key to the right, it won't only be Bane who dies, but all the fatemarked."

For a moment, the truth didn't register in Grey's mind. So what? He didn't know any of the fatemarked in all those distant lands, and they'd still be ridding the world of a madman, a merciless killer without a soul.

But then it hit him:

Erric was fatemarked.

Shae was fatemarked.

They would die, too.

"You're not turning the key to the right," Grey said, for the thousandth time.

Though it was risky, they'd stayed another night on Pirate's Peril. Everyone agreed that given the new information, they all needed to sleep on things and see what the morning would bring. Thankfully, the Drahma were apparently still licking their wounds, and hadn't attacked again.

For Grey, the morning was much the same as the day before, and it most definitely did not involve his baby sister committing suicide by fatemark.

"It is *our* choice," Shae said. Grey hated how she kept throwing around words like *our* and *we* and *together* when referring to she and Erric. Those were words that used to define them as siblings, not she and some random pirate king they'd just met.

"The whole thing is ridiculous," Grey said, biting down hard on a hard heel of rye bread. "Why would the Western Oracle give each of you half of a key—"

"The halfmarks," Shae interrupted. "That's what they're called."

"Whatever," Grey said. "Why give you these halfmarks just so you can kill yourselves and all the other fatemarked?"

"It's a failsafe," the king explained. Truth be told, the night of rest had done little for him—he had dark circles under his eyes. "The Oracle didn't know exactly what would happen once she unleashed the fatemarked. She could only create us, not control us. Bane was a risk—she hoped he would kill the most violent of the rulers and leave the peaceful ones, but now he's just killing everyone. And most of the other fatemarked aren't helping matters either. Most of them are used in war, and either killing each other, or killing other people."

Grey scowled. "How do you know any of this?"

Shae sighed. "We just do," she said. "We saw things and we understood."

"Things you couldn't know until you met a pirate king." Grey knew he was being unfair, but he didn't care. The whole thing was madness. "What pathetic sort of power is it to kill yourself? Godsdamn, I can even do that! Give me a high enough cliff and I'll pretend to be a bird!"

"We already *did* that on the Dead Isles, remember Grey?" Shae said. "Didn't kill us, did it?"

Though Grey was still frustrated and angry, he was impressed by her wit. "But why should a fourteen-year-old girl have to die? A pirate king, maybe, but a little girl?"

"Grey…" the pirate king said.

"You stay out of this," Grey fired back.

Shae's teeth ground together. "I'll have you know I'm a woman flowered, Grey Arris."

The last thing Grey wanted to hear about was the flowering of his little sister. "You're a child."

"Grey…" Erric tried again.

"Shut it," Grey said, pointing a finger at the pirate.

"If anyone is acting like a child, it is *you!*" Shae said. She stood, stomping from the room, slamming the door shut behind her.

Grey started to go after her, but Kyla grabbed his arm. "Wrath, you can be difficult sometimes. And stubborn."

"You forgot pig-headed," Grey quipped.

"And the countenance of a mule," Erric added helpfully.

661

Grey fired a scathing look his way and the king snapped his mouth shut.

He looked back at Kyla. "We're talking about my sister's *life* here," he said. "Not whether she wants to run away to sea and marry a sailor."

"And you would support her if she wanted to do the latter?" Kyla asked, hands on hips.

"Well, no. But I would oppose it less vehemently."

"Ha!" Kyla said. "After you told me about your criminal past, you couldn't stop going on about how you'd *changed*, how you were supporting your sister in her quest to find the meaning of her fatemark. But that was all a bundle of bollocks, wasn't it? You haven't changed a bit, not when it comes down to the meat of it."

Grey took a deep breath. Was she right? Was he still Grease Jolly, just going by a different name? Was that who he would always be? He remembered the pain of losing his hand, dwarfed only by the torment in his soul when he realized the furia had taken his sister to the Dead Isles. It was then he had decided to change, to be someone Shae could be proud of. He could still be that brother, that man. "No," he said. "I am not that fool anymore."

"Then start *listening* before opening that big mouth of yours. Erric has been trying to speak for some time."

Grey looked at Erric, who smiled at him and waved. Grey sighed. Said, "I'm sorry. I was cruel. I was angry. Shae is the only family I have left."

Erric nodded, his mouth pulled into a tight line. "I understand. I never had a sibling, but when my father died…it took me months before I could pull my head from the sand and carry on his work."

"What were you trying to say?"

"We already made our decision," Erric said. "Last night, while you slept."

Heat rose inside Grey's chest once more, but, determined not to blow up again, he tempered it. "And?"

"And we're leaving Pirate's Peril. Today. Like you suggested."

Grey was dumbfounded. Why hadn't Shae just said that? It dawned on him. From the moment he'd woken up, he'd hounded her about the foolishness of killing herself to kill Bane, about how he wouldn't *allow* her to do it, how it wasn't really *her choice*. He'd mocked and he'd berated and he'd acted like a child. Just like Shae had said. "I'm a fool," he said.

"Aye," Kyla said. "A pig-headed, stubborn, mulish one. But I still love you all the same."

He found Shae near the edge of the cliffs, sitting on a rock.

She must've seen him approach, but she didn't acknowledge him.

"I'm sorry," he said, clambering up and plopping down next to her.

"Why?" she asked. She was tracing her palm with her finger. *The mark*, he realized. *She knows exactly where it is, even when it can't be seen.*

A revelation rippled through him, something he'd never really thought about: *Shae's had to live with her mark her entire life.* How hard that must've been, especially not knowing what it meant. Grey, on the other hand, had preferred to pretend as if it didn't exist, only worrying about the risk of it being discovered.

"Because it *was* your choice. It still is. I shouldn't have tried to bully you into my way of thinking."

Her eyes flashed with anger, pinning him in place. "You're only saying that because we decided not to do it."

He shook his head, his lips beginning to tremble as the words took shape. Tears blurred his vision. "Shae, I love you more than anything. I know I don't always know how to show it, and most of the time I say and do the wrong thing, but it doesn't change the fact that you're my sister. I just want you to be happy. If you *need* to do this, if you *need* to use your mark to kill Bane and the rest of the fatemarked, then I'll support you. But godsdamnit, Shae, I will miss you more than if the sun were to fall from the seventh heaven and crash into the sea."

Tears were dripping from his chin now, and Grey blinked to clear his vision only to find that Shae was crying too. She fell into him and he held her as she sobbed into his shoulder. "We could save *lives*, Grey," she said, her voice muffled against his shirt. "We could do good. But I'm too scared. I don't want to die."

He remembered the fear she'd tried to hide the night before. The only reason she would've been scared was if she was seriously considering using her key, her halfmark, along with Erric. "I know, Shae," Grey said now, holding her tight. "I know."

He held her for a long time, until she finally straightened up and looked at him. "There's another way, you know. We can use our key another way."

Grey was beyond being surprised at this point. "How?"

She spoke slowly, thoughtfully. "Our key can also strengthen the powers of the other fatemarked, if we're close enough. We might be able to help the ones that are trying to do the right thing, who are on the right path."

Grey nodded. Something about this felt right. "How do you decide who to help?"

She smiled. "We just know, Grey."

Captain Smithers was in mourning. Though he was still dreadfully ill from the Drahma poison, he managed to fight to his feet to make his last stand, begging the pirates to help repair *The Jewel* so it could sail with the rest of their fleet. According to one of the pirate carpenters, the fix would take months. *Impossible*, was the word he'd used.

"You can stay here with her," King Erric said, calling the old man's bluff. "Or you can command this beauty instead." He pointed at a medium-sized ship with crisp, white sails and fine, curving lines. In Grey's estimation, it put *The Jewel* to shame. It was one of many ships without captains after the Drahma attack. Many of them were without crew as well, and would be left behind.

Though Captain Smithers sniffed at the ship, and immediately began criticizing its 'numerous deficiencies,' he boarded it without question, allowing two of his crew to help him below decks to locate his new quarters.

Kyla laughed and followed.

Grey began to as well, but stopped when Erric said, "You're welcome on my ship." His ship was, of course, the largest in the fleet, the enormous monstrosity they'd seen when they first sailed in and sunk in the cavern harbor. He'd since learned she was called *The Pirate Queen*.

"Thanks, but no thanks," Grey said. "I belong with them. And we'll be in close enough proximity, right?"

"Of course."

Grey said, "I'm sorry. I know this place is your home. I'm sorry we ruined it for you."

Erric said, "Like your woman said, stop being sorry. I'm not. We've relied on this place for too long, and we were always in danger from the Drahma, even if we didn't want to admit it. It's high time we left and did more than steal from the rich and give to the poor. It's time we fought for the abused, for the slaves of Phanes."

"Is that where we're going?" Grey asked. "To Phanes?" He gestured across the ocean, to where a long smudge of red sat between water and sky. The blade still strapped to his wrist slashed the air to ribbons. He'd considered removing the knife from his stump after they'd passed the Drahma archway, but decided against it. Truth be told, he'd grown accustomed to having it.

"Aye," the king said.

Grey nodded. "I've always wanted to see the red rocks close up. C'mon Shae." He beckoned to his sister, who had been watching the exchange with interest.

She shook her head. "I'll be fine here."

Grey's first instinct was to argue, to force her to join him on Smithers's new ship, but he managed to bite his tongue, barely. "Good," he said. "May the wind be at your back. I'll see you on the high seas!"

Shae broke into a smile, for once looking exactly like the fourteen-year-old girl that she was. She charged across the deck and crashed into him, squeezing him tight. He was very careful not to impale her with his blade-hand as he hugged her.

There was only one obstacle left before they reached the open waters of the Burning Sea:

The Drahma archway. It was especially dangerous because only one ship could fit through at a time, which meant they lost any semblance of strength in numbers. They'd taken every precaution, with all hands on deck, armed and ready, but if the creatures attacked in droves, they would most likely be overwhelmed.

"Think they'll come?" Grey whispered to Kyla.

"They hate us now, Grey," she said. "Hatred can drive even the noblest of creatures into irrational decisions."

He was hoping for a simple "no." He gripped her hand, leaning his blade on the railing of Smithers's new ship, which he'd renamed *The Jewel II*. His blade cut a thin, narrow path into the wood.

Grey held his breath as the first ship, the king's massive vessel, sailed through unmolested. Another ship passed beneath the arch, then another. It was their turn.

Grey peered up at the carvings in the stone, trying to remember how it felt when he'd first seen them, what kind of man he was. *Am I any different?* he wondered. *Does it even matter?*

And then they were past, headed out to sea, the cliffs of Pirate's Peril growing smaller in their wake. *Yes*, he thought. *It does matter and I am different.* For what was the point of swimming to the darkest depths of the ocean if you couldn't rise again and take a breath, see the sunlight shining down? *I have to change*, he thought. *I have to be better, each and every day. We all do.*

He roped an arm around Kyla's shoulders, pulling her close. She leaned back to look up at him, her lips parting slightly, temptingly.

He eased forward and kissed her.

"Get a cabin!" one of the crew shouted, the rest of them exploding into laughter.

Ninety-Six

The Southern Empire, Phanes,
a remote part of Phanea
Bane Gäric

The slave army was spread before them like an ocean of human flesh, ten-thousand strong. They were primarily of Teran descent, their skin as red as the western cliffs, gleaming under the high noonday sun. They trained in battle leathers, practicing the art of phen ru, a martial art Bane was beginning to despise. Why waste so much energy on a series of acrobatic maneuvers when a simple slash to the throat would end an enemy's life just as well?

Still, they were a marvel to behold, as they moved together, perfectly coordinated, not getting in each other's way as they flipped and spun and pretended to slash each other to ribbons. The spikes attached to their boots and the blades strapped to their wrists were dull, and wouldn't do more than bruise. In a real battle, however, these men and women would *devastate* their foes, tearing through them like a spear thrust through wet paper.

"Do you understand now why we have to do this?" Bane asked Chavos, who he was beginning to think of as his apprentice. He didn't want this to turn out like the last time, when Chavos hesitated at the last moment and tried to kill himself rather than releasing his plague on the Phanecians.

"Yes," Chavos said. "Killing these slaves seems like a horrible thing to do, but if we don't, they will kill hundreds of thousands on behalf of the emperor. We are *saving* lives, not ending them." Though his friend spoke truly, Bane was disappointed that it sounded as if he were reading from a book. The words lacked his own conviction. *Ah well, that will come with time, when he sees the fruits of his labors,* he thought. At least he was here; at least he was trying. It was progress—a step forward.

"Also, as the plague spreads, it will kill many of the slave masters," Bane reminded him. "Maybe even the emperor!" The latter was a longshot, and Bane was more than capable of ending Falcon Hoza on his own, but he wanted Chavos to feel the power of what he was about to unleash.

Chavos nodded. Murmured, "The emperor." Began removing the two pairs of gloves he wore to protect the world from his touch.

Bane knew his friend was somewhat naïve, but he didn't feel bad about manipulating him. His cause was too important for regret. No cost was too great to achieve peace.

"Are you ready?" Bane asked.

"I think so."

"What?"

"Yes," Chavos said more firmly. "I'm ready."

"Good." Bane, as he had done so many times since he'd started this partnership with Chavos, reached across to grasp his arm. The only difference this time was that Chavos no longer wore his gloves.

With the speed of a striking snake, Chavos lifted his hand and touched Bane's face.

Ninety-Seven

The Southern Empire, Phanes,
a remote part of Phanea
Bane Gäric

Bane was rarely surprised anymore, but when Chavos touched him with his bare skin on Bane's bare face, he was so stunned that for a moment he did nothing but stare at the man he'd called friend, brother. Companion.

Chavos didn't offer a gloating smile, or an angry snarl, or a bitter scowl. No, he just looked sad, even as Bane felt the plague ripple across his skin, sinking into his bloodstream, contaminating his body.

"I'm sorry, Bane," Chavos said, sounding utterly sincere. "It was the only way I knew how to stop you. I may not know much of the world, but I know what you're doing isn't right.

Peace isn't achieved through more killing. And I won't infect the innocents below."

Bane was also surprised to find that he wasn't angry at his friend. If anything, he was proud of him. For the first time, Chavos had done what *he'd* wanted to do. What he felt was right. And it didn't involve killing himself.

But that didn't change what Bane needed to do next. *Even a friend can be an enemy,* he thought bitterly. *This is the world we live in. Fatemarked killing fatemarked.*

In a flash, he drew his blade and shoved it into Chavos's gut.

Just as quickly, he roped his arms behind his friend's head and back before he could fall, and laid him gently on the ground. Chavos's mouth was open in a silent gasp, the blood beginning to trickle from one corner of his lips. He seemed to be trying to say something, but Bane said, "Shhh. It doesn't matter anymore, friend. You go to meet your creator, wherever she is. The Oracle will see your heart, and know that it is true."

Chavos died. Bane wondered how long it would be before he followed him.

Bane was still trying to figure things out. He wasn't dead, so that was good. Though he could *feel* the plague inside him, sometimes burning, sometimes cold, it had little impact on his movements. Thus far, he'd seen few of the standard effects of the plague—no red bumps, no fever, no chills, no hallucinations. A little weakness perhaps, but none of the severe muscle deterioration so often seen in plague victims. All things considered, Bane was in good spirits.

He suspected his deathmark had everything to do with it. Either his mark was holding the plague at bay, or slowing its progress. It might kill him eventually, he knew, but not today. Nor tomorrow. And there was still work to be done.

The plague also gave him a potential opportunity. That was why he was creeping amongst the thousands of sleeping forms. That was why he'd chosen a victim near the middle of the group. It would only take one, he knew, and the plague would do the rest.

The slave soldier, like all of them, was young—perhaps fourteen. Young, yes, but a deadly weapon in the hands of his masters. He felt no remorse at what he was about to do. He wished it wasn't necessary, but this boy's life had been forfeit from the day he was born. He would be another sacrifice for the greater good. Slowly, carefully, Bane touched him on the ear. The soldier stirred but didn't awaken.

Bane waited.

Nothing happened.

He touched him again, this time on the cheek. The boy's eyes fluttered open, but in the dark he wouldn't really be able to see Bane the way Bane could see him. "Hello?" he said. "Is someone there?"

Bane said nothing, silencing his own breathing.

Still, nothing happened.

Bane vanished, returning to his hideaway, the one he'd once shared with Chavos. Whatever his deathmark was doing to stop or slow the plague was also preventing him from spreading the disease. A pity. A tool like that could've come in handy. No matter, he had plenty of his own powers to use. But he would need to move up his timelines, just in case the plague killed him sooner than he thought it would.

And he needed another ally. A stronger one. One who was striving for the same thing as he was but perhaps in a different way. An ally who might even be able to save his life.

Yes. He could sense the violence brewing, like the tingling sensation in the air before a major storm. Not here, but somewhere else…

He shifted to Calypso, to the palace, but it was remarkably empty. A lone guardsman spotted him and called out, but he was already gone, moving to the next likely place for a battle. The east. Ferria. Grian Ironclad had been stirring all kinds of pots as of late.

He reappeared well away from Ferria, just to be safe. The Iron City looked peaceful in the early morning light. There were no shouts, no cries of battle, no smell of blood in the air. Then again, there was something…

He turned to face the sea. *There!*

He spotted them closing in. From this distance they were small enough to be birds. Below them were ships. Dozens of ships, each bearing the Calypsian dragon. Warmongers and destroyers of peace.

Where there was battle, there would be fatemarked. *With any luck, I'll find the one I'm looking for*, Bane thought.

Ninety-Eight
The Southern Empire, Phanes
Falcon Hoza

Falcon's brothers had heard rumors of the previous night's disturbance in the slave quarters, and they wouldn't let it go, prattling on about how weak he was and how "Our father would never have allowed such a mockery to be made of the Hoza name."

Falcon tuned them out, his mind still clicking through the events that led to his decision to concoct the story. Shanti's words replayed over and over again in his head. *We would have been killed. Unless...*

Unless...he did something. Which he did. But he hadn't saved them, not really. If not for his rash actions they never would've been in that position in the first place. Still...she'd made her point in dramatic fashion.

He *was* emperor, and he did have power. But could he really do anything for the slaves' plight? He shook his head. He could, but he knew the Phanecians would never allow it. They were too accustomed to the slaves, too happy to be served, to have the worst jobs done for them while they ate and drank and carried on their slothful lifestyle. There would still be a rebellion, only it would be his own people rising up against him.

"Are you even listening, brother?" Fang shouted, finally breaking through the fog.

"Yes, yes, it was a foolish decision, I heard you," Falcon said, hoping they would go away.

"That's not what he said," Fox said, rounding the other side of the throne. He was holding something—a book. The book Shanti had given him. The last page was ripped out and clenched against the front cover.

Falcon frowned. His brothers were being insolent, even for them. "You ransacked my quarters?"

Fang said, "I was looking for an emperor, but there's none to be found in all of Phanes."

"You have crossed a line."

"No, brother, we are on the *same side* of the line. It is you who has crossed over, and this is the final piece of proof. Father would be ashamed of you."

Anger boiled up inside Falcon. "Father was a tyrant!" He instantly regretted the words, not because they weren't true, but because of the risks associated with speaking them. Thankfully, no one but his brothers were around to hear.

"Father made Phanes great again. You are disassembling it stone by stone."

677

Falcon could sense something else lingering on the tip of his brother's tongue. "Say your piece, brother. I am all ears."

Fang hesitated for the briefest of moments, and then said, "I. Challenge. You."

"On what grounds?" Falcon growled. Inside, his heart was beating too fast. *This is it. It came sooner than I expected...*

"Right to rule. You are the eldest, but not the strongest," Fang said.

"I've defeated you both numerous times in combat." Falcon pointed out, using the same argument he'd relied on time and time again. *Please back down.* Inside, however, he knew they wouldn't, not now that the challenge had been issued.

"Not at the same time," Fox said, grinning. "Songs will be sung of this fight."

"You're *both* challenging me?" It wasn't unprecedented, but he didn't expect it in this case. The challenges were always to the death—only one emperor could emerge from the circle. He'd thought Fox would back down and let Fang rule.

Fang said, "Either of us would be better than you, and two of us improves our odds."

"But at least one of you will die, too."

"True," Fang said. "But we're willing to risk it for the good of Phanes."

For the good of Phanes, Falcon thought wryly. Strangely, he felt no fear, only resignation. This day was inevitable from the moment his younger brothers had been born with malice in their hearts.

"May the strongest emperor survive," Falcon said, leaving them in his wake.

Shanti came to his quarters on her own terms, just after the evening meal. News of the challenge had swiftly spread throughout the palace, and then through all of Phanea, if not the entire empire. With the stream network, the Four Kingdoms would know soon, too. A palace officiant had informed Falcon several hours earlier that the challenge would take place the following day, on neutral ground.

Shanti said, "I heard," and closed the door.

"You're not happy? I thought you would be."

"You're the best thing that's happened to Phanes in a long time," she said.

Her compliment, though undeserved, sent a thrill through him. "Says a rebel slave."

"Yes, I do. And I do not make such statements lightly."

"Is that why you kicked me in the face?"

She cringed. "Sorry, but I needed to be certain."

"Of what?"

"Of you."

He mulled over her words, remembering the man who'd come to help her, who'd tried to kill him. "Who was—"

"You didn't recognize him?" she interrupted. "That was Jai Jiroux."

"What? But he had—" Red skin, narrow eyes, a slight limp. Falcon shook his head at his own prejudice. He'd sized up the man as a faceless slave using three very vague details, even though he'd known there was something familiar about him. "A disguise," he said.

"In fairness, it is an effective one. I had to look twice to make certain my eyes didn't deceive me."

"You know him from the Garadia escape," Falcon said. A statement, not a question.

She nodded anyway. "Yes. We are…close."

"Lovers?" Falcon said, forcing a thin smile. He wondered how the former Garadia Mine Master had managed to infiltrate the palace. Then he realized he didn't really care.

"None of your business," she said, but it wasn't a reprimand. There was a brief moment of silence as she stood inside the door. "I'm sorry I pushed you so hard. I was hoping you would be able to make a difference without bloodshed."

"It's fine," Falcon said, and he was surprised how much he meant it. The last fortnight had been more interesting than the last eighteen years of his life. "But there is always bloodshed. That's something I learned as a boy."

"What will happen?" she asked.

"My brothers and I will fight to the death. Two will die, one will emerge the emperor."

"When?"

"Tomorrow."

"So soon?"

"We can't leave the empire perched on the edge of a knife. There are kingdoms to conquer, wars to be won!" The only solace Falcon took from any of it was that the spectacle would not be public.

"Perhaps I can do something."

"You might not want to," Falcon said, taking a deep breath. He felt as if a giant weight was crushing him into the floor.

"Why not?"

"Because I have something to tell you. A truth, long kept from you."

Her eyes narrowed. "What truth?"

"It's about your mother," he said.

There was a slight tremble of her lip as he began to tell the story of how her mother had died.

When he finished, Shanti said nothing, but he could sense the grinding of her teeth behind her pursed lips. She had to be saddened by the news, but only anger showed in her posture, her expression. After a moment in which her fierce green eyes seemed to bore *through* him, impaling him on a spike, she turned, opened the door, and left, slamming it behind her.

And Falcon knew, whatever she'd been considering doing to help him on the morrow had been lost the moment he told her the truth.

Despite that, he felt relieved. Exhausted, but weightless, as if his feet were lifting from the floor.

Ninety-Nine
The Southern Empire, Phanes
Jai Jiroux

Jai had gone to sleep as soon as his evening work was finished, but found himself being shaken awake. "Jai!" Shanti hissed.

"Erm?" he replied.

"If you want to kill the emperor, I will allow it." She spoke the words directly in his ear, so that any of the other slaves who were pretending to sleep couldn't hear.

He jolted up, fully awake in an instant. She put a finger to her lips, motioning for him to follow. They snuck from the quarters and into the corridor. The guards patrolled this area regularly, so they wouldn't have long.

"What happened?" Jai asked.

"Nothing," she said, but her eyes were a moving target.

"Tell me," he said, placing a steadying hand on her shoulder. Like a brittle stalk blown over by the wind, she fell into his arms. Her body shook silently, her tears wet against his neck.

"She's dead," she sobbed. "My mother is dead."

For a moment he was stunned, thinking of his own mother, how beautiful she had looked as she danced phen sur—just as he remembered her. Then he remembered the story of how Shanti's father and sister had been murdered, how only she and her mother had survived. If her mother was dead, it was only her left. He felt his own eyes welling with tears, his heart cracking to see her in such pain.

"I wish I could have met her," he said, immediately wondering whether it was the right thing to say. He shook his head. "Not just her. All of them."

She looked up at him, her eyes moist with tears, mixing with the black ones etched on her cheeks. Though her pain flowed over her like a waterfall, she was as beautiful as he'd ever seen her. "Me too," she said, raising a hand and wiping one of his tears away with the back of her thumb. He hadn't even felt it drip from his eye.

Jai's expression turned serious. "How?"

She shook her head, and the sadness seemed to disappear, replaced by anger. "The wound is too fresh. Perhaps one day I will be able to speak of it..."

Jai remembered what she'd said before, about killing the emperor. "I am yours to command," he said.

"I—" She hesitated, biting her lip. "You heard about the challenge from Fang and Fox?"

"It's all anyone is talking about," Jai said. "Tomorrow the world will be two Hozas better."

683

"The frustrating thing is, Falcon was *honest* about my mother. He could've told any lie, or said nothing at all, but he *chose* to tell me, so that I wouldn't protect him anymore."

Jai's eyes narrowed. "I've known the Hozas for a long time, Shanti. It's a trick. It's what they do. Falcon is the same as the others; he's not what he appears to be."

She blew out a breath. "You saw what he did last night, how he *saved* us. I gave him the ultimate test and he passed."

Jai had thought of nothing else since it happened. It was…strange. And unexpected. Jai had originally believed it was because Falcon seemed to have feelings for Shanti, but that didn't make sense. If that's all it was he could've had Jai executed for trying to kill him.

"There's more," Shanti said. Jai raised his eyebrows, waiting. "I told him who you are."

"You did *what?*"

"He barely batted an eye. He almost seemed to have expected it."

"Then why am I still here? He should've had his guards take me back to Garadia, or worse." Falcon Hoza showing some kindness toward a pretty slave girl was one thing, but sparing Jai was something else entirely.

Shanti said, "I know you don't trust him, and neither do I, not fully, but there's more to him than you think. He's a brilliant actor playing the role he was born to play, but behind closed doors he's kind and insecure and always seeking an escape from his real life."

Behind closed doors. Jai tried to control the flush of jealousy, but found it impossible.

"*Jai*," Shanti said, reading his expression. "We have only talked, I swear by the light of the sun goddess." She touched his cheek, grazing her lips against his. It sent shockwaves through his very soul. "My heart is broken, else I would give myself to you this very moment."

Jai swelled with happiness and desire, tempered only by his remembrance of the pain she was in. He held her against him, their heartbeats falling into step until they felt like the rhythm of a single heart.

And though Jai had only seen the dark side of the emperor, he trusted Shanti's instincts implicitly. They'd been through too much together for him to do anything different. A plan began to form in his head.

"If Falcon is winning against his brothers, we shall let him win," he said. "But if he is losing…we will crush his brothers as soon as they defeat him." It was the best compromise he could offer.

"Thank you," Shanti said against his neck.

"I want to show you something," Jai said.

One-Hundred
The Southern Empire, Phanes
Falcon Hoza

Falcon had a feeling the "neutral" location for the challenge had been planned by his brothers, and perhaps his own generals too. It was clear from their expressions that they were tired of being blocked by the emperor, and would be happy for a change of rule. Yes, they'd each wished him support from the gods, but their hearts weren't in it.

The fight, of course, would take place in the large canyon where the slave army had been hidden away for years, living and training for the day when they would finally be set loose on Phanes' enemies.

The slaves had formed a giant circle around the "ring," and were charged with pushing any of the competitors back into the fray if they attempted to flee. Only victory would allow them to step without. Falcon remembered a story his father had loved to tell, about how one of his brothers had once challenged him. Needless to say, Vin Hoza had come out on top, and was never challenged again.

Falcon had seen Shanti and the crippled slave he now knew to be the infamous Jai Jiroux boarding the large slave chariot. They would be in attendance, serving the many important men and women who had been invited to the private battle. Falcon had tried to catch either of their eyes, but they'd both ignored him completely.

It is better this way, he thought. *It shall be easier to die knowing I have no one on my side.*

And die he would, he knew. Though he was a master of phen ru, his brothers were too. One on one, he'd defeat either of them eight times out of ten, but facing them together...his chances were slim. The odds makers were giving him one in sixty, which he thought was generous in his favor. *Perhaps I should have bet on myself*, he thought wryly. *It's not like I'll need my wealth where I'm going.* And it would mean less wealth for one of his brothers to inherit.

Beyond the army of slaves, the canyon walls stood like massive sentinels, or perhaps witnesses, their heads heavy and downcast. The sun had not yet breached their guard, and the ring was shrouded in shadows.

Fang approached him. He raised the fist that was meant for brothers, one of the Three Great Pillars of Phanes. Falcon just stared at it, for fists would be the least of his worries today. All three of them were strapped with blades on their wrists and feet, in the traditional Phanecian manner. Fang only laughed, mimicking the gesture to Fox, who returned it.

Fox said, "May the gods—"

"Save it," Falcon said. "This is the work of men, not gods."

Fox said, "It didn't have to be this way, brother."

"I am no longer your brother. May you die quickly and with great pain." Falcon was surprised at his own words, at the intensity of the heat rising within him. It was borne of a realization of how foolish he'd been his entire life, how much time he'd wasted on pretending to be someone he wasn't. His brothers had always fit the mold, while he didn't seem to be meant for a mold at all.

Fox forced out a laugh, but he could see the fear in his youngest brother's eyes. Almost certainly it was Fang who'd bullied him into this—as children, he was always the one coming up with schemes. And Fox *always* went along with them, trying to impress his older brothers. *I'm as much to blame as anyone*, Falcon thought. Instead of being a good example to Fox, he'd become his father in miniature, at least when anyone was watching.

Now, abruptly, the intense anger he felt just a moment ago, evaporated completely, leaving him melancholy. And, he realized, despite everything:

He didn't want to kill them.

Not even Fang, who'd forced them both into this situation. Even if it meant Phanes was doomed to repeat the same cycle again and again. He would fight, but not to the death.

As the officiant raised his arm to signal the beginning of the bout, Falcon began unstrapping his weapons.

Jai Jiroux

"What the Void is he doing?" Jai said, watching as each blade dropped to the ground. The officiant seemed to be in shock, too, his arm still raised. He seemed uncertain as to whether to start the fight, what with the emperor having discarded his weapons like rusty butter knives.

Shanti said, "I told you he's different." She didn't look pleased, only thoughtful.

She *had* told him, and Jai had believed her, but this wasn't just different—it was suicide.

"Begin!" Fang shouted at the officiant. "If my brother chooses to make this more challenging, so be it. We all make our choices."

Fox looked less convinced, eyeing his own blades, as if considering whether he should follow his eldest brother's lead. In the end, he tightened them instead.

Jai felt his justicemark give a faint pulse, the first since he'd arrived. He had a role to play on this day, and it was fast approaching.

The officiant, sweating profusely in the canyon heat, closed his eyes and dropped his hand.

Fang didn't waste any time, springing off his hands and launching himself through the air, his body twisting all the way around twice, his bladed feet slashing the air to ribbons.

Falcon sprang forward, performing a perfect somersault beneath the flipping Fang, catapulting out of it into a kick that caught Fox in the throat before he could defend himself. Gagging, the youngest brother stumbled back, clutching his neck with one hand while sweeping a rounded kick before him to keep Falcon at bay.

By then, Fang had landed, turned, and cartwheeled back toward his brothers. He lashed out with both wrist blades in short succession, a series of deft swipes that would've given most martial artists more than they could handle. But Falcon truly was a master of phen ru, dodging each blow by ducking, sliding, and, once, blocking his brother's wrist with his own hand, while avoiding being sliced open. He twisted Fang's arm back, and the middle brother cried out in pain. Falcon followed it up with a powerful knee to his abdomen.

Unfortunately, Fox had regained his breath and was charging in from behind. At the last moment, the emperor seemed to sense it, dropping flat to the ground and kicking both legs upward to propel his brother into the air.

Fox, however, managed to control his body in midair, landing on his feet. He kicked toward Falcon's head, but he rolled over, once more regaining his feet.

There was a lull in the action, as each caught their breath, circling like vulzures. Something about Fang's and Fox's nearness made it obvious they were in league, at least until their older brother was dead.

Jai scanned the sea of slaves, watching their faces for any signs of emotion. Any evidence that they *cared* what happened in the ring. Instead, all he saw were blank faces, devoid of expression. His heart broke for them, for they had never been given the chance to live.

His justicemark began to heat up.

He caught Shanti's eyes, and nodded at her once. The night before, he'd told her about his mark, about how it told him when someone was lying, how it gave him insights into the

690

justices—and injustices—of the world around him, helping him see the truth where lines began to blur. She'd taken the news well, all things considered. He also told her about what else he thought it might help him do, a power he was only beginning to understand.

The power of persuasion.

He refocused on the match, where Fang and Fox were simultaneously flanking the emperor, each trying to distract him while the other attempted to infiltrate his defenses. Jai, with his training in the defense art of phen lu, could see a dozen opportunities for them to breach Falcon's defenses, but they could only seem to focus on his fists and feet. Still, bit by bit, strike by strike, they wore him down, until he was breathing heavily as he retreated across the circle.

"Tighten the net!" the officiant commanded, after a set amount of time had passed with no one dead or wounded.

Without question, the slave soldiers began to march forward, until the large ring was cut in half. Falcon was forced to sprint full speed around its edge to avoid being trapped by his brothers.

"He can't win this," Shanti said. "Especially without weapons."

As if in response to the truth of her words, Fang performed a front flip, unfastening one of his blades from his wrist in midair, and throwing it as he landed. Having not expected the unorthodox maneuver, Falcon was only able to save himself by twisting his body at the last moment, grunting as the blade entered his shoulder.

Fang grinned. "We haven't fought in a while, brother. I've learned a few new things."

Jai watched Fox closely during the exchange; could see the way his face twitched as he realized that once Falcon was dead, he would be next.

Shanti leaned forward, as if considering joining the battle, the first ever slave woman to protect an emperor. "No," Jai said. She looked at him, biting her lip. "Do you trust me? Do you believe what I told you last night?"

"Yes," she said. "I believe *you believe* what you said. But what if this doesn't work?"

"Then gods help us all," Jai said.

Back in the ring, Falcon had wrenched the blade from his shoulder, blood pouring down his arm. Like before, he tossed the weapon aside. Fang said, "You're making this far too easy, brother."

"I shall try harder," Falcon said between clenched teeth, clutching his shoulder and trying to stem the flow of blood.

The officiant called, "Tighten the net!"

Once more, the slaves marched in formation, cutting the size of the fighting area to a quarter of what it had been to begin with.

Fang lashed out and Falcon dodged. Fang started a kick, but at the last moment twisted it to the side at Fox, catching him in the midsection, the blade sinking into his flesh. He hadn't expected it at all, a final betrayal by a brother he'd seemed to look up to.

A stunned look in his eyes, he dropped to his knees, blood spilling between his fingers. "Falcon?" he said, his words slurring, his eyes finding the emperor.

"Yes, my brother," Falcon said, sadness in his eyes. "I am here. Go meet the gods."

Fox Hoza collapsed as life left him.

Jai's mark sang; an enemy to justice had perished.

Falcon Hoza

Though Fox had become a miniature version of Fang, he still didn't want him to die. Seeing his lifeless body lying in the dust made his chest squeeze his heart. *What a waste*, he thought. *Why do we waste lives like so much rotten fruit?* It was a question he knew there was no answer to.

Determination poured through him, lending his body a jolt of strength. *I will not kill Fang.*

With their brother dead on the ground, the battle continued, Fang charging at him, slashing his remaining wrist blade from side to side, intermittently launching a front kick to keep him guessing.

Falcon did his best to dodge the blows, but his body felt weakened, by loss of blood perhaps. He performed a side flip to escape a killing slash, but wasn't able to complete the rotation, landing awkwardly on his ankle.

A moment later, pain roared through his shoulder and he felt a strange sensation pouring through his arm, chasing the agony away. A dull numbness set in. No, it was more than that. Paralysis.

I can't move my arm! he thought.

Wait. The feeling was spreading through his chest, into his other arm, his legs. His entire body felt like it was made of rhubarb jam. He tried to stand, but his legs gave way and he collapsed.

693

His mind felt clouded over, a thunderstorm brewing. Everything was spinning, his brother's face appearing overhead, circling him. A grim smile of victory.

A ray of light burst through the fog—a realization. *The knife my brother threw. It was poisoned.* Jade hemlock had been known to cause paralysis over a period of time, an effect that occurred faster during periods of strenuous activity. It wouldn't kill him, but Fang didn't need it to. Disabling him would allow Fang to finish Falcon off with ease.

I am sorry I failed you, Shanti, Falcon thought. *I am sorry I wasn't the man you thought me to be. I am sorry about your mother, your father, your sister, your life. I wish...*

A blade flashed overhead, sparking as the light crested the cliffs, catching its edge. Fang, being overly dramatic as he finished off his wounded prey.

Falcon closed his eyes.

Jai Jiroux

From the moment Fox Hoza had taken his last breath, Jai's justicemark had been growing hotter and hotter on his heel, until smoke had begun to curl from his slave moccasins, a hole having burnt through the thin sole.

It is time, Jai thought. He could feel the raw power filling him, making his heart pound. Not strength. Not magic of the conventional kind, but magic nonetheless, not altogether different than that the Slave Master, Vin Hoza, had wielded. The thought made Jai uncomfortable, but with the emperor lying prostrate on the ground, he had little time to contemplate the choice he was about to make.

"You don't have to save him," Shanti said, her voice angry, tears brimming her eyelids. Though her words were filled with vengeance, Jai could see the truth behind the mask:

She didn't want Falcon Hoza to die—still *believed* he was more than the world thought him to be. Jai didn't want to kill him either, not from the time he'd unstrapped his weapons and refused to kill his brothers.

Fang sauntered over to the fallen emperor, the confidence of certain victory spreading across his face. He raised his blade with a flourish, knowing all eyes were on him, the man about to become the new emperor, the most powerful man in all of Phanes.

Jai stood to his full height, a hunch-backed cripple no longer. In fact, he felt no pain at all, his festering injuries granting him a respite. At the penultimate moment, when Fang's blade reached its apex and, inevitably, must come slicing down toward his brother's heart, Jai raised his voice and spoke:

"Soldiers!" he shouted, his voice thunderous, echoing through the canyons. He could feel the raw, unnatural power in each syllable, and all heads turned his way. Fang's blade hung in midair, his eyes flicking to where Jai stood, narrowing in anger at the one who would interrupt his moment of glory. "Your generals have clouded your minds, forcing you to obey them by the threat of the whip," Jai continued. He was aware of several men—guards from the palace—rushing his way to put an end to his outburst, but he ignored them. "But you are theirs no longer. No..." He shook his head, not reacting as one of the guards reached him, tried to grab him. He trusted Shanti, and she did not fail him, performing a maneuver graceful enough to be part of a dance, her leg lifting high, swooping over the guard's head, and then crashing down on his spine. He collapsed in a heap.

Jai could sense the minds of each and every slave soldier, more than ten thousand strong, waiting for him to speak the words, already anticipating it. His words were justice—perhaps not the kind he wanted the most, but that could come later. He had to believe that.

"Now," he said, "you are *mine*."

On the final word, there was a thunderclap, though the sky was clear. The earth shook, and rocks tumbled from the canyon walls. Several large stones crashed into the helms of the generals, knocking them senseless, perhaps even killing them.

The soldiers raised their fists to their chests. In one voice, they boomed, "What is your command?"

Jai said, "Save the emperor."

Falcon Hoza

Falcon's eyes fluttered open when he heard the voice. Something was happening, though it was difficult to determine what. All he knew was that, inexplicably, he wasn't dead—at least not yet.

Above him, that sparkling scythe hung, like the green moon god in early spring. Not falling, but threatening. His brother's attention was drawn elsewhere, most likely to the powerful voice echoing through the canyons.

Frantically, Fang's eyes shot downward, meeting Falcon's in a shattered instant. He saw the uncertainty, the remorse, the fear, and then, the decision.

I don't want to die, Falcon thought, pushing any energy he had left against the paralyzing poison flowing through his bloodstream. "Argh!" he yelled, rolling halfway to the side, just far enough for the blade whooshing down to scrape against his flesh but not impale him. He heard it *thunk* into the ground as all strength left him.

Darkness swarmed over him.

One-Hundred-and-One
The Southern Empire, Phanes
Jai Jiroux
One week later

Jai could still remember how it had felt as the soldiers had swarmed Fang Hoza, taking him apart bit by bit. Next, on Jai's command, they had taken the guards and the generals. He had spared the lives of the wealthy spectators, though he had captured them.

It had felt powerful. Though he knew justice was being served—his justicemark proved that—something about it had felt *wrong*. Maybe it was that he was controlling the slaves with naught but his voice, convincing them he was their commander. Or maybe it was that he was rounding up people he didn't even know, stealing their freedom, chaining them together and marching them back to the palace.

From there, things had only gotten messier. The army had taken Phanea with ease. Though one general had remained back at the palace with a contingent of guards and soldiers, when they'd seen the thousands of soldiers marching on them, they'd tried to flee. Jai had the soldiers catch each and every one of them before they could spread the word about what had happened.

The wealthy slave owners were next. Few of them fought back, and those that did were subdued and chained using the metal links of their own slaves, who were released.

The last week had been chaos.

There were released slaves living in the dwellings of those they used to serve. The prisons were overflowing with the previously wealthy, whom Jai now had to worry about feeding and caring for. And, despite their efforts, someone had escaped to spread the news around Phanes. Stories of mine masters being overrun by their slaves were coming in each day. Some of those very slaves—well, not slaves any more—had begun wandering into Phanea looking for shelter and food. There were rumors that the war cities along the Southron Gates were already raising their armies and preparing to march on Phanea.

However, of all the challenges, the one that troubled Jai the most was that he hadn't been able to find his mother anywhere in the palace. He was beginning to wonder whether he'd imagined her.

Jai hadn't gotten a lot of sleep, and there wasn't much more on the horizon.

Despite all of that, he knew he'd make the same choices again in a heartbeat.

Watching Shanti approach, her muscular stride commanding the attention of all she passed, Jai couldn't hold back a smile.

"More good news?" he said sardonically. He was standing just outside of the room he'd been bedding down in, one of the general's, deciding whether to try to take a nap.

She touched him lightly on the chest, rose onto her toes, and kissed him deeply, stealing his breath.

Any thoughts of a nap flew out of his mind.

She pulled back, laughing. "A kiss seems like such an easy thing now," she said.

"True," he agreed, curling a hand behind her back. "We should do it more often."

"Gladly." Her lips brushed his cheek before finding his once more, parting to allow their tongues to meet. He tugged on her shirt, drawing her toward his door.

Still kissing her, he fumbled to get it open. When it finally burst free, he was barely able to kick it closed before she'd shoved him onto the bed, her hands burning their way under his shirt, drawing it over his head.

This he needed, not only because his feelings for her were lightning and thunder bottled, but because it was a reprieve from the challenges of fighting a civil war against his own people while trying to rebuild an empire from the bottom up.

As her lips kissed a path from his abdomen to his neck, he worked on her shirt, eventually figuring out the complex ties to unravel it over her head.

Her lips found his once more, and any thoughts of war or rebellion or justice disappeared into Shanti.

Shanti lay against him, skin on skin, so warm, so full of life. His heart beat with hers, their breaths naturally falling into sync.

Her face was perfection in sleep, smooth red stone carved into a statue of a goddess. Her black tears shone in the waning afternoon light. He spotted one that was slightly darker than the others.

It's new, he thought. *For her mother.*

The thought made him sad. It also made him long even more for his own mother. Perhaps he'd only thought he'd seen her. He almost laughed at his own foolishness. He hadn't even seen the woman's face, only assumed it was his mother based on the beauty of her dance of phen sur. The last time he'd seen his mother dance was as a boy. In fact, it was probably the imagination of a child that had built his mother's artistry to such a high level.

No, he thought, chiding himself. *It was her. I could feel it in my bones. And I will find her.*

Sonika Vaid and her Black Tears arrived the very next day, all smiles and congratulations on the monumental victory the rebellion had won.

"You will be emperor," the dark-haired Phanecian said. Not a question or a suggestion—a statement.

Though several others had suggested the same thing— Shanti included—Jai had waved off the idea as nonsense. In his mind, Phanes could become anything they wanted now. It didn't have to remain an empire.

"We have plenty to worry about first," he said neutrally, not wanting to ruin the moment with an argument. "I'm just glad you and the Tears are alive."

"We didn't lose a single warrior when we returned to Garadia," Sonika said proudly.

A thrill shot through Jai. Garadia. In all the chaos, he'd forgotten about his original home, the one mine he'd wanted to liberate more than any other. "Where are they? Where are my people?"

"Surprise," Sonika said, smiling.

Around the corner, they came in droves, led by Jig and Viola and their mother, Marella. Jig practically tackled him, while Viola—who was fast becoming a woman—offered a shy smile and a kiss on the cheek. Marella's hug was warm and thankful, and Jai's eyes overflowed. More and more came, old friends and new ones, the people he'd lived and breathed with for five long years. The people he'd mourned with. The people he'd once failed.

When the reunion was finished, and Shanti left to guide them to where they'd be able to shelter in the short term, Jai turned to Sonika. "Thank you. You have done well."

"As have you," she said. "And it seems you've done well with Shanti, too."

Jai blushed. "How could you tell?"

"A woman knows," she said. "And I know Shanti better than most. She is happy, despite the news of her mother."

Jai nodded. "She is the strongest woman I have ever met, save for you perhaps."

Sonika laughed at that, but didn't contradict him. She knew her strengths. "What news from the other mines?"

"First I want to hear about Garadia. Where are the mine masters? Where is Axa? Have they been taken to the prison yet?" Jai wanted to see the man he'd once despised, who had grudgingly become his friend and coconspirator.

Sonika frowned. "The Tears are efficient," she said. "Don't you remember? We leave none living who are not deserving."

Oh gods. Jai closed his eyes. He should've known. In truth, he'd not even considered the fact that Axa would be caught in the path as the landslide of rebellion rumbled over the empire.

"I—" Jai opened his eyes.

"Did we do something wrong?" Sonika said, still frowning.

"No," Jai said. "It is just hard when so many have to die for change to occur. I wish it wasn't so." *Goodbye, Axa,* he thought. *And thank you. For everything. You have more than redeemed yourself in the eyes of the gods, of that I am certain.*

Jai hoped that whatever came next, that no more of the people he loved would be caught in the crossfire. "I want to show you something," he said.

The army continued to live in the canyon they'd grown up in. Several times Jai had tried to persuade them to relocate, but not using the power of his justicemark. He didn't want to force them when he could help it. That being said, he knew they would have to fight again, and he would have to command them.

As soon as the empire was won, however, he would release them from this duty to do as they wished.

"There are so many," Sonika said, her voice filled with awe. "How did Hoza keep them hidden for so long?"

Jai shrugged. "The canyons are a maze, and no one ever had any reason to venture this far inside them. Too dangerous."

"And they will fight for you?"

Jai didn't like the way that sounded, but it hit closer to the truth than any other wording. "Yes."

Sonika nodded. "Then we will win. We killed the Hozas, and next we shall take all of Phanes."

Jai bit his lip—Shanti, apparently, hadn't told her old friend everything that had transpired.

"We killed all the Hozas but one."

"What?" Her eyes were as sharp as twin daggers.

"I thought you knew. Falcon Hoza survived. Fang poisoned him with jade hemlock, but wasn't able to finish the job before the soldiers swarmed over him."

"Interesting," Sonika said, a light entering her gaze, one he'd seen before. "A public execution would be an effective way to solidify our victory. We can make an example of him."

Jai cringed. "We're not going to kill him."

"Why not?"

"Because, for now, he's still the emperor, and we need him to convince the Phanecians to change."

One-Hundred-and-Two
The Southern Empire, Phanes
Falcon Hoza

Feeling was slowly beginning to come back to his extremities, though he could do little more than wiggle his fingers and toes. Typically, the effects of the poison didn't last this long, but Fang hadn't taken any risks, using an especially potent form of the liquid.

Fang, Falcon thought. *Fox.*

I am all that's left of my family, save for Raven and Whisper. He vowed to send a stream to Calypso as soon as he was well enough, telling them everything and begging for an end to the civil war. Assuming Jai Jiroux and the other rebels allowed it. Assuming they didn't still plan to kill him.

He startled when he realized there was a dark form on the edge of his vision, watching him. "Hello?" he said.

"Emperor," Shanti said. "Are you comfortable?"

He breathed a sigh of relief. He'd expected it to be an assassin. He deserved as much. "I can't feel much, so I don't rightly know. I'd rather be on the floor." When he'd first emerged from unconsciousness, still paralyzed, he'd found himself on his father's bed—he still didn't think of it as his own—where he'd remained since. Three times a day someone would enter his room and spoon a liquid meal down his throat and change the wrappings about his loins. (The latter was embarrassing each time.)

This, however, was the first he'd seen of Shanti, and he felt a slight flutter in his chest at her presence.

"Do you want to know what's happening in your empire?" she asked.

He tried to shake his head, but even that wouldn't work. "No," he said. "And it's not my empire, not anymore. It never really was. It's the people's empire."

"Which is exactly why you should be the emperor. At least for a while longer."

He laughed, his fingers twitching erratically. "I'm certain the freed sleeves will disagree, as will the rebels."

"Jai Jiroux agrees, at least in principle."

"He bears a tattooya, does he not?" The last week had given Falcon time to piece his memories together, eventually determining that it was Jai's voice that had commanded the slave army to save him.

Shanti shifted, standing, moving to the front of his father's bed, where he could see her better. "He does. The justicemark he calls it. He showed it to me the other day. It's on his heel. The scales of justice."

Falcon pursed his lips. This was the kind of man the empire needed. A good leader. A strong leader, capable and honorable and unjaded by living a false life. Then again, Falcon remembered, Jai Jiroux *had* pretended to be a loyal mine master to his father. *Perhaps we aren't as different as I think.* "You and Jai are…"

"Yes," she said, understanding. "We are."

"He is fortunate indeed."

"Thank you for saying that. Would you like me to read you a book?"

The offer was perhaps the kindest thing anyone had ever done for Falcon. "Please. So long as it isn't the last book. Too tragic, even for me."

She laughed. "Fair enough. I have a whole stack for you, though you don't have to hide them in your bedroll any longer."

Something about that truth, more than anything else, made Falcon's heart swell with excitement. It was a bold, brave new world, and he had the chance to be a part of it.

Shanti settled in at the foot of the bed, cracked a book, and started to read.

One-Hundred-and-Three
The Eastern Kingdom,
approaching Ferria from the sea
Raven Sandes

Goggin and his guanero had been placed on ships and sent well ahead of the dragonia, allowing a week for them to sail northward, curling a path out of sight from land before turning sharply toward Ironwood and Ferria. It was a tactic used once before, long before Raven had been born.

It will work again, she thought now, watching the water for any sign of the ships. The land was somewhere to the west, but out of sight for the moment.

She felt Roan Loren's arms around her waist, his grip lessening with each mile that passed as he grew more accustomed to flight. To either side, the dragonia flanked her, flying in perfect formation, their leather armor strapped around their scales, adding a second layer of protection to their vital areas.

Roan hadn't spoken in a while, having given up his endless attempts to change her mind. She suspected he'd fallen asleep, but then he said, "There," pointing past her toward the ocean's whitecapped surface.

She saw it. The first of the ships, its sails full as it churned westward. The other vessels came into view, each bearing the Calypsian sigil. Seven seaworthy dragons to add to the twelve in the sky.

Roan said, "It's not too late."

"You've said your piece. Now please, be silent or I shall dump you in the sea."

"Dump away. My voice is all I have to give."

"You cannot stop a dragon once it spies its prey," she said.

"No, *I* can't. But *you* can. It is you who sits on the dragon throne. It is you who can change the way your people think."

She had to hand it to him—he was as persistent as a starved hound begging for scraps at its master's table. "Can a dragon change their nature? Can a snake subsist on fruit and straw?"

"You are human," Roan said.

"I am. And we are worse than both dragons *and* snakes."

"The sins of the past don't justify those of the future."

"You've been spending too much time with my Aunt Windy."

Still, something about what he was saying broke through her stubbornness. Was this really what she wanted? Yes, she had to avenge the deaths of her warriors, of the innocents at Kesh, but how many more would die in a direct attack on a city built—assuming Roan was correct—to defend against dragons and guanik?

For the first time since they'd departed Calypso, she felt unsure of herself.

I can't lose you, too. Whisper's words, from the last time they'd spoken. Twice Raven had tried to speak to her sister again, but she wouldn't see her, not even to say goodbye. It had left a pit in Raven's chest, but she'd filled it in with anger and bloodlust.

Roan said, "Turn them around. Give the order for the ships to return to Calypso. The dragonia will follow. Prepare your defenses at home. If the easterners attack, then fight."

The thought of such a decision took her breath away. She could picture the joy on Whisper's face, the bridge it would create between them. Her soldiers would be angry for a time, yes, but they would have no choice but to move on—she was the empress.

"Impossible," she said. "It's impossible."

"It's not," Roan said. "I promise you."

His words seemed to break through the cloud cover, rays of sunlight bathing her face in warmth. *A sign. Oh gods, what am I doing?*

An excited thrill churned through her as she contemplated what she was about to do. That, more than anything else, convinced her it was the right decision.

"Rider. Shanolin," she shouted, raising her voice to be heard over the beating of wings, the rush of wind.

Her dragon masters angled their heads in her direction, awaiting her command. "Call off the attack," she said.

Rider's eyes widened. Shanolin's narrowed. "I misheard my empress," Shanolin said.

"You did not. This ends now. We're returning to Calypso. Spread the word. Tell the ship captains to reverse their course."

710

Rider said, "It shall be done," her eagerness obvious as she broke formation.

Shanolin, on the other hand, said, "No."

"What?" Though the dragon master had, at times, been difficult, insolent even, he'd never so directly challenged her command.

"You foolish girl," he growled. "You think because you sit on the dragon throne that you control the dragonia?" He shook his head, grasping the reins tighter. "Even Rider is blind to the power I've been building over the years. Save for Siri and Heiron, the dragons will answer to me, and me alone."

Oh gods. Rider was right. I've been a fool. I am the blind one.

With a barked command, Cronus dove after Rider and Heiron. To Raven's shock, the rest of the dragonia followed in perfect attack formation. She shouted the command for *halt*, but her order was ignored.

Raven didn't have time to think, to consider the magnitude of Shanolin's treason—she only had time to act.

"Dive!" she roared, though Siri was already angling herself lower, her wings cutting through the air like twin knives. Dead ahead, the dragonia were closing in on Rider and Heiron, who were oblivious to the danger. Instead, Rider was standing, motioning to the ships, giving them the signal to reverse course and head for home.

And then, to Raven's horror, Cronus was upon the dragon master, his clawed feet ripping her from the saddle, tossing her into the air. Heiron, having felt the impact, wheeled around, releasing a powerful roar laced with shimmering flames. The enormous dragon tried to plunge downward, but Cronus blocked his path, his giant maw open to reveal teeth as black as charred wood.

Heiron, now riderless, launched himself at Cronus, biting at his neck. Cronus dodged, releasing a shriek, clamping his teeth on Heiron's foot. Heiron kicked with his other powerful claw, landing a blow on Cronus's head, knocking him loose.

That was all Raven saw, for Siri had now streaked past the dragon brawl, plummeting for the ocean in a freefall. Rider's small form twisted and spun, battered by the wind. Siri closed in, grunting in determination. Though Raven was her rider, she'd always had a certain affection for Rider, who never failed to give her special attention when Raven wasn't around to do so herself.

The ocean, however, grew ever closer. A fall from this height, Raven knew, would be the equivalent of dashing one's body against a slab of stone. "GO!" she screamed, though Siri was doing just that. She could feel Roan clutching her from behind, but barely registered the additional pressure, her entire focus on her friend.

Just before the moment of impact, the dragon swooped beneath Rider, a red blur, catching the dragon master softly on her leather wing.

"Rider!" Raven shouted, but her friend lay still, unmoving. Blood leaked from a wound somewhere near her abdomen. "Siri, roll her to me." She knew it might be dangerous to move the dragon master's body, but there was no other choice.

Siri understood, angling her wing so that the dragon master slid along its broad expanse. Raven caught her with both hands, tipping her head back to look at her face, which appeared so peaceful she might've been sleeping, her eyes closed. A trickle of blood oozed from one corner of her mouth. Raven was unaware of whatever was happening above her, arrow-focused on the dragon master. Her friend.

"I can help her," Roan said.

"How?"

"I can *heal* her."

"You are trained?"

"Something like that."

"Rider, can you hear me?" Raven asked.

The woman's eyelids fluttered open, her gaze wild and unfocused for a moment before landing on Raven. "Empress?" she said.

"Are you in pain?"

A sly smile. "Pain? No. I was dreaming. I dreamt I was flying like Heiron, the two of us side by side. I was a dragon, too."

A sudden look of horror crossed her face. "NO!" she screamed, her eyes painting a path past Raven, toward the sky.

Raven looked up to find Heiron locked in battle with not only Cronus but the rest of the dragonia, which had the black dragon surrounded, snapping from all sides. The largest dragon in the brood was already bleeding from a dozen places.

"Heiron?" Rider said. "Heiron?" The confusion was evident in her tone—she didn't have any recollection of what had transpired.

Raven had an impossible choice. If she ordered Siri to help Heiron, she would likely be killed too. But if she didn't...

"Fly, my beauty! Fly!"

"Raven!" Roan shouted, but his voice was sucked away by the wind as Siri shot upward, gusts buffeting her sides, a trickle of flame licking the corners of her mouth. Siri hit the first dragon she encountered from the side, biting and scratching, tearing off chunks of leather armor and scales, spewing flames at the rider. Neither the dragon nor its rider stood a chance,

713

blood spraying in all directions as they fell toward their watery grave.

Raven had not been idle, managing to unhook a whip from the saddle as they spun and twisted, finding a target, snapping the long weapon. She caught the rider around the neck, yanking back, watching with satisfaction as the treasonous bastard was ripped from his saddle, slamming against Siri's scales, bouncing off, and falling away with a scream.

Amidst the melee, Heiron continued to fight for his life, roaring, slapping his spiked tail at anything and everything. One dragon took a long spike to the face and it broke off in its eye. It screamed, but the ear-shattering sound was cut off when Heiron crunched its enormous jaws on the dragon's neck. Flames shot from the dozen or so puncture wounds. The dragon tried to flap its wings to stay aloft, but some connection between brain and limbs had been severed, and it only served to spin in a wild circle before dropping from the sky.

Watching the dragons Raven had once loved destroy each other twisted something inside her chest.

And yet the worst was still to come.

Rider rasped, "Please. Help him." She was dying, and her entire focus was on her dragon, her friend, her blood ally.

Raven remembered what Roan had said earlier, about being able to heal. She twisted her head to look at him. "*Save her*," she said. He nodded, eyes wide. Just as she started to turn back around a light caught her eye through his shirt. She shook it off and refocused.

Siri's path was barred by three dragons. Beyond them, Cronus took Heiron from behind while the large dragon was distracted by other foes. Cronus's claws slid around Heiron's long neck, clamping tight. He began to tear into him.

Raven had to look away. The sound that burst from Rider's mouth sent shivers down her spine. It was a cry of one's soul being ripped away, shredded into a thousand pieces. Raven understood—she couldn't imagine losing Siri—but the sound still made her cringe.

Broken, bleeding, Heiron fell from the sky. Time seemed to stop, the dragon's eyes finding its master's as it dropped, locking on Rider in a final shared connection.

And then the sea swallowed him.

The mighty dragon was lost.

"Oh gods," Roan breathed from behind.

Raven had no choice but to flee.

Rider was dead in her arms, the final blow dealt when she watched the murder of her dragon.

"I thought you said you could save her!" she screamed at Roan.

"She didn't want to be saved," was all that he said in reply, sadness in his tone.

The dragonia gave chase, but quickly stopped—Siri was the fastest, outdistancing them as she charged northward.

Once they were alone again, Raven halted her flight, commanding her to hover in place as she took in the hopelessness of the situation.

She was certain the ships had seen the command from Rider, but they continued to churn westward. Evidently Shanolin's treason extended to her captains. *How could I have been so blind?* She'd been so focused on Whisper, on the decisions she had to make, that she'd become complacent. She hadn't spent nearly as much time with her soldiers and dragon masters as she should have. And the entire time Shanolin had been whispering in their ears, probably promising them riches and power and who knows what else.

One ship did, however, turn away from the rest, angling south, as commanded. Even from this height, she could make out the reptilian beasts on deck.

The guanero.

"Goggin," she murmured.

Roan said, "You still have an ally."

Even as she realized the truth of his words, the dragonia launched themselves at the ship, streaking past it, shooting bursts of flame across the wooden vessel. When they were finished, the ship was an inferno and Raven's heart was a smoldering wreckage.

This is my fault, she thought, sickened by the sight of men, women, and guanik leaping from the sides of the ship. The dragons left the ship to burn, the guanero and guanik to drown, speeding after the ships.

"Siri, turn around," she said, barely loud enough for the dragon to hear. "We have to save as many of them as we can."

Even as the dragon began to wheel about, Roan said, "No."

"What?"

"You can try to come back for them later. There's no time. Go to Ferria. Stop this before they're all dead."

But Goggin. But my loyal warriors.

I am the empress.

I am a sacrifice.

Whisper's words: *I couldn't lose you, too.*

"I'm sorry, sister. I'm so sorry."

She gave the command and Siri soared westward. Soon the shimmering, iron-sheathed trees of Ironwood came into view.

At long last, she'd reached Ferria.

It was here, she knew, that she would die.

PART III

Gwendolyn ⬥ Bane ⬥ Roan
Gareth ⬥ Goggin ⬥ Rhea

In the beginning, there shall be Death and there shall
be Life.
And they shall be two sides of the same coin.
The Western Oracle

One-Hundred-and-Four

The Eastern Kingdom, Ferria
Gwendolyn Storm

Gwen raced outside, feeling a strange calm set in as her heromark flared on her cheek.

Somehow she knew this day would come, as if she'd been preparing for it her entire life. The events of the Dragon Massacre—more than eight decades past—flashed through her mind, frozen images of the worst day of her long life. The last image was of Alastair, her warrior poet, his final words sliding from his tongue, warming her, destroying her.

The beat of dragons' wings. Shouts from the castle. Screams from the village.

Not this time, she thought, bounding down the iron steps, ignoring shouts from Gareth and Grian behind her. Their orders applied to their captains, their legionnaires, not to her.

They could fight for control, for power, but she was of a single mind in this moment.

Save them. Save as many of them as she could.

Their dark, sinewy forms streaked across the sky, blotting out the sun, casting dark shadows upon the world. Though Gwen knew the dragons could attack any part of the castle from any direction, it was the second wave she was more concerned with, and they could only come through the front gates.

She ran.

Men and women garbed in armor fell behind her as if they weren't moving, though they too were running. Those on horseback were no match for her speed either, the horses' eyes wide as she accelerated past, skidding and changing direction as she passed through each inner gate.

And then the front gate stood before her, a large group of legionnaires behind it, awaiting the enemy.

THUD! The battering ram shook the iron gate. Gwen had to get the legionnaires away, spread them out. The soldiers knew this from their training, but old habits were hard to change, and none of these men and women had ever faced a dragon, much less the several that swooped down now from above.

THUD! The ground under her feet shook as she raced forward, waving her arms. "Disperse!" she shouted. "Spread out!"

Numerous faces turned halfway toward her, torn between the threat behind the iron gates and her barked command. And then their training kicked in. They scrambled around each other, heading in all directions, filling the courtyard, leaving several arm's lengths between each of them.

Good, Gwen thought. It would at least give them a chance. The dragons would try to herd them, as they did eighty-four years ago, like sheep, but it would be harder now that they weren't gathered in bunches.

She spotted an Orian atop the wall, manning the gate. With a burst of speed, Gwen raced directly toward the wall, throwing herself up it. She ran *up* the wall, reaching the surprised Orian's side in an instant. The woman was protected by a metal chamber flanking the gates. Another Orian waited in a similar position on the opposite side.

"Situation?" Gwen asked. The purple-eyed woman was clearly one of the hundred or so channelers responsible for the iron defenses that had been implemented since the tragedy of the Dragon Massacre. She glanced at Gwen's cheek, where she could feel her fatemark continuing to burn.

The Orian shook away her surprise and said, "Gwendolyn Storm. Thank Orion you are here. They made landfall right on top of us, pouring from the ships. They are still coming."

"What are you waiting for?"

"Orders."

Gwen thought of the two brothers barking commands at the captains in the throne room. The situation was chaotic enough without adding a power struggle to it. "I've got your orders. Initiate all ore defenses."

The woman hesitated for a moment. Gwen was somewhat famous given her fatemark but she wasn't in the chain of command. Her eyes snapped to the gates as another heavy *THUD!* reverberated through the wall.

Gwen grabbed her shoulders, steadying her eyes back on her. "I have *lived* through this before. These Ironclads have not. Your captains have not. Listen to me."

The woman, seeming to realize the truth of her words, nodded. Then she raised a hand, spinning in a circle. Gwen watched as, from dozens of other protected areas of the castle, Orians raised their hands in recognition of the signal.

She dropped her hand, placing it on the wall of the iron chamber and closing her eyes. Concentrating.

The iron rippled and then began to move.

Gareth Ironclad

Gareth knew now wasn't the time to argue with his brother, but several of the captains were turned toward him, awaiting orders.

He opened his mouth to speak. His teeth clamped shut, nearly biting off his tongue, when Grian barreled into him from the side.

He hit the metal floor heavily, the breath gasping from his lungs. They rolled several times before coming to rest. He was vaguely aware of the captains brawling nearby, half for him and half for Grian. The recognition made him ill. They were under attack and their captains couldn't even save their petty differences for another time. Neither could his brother, it seemed.

Grian held him down. "I warned you, brother. You should've stayed away."

Gareth couldn't breathe, couldn't speak. But that didn't mean he was defeated, though he pretended he was, letting his shoulders slump, his eyes close...

He bucked his head forward as hard as he could, smashing his forehead into Grian's nose. Blood spurted out and his brother howled, clutching his face.

But he wasn't done. He'd promised to be the Sword, and that's what he would be. He grabbed Grian by the collar of his shirt, hefting him up, slamming him against the wall. "We are *all* going to die. We'll discuss the throne later. For now, *I* am king. Agreed?"

Shocked, his brother nodded, his eyes wide.

"Say it."

"You are king," he said, blood dripping from his lips.

Gareth released him, and his brother slumped to the floor. He turned to face his captains, who had stopped their fighting to watch the brothers do battle. "You all heard him?"

They nodded.

"Then go. Do your duty. Dragon defenses. We have a castle to save."

As they hustled for the exit, Gareth released a breath. He only hoped there was still time. Grian stood, spitting a wad of blood in his direction. "This changes nothing," he said. He strode from the room, following the captains that were no longer his.

A dark-cloaked form appeared before Gareth. "You escaped me once," Bane said. "But not again."

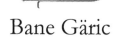

Bane Gäric

The true King Ironclad plucked a sword from a rack mounted to the wall.

Bane knew it wouldn't be enough, despite the weakness he felt in his blood, the plague flowing through him—Chavos's curse.

He strode forward, drawing his knife. There wasn't time to waste—he could *feel* the presence of his nemesis, his opposite, drawing near.

Gareth swung, a graceful arc of steel slashing through the air. Bane sidestepped nimbly, feeling his deathmark burst to life atop his skull. Before the king could finish his stroke, Bane leapt forward, thrusting his knife into his midsection.

Clang!

Surprised, Bane barely managed to maintain his balance as Gareth shoved him back. His sword had blocked the strike, somehow sweeping across in time to protect him.

Bane grinned. This almost made the entire event all the sweeter. Death was death, but there was something to be said for a death truly *earned*. He danced forward, dodging another expert blow from Gareth. He lashed out with a foot, kicking the king in the knee, hearing a satisfying crunch as he fell to one knee, hobbled.

He dropped his knife, punching Gareth in the face five times in short succession. Ironclad fell back, his sword skittering from his hands.

Bane retrieved his knife. It felt cold against his warm palm. He stood over Gareth, whose face was a bloody mess, one eye already closed from the swelling. "Now you die," Bane said, plunging the knife down toward the king's chest.

Gareth rolled unexpectedly, and the knife missed, slamming into the metal floor. Bane's stroke was so powerful that the blade not only bent, but snapped, its point clattering away.

Slightly annoyed now, Bane dropped the blunt weapon, turning to face his resourceful foe, who was back on his feet, fists raised and ready for a fight. Gareth spat out a wad of blood and said, "Come on, Bane. What else you got?"

If you only knew, Bane thought. He was about to finish him, when there was a heavy sound as something landed on the roof.

A thrill ran through him.

He's here.

Roan Loren

Roan had sensed his cousin's presence the moment they'd come within range of Ferria. It was like a dark cloud in his mind, a swarming feeling of nothingness.

He'd told the empress to steer Siri toward the castle apex. To his surprise, she continued to follow his advice. The pain of those she'd lost had made her numb. He felt awful he'd been unable to save her dragon master, but the woman's will died the moment her dragon had fallen.

As they'd soared over the castle, Roan had taken it all in:

The other dragons launching themselves at the walls, most gathering at the gate, trying to melt it down as the foot soldiers smashed it again and again with a battering ram; the castle defenses coming alive as the Orian channelers wove their magic, iron spikes bursting from the walls, killing soldiers in waves; the dragons recognizing the threat, taking to the sky, but not before one was pierced in the breast by an enormous steel shard; the dragon fell, landing with a thunderous crash amidst the eastern legionnaires, who fell upon it with sword and lance. The residents of Ironwood were not idle either, ore panthers bursting from the foliage, falling upon the Calypsians with claw and tooth. Ore hawks appeared, too, doing battle with the dragons in the sky. Fiery plumes erupted from the dragons' mouths, vaporizing several of the hawks, while others managed to slip past, pecking and clawing at the beasts' necks. All in all, it was war: chaotic, furious, violent.

And then he'd seen her:

Gwendolyn Storm, a flash of steel armor and silver hair, racing along the wall, cutting down the dozens of Calypsians that had already scaled their way into the castle.

How? The last time he'd seen her she was imprisoned by his sister, Rhea Loren, in Knight's End, her fate tied to his own mission.

And yet she was here, and, with a shock, he realized he'd always expected her to be, just as he expected to see Gareth. *It's why I'm here,* he thought. Rivers of fate coming together, joining, coalescing…

The urge to stop, to go to her, to show himself…it was a force of nature—a lightning strike in his brain—but he resisted. If any of them survived this, there would be time for tearful reunions later.

Darkness closed in as Siri landed atop the throne room.

Roan grabbed Raven's shoulder, forcing her to look at him. Her eyes were vacant, each blink slow and tired. "All is not lost," Roan said. "Until we are dead, there is hope. Never forget that. Now go, save your people."

"I should've listened to you," she said, her eyes casting over the castle. "I've destroyed everything."

Roan shook his head, feeling a sudden tenderness toward this broken woman, a victim of circumstance and the pressure

726

of an entire empire weighing on her shoulders. "It's not your fault. You made the right decision. Shanolin betrayed you. This is on him." He cupped her cheek softly. "May we meet again."

He flung his foot over the dragon, dropping the distance to the roof, landing in a crouch. Without looking back, he slid down the domed roof, cringing in pain as his ankle turned when he fell onto the top of the stairs in front of the throne room.

He pushed healing into his leg, his chest instantly warming. Light crept from the edges of his shirt.

Inside, two men stared at him.

"You need a haircut," Gareth said, somehow managing one of his token smirks despite being battered, bloody, and bruised. One of his eyes was hidden behind a mound of swelling.

"You look like hell," Roan returned.

Bane said, "That's where you're both headed."

"Hello, cousin," Roan said, stepping inside the throne room.

"Peacemaker. It's been a long time."

"Not long enough." Despite his easy words, Roan felt a slash of fear burrow through him. Bane was unpredictable, and his very presence felt like a harbinger of doom. There was something different about him. It was subtle, but Roan could see the way his hands shook.

Before he could contemplate the meaning, Bane said, "Good luck," and whirled, grabbing a sword from a rack on the wall, spinning it deftly toward Gareth.

Roan leapt into action, weaponless, naught but his fatemark to protect them both. Instinct drove him to thrust out his arms and a burst of light shot from his fingers. When Bane's blade hit the light, it stopped and stuck. He tried to yank it back, but doing so only caused it to shatter into a thousand shards, each tinkling to the floor like broken glass.

"I see you've learned a few new tricks," Bane said. "But so have I." His slammed his foot to the floor, which cracked, the metal separating in a jagged vein, quaking as it broke apart.

Roan dove to the side, narrowly avoiding being sucked into the widening void. The roof above them began to crumble, ragged chunks of iron breaking away and tumbling into the abyss. Now Bane and Gareth were on one side, Roan on the other.

Oh gods. He's dead. I've failed him.

Gwendolyn Storm

The spiked, crimson dragon that had flown over her head had borne two passengers. One was dark-skinned, a Calypsian. But pressed against her back was another, his skin fair, his long blond hair windblown behind him.

Something about him was as familiar as the sunrise.

Roan.

She didn't take the time to ponder the impossibility of his sudden appearance, or why he would be riding a Calypsian dragon, instead leaping from one wall to the next, her momentum carrying her across the battle-scarred landscape beneath her.

Despite the efforts of the channelers, the invaders had broken through the gate. Hundreds of Calypsians had died, but many more were behind them. The dragons seemed to be everywhere, raining fiery hell from the sky. The ore hawks had appeared moments earlier, the ore panthers, too, but the dragons were winning—powerful, well-trained beasts born to kill.

Gwen danced along the wall, deflecting arrows shot her way with her armor, catching a spear in midflight, launching it back from whence it came. The next gap between walls was too great a distance even for her, so she dropped to the ground. This far inside the castle's walls, the fighting was less fierce. Still, she took the time to slash down three invaders who had surrounded a single legionnaire. The man nodded his thanks before racing off to find another foe.

Several other legionnaires sprinted past her, followed closely by a shadow. The dragon released its flames and they died, cooked within their own armor, naught but charred corpses before their bodies hit the ground. The dragon landed before her, roaring.

It was gray, the largest dragon she'd ever seen, its tail a mess of spikes and its teeth dripping black blades. The dragon's rider was male, his dark eyes pinning her with a stare. He barked a command and the dragon reared back.

Gwen felt no fear. Not here, not in her home. She focused on her armor, on the connection she felt to the ore while in Ironwood. She could feel the ore melting, shifting, *changing*. She didn't move, not even as the dragon opened its maw, thrusting itself down upon her.

As darkness surrounded her, Gwen thought, *This is for you, Alastair. May we meet again.*

Raven Sandes

Siri took to the air, soaring over the carnage. She saw Cronus and Shanolin. Killing, killing, so much killing. She saw three dead dragons, too, their enormous forms broken on the ground. *Oh gods, we're* losing, she realized. It was just as Roan had said would happen. She watched as another dragon fell, a long metal spike having burst from the top of a wall, impaling it through the chest.

Yes, they'd breached the gates, but the legionnaires were spread out enough to prevent the dragons from killing them in bunches. And the easterners fought back fiercely, holding the invaders at bay, helped by the Orian defenses, which launched blades and arrows from the face of the walls, hitting only enemies.

There is nothing I can do, she thought. This fight was over before it ever started, a preordained defeat.

"Siri!" she cried, her thoughts turning to Roan. The dragon stirred beneath her, its wings undulating in broad strokes as it wheeled about. An ore hawk, its broad wings and sharp beak armored with iron, dove toward her, but Siri melted it with a blast of heat. Molten drops of ore fell like rain.

Raven steered Siri back toward the castle apex. She couldn't save her soldiers—who weren't really her soldiers anymore—nor could she save the dragonia. When Shanolin had betrayed her, he had sealed their fate. But she could save Roan. He had tried to help her and she would return the favor. It was this thought alone that kept her from throwing herself from Siri's back.

For the second time, Siri landed atop the iron dome, her claws skittering for purchase. "Down," Raven commanded, and her dragon slid to the steps below, maneuvering its head through the doorway. Raven leapt to her feet and ran along the dragon's neck, dodging spikes. Standing atop Siri's head, she took in the situation.

A wide crack ran down the center of the space, tearing the throne itself in half. On one side was darkness, a dark-cloaked form seeming to suck away all light. He had his hands clamped around another man's neck. The man's face was turning red.

On the other side was Roan, surrounded by light, which was pouring from his fingertips. The light shot across the chasm, crashing in waves against the darkness. But again and again and again it was repelled. Roan's eyes were focused but full of fear.

He bears a tattooya, Raven thought. *Like Fire*. For some reason this fact didn't surprise her.

Raven didn't know who either of the forms on the opposite side were to him, but this was her debt to repay.

She snapped her whip at a cleft in the metal ceiling, felt it catch, and then swung forward, letting her momentum carry her toward the cloaked form. Behind her, she heard Siri shriek, although the meaning of the sound didn't register in her brain, which was fully focused ahead.

She leaned back and smashed her heels into the center of the cloak, surprised by the force of the impact, which was like hitting a stone wall. Still, the form toppled over and she landed on top of him. His fingers were ripped from the other man's throat and a gush of breath exploded from the man's lips as he twisted to the side, gasping and coughing.

731

And then the dark-cloaked form was upon her and she could see his face—her mouth opening in surprise when she saw the young face, barely older than that of a boy, his smooth pale cheeks like frosted glass. Something burned atop his head. A marking that instantly reminded her of Fire, her sister.

And she knew:

This was the deathmarked boy everyone was talking about.

He touched her and the world spun away.

Everything was still; everything was silent.

She blinked against the brightness of the sun. A pile of ashes rested nearby. *The Unburning Tree*, she thought, which had been burned to ash the moment of Fire's death. *I'm back in Calypso. Impossible.*

She stood, looking around, feeling as if she were in a dream. *Where are the guards?* she wondered. And then:

Whisper!

She charged across the dusty landscape, barreling into Whisper's quarters.

Empty.

Whirling, she raced back the way she'd come, this time entering the council room from the private, rear entrance. The head of the dragon throne rose before her, golden scales shimmering.

Thank the gods, she thought, seeing Whisper past the throne, kneeling before it. Her eyes were downcast and she seemed to be praying. When she lifted her head, her eyes were brown pools. Their eyes met. "I'm sorry, Raven," Whisper said.

The apology sent a shiver of fear through Raven, though she wasn't sure why. "Sister," she said. "You have nothing to apologize for." Her own tears dribbled from her eyes as the events of the last day finally sank in, catching her from behind.

Rider dead. Heiron dead. Siri's scream, which she only just realized was one of pain. Goggin, left behind to drown. Her dragonia, her soldiers, all dead or dying.

I have nothing, she realized, her tears flowing faster.

Movement in the throne made her recognize they weren't alone, that Whisper hadn't been praying to an empty chair, but bowing to the seat's occupant.

A familiar face peered around at her. "Ahh, my dark-haired niece," the woman said. "How I've missed you. And my throne."

Aunt Viper.

Strong hands grabbed her from behind, shoving a sack over her head.

Whisper screamed.

One-Hundred-and-Five
The Eastern Kingdom, Ferria
Bane Gäric

After transporting the Calypsian Empress back to her palace, Bane reappeared in Ferria. He still had some unfinished business to attend to. He stumbled, his energy flagging, even more so because of the plague now working its way through his body.

Roan had found a way to cross the chasm and was now helping Gareth Ironclad to his feet, supporting his weight as the king gasped for breath. Angry red finger marks ringed his throat.

To his surprise, Bane felt no satisfaction.

Roan finally noticed his presence, and said, "Did you kill her? Did you kill Empress Sandes?"

"No." Although Bane had been tempted to end Raven Sandes the way he'd ended her mother, something had told him doing so would've sacrificed any opportunity he had to talk to the Peacemaker. And that was his priority.

Roan nodded thoughtfully. "I won't lie. I'm surprised. Still, I was hoping you were gone." There wasn't anger in his tone, not exactly. More like tiredness. Exhaustion. Bane understood. He was feeling exhausted himself. Using his fatemark always did that to him. He'd need a long sleep after today.

"I'm glad I got your attention."

Roan sighed. Gareth's eyes were fluttering. It seemed everyone was tired. "What do you want, Bane? Are you going to try to kill the king again? If so, get on with it."

Bane managed to laugh, though he really did feel on the verge of collapse. "I wasn't really going to kill him."

At that, Roan's eyes narrowed. "So you were just strangling him for your own amusement?"

"I was seeing how far you'd go for him. I was seeing how committed you are to your role as Peacemaker."

"You were... *testing* me." The words came out cold.

"Yes. You see, cousin, we are one and the same, two sides of the same coin. Death and Life. Dark and Light. Violence and Healing. Without one, the other cannot exist."

"I am nothing like you."

"Oh? You mean your quest hasn't taught you the truth yet? I can prove it. The Western Oracle breathed life into both of us from the same fatemark. That coin I mentioned? She split it in half."

Bane saw the light enter Roan's eyes, and he knew he had him. The Loren prince was hungry for knowledge, and Bane was more than willing to show him one version of the truth.

"Let me show you," Bane said. "And then you can decide for yourself. Take my hand."

One-Hundred-and-Six
The Eastern Kingdom, Ferria
Roan Loren

Roan knew it might be a trap, but he had to walk into it anyway. His body was bone-weary, but his mind churned with the need for information. Thus far, he'd discovered nothing of substance in Citadel, and he was at the end of his patience. Bane, despite seeming so straightforward at first—*I kill rulers,* had seemed to be his mantra—was fast becoming an enigma, another question with no answer.

He could've killed Gareth. He could've killed Empress Sandes.

But he didn't.

Roan needed to find out why.

He lay Gareth gently on the ground, and then pushed some more of his healing power into him. Gareth's eyes fluttered open. "I thought I was dreaming," he said.

"Do you dream about almost dying a lot?" Roan asked, cupping his hand to the king's cheek. His skin felt warm, and Roan longed to feel it with his lips. In a perfect world, Bane would disappear and never return and they could be happy.

But it wasn't a perfect world—far from it.

Gareth said, "It seems to happen to me a lot."

"You should really be more careful," Roan quipped, his heart swelling with love for this man.

Gareth said, "You found me."

"Yes," Roan said, but Gareth's eyes were already closing. "I will always find you."

"Promise me."

"I promise." Roan spun his finger in an arc, releasing shreds of light as he moved, creating a white shield around Gareth's sleeping form. The effort took so much out of him he almost curled up in a ball next to the king.

Taking deep breaths, he fought to his feet, where Bane continued to hold his hand out toward him. An offer. Something about his expression surprised Roan. He almost looked…sad.

Roan took a step forward, breathing in and out, preparing himself for whatever was to come.

And then he took Bane's hand.

The world he stepped into was a shadow world without beginning or end. Roan seemed to be floating or sinking or something else he couldn't describe. His exhaustion had fallen away, leaving him strangely energized.

Bane was there, watching him carefully, their hands still entwined. He, too, seemed refreshed, the weary lines on his brow having smoothed themselves out. "Watch. Listen. Remember."

The shadows vanished and all around him were words, clarifying and fading like inkreed messages dipped in water. He couldn't read them fast enough to make any sense of what they said.

And then she was there, a woman garbed in all red after the manner of the furia. Even without Bane telling him, Roan knew who she was.

The Western Oracle.

A boy was writing furiously at a table as she spoke, her eyes rolled back into her head. Instinctively, Roan knew he was her son, later to become the man who called himself Bear Blackboots.

Bane motioned toward the table, which was lit by a flickering lantern. *Look*, he said, though his lips did not move.

Roan craned his neck, anxious now. This was what he'd been searching for. This was the answer to all his questions about his origin and his purpose and the path to achieve peace in the Four Kingdoms!

The words came into focus, the ink still wet, glistening darkly under the lantern's glow.

In the beginning, there shall be Death and there shall be Light.
And they shall be two sides of the same coin.

Roan felt as if he was falling as the scene faded, replaced by shadows once more. *No!* he tried to scream, though he failed to make a sound.

Do you see now? Bane asked. *Do you see the truth? We are bound to peace. Only together can we achieve it.*

I don't believe you, Roan said. *This is a trick.*

I am not a trickster, Bane said. *You should know that by now. I kill because I must; because the deaths I choose will pave a path to peace. Just as the lives you save are necessary for the greater good.*

Something about his words rang true, and yet Roan couldn't contemplate a world where Bane was necessary for the greater good. *I don't want to hear anymore.*

You would choose blindness over truth?

I would choose life over death.

There it was again—that sadness. The boy's eyes were full of it, deep pools of melancholy as fathomless as the depths of the ocean. He blinked and they were gone, replaced by dark arrogance and casual indifference. A mask, or simply another face?

What is happening to you? Roan asked.

Nothing of concern to you, Bane said. *Take this.* It was a round, black marble, its surface swirling as if filled with restless storm clouds. *It is infused with a measure of my power. You may use it only once to go wherever you will. I hope, however, that you will choose this place, where you will find me. We can talk at length as we rest. I can teach you all that I know.*

Roan knew it was a gift, even if Bane offered it only out of his own self-interest. Bane's hand shook as he gave it to him. *Thank you,* Roan said. *Though I shall not return.*

We shall see.

The shadows disappeared and Roan was, once more, beside Gareth, the glowing ethereal shield casting a gentle white light across his sleeping form.

Outside, a dragon released a mournful cry. Roan sensed the battle was nearly over.

Roan considered Bane's offer, and was sorely tempted. The boy, his cousin, despite the darkness inside him, knew much of the Western Oracle and her teachings. He could return to him and ask any question he wanted.

But at what cost?

He looked at Gareth, drawing his hand across his hair, brushing his dark locks away from his face. *He is so peaceful*, he thought. *My presence here will only bring Bane back.*

As much as he wanted to linger in Ferria, to spend time with Gareth and Gwendolyn beneath the shade of the Iron Forest, to jape and tell stories about how they came to be here, he knew he could not stay.

He was spent, the last of his energy drained, and he knew if he didn't act fast, he would fall into a deep sleep. He held the dark, storm-filled marble in his hand, staring into it. And then he made a decision.

When he blinked, Ferria disappeared, along with the marble.

NO! a lonely boy cried.

I am sorry, Roan thought.

The world came into focus once more. A familiar room stacked with piles of paper, maps, scrolls, and, of course, smelling strongly of thick, horrid tea surrounded him now.

"I was hoping you'd return," a voice said. He turned to find Lady Windy Sandes watching him with interest. She didn't look surprised, as if she'd been expecting him to appear from thin air at exactly this moment. "There is something I need to show you."

"Tomorrow," Roan said, his words slurring. "Or the next day." Finally, his legs failed him. He slumped to the floor and slept, the light of his lifemark fading into the dusky darkness.

One-Hundred-and-Seven
The Eastern Kingdom, Ferria
Gwendolyn Storm

The moment before the dragon's enormous maw had closed over her, Gwen had sheathed her entire body in ore, infusing it with power from her heromark. At the same time, she'd taken a deep breath, holding it in her chest as she felt the blade-like teeth crunching down upon her, clacking and clanking off her armor.

The clanking stopped and the searing, burning heat arrived, seeming to surround her, as if she were standing in the direct center of a fiery inferno.

I've been swallowed whole, she thought, feeling a shred of fear run through her at the realization that her insane plan had actually worked.

Her lungs were starting to burn, so she figured she'd better get started with the next phase.

She lifted her sword and started cutting.

The dragon's roar was more of a rumble this deep inside of the beast, but Gwen still felt it in her bones. It was like she was a part of it now—its pain was her pain. But still she hacked and slashed, her strokes becoming more vigorous as she gained more room.

And then, with a final enormous swing, she felt its flesh give way and she spilled out. She channeled her ore away from her mouth and nose, sucking in beautifully cool air. Next, she uncovered her eyes. Thick, dark blood and ichor covered her, dripping from her armor, pooling on the ground. On either side of her was the dragon, split into two pieces, its chest ripped open, its enormous eyes staring at her but seeing nothing. Its spiked tail, to her disgust, continued to twitch, some kind of post-death involuntary reflex.

The attack came from behind, though she sensed it well before it arrived, diving to the side, feeling the whoosh of a blade rush past. Her foe landed deftly on his feet, pivoted, and then came at her again. Due to the vigor with which he attacked, she knew this was the dragon rider. It was said the riders and dragons were connected by some mystical tether, bound to each other by something stronger than blood.

And this man was supremely pissed she had killed his dragon.

But that wouldn't save him.

He fought valiantly, but, as she always did, Gwendolyn Storm emerged alive.

Shanolin, however, dragon master and traitor, did not.

One-Hundred-and-Eight
The Eastern Kingdom, Ferria
Gareth Ironclad

He awoke to the lingering warmth of lips on his cheek.

"Roan," he whispered, willing it to not have been a dream. Willing him to still be there, by his side.

The throne room was empty, a large crack running down its center, the iron throne itself decimated, half of it missing. Above, the ceiling and roof were torn in two, the darkening evening sky beginning to fill with stars, some of which streaked across Orion's Great Forest. Smoke hung like fog in the air.

Everything was strangely silent. Too silent for the battle that had been raging earlier.

Gareth stood, and noticed something was lighting the room. He searched for the source, only then realizing the light was all around him, moving as he moved. Like a full-body shield. Even as he stared at it in awe, it slowly disappeared.

"Roan," he said again, feeling the emptiness caused by the departure of a loved one. Wondering whether it could ever be filled.

A croaky voice broke the silence. He craned his ear, trying to determine the source. It sounded close. He stepped outside, his mouth falling open, his eyes widening.

For he'd come face to face with a dragon, its fierce red eyes boring into him. Its body jerked as it tried to move, to lunge at him, but was held firmly by dozens of ore chains attached to various parts of the castle.

Ah, he thought. *The final Ferrian defense against dragons worked.* Beyond the dragon, fires burned here and there, but all in all, the castle seemed to be intact. *We've won. Or, at least, survived.*

And they'd captured a dragon in the process. He was pretty sure he knew whose dragon it was, in fact, though he didn't yet know how to feel about that.

The croaky voice came again, and this time it was even closer, and he was able to make out the word. His name. "Gareth?"

He peered into the gathering darkness, a chill running through him when he realized who had spoken.

Grian, lying awkwardly against the metal steps, pinned by the dragon's powerful foot. One of its claws vanished between his shoulder blades. It was obvious to Gareth what had happened. After fleeing the throne room, Grian had changed his mind. He'd returned, perhaps hoping to find Gareth.

His twin said his name again. "Gareth."

"I'm here, brother," he said. "I'm going to get you out of there."

"No," Grian rasped. "You'll only get yourself killed."

"Then I'll get help."

"We both know it's too late for that. It's also too late for this, but I want to say"—he swallowed a cry of pain as the dragon shifted its foot slightly—"I want to say I'm sorry."

"Grian, none of that mat—"

"It *does* matter. I was a fool, blinded by my own"—another wave of pain—"ambition and loss."

Loss. That word, now more than ever, seemed to echo through the night like the beating of a great heart.

Grian took one final breath, shuddering, and his body went still.

One-Hundred-and-Nine
Off the coast of the Eastern Kingdom
Goggin

Men like Goggin were not supposed to swim. It was a simple matter of bone density, muscle mass, and his inability to move his arms and legs in a manner graceful enough to keep his enormous bulk afloat.

And yet, after ripping off his weapons belt and letting his knives and scimitars sink to the bottom of the ocean, he clung to the wooden door with all his strength, long after the cries of his fellow guanero had ceased, the dragon shrieks and beating wings fading away, the smoke from the burning ship dissipating, joining the clouds.

The clouds, Goggin thought, as he stared up at the sky. He'd never really looked at them before. Sure, he'd seen them, perhaps even commented on their shape or the effortless way in which they blocked the harsh southern sunlight. But he hadn't *seen* them the way he saw them now.

For they were each a one-of-a-kind creation, beautiful in the manner in which they moved, changed, adapted to the ever-shifting winds. He saw one that looked like a dragon, and it almost made him chuckle.

Then came the stars, as infinite and innumerable as the individual grains of sand in the Scarra. How they twinkled like winking gold coins. How they exploded, green bursts of color. How they soared across the night sky, crimson comets of light and beauty.

The full moons rose from opposite ends of the sky. The red god, Ruahi. The green goddess, Luahi. Their paths, on nine-hundred-and-ninety-nine nights out of a thousand, were destined to miss, their hands outstretched and reaching, but passing, their loving touch unfulfilled.

It felt like a metaphor for Goggin's own life, which suddenly felt small and meaningless. How many times had he thought he found love, only to have it blow up in his face? How many times had he drunken the pain away, laughed it away, japed it into oblivion?

I have never known true love, he realized, and the thought brought a tear to his eye, the first in years, perhaps decades. His vision blurred and the moons wobbled. He blinked and breathed and listened to the beat of his own heart, watching them as they climbed, higher and higher, pulling themselves up by, it seemed, sheer strength of will and desire.

Love raised them up.

And then, his breath catching in his lungs, they kissed. A peck at first, and then something deeper, more passionate. Goggin looked away, feeling like an intruder.

Clinging to his floating wooden door, he drifted away.

When he awoke, squinting, the moons and stars were gone, fading into a day as bright as it was hot. *Too hot to be the east*, he thought, which meant the currents had pulled him south.

But how far?

Truth be told, he was surprised to be alive.

I am, he thought, clinging to that thought the same way he'd clung to his wooden door as dragonfire had rained down upon them.

His shirt had already dried in the sun, and now he tugged his sleeves down to cover his hands, pulled his collar up to block as much of his face as possible. This was a sun that would eat a man alive if he wasn't careful.

He remembered seeing the signal from Rider to change course, to return home. Grudgingly, he'd given the order to his ship's captain, though he longed for a fight, for a chance to avenge his fallen guanero.

Then the unthinkable had happened—they'd been attacked by the rest of the dragonia. Now *all* his guanero were gone.

Bastards! he thought angrily. He suspected Shanolin, but it could've been any of the dragon masters, really. Any of them except Rider, of course. She was as loyal as they came. Now she was probably dead.

He wondered if Raven had survived her dragon riders' mutiny. She was a good empress, less cold then her mother and more patient than Fire. Strong but kind. Beautiful but humble. Capable but aware of her own weaknesses.

749

The level of his own admiration for her took him by surprise. How long had he felt this way? With an unexpected reddening of his cheeks, he felt embarrassed at the many foolish acts he'd committed in her presence. The drunken singing, the half-naked japing, the gorging and swilling and dancing and carrying on with other women...

Why do I act like that? he wondered.

He laughed at his own pointless thoughts. Evidently it took being shipwrecked and floating aimlessly in a vast ocean to get him to reflect on his past.

Still, his thoughts of Raven kept him from falling into despair. He searched the horizon in all directions, trying to get his bearings. Nothing. No sign of land or life.

I need food. I need water. Water more than food.

Another laugh burst from his throat. "The irony," he muttered, his voice coming out a croak. Being thirsty and surrounded by water but unable to drink any of it.

With nothing better to do, he closed his eyes and slept.

He awoke to darkness. For a moment, he thought he was underwater and he held his breath, thrashing about to try to force himself to the surface. Pain shot through his knuckles and elbows as they smashed against his makeshift wooden craft.

Slowly, his breathing returned to normal, his eyes settling on the comforting sea of stars above. The moons were nearly at their peak, but tonight, like most others, they wouldn't kiss, the previous night's passion already a fading memory.

So sad, Goggin thought, to live one's life in sight of love but rarely able to act on it.

He snorted. *I am no poet*, he thought. *I should stick to hitting and stabbing things.*

Too bad all his weapons were resting at the bottom of the ocean.

Though hunger twisted his stomach in knots, the thirst was far worse, a fire raging in his throat, turning his mouth to scorched desert sand. Water lapped against the sides of his boat, and he was sorely tempted to cup his hands and drink. He stayed his hands, however, knowing all too well that the saltwater would only dehydrate him faster, hastening his death.

Maybe I'll sleep some more, he thought. So he did.

When he awakened, a white-feathered, yellow-beaked seabird was sitting on his chest, pecking at his arm.

Hello, little bird, he tried to say, but all that came out was "Unghhhh." The bird flew away.

Sleep claimed him once more.

Mmmm. Water, he thought. It might've been simpre, as good as it tasted. It even burned on the way down, though in a good way.

Choking drowning dying can't breathe can't breathe can't—

He spluttered and gagged, sitting up sharply and vomiting all over his own lap.

"Slowly, my friend," a voice said. A hand patted his back gently.

I'm dreaming, Goggin realized, blinking, looking around. A sparkling silver ocean lapped against a sandy shore. Squat, barrel-like trees with broad white leaves lined the beach. A gray-skinned man, his forehead broad and flat, his chin square, looked at him with concern.

"Where am I?" Goggin asked.

The man said, "Welcome to the Dreadnoughts. You are lucky to be alive."

Alive, yes, Goggin thought. *Lucky, not so much.*

He accepted another drink from the man's cup. This time he sipped it.

It was a small step for a large man. Then again, it was probably the largest step he'd ever taken in his life. He vowed it wouldn't be the last.

He would find a way to return to Calyp.

And he would have his revenge on the traitors that took everything from him and his empress.

One-Hundred-and-Ten
The Eastern Kingdom, Ferria
Gareth Ironclad
One week after the Dragon Defense

An eventful week had passed, and Gareth had yet to encounter Gwen, so eventually he decided to go looking for her. As king, he'd been busy organizing the rechanneling of several castle walls that had been melted down by the dragons. The dragon carcasses also had to be removed, as well as the corpses of their enemies. The lot of them had been buried in an enormous pit dug on the plains, well away from the edge of the forest.

The eastern dead had also been buried, but within the wood. It was a time of celebration, of victory, but also a time of mourning and sorrow for those they'd lost.

Gareth didn't mind staying busy; it kept him from thinking too much about Roan.

And, of course, there was the captured dragon to deal with. For now, he'd repositioned his hundred Orian channelers around an enormous iron hovel they'd created to imprison the beast. *Empress Sandes' dragon*, he thought now, as he approached the gate to Gwen's forest dwelling. He shook his head. Never in a million years did he think his first prisoner as king would be a leather-winged, fire-breathing monster.

He halted at the gate, turning back to the dozen guards that had been following him. "Stay here," he said.

They obeyed, and he marveled at how everything had changed the moment his brother had died. Even those who viewed Gareth as a failed Shield couldn't deny the fact that his claim on the throne was complete.

As expected, he found Gwen enjoying the comforts of her own home, a beautiful ore-sheathed tree in the midst of Ironwood. She looked so content leaning back with her eyes closed, her back supported by an enormous iron leaf that seemed to form to fit her body, that Gareth almost turned around and left, so as not to disturb her much-deserved rest.

"Don't you think we've spent enough time together?" she said, just as he was contemplating leaving. Her eyes remained closed. It was a jape, although there was some truth to it.

"I heard you killed a dragon," Gareth said.

She shrugged.

"A big one."

She opened her eyes lazily. Looked at him pointedly. "They're all big."

"From the *inside*."

At that, she laughed. "Just because I'm an old woman by human standards doesn't mean I can't learn a few new tricks."

Gareth grinned. "Thank you."

"For the dragon? It was my pleasure."

"Not just for that. For everything. For believing in me. For not giving up on me."

"You're welcome, but I did it for Roan, not you."

"Really?"

"No. Not really."

"Speaking of Roan…"

"He was here, in Ferria—I *know*."

He tried to hide his surprise, failing miserably. "Did you talk to him?"

She shook her head. "I didn't find the time. Too many dragons flying about."

"He saved me, you know. Again. But it wasn't just him."

Gwen's interest seemed to perk up. She shifted on her perch. "Oh? Don't tell me your brother finally manned up and did the right thing."

Gareth laughed, despite the mention of his brother. Did she not know he was dead? "Grian? It's not in his blood. And he was knocked out. I may or may not have had something to do with that. Believe it or not, when Bane and Roan were doing their whole my-darkness-is bigger-than-your-light thing, Empress Raven Sandes showed up out of nowhere and tackled Bane. He was choking the life out of me at the time. She saved my life."

Gwen's yellow eyes met his, narrowed, cat-like, but then rolled away. "I suppose we should invite her over for tea then."

He shook his head. "I'm not saying it's the beginning of some kind of an alliance, that would be impossible considering they just attacked us with a horde of dragons."

"A brood."

"What?"

"They call it a *brood* of dragons."

"Yes, well, I'm certain our good citizens would frown upon an alliance with the Calypsians."

Gwen's fingers danced over the branch, making ore flowers grow and then disappear. "I don't care much for the Calypsians, but I *despise* the Sandes."

"I know."

There was silence for a few moments, each lost in their own thoughts, and then Gwen asked, "Why do you think Raven Sandes would save your life? It makes no sense to attack your castle and then protect you from Bane."

Gareth considered the question. It was one he had been pondering ever since Roan left. "I don't think she was completely in charge of what happened. It was almost as if she had doubts about the attack but was powerless to stop it."

"You're defending her?"

"All I'm saying is there are some strange circumstances."

"Such as…"

"A dragon corpse washed up onshore. It was a big one, even bigger than the one you killed. No dragons were killed over the water by us, at least none that we know of."

Gwen frowned, but didn't say anything.

Gareth continued: "And now evidence of a shipwreck has been appearing. Planks, barrels, torn sails."

"Those could've drifted in from anywhere."

"They are charred. Burnt. The damage looks to be from dragonfire. And the remnants of the Calypsian sigil are on the sails—the dragon."

Gwen chewed on that for a minute. "What are you going to do?"

"I don't know yet. Even with our new defenses, we were lucky to survive the attack. We were even more fortunate the dragons ignored the village. They probably thought they could do what they wanted later, after the castle had fallen. The first thing I'm going to do, however, is cease all military actions on our borders. For now, we defend only."

"Do you think Grian will go for that?"

It was a mistake coming here, he thought. *My problems are not hers.*

"You don't know? Grian is dead."

With that, Gareth stalked off. He was tired of talking.

One-Hundred-and-Eleven
The Eastern Kingdom, Ferria
Gwendolyn Storm

She probably should've gone after him immediately, but it was pretty clear he needed some alone time of his own. So she waited a day. Thinking. Catching up on sleep. Gwendolyn felt bad about how she'd handled the aftermath of the battle that was being called the Dragon Defense. She should've gone to Gareth, offered her help. Then she would've known Grian was dead. She could've helped him through that, too. Instead she'd slipped through the dead and living, until she spotted Gareth, looking no worse for wear. Once she was certain has was not seriously injured, she snuck away.

For a week she'd mourned Alastair's death all over again. It was strange, feeling that sharp pain, like a knife to the chest, all these years later. She'd thought killing a dragon would give her

758

closure, but it had had the opposite effect, reopening wounds she thought had long healed, their scars fading.

Finally, however, she returned to the castle, eventually bullying several guards into allowing her to visit the king in his private quarters, where apparently he'd been holed up ever since he gave the command to pull back all legionnaires currently across the borders.

Gareth sat in a wooden, high-backed chair, his head in his hands, his long dark hair falling in waves across his face.

Gwendolyn entered the room silently, taking a seat. Listening to Gareth's breathing, his deep, mournful exhalations. He'd lost a family. Not two years ago, he was one of five. Not two months ago, he was one of four. Not two weeks ago, he was one of two.

Now he was one.

The only Ironclad left in the Four Kingdoms, save for a single cousin, Hardy. The end of a long line of strong rulers that had protected their people from being overrun by their enemies over the centuries.

Gwendolyn could relate. When she lost her mother and father in short succession, far too soon in the lifespans of Orians, it had broken her in half. If she was in Gareth's shoes—and she had been, once—she wouldn't want to hear condolences. No, she wouldn't want to hear much of anything, save for the beating of her own heart to remind her she was still alive.

A distraction, she remembered. Distracting herself had been the only way she'd been able to cope with the deaths of her loved ones. She'd thrown herself into helping others, using the Orion-given abilities she'd been blessed with to do as much good as she could. At the same time, she'd closed her heart off from the world, sheathing it in iron.

"Go away," Gareth said, his face still hidden.

"No," Gwen said.

Gareth looked up, his eyes tired but dry.

Gwen said, "What? You can visit me at home but I can't reciprocate?"

"Suit yourself. Wallow with me."

"I would, but I'm all wallowed out."

Gareth snorted. His fingers pulled at his sweat-soaked tendrils of black hair. "I don't know why I even *care*," he said after a few moments of silence.

"Because he was your brother."

"Aye, and a shite brother he was. Growing up, he mocked me mercilessly. He had a huge iron chip on his shoulder at having been born third, and he was always trying to compensate for it. I think that's why he did what he did. Why he disowned me and waged war on three sides at once."

"None of that matters now."

"Because I'm the king?"

Gwendolyn shook her head. How to explain… She wanted to scream at him: *You've been the king since the moment your father took his last breath, you dolt!* But she suspected berating him would be counterproductive. Something her father once told her, an old story, sprang into her mind at that exact moment, catching her by surprise. She hadn't thought of the story in decades, and yet she remembered her father's tale word for word, a perfect recollection. After he'd finished the story, Gwen had begged him to tell her again, but he'd refused. "It's a story to be heard once," he'd said.

"Have you ever heard the *Story of the Telling Tree?*" Gwen asked.

Gareth frowned. "Does it involve war, drinking, and tickling fair maidens?" he asked. "Because those are the only kinds of stories my father told us growing up."

"No."

"Then no, I have not heard it."

"Good. I shall tell you. Many years ago, long before the Crimeans discovered the Four Kingdoms, the Orians lived in Ironwood. My ancestors were very different in those times. They felt connected to the forest, but they couldn't exactly explain why. Back then, the forest appeared just like any other. There were trees and plants and animals—panthers, hawks, squirrels—"

"Monkeys?"

Gwen didn't miss a beat. "Aye. Frisky monkeys that would steal your food between your plate and mouth."

Gareth nodded, as if the story was suddenly becoming more familiar.

Gwen continued: "The Orians called themselves the Tellers. They knew nothing of Ore, or Orion, or channeling." Gareth cocked his head to the side. "It's true. You wouldn't recognize us or Ironwood. We were a peaceful people, deeply attuned to the whisperings of nature. There was a tree, deep in the heart of the forest, the largest of them all, broader and taller than any other in Ironwood. It was known as the Telling Tree, and it was worshipped by the Tellers."

Gwen could tell Gareth's interest was piqued, his body language having changed. He leaned toward her. "Go on."

"The Telling Tree was where my ancestors went to pour out their problems. They kneeled on a bed of sharp stones,

761

which cut into their knees. The purpose of these stones was to remind them to make the most of their time with the Telling Tree. The most determined, those Tellers who could ignore the pain, would earn their just rewards."

"What rewards? More time talking to a tree?"

"That's just the thing. It wasn't just the telling that was important. They received *answers*."

Gareth rolled his eyes. "I should've known it would be a talking tree."

"Not exactly. After telling their problems to the Telling Tree, they would arise and be filled with answers. Maybe it was the tree's doing, a reward for them having suffered great pain to speak with it, or perhaps the answers were already there, simply unlocked because of their faith."

"Which is it? Was it a magical talking tree or not?" A hint of mocking had entered Gareth's tone. Gwendolyn viewed it as a good thing. She ignored the question and continued the story.

"One day, a Teller who had lost everything kneeled before the tree, pouring out his problems. The stones bit into him, but he ignored them, talking and talking throughout the day. He didn't stop until long after the sun was gone and the stars twinkled in the night sky above the forest." She paused, recalling her father's exact words. "When he arose, streams of blood running down his knees, pooling at his feet, he heard the tree's answer in his head."

"What did it say?" Gareth asked, and she almost laughed because as a young girl she'd voiced the very same question at that very same moment.

"Give up," Gwen said. "The Teller was very angry. He'd suffered day and night before this tree to find a way to solve all his problems, and the Telling Tree had told him to give up? Rage boiled within him, spilling over. He withdrew a sharp instrument that his people used for cutting thick branches when they fell from the trees. And then he began cutting."

"If the tree was as big as you say it was, he probably didn't get very far."

"Wrong. This was a determined man. He cut all night and into the next day. When people gathered to tell their problems to the Telling Tree, he threatened them with the blade. They backed off, unaccustomed to dealing with such violence. They were scared and uncertain. For days on end he cut and hacked and sawed, until he reached the tipping point, where the weight of the tree above could no longer be supported by the diminishing base.

"But the man didn't notice. Sweat was pouring into his eyes and he was blind to anything but cutting, cutting, cutting…the base snapped, clamping down upon his blade and his arm, cracking them both in half. He howled, watching as the tree shifted, raining leaves and branches from the lofts of its uppermost boughs. Any satisfaction as to the progress he'd been making was lost to his fear and pain as the tree began to fall."

"Poor bastard."

"Aye. The tree fell on him and he died. It destroyed hundreds, if not thousands, of other trees, too. Thankfully, none of the other Tellers were hit. Perhaps it was luck. Perhaps it was some other power, a final gift from the Telling Tree.

"When the dust cleared and the Tellers began to gather at the tree's base, the strangest thing happened. The ground opened and took the fallen tree into it, swallowing it whole. Any signs of the man were gone as well, leaving only a stump as broad as a plateau. One by one, the Tellers climbed onto it, their mouths gaping in amazement.

"For there, written upon the endless rings were their stories, their problems laid bare. That's when they realized that the answers had never come from the tree—which merely collected their problems, taking the weight of them from their shoulders—but from their own hearts, their own perseverance. The determined man who had cut down the tree had received the only answer his heart could give him: to give up. He was determined to tell his problems, but not to solve them. He wanted an easy solution, not the truth, which was that it would require a lot of hard work and time to overcome the adversity he faced."

Gareth groaned. "I'm sensing a moral, but I think I'd rather take a punch in the face."

"As satisfying as that would be," Gwen quipped, "I think you've taken enough hits lately."

"This isn't a true story, is it?"

"Why would you say that?"

"Because I've never heard about a stump in Ironwood. All the trees are huge and unbroken."

"Just because you haven't seen it doesn't mean it doesn't exist. After the people finished reading their problems from the top of the stump, they departed. That's when something magical happened. The deposits of ore that had been hidden beneath the forest were drawn into the Telling Tree's roots, becoming a part of the stump, sheathing it in armor. The other trees took note, realizing it was the answer to their own problems: that they were susceptible to being chopped down, a fact they'd never realized until now. Soon the entire forest was protected by the ore, and so it remains to this day.

"My ancestors adapted, beginning to worship the Ore, learning how to channel it. Becoming one with it, a mutual respect developed over time. In short, they became the Orians."

"Wait, am I supposed to be the stubborn dead guy, the Telling Tree, or the ore monkey?"

"That's for you to decide," Gwen said, allowing herself a wry smile.

"All three," Gareth said. "At one point in my life or another. I've been many things in my life. An arrogant prince, a royal prisoner, a disowned brother..."

"And now?"

"A king," he said. "Now I am a king."

One-Hundred-and-Twelve

Unknown location

Bane Gäric

Bane felt numb. He'd opened the door to his secret place to the Peacemaker, and all Roan Loren had done was close it in his face.

He'd tried threats. He'd tried violence. He'd tried fear.

He'd tried truth.

Each time, the same result. He was alone.

He didn't understand. He'd offered Roan everything he was seeking, and still, he'd turned him down. The Western Oracle had intended for them to work together, hadn't she?

Chavos's body seemed to glow in the lanternlight. He looked so peaceful he might be sleeping. For a moment, Bane pretended he was, and that he'd soon open his eyes and they'd eat and talk, and then Bane could fall asleep and not be alone.

The man had been too weak-stomached and soft-hearted for the work that needed to be done. He was the same as Roan, but without the courage and valor. He shook his head. No, that wasn't true. Chavos *had* been courageous, in the end, even if that courage was misguided.

Bane knew the plague would eventually kill him, unless he could convince Roan Loren to save him.

This world doesn't want peace, he thought, turning away from his dead friend.

And I have no one.

This was supposed to be his purpose, the entire reason he'd been put on this earth, in these lands, in this time, being deathmarked and raised in a cold cave with Bear Blackboots. Even his own father had abandoned him.

No more.

The two words surprised him, because he'd never considered them, never truly contemplated a different path. No, his destiny had been placed before his feet long before he was born, and he had no choice but to follow it. Right?

But what if there was another way? What if, despite the Western Oracle's best intentions, the fatemarks were unable to achieve the peace she'd envisioned? She was, after all, a human, and capable of error. Of failure.

But you haven't failed, thought Bane, hoping she could hear his mind, wherever she was. *I won't fail you.*

Achieving peace would simply require a different approach. Yes, killing the foolhardy, warmongering rulers was a necessary evil, but new rulers only arose to take their places. Unless there was one strong, peace-loving ruler to oversee *all* of the Four Kingdoms, the cycle of war and violence would continue forever, or until everyone was dead.

Yes, he thought. *The Four Kingdoms shall become one.*
And I shall be their king.

With that last thought circling his mind like a hungry vulzure, Bane fell into a deep sleep with the beginnings of a smile on his face. The thrum of the plague through his blood faded into a dull beat eclipsed by the hammering of his heart.

One-Hundred-and-Thirteen
The Western Kingdom, Knight's End
Rhea Loren

Wrath, why does everything have to be so difficult? Rhea wondered, as she stood atop the wall, watching the fires burn ever closer.

Wrath had forgiven her for lying to her people, right? Wrathos could've killed her in an instant, but instead she'd been spared. All for what? To go up in flames with the rest of her kingdom?

Ever since that day of triumph on the banks of the Bay of Bounty, the refugees had begun to arrive, a trickle at first, and later a waterfall. They brought news of the wildfire, which had somehow managed to leap from the Tangle into the dry grasslands, swarming furiously across the plains. *Unnatural,* they called the fire, as if some demon spurred it ever onwards.

Rhea called is a bad stroke of luck. She, of course, welcomed the refugees with open arms, providing her soldiers to set up a makeshift camp for them. There wasn't room inside the walls of Knight's End, so they would be the first to burn when the fires arrived. She had a feeling that the walls wouldn't stop the flames anyway.

So far nothing had, though they'd tried all the usual methods relied on during the dry season. Controlled fires had been set, burning the grass away until there was nothing left for the flames to eat. And yet, the wildfire had simply streamed across the dirt, unflinching. Next, trenches had been dug, but the flames simply released sparks, which were carried on the wind, landing across the ditches, bursting into flame once more. Several determined farmers had even attempted to form a water brigade, passing barrels down a line and dumping them on the flames.

Many had lost their lives in the attempt, before the survivors eventually fled, joining the other refugees at Knight's End.

Perhaps the fires are *unnatural,* Rhea mused. *Perhaps it is the punishment we have earned.*

Closer and closer the flames came, like a merciless army clad in burning armor.

The refugees on the outskirts of the walls began to scream and run, knocking each other over to try to escape to the ocean. Others attempted to infiltrate the city via the gates, but they'd already been closed for the night. The guards were under strict orders not to open them for anyone, lest the flames find a way into the city.

The camp was taken by the fire. Flames licked at the walls, and then began climbing.

"Your Highness, we have to go," one of her Furies said, grabbing her arm.

Her eyes darted to the woman's strong grip, and she slowly released it. "Please. We'll all perish if we stay here."

"Wrath will save us," Rhea said. He *had* to, else what was the purpose of her great victory in the Bay of Bounty, her defeat of Darkspell, her conquering of Wrathos? What was the purpose of any of it?

"What of the people?" the Fury asked. "The streets are flooded. They are demanding for the gates to be opened, so they can flee to the ocean."

In a way, it was amusing. People on opposite sides of the gates, all pounding. Some to get in, some to get out. "Do *not* open the gates," Rhea said. "Tell them to return to their homes. Wrath will save them on this night. Tell them to have faith."

The faithless Fury nodded and left. Rhea continued to watch the carnage, the chaos, with interest. *Fear is a greater enemy than any other*, she realized. *Faith is the only shield in dark times.*

The fires reached the tops of the walls, streaming down the opposite side, spurred by a stiff breeze brought by an armada of clouds blowing in from the north.

Rhea stared at the sky, feeling her skin start to tingle. *Could it be?*

Screams. The slap of feet. Cries of fear. The first homes began to catch fire, the stone itself burning like dry wood. The castle, too, was afire now, the walls springing flaming leaks.

But Rhea only had eyes for the sky, the boiling cauldron of gray clouds billowing like smoke.

The first raindrop hit the back of her hand. As she reached down to touch it, the second hit her nose, making her laugh.

She stuck out her tongue and caught another there, tasting its sweetness. The answer it contained.

The seventh heaven opened, emptying its contents, beginning a new season. *Wrath's Tears*, it was called, when their god cried for the sins of the people, the souls lost, the souls claimed. All else had failed to extinguish the flames, but now, in the steady downpour, the fires began to disappear, a few at first, and then across the board.

Rhea was soaked to the skin in an instant, the water pouring from her round belly, but she didn't care. Once again, Wrath had saved her. Her child, too.

Wrath's vengeance was headed south, and she would be its bearer.

Want to know more about your favorite characters from Fatemarked? Grab *Fatemarked Origins Volume I* and *Volume II* for eleven short stories from the Four Kingdoms, featuring the origin stories of Gwendolyn Storm, Tarin Sheary, Shanti Parthena Laude, and Bear Blackboots!

And watch out for more Fatemarked Origins stories, as well as the continuation of the Fatemarked Epic, coming SOON.

A personal note from David...

If you enjoyed this book, please consider leaving a positive review on **Amazon.com**. Without reviews on **Amazon.com**, I wouldn't be able to write for a living, which is what I love to do! Thanks for all your incredible support and I look forward to reading your reviews.

THE FATEMARKED
(d)=deceased

***For a complete online listing of sigils, symbols and fatemarks from The Fatemarked Epic:
http://davidestesbooks.blogspot.com/p/fatemarked-sigils-symbols-and-fatemarks.html

 Lifemarked- Roan Loren (the Peacemaker)

 Deathmarked- Bane Gäric (the Kings' Bane)

 Halfmarked- Shae Arris

 Halfmarked- Erric Clawborn (the Pirate King)

 Swordmarked- Sir Dietrich

 (d) Icemarked- the Ice Lord

 (d) Ironmarked- Beorn Stonesledge

 Heromarked- Gwendolyn Storm

 (d) Firemarked- Fire Sandes

 (d) Plaguemarked- the Beggar

(d) Slavemarked- Vin Hoza

 Justicemarked- Jai Jiroux

 Soulmarked- Lisbeth Lorne

ROYAL GENEALOGY OF THE FOUR KINGDOMS
(three generations)

(d)= deceased

The Northern Kingdom (capital city: Castle Hill)

(d) Wilhelm Gäric (the Undefeated King)
(d) Ida Gäric

Born to Wilhelm and Ida:
Helmuth Gäric (the Maimed Prince)
(d) Wolfric Gäric (the Dread King, political marriage to western princess, Sabria Loren)
(d) Griswold Gäric (usurper)
Zelda Gäric (childless)

Born to Griswold:
(d) Dirk Gäric

Born to Wolfric and Sabria:
Annise Gäric
Archer Gäric
Bane Gäric (The Kings' Bane)

The Western Kingdom (capital city: Knight's End)

(d) Ennis Loren
(d) Mira Loren

Born to Ennis and Mira:
(d) Gill Loren (married to Cecilia Thorne Loren)
(d) Ty Loren
(d) Sabria Loren (political marriage to Wolfric Gäric)

Born to Ty:
(d) Jove Loren
Sai Loren
Wheaton Loren
Gaia Loren
Ennis Loren

Born to Gill and Cecilia:
Roan Loren
Rhea Loren
(d) Bea Loren
Leo Loren

The Eastern Kingdom (capital city: Ferria in Ironwood)

(d) Hamworth Ironclad
(d) Lydia Ironclad

Born to Hamworth and Lydia:
(d) Coren Ironclad (Thunder)
(d) Oren Ironclad (the Juggernaut, married to Henna Redfern Ironclad)

Born to Coren:
Hardy Ironclad

Born to Oren and Henna:
Gareth Ironclad (the Shield)
(d) Guy Ironclad
(d) Grian Ironclad

The Southern Empires
Empire of Calyp (capital city: Calypso)

(d) Jak Sandes
(d) Riza Sandes

Born to Jak and Riza:
(d) Sun Sandes (the First Daughter, marriage union to Vin Hoza, emperor of Phanes, now severed)
Windy Sandes (the Second Daughter, childless)
Viper Sandes (the Third Daughter, childless)

Born to Sun and Vin:
Raven Sandes (the First Daughter)

(d) Fire Sandes (the Second Daughter)
Whisper Sandes (the Third Daughter)

Empire of Phanes (capital city: Phanea)

(d) Jin Hoza
(d) Dai Hoza

Born to Jin and Dai:
(d) Vin Hoza (marriage union to Sun Sandes, empress of Calyp, now severed)
(d) Rin Hoza
(d) Shin Hoza

Also born to Vin and Sun:
Falcon Hoza
(d) Fang Hoza
(d) Fox Hoza

Acknowledgments

And yet another book longer than the last comes to a close. I will *attempt* to not continue the trend, else this series might never end.

Have you all seen the cover? AWESOME. Yeah, that's Piero's work; he's my artist for all things epic, and I think you can see why. Thanks Piero, keep on doing what you do best!

Betas! Laurie Love, Elizabeth Love, Karen Benson, Kerri Hughes, and Terri Thomas. The more complex this series gets, the more you rise to the occasion and conquer my plot holes. I feel like I have my own personal squad of fatemarked!

Readers readers readers...YOU are the reason this series keeps getting better. You inspire me, motivate me, and teach me of the goodness of the world. Thank you, my friends!

The saga continues in other books by David Estes available through the author's official website: http://davidestesbooks.blogspot.com or through select online retailers including Amazon.com.

High Fantasy Novels by David Estes

The Fatemarked Epic:
Book One—Fatemarked
Book Two—Truthmarked
Book Three—Soulmarked
Book Four—Deathmarked (coming soon!)
Book Five—Lifemarked (coming soon!)

Fatemarked Origins:
Volume I
Volume II
Volume III (coming soon!)
Volume IV (coming soon!)
Volume V (coming soon!)

Science Fiction Novels by David Estes

Strings (*also available in audiobook*)

One of "15 Series to Read if You Enjoyed The Hunger Games"—Buzzfeed.com
The Dwellers Saga (*also available in audiobook*):
Book One—The Moon Dwellers
Book Two—The Star Dwellers
Book Three—The Sun Dwellers

Book Four—The Earth Dwellers

"Fire Country is a fast, fierce read."—Emmy Laybourne,
author of Monument 14
The Country Saga (A Dwellers Saga sister series)(*also available
in audiobook*):
Book One—Fire Country
Book Two—Ice Country
Book Three—Water & Storm Country
Book Four—The Earth Dwellers

"The Walking Dead for teens, with ruthless witches instead
of bloodthirsty zombies."—Katie Reed, agent at Andrea
Hurst & Associates
Salem's Revenge:
Book One—Brew
Book Two—Boil
Book Three—Burn

"Someone must die before another can be born…"
The Slip Trilogy:
Book One—Slip
Book Two—Grip
Book Three—Flip

About the Author

David Estes was born in El Paso, Texas but moved to Pittsburgh, Pennsylvania when he was very young. He grew up in Pittsburgh and then went to Penn State for college. Eventually he moved to Sydney, Australia where he met his wife and soul mate, Adele, who he's now happily married to.

A reader all his life, David began writing science fiction and fantasy novels in 2010, and has published more than 20 books. In June of 2012, David became a fulltime writer and is now living in Hawaii with Adele, their energetic son, Beau, and their naughty, asthmatic cat, Bailey.

Made in the USA
San Bernardino, CA
13 May 2020